The
Covenant
of
Water

Also by Abraham Verghese

Cutting for Stone

The Tennis Partner

My Own Country: A Doctor's Story

The Covenant of Water

A Novel

Abraham Verghese

Grove Press
New York

This book is a work of fiction. Any resemblance between these fictional characters and actual persons, living or dead, is purely coincidental.

FIRST EDITION

Published simultaneously in Canada
Printed in the United States of America

First Grove Atlantic hardcover edition: May 2023

This book was designed by Norman E. Tuttle at Alpha Design & Composition.
This book is set in Janson Text 10.8-pt.
by Alpha Design & Composition of Pittsfield, NH.

Library of Congress Cataloging-in-Publication data is available for this title.

ISBN 978-0-8021-6217-5
eISBN 978-0-8021-6218-2

Grove Press
an imprint of Grove Atlantic
154 West 14th Street
New York, NY 10011

Distributed by Publishers Group West

groveatlantic.com

23 24 25 26   10 9 8 7 6 5 4 3 2

For Mariam Verghese

In Memoriam

And a river went out of Eden to water the garden.
—Genesis 2:10

Not hammer-strokes, but dance of the water,
sings the pebbles into perfection.
—Rabindranath Tagore

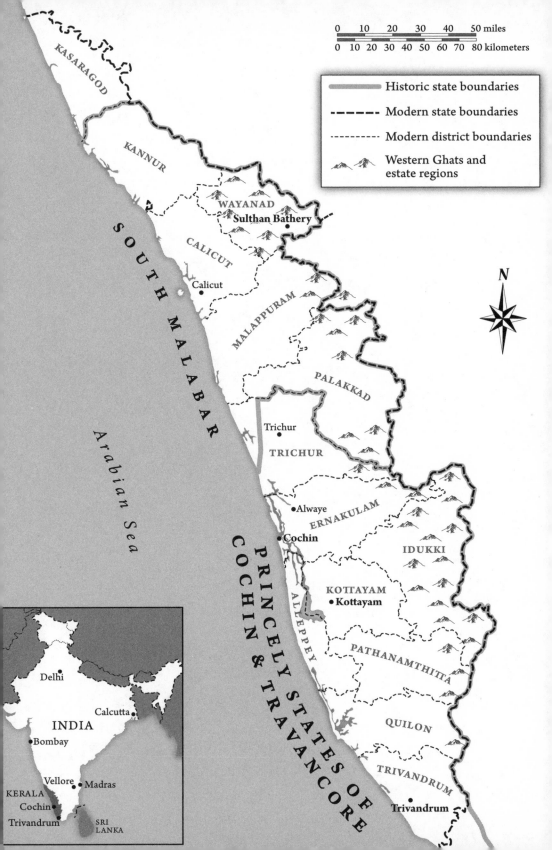

KASARAGOD

KANNUR

SOUTH MALABAR

WAYANAD
● Sulthan Bathery

CALICUT

● Calicut

Arabian Sea

MALAPPURAM

PALAKKAD

Trichur ●
TRICHUR

● Alwaye
ERNAKULAM
● Cochin

IDUKKI

ALLEPPEY
KOTTAYAM
● Kottayam

PATHANAMTHITTA

QUILON

TRIVANDRUM

● Trivandrum

PRINCELY STATES OF COCHIN & TRAVANCORE

| | 0 | 10 | 20 | 30 | 40 | 50 miles |
| 0 | 10 | 20 | 30 | 40 | 50 | 60 | 70 | 80 kilometers |

——— Historic state boundaries

– – – – Modern state boundaries

- - - - Modern district boundaries

Western Ghats and estate regions

N

INDIA

Delhi

Calcutta ●

Bombay ●

Vellore ● Madras

KERALA
Cochin ●
Trivandrum ●

SRI LANKA

Part One

CHAPTER 1

Always

1900, Travancore, South India

She is twelve years old, and she will be married in the morning. Mother and daughter lie on the mat, their wet cheeks glued together.

"The saddest day of a girl's life is the day of her wedding," her mother says. "After that, God willing, it gets better."

Soon she hears her mother's sniffles change to steady breathing, then to the softest of snores, which in the girl's mind seem to impose order on the scattered sounds of the night, from the wooden walls exhaling the day's heat to the scuffing sound of the dog in the sandy courtyard outside.

A brainfever bird calls out: *Kezhekketha? Kezhekketha? Which way is east? Which way is east?* She imagines the bird looking down at the clearing where the rectangular thatched roof squats over their house. It sees the lagoon in front and the creek and the paddy field behind. The bird's cry can go on for hours, depriving them of sleep . . . but just then it is cut off abruptly, as though a cobra has snuck up on it. In the silence that follows, the creek sings no lullaby, only grumbling over the polished pebbles.

She awakes before dawn while her mother still sleeps. Through the window, the water in the paddy field shimmers like beaten silver. On the front verandah, her father's ornate *charu kasera*, or lounging

chair, sits forlorn and empty. She lifts the writing pallet that straddles the long wooden arms and seats herself. She feels her father's
ghostly impression preserved in the cane weave.

On the banks of the lagoon four coconut trees grow sideways,
skimming the water as if to preen at their reflections before straightening to the heavens. *Goodbye, lagoon. Goodbye, creek.*

"*Molay*?" her father's only brother had said the previous day, to
her surprise. Of late he wasn't in the habit of using the endearment
molay—daughter—with her. "We found a good match for you!" His
tone was oily, as though she were four, not twelve. "Your groom
values the fact that you're from a good family, a priest's daughter."
She knew her uncle had been looking to get her married off for a
while, but she still felt he was rushing to arrange this match. What
could she say? Such matters were decided by adults. The helplessness on her mother's face embarrassed her. She felt pity for her
mother, when she so wanted to feel respect. Later, when they were
alone, her mother said, "*Molay*, this is no longer our house. Your
uncle . . ." She was pleading, as if her daughter *had* protested. Her
words had trailed off, her eyes darting around nervously. The lizards on the walls carried tales. "How different from here can life be
there? You'll feast at Christmas, fast for Lent . . . church on Sundays.
The same Eucharist, the same coconut palms and coffee bushes. It's
a fine match . . . He's of good means."

Why would a man of good means marry a girl of little means, a
girl without a dowry? What are they keeping secret from her? What
does *he* lack? Youth, for one—he's forty. He already has a child. A
few days before, after the marriage broker had come and gone, she
overheard her uncle chastise her mother, saying, "So what if his aunt
drowned? Is that the same as a family history of lunacy? Whoever
heard of a family with a history of drownings? Others are always
jealous of a good match and they'll find one thing to exaggerate."

Seated in his chair, she strokes the polished arms, and thinks
for a moment of her father's forearms; like most Malayali men he'd
been a lovable bear, hair on arms, chest, and even his back, so one

never touched skin except through soft fur. On his lap, in this chair, she learned her letters. When she did well in the church school, he said, "You have a good head. But being curious is even more important. High school for you. College, too! Why not? I won't let you marry young like your mother."

The bishop had posted her father to a troubled church near Mundakayam that had no steady *achen* because the Mohammedan traders had caused mischief. It wasn't a place for family, with morning mist still nibbling at the knees at midday and rising to the chin by evening, and where dampness brought on wheezing, rheumatism, and fevers. Less than a year into his posting he returned with teeth-chattering chills, his skin hot to the touch, his urine running black. Before they could get help, his chest stopped moving. When her mother held a mirror to his lips, it didn't mist. Her father's breath was now just air.

That was the saddest day of her life. How could marriage be worse?

She rises from the cane seat for the last time. Her father's chair and his teak platform bed inside are like a saint's relics for her; they retain the essence of him. If only she might take them to her new home.

The household stirs.

She wipes her eyes, squares her shoulders, lifts her chin, lifts it to whatever this day will bring, to the unloveliness of parting, to leaving her home that is home no longer. The chaos and hurt in God's world are unfathomable mysteries, yet the Bible shows her that there is order beneath. As her father would say, "Faith is to know the pattern is there, even though none is visible."

"I'll be all right, Appa," she says, picturing his distress. If he were alive she wouldn't be getting married today.

She imagines his reply. *A father's worries end with a good husband. I pray he's that. But this I know: the same God who watched over you here will be with you there,* molay. *He promises us this in the Gospels. "I am with you always, even unto the end of the world."*

CHAPTER 2

To Have and to Hold

1900, Travancore, South India

The journey to the groom's church takes almost half a day. The boatman steers them down a maze of unfamiliar canals overhung by flaming red hibiscus, the houses so close to the edge she could touch a squatting old woman winnowing rice with flicks of a flat basket. She can hear a boy reading the *Manorama* newspaper to a sightless ancient who rubs his head as if the news hurt. House after house, each a little universe, some with children her age watching them pass. "Where're you going?" asks a bare-chested busybody through black teeth, his black index finger—his toothbrush—covered in powdered charcoal, frozen in midair. The boatman glares at him.

Out from the canals now, onto a carpet of lotus and lilies so thick she could walk across it. The flowers are opened like well-wishers. Impulsively she picks one blossom, grabbing the stem anchored deep down. It comes free with a splash, a pink jewel, a miracle that something so beautiful can emerge from water so murky. Her uncle looks pointedly at her mother, who says nothing though she worries that her daughter will dirty her white blouse and *mundu*, or the *kavani* with faint gold trim. A fruity scent fills the boat. She counts twenty-four petals. Pushing through the lotus carpet they emerge onto a lake so wide that the far shore is invisible, the water still and smooth. She wonders if the ocean looks like this. She has almost forgotten that she's about to marry. At a busy jetty they transfer to a giant canoe poled by lean, muscled men, its ends curled up like dried bean pods. Two dozen passengers stand in the middle, umbrellas countering the sun. She realizes that she's going so far away it won't be easy for her to visit home again.

The lake imperceptibly narrows to a broad river. The boat picks up speed as the current seizes it. At last, in the distance, up on a rise, a massive stone crucifix stands watch over a small church, its arms casting a shadow over the river. This is one of the seven and a half churches founded by Saint Thomas after his arrival. Like every Sunday school child she can rattle off their names: Kodungallur, Paravur, Niranam, Palayoor, Nilackal, Kokkamangalam, Kollam, and the tiny half-church in Thiruvithamcode; but seeing one for the first time leaves her breathless.

The marriage broker from Ranni paces up and down in the court-yard. Damp spots at the armpits of his *juba* connect over his chest. "The groom should have been here long before," he says. The strands of hair he stretches over his dome have collapsed back over his ear like a parrot's plume. He swallows nervously and a rock moves up and down in his neck. The soil in his village famously grows both the best paddy and these goiters.

The groom's party consists of just the groom's sister, Thankamma. This sturdy, smiling woman grabs her future sister-in-law's tiny hands in both of hers and squeezes them with affection. "He's coming," she says. The *achen* slips the ceremonial stole over his robes and ties the embroidered girdle. He holds out his hand, palm up, to wordlessly ask, *Well?* No one responds.

The bride shivers, even though it is sultry. She isn't used to wearing a *chatta* and *mundu*. From this day on, no more long skirt and colored blouse. She'll dress like her mother and aunt in this uniform of every married woman in the Saint Thomas Christian world, white its only color. The *mundu* is like a man's but tied more elaborately, the free edge pleated and folded over itself three times, then tucked into a fantail to conceal the shape of the wearer's bottom. Concealment is also the goal of the shapeless, short-sleeved V-neck blouse, the white *chatta*.

Light from the high windows slices down, casting oblique shadows. The incense tickles her throat. As in her church, there are no pews, just rough coir carpet on red oxide floors, but only in the front. Her uncle coughs. The sound echoes in the empty space.

She'd hoped her first cousin—also her best friend—would come for the wedding. She had married the year before when she was also twelve, to a twelve-year-old groom from a good family. At the wedding the boy-groom had looked as dull as a bucket, more interested in picking his nose than in the proceedings; the *achen* had interrupted the *kurbana* to hiss, "Stop digging! There's no gold in there!" Her cousin wrote that in her new home she slept and played with the other girls in the joint family, and that she was pleased to have nothing to do with her annoying husband. Her mother, reading the letter, had said, knowingly, "Well, one day all that will change." The bride wonders if it now has, and what that means.

There's a disturbance in the air. Her mother pushes her forward, then steps away.

The groom looms beside her and at once the *achen* begins the service—*does he have a cow ready to calve back in the barn?* She gazes straight ahead.

In the smudged lenses of the *achen*'s spectacles, she glimpses a reflection: a large figure silhouetted by the light from the entrance, and a tiny figure at his side—herself.

What must it feel like to be forty years old? He's older than her mother. A thought occurs to her: if he's widowed, why didn't he marry her mother instead of her? But she knows why: a widow's lot is only a little better than a leper's.

Suddenly, the *achen*'s chant falters because her future husband has pivoted to study her, his back turned—unthinkably—to the priest. He peers into her face, breathing like a man who has walked rapidly for a great distance. She dares not look up, but she catches his earthy scent. She can't control her trembling. She shuts her eyes.

"But this is just a child!" she hears him exclaim.

When she opens her eyes, she sees her great-uncle put out a hand to stop the departing groom, only to have it flicked away like an ant off a sleeping mat.

Thankamma runs out after the runaway groom, her apron of belly fat swinging side to side despite the pressure of her hands. She overtakes him near a burden stone—a horizontal slab of rock at shoulder height, held up by two vertical stone pillars sunk into the ground, a place for a traveler to set down a head load and catch their breath. Thankamma presses her hands on her brother's considerable chest, trying to slow him down as she walks backward before him. "*Monay*," she says, because he's much younger, more like her son than her brother. "*Monay*," she pants. What has transpired is serious, but it is comical how her brother pushes her as if he were a plowman and she the plow, and she can't help but laugh.

"Look at me!" she commands, still grinning. How often has she seen that frowning expression on his face, even as a baby? He was just four when their mother passed away and Thankamma took over her role. Singing to him and holding him helped unfurrow his forehead. Much later, when their eldest brother cheated him of the house and property that should have been his, only Thankamma stood up for him.

He slows down. She knows him well, this hoarder of words. If God miraculously unlocked his jaw, what might he say? *Chechi, when I stood next to that shivering waif, I thought, "This is who I'm supposed to marry?" Did you see her chin trembling? I have my own child still at home to worry about. I hardly need another.*

"*Monay*, I understand," she says, as if he *had* spoken. "I know how it looks. But don't forget, your mother and your grandmother married when they were just nine. Yes, they were children, and they kept being raised as children in another household, until they were no longer children. Does this not produce the most compatible and best of marriages? But forget all that and just for a moment think about that poor girl. Stranded before the altar on her wedding day? *Ayo*, what shame! Who'll marry her after that?"

He keeps walking. "She's a good girl," Thankamma says. "Such a good family! Your little JoJo needs someone to look after him. She will be to him as I was to you when you were little. Let her grow up in your household. She needs Parambil as much as Parambil needs her."

She stumbles. He catches her, and she laughs. "Even elephants struggle to walk backwards!" Only she would construe the faint asymmetry on his face as a smile. "*I* picked this girl for you, *monay*. Don't give that broker too much credit. *I* met the mother, and *I* saw the girl, even if she didn't know I saw her. Didn't I choose well the first time? Your blessed first wife, God rest her soul, approves. So now, trust your *chechi* once more."

The marriage broker confers with the *achen*, who mutters, "What kind of business is this?"

The Lord is my rock, and my fortress, and my deliverer. Her father taught the young bride to say that when she was scared. *My rock, and my fortress.* A mysterious energy emanating from the altar now settles on her like a surplice, bringing a profound peace. This church is consecrated by one of the twelve; he stood on the ground where she stands, the one apostle who *touched* Christ's wounds. She feels an understanding beyond imagination, a voice that speaks without sound or motion. It says, *I am with you always.*

Then the groom's bare feet reappear beside her. *How beautiful are the feet of the messengers who preach the gospel of peace.* But these are brutish feet, callused and impervious to thorns, capable of kicking down a rotting stump, and adept at finding crevices to clamber up a palm tree. His feet shift, knowing they're being judged. She can't help herself: she peeks up at him. His nose is as sharp as an axe, the lips full, and the chin thrust out. His hair is jet black, with no gray, which surprises her. He's much darker than she is, but handsome. She's astonished by the intensity of his gaze as he stares at the priest: it's that of a mongoose awaiting the snake's strike so it can dodge, pivot, and seize it by the neck.

The service must have gone by faster than she realized, because already her mother is helping the groom uncover her head. He moves behind her. He rests his hands on her shoulders as he ties the tiny gold *minnu* around her neck. His fingers brushing her skin feel as hot as coals.

The groom makes his crude mark in the church register then passes the pen to her. She enters her name and the day, month, and year, 1900. When she looks up he is walking out of the church. The priest watches his receding form and says, "What? Did he leave the rice on the fire?"

Her husband is not at the jetty where a boat bobs and strains impatiently against its mooring.

"From the time your husband was a little boy," says her new sister-in-law, "he's preferred his feet to carry him. Not me! Why walk when I can float?" Thankamma's laughter coaxes them to join in. But now, at the water's edge, mother and daughter must part. They cling to each other—who knows when they will see each other again? She has a new house-name, a new home, unseen, to which she now belongs. She must renounce the old one.

Thankamma's eyes are also moist. "You don't worry," she says to the distraught mother. "I'll care for her as if she were my own. I'm going to stay at Parambil two or three weeks. By then she'll know her household better than her Psalms. Don't thank me. My children are all grown. I'll stay long enough for my husband to miss me!"

The young bride's legs wobble when she peels away from her mother. She might fall if not for Thankamma swinging her onto one hip like a baby, then stepping into the waiting boat. She instinctively wraps her legs around Thankamma's sturdy waist and presses her cheek to that meaty shoulder. From that perch she gazes back at the forlorn figure waving from the jetty, a figure dwarfed by the giant stone crucifix rising behind her.

The home of the young bride and her widower groom lies in Travancore, at the southern tip of India, sandwiched between the Arabian Sea and the Western Ghats—that long mountain range that runs parallel to the western coast. The land is shaped by water and its people united by a common language: Malayalam. Where the sea meets white beach, it thrusts fingers inland to intertwine with the rivers snaking down the green canopied slopes of the Ghats. It is a child's fantasy world of rivulets and canals, a latticework of lakes and lagoons, a maze of backwaters and bottle-green lotus ponds; a vast circulatory system because, as her father used to say, all water is connected. It spawned a people—Malayalis—as mobile as the liquid medium around them, their gestures fluid, their hair flowing, ready to pour out laughter as they float from this relative's house to that one's, pulsing and roaming like blood corpuscles in a vasculature, propelled by the great beating heart of the monsoon.

In this land, coconut and palmyra palms are so abundant that at night their frilled silhouettes still sway and shimmer on the interiors of closed eyelids. Dreams that augur well must have green fronds and water; their absence defines a nightmare. When Malayalis say "land" they include water, because it makes no more sense to separate the two than it does to detach the nose from the mouth. On skiffs, canoes, barges, and ferries, Malayalis and their goods flow all over Travancore, Cochin, and Malabar with a swiftness the landlocked cannot imagine. In the absence of decent roads and regular bus transport and bridges, water is the highway.

In our young bride's time, the royal families of Travancore and Cochin, whose dynasties extend back to the Middle Ages, are under British rule as "princely states." There are over five hundred princely states under the British yoke—half of India's land mass— most of them minor and inconsequential. The maharajahs of the larger princely states, or "salute states"—Hyderabad, Mysore, and Travancore—are entitled to anywhere from a nine- to a twenty- one-gun salute, the number reflecting a maharajah's importance in the eyes of the British (and often equaling the count of Rolls- Royces in the royal's garage). In exchange for keeping palaces, cars, and status, and for being allowed to govern semiautonomously, the maharajahs pay a tithe to the British out of the taxes they collect from their subjects.

Our bride in her village in the princely state of Travancore has never seen a British soldier or civil servant, a situation quite unlike that in the "presidencies" of Madras or Bombay—territories admin- istered directly by the British and teeming with them. In time, the Malayalam-speaking regions of Travancore, Cochin, and Malabar will come together to form the state of Kerala, a fish-shaped coastal territory at India's tip, its head pointing to Ceylon (now Sri Lanka) and its tail to Goa, while the eyes gaze wistfully across the ocean to Dubai, Abu Dhabi, Kuwait, and Riyadh.

Push a spade into the soil anywhere in Kerala and rust-tinged water wells up like blood under a scalpel, a rich laterite elixir that nour- ishes any living thing. One can dismiss the claims that aborted- but-viable fetuses cast away in that soil grow into feral humans, but there's no arguing that spices flourish here with an abundance unmatched anywhere else in the world. For centuries before Christ, sailors from the Middle East caught the southwesterlies in the lateen sails of their dhows, to land on the "Spice Coast" and buy pepper, clove, and cinnamon. When the trade winds reversed, they returned to Palestine, selling the spices to buyers from Genoa and Venice for small fortunes.

The spice craze swept over Europe like syphilis or the plague and by the same means: sailors and ships. But this infection was salutary: spices extended the life of food and whoever consumed it.

There were other benefits. In Birmingham, a priest who chewed cinnamon to mask his wine breath found himself irresistible to female parishioners and pseudonymously penned the popular pamphlet *Newe Sauces Swete and Sharp: A Merrie Gallimaufry of Couplings Uncouthe and Pleasant for Man and his Wyf.* Apothecaries celebrated the miraculous cure of dropsy, gout, and lumbago by potions of turmeric, kokum, and pepper. A Marseilles physician discovered that rubbing ginger on a small, flaccid penis reversed both states, and for the partner procured "such pleasure that she objects to him getting off her again." Strangely, it never occurred to Western cooks to dry roast and grind together peppercorn, fennel seed, cardamom, cloves, and cinnamon, then throw that spice mix into oil along with mustard seed, garlic, and onions to make a masala, the foundation of any curry.

Naturally, when spices fetched the price of precious jewels in Europe, the Arab sailors who brought them from India kept their source a secret for centuries. By the 1400s, the Portuguese (and later the Dutch, the French, and the English) made expeditions to find the land where these priceless spices grew; these seekers were like randy youths who'd caught the scent of a loose woman. Where was she? East, always somewhere east.

But Vasco da Gama went west from Portugal, not east. He sailed along the West African coast, rounded the Horn of Africa, and came back up the other side. Somewhere in the Indian Ocean, da Gama captured and tortured an Arab pilot who led him to the Spice Coast—present-day Kerala—landing near the city of Calicut; his was the longest ocean voyage yet undertaken.

The Zamorin of Calicut was quite unimpressed by da Gama, and by his monarch who sent sea corals and brass as tributes, when the zamorin's presents were rubies, emeralds, and silk. He found it laughable that da Gama's stated ambition was to bring Christ's love to the heathens. Did the idiot not know that fourteen hundred years before his arrival in India, even before Saint Peter got to Rome, another of the twelve disciples—Saint Thomas—had landed just down the coast on an Arab trading dhow?

Legend has it that Saint Thomas arrived in 52 AD, disembarking close to present-day Cochin. He met a boy returning from the temple. "Does your God hear your prayers?" he asked. The boy said his God surely did. Saint Thomas tossed water into the air and the droplets remained suspended. "Can your God do that?" By such displays, whether magic or miracles, he converted a few Brahmin families to Christianity; later he was martyred in Madras. Those first converts—Saint Thomas Christians—stayed true to the faith and did not marry outside their community. Over time they grew, knitted together by their customs and their churches.

Almost two thousand years later, two descendants of those first Indian converts, a twelve-year-old bride and a middle-aged widower, have married.

"Happened is happened," our young bride will say when she becomes a grandmother, and when her granddaughter—her namesake—begs for a story about their ancestors. The little girl has heard rumors that theirs is a genealogy chock-full of secrets and that her ancestors include slavers, murderers, and a defrocked bishop. "Child, the past is past, and furthermore it's different every time I remember it. I'll tell you about the future, the one *you* will make." But the child insists.

Where should the story begin? With "Doubting" Thomas, who insisted on seeing Christ's wounds before he'd believe? With other martyrs to the faith? What the child clamors for is the story of their own family, of the widower's house into which her grandmother married, a landlocked dwelling in a land of water, a house full of mysteries. But such memories are woven from gossamer threads; time eats holes in the fabric, and these she must darn with myth and fable.

The grandmother is certain of a few things: A tale that leaves its imprint on a listener tells the truth about how the world lives, and so, unavoidably, it is about families, their victories and wounds, and their departed, including the ghosts who linger; it must offer instructions for living in God's realm, where joy never spares one from sorrow. A good story goes beyond what a forgiving God cares to do: it reconciles families and unburdens them of secrets whose bond is stronger than blood. But in their revealing, as in their keeping, secrets can tear a family apart.

CHAPTER 3

Things Not Mentioned

1900, Parambil

The new bride dreams that she's splashing in the lagoon with her cousins, piling onto their narrow skiff, deliberately capsizing it, and clambering on again, their laughter echoing off the banks.

She awakes confused.

A snoring mound beside her swells and subsides. Thankamma. Yes. Her first night at Parambil. That name rubs awkwardly over her tongue like the edge of a chipped tooth. From next door, her husband's room, she hears nothing. Thankamma's body hides a small boy—she sees only the shiny tousled hair on his head, and a hand, palm up, resting just beyond it.

She listens. Something is missing. The absence is disquieting. It comes to her: she cannot hear water. She's missing its murmuring, soothing voice, and so she manufactured it in her dream.

Yesterday the *vallum*, a dugout buttressed across with planks, dropped her and Thankamma at a small jetty. They crossed a long field dotted with towering coconut palms laden with fruit. Four cows grazed, each tethered on a long rope. They walked through rows of banana trees, the floppy leaves nuzzling and knocking against each other. Bunches of red bananas hung down. The air was perfumed by a *chempaka* tree. Three well-worn, polished rocks served as stepping-stones across a shallow stream. Further up, the stream broadened into a pond whose banks were overgrown with pandanus shrubs and dwarf *chenthengu* palms laden with orange-colored coconuts. An inclined washing stone sat near the pond's edge; Thankamma said that spot was where she should come to bathe. The stream's burble was a sound that augured well. She'd looked for the house when they landed at the jetty, but it wasn't there by the river, so surely it must be by the stream . . . but she saw nothing. "All this land, over five hundred acres," Thankamma said proudly, pointing left and right, "is Parambil. Most of it is wild, hilly, not cleared. Of the part that is rough-cleared, only a portion is cultivated. Before your husband tamed it, this was all jungle, *molay*."

Five hundred acres. The home she'd known till yesterday sat on barely two.

They'd continued through a trail flanked by tapioca. At last she saw the house, high up on a rise, silhouetted against the light. She stared at what would be her home for the rest of her life. The roofline had the familiar sag in the middle, curving up to the ends; the low overhanging eaves blocked the sun, and shaded the veran-dah . . . but all she could think about was *Why up there? Why not by the stream? Or by the river that brings visitors, news, and all good things?*

Now, lying on her back, she studies the room: the oiled, pol-ished walls are of teak, not wild jackwood, with crucifix-shaped openings at the top through which warm air can escape; the false ceiling is also of teak, a buffer against the heat; thin wooden bars across the windows allow the breeze to pass freely; and of course, there's a split door leading out to the verandah, the upper half now open to admit the breeze, the lower half closed to keep out chick-ens as well as all legless creatures—it's much like the house she left behind, only bigger. Every *thachan*, or carpenter, follows the same ancient *Vastu* rules, from which neither Hindu nor Christian will deviate. For a good *thachan*, the house is the bridegroom and the land is the bride, and he must match the two with as much care as the astrologer matches horoscopes. When tragedy or a haunting hangs over a household, people will say it's because the dwelling was inauspiciously sited. And so she asks herself again: *Why here, away from water?*

A rustle of leaves, a tremble transmitted through the ground, sends her heart racing. Something near the door blocks the starlight. Is this a household ghost coming to introduce itself? Next, a leafy bush seems to grow into the room through the upper half of the door. A huge snake coils around the bush. She can neither move nor scream, even though she knows something terrible is about to happen to her in this mysterious, landlocked house . . . but would death smell like jasmine?

A swatch of uprooted jasmine hovers above her, held fast by the trunk of an elephant. The florets sway over the sleepers, then pause over her. She feels a warm, moist, ancient breath on her face. Fine soil particles fall on her neck.

Her fear subsides. Hesitantly, she reaches for the offering. She's surprised that the nostrils look so human, fringed by paler freckled skin, as delicate as a lip, yet as nimble and dexterous as two fingers; it snuffles at her chest, tickles her elbow, then traces a path to her face. She suppresses a giggle. Hot exhalations puff down on her like benedictions. The scent is something out of the Old Testament. Noiselessly, the trunk withdraws.

She turns to find she has a startled witness. Two-year-old JoJo sits staring over Thankamma's midriff, his eyes wide. She grins, rising, impulsively beckoning him and lifting him to her hip, and they head outside, following the apparition.

She senses spirits everywhere in Parambil, just as in any house. One paces outside on the *muttam*. The darkness flickers with invisible souls as plentiful as fireflies.

In a clearing by a towering palm, hovering over a stack of coconut fronds, the retinal glow of an eye sways like a lamp in a breeze. As her vision adjusts, a mountain of a forehead emerges, then languidly flapping ears . . . a sculpture carved from the black stone of night. The elephant is real, not a ghost.

JoJo absentmindedly encircles her neck with one arm, his fingers clutching her earlobe, comfortably settled on her hip as if he's never known any other. She wants to laugh; just yesterday, *she* was the one clinging to Thankamma. They stand still, two half-orphans. The spirits take their orders from the jasmine-giver and retreat into the shadows that yield to the dawn.

In her short life she's seen temple elephants worshipped and pampered with treats; she's seen logging elephants lumbering through villages on their way to the forest. But surely this beast blocking out the stars is the world's biggest elephant. To watch its leisurely chew, the graceful dance of the trunk as it folds leaves into a grinning mouth, soothes her.

On the elephant's leeward side, just beyond the mud bund that creates a moat around every coconut tree to keep water and manure from draining away, a man sleeps on a rope cot.

Her husband's elbows and knees jut from the sagging wooden frame. In the posture of his powerful left arm, curled to make a pillow for his cheek, the fingers gathered to a point, she sees echoes of her jasmine-bearing visitor.

CHAPTER 4

A Householder's Initiation

1900, Parambil

Inside the kitchen, the packed-earth floor feels cool on her soles. The walls are dark from smoke, and they enfold mouthwatering scents; she is immediately at home in this shady sanctuary. Thankamma, bent over, blows through a wide metal tube, her cheeks ballooning as she coaxes the overnight embers in the *aduppu* back to life. Of the six brick slots in this raised hearth, pots are sitting on four. She marvels at how fast Thankamma moves for a big woman, her hands a blur, feeding dry coconut husks under the pan with the frying onions here, and flattening embers there so the rice can now simmer. Thankamma pours the bride coffee brewed in milk and sweetened with jaggery. "I made *puttu*," she says, pushing a spongy white cylinder of steamed rice flour out of its wooden mold and onto her banana leaf plate. For JoJo she mashes it with banana and honey. She's warmed up the beef fry—*erechi olarthiyathu*—and the fiery fish curry—*meen vevichathu*—from the previous night. "Isn't the fish tastier in the morning? That's the beauty of this clay pot! Treasure it and never use it for anything but *meen vevichathu*, all right? Every year, your curry will get better. If there's a fire in my house and I must choose between my husband and my clay pot . . . well, all I can say is he's lived a good life. The curries I will make in my pot will ease my widowhood!"

Thankamma's laughter rings out. The bride sits dazed, cross-legged, contemplating her first breakfast at Parambil: it is lavish, and more nourishing than what she and her mother ate in a week.

"Your husband ate standing, as usual. He's already gone to the field."

Thankamma insists that a bride should do nothing but let herself be spoiled. She tries, but it is against her nature. She watches Thankamma's fingers, trying to keep track of the ingredients they toss into the curries, but it's hard when there are never fewer than two dishes being made at the same time. Thankamma's hands must have a memory of their own, she thinks, because their owner pays no attention to them as she chatters away. JoJo drags her away, proud to be her guide, walking her through every room, forgetting he just did it two hours before. The house is L-shaped, one limb being the older, original house, sitting well off the ground on a high plinth, and constructed around the strongroom, or *ara*, in which a family's wealth—money, jewelry, and paddy—are stored. A cellar sits below the *ara*, while an unused bedroom and a large pantry flank it; next to the pantry is the kitchen. A narrow outer verandah connects everything. The newer limb of the house is lower to the ground, with a broad, inviting verandah on three sides. It has a sitting room that gets little use, then two adjacent large bedrooms—her husband's and the one she, JoJo, and Thankamma sleep in—and another room that is used as a storeroom.

Old and new limbs embrace a rectangular *muttam*, or courtyard, surfaced with yellow, gold, and white pebbles hauled from a riverbed. Each morning a *pulayi* woman, Sara, sweeps the *muttam* with a stick broom, leaving a fan-shaped pattern as she clears away dead leaves while evening out the pebbles. The *muttam* is where mats are rolled out to dry boiled paddy, where clothes hang on a line, and where JoJo kicks his ball.

After lunch, she, JoJo, and Thankamma take long naps. Her husband never naps and spends most of his time outdoors working the land. When she catches a glimpse of him in the fields, he's always accompanied by a few *pulayar*, standing out from them because of his height, and because compared to theirs his skin looks fair. In the evenings, Thankamma puts her feet up and the three of them sit in the breezeway outside the kitchen, as the older woman tells endless stories while spoiling JoJo and her with treats from the cellar. Belatedly it occurs to her that Thankamma's stories are a form of instruction. She tries to recall them at night when she lies down to sleep, but that's also when homesickness clutches at her insides, and her every thought turns homeward. Thankamma's affection is so reminiscent of her mother that it can accentuate her sadness. She allows herself to cry only when she's certain everyone is asleep.

On her second morning, when they hear the fishmonger's yodeling cry in the distance, Thankamma asks the bride to hail her. Five minutes later the woman is outside the kitchen, the scent of the river clinging to her. Thankamma helps her lower the heavy basket off her head.

"*Aah*, and this is the bride!" the fishmonger says, brushing scales off her forearms and squatting down. "For her only I brought special *mathi* today." She removes the sackcloth covering the basket as though uncovering precious jewels.

Thankamma sniffs a sardine, squeezes it, then slaps it down against its mates. "Just for the bride, is it? Keep it if it's that special. What's under that cloth? *Aah!* See that! Who's that *mathi* for? Was there another marriage I didn't know about? Give it here! Not a word!"

The next day, the bride sees Shamuel *pulayan* crossing the *muttam*, straining under a headload of coconuts in a wide basket. Thankamma had pointed him out as Parambil's foreman and her husband's constant shadow; Sara, who sweeps the *muttam*, is his wife. Shamuel's family has worked for them for generations, Thankamma said; his forebearers were probably indentured to the family in ancient times, before that was outlawed. The *pulayar* are the lowest caste in Travancore, rarely owning their own property, even their huts belonging to the landlord; the sight of them is enough to pollute a Brahmin, who then must take a ritual bath.

Under the weight of his basket, Shamuel's neck and arm muscles are taut cables on his small, compact frame. His bare chest heaves, his ribs appear to be more out of the skin than in; his body is quite hairless save for stubble on his cheek and above his lip and a cropped head of hair, graying at the sides. He looks her husband's age, though Thankamma said he's younger.

When Shamuel spots her, a huge smile transforms his face, his cheekbones shining like polished mounds of ebony and the white, even teeth highlighting his fine features. There's a childlike quality to his excitement at getting to welcome the new bride. "*Aah!*" he says—but there's a practical matter to deal with first: "*Molay*, could you ask Thankamma *chechi* to come out? This basket might be too heavy for you to help me."

Once Thankamma helps him lower the basket, he removes the *thorthu* coiled atop his head, shakes it out, then wipes his face, neither his smile nor his eyes leaving the new bride. "More baskets coming. We've been climbing all morning, the *thamb'ran* and me." He points and she sees her husband in the distance, arms crossed, sitting astride a crooked palm at a spot where the trunk is almost horizontal. His legs dangle carelessly, and he looks lost in thought. The sight makes her shudder involuntarily, stirring up her fear of heights. She can't imagine a landowner risking his life like that when there are *pulayar* to do that work.

"How come you let the *thamb'ran* up there so soon after his wedding?" Thankamma says, acting cross. "Tell the truth—if he climbs, it's half the work for you."

"*Aah*, you try to stop him. He's like the little *thamb'ran* here," he says, prodding JoJo's belly. "Happier in the sky than on the ground." JoJo is pleased to be called the little master.

Shamuel's bare chest is flecked with bark. Still grinning at the *thamb'ran*'s wife, he fastidiously pleats his blue-checked *thorthu* lengthwise and then drapes it over his left shoulder. She turns shy and drops her eyes, noticing his deformed right big toe, flattened out like a coin, the nail gone.

Thankamma says, "*Aah*, Shamuel, please husk three coconuts for us, then. After that, wash up and come eat something. Your new mistress will serve you."

Shamuel has his own clay dish hanging from a hook under the overhang of the roof at the back of the kitchen and that's where he will eat, on the back steps. *Pulayar* never enter the house. Sara cooks for him at home, but a meal at the main house spares his store of paddy. After rinsing out his dish, he fills it with water and drinks it all, and then squats on the step. The bride serves him *kanji*—soupy rice in its cooking water—with a piece of fish and lime pickle.

"You like it here, then?" he asks, a big ball of rice bulging his cheek. She stands shyly before him and nods. Her finger absent-mindedly traces ആ, the first letter in *āna*, or *elephant*, a letter she thinks somehow manages to resemble an elephant. "I was younger than you when I came to Parambil. Just a boy, you know," he says. "Before there was even a house. I feared we'd be trampled as we slept. A house protects you. The secret is the roof, did you know? Why do you think we always build it this way?"

To her eyes the roof is like any other. Only the front gable—the face of the house with its pattern of carved openings in the wood—is unique to every home. Everywhere else, the thatch eaves flare out, as though the roof intends to swallow the dwelling. Shamuel points. "When the rafters stick out like that, an elephant has no flat surface on which to lean. Or push." He's like JoJo in his pride in instructing her. She takes to him.

"The elephant came to greet me on my first night," she offers in a small voice.

"Did he? Damodaran!" Shamuel says, laughing, shaking his head. "That fellow comes and goes as he pleases. I was about to sleep but I felt the ground shake. I knew it was him. I went out and there was Unni sitting atop of him, grumbling because Damo chose to come from the logging camp when it was already dark. *Aah*, but Unni didn't complain too much. Whenever Damo is here, Unni gets the nights off to be home with his wife. And the *thamb'ran* sleeps next to Damo. They talk."

Keeping an elephant, she has heard, is expensive. Not just paying for Unni, who must be the mahout, but the cost of feeding Damo.

"Is Damodaran ours?"

"Ours? Is the sun ours?" Shamuel waits like a schoolmaster for her to shake her head to say no. "*Aah aah*, just like the sun, Damodaran is his own boss. I tease Unni that Damo is really the mahout, even if he lets Unni sit on top and pretend to steer him. No one told you about Damo? *Aah*, let Shamuel tell you. Long before there was this house, as the *thamb'ran* and my father slept outside, they heard terrible cries. Trumpeting. The ground shook! The sound of trees cracking was like thunder. My father thought the world was ending. At dawn they found young Damodaran just over there, on his side, one eye gone, bleeding, with a broken tusk sticking out between his ribs. The bull elephant that attacked him must have been in musth. The *thamb'ran* tied a rope around that tusk and then, standing far away, he pulled it out. You've seen the tusk? It's in *thamb'ran*'s room. Damodaran bellowed in pain. Bubbles and blood poured out of the wound. *Thamb'ran*—so brave he is—climbed up onto Damo's side and plugged the hole with leaves and mud. He poured water little by little into Damodaran's mouth and sat there talking to him all that day and night. He said more to Damo than he has to all the people in his life put together, that's what my father said. After three days, Damodaran got up. A week later he walked away.

"A few days after that, the *thamb'ran* and my father cut a big teak tree and were trying to lever it to the clearing. Damodaran stepped out from the forest and pushed it for them, just like that. Elephants like to work. He became so good with logs. Now he works in the teak forests with the loggers, but only when he feels like it. Whenever he decides, he comes back here. He came to see the *thamb'ran*'s new wife. That's what I think."

Under Thankamma's guidance, she slowly eases into her new life at Parambil. With every passing day, she feels the home she left behind fade, which makes her longing more acute. She doesn't want to forget. After breakfast, Thankamma says, "Today, I thought we can make jackfruit *halwa* together. Because JoJo and I are craving it!" JoJo claps his hands. "*Molay*, the sweetness of life is sure in only two things: love and sugar. If you don't get enough of the first, have more of the second!" Thankamma has already boiled pieces of jackfruit and now she mashes them with melted jaggery. "Here's a secret: as you mash the jackfruit, close your eyes and think of something you want from your husband." Thankamma screws her eyes shut, grinning from the effort, and showing off the gap between her front teeth. "Now a pinch of cardamom, salt, and a teaspoon of ghee. Ready! It must cool more now. Taste it. Isn't it wonderful?" She lowers her voice. "I'm serious, *molay*. This is the key to a happy marriage. Make your wish and then feed your husband this *halwa*. Whatever you want will come true!"

Her pride in getting into the rhythm of the household, of making a few dishes under Thankamma's watchful eye, is undercut by the knowledge that Thankamma must soon leave. When Thankamma lavishly praises her chicken curry, she glows with pride, but in the next moment she finds herself clinging to Thankamma, burying her face on that well-padded shoulder to hide her tears. *Please stay! Never leave!* But already she loves Thankamma too much to say it. Thankamma has her own house to run, a husband who awaits her. She mumbles, "I will never forget your kindness. How can I ever thank you?" "*Aah*, when you have a daughter-in-law, treat her like a jewel. That's how you can thank me."

*　*　*

The day before she is to leave, Thankamma steps out of the kitchen and peers up at the sun, finding it directly overhead. "*Molay*, cut a banana leaf and pack a lunch for your husband. Let him taste your bean *thoren* and also the *mathi* we fried. Put plenty of rice. He's out there somewhere with Shamuel no doubt, always surveying his land. See that tall coconut palm? He'll be somewhere there." The bride obediently ladles the food onto a banana leaf, folds it, and secures it with string; she picks up a small brass vessel with *jeera* water—water boiled with cumin seeds—and heads out. She's anxious about Thankamma's imminent departure. That morning she discovered that no paper or pen existed at Parambil. Her hopes of writing down some of Thankamma's recipes are dashed. What if she forgets them?

The footpath is lined by tall grass that reaches her shoulder; Thankamma had said it was once so overgrown that neither God nor light could penetrate, and the undergrowth was alive with scorpions, cobras, giant rats, and biting centipedes. "What Hindu or Christian would be mad enough to try to settle here?" Thankamma had said. "Your husband came here after our oldest brother tricked him out of the family home by getting him to make a mark on a piece of paper." Shamuel's father, Yohannan *pulayan*, came along, seeing it as his duty to serve the rightful heir; later Yohannan brought his wife and son. The two men built a rough shelter. "Can you imagine my brother sleeping under the same roof as his *pulayar*? Eating with them? All barriers of caste vanish when you enter hell, is it not? Only the saints kept them alive. The first week a tiger carried off their only goat. They had more days with fever than without. But they dug, drained the marsh, never stopped clearing. *Molay*, I tell you this not just because I'm proud of my little brother, but so that you know his ways are not the ways of everyone. Yohannan was like a father to him. And like that only, his son Shamuel will be there for you and your family for a lifetime." Thankamma said her husband enticed a skilled Hindu *thachan* and a blacksmith to move to the area by offering them cleared plots by the stream, and ensuring that the *pulayar* huts would be downstream, so these crafts-men couldn't complain of ritual pollution. The potter, goldsmith, and stone mason came later. After his house was built, her husband gave one- to two-acre plots to a number of his relatives. Once they cultivated their land and sold their harvest, these relatives could buy more land from him if they wanted. "You understand what I'm telling you, *molay*? He *gave* the land outright! They can pass it to their children. He wanted this area to prosper. He's not done. Who knows, next time I come to visit there might be a proper road, provi-sion stores, a school . . ."

"A church?" she'd suggested, but to that Thankamma made no answer.

She finds her husband gazing up at a tree, his bare chest flecked with bark, a fierce *vettukathi* hanging from his waist, the billhook pointing back. He's surprised to see her. He takes the food. "That Thankamma!" The smile is in his voice, not his face. He sits, resting against the tree, but not before spreading his *thorthu* for her to sit on. He wolfs down the food. She doesn't say a word. She's astonished to realize that her shyness is matched by his.

When he's finished, he rises and says, "I'll walk back with you."

She hears shouts and laughter. On their left in the distance a log straddles a rivulet she hasn't seen before. On the other bank in a clearing sits a large burden stone. These crude structures stand like primitive monuments along well-traveled footpaths, allowing a traveler to ease their heavy headload onto the horizontal slab and rest for a while. She sees a young man push and rock the horizontal beam of the burden stone, while two friends egg him on. All three have streaks of sandalwood paste on their foreheads. The one doing the pushing is powerfully built, his head shaved except for a knot-ted tuft in the front. The horizontal slab comes off its supports and hits the ground, raising a cloud of red dust. The miscreant's face is flushed with pride and excitement.

She pictures Shamuel returning from the mill, balancing a heavy sack of ground rice flour on his head, anticipating the burden stone where he can bend his knees just enough to slide the sack onto the horizontal slab. He would be forced to go on, or else to drop the sack and wait until someone came by to help lift it back onto his head. In a land where most everything is transported in this manner, where roads are regularly washed away or too rutted for bullock carts, and where only the footpaths are reliable, a rest station like this is a blessing.

The young men spot the couple and turn silent. They look well-fed, the sort who never have to carry a load or require a burden stone. By their dress and appearance she thinks they are Nairs. A large Nair family lives along the western edge of Parambil. The Nairs are a warrior caste, employed by generations of Travancore maharajahs to defend against invaders. Her father's Nair friend had looked the part, sporting a fierce mustache to go with his strong physique. Under British rule, the maharajah had their protection and no longer needed his Nair army. Govind Nair had been bitter. "How can he call himself ruler of Travancore? He's a puppet who hands over our taxes to the British. The British 'protect' him from what? Isn't the enemy already inside the walls?"

Her husband half-hitches his *mundu*, exposing his knees as he marches to the log bridge, but reaching it, he crosses very gingerly. The youths snigger at this, but still, they brace themselves as this older bull elephant approaches. Her stomach churns. To her astonishment, her husband ignores them and squats down to the stone instead. "So, you're strong enough to push it over. Are you strong enough to put it back?"

"Why don't you?" the boy says cheekily, but with a quaver in his voice.

Her husband gets his fingers under one pole of the fallen beam, heaves it to waist height, and walks it upright. Then he lets the stone beam tip back on the fulcrum of his shoulder, where it seesaws. His quivering thighs are like tree trunks and his neck muscles are thick ropes as he maneuvers one end and then the other back atop the vertical pillars. He leans on the restored slab to catch his breath. With a sudden thrust he pushes it off its support again. It thuds to the ground and rolls to the youths, who must leap back. Flicking his eyebrows up, he challenges the tall youth. *Your turn.*

An unnatural quiet hangs over the clearing, like water suspended in the air. At last her husband calls out to her, "They're just dressed like men. This boy's father and I put up this stone before this one was born. Now in his old age, Kuttappan Nair must clean up behind his calf, but he'll lift this stone as if it is a toothpick." He turns his back to them and returns.

The topknot falls forward as the young man bends and tries to lift the stone, grimacing, veins popping out like snakes on his forehead. When he gets it upright, his muscles fail him and his friends rush forward to keep it from crushing him. When he tries to ease it onto his shoulder it sways wildly. They restore the beam, but all three look ruffled and bruised, and the tall one's shoulder bleeds. Her husband sees none of this, arriving beside her, his face thick with anger, terrifying her. With a quick tilt of his head he conveys his thanks for lunch and his need to get back to work. She runs home.

Thankamma takes one look at her face and sits her down. "Those boys are lucky that he controlled his temper," Thankamma says after hearing what happened. Her words are hardly reassuring, and the cup of water in the bride's hands shakes. "*Molay*, don't worry. He'll never be angry without cause. And never at you. He would never mistreat you." Thankamma puts an arm around her. "I know this is all new and frightening. When I got married, my husband and I were only ten. He was a naughty brat. We ignored each other. We were just children in a big house, and there were so many of us. The boys were all mean. One time I saw him sitting on a log looking at the stream. I came up quietly and I pushed him into the water!" Her laugh is infectious and the bride cannot help but smile. "He likes to remind me of that day even now! Yes, we disliked each other. But see, things don't stay the same. Don't you worry." Thankamma looks at her and adds earnestly, "What I'm trying to say is that my brother is like a coconut. The hardness is all on the outside. You're his wife, and he cares for you as Thankamma cares for you. You understand?" She tries to. Thankamma, who's never at a loss for words, seems uncomfortable saying even this much. "There's nothing you have to do. Don't worry. It'll all unfold in its own time."

CHAPTER 5

Husbandry

1900, Parambil

In the wake of Thankamma's departure, silence descends on the house, a feeling of being underwater with too little light filtering through. JoJo, unsettled, doesn't let his stepmother out of his sight; even in sleep his small fingers are curled in her hair. Their first night alone, she's awake, not because of her husband's snores from the adjacent bedroom but because she has never slept without an adult beside her. His snores, though distant, are reassuring; they are punctuated occasionally by a cough and then a disgruntled rasp, as if someone prodded a slumbering tiger. He talks in his sleep, more words than he's said to her since her arrival. Seeing him be so playful with Damodaran, who has left as mysteriously as he came, she knows there's a childlike side to him. Still, she only dares speak to him to tell him dinner is ready.

Shamuel comes by several times during the day to ask if she needs anything and is disappointed if she doesn't. She's touched by his concern.

"Shamuel, there is something I need."

"*Ooh-aah*, anything!"

"Paper, envelope, and a pen to write to my mother."

The eager smile on his face fades. "*Aah.*" He clearly has no experience with those commodities. Still, he surprises her when he returns from the market, proudly retrieving envelopes, paper, and a pen from the collapsed sack on his head.

My Dear Ammachi,
  May this letter find you in good health. Thankamma was here all this time. I manage well. I cook several dishes.

Not long after her father died, her mother lost her dominion in the kitchen; she bemoaned the fact that she hadn't taught her daughter to cook before her wedding.

It's just me and JoJo now. He is my shadow. Without him I think I would miss you so much more. The only trouble he gives me is when I want to bathe him.

When she first tried it, JoJo fought her. Still, she poured water over his head, but then he turned pale, his eyelids fluttering like a moth's wings and his eyeballs rolling in their sockets. She was terrified, thinking he was about to have a convulsion. She never poured water on his head again, resorting instead to a washcloth for his hair and face. Even so, it's a daily battle. There's a war, she now sees, between the men of Parambil and the waters of Travancore. She won't share this with her poor mother. Maybe she already knows?

How can I be a better householder, a better mistress of the house?

She wishes she could erase that sentence, because her mother is no longer the householder or the mistress of the house. Her trials in the joint family home began soon after she became a widow, her brother's and sister-in-law's characters changing. Her mother likely sleeps on the verandah now and is bullied and treated like a maid. Meanwhile, at Parambil, her daughter lacks for nothing; grain threatens to spill out of the *ara*, and the lockbox is never short of coins.

When I pray in the evening, I say to myself, "My Ammachi is also praying right now." That way I feel close to you. I miss you so much, but I cry only at night when JoJo can't see me. I wish I'd brought my Bible. There isn't one here. I know Parambil is far, but please, Ammachi, come visit me. Come stay a few nights. My husband doesn't like to travel by boat. If you can't come, maybe I will try to come. I'll have to bring JoJo . . .

She pictures her mother reading the letter, her mother's tears staining the page just as hers do. She imagines her folding the letter under her pillow, then keeping it with her few possessions in her bedroll. Then, in her thoughts she sees a hand—her aunt's— probing in the bedroll while her mother bathes. It keeps her from asking her mother if she's eating better now that there's one less mouth to feed. A part of her *wants* those prying eyes to read those words and recognize the injustice in their souls. But it would only make things more difficult for her mother.

A reply comes in three weeks through the *achen* who performed the marriage and who travels to the diocese office in Kottayam every two weeks; there he mails and collects letters if there are any. A boy brings it over to the house. In her letter her mother showers her with love and kisses and says she's proud to imagine her daughter stepping into the role of householder thanks to Thankamma's coaching. At the end of the letter, her mother uncharacteristically and strongly dissuades her daughter from coming back to visit, giving no explanation. And she doesn't respond to her daughter's impassioned request that she please visit Parambil. The letter only makes her worry more about her mother's welfare.

Thankamma's homilies run wild in her head like braids that have come unraveled. *The bottom tier of a banana bunch always has an even number and the tier above is odd.* If someone tried to sneak off with just one, Thankamma would know; to maintain the pattern, they would have to remove a banana from each row and that would be obvious. But then again, who would steal? *Be observant*—that must have been Thankamma's lesson. Yet that morning, she isn't. She ignores a speckled hen's urgent clucking and its repeated and determined forays into the kitchen, shooing it away.

"She's ready to lay an egg, Ammachi!" JoJo says.

Did JoJo just call her "Ammachi"? *Little Mother*? Her chest swells with pride. She hugs him. "What would I do without you, little man?"

She grabs the hen and sets it on a sack in the pantry, then inverts a wicker basket over it. The hen fusses indignantly at her from the dark. "Forgive me. I'll be listening for when you're done, I promise."

There are few visitors. She feels very alone. She daydreams of her mother strolling up from the jetty, surprising her with a visit; she conjures this up so often that she finds herself glancing in the direction of the river several times a day.

The only visitors she's met properly are Georgie and Dolly from the tiny house closest to Parambil on the south side. It was Thankamma they came to see, and they came just once. Georgie is the son of her husband's brother, the one who tricked him out of his birthright. Their house sits on a two-acre plot that her husband gave to his nephew, because in the end Georgie's father died destitute, leaving Georgie and his twin brother nothing but debt. She liked Dolly *Kochamma* at once. (Since Dolly is at least five years older, *kochamma* is how she addresses her.) Dolly is fair, with doe eyes, a quiet woman who feels no pressure to speak, her expression one of saintly patience. Georgie is the lively, gregarious type, surprising the new bride by happily crowding into the cozy kitchen with the women, something her husband would never do. She wonders why her husband would generously rescue his nephew yet have so little to do with him. Shamuel says that Georgie isn't much of a farmer, not like the *thamb'ran*; but if her husband is the standard, no one measures up. Perhaps Georgie feels unworthy of his uncle's gift.

JoJo never lets his "Ammachi" out of his sight except when she goes to the stream to bathe, or when she goes to the river near the jetty and plunges in, something she loves to do. JoJo waits anxiously at home for her return. For JoJo, "bath" in any form remains a daily battle. She loves her bathing spot where the creek broadens, forming a pool, the water so slow and clear she sees tiny fish swimming in it, yet deep enough that her toes barely touch the bottom. The inclined washing stone squats on the bank beneath the shade of a rambutan tree, whose hairy red fruits hang down like ornaments.

Parambil is bursting with mangoes. Shamuel *pulayan* and his helpers bring in basket after basket, forming a mountain in the foyer outside the kitchen. Even after dispatching full bags to the *pulayar* huts, to the craftsmen, to their relatives, there are too many left. The sweet, fleshy varietal that comes in hues of yellow, orange, and pink fills the kitchen with a fruity perfume. JoJo's chin is raw from the juice that drips. She pulps as much as she can for syrups and jams. With the remaining pulp she makes *thera*—mango-fruit jerky. First she cooks it with sugar and roasted rice flour. She spreads this paste onto a woven mat as long and as wide as a door and places it in the sun. JoJo's task is to chase off birds and insects. After it dries, she adds more layers, waiting for each one to dry before spreading the next, until it is an inch thick and can be cut into strips. She's thrilled to see her husband carry away a plug of *thera* after breakfast and lunch, chewing on it as he works.

As a treat for JoJo she carves an unripe mango, splaying it open like a lotus flower—a trick her mother taught her—then sprinkling it with salt and red chili powder. JoJo finishes every last sour and spicy morsel and then walks around sucking air through pursed lips, his mouth on fire, but begging for more.

The *ara*—the central, windowless room of the old part of the house—is built like a fortress. Its one-piece door is three times as thick as a regular door, and it is protected by a huge lock for which she has the key. The sill is so high (to contain the paddy in there) that while her husband steps over it, she must climb over. Inside, her feet sink into the grain that reaches her knees. She opens the *ara* at least once a week to get money from the strongbox, and less often to remove paddy or to store it. Beneath the *ara* and accessed by small stairs from the adjacent unused bedroom is a dark, musty cellar where she keeps her preserves in tall porcelain jars. Razor-thin shafts of light come through the ventilation grille cut into the wood. Every house has its indoor and outdoor ghosts, and those in the Parambil house are still new to her. She resolves to speak to the one who inhabits the cellar because she has reason to suspect that it has an awful sweet tooth. She feels it hiding in the corner, behind the cobwebs, a gentle, sad, and perhaps frightened spirit, more wary of her than she of it. "Help yourself to anything you choose. I don't mind, but do put the lid back on tight," she says, standing bravely before it. She had planned to add, *Please don't try to bother me*, but just then JoJo's indignant voice rings out, "Amma-chi? Where are you? When you play hide-and-seek you have to hide where I can see you, or it's not fair!" She can't help giggling. A sudden lightness in the closed air of the cellar tells her the ghost is laughing too. Only after she emerges does she wonder if this spirit might be JoJo's deceased mother.

When the monsoon arrives and the clouds open, she's ecstatic. In her father's house, she and her cousin would oil their hair and step out into the downpour with their soap and coconut-fiber scrub, delighting in the heavenly waterfall. They anticipated the monsoon as much as they did Christmas, a time when body and soul are cleansed. The dust and the shed skins of insects cemented to stalks are swept away, leaving a brilliant shine on leaves. Without the monsoon, this land whose flag is green and whose coin is water would cease to exist.

When people grumble about flooding, about flare-ups of gout and rheumatism, they do so with a smile.

The rain never holds anyone back. Her umbrella becomes a halo that goes wherever she goes outdoors, while her bare feet happily slosh through puddles. Shamuel fashions a cap from palmyra bark that allows water to sheet off his head. But rain confines her husband in a way that baffles her; she's not brave enough to probe. She gradually gets accustomed to seeing him sitting for hours and sometimes all day on the verandah like a child forbidden from play, subdued, glowering at the clouds, as though that might persuade them to reverse their course. He has JoJo for company because JoJo is the same way. Once, an unexpected rain squall caught her husband unawares, without an umbrella as he approached the house; the raindrops seemed to make him stagger, his legs turning wobbly as he ran for shelter, as if stones and not water had fallen on his head. Another evening she sees him seated near the well, bathing by soaping and rinsing his body in sections. He doesn't see or hear her; she's tempted to run away but is too mesmerized by this sight of his body to move. She roils with emotions: guilt for spying on him; a terrible urge to giggle; embarrassment, as if she were the one naked; and a fascination with this sight of her husband fully revealed. He has never looked more powerful and frightening, even if this piece-meal bathing renders him childlike. There's a practiced ease and elegance to his miserliness with water, but the element missing from his movements is pleasure.

Every morning when she reawakens the embers in the hearth, the kitchen welcomes her like a sister with no secrets, and it makes her happy. She's come to believe this has everything to do with the benevolent presence of JoJo's mother. The cellar may be the spirit's preferred haunt and the place where what is amorphous comes as close as it can to taking physical form, but her spirit also drifts up here, drawn by the crackle of the hearth fire, or the voice of her child conversing with his new Ammachi. Why else do the bride's dishes turn out better than she has any right to expect, since Thankamma's recipes are hopelessly muddled in her head? She cannot give all the credit to the seasoned clay pots. No, she's being rewarded for taking loving care of JoJo. She feels one with the rhythm of the house and has the sense she is running it well.

CHAPTER 6

Couples

1903, Parambil

In the three years since her arrival, she's transformed the covered breezeway outside the kitchen into her personal space; she has a rope cot here where she and JoJo nap after lunch and where she teaches the five-year-old his letters. It allows her to keep an eye on the pots on the hearth and the paddy drying on mats in the *muttam*. While JoJo sleeps she sits on the cot, rereading the only printed material in the house: an old issue of the *Manorama*. She can't bring herself to throw the paper away. If she does, there'll be nothing, no words on which her eyes might rest. She's tired of chastising herself for not bringing a Bible with her to Parambil; instead, she directs her annoyance to JoJo's mother. It's unthinkable for a Christian household not to have the Holy Book.

JoJo stirs just as she sees Shamuel returning from the market with the shopping, a sack balanced on his head. He squats before her and empties the sack before folding it away.

Shamuel mops his face with his *thorthu*, his eyes falling on the newspaper. "What does it say?" he asks, pointing with his chin as he smooths out his *thorthu* and drapes it over his shoulder.

"Do you think something new crawled in there since the last time I read it to you, Shamuel?"

"*Aah, aah*," he says. His graying brows frame eyes that like a child's cannot conceal his disappointment.

The next week when Shamuel returns from the provision store and empties his sack, he says in his usual manner, "Matches. Two is coconut oil. Three is bitter gourd. Garlic, four. *Malayala Manorama*—" setting the paper down as though it's another vegetable. He can barely conceal his delight when she clutches the paper to herself, elated. "Weekly it will come," he says, proud to have pleased her. She knows that only her husband could have arranged this.

Later that morning, she spots her husband not far from the house, but ten feet off the ground, seated in the fork of a *plavu*, or jackfruit tree, his back against the trunk and his legs extended along the branch, a toothpick at the corner of his mouth. She's tempted to wave the newspaper to convey to him how grateful she is. She still marvels at his choosing these lofty perches instead of putting his legs up on the long arms of his *charu kasera*; his particular chair is striking in size because it is made to his proportions, yet it sits unoccupied on the verandah. She observes him up there; his face in profile is handsome, she thinks. A *pulayan* below him and out of her sight says something that makes her husband remove the toothpick and grin, showing strong, even teeth. *You should smile more often*, she thinks. He yawns and stretches, adjusting his position, and her stomach turns cold. A fall from even this modest height would be devastating. Whenever she spots him so high up a distant tree that he's no more than an eccentric bump marring a smooth trunk she cannot bear to look. Shamuel says that it's from that vantage point that he reads the land, plans the direction of irrigation ditches or new paddy fields.

In the evenings after she serves dinner and while her husband eats, she reads the *Manorama* to him. He never picks it up himself. The newspaper brightens her days, but it does nothing for a profound loneliness that she's ashamed to acknowledge. Thankamma, who had promised to return, writes that her husband has taken ill and is bedridden, so she has put off her visit indefinitely. As for her mother, three monsoons have come and gone and they have yet to see each other! Her mother tells her not to visit. Even if she wanted to, a young woman doesn't make such a journey alone. JoJo, who clings to her like a bracelet, won't go near the boat jetty, let alone climb into a boat. She suspects her husband is the same way.

When her formal evening prayers are done, she converses with the Lord. "I'm so happy about the newspaper. My husband clearly cares about my needs. Should I mention the other matter? I don't mean to complain, but if this is a Christian house, why don't we go to church? I know you've heard this before. If my mother could only come here, I wouldn't bother you. I could talk it over with her."

Perhaps in answer to her incessant prayers, at last a letter comes from her mother after long months of silence. Shamuel calls at the church on his way to the mill and this time he comes back excitedly holding the letter with both hands because he knows how precious it is; his excitement is nearly a match for hers.

My darling daughter, my treasure, how it warmed my heart to see your letter. You won't know how many times I kissed it. Your cousin Biji is getting married. I go to the church every day. I visit your father's grave and I pray for you. My most precious memories are with him, and then with you. What I am saying is please treasure each day you are in your marriage. To be a wife, to care for a husband, to have children, is there anything more valuable? Keep me in your prayers.

She revisits the letter many times in the ensuing days, kissing it each time like a sacred object. No matter how many times she reads it, it does nothing to diminish her worry. She resists the reality of life: a married woman gives up her childhood home forever, and a widow's fate is to remain in the home she married into.

*   *   *

The calendar on the wall—a pullout from the newspaper—looks like a mathematical table and astronomy chart. It shows lunar phases, the times each day that are inauspicious for setting out on a journey. Now it tells her this is the start of Lent, the fifty-day fast leading up to Good Friday. She will give up meat, fish, and milk, but on the first day she doesn't eat even a morsel.

When her husband sits down to dinner that evening she puts the freshly cut banana leaf and the *jeera* water on the table. He smooths out the leaf. She frames the words she's rehearsed. Just as she opens her mouth to speak, he flattens the spine of the banana leaf with his fist—*Crack! Crack!*—startling her. He splashes *jeera* water on the green mirrored surface, brushing the excess off in the direction of the *muttam*. The moment is gone. She quietly serves the rice, the pickle, the yogurt . . . then she approaches with the meat, to see if he'll wave it off on this first day of Lent. But no, he's impatient for it. What made her think this year would be different from previous years?

In the days that follow, neither meat nor fish crosses her lips; she misses the companionship of a household that is fasting, but her loneliness only strengthens her determination.

"You should eat more," Shamuel says, halfway through Lent. "You're getting too thin." It's forward of Shamuel to speak this way. "The *thamb'ran* says so. He's worried." She feels like the people on a hunger strike pictured in the paper, camped outside the Secretariat: becoming more diminished in order to be seen.

"If the *thamb'ran* thinks so, he should tell me."

That night she puts off prayers and putters around with other things. At last, when she's sleepy, she covers her head and stands facing the crucifix on the east wall of her bedroom, following tradition, because the Messiah would approach Jerusalem from the east. No prayers, no words will come to her mouth. Does God not feel her disappointment? Eventually she says, "Lord, I'm not going to keep asking. You see the obstacles in my path. If you want me in church, then you must help. That's all I'll say. Amen."

Thankamma had said that the secret to getting what you wanted from your husband was to make a wish as you prepared jackfruit *halwa*. But it isn't halwa that opens the door, it's her *erechi olarthi-yathu*. She prepares it in the morning by roasting and then powdering coriander and fennel seeds, pepper, cloves, cardamom, cinnamon, and star anise in a mortar and rubbing this dry mix into the cubes of mutton to marinate. In the afternoon she browns onions along with fresh coconut slivers, mustard seeds, ginger, garlic, green chilies, turmeric, and curry leaves and more of the dry spice mix, then adds the meat. She flattens the fire to embers, uncovering the pot so the gravy thickens and covers each cube of meat with a heavy, dark coating. That night, once she sends JoJo to say to his father "*choru vilambi*"—*rice is served*—she finishes the dish by refrying the meat in coconut oil with fresh curry leaves and diced coconut. She brings it out sizzling, the oil still spitting on the blackened meat's surface. Before she's done ladling it on his banana leaf, he's popped a piece in his mouth. He can't resist.

She stands quietly to one side as he eats, but closer than usual. She's already read the newspaper to him in the past few nights and must await the new edition. God suddenly gives her the nerve to speak.

"Is the meat all right?" she asks. She knows it has never tasted better.

The words have left her mouth like water from the long spout of a *kindi* and she watches them arrive at the cup of his ears. It's as though another human being has spoken, not she.

Just when she thinks he's annoyed at her boldness, the big head sways from side to side, signaling his approval. The surge of pleasure she feels makes her want to clap, to dance. For once, he sits after he finishes, not rising to rinse off his hands from the *kindi*.

Can he hear the hammering of her heart?

JoJo, who peeks at them from behind a pillar, is astonished to hear her speak to his father. He whispers much too loud, "Ammachi, don't tell him! Tomorrow I promise I'll bathe."

She clamps her hand to her mouth, but not before a giggle escapes.

There's a terrible pause and then a strange explosion; an impossibly loud and unexpected laugh emanates from her husband. JoJo emerges into the light, puzzled. When he realizes that they are laughing at him, he races up and smacks her on the thigh, crying and furious, running away before she can grab him. This only renews her husband's guffaws, and he throws himself against the back of his chair. The laughter transforms him, revealing a side of him she has not seen.

He wipes his eyes with his left hand, still smiling.

And words come tumbling out of her mouth. She tells him that when it was time for JoJo's bath that afternoon, she'd looked everywhere for him, eventually finding him high up in the jackfruit tree, stuck there on the *plavu*. Her husband's bright smile is still there. She goes on: JoJo is learning his letters and his numbers, but only if she bribes him with a treat of raw mango dotted with chili powder. She herself prefers the varietal of plantain that Shamuel brought today . . . She hears herself prattling and stops. The crickets fill the void, and now a bullfrog joins the chorus.

Then her husband asks her a question that he might have asked a long, long time ago: "*Sughamano?*" *Is everything good for you?* He looks directly at her. It's the first time he's studied her so intently since he stood before her in church almost three years ago.

She tries to meet his gaze; in his eyes is a force as powerful as that of the altar in the church where they married. She recalls the line in her wedding service: *As Christ is the head of the church so also the husband is the head of the house.*

Suddenly she understands why he has kept his distance since the day of their marriage, saying little, but from afar ensuring her needs and comfort; it isn't indifference but the opposite. He recognizes that he's someone who can so easily make her fearful.

She drops her gaze. Her ability to speak has flown away. But she's been asked a question. He's waiting.

Her legs feel unsteady. She has a strange impulse to go to him, to brush that knotted forearm with her fingers. It's an urge for affection, for human touch. At home she had daily hugs and kisses, her mother's body to warm her at night. Here, but for JoJo, she'd wither to nothing.

She hears his chair scrape back because he has given up on a response. She says softly, "I miss my mother."

He raises his eyebrows, perhaps unsure whether he imagined the sound.

"And it would be nice to go to church," she says in a voice that is unnaturally loud.

He seems to turn this thought over. Then he rinses his hands with the *kindi*, steps down to the *muttam*, and is gone. Her heart contracts. *Foolish, foolish to have asked for so much!*

Later that night, once JoJo is asleep, she goes back to the kitchen to clean up, and to cover the embers with a coconut husk, allowing them to survive till morning. Then she returns to the room where she sleeps with JoJo, her heart heavy.

She's startled to see an open metal trunk on the floor. The stack of folded white clothing inside must belong to JoJo's mother. All she brought with her to Parambil was her wedding *chatta* and *mundu* and three extra sets, all the same bright white, the traditional Saint Thomas Christian woman's garb. She left behind the colorful half-saris and skirts of childhood. Her *chattas* are tight at the shoulders and they faintly outline her budding breasts, when the formless garment is meant to suggest that there's nothing there at all. She'd taken to wearing an oversized and threadbare *chatta* and *mundu* that Thankamma left behind. The *chattas* in the trunk, which must belong to JoJo's mother, fit perfectly. She studies herself in the mirror. Her body is changing; she's taller and has put on weight. Over a year ago, she bled for the first time. It scared her, even though her mother had warned her it would happen. She brewed ginger tea for the cramping and she fashioned menstrual cloths, calling on her memory of seeing them hanging on the line. When she put her laundered menstrual cloth out to dry, she camouflaged it with towels and linen. For four days she felt ill at ease, so distracted while trying to carry on. There was no one she could commiserate with, or celebrate with, for that matter. Even now, those four or five days are a great trial.

At the very bottom of the trunk, she finds a Bible. *You had a Bible all these days and never told me?* She's too excited by this find to be annoyed for very long, but she resolves to mention it the next time she visits the cellar.

When Sunday comes she's surprised to find her husband in his white *juba* and *mundu*—his wedding clothes. She's so accustomed to seeing him bare-chested, his *mundu* half hitched, and a *thorthu* over his left shoulder, indistinguishable from the *pulayar* who work for him. Only his height and breadth set him apart, a sign that he grew up in a house where there was ample food. He calls out to Shamuel: "Ask Sara to come stay with JoJo till we come back from church."

She races to get dressed. "Lord, I'll thank You properly once I'm in Your house."

They set off over land, heading the opposite direction to the boat jetty. She clutches the Bible, scurrying to keep up, taking two steps for each of his. She's so excited that her feet barely touch the ground. After a bit they come to the rivulet with its single-log bridge, slippery with moss. "You go first," he says, and she scampers over. He follows, feet planted carefully, his jaws clenched. Once across, he rests a hand on the burden stone, gathering himself before they head on. Their walk to church is much longer than if they had gone by boat; eventually they cross the river on a bridge wide enough for carts.

The sight of people streaming into church thrills her, though she knows no one. "I'll be waiting there," he says, pointing to a spreading *peepal* with aerial roots hanging down like whiskers over the church's graveyard. She's too excited to do anything but go on into the church, pulling her *kavani* over her head. She's forgotten what it's like to see so many at worship, to feel bodies all around, to be part of the fabric instead of a thread torn from the whole.

The men are on the left, women on the right, an imaginary line separating them. She relishes the familiar phrases of the Eucharist. When the *achen* raises the veil and shivers it in his hands, she feels God's presence, feels the Holy Spirit wash over her, wave after wave, lifting her off her feet. Joyful tears blur her sight. "I'm here, Lord! I am here!" she cries silently.

When the service is over, she comes outside and spots her husband emerging from the graveyard, his expression brooding. Excited conversation and laughter from the jetty and in the ferryboats reach their ears. They head back in silence.

"It's five years ago that she died . . ." he says suddenly, his voice laden with emotion.

JoJo's mother. It's strange to hear him speak of her with such feeling. Is it envy she feels? Is she hoping that he might speak about her one day with the same passion? She's silent, fearful that anything she says will stop the flow of words.

"How can you forgive a God," he says, "who takes a mother from her child?"

The spaces between his sentences feel as wide as a river. This time when they ford the log bridge, he goes first. He waits on the other side, studying his young wife who wears the clothes of his late wife, as though seeing her for the first time.

"I wish she could see us," he says, standing still. "I wish she could see how well you care for JoJo. How much love he has for you. That would make her happy. I wish she could see that."

She feels dizzy from the praise, clutching the Bible that once belonged to the woman he just invoked. She is standing close to him and cranes up to see his face, feeling she might topple back.

"I *know* she can see us," she says with conviction. She could tell him why, but he doesn't need explanations, just the truth. "She watches over us in everything. She stays my hand when I want to add more salt. She reminds me when the rice boils over."

His eyebrows go up and then his face relaxes. He sighs. "JoJo has no memory of his mother."

"That's all right," she says. "With her blessing, I'm his mother now. There's no need for him to remember or to grieve."

They haven't moved. He peers down at her with his intense gaze. She doesn't flinch. She sees something giving way in him, as though the door to the locked *ara*, to the fortress of his body, has swung open. His expression turns to one of contentment. The trace of a smile seems to signal the end of a long torment. When he resumes walking, it's at an easier pace, husband and wife in step.

The following Sunday, he suggests she go alone to church by boat—since he's not coming, she doesn't need to make the long walk. He escorts her to the jetty, where a few other women and couples are gathered. As the boatmen pole the boat off the bank, she looks back and sees her husband standing in a cluster of areca nut trees, their narrow, pale trunks a contrast with his thick, dark one. He's rooted to the ground more firmly than any tree. Not even Damodaran could dislodge him.

Their eyes lock. As the boat pulls away, she registers his expression: sadness and envy. She aches for him, a man who won't travel by water, who perhaps has never heard the sound of water parting before the prow, never felt the exhilaration of being carried by the current, or the spray as the boatman's pole clears the water. He'll never know the bracing sensation of diving headfirst into the river, the roar of entry followed by enveloping silence. All water is connected, and her world is limitless. He stands at the limits of his.

On her sixteenth birthday, she hears a commotion outside the kitchen and the excited voices of children. The ducks clustered around the back steps squawk and struggle to take flight, forgetting their clipped wings. She knows who it is even before she hears the clink of a heavy chain and before she turns to see the ancient eye that somehow peers in through the kitchen window. She laughs. "Damo! How did you know?" This is a new sensation: to gaze at that eye without the distraction of the immense body. She marvels at his tangled eyelashes, the delicately patterned, cinnamon-colored iris. Suddenly she's gazing into Damo's soul . . . and he into hers. She feels his love, his concern, just as when he greeted her on her first night as a bride.

"Give me a moment. I have a treat for you." She's at a delicate phase in making *meen vevichathu*. She lowers the seer-fish fillets into the fiery red gravy that simmers in the clay pot. It owes its vibrant color to chili powder, and its muddy consistency to the cooked-down shallots, ginger, and spices. But the key to its signature flavor is kokum, or Malabar tamarind. She must taste it repeatedly, balancing tart with salt, adding kokum water if the curry isn't sour enough, and removing kokum pieces if it's too sour.

The impatient giant stamps his foot, shaking dust from the rafters.

"Stop! If my curry turns out badly, I'll tell the *thamb'ran* who's responsible."

She emerges with a hastily mixed bucket of rice and ghee. Damo's grin reminds her of JoJo at his naughtiest. Caesar, the pariah dog, dances excitedly but is careful to stay clear of the giant's feet. Damodaran pinches the lip of the bucket, lifts it from her hands, and inverts its contents into his mouth as if it were a thimble. He sweeps its edge with his tongue, then puts it down and probes with his trunk for anything he has missed.

Unni, perched on Damo's neck, his bare feet hooked behind the huge ears, looks like a cat stranded up a tree. The mahout's frown is hard to see on his dark, pockmarked face, but his thick eyebrows are crossing in the middle.

"Look!" Unni says, pointing to the mess on the *muttam*. "I tried to steer him to his spot by the tree, but no, he had to come by the kitchen first."

She leans her hand on Damo's trunk. "He came for my birthday. No one here knows, but somehow he does. God bless you for coming, my Damo." Suddenly she feels shy—she doesn't speak to her husband in such loving tones. Damo curls his trunk into a salute.

When she finishes in the kitchen, she goes to Damo at his usual spot by the oldest palm. Unni has chained Damo's back leg to a stump, but it's more reminder than restraint. Damo can snap it as easily as a child breaks a twig, and he often does. As usual, every child around Parambil has come running, word having spread that Damo is home. The toddlers wear just the shiny *aranjanam* around the waist, not the least self-conscious about their nakedness, though wary of Damo as they hide behind the older children. She spots JoJo, one arm around the shoulder of the blacksmith's son, who is also six years old, but JoJo is a head taller. She stands back observing, as intrigued by the children as by the elephant.

Damo dips his trunk in the bucket of water and sprays his spectators. The little ones scatter, shrieking happily. When they regroup, he does it again.

Damo is fastidious. Unlike a cow or goat, he won't eat if his excrement is lying around. If Unni wants him to stay in one spot, he must keep shoveling away whatever pushes out of Damodaran's rear end. It's a never-ending task for Unni, and endlessly fascinating to the young audience.

"What's that?" the blacksmith's daughter says, pointing to the thick, crooked club hanging down from Damo's belly, its blunt end a mossy green. She's seven years old. "Is that another trunk?"

"No, silly," her brother says, speaking with authority despite being a year younger than her. "It's his Little-Thoma."

The boys laugh. The toddlers, who don't understand, laugh loudest of all.

"Ha!" the blacksmith's daughter says huffily. "It's not so little then, is it? If you ask me, his trunk looks more like a Little-Thoma than that funny thing."

There's a silence as the children consider this question. The brother turns to examine the goldsmith's two-year-old grandson, a bow-legged, befuddled, and potbellied baby who has one finger in his nostril; all of them now study this little fellow's uncircumcised, puffy penis that ends in a wrinkled pout; then they compare it to Damodaran's trunk.

"I suppose it does," the blacksmith's boy says.

Damo's swaying trunk seems to exist independently of its owner, its movements decidedly human. While his forefoot pins down a coconut branch, the pincer tip of Damo's trunk strips off the leaves in one graceful stroke. He smacks the bundled leaves against the tree to rid them of insects, then folds them onto his lip. As he chews, his trunk swings back down, but then, like a restless, playful schoolboy, he snatches the towel off Unni's shoulder and waves it like a flag before Unni snatches it back.

"If only *my* Little-Thoma could do all that his trunk does," she overhears the blacksmith's boy say, "I'd reach up and pluck mangoes or even coconuts." She watches JoJo listening intently, one hand discreetly feeling between his legs. She slips away, hand over her mouth, waiting till she's out of earshot before she collapses with laughter.

That evening she serves her husband the *meen vevichathu*. He nods approvingly after tasting it. It will soon be five years, but she still worries about her cooking.

"As I was making it, Damo came and put his eye to the kitchen window."

He laughs and shakes his head. "Do you have ghee rice I can take to him tonight?" His expression is like JoJo's asking for another raw mango.

"But he had one bucket when he came," she says.

"Oh, did he? Well, then . . ."

"But I can get more."

He looks pleased. He clears his throat. "Damo's never gone to the kitchen before. Means he likes you," he says, looking up with a shy, teasing glance. She sets the newspaper down and heads to the kitchen to prepare the ghee rice.

Yes, I know Damo likes me. He came to greet me on my birthday. I know what he's thinking. It's you whose thoughts I never know.

When she returns with the ghee rice, her husband ignores it. With his eyebrows he invites her to sit; he places a tiny cloth bag with a drawstring on the table before her. She pulls out two huge, heavy gold hoop earrings, intricately worked on the outside but hollow within, otherwise their weight would tear through the ear. A filigreed nut hides the post and screw. She stares in disbelief. Is she truly the owner of these *kunukku*? So that's why she's seen the goldsmith trudging back and forth over the last month. All her life she's admired *kunukku*. They don't go into the fleshy part of the ear, but through the curling rim on top where it thins out like the lip of a seashell. She'll need to pierce the cartilage and then enlarge the hole by packing it with areca leaves until it's big enough to accept this thick post and screw. Many women wear just the post and screw; on special occasions when they connect the hoops, they project out from the ear like a cupped hand.

Unlike many brides who come with jewelry as part of their dowry, all she has is her wedding ring, the tiny gold *minnu* that he tied around her neck in the ceremony, and two small gold studs that were hers when her ears were first pierced at the age of five.

She can't believe he remembered her birthday when he had never done so before. Now she's the one with no words. Her husband never picks up the paper but as a farmer he's acutely aware of dates and seasons. In the distance she hears leaves smacking against a tree, the sound of Damo feeding. Not for the first time she wonders if the two giants are in league.

When she can bring herself to meet his gaze, her husband is smiling. He leaves without a word, taking the bucket with him; he'll sleep on the cot next to Damo while Unni heads home to visit his wife.

When Damo is at Parambil, the ground vibrates with his movements. The sounds of his feeding—the snapping of branches, the crushing of leaves—soothe her. But a few days later, Damodaran returns to the logging camp; like the *thamb'ran*, he's happiest when working. In his absence the quiet of Parambil feels exaggerated.

That night, just as she's drifting off to sleep, her husband appears. She sits up, alarmed, wondering if something is wrong. His frame fills the doorway, blocking out the light. His expression is calm, reassuring. All is well. He holds the tiny oil lamp in one hand and now he extends the other.

She eases free of the sleeping JoJo, takes the proffered hand, and he pulls her to her feet effortlessly. Her fingers remain coddled in the nest of his palm as they step out. This is a new sensation, to be holding hands; neither of them lets go. But where to? They turn into his room.

Suddenly the hammering of her heart is so loud that she's sure it echoes under the rafters and will wake JoJo. Blood surges into her limbs, as though her body knows what's about to happen even if her mind is five steps behind. At that moment she cannot know that the nights when he comes silently and leads her away will come to be so precious to her; she doesn't know that instead of her lips quivering, her body trembling as it does now, instead of her insides turning cold and her legs threatening to buckle, she'll feel a surge of excitement and pride, a longing when she sees him standing there, his hand extended, wanting her.

But what she feels now is panic. She's sixteen. She has some notion of what's supposed to take place, even if that knowledge is inadvertent and from observing God's other creatures in nature . . . but she's unprepared. How exactly does it happen? If she could have brought herself to ask that question, whom might she have asked? Even with her mother it would have been so awkward.

He gently guides her to stretch out beside him on his raised teak bed; it doesn't escape him that she's frightened, shivering, on the verge of tears, and that her teeth are chattering. In lieu of spoken reassurances, he gathers her to him, one arm under her head, enfolding her, holding her. Nothing more. They lie this way for a long time.

Eventually her breathing slows. The warmth of his body stops her shivering. Is this what the Bible meant? *Jacob* lay *with Leah. David* lay *with Bathsheba.* The night is still. At first, she hears only the hum of the stars. Then a pigeon coos on the roof. She hears the three-note call of the bulbul. A faint scuffle in the *muttam* and soft padding sounds must be Caesar chasing his tail. Also a repetitive drumming that she cannot place. Then it comes to her: it's his heartbeat, loud, and almost synchronous with hers.

That low-pitched, muffled thud reassures her, reminds her that she's in the arms of the man she married almost five years ago. She thinks of the quiet ways he's attended to her needs, from arranging for the newspaper to escorting her to church for the first time, and now walking her to the boat jetty every Sunday. He expresses his affection indirectly in those acts of caring, in the way he looks at her with pride as she talks to JoJo, or as she reads the paper to him. But on this night during dinner he conveyed his feelings directly but wordlessly through precious earrings that are the sign of a mature woman, a wise wife. This moment could have come at any time in the last few years, but he waited.

After a while, he lifts his head up to look into her face; he raises his eyebrows and tilts his head questioningly. She understands he's asking if she's ready. The truth is she doesn't know. But she knows she trusts him; she has faith that if he brought her here it's because he knows she's ready. For once she doesn't look away; she holds his gaze and peers into his eyes, seeing into his soul for the first time in the four years she has been his wife. She nods.

Lord, I am ready.

He hovers over her, guides her to receive him. She bites her lips at the first sharp pain, muffling the cry that escapes. He pauses and retreats out of concern, but she pulls him down, hiding her face against the valley between his shoulder and chest so that he might not witness her shock, her disbelief at what is happening. Until that moment when he held her hand and led her to this room, they had never touched, not even by accident. Neither holding his hand nor lying in his arms prepared her for this. She feels stupid and ashamed for not knowing, for never imagining that what was supposed to "unfold in its own time," as Thankamma once said, meant this breach of her body, meant taking him wholly into her insides. She feels betrayed by all the women who withheld this knowledge from her, who might have better prepared her. His extreme gentleness, his consideration for her is unnaturally paired with that first searing pain, then the dull discomfort it gives way to. His repetitive thrusts intensify, the pace quicker. How does this end? What must she do? Just when she fears he will break her, just when she wants to cry out for him to stop, his body stiffens, his back arches, and his expression becomes unrecognizable, pained—as though she inadvertently broke him. She is naïve participant and horrified observer. He tries to stifle an agonal moan but fails . . . and comes to a shuddering stop. He lies on her, spent, a dead weight, his skin wet with perspiration.

Her thoughts are in turmoil, but she rejoices as it dawns on her that she has survived the ordeal. She has an urge to giggle at being pinned like this, by his sudden helplessness. She has not just endured, but it is her body, her contribution to what transpired that has left him robbed of all strength and rooted to her. Belatedly, as she slowly recovers her composure, she recognizes that she has blundered into full womanhood. The seconds tick by, and his weight crushes her so she can barely breathe, yet paradoxically she doesn't want him to move, doesn't want her feeling of power, of pride, and of ascendancy over him to end.

In later years, on the rare occasions when his appearance at her door, hand extended, is inconvenient, she never refuses, because in his tender embrace and the inelegant act of what follows, he expresses what he cannot say and what she needs to hear and what she begins to feel now for the first time lying under him: that she's integral to his world, just as he *is* her world. She cannot imagine now that the pleasure she sees on his face will be something she too will experience from time to time, or that she'll unobtrusively find ways to guide him in a manner that pleases her. For now, she's so full with him she feels he has split her in two, and yet for the first time since her marriage, she is whole, complete.

Gradually, she feels a loosening, a slackening of his grip of her insides, and at last he rolls to one side, just his slab of a thigh over hers. His withdrawal leaves her insides smarting, leaves her exposed, and leaves a void between her legs in a place once sealed to the world. She's no longer sure of this most intimate part of herself that feels forever altered. There's wetness trickling down her thigh. She wishes to bathe, and yet, despite the raw, throbbing pain, she is reluctant to leave, relishing this sensation of her husband fast asleep, unconscious next to her, his head nestling against her, a hand draped over her chest, much in the manner of his son.

In the days that follow she feels free to say much more to him at dinner, not just the events of the household, but her thoughts, her feelings, and even her memories, without worrying about his response. Listening *is* talking for him; there's an eloquence to this kind of attentiveness; it's rare, and yet he's generous with it. He alone amongst all the people she knows uses his two ears and one mouth in that exact proportion. She loves him in a way she didn't know she could before. Love, she thinks, isn't ownership, but a sense that where her body once ended, it begins anew in him, extending her reach, her confidence, and her strength. As with anything so rare and precious, it comes with a new anxiety: the fear of losing him, the fear of that heartbeat ceasing. That would mean the end of her.

Parambil settles into its rhythm: mouths to feed, mangoes to pickle, paddy to thresh, Easter, Onam, Christmas . . . a cycle she knows so well and by which she measures her days. To an observer, everything is the same. But after that night, all distance between husband and wife vanishes.

"Lord, thank you . . ." she says in her prayers. "I won't mention specifics. After all, what don't you know about my life on earth? But I have a question. When my husband fled the altar four years ago, I heard your voice say to me, 'I am with you always.' Did you speak to him too? Did you say, 'Turn back'? Did you say, 'She is the one I chose for you'?"

She waits. "Because I am, Lord. I am the one."

CHAPTER 7

A Mother Knows

1908, Parambil

One morning, in her nineteenth year on earth, she wakes unrested, unable to rise, weighed down by a blanket of melancholy. JoJo tries to cheer her up, weaving her a ball from coconut fronds. "Over-under, over-under, then *under*-over, *under*-over, all right?" he says, forgetting who taught him. He is ten and already taller than his Ammachi, who will soon be twice his age, but whenever they are alone he reverts to acting much younger. An anxious JoJo helps her to the kitchen, but the simple act of blowing on the embers leaves her breathless.

After lunch she retreats to her bedroom and only wakes when her husband's cool hand strokes her brow. She is shocked to see the sun is going down. She has done nothing for dinner; she bursts into tears. He sends JoJo away with a glance.

Why the tears? he asks with his eyebrows.

She shakes her head. He insists.

"You must forgive me. I don't know what's come over me." His expression says he knows there's more to it.

Ever since their marriage was consummated, she confides freely in her husband except when it comes to her mother. She's ashamed for him to know just how impoverished her life had been before her marriage. When she was sixteen, she'd found the courage to beg Shamuel to accompany her on a trip to see her mother; she had Shamuel ask the *thamb'ran*'s permission. The *thamb'ran* agreed. She'd used Shamuel because she didn't want to put her husband into a position of saying no to her. She wrote to her mother giving her the date of her visit. She had made up her mind that if she found her mother miserable, she would bring her back to Parambil. She could only hope her husband understood; a husband had no obligation to care for his mother-in-law. Two days before she was to leave, her mother's letter came, emphatically forbidding her from visiting, saying it would only make matters worse. Her mother added that her brother-in-law promised that they would all visit Parambil very soon. Of course that never happened.

"I worry about my mother," she says at last, weeping, relieved to finally confess what she has kept from him. "I know in my bones she is being mistreated, even starved. After my father died, my uncle wasn't kind to us. My mother's letters talk of everything but herself. I can feel her suffering."

Her husband's anvil-like hand remains on her brow but his face is very still.

The next day, he and Shamuel are gone before she wakes. There's no sign of them all day and by nightfall they have not returned. She is beside herself with worry.

The following afternoon, a bullock cart jolts up the path from the boat jetty, brushing past the overgrown tapioca. Shamuel sits in front with the driver. A familiar figure peers over his shoulder.

She'd forgotten her mother's tall forehead and her pinched nose, both of which are exaggerated because she's so thin, her hair white, and her cheeks collapsed from missing molars. It's as though fifty years and not eight have gone by. Her mother clutches her meager belongings: a Bible, a silver cup, and a bundle of clothes, as she descends stiffly from the cart. Mother and daughter cling to each other, their roles reversed: it's the mother returning to the safety of her daughter's arms, crying into her bosom, no longer hiding the misery of the intervening years.

"*Molay*," her mother says, when she can finally speak, "God bless your husband. At first, when I saw him, I thought something happened to you. He took one look around and he understood. 'Come, let's go,' he said. *Molay*, I was so embarrassed, because your uncle wasn't pleasant—didn't even offer water. Then *she* pipes up behind him to say I owed them money for . . . for breathing, I suppose. Your husband raised his finger." And she holds up a digit as if testing the wind. "'Not another word,' he said. 'This isn't how my wife's mother should be living.' I shook that dust from my feet and didn't look back."

Shamuel, grinning, nevertheless scolds the daughter. "Why didn't you say something to the *thamb'ran* before? Your mother was living like the women seeking alms outside the church! Just a tiny corner of the verandah for her sleeping mat."

Her mother drops her head, ashamed. She says, "Your husband put us on the boat. He said he'll come another way."

In the room they will soon share she watches her mother take in the teak *almirah* where she can put her clothes, the writing desk, the dresser with the mirror. Her mother sees her own reflection and self-consciously tucks white strands of hair behind her ears. In the kitchen she serves her mother tea, then quickly grinds coconut, retrieves eggs from the pantry, reheats a fish and a chicken curry, chops beans for a *thoren*, telling Shamuel not to leave before eating. "Oh, my baby," her mother says when she's served, tears trickling down her cheeks. "When have I seen meat and fish and egg together on the same leaf?"

Later, her mother sits on the rope cot watching her. She grabs her daughter as she rushes to and fro. "Stop! No *halwa*, no *laddu*, nothing. I want nothing more! Just sit here and let me see you, let me hold you, my precious." In the way her mother looks at her she sees how much she herself has changed, no longer the child bride her mother last saw, but the capable mother of JoJo, and the mistress of Parambil. Her mother runs her fingers through her daughter's thick hair that she has missed combing and braiding; she turns her daughter's face this way and that in front of the lamp. "My little girl is a woman now—" Abruptly her mother pulls back, her eyebrows rising as she takes in the discoloration of the cheeks and across the bridge of the nose, like bat wings. Wide-eyed, she exclaims, "My goodness, *molay*! You're with child!"

She knows at once that her mother must be right. Perhaps it isn't strange that her heart called out for her mother, now that she's to be one.

At midnight she's pacing the verandah alone, rejoicing at a reunion she dreamed about, but also praying and worrying. At one in the morning, she sees a distant glow from a torch made of dried, tightly bundled palm fronds.

She runs to greet her husband as if he's been away for years. She can't help herself, jumping into his arms like a child, and wrapping her legs around a body that feels like an overheated furnace after his two-day march. He throws aside the torch, and it sparks out against the ground. He holds her. She buries her head against him, overcome with relief. She pleads silently, *Never grow old, never die*, knowing it's too much to ask. *My rock, my fortress, my deliverer.*

He washes by the well. His lids are heavy as he eats dinner. He recounts his route, and she traces his circuitous path on her palm. He has walked for eighteen hours and over fifty miles.

He heads to his bed, too tired to even carry his lamp. She follows him past the threshold of his room. She's rarely in there without his leading her in. She lies next to him. She takes his hand and puts it on her belly, and smiles at him. He's puzzled. Then, ever so slowly, understanding shows on his weary features and he smiles. She hears a low exclamation. He squeezes her to him, but then catches himself, fearful of being too rough in his embrace. If God gave her one moment in time that she could stretch out for as long as she lives, this would be it.

She hears his breathing become deeper, steady. His expression is still joyful in sleep, and his hand stays on her belly, cupping his child. In that sheltered, sacred nook between his arm and chest, she's at peace. "Forgive me, Lord." She thought her prayers were unanswered. But God's time isn't the same as hers. God's calendar isn't the one hanging in her kitchen. *To everything there is a season, and a time to every purpose under heaven.*

It's pointless chastising herself for not rescuing her mother sooner. *Happened is happened*, she thinks. The past is unreliable, and only the future is certain, and she must look to it with faith that the pattern will be revealed.

The girl who shivered at the altar, who now lies beside her husband, who is now with child, cannot see that one day she will be the respected matriarch of the Parambil family. She doesn't know that in time she'll earn the label with which JoJo has christened her, the first English word the little fellow learned, and at once offered her, not to tease her about being tiny, but in tribute: "Big." He called her "Big Ammachi." She doesn't know that she'll soon be *Big* Ammachi to one and all.

CHAPTER 8

Till Death Do Us Part

1908, Parambil

With the birth of her daughter, her previous life is swept away. Her body is at the beck and call of a beloved tyrant who rudely summons her from sleep, demands access, and by sheer force sucks milk from her breasts that are so swollen that she struggles to recognize them as her own.

She finds it hard to remember those nights when it was just JoJo and her, sleeping coiled together, his fingers woven into her hair to ensure that she didn't abandon him to his recurring nightmare of being adrift on the river. Was there really a time when she had three pots on the fire, one ear cocked for the hen about to lay its egg, and the other for the rustle of rain, so that the drying paddy could be brought in? And all the while pretending to be a tiger for JoJo? Now, she hardly leaves the old bedroom next to the *ara*, which they had put to use for her labor. Her connection to Parambil feels doubly cemented with a daughter who'll claim this as home, at least till she marries.

Dolly *Kochamma*, without being asked, moved in during the last stages of her confinement, to help with the household tasks and with JoJo. Quiet and easygoing, Dolly never speaks of the challenges she and Georgie face. On his small plot of land, the gregarious Georgie should grow enough coconuts, tapioca, and bananas to live on, and even have a small profit, but somehow, they barely get by. Shamuel says it is from poor planning, along with his weakness for schemes such as planting wheat instead of rice, because it was less work, only to find wheat grew poorly and there was little market for it. Georgie must know he is a disappointment to his uncle and so he stays away, but every morning, when the baby falls asleep after her ten o'clock feeding, Dolly *Kochamma* oils the new mother's hair, and massages her with spiced coconut oil. When Big Ammachi thanks her profusely, Dolly says, "Your husband rescued us when we had nothing and I was pregnant with my first child. JoJo's mother did this for me. Now, you're doing me a favor, allowing me to be of use." Dolly encourages her to go to the stream and bathe properly. "Don't worry. Baby *Mol*"—for now the child has no name other than "Baby Girl"—"won't stop breathing in your absence."

Meanwhile her mother has taken over the kitchen. The hollow-cheeked, gray-haired woman who stepped down so gingerly from the bullock cart has a decade's worth of bottled-up thoughts to share, even if she doesn't have quite the energy she once did.

JoJo doesn't understand why his Big Ammachi spends so much time with the baby, or why he must be quiet when the baby sleeps. One morning his jealousy drives him to climb high up the *plavu* and cry for help as though he's stuck up the tree. When he's ignored, he's furious, and comes down, wraps his valuables in a *thorthu*, and announces his permanent relocation to Dolly *Kochamma*'s house. Dolly and Georgie indulge him; their children spread a mat for him next to theirs. This is how JoJo spends his first night away from Parambil, praying the place will fall apart in his absence.

When word comes the next day that his Big Ammachi misses him, JoJo races back, but he slows at the threshold, pretending he's returning only under duress. His mother smothers him with kisses till he's forced to give up his façade. "You're my little man! How can I go down to the cellar for pickles without you? That ghost welcomes me as long as you're there." Her little man invites his new friends over, and soon the *muttam* echoes with the sounds of children laughing and playing; the cacophony reminds her of her own childhood, surrounded by the constant sounds of cousins and neighbors. Thankfully, Baby Mol sleeps through most anything. Now and then, while nursing Baby Mol, she'll hear one of the children wailing. In the past, she'd have raced out to investigate, but now she tells herself, "A crying child is a breathing child."

After a month she moves back to her bedroom, preferring the familiarity of the bamboo mat she unrolls on its floor to the raised bed in the original bedroom next to the *ara* where she gave birth. Baby Mol is beside her atop a folded towel, while JoJo and her mother sleep on their mats on her other side. In the mornings, each mat is rolled up around its pillow and the bedrolls stacked on a raised ledge.

Every evening, after his bath, her husband appears at the threshold of her room. Her mother, if she's there, feigns a task in the kitchen and disappears. Words may escape the mountain, but only when he's alone with his wife. His biceps bulge as he brings the bundle of cloth and flesh that is his infant to his bare chest, while the new mother marvels at the sight of Baby Mol swallowed by his huge, callused hands. "Are you eating well?" she asks. "Yes, 'Big Ammachi,'" he says, teasing her. "But your mother's *erechi olarthiyathu* isn't as good as yours." He isn't aware that he's paid her a compliment she cherishes.

She recalls Thankamma saying her brother was like a coconut: fibrous and forbidding on the outside but with precious layers within; its water soothes babies with gripe, while the tender white flesh is vital for every Malayali dish; that same flesh when dried and pressed—copra—yields coconut oil; the discards from pressing copra are fodder for cattle; the hard shell makes a perfect *thavi*, or ladle; and the thick outer cover, when dried and spun, yields coir rope. Life would cease in Travancore without the coconut, just as Parambil would stop without her husband. But his saying her mother's *erechi olarthiyathu* is "not as good as yours" is his way of saying that he misses her.

At night, after she puts the baby to sleep, her blouse sodden and smelling of her own milk, she wonders if there are nights when her husband comes seeking her while she's asleep. Does he touch her, try to shake her awake? Or does the sight of her mother and the two sleeping children halt him at the door? The truth is, she isn't ready for him. The ordeal of labor is fresh in her memory. She was left with a tear that is finally less painful, but her body is still offering strange new embarrassments that thankfully seem to diminish with time. It will be a while before she's fully healed. Every month some story reaches her of a birth gone awry, a woman bleeding to death, or a baby stalled during its exit, an event that is fatal to mother and child. "Thank you, Lord, for bringing me through this unscathed." She doesn't share with the Lord that she misses the closeness with her husband, misses the excitement of getting on his bed, her heart pounding, and hearing his heart do the same. "Well, you can't have one without the other," she says, but just to herself. There are certain things that God does not need to be told.

The rhythm of Parambil is one of constancy and constant change. JoJo excitedly reports that Georgie's twin brother, Ranjan, along with his wife and three children, appeared in the night with all their worldly possessions. Big Ammachi can hardly imagine Dolly's plight with so many crammed into her tiny house. Ranjan, like Georgie, was left nothing by his father. He found a decent job as an assistant manager on a tea estate in Coorg. The pay was good, but theirs was a lonely existence in the Pollibetta hills. Something happened that caused the wife to restrain her husband with rope, throw him in a cart, and bring the family down the mountain and eventually descend on Georgie and Dolly *Kochamma*. The wife, a stout woman with a square jaw, and the habit of squeezing her eyes shut before speaking, appears formidable, more so because she wears a large wooden crucifix that would look better nailed to a wall than hanging over her bosom. She carries a Bible tightly clasped in her hand as though fearful someone will rip it free. Dolly's children secretly call her "Decency *Kochamma*," because (according to JoJo) everything looks indecent to her. If she isn't railing against a sin the children have committed, she's railing against one they're about to commit.

A few days later, Big Ammachi sees the twins walking up to call on their uncle, holding hands the way close friends do. They are identical, but Ranjan looks rougher for the wear. He shares his brother's boyish fidgetiness, as though an eccentric wheel turns within, producing a restless dance of his lips, eyebrows, eyes, and limbs and affecting his gait. Both men have the same expression of unwarranted optimism, despite their circumstances—an admirable trait. They try to act solemn just before they go in to see her husband, but when they emerge, they are elated, bouncing off each other like boys let out of school. She learns later that her husband has deeded Ranjan a small, sloped, uncleared plot that sits adjacent to Georgie's. He'd probably decided on it when he first heard of his nephew's return; so now he has provided for Ranjan as well as Georgie. She admires her husband's generosity, but he struggles to match it with warmth, or with the kind of wise counsel that might help his nephews be more successful. That is not his way.

JoJo reports that the twins have decided to tear down Georgie and Dolly's small home and build a new joint dwelling using the best wood and good brass fittings—just the sort of house that the long-suffering Dolly *Kochamma* deserves, but it's happening only because Ranjan and Decency *Kochamma* are throwing in their savings. The new foundation will sit mostly on Georgie's plot, which has the well and the best drainage; most of Ranjan's plot will go to a new approach road, and to grow *kappa* and plantain. A shared kitchen will sit between the two wings of the house. Big Ammachi can't help worrying for Dolly *Kochamma*.

JoJo has outgrown the house. Since he avoids water, he cannot challenge the other children in diving or swimming; instead, JoJo rules the heights. Trees are his domain, and he tops the others in his daring and recklessness. He puts monkeys to shame in the way he scampers along a high branch of a tree, jumps to its neighbor, or dismounts by swinging off a vine and doing a backflip before landing on the dead leaves below. That last stunt makes him a hero to the younger children.

On a Tuesday, after being confined by two days of rain, the older children race outside to swim in the river. Only the toddlers are there for an audience as JoJo clambers up a tree, grabs a vine, and swings out. But his hands slip off the wet vine, throwing off his backflip. He's leaning too far forward when he lands, his momentum forcing him to race forward before he falls facedown into a shallow drainage ditch filled with rainwater. The toddlers applaud the splash, and the added comical touch of JoJo choosing not to stand up and instead to thrash in the puddle like a hooked fish. The little ones are in hysterics, clutching their bellies. *That JoJo! The things he can do!* But they get bored when JoJo doesn't get up, and they gradually drift away.

"JoJo is hiding in the water, and he won't play," one of them reports to Big Ammachi.

Lulled by feeding Baby Mol, she smiles.

Seconds later, she rips the baby off her nipple. Its arms fly to both sides as if to break a fall. She puts the baby down. "What water?" she screams. "Show me! Where?" The child is startled, but points in the direction of the irrigation ditch and she runs.

She sees JoJo's shoulder blades and the back of his head cresting the water, his hair wet and glistening, hair that's such a struggle to wash. She leaps into the turbid ditch, jarring her spine because of its unexpected shallowness—it barely reaches her knees—and flips him onto the ground. She pushes on his stomach and mud surges out of his mouth. She cries, "Breathe, JoJo!" Then she screams. "*AYO*, JOJO, FOR GOD'S SAKE! BREATHE!" The sound pierces the air, and it carries for a mile. She hears footsteps pounding over wet leaves. Her husband slides down to her, on his knees. He squeezes his son's ribcage, pushes on the belly. Shamuel arrives breathless and kneels across from the pair, reaching into JoJo's mouth to sweep out mud, and more mud, but still he doesn't breathe. Georgie suspends JoJo by the ankles while Ranjan pumps JoJo's arms up and down and water pours out, but he won't breathe. Ranjan covers JoJo's lips with his and blows into his lungs as JoJo hangs upside down, his arms alongside his ears like a fish being weighed . . . but he doesn't breathe. They lay him down and take turns breathing into his mouth, thumping on his back, pushing on his belly. She circles them like a madwoman, tearing at her hair, crying out in disbelief, screaming at them, "Don't stop! Don't stop!" But JoJo, stubborn in life, is more stubborn in death and will not breathe for her, or his father, or Shamuel, or all others who try; he will not breathe to save their broken hearts. Their efforts seem to be violating his limp body. At last, her husband pushes them away and holds his son to him, groaning, his body shaking.

She registers a distant shrill wail that empties a pair of tiny lungs, then a gasp for air, then another shriek. She has completely forgotten Baby Mol! *If you're crying, that means you're alive.* She backs away, afraid to leave JoJo. She runs back to her room and picks up the infant. She lifts her *chatta*, shoves a nipple at the baby, alarming it by her brusqueness, making it only wail more. She studies the infant's face, the bared gums, the ugly mask of its discontent; she resents its blind need for her teat. At last, it latches on.

With the baby at her breast, she stumbles out to see her JoJo, her faithful shadow and companion for eight of his ten years, her little man, lowered down on the verandah bench by his father, the boy's belly grotesquely distended. Her shattered husband turns and leans his raised arms against a pillar, as if to push it down, but the pillar is the only thing keeping him upright. The expression on JoJo's face is one of puzzlement. She squats by her son, her hand on his cold forehead, and she wails. Baby Mol's eyes roll up in fright and she bites sharply on the nipple. *Lord,* Big Ammachi thinks, *I'll willingly trade this new life if you give me my JoJo back.* This thought shames her into a measure of sanity. She reaches out to her husband, still chained to the pillar, as silent in grief as he is in joy.

CHAPTER 9

Faith in Small Things

1908, Parambil

"Drowning on land" is how she thinks of it. In its aftermath she has a recurring nightmare: she's carrying her children, her mother, and her husband on her head, staggering under the weight, in danger of sinking into the soil if she stops moving, mud filling her mouth. When she arrives at the burden stone, the horizontal slab is on the ground, useless. She looks up and down the road for help, but she's alone.

Somehow, she goes on, so that Parambil can go on. If her father were there, he'd encourage her to be "faithful in small things." Nothing ruffled him, not even his own suffering. But she resists this verse. She's furious with her God. "How can I be faithful in small things if you can't be faithful in big ones?"

She's surprised to feel anger toward her grieving husband. It builds within her. At first, like a hornet's nest, it's no more than a fleck of mud in a wooden joist. But it grows, and portholes appear, and soon a steady drone can be heard within. She prays for her fury to be lifted. She prays, even though God has failed her, because what else can humans do in such circumstances but pray? "I've never seen his lips touch toddy. No one can accuse him of sloth, or miserliness.

He has never hit me, and never would. Lord, he doesn't merit my wrath. He lost his child too. Why do I feel this way?"

She goes to his room after his bath, entrusting the baby to her mother. At this hour, just before dinner, he's often recumbent, his hand draped over his forehead, as if the act of bathing exhausts him. She recognizes his mannerisms but never truly knows what they signify.

To her surprise, he isn't lying down but seated on the bed, his shoulders back, his head up, as if he expects her and has steeled himself for what must come.

"I need to know," she says simply, standing in front of him, their faces on the same level. He tilts his right ear to her. She's been aware for a while that he hears poorly, but his silence makes it less obvious. She says it again. He watches her lips to see if there's more.

Any other man would have said, *Know what?* But not him. She doesn't wait. "I need to know about"—she wrings her hands in exasperation—"about the Condition."

She has just christened it. Surely that's the first step. She's named this thing that she has sensed from the time the marriage was proposed: the whispers about drownings running in the family, the house built away from water, his distaste for rain, his strange way of bathing—the very things that afflicted their son. *The Condition.* You can't ask how to hunt a snake if you don't have a name for it.

He doesn't feign ignorance, but he doesn't move. Seated, he's still taller than she is, but to her their age gap feels narrower than ever.

"For our daughter's sake," she says. "So I can protect her. And for the other children we'll have, God willing. I need to know what you know. Why was JoJo so fearful of water? Why won't you, my husband, get on a boat? Does Baby Mol have the Condition too?"

He stands up, towering over her, and her heart races. He's never come close to threatening her. She braces herself. But he steps past her to reach up and retrieve a parcel wedged on the ledge just under the ceiling. It's wrapped in cloth and tied with a string. He holds it outside the door and shakes off the dust.

"It was hers," he says, as though that's sufficient explanation. He sits beside her and unwraps the disintegrating coarse hemp cloth around it. The second layer is the cloth of a fine *kavani*. She gets the scent of a bygone era, and of another woman, the same scent that is in the cellar at times, and that was on the stored garments he gave her when he first took her to church. JoJo's mother. On top of the pile is a gauzy, transparent cotton pouch that she can see holds a wedding ring as well as the *minnu*—the tiny, gold pendant in the shape of a tulsi leaf, with gold beads forming a crucifix on its surface. He tied this around his departed wife's neck when they married, just as he tied her own *minnu* around her neck on their wedding day.

He moves the pouch aside and hands her a small square sheet: JoJo's baptismal record. She's wrenched with guilt seeing this, as though at this moment she's breaking the news to JoJo's mother of her son's death. She fights back tears. She doesn't dare look at her husband. Her anger has vanished.

Now his big hand lifts out a folded wad of papers, crumpled at the edges. The silverfish have chewed at the corners, while the paper beetles have made crescent-shaped fenestrations through it. Gingerly he unfolds the fragile parchment. It is an outsized map or chart made up of papers glued on their long sides, but the rice-paste glue, so delicious to silverfish, is largely eaten away. He spreads it out over both their laps. The writing is faded. A few more years and these papers will be just dust.

A tree. The thick, dark trunk is crooked, and on the branches are a few leaves. The leaves have names, dates, annotations. She recalls a similar genealogy drawn by her father. She'd sat on his lap as he explained. "Matthew gives us the genealogy of Jesus beginning with Abraham. Fourteen generations to David, then fourteen from David to the Babylonian Captivity, and another fourteen from the exile to the birth of Jesus." Her father was convinced Matthew had omitted two generations. "He was a tax collector. He liked the symmetry of fourteen repeated thrice. But it's inaccurate!"

The tree on her lap lacks symmetry and is devastatingly accurate. She understands at once that it is a catalog of the malady that has shattered the Parambil family, but unlike Matthew's gospel, this is a secret document, hidden in the rafters, to be viewed only by family members, and only when they absolutely must see it. Did it take the loss of their son for her to earn the right to this knowledge? She's had a child with this man! They are bound by blood, yet he kept this from her.

She brings the lamp as close as she dares. Surely this fresher writing that recorded JoJo's birth must be JoJo's mother's—why was *she* allowed to see this? Did she already know of the Condition and ask? Other hands, some old and tremulous, as evidenced by the hitches in the loops, coils, and uprights of the Malayalam script, have laboriously penned entries too. Perhaps her husband's mother, or his grandmother? And someone else before that, and before that. There are also smaller slips of ancient, coarse paper inside the folded map.

He peers over her shoulder, his hands clenched.

Using JoJo's name printed on a branch as anchor, she sees that the Parambil lineage goes back at least seven generations (not counting the slips of paper) and forward two. She is entering unfamiliar backwaters. The past is as murky as the ghostly faint ink, the crumbling paper. The ancestral family boasts slave traders, two murderers, and the apostate priest Pathrose—it says so here. Next to one name she reads, "Just like his uncle, but younger"—she struggles to decipher the letters so closely crammed together—"and so never married." An annotation next to a "Pappachen" three generations before her husband says, "His father, Zachariah, also deaf and staggered when eyes closed from the age of forty." A loose note says: "Boys suffer more often than girls. Watch for exuberant children, fearless except for water. By the time they are taken to the river, all you mothers will know."

They're describing JoJo. Which mother wrote this warning?

She turns back to the tree, to a symbol that recurs on some branches.

"What are these squiggles under this strange crucifix?" she asks. "Are they not words?" he says softly.

She turns to him, stunned. For the longest time she has read the paper to him at the dinner table, but has never seen him read. She assumed he never cared to. He cannot read! How could she not know this till this moment? The innocence of his question reminds her of JoJo when she first met him, and she fights back tears.

She shakes her head. "No. It's not words." He says, "Then it looks like water. With a cross."

She is in awe of her husband. He is illiterate, yet he saw it for what it was, just as he might see a dusting of mold on a tree trunk. "True," she says softly. "A cross over water. A sign they died by drowning."

He says, "Is Shanthama there? My father's older sister?" She finds her, and points: the cross on water is by her name. "She drowned before I was born."

Which grief-stricken mother thought up this symbol? Under the dancing flame of her lamp, the crucifix atop the wavy lines also resembles a denuded tree at the head of a fresh mound of dirt: a grave.

"There's a death by drowning every generation," she says, tracing with her finger. A few of the crosses have annotations, and she reads aloud: "In the lake . . . the stream . . . the Pamba River . . ."

Her husband points with his chin in the direction of their sorrow. "Irrigation ditch." It will be her task to write those words.

How much did the marriage broker know about the Condition? What about her mother or uncle? Did they know and conceal it from her? Or dismiss it? But of course her husband knew. She doesn't want to hate the man she loves. But she has to get it off her chest.

"I wish you'd told me what you knew," she says. "We could have protected JoJo, forbidden him from swinging on those things, climbing trees so—"

"No!" her husband says so vehemently that she almost drops the papers. He stands. She's seen this kind of anger directed at others, but never at her. "No! That's what my mother did. Kept me on the property, a prisoner, when all I wanted to do was run, jump, climb. And after my mother died, Thankamma and my brothers did the same. When I look at this I can only see squiggles," he says, jabbing the papers with a finger. "You know why? She never let me go to the church school because it was across the river. She didn't even want me to walk next to it. What I know now is there's always a way to get somewhere, it's just longer. My brothers and sisters have no problem with water. They went to school. Once, I ran away. My brothers and Thankamma locked me up. Out of love, they claimed! But it was out of fear. Out of ignorance!" His tone softens. "My mother and Thankamma meant well. They wanted to protect me like you wished to with our JoJo. But it made me weak. My brother cheated me because I couldn't read." He's pacing the room. "Believe me, no one had to tell me or JoJo to stay away from water. If we can't swim, we can do plenty of other things. We walk. We climb. Do you think I don't mourn my only son? But if I had the chance to do it again, I'd change nothing. JoJo wasn't on a leash. My son lived like a tiger the few years he had on this earth. He climbed. He ran fast. He made up for the one thing he could not do." His voice breaks. He gathers himself and goes on. "I didn't hide it. I assumed you knew. Your uncle certainly knew. I'm sorry if you didn't. You only had to ask. But I don't go around with a bell like a leper to announce it. This is a part of me. Like the goldsmith's wife whose face is scarred by smallpox, or the potter's son whose foot is turned. This is me. This is who I am."

She's forgotten to breathe. He's said more words of significance in one evening than in their last eight years together. The
crowd that is within him—small boy, father, and husband—rage and
grieve together.

His expression softens. "You could have married better."

She reaches for his hand, but he pulls away and leaves the
room.

Her mind is in a whirl. Thus far, nothing suggests Baby Mol
has any fear of water. Even if Baby Mol doesn't have the Condition,
she'll be considered tainted, capable of passing on this bad seed.

With a shaking hand she records the year JoJo's mother died.
She draws a new branch arising from her husband's name. She
writes in her name and the date of her marriage, then a branch from
their union where she writes "Baby Mol"; she will have Baby Mol
baptized before she is six months and then she will enter her proper
name and birth date. How many branches will lead down from Baby
Mol once she marries? "I'm on the inside now, Lord," she says. "The
Condition is mine as much as it is his. How can I cast blame?"

Under JoJo's name, she writes the year of his passing. She
draws the three wavy lines, easy enough to do with her trembling
fingers. How cruel, how viciously unfair that JoJo should die from
the one element he worked so hard to avoid. Atop the wavy lines she
draws the cross, which looks like a tree on the hill of Calvary, the
three points breaking into sub-branches, reminiscent of the Saint
Thomas cross, but also looking like tree branches that have been
cleaved off, leaving the pointy ends clawing at the sky. She grieves
now with JoJo's mother. *I know he was yours, but he was mine too and I
had him longer. I loved him so much.* Her pen touches the paper, struggling to fit the loopy shapes and tails and comebacks of Malayalam
script in the small space: DROWNED IN IRRIGATION DITCH. Her mind
swims with images of a much younger JoJo, his smile full of holes—
if only she'd kept those baby teeth, then she'd still have something
of his! He'd insisted on planting them to grow a tusk, and then he'd
forgotten where.

She stares at the parchment when she's done; the Water Tree, she might call it. Is the Condition a curse? Or a disease? Is there really a difference? She knows of a family in which the children have bones that break easily, and the whites of their eyes have a light-blue tinge. They grow out of it, and as adults, they seem almost normal. But when two first cousins eloped and moved away, their child suffered fractures in its journey out of the womb, and by its second year of life its legs were drawn up like a frog's, its chest squashed, and its spine twisted. It died before it was three.

She reassembles the papers, ties a ribbon in place of the string. She takes the Water Tree to her room. It's hers now. She will be the one henceforth to repair and preserve this genealogy, to annotate it and to pass it on.

At dinner, he doesn't meet her eyes when she serves him. Her mother made an egg curry in a thick red sauce, scoring the hard-boiled eggs with three slashes so the sauce can seep in. Her red-eyed mother never asked about the voices raised in her husband's bedroom behind the closed door.

That night, mother and daughter pray together. "May the living and the departed together cry out: 'Blessed is He who has come, and is to come, and will raise the dead.'"

After she uncovers her head and snuggles with Baby Mol, feeling the emptiness where JoJo would have been, she feels entitled to speak frankly to God.

"Lord, maybe You don't want to cure this for reasons I don't understand. But if You won't or can't, then send us someone who can."

Part Two

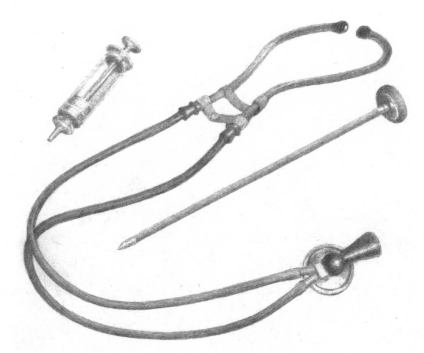

CHAPTER 10

A Fish under the Table

1919, Glasgow

On Saturdays, Digby's mother takes him to the Gaiety, Glasgow's best. Years later, when he remembers those afternoons his nose will itch, as though he's inhaling the Jeyes Fluid wafting off the seats. But that pungent cleaner never managed to dampen the smell of stale tobacco exuding from the floors and walls.

Johnny the ticket seller's eyes are on different floors from his prizefighting days. He no longer remarks that a boy of ten shouldn't be at a variety show. The dancing girls open the matinee and his mother's hand stays clamped over Digby's eyes until the second-spot magician appears. The floaters in Digby's vision don't clear till the next act, which is either the sword swallower or the juggler.

The audience is louder and less forgiving after intermission, tanked up on pints of heavy. The roll-your-own haze is thicker than morning fog on the Clyde. The comics come out like gladiators, but brandishing cigarettes instead of maces. Eight minutes is what it takes for the dout to burn their fingers, and that's how long they have on stage. Most are booed off in under five.

His mother is stone-faced the whole time, her thoughts far away in a manner that always worries Digby. Is she recalling being on stage here herself? She gave up a theatrical career, and fame, perhaps, because she was carrying him. Or is she thinking of the man she met here who ruined it all? Digby studies the performers. He never met his father, but Archie Kilgour was of this tribe, traveling from town to town, haunting the same pubs in each city (in Glasgow it was the Sarry Heid), the publican's face more familiar to them than their own bairns, and bedding down in the same theatrical digs like Mrs. MacIntyre's. Digby's mother once said Archie Kilgour had nailed a kipper to the underside of the dining table when Mrs. MacIntyre denied him credit. Digby asked why under the table. "Gie it a thought, Digs. Yon's the last place onybuddy wid look fur something rotten. That's him all over. So low he could slide under a snake's belly wearing a lum hat."

Some say Archie sailed for Canada, others that he never left. Archie Kilgour's real talent was in disappearing. All Digby really knows is that he's the sort who leaves a fish pinned under the dining table, and he left Digby pinned in his mother's womb. Digby imagines half-siblings he surely has in the other towns on the circuit: Edinburgh, Stirling, Dundee, Dumfries, Aberdeen . . .

The rousing finale is always "There's a Girl for Every Soldier," and it rings in Digby's ears as they emerge. He feels buoyant, lighter than air, only wishing his maw could feel the same way.

Digby can't imagine a more exciting time to be alive. The Wright brothers made the first heavier-than-air flight in 1903, but, as every Scottish schoolboy knows, the Barnwell brothers did the same at Causewayhead soon after. He dreams of steering a biplane, of becoming lighter than air! He'll fly his maw over Glasgow and away. He'll make her smile. He'll make her proud.

On Wednesdays, the two of them have a midweek treat: tea at Gallowgate. Digby waits for her and thousands of "Singers" to pour out of the factory at the end of the shift. The Proddies will emerge first. Catholics like his mother come after; they are the lowest paid and do the roughest jobs. Her supervisor is a Proddy and a Rangers supporter, of course. Glasgow, like most Scottish cities, is violently split by religion. His grandparents were in the Irish wave that came after the Famine, turning the East End into a Catholic bastion (and the home of the Celtic football team).

Digby loves to stare up at the square clock tower that stands six stories high. The factory buildings extend on either side of it like trains a mile long. Each face of the tower, which is Glasgow's most famous landmark, has a massive clock weighing two tons, with SINGER in giant letters above each dial, visible from anywhere in the city. Digby could spell SINGER before he could write his name. Standing this close and looking up, Digby feels he's in the presence of God, whose name is SINGER. God has his own trains and railway station to run parts from the foundry to Helensburgh, Dumbarton, or Glasgow. God churns out a million sewing machines a year and employs fifteen thousand people. God lets his mother splurge on drawing paper and watercolors for Digby. God allowed his mother and him to move out from Nana's and live on their own, and be silly and loud and have jam with their tea every day if it pleases them, and it does.

The rumble of hundreds of hobnail boots sound as they descend the factory steps. Soon he spots his mother, red-haired and beautiful. Men look at her in a way that makes him angrily protective. "Away! I'm done with men, Digs," she said after cutting down a suitor. "A mooth ta eat and ta tell lies, that's all."

She's not smiling when she comes to him. "They've gone an' cut the assemblers tae only a dozen and the rest o' us are meant to pick up the slack. Ah was burstin'—hardly time to take a pee. An it's aw fur the sake of 'industrial efficiency'!" There'll be no tea today. Instead, her coworkers gather around his mother's dining table, planning a strike. Digby hears them say that God—Mr. Isaac Singer—is really the Devil. God is a polygamist with two dozen children by various wives and mistresses. God sounds a lot like Archie Kilgour. For the next week, his mother is off to meetings every night, rallying support, returning late, bright-eyed but pale with fatigue.

*   *   *

He's slicing bread for their tea when he hears her steps on the stairs much too early. He has a terrible foreboding. "They give me ma book, Digs. Kicked yer maw oot. They found cause." If she expects her friends to strike in her support, she's disappointed. Since she's no longer employed, the strike fund won't pay her.

There's nothing to do but move back in with Nana, a flatulent hypochondriac who crosses herself when she hears church bells and refers to Digby as "the bastard." Digby and his mother sleep in the front room—no more jam, and sometimes no bread. His mother has the covers over her head when he leaves for school, and she's that way when he returns. Her dull eyes remind him of the haddock lined up on ice at the Briggait Fish Market. "Thar's nae good that e'er came out o' the Gaiety," Nana says to her daughter with satisfaction.

This is how a boy's world crumbles. On his walks back from school, the four-eyed monster in the tower tracks his every movement. No show tunes play in his head. He and his mother are intruders in a house that holds the coffin gases of a "pernickety old pharisee of a wummin," as his mother is wont to say.

The doctor who came to the mean little flat called his mother "catatonic." When she rallied, Digby walked her from factory to counting house to drugstore. Work, any work, would be healing. But she might as well have been wearing a sign that said GINGER FENIAN AGITATOR. That was what a butcher called her. She cleans houses when she can; an invalid herself, she's hired to care for invalids.

Winters are so cold Digby keeps his hat on indoors, but he must remove one glove to do his essays. Nana hounds her daughter. "Get yirsel' oot. We've nae coal, and gey little food. If ye'te beg, if ye'te spread yer legs, do it. That's how you got yirsel' into this mess."

*   *   *

Seven years after she was let go, they are still at Nana's. After school, by habit, he keeps watch over his mother, sitting beside her, sketching on water-stained ledgers a neighbor gave him. He spins out a rich and sensual world in pen and ink. Beautiful women wearing heels that turn their calves into erotic pillars, women with slim shoulders and full hips in fancy hats and fur shrugs. Here and there a breast pops out from a blouse. Newspaper advertisements are good for perfecting form. The eyes he sketches are getting better; the tiny square of reflected light over the iris brings his creations to life, allows them to behold their creator. When he discovers an anatomy text in the Clydebank Library on Dumbarton Road, the women in Digby's sketches begin to have transparent skin that reveals their bones and their articulations. He's reassured to think that no matter how disappointing humans can be, the bones, the muscles, and the viscera are constant, an unchanging interior architecture . . . except for the "external genitalia." A woman's privates are rather less than he expected to see: a furry mound, a lipped portal that further conceals and leaves him with more questions.

His mother was once the most glamorous woman he knew. But now, so many years after losing her job, she makes little effort, speaks not at all, and still spends hours in bed. Even so, in the line of her arm draped over her cheek, in the angle between forearm and wrist, and again between palm and fingers, she has innate grace. Her red hair no longer looks on fire, and her forelock of gray suggests she's brushed up against wet paint. At times she stares at her son, punishing him with a look that makes him feel responsible for all her troubles. She's aged, but he can't imagine she'll ever look like Nana, with those inflamed fissures at the corners of her lips, bookends for a foul mouth.

The only time his mother ever turns on him is when Digby proposes to leave school, to get work. "Do that and ah'm deid," she says, furious. "It's only you bein' top o' the class that gets me through this hell. I dream o' yer success. Dinnae disappoint me."

*   *   *

In the end, she disappoints him. By then he's almost a man, with a Carnegie College scholarship, secured against all odds. He plans to study medicine, drawn as he is to the body and its workings.

He comes home on a Sunday after an all-day tutoring session. Nana is out. Above his desk, his mother sticks her tongue out at him obscenely, a tongue three times its normal size, and blue. Her frog eyes mock him. The smell in the room tells him that she's soiled herself. She dangles from a rafter, her toes barely off the ground. His school tie bites into the blue flesh of her neck.

Digby falls back against the door, dropping his books. This is why he kept vigil. This is what he feared, though he never dared put words to it. He's too terrified to approach the body and take it down.

He lets the old woman make her own discovery. Nana screams, and then her sobs spill out of the room. The *polis* take the body down. The neighbors gawp at the sheeted form. His mother's soul has been dead for years and her body has now followed.

Digby steps outside. It's the twenty-second of May, a quarter of the way into the century, a decade after a war wrought terrible slaughter. One more death hardly matters, but it does for him. His feet carry him away. He wants to find people, lights, laughter. Soon he's in a pub, thick with revelers. He has to shout at the barmaid for his two pints. "For the granda and his mate," he says, nodding to the back room. The taste is vile. He thinks of Archie Kilgour. *Are you drinking tonight, you jakey? Yer a widower, did you know?* As for his mother, he has no tears, only angry words. *Did you think of me, Ma? Do you think you're off to a* better *place?*

He gets thrown out of the pub; he's not sure why. Next, he's in a small, dark, beery room where the drinking is serious and silent. He shoves in next to a group of lads who give him the evil eye. "Two pints for the granda," he says again, but doesn't bother to move to a table, drains his first glass at the bar. He notices the blue-and-white bunting on the wall facing him, then sees those colors echoed on the scarves of morose men. *Fuck me, I'm in a Rangers' pub!* He's trying not to laugh, but he can't help it. "Fucking Rangers!" He shakes his head. Did he say that out loud?

A man tells Digby to come outside. Digby has a better idea: he'll drink the second pint right where he is.

A fist hits him on his ear. A bottle is smashed, and something sharp flicks at the corner of his mouth. The publican comes around the beer-puddled counter and heaves him out on the pavement. "Bugger off before they finish yer smile, and you with it!" Digby stumbles round the corner, sobered by the recognition that these silent men might find killing him more diverting than drinking.

At the newsstand on the corner, a hundred identical handsome faces jeer at him, triumphant. LINDBERGH'S CROWNING HOUR, the banner headline reads. THE HERO OF AMERICA. The wetness trickling into his mouth tastes faintly sweet, faintly metallic. His sleeve is red. His eyes don't want to focus. Could a man really have flown across the Atlantic? Yes! Says so in big letters. In a plane called the *Spirit of St. Louis*. Lindbergh landed, his mother aloft. He feels no pain at all.

CHAPTER 11

Caste

1933, Madras

"Travel broadens the mind and loosens the bowels." A street vendor's lamb kebab in Port Said drops Digby to his knees, confining him to his cabin for two days, enough time to appreciate Professor Alan Elder's parting words in Glasgow. By the time he recovers, they're out of the Suez Canal and passing through the Bab-el-Mandeb, the Gate of Tears. This narrow strait, barely eighteen miles across, connects the Red Sea with the Indian Ocean. Off one bow, he sees Djibouti; off the other, Yemen. Save for a three-month posting in London, he has spent his twenty-five years on earth in Glasgow and might have spent the rest of his life there, never seen this confluence of waters, never discovered for himself that the English Channel, the Mediterranean, the Red Sea, and the Indian Ocean, despite their individual personalities, are one. All water is connected and only land and people are discontinuous. And his land is a place where he can no longer stay.

Under his feet, the ship is alive, making groans and sighs. He paces the deck in a broad-brimmed hat, though it can't keep the sunlight from bouncing off the water and tanning his face, highlighting the pale, jagged scar that creases his left cheek from the corner of his mouth to his left ear. The shifting moods and colors of the Arabian Sea—azure, blue, and black—mirror the ebb and flow of his thoughts. The horizon rises and then dips; the salt spray is cool on his face; he has the sensation of standing still while plunging toward his future.

He peeks into a first-class stateroom, ashamed of his curiosity yet awed by the sofas and plush chairs, the thick brocade curtains and the pocket doors that allow valets and maids to attend to their employers. A maharajah is on board; he and his retinue have booked all of First Class. Digby is one class below, with his own tiny cabin. There are two classes below his, the segregation so complete that he hears rather than sees them.

A rough sea brings on what is either seasickness or a relapse of the ailment from the lamb kebab. Being a doctor means he has no objectivity about his symptoms. When he's absent from the dining room for two seatings, Banerjee, who has a seat at the same table, comes to check on him.

Alarmed to see that Digby is barely able to lift his head, Banerjee returns with broth and paregoric. The tincture's camphor-and-anise odor settles in the cabin and quietens his stomach. Banerjee—or Banny, as he asks Digby to call him—is in his late twenties, baby-faced, with the complexion of a boy raised on milk and cream, with meat never having touched his palate; his light-brown skin, which he assiduously protects from the sun, is fairer than the tanned Digby's. Banny seems too young to be the barrister he is, called to the bar after four years of study in London. The path he has taken is much like Gandhi's at the tail of the previous century, an observation Banerjee makes quietly but with pride.

When Digby rejoins the dinner table, Mrs. Ann Simmonds, the wife of a district collector in the Madras Presidency, says, "Duck tonight," as if unaware of Digby's previous absence. Her wide face has no edges, no angles; she reminds Digby of a bulldog, and has the moist, sagging eyes to match. From their first day she took command of their table, acting like a stateroom passenger choosing to dine with the masses out of her largesse. Listening to her hold forth, as he has every night, Digby is reminded of his three-month posting at Saint Bart's Hospital in London—the prize for a medal exam he topped in Glasgow in his third year of medical school. Until he got onto the Bart's wards, he wasn't aware that he had an accent, or that it made others assume that he was provincial and stupid. It was a rude awakening. He couldn't shed the accent entirely but one could soften it; he had worked hard to stay clear of those words or phrases or pronunciations that typecast him. Not that such efforts have fooled Mrs. Simmonds, who largely ignores him. Now he overhears her say to the diner across from her, "We English know what's best for India. When you get there, you'll see."

Later that night, Digby strolls the deck with Banny. Despite the bond they've formed, they haven't discussed politics. Digby confesses his ignorance of the world outside of Glasgow, or even outside of the hospital. "I lived in the infirmary these last few years. I had no cause to read a newspaper unless it appeared under a wound dressing, or in a belly I was opening." He's been making up for it by studying the papers in the ship's library. The headlines are about Germany's intention to rearm despite the Treaty of Versailles. A belligerent new chancellor promises to lead the country out of its economic devastation. But there's little news of India.

"You could ask Mrs. Simmonds."

"No, thank you," Digby says.

Banny smiles, polishing his lenses and squinting at Digby. "Why go to India, Digby?"

Digby sees clouds in the distance, arranged as though along a plumb line. He imagines land beyond. They're alongside the west coast of India, passing Calicut or Cochin. "A long story, Banny, I'm afraid. I fell in love with surgery. I was a good student, then a good houseman in surgery. Eager. Dedicated. When I wasn't on duty, I loitered in Casualty, hoping to scrub in on accident cases. But when it came time to be selected for a surgical postgraduate post in Glasgow, turns out I wasn't in the right pew. Outside of Glasgow there wasn't a chance. So I joined the Indian Medical Service, hoping to develop as a surgeon."

"Being a Catholic, was that it? How did they know?" Banerjee asks. "Your name?"

"No. Mine could be Protestant or Catholic. Now, Patrick or Timothy or David would be a giveaway. But I'd gone on scholarship to St Aloysius' College. A Jesuit institution. I could hardly hide that. But even without that, it's as if I'm giving out secret signals." Digby looks at his companion uncertainly. "I'm sure it's hard to understand."

Banerjee laughs. "Not at all. It's quite familiar."

Digby is embarrassed. It's a stupid thing to say to a man who has lived under the yoke of British rule from birth. But Banny can sound and seem more British than Digby. "I'm sorry—"

"Why be sorry, Digby? You're the victim of a caste system. We've been doing the same thing to each other in India for centuries. The inalienable rights of the Brahmins. And the absence of any rights for the untouchables. And all the layers in between. Everyone who is looked down on can look down on someone else. Except the lowest. The British just came along and moved us down a rung."

The ship rounds the southern tip of India and heads up the Coromandel Coast. At midnight, Digby stands alone on deck. The black waves turn a fluorescent green and blue, as if a fire rages deep in the ocean. He's the only witness to an utterly beautiful yet mysterious spectacle. (Only the next day does he learn from the steward that it was phosphorescent plankton, a rare sight.) It seems to underline for Digby that he has in the course of this voyage peeled off his past like a soiled glove. More so than ever, he has shed a Glasgow shattered by the Great Slump, shed its patter, shed his last living relative, shed everything but the festering wound it left on him. The only industry that thrived in Glasgow was violence. It bubbled out of the Gorbals behind the infirmary and from elsewhere in the city; it showed up

in the casualty ward every night. As a houseman, Digby sewed faces
that had been expertly sliced by the warring razor gangs, the Billy
Boys or Norman Conks, always a symmetrical pair of slashes hook-
ing up from the corners of the mouth to the ears, marking the victim
for life with a "Glasgow smile." Digby feels fortunate that his own
scar is just one-sided; the smashed bottle was duller than a razor
and left him with a jagged dimple next to his natural one. It is a pale
stigma of a life he wants to forget. He could have forgiven Glasgow
his scar, his disappointments, his mother's suicide. That was hardly
reason to leave; even misery, when familiar, has its own comfort.
What he couldn't forgive was that after all his slaving, after his sin-
gular and almost maniacal devotion to surgery, he'd come to the
manned door and was denied the password. His mentor, Professor
Elder, a man beyond caste, albeit from upper-caste Edinburgh, did
his best to help, suggesting a way out. "I know a place where you'll
get tremendous experience, and with luck find great mentors in surgery. Have you considered the Indian Medical Service?" *What's fur
ye won't go by ye*, Digby thinks. It was a phrase his mother would use:
whatever is in his destiny will come to him, regardless.

When he disembarks in Madras, he feels he's arrived on a new planet.
The city has a population of six hundred thousand, and most of them
are at the quay, or so it appears to Digby from the cacophony, the
confusion, and the heat. He breathes in the odors of cured leather,
cotton, dried fish, incense, and salt water, the top notes of the an-
tique scent of this ancient civilization.

Stevedores pour from the ship's hold like a column of ants,
bent forward from the weight of gunnysacks held over a shoulder
with a grappling hook, sweat glossing their black skins. Women
clustering outside customs make a bouquet of bright green, orange,
and red saris with bold patterns. He's entranced by the punctuation
of a glittering stone in the nose, a red dot on a gleaming forehead,
gold dangling from the ears and echoing the heavy borders of the
fabrics. The rickshaws and carriages lined up outside are painted

in every color of the rainbow. The vibrant, uninhibited palette of Madras is a revelation. Something clenched within him unwinds.

In the customs shed, he watches Mrs. Ann Simmonds greet a small but stocky man, presumably her husband, the district collector: little joy is evinced by either party at this reunion. She marches off to a small car, her chin in the air, her stubby nose pointed in the direction of Westminster, and with a royal's expression on her face.

"*Oi*! I said no! You insolent *babu*! Do you want a thrashing?"

Digby swivels around to see a red-faced Englishman rise from behind a customs desk to loom over Banerjee. The tableau sends a chill through him, a wrenching recognition that he is, by virtue of arrival, one of the occupiers; his is the inalienable right to be first off the gangway, receive a quick stamp of his papers, and not be talked to in this manner.

In the humid customs shed the hands of the clock have paused, waiting to see what's next. Digby's breath quickens in the hothouse air, and reflexively he takes two steps to intervene.

Just then, another customs official intercedes. All Banerjee seeks is to disembark for the twelve hours that the ship is berthed, so he can visit a friend in Madras before continuing north to Calcutta. The senior official gives his subordinate an impatient look, stamps Banerjee's papers, and lets him leave. Banny's gaze falls on Digby. His hooded eyes have turned hard as stone, expressing the dogged resentment and the unwavering resolve of a subjugated nation that bides its time. Then the look vanishes. He bestows a stoic smile on Digby and heads for the separate exit for non-whites. He doesn't wave farewell.

CHAPTER 12

Two Big Ones

1933, Madras

The clerk from the hospital who meets him at the port is shocked that Digby has no trunk, just a shabby suitcase. They travel in a rickshaw pulled not by a beast of burden but by a man. The heat and a touch of *mal de débarquement* leave Digby disoriented, taking in the cow loitering in the middle of the broad avenue, the blur of dark faces on either side, the cobbler at work on the dusty pavement, the low-slung whitewashed buildings with hand-painted signboards, and the cluster of huts on the edge of a stagnant pond of water. They pull up at a bungalow not far from the harbor and close to Longmere Hospital, his new place of employment.

A short man in a white shirt, white trousers, and bare feet slips a jasmine garland over Digby's head, then bows, his palms held together at chin level. Muthusamy is to be Digby's cook and housekeeper. For someone who is used to calling a tin of sardines his breakfast, lunch, and dinner, Digby can't fathom the notion of his own cook, let alone one who garlands him. Muthu's white teeth are a beacon in his coal-dark face; his forehead has three horizontal streaks of ash—a *vibuthi*, as Digby learns later, a sacred Hindu marking that Digby will soon observe him apply each morning after lighting camphor and praying before the small icon of a god tucked in a kitchen shelf. Muthu's salt-and-pepper hair is parted in the middle and oiled back; he radiates kindness. Digby bathes and then sits down to the meal Muthu has prepared: rice with what Muthu says is "chicken korma"—chicken in an orange-colored gravy. Digby is famished and the korma mixed in with the rice is delicious, a riot of completely new flavors on his palate. He finishes most of it before he belatedly notices that his mouth burns and his forehead blossoms with sweat. After dousing the flames with ice water he lays down on his bed under a sluggish ceiling fan. His last waking thought is that he must ask Muthu to tone down the combustible ingredients in his dishes until he is more used to them. He sleeps for eleven straight hours.

The next morning, Assistant Civil Surgeon Digby Kilgour shows up for duty at the cluster of two-story whitewashed buildings that is Longmere Hospital. It is close enough to the harbor for the smells of tar and brine to waft into the wards. He reports to Civil Surgeon Claude Arnold, who he discovers is not one to keep civil hours. One hour passes, with Arnold's office manager periodically offering the curious phrase "Doctor Arnold is just presently only directly coming now, sir." The manager, along with the Anglo-Indian secretary and the barefoot peon, smiles at Digby. "Having tea, Doctor? Or taking degree coffee?" "Degree coffee" turns out to be sweet and delicious; it is coffee brewed in hot, frothy milk. It gets its name, he's told, from the markings on the hydrometer or lactometer used to ensure the milk isn't too diluted with water.

The ceiling fans rustle the free edges of papers held down by stones. Nothing else stirs. The three employees show languorous skill in the art of not moving a muscle in the stifling heat. The pretty secretary's eyelids flutter each time he glances her way, a kind of Morse code, Digby thinks. Her lovely arms are dark, but her heavily powdered face is chalky white and stands out against her blood-red lipstick and varnished black hair. She brings to his mind a showgirl under stage lights.

Close to noon, the office staff suddenly shuffle papers; the peon stands. They've received a secret signal. Minutes later, a blond Englishman in his forties, in a dapper white linen suit and brown shoes with a mirror finish, materializes in the doorway, the peon grabbing the pith helmet from his extended hand. He registers Digby's presence with a raised eyebrow. His wide shoulders suggest a former sportsman; he's good-looking, but his sallow complexion and puffy, bloodshot eyes hint at the dissolute. The small mustache is darker than his hair, and to Digby it seems faintly ridiculous.

Senior Civil Surgeon Claude Arnold takes the measure of his fresh-off-the-boat subordinate: he sees a young man with a widow's peak marking his thick hair, a strange, irregular dimple on his left cheek, a crumpled blazer over his arm, and woolen trousers that only a masochist would wear in Madras. Digby squirms under this scrutiny. Claude Arnold has the confidence of a public-school boy encountering his social inferior. He studies Digby's documents, the papers trembling slightly in his hand. He offers a cigarette; the eyebrow goes up again when Digby declines, as though the new man has failed another test. Eventually, after his coffee, Arnold stands and motions for Digby to follow.

"You'll be responsible for two surgical wards. Under my supervision, of course," Arnold says over his shoulder. "Both are for natives. For your sins, old fellow. I run the Anglo-Indian and British wards. Two LMPs will be working for you, Peter and Krishnan." He drags with relish on his cigarette, as if to show Digby what he's missing. "I don't care for LMPs. I'd rather have a real doctor than a *babu* impersonation." Digby knows that Licentiate Medical Practitioners pass an abbreviated two-year diploma course and can practice medicine. "But it's India, you know. Can't do without them, or so they tell us."

Arnold stops at the male native ward. "Where's Matron Honorine?" he asks irritably of the brown-skinned nurse who rushes to greet them with a ready smile. Matron is gone to the pharmacy.

Patients occupy the beds on either side of a long, high-ceilinged room, and others lie on mats between the beds. Outside is a covered porch with more patients on mats. A man with a grotesquely swollen belly, and a hollowed face that emphasizes his cheekbones, sits on the edge of a bed, his stick arms propping him up. Meeting Digby's gaze, he smiles, but his face is so wasted that he appears to bare his teeth. Digby nods. The sight of suffering is familiar; its language transcends all borders. The native female ward is across the hallway, and it too is full.

Dr. Claude Arnold's Anglo-Indian ward currently is populated by one patient, plus a lone probationer presiding over him. The other carefully made beds all stand empty. Arnold doesn't take Digby to the British ward. The latter, he will learn later, is a collection of six private rooms on the upper floor, all unoccupied. British and Anglo-Indian patients in the know choose the General Hospital near the railway station, or else the Royapettah Hospital, for their surgical problems.

On the second floor, two operating theaters lead off from the scrubbing station. "Today is operating day for your wards," Arnold says. "You get Tuesdays and Fridays. The native side hasn't had a surgeon for a while. Well, we have the LMPs. They could do some major surgery if I were to let them. But then, before you know it, they'll set up shop in some small town and call themselves surgeons." Arnold points to the corkboard. "Take a look," he says, and then he slips out of sight.

The surgical list for the day is impressive in length: two amputations, a string of hydroceles and hernias, and four I&D's—incision and drainage for tropical abscesses. But Digby sees no major surgeries posted. Claude Arnold returns with a brightness in his eyes that was absent before. Digby picks up a medicinal odor on the senior civil surgeon.

"So, you're a surgeon," Arnold says suddenly, turning to Digby with unexpected charm, almost smiling.

"Well, not quite, Dr. Arnold. I did a total of a year and a—"

"Nonsense! You're a surgeon! Call me Claude, by the way."
His new congenial tone is that of the captain of the cricket team
needing ten runs from the last batsman. "You learn by cutting.
Remember, Kilgour, for these people the choice is you or nothing
at all. Be bold!" The corners of Claude's mouth turn up, as though
he's let Digby in on a trade secret, or perhaps a joke. "You might as
well plunge in," Claude says. Then to the waiting theater boy, "Get
Doctor Kilgour a locker and whatever else he needs." There's to be
no further orientation.

Before he knows it, Digby is scrubbed, gowned, and gloved. The
redolence of this theater, a continent away from Glasgow, is familiar: ether, chloroform, phenol, and the lingering feculent odor of an
abscess recently drained. But the similarity to Glasgow stops there.
Digby stares at the most astonishing sight framed by the surgical
towels: a scrotum ballooned beyond the size of a watermelon, now
reaching the kneecaps. The penis is buried in the swelling like a belly
button in an obese abdomen. When he read "hydrocele" on the surgical list, this wasn't what he pictured. He expected to see a modest
collection of fluid in the space enclosed by the *tunica vaginalis* that
covers the testis. He'd operated on a unilateral hydrocele in a child,
a straightforward procedure. But that gentle, lemon-sized scrotal
swelling of memory has no relationship with this brown, corrugated
behemoth. In the adjoining theater, an amputation is in progress.
It'll be a while before the LMP on that side can help. Claude has
vanished. And Digby is living the recurring nightmare of every surgeon: the patient under ether, the body cavity open, but the anatomy
unrecognizable. His legs feel weak.

The Tamil scrub nurse across from him smiles through her
mask.

"It's . . . a large one," is all Digby can manage, his gloved hands
locked together in the manner of a prelate.

"*Aah*, yes, Doctor . . . Big only," the scrub nurse says agreeably,
her tone implying that "big only" is something to celebrate, and

small isn't worthy of her theater. Her head movements, like those of Muthu, confuse him: what's a "no" in Scotland becomes "yes" here, as long as there's a little yaw and twist with it. "But above the knee only," the nurse adds, striking a note of slight disappointment. It takes Digby a second to understand that hydroceles (and groin hernias too, he will later learn) are classified here as "above the knee" or "below the knee" and the latter alone are truly deserving of being called "big only." If the specimen were a fish, she might fling it back in the river.

Digby is pouring sweat. A hand mops his brow before he drips onto the patient—it's the barefoot orderly who's also in charge of the ether mask. The scrub nurse uncovers the tray of instruments, waiting for his order.

"Actually, I've never seen anything this big," Digby says, stalling.

"Big only," she repeats, but with less enthusiasm, puzzled that the doctor doesn't plunge in. Her grizzled counterparts in Glasgow might have responded with "Aye, it's a stoater of a scrotum and ye've said it twice already, but ye'll not shrink it by gabbin', so g'wan and take yer knife to it."

CHAPTER 13

Magnification

1933, Madras

A large white woman bustles in, gnarled fingers pressing the surgical mask to her face, forgoing the ties in her haste. Gray hair shows at the edges of a surgical cap that sits askew. "Aa'm Matron Honorine Charlton. Just missed you on the ward." She's out of breath. "Oh dear, I see Claude's thrust ya right into the fray. Goodness! He could've let you get your land legs, mind," she says, in a thick, familiar accent that marks her at once as a Geordie.

He steps back from the table. "Matron, I . . ." Her blue eyes, framed in a nest of fine wrinkles, take it all in.

She comes around to his side, her voice a whisper. "Is everything all reet, then?"

"Yes, yes! Thank you . . . Well, no . . . I'm in a wee bind," he whispers back. "I wish I'd examined the patient first. If I'd only had a chance to think about the operation, to review the steps . . . I've operated on hydroceles, but Matron, this—I hardly know where to begin."

"Aye, of course!" she says soothingly. "Peter or Krishnan could have learnt you, but they're both busy. I'll tell you what—you divven't *need* an assistant, but this being your first day, if you don't mind, I'll scrub in myself."

He could kiss her, but she's gone. Digby unclasps his hands and re-drapes the towels around the brown melon for want of anything to do. The scrub nurse nods approvingly. Digby's not used to such deference from the staff. In Glasgow he was bullied by the scrub nurse and was fodder for the senior registrar or the consultant. It had nothing to do with religion, just medical hierarchy, although they weren't above asking "What school d'ya go tae?" or fishing for his football loyalty with "Who d'ye follow?" He's ashamed to realize that here in British India, he's white and that puts him above anyone who is not. The nurse will do nothing to add to his embarrassment.

She asks politely, "Tenelevenfifteen, Doctor?"

"He says he'd like the eleven blade, thank you, Sister," Matron Honorine says, appearing on the other side just in time to decipher the question, and now speaking in an accent worthy of the BBC.

Honorine grips the scrotum with both hands, as though placing a rugby ball on the goal line. "We have so much filarial infection in Madras. It clogs the lymphatics. The swollen legs—the elephantiasis—gets all the attention, but there's fifty of these beauties for every big leg." She squeezes to make the skin taut. "I'd make a longish vertical skin incision here first." She points just to the right of the median raphe, the dark streak over the septum that divides the scrotum into two compartments.

The skin parts under his blade and blood wells up at the edges. Digby finds his rhythm as he ties off bleeders. His heart rate slows. Order is restored.

On her advice, he wraps gauze around his index finger and pushes the scrotal skin off the tense balloon, working all around until the fluid-filled sac is delivered fully from that half of the scrotum, a shiny, huge Fabergé egg.

"You can drain it now. I'll get a basin," she says, turning aside.

But Digby has already stabbed the balloon. A jet of clear yellow fluid hits him in the face before he can jerk his head away. Honorine grabs the scrotum and points the fountain to the basin. "Well, you've just been christened, you have there, pet," she says, laughing. The orderly wipes his eyes for him.

Once the balloon is flaccid, Digby trims the redundant sac off the testes, leaving just a fringe, and then oversews the cut edge. "You could make a bonny bloose out of that," Honorine says, holding up the shiny excised tissue.

He repeats the procedure on the other side of the scrotum and closes both skin incisions. "Most grateful, Matron. Don't know what I'd have done without you."

"Call us Honorine, pet," she says. "You did famously. It's the same operation as you did in Scotland, just that the pathology is magnified."

That word captures Digby's first impression of India. It's a term he'll use often when a familiar disease takes on grotesque proportions in the tropics: "magnified."

Digby rides a bicycle to work each day because he can't abide being pulled in a rickshaw when he is able-bodied. This morning, on the small street outside his bungalow he finds a carpet of yellow blossoms from the towering copper pod. He turns onto the dusty macadam thoroughfare and overtakes a dhobi with a huge laundry bundle on his bicycle rack. The banyan tree on Digby's route is a hive of industry. Already the letter writer is busy, sitting cross-legged with a square of cardboard balanced on his thighs and serving as his desk, as he takes dictation from a woman. A hawker lays his plastic bangles on a sheet on the ground; the earwax remover waits for customers. On the other side of the tree, the saffron-robed fortune-teller fans his deck of cards, warming up for business, his birdcage beside him. Digby has seen previously how the parrot emerges to pick the card that reveals the customer's destiny; then the bird cocks a wistful glance to the sky before returning to its cage.

Passing a tea stall, Digby notices a customer squinting to see past milky-white corneas. Digby takes in the prominent brow and the collapsed, saddle-shaped nose—the man has congenital syphilis, without a doubt. If Digby had anyone at home to write to, he might catalog these morning sights, describe the small-framed, handsome Tamils with their sharp Roman features, bright glittering eyes, and ready smiles. Next to them he feels pale, blotchy, and much too vulnerable to the sun.

Digby immerses himself in running the native surgical wards. His LMPs, Peter and Krishnan, are masters of the minor operations: hydroceles, circumcisions, amputations, urethral strictures, draining abscesses, removing lipomas and cysts. They pass on their skills to him quite generously. He emulates his LMPs in other ways, drinking gallons of water a day, along with a salt tablet or a salt lassi. The heat and humidity are constant. There is a short rainy season, so he's told, though most years it hardly merits its name.

Before Digby arrived, native patients needing major surgery—thyroidectomies, mastectomies, surgery for duodenal ulcers, and head and neck tumor resections—were sent on to the Madras Medical College and General Hospital. Now, Digby takes on just a few major operations that he feels comfortable performing; of these, the operation to cure peptic ulcers is the most common. It's pointless to prescribe daily antacid therapy to a long-suffering patient who barely earns enough for food. During surgery, Digby leaves the ulcer in the scarred duodenum alone and instead removes a chunk of the acid-producing part of the stomach—a partial gastrectomy. Then he connects the remnant of the stomach to a loop of jejunum, thus bypassing the ulcer. He feels Professor Elder's eyes on him, hears his voice at every step, as Digby sutures bowel: "If it looks all right, it's too tight. If it looks too loose, it's all right." The results are dramatic, with patients quickly pain-free and able to eat. On theater days he'll speed through three of these operations before he gets to anything else.

One of his peptic ulcer patients on the fourth post-op day hasn't recovered bowel function. Digby says to Krishnan, "I don't understand. The surgery went well, and his pulse and temperature are fine, the wound is good. Why are his bowels so silent?"

"Maybe he needs you to reassure him, sir. Say it with full feeling. I will translate."

A skeptical Digby squats by the bed. "Senthil, we cured the ulcer. Everything looks perfect inside you." The man's eyes are on Digby's lips, ignoring Krishnan, as if the Tamil comes off Digby's tongue. "Soon you can eat anything." Senthil looks relieved; his wife tries to touch Digby's feet. Digby feels quite silly.

At the end of the day, while Digby, Peter, Krishnan, and Honorine take tea in her office, the probationer pokes her head in to say, "Matron! Patient Senthil is passing flatus only!"

"Praise the Lord," says Honorine. "He who farts, lives!"

Digby coughs out his tea.

Arnold is rarely to be seen and his wards are largely empty. When he and Matron are alone at the end of a long day, seated in her office and resting their feet, Digby cannot stop himself from saying, "Honorine, I'm puzzled about Claude. I mean . . . I don't understand. Why is it that his ward . . . I mean, why doesn't he . . . ? That is to say . . ."

Honorine waits, relishing his embarrassment. "Well! You waited a long time to ask, didn't you, Digby Kilgour. Ah, you'll hear it soon enough, you will. And then it might be exaggerated. What is it about Claude Arnold? Who but Claude can ever say? Did you kna'a he's the oldest of three brothers, all in India? The youngest is a governor up north. The man rules over territory bigger than England, Scotland, and Ireland put together. The middle one is first secretary to the viceroy. In other words, they're both at the very top of the ICS." The Indian Civil Service, or ICS, is the machine by which a mere thousand British administrators control three hundred million people, a miracle of management. "As to why Claude hasn't reached those heights hissel', well that's a mystery to we all. Alcohol's a big part of it, but that may have come later. All three of them brothers are Old Etonians, or Old Harrow—Old something.

A public-school boy, 'n other words, a reet bobby dazzler, except he's not thrived as he should," she growls in the Geordie accent she retreats to when it's just the two of them. "Public school education is the very heart and soul of the Raj. Have you went to public school then, pet?"

Digby laughs. "You wouldn't ask if you thought I had."

"Believe it or not, I was almost engaged to an Old Boy from Rugby. The public schools give them boys three tools, Digby. Knowledge, ceremony, and sport. Me Hugh knew his classics, his Latin, and his *History of the Peloponnesian War*. But he'd have to scratch his heed to draw a map and put our Newcastle on it, wouldn't he! It's all about 'We must strive, and we must win.' Them bairns are taught their destiny is to rule the world. Look at the magnificent buildings we have here. Or d'ya remember the durbar to celebrate Queen Victoria as Empress of India—not that she came for it, mind. It works wonders in cowing the natives. But it only works because those ICS types, to a man, *believe* they're doing good. They're civilizing the world."

Digby is taken aback at her breathless anger against the mission of the British Empire. When he signed up he hadn't given much thought at all to the mission. But from the outset he's felt guilty about his newfound privilege. He doesn't ask Honorine anything more about her Hugh, and she doesn't volunteer. Her mood has turned sour.

She pulls out a bottle of sherry and, ignoring Digby's raised eyebrow, fills two tiny glasses. The nutty, caramel-like flavor and the sweetness are a revelation. His glass is soon empty.

"Are we not doing *some* good here, Honorine?" he asks gently.

She looks at him kindly. "Aye, bonny lad, you are! Us all are! Our hospital, the railways, and telegraphs. Plenty good things. But it's *their* land, Digby, and we take and take us. We take tea, rubber, take their looms so they must buy our cotton at ten times the cost . . ."

"I met a young Indian barrister on my ship," Digby says. "Lovely man who nursed me when I was ill. He said that our leaving India is inevitable."

Honorine stares at her glass as though she doesn't hear him.

"Ah, well, there you gan," she says after a bit. "Now off with you," she adds, taking his glass from him. "No, don't argue. I can't gan yem if you're still here. You did a good day's work. Gan over to the club like a good sahib. You deserve a drink—a proper one."

CHAPTER 14

The Art of the Craft

1934, Madras

In the morning as Digby turns into the native ward, a giant goiter leaps up in front of him. It bulges from collarbone to chin, swallowing all the landmarks of the neck. The face above it sits like a pea atop a toadstool. Aavudainayaki is a thin woman with a broad smile that makes up for the rudeness of her goiter. Palms clasped, she greets him with "*Vanakkam*, Doctor!" When she first arrived, her overactive goiter caused her palpitations and tremors and made her intolerant of heat. Two weeks of oral saturated solution of potassium iodide drops—SSKI—have reversed her symptoms, and she's thrilled. But SSKI has done nothing for the enormous, lumpy swelling that stretches taut the skin of her neck, revealing the lattice of engorged blood vessels on the goiter's surface.

"*Vanakkam*, Aavudainayaki!" He feels bad that he's unable—or isn't foolhardy enough—to tackle her goiter, but he's taken pains to master her formidable name. To remove her goiter he needs a skilled surgeon to teach him. The same is true if he is to tackle the exceedingly common cancers of the tongue or of the larynx that are related to the unsightly habit of chewing *paan*. He referred Aavudainayaki to the Madras Medical College, but she refused. No one

but "Jigiby Doctor," who gave her the miraculous drops, may operate. Krishnan translated her thoughts: "She says she has faith only in
you, and she'll wait until you agree."

"Honorine," Digby says when he enters the ward, "stop feeding that goiter. I swear it's grown overnight."

"It won't get smaller with yer complaining. I've canceled your
clinic on Tuesday. We're meeting Ravi. Dr. V. V. Ravichandran at
General Hospital. He's brilliant . . . The first Indian full professor in
surgery at the Madras Medical College. When the governor needed
surgery, his wife quietly sent for Ravi. Everyone knows he's the best,
but on top of that he's a lovely man and a good teacher. I knew him
when we were posted together in Tanjore."

"Well, well! What's this?" An Indian in white slacks and a white
short-sleeved shirt breezes into his own office, three junior doctors in tow, his high-pitched laughter preceding him as he exclaims,
"Claude Arnold's assistant wants to learn? A miracle! Most want to
flee Claude only!" His excited demeanor is that of a man perpetually
on the verge of hysterical laughter, his eyes buried in round, smiling cheeks. Digby finds himself grinning. Dr. Ravichandran grasps
Honorine's and Digby's hands at the same time. His prematurely
gray hair is slicked back and receding. On his convex forehead his
namam is a vertical, three-pronged fork, the center stripe red and the
flanking two white. It signals he's a Vaishnavite, holding Vishnu to be
the supreme god in the pantheon.

Ravichandran releases Digby's hand but not Honorine's; his
full lips are pulled back into a disarming grin that Digby soon understands is a permanent state. "Dr. Digby, but for this remarkable lady
I would have collapsed and been cremated in Tanjore, such was my
busy-busyness, daily, from morning to night." His lilting speech
reminds Digby of the Carnatic music teacher next door to his bungalow, who drills his students in the army of intermediate notes
between the Western do-re-mi. "But Madam Honorine stepped in,
no discussion. She made a schedule. Including tea together each day,

no matter what, at four thirty. Then I was to go home. Private practice could only begin at seven *pee yem*. Not only that, she decreed that practice must be away from my house, so I'd have some sleep!"

"Fat lot of good that did, Ravi, when you kept giving patients your home address."

Ravi guffaws at his own helplessness. "*Ayo*, Honorine, those Tanjore patients are still coming two hundred and fifteen miles to see me, though I try to dissuade them!" His professional vanity is strangely charming.

The bearer sets down tea and butter biscuits; the stenographer pushes a stack of forms before Ravi and he signs without looking down. A limping barefoot man in a blue uniform, who Digby learns later is Veerappan, Ravi's former patient and driver, sets a colossal six-tiered silver tiffin carrier on Ravi's cluttered desk. He unlocks the frame by sliding the long spoon-bolt out of its rings, then unstacks and displays each dish for Ravi to peer at and sniff before Veerappan reassembles it all and departs, having filled the room with the scent of coriander, cumin, and lentils.

"Some things haven't changed, I see," Honorine says. "How's yer muther, then?"

"My mother is well, thanks be to the Divine," Ravi says. "Digby, no other hand but my mother's prepares my food, as I am her one and only issue." He giggles mischievously. "If she knew that I am giving it away to patients in the septic ward, she would have to destroy the cooking vessels, bathe in the temple thrice a day, and live on barley and ghee for five days. But she is suspicious. When I get home, she'll ask, 'How was the bitter gourd?' knowing fully well there was no bitter gourd! Veerappan has a second tiffin carrier in the car whose existence is unknown to Mother. I eat when I go later for house calls. I give in to my weakness for mutton korma with paratha. Beloved Matron Honorine only was my temptress and corrupter. Her pease pudding with ham—that was how my flesh-eating life began. One day, I will atone by giving away all my possessions—wear saffron robes, go to Benares, and pass from the world."

All this while, an audience of junior doctors looks on, and an office boy hands Ravi a stack of chits, each of which he manages to scan without losing his train of thought.

"Glasgow, is it? Oh, Digby, so much I wanted to visit. Glasgow! Edinburgh! Hallowed names for surgeons, are they not? How wonderful it would have been to sit for the exams. To put the magical FRCS behind my name . . . Fellow of the Royal College of Surgeons! *Ayo*, I even had my steamer ticket!"

"What stopped you?" Digby asks hesitantly.

"Three thousand years of history," Ravi says gravely. "We Brahmins believe the ocean is polluted, and in crossing to a foreign land over water the soul putrefies; one is damned for all time—"

"Tell him the truth, Ravi," Honorine says. "It was your mother."

He bursts out laughing. "Correctly only Honorine is telling. *Ayo*, my saintly mother . . . it would kill her. If I went overseas that would be matricide. Supposing she survived, her only issue would return so polluted that even if he stood out of sight, she could not speak to him ever again. Thus only, I stayed. But tell me, Digby, what made *you* risk eternal damnation and cross the water? What are you running from? Or to?"

Blood surges around Digby's scar. Ravichandran's grinning gaze settles there with curiosity and compassion. Digby searches for words.

"A blushing surgeon is better than the other kind," Ravi says to Honorine. "I won't add to the discomfort of a man who is already having Claude Arnold as his superior. Digby, did you know a Rolls-Royce sits in front of Claude's house? Why he bought it? Because I have one! My Rolls was the first in Madras and has been a splinter under the dermis of your countrymen! 'The impertinence of this *babu*!'" Ravi says, trying to mimic a posh English accent. His laughter interrupts his narrative. "The governor had to get one. Much later, Claude Arnold too. But Claude's doesn't move. It decorates the house like the *pottu* on my mother's forehead. Digby, I am unmarried. I work very hard. For the profession I am giving up the necessities, but should I give up the luxuries? In my own land, am I not to come and go as I please?"

Ravi suddenly shouts over Digby's shoulder at someone in what sounds like coarse and vulgar Tamil, his smile fading. "Impatient people!" he says, the smile slowly returning. "Always rushing. I am so behind that yesterday catches up with tomorrow. Anyway, Digby, if saintly Honorine likes you, then I am liking too. Come. My first case is a stomach resection for a likely gastric cancer. If it's not too far gone."

In the theater, Digby assists, anticipating Ravichandran's movements, yet careful not to get in the way. There's a rock-hard mass in the antrum, just above the pylorus where the stomach empties, a location where even a small tumor comes quickly to a patient's attention because they feel full after a few bites. Ravi runs his hand over the surface of the liver, then pulls out the small bowel, all twenty feet of it, feeding it through his hands, looking for metastasis. Then he inspects the pelvis. "No spread. We'll do a distal gastrectomy. Switch sides. I will be your humble servant." Digby cuts out half of the stomach. Having Ravichandran as his skilled assistant, subtly improving his view and access, makes Digby feel like a far better surgeon than he really is. When he's done, they're left with a stump of the duodenum—into which bile and pancreatic juice pour—and the stump of the stomach remnant.

"What now, my young friend?"

"I'll sew off the duodenum, leaving a blind stump. Then I'll connect a loop of jejunum to the remnant of the stomach." It's the same familiar procedure he does for peptic ulcers at Longmere.

"A gastrojejunostomy, is it? Why not join the stomach directly to the duodenum? A Billroth One? Why not keeping the normal continuity? And then no duodenal stump to leave behind that might leak."

Digby clasps his hands together, his gloves bloody past the knuckles, the open belly awaiting his decision. "To be honest," he stammers, "I've done many more gastrojejunostomies at Longmere. For me it would be trickier to connect what's left of the stomach to the scarred duodenum than to do what I am familiar with and know I can do safely. Yes, it would leave behind a blind duodenal stump, but that has less chance of leaking than if I tried to connect the stomach to the duodenum. In my hands."

"Good answer! The best possible operation is not the same as the best operation possible! Of course, if the cancer returns, all this is moot. Go ahead."

Operating weekly with Ravichandran at General Hospital is precisely the surgical education Digby sought when he came to India. He sops up every pearl the brilliant surgeon offers, and lingers to watch Ravi as he operates with others. Meanwhile, Aavudainayaki waits, unwavering in her determination that "Jigiby Doctor" take out her goiter. She earns her keep on the wards by being a willing helper to Matron and the nurses, and a support to new patients. She has become family.

Five weeks after first meeting Ravichandran, Digby takes Aavudainayaki to General Hospital in the early morning in a rickshaw. Ravi greets her graciously in Tamil. After palpating her goiter, he has her raise her arms and keep them up, her biceps bracketing her cheeks. Soon, her face gets dusky colored and congested, and she becomes breathless. "See that, Digby? Call it 'Ravi's sign.' It means this goiter extends into her chest. If we can't get at it from the top, we'll be sawing through the sternum. Nothing routine about this, I assure you."

The anxious patient is eager to convey something in Tamil to Ravi, who reassures her. He says drily to Digby, "I've assured her that the white man only is performing the surgery. I am merely assisting the great Jigiby Doctor."

Ravi fusses after the patient is under anesthesia, asking first for a bigger sandbag between the shoulder blades to throw her neck forward, and for the foot of the table to be lowered further to help the engorged neck veins drain better. "Small things make a big difference, Digby. God is in the small things."

Soon after they start, the operative field is cluttered with hemostats and they pause to tie off all the bleeders. As Ravi predicted, Aavudainayaki's goiter extends down into the chest; not even his long fingers can retrieve it. "Ravichandran's Spoon, please," he says, turning to the scrub nurse. The long instrument she produces is new to Digby. Ravi eases it under the breastbone. Blind, by feel alone, he levers the lower pole of the goiter out of the chest. "You recognize my instrument, Digby? It's the spoon that slides through the side slots of my tiffin carrier and bolts the stacked dishes together. My mother blames the driver for losing our spoons. Truly it is multi-purposeful, is it not? Eating fish curry or fishing out goiter!" When they're done, Ravi is concerned. "The first night is the most dangerous. Essential to have a tracheostomy tray and a nurse at the bedside, please." There's reason to worry: the cartilage rings of the trachea normally prop the airway open, but Aavudainayaki's are thinned out from long-standing pressure from her goiter. Postoperative swelling presents a real danger of the rings collapsing.

Digby has a full day of clinic and rounds at Longmere. But after dinner, he cycles to General Hospital again. Aavudainayaki's smile has greeted him each morning for weeks now. For all her faith in Jigiby Doctor, he's terrified of it ending badly.

At night all hospitals become hushed, sepulchral, the silence punctuated by a few coughs or moans. Digby's footsteps echo in the hallways as he passes the open wards. A nurse sitting under a dim lamp looks up, surprised; she smiles shyly. Her smile stays with him. He feels a longing to be close to a woman.

Aavudainayaki sleeps comfortably, a tracheostomy kit at her bedside, but no nurse is to be seen. A sluggish, slovenly probationer returns after an hour, startled to see Digby. He dismisses her. He'll keep vigil himself. To pass time he tries to depict the stages of the operation in his sketchbook.

* * *

Digby wakes to a high-pitched mewling noise and the sight of a desperate Aavudainayaki laboring to pull in air. That frightening sound—stridor—signals airway obstruction. He leaps to her side, ashamed that he fell asleep. Her terror-stricken face shows no joy at seeing Jigiby Doctor; she senses her imminent death. Digby tears open the tracheostomy tray while yelling for help. This is his worst nightmare: a tracheostomy in bad lighting with a struggling patient. He slashes through her dressings and is stunned to find her neck no longer flaccid as it had been after surgery—but swollen as though the goiter has returned with a vengeance! He cuts away three skin sutures and a huge blood clot slithers out past his fingers onto the bedsheet, a leering, jellylike blob. Aavudainayaki's distress eases at once. Others arrive and flashlights shine onto the wound, which shows no active bleeding. The trachea is exposed and he could easily do a tracheostomy. But he sees no fresh bleeding and Aavudainayaki's breathing is steady, her face calm. She even tries to smile.

He should take her back to the theater and under anesthesia explore the wound, find the bleeder if it's still oozing. But it's four in the morning. For an outsider to get the theater up at that hour will require an act of God. He's loath to phone Ravi. He lets the skin flap back down without suturing it, just covering it loosely with gauze. *If there's the slightest sign of fresh blood, I'll take her back.*

In the morning, the surgical team arrives for rounds, Ravi at its head. He eyes the large liquefying clot in the basin. Aavudainayaki's smile is back, but Dr. V. V. Ravichandran is unsmiling. He examines the wound. The entourage of interns and assistant surgeons shift their feet nervously. "Which one of you checked this patient in the night?" Silence. "Good thing you were here, Digby. But when that clot came out, she belonged in the theater. You should have called me at once."

"Her breathing improved. If—"

"No ifs, buts, and *baingan bhartas*!" Ravi says sharply, cutting him off. "In the interest of a patient you may wake me and Jesus Christ himself. To wake the anesthetist, you will need divine assistance. But take patient to theater. No discussion!" He glowers at Digby for a few seconds, then his expression softens. He picks up Digby's open sketchbook. "*Aah*, nice only. Those surgical atlases never bleed, do they?"

As Ravi and the surgical crew are about to exit the ward, he stops and turns around so suddenly, his retinue pile into one another. His voice fills the ward. "Dr. Kilgour. Good surgeons can do any operation. Great surgeons take care of their own complications."

Digby colors with the praise.

CHAPTER 15

A Fine Catch

1934, Madras

"Aa' never seen so many uniforms in the city," Honorine says. She and Digby are in the New Elphinstone Theater, taking refuge from a blazing sun. The Saturday matinee crowd is a sea of regulation haircuts and khaki. "Here I was hoping Longmere would be me last posting. If it's war again, they'll drag we from the Civil Branch to the military. Of course, I'll do me part. But the world's gone mental, if you ask me. Japan invading China? What if they decide India's next? Not to mention them Germans, the new chancellor. I don't trust him, me."

"It feels inevitable when you read the papers—war, I mean." Digby was astonished to learn that a million Indian soldiers had fought in the Great War, and as many as one hundred thousand had died. Editorials opine that if Indians are to be conscripted into the British Indian Army to fight again, they won't settle for anything less than freedom in return.

"Inevitable? God, na divven't say that!" She scrabbles in her large wicker bag. She gives up, then snatches the kerchief Digby proffers and dabs her eyes. "I lost my older brothers in that war. It was the death of me poor mam. These politicians? They're all gadgies, Digby," she says bitterly. "If women were in power, you'd not see us sending lads to their death."

If there's war, Digby will be posted to a military unit. He recalls Professor Alan Elder in Glasgow saying that war was the only proper school for surgeons. It's not a thought Digby will share with Honorine.

The triple feature ends with *City Lights*. Chaplin's physical comedy has them convulsing in laughter. The wistful sweetness of the story—a tramp who falls in love with a blind girl and raises money for an operation to restore her sight—is the ideal antidote for the talk of war.

They emerge after what seems a lifetime. Though it is dusk, it is blisteringly hot, the air still. Instantly, Digby feels sweat beading on his lip and his brow. Despite the smells of frying *vada* from a roadside stall, the heat has erased his appetite.

"Marina Beach," Honorine says decisively to a *jatka* driver whose long, betel-nut-stained teeth resemble those of his nag; neither man nor horse is enthusiastic about moving.

"Chaplin redeems all men," Honorine says, her mood improved. "True love wins the day. I'd take him back to mine if I could."

"Not much of a conversationalist though, is he?"

"And that'd be the blessing of it and all!" Honorine says.

On Wallajah Road, the horse whinnies, picking up its pace. The driver sits up. Honorine closes her eyes and inhales. Digby feels the first stirrings of hunger.

By such subtle signs, like an orchestra tuning up, the daily event that is central to life on the Coromandel Coast announces itself: the evening breeze. The Madras evening breeze has a body to it, its atomic constituents knitted together to create a thing of substance that strokes and cools the skin in the manner of a long, icy drink or a plunge into a mountain spring. It pushes through on a broad front, up and down the coast; unhurried, reliable, with no slack until after midnight, by which time it will have lulled them into beautiful sleep. It doesn't know caste or privilege as it soothes the expatriates in their pocket mansions, the shirtless clerk sitting with his wife on the rooftop of his one-room house, and the pavement dwellers in their roadside squats. Digby has seen the cheery Muthu become distracted, his conversation clipped and morose, as he waits for the relief that comes from the direction of Sumatra and Malaya, gathering itself over the Bay of Bengal, carrying scents of orchids and salt, an airborne opiate that unclenches, unknots, and finally lets one forget the brutal heat of the day. "Yes, yes, you are having your Taj Mahal, your Golden Temple, your Eiffel Tower," an educated Madrasi will say, "but can anything match our Madras evening breeze?"

The sandy beach that comes into view is so wide that the blue of the ocean is a narrow ribbon melting into the horizon. They're coming to the very spot where the British got their first toehold in India in the form of a tiny trading post, the forerunner to the East India Trading Company. By the 1600s, the depot needed a military fort—Fort Saint George—to store the spices, silk, jewelry, and tea bound for home, and to keep these goods out of the hands of local warlords, and the French, and the Dutch. The city of Madras blossomed on either side of the fort. Digby is becoming more familiar with the city, exploring it by bicycle, and puzzling out its neighborhoods. The old "Blacktown" near the fort changed its name to Georgetown when the Prince of Wales came to visit. Anglo-Indians cluster in Purasawalkam and Vepery, while foreigners choose Egmore or the fancier suburbs of Nungambakkam. The Brahmin enclave is Mylapore, while the Muslim population is concentrated in the vicinity of Gosha Hospital and Triplicane. He and Honorine have arrived at Madras Marina, conceived of by a former governor with the improbable name of Mountstuart Elphinstone Grant Duff. The grand promenade runs for miles in either direction.

Along the marina and facing the sea is a succession of massive edifices, built for the ages. Freed by distance from the constraints of Whitehall, it appears to Digby that the architects indulged their Oriental fantasies, building these sculpted temples to the Empire. He and Honorine dismount by the University Senate Building. Its tall minarets appear to have mated and given birth to a brood of junior spires all crowned with snowcaps. Digby sees Renaissance, Byzantine, Muslim, and Gothic elements all battling each other in one structure. It's meant to fill the natives with awe, Digby thinks. Like the Singer clock tower.

"I *should* hate these buildings," Honorine says. "But I'll miss them when I leave, I will."

Digby is puzzled. Honorine has lived longer in India than in England.

Seeing his expression, Honorine laughs. "Oh Digby, I love this city. Love living here. But the country'll be free soon. I divven't talk about it because it'd be heresy, wouldn't it? Of course, if the Indians lets us stay, I will."

They make an odd pair, strolling barefoot in the sand: the lumbering, gray-haired woman on the arm of a gaunt, younger man whose dark hair has a reddish tinge, as though he's rubbed henna into it. His scar makes him look boyish. They sit gazing out to sea. Three fishermen squat in the shadow of a catamaran, smoking, their backs to the water.

"I'm embarrassed how little I knew of India when I signed up," Digby says suddenly. "All I thought about was getting surgical experience—as if the Indian Medical Service existed to serve me." He must raise his voice over the roar of crashing waves. "I doubt I'll get used to the privileges I have here. I fear what might happen if I did."

A young couple strolls past, pressed against each other. The jasmine in the woman's hair leaves a perfumed trail. Matron regards them and sighs. "What are you doing hanging round old Honorine, Digby? You know my nurses all have you in their sights."

He laughs self-consciously. "I'm not quite ready for that. Too complicated."

"Ah, yes, well, you're safe with me."

"I meant—"

"The thing about my Anglo-Indian girls, Digby, my nurses, and the secretaries? They're at the short end of the stick. Some may look whiter than you or me, but a fat lot of good that does. They imagine if they were to marry someone like you, they'd *become* British. But the truth is you'd have a hard time bringing them into the Madras Club. And your bairns would still be Anglo-Indians and face the same obstacles. You have a wounded air about you, pet, and yer a canny surgeon. Makes you attractive. Be cautious, is all I'm saying."

Digby laughs nervously, thankful that in the twilight she can't see him blush.

"Nothing to fear, Honorine. My solitude is a state I've gotten used to. It feels safer than . . ." He can't bring himself to utter the alternative.

Honorine's face shows sadness, or is it pity? "Forgive her, Digs. Let her go."

For a moment he's at a loss. She's the only person in Madras to whom he's volunteered the story of his mother's death, the hard years before and after. Secrecy lives in the same rooms as loneliness. His secret—and his failing—is that after his mother's betrayal, he cannot risk love.

"I have, Honorine."

"Ah, well," she says, looking out to sea, the breeze blowing her hair back. "It's not me you have to convince, is it, pet?"

Before Christmas, as Digby is about to head home, Honorine rushes into his ward, a tall, stocky white man in tow. "Digby, come with us. This is Franz Mylin. Doctor Arnold admitted his wife two days ago. She's not doing well."

Mylin is built for rugby, with a huge neck and upper body. He is carrot-topped, and at this moment his face, contorted with anger, is also red. They head upstairs while Honorine recounts the essentials, couching her words for the husband's sake: the Mylins just returned by steamer from England and on the last three days of the journey, Lena Mylin developed abdominal pain and vomiting that became worse. On disembarking they came directly to Long-mere. Claude Arnold's admitting diagnosis was dyspepsia. "That was thirty-six hours ago," Honorine says.

Mylin bursts out, "He barely touched her when she came in. Haven't seen him since! She's just been lying there, getting worse by the hour."

The British ward is empty but for the birdlike figure of Lena Mylin, lying very still in bed, her breathing rapid. Strands of dark curly hair are glued to her forehead. She watches Digby's approach with apprehension. Franz says, "Please don't jar her bed. The slight-est movement makes the pain worse."

That statement alone speaks of peritonitis from an abdominal catastrophe, which Digby's exam confirms: the right side of her belly is rigid. He registers her dry tongue and parched lips and the tint of jaundice in her eyes, and her clammy skin. When he asks her to take a deep breath while he gently probes below her ribs on the right side, she winces and arrests her inhalation. Her inflamed gallbladder has met Digby's fingers. He doesn't mince words. "I'm pretty sure a stone is obstructing your gallbladder and now it's dis-tended with pus." He avoids the word "gangrenous," so as not to alarm them further. "It's urgent we operate."

"The bastard called it seasickness!" Franz says bitterly. "Where is he? This is criminal!"

In the theater, as soon as Digby opens the abdomen, he sees what he feared: a distended, angry-looking gallbladder with dusky patches of gangrene. *There's your dyspepsia, Claude.* He makes a small hole in the engorged sack. A sludge of yellow pus, green bile, and small pigment stones spills out onto the gauze pads and into the suction apparatus. He unroofs as much of the gallbladder as he can, leaving only the part stuck to the liver. He avoids the cystic duct where the gallbladder empties. Dissecting there with all this inflam-mation is hazardous. Lena's tissues bleed vigorously. Before closing the belly, he leaves a rubber drain near the liver bed. After surgery

Lena Mylin looks very pale and has low blood pressure. Digby hurries to the "blood bank"—a closet with a refrigerator, really—where, using typing serum, he establishes that hers is B blood group, a rare one. The blood bank is his innovation, one of the areas in which they are ahead of the other city hospitals. After a pint of blood, Lena's blood pressure rises and color returns to her face.

"Whose blood was that?" Franz asks.

"Mine," Digby says. His blood group makes him a universal donor. Luckily, he had two units of his own blood in storage for just such a need. "I'm going to give her a second bottle."

Digby keeps vigil with Franz. By morning Lena is clearly improved. He learns that the Mylins have an estate on the other coast, near Cochin. Franz's face relaxes when he describes their home of many years in the Western Ghats, where he grows tea and spices. "You must come and visit, Doctor Kilgour."

At noon Digby returns to find Claude Arnold at the foot of the bed, examining Lena's chart while Franz stands there, arms crossed, glowering, bursting to speak. Lena's face is averted.

"Well," Claude says, registering Digby's presence, "Dr. Kilgour saved the day, it seems—" and with that he slips past Digby and walks out before they can react. Digby pacifies an apoplectic Franz.

Later, when Digby emerges from the ward, Claude appears from his rear. He must have waited behind a pillar. If Digby imagined that Arnold might be sheepish, or even grateful to his junior, he's quickly disabused of that notion.

"You should have just put in a drain and come out. Nibbling away pieces of the gallbladder? Hardly standard practice." Claude's back is turned to the ward entrance and he misses Franz Mylin emerging to loom just behind him. "I call that irresponsible and foolhardy, Digby."

Before a stunned Digby can think of a rejoinder, Claude once again walks away. But this time, with an oath, Franz lunges and slams a meaty hand on Claude's shoulder, spinning him around. Claude's supercilious expression is replaced by one of surprise and fear. Digby leaps between them as Franz swings, so the deflected punch hits Claude's chest. Arnold flees. Franz roars at the retreating figure of Longmere's chief surgeon: "Come back, you fucking coward! Who are you calling irresponsible? You're not half the surgeon Kilgour is!" The words echo on Claude's empty ward. For the rest of Lena's stay, Claude stays away.

Lena turns out to be the more sociable and talkative half of the couple. She knows every probationer's name and they cannot do enough for her. The drain is out in three days, and ten days after her surgery, she is ready for discharge.

When it's time to say goodbye, Franz grasps Digby's shoulders and squeezes; the big man is too moved to speak.

Lena takes Digby's hand. "Digby," she says, surprising him by using his first name. "How can I repay you? You saved my life. We'll be offended if you don't visit us at the estate. You need a holiday. Please promise you'll come?" Digby's sputtering reply isn't convincing. "Digby," she says, "do you have relatives in India?"

"No, I don't."

"Oh, yes you do. We're blood now."

CHAPTER 16

The Craft of the Art

1934 Christmas, Madras

Nungambakkam, where Claude Arnold resides, is a vision of England rendered on the canvas of southern India. Tree-lined avenues carry names like College Road, Sterling Road, and Haddows Road. The topiary outside the garden homes and bungalows is Bird-on-Pyramid, Ball-atop-Ball, and Bunny Rabbit, with little variation; Bunny Rabbit is the most popular. Digby thinks it's the work of one itinerant *maali*, if for no other reason than that every Bunny Rabbit looks a little like a mongoose.

This fantasy of Belgravia in Madras must ignore the reality of the pariah dog's corpse in the middle of College Road; it must stubbornly hold that this is indeed the eighth day of Christmas despite humidity that would dissuade eight maids a-milking from doing any such thing, and heat so relentless that the pariah dog, it turns out, isn't dead, just felled by sunstroke. It staggers to its feet, forcing Digby to swerve around it on his bicycle.

Claude's porcelain-white home stands out against the red clay of the circular driveway that is packed with vehicles. Oil lamps placed between the balustrades on the second-floor balcony and between the colonnades of the ground floor give it an ethereal glow as the sun approaches the horizon. "If only you brought this much attention to detail to your hospital work, Claude," Digby mutters. He'd debated coming to the Christmas party; in the end he felt it would only worsen their fraught relationship if he stayed away.

A shiny black-and-green Rolls-Royce sits under the portico. Before Digby can lean his bicycle against the wall, a servant grabs it, assuring him by his smile that it will be swiftly hidden and no one will be the wiser.

The living room is overflowing. A Christmas tree rises above the bobbing heads; on its limbs the cotton-ball "snow" droops in the soggy air. The women are in long gowns, some backless, all sleeveless, with silk wraps draped over their shoulders.

Digby, sweating from his ride, would like nothing more than to remove the blazer he put on just before stepping inside. He passes behind three women, their backs to him, their floral perfume evoking Paris or London. He hears Claude's voice, the words slurring just the slightest bit: "—the back seat was the only place the maharani could drink, hidden behind the curtains, while her driver circled the estate." A woman asks a question that Digby doesn't catch, but he hears Claude's reply: "A Rolls never breaks down, my dear. Rarely, it may fail to proceed."

Digby moves past a cabinet packed with sports trophies and framed pictures of two boys at various ages, lately as teenagers. A bearer proffers whisky; Digby takes a napkin instead. He slips into the dining room to discreetly mop his face and neck; he feels shabby and out of place. The heavy oak dining table, the goblets and metal plate holders evoke for him the knights of King Arthur. His back to the festivities, Digby stands before three large, framed landscapes, still sweating energetically. He's angry at himself for being here.

Right, Digs. In two minutes ye'll dive right back in amongst them, shake the bastard's hand, wish him the merriest o' merry Christmases and, since you won't see him in hospital before the bells o' Hogmanay, top it off with an all the best for auld lang syne an' a guid new year tae him and his.

But cool off first, Digs, mop that brow and get in behind that collar. Admire his fancy painting—pasture, is it Claude? Say "very nice" to his pathetic wee lake with its wildflowers. No, no one ever thought of that critique before. And this last painting . . . a dark forest, he says? A dark . . . midden, says I. They're rubbish, thank you very much. Fancy, gilded frames that cry "We belong in a museum" . . . but rubbish they are, and rubbish they'll aye be. No matter how loud anyone cries . . .

"They're not much, are they?" a husky female voice says. He spins around, finding himself uncomfortably close to a woman; she is striking, a shade taller than he. They both step back. Her musky attar with notes of sandalwood and lost civilizations is the opposite of a Parisian scent. He feels transported to a maharani's boudoir. "The bearer said you didn't want whisky. I brought you some pomegranate juice. I'm Celeste," she says, smiling.

Oh, please don't be! Not his wife.

"I'm Claude's wife." She holds a cup in each hand.

Her brown hair is held back with a silver band and pinned in a chignon above her neck. She has a triangular face and a slight overbite, which makes her lips appear to pout. Head on, her features are handsome, faintly androgynous. She's Claude's age, early forties. Three rubies float down over her breastbone, the chain barely visible as it crosses her clavicles.

"Digby Kilgour." He offers his hand. But her hands are occupied. He takes his cup.

"Claude says you're quite the artist."

How the bloody hell would he know? She waits expectantly.

"More an admirer of art," he says, his cheeks burning. "Just trying to capture the things I see."

Her large eyes, the color of chestnuts, are warmed by the glow of the rubies. If Claude is distant, aloof, she's the opposite, her gaze direct and curious. But he sees a hardness around her mouth that vanishes when she smiles.

"Oils?"

"Watercolors," he says. She waits. "I . . . uh, I like the mystery, the unpredictability of what emerges."

"Do you do portraits?" she says, cocking her head. Does she know she is posing? She isn't seeking to cause discomfort but to remedy it.

"Sometimes, yes. I . . . there's so much to see in Madras. Faces on the streets, women in their saris. Banyan trees, landscapes . . . ?" He gestures at the framed paintings. He's babbling.

She leans closer to whisper, "Digby, your honest opinion on these paintings?"

"Ah, well . . . they're not so bad."

"So you like them?" The chestnut eyes fix on him. He cannot lie to her.

"Ah, I wouldn't go that far."

She laughs happily. "They belonged to Claude's parents. I loathe them—the paintings, you understand."

For the first time that evening he feels at ease.

She cocks her head again. "May I show you something?" She walks away, not waiting for an answer. He follows, his eyes on the nape of her neck where fine hairs form an arbor pattern. In the parlor near the stairs hangs a simple painting on beige cloth. It's perhaps twelve inches by sixteen, in a crude wooden frame: a seated Indian woman, her head turned in one direction, her shoulders in another. The style is childlike, simple, yet artful and colorful. It doesn't try to be anatomically correct or realistic, yet it convinces utterly. He takes his time studying it.

"It's extraordinary!" Digby says. "What I mean is with just that line for a nose and ovals for the eyes . . . and curves that convey the sari, the body posture"—he uses his hand to trace the outlines in the air—"and only three colors, the woman emerges! It's uncompli-cated, yet skillfully done. Did you paint this?"

That bright laugh again. The curving line of her neck echoes the painting. The impression of height she gives resides largely in that line, and in her lanky arms. Her grace borders on the awkward, which he finds quite beautiful.

"No. I didn't paint it. But it *is* mine. I've had to fight to display it. It's a *kalighat* painting, a type I saw as a young girl growing up in Calcutta. They churn these out for the pilgrims coming from great distances to the temples. Typically, they portray a character from the *Mahabharata* or *Ramayana*. If it were up to me, I'd bin those old monstrosities and put these up instead." They laugh together. "Yes, I'd have a roomful of *kalighats*." She raises her arm, the wrist angled back as she fans her fingers out, tossing *kalighats* over the walls. His eyes glide off the arc of her triceps, the slope of her forearm, her pronated wrist, the curve of her knuckles, and off her buffed nails and then onto the wall. In his mind's eye he can see a room covered with these vivid and unique portraits.

He forces his eyes back to the painting. With a finger he traces the figure, trying to memorize it.

"There's a lyricism here," he says. "Even if the artist is churning them out. A simple but eloquent vocabulary."

"Precisely! What I find fascinating is that a villager makes a once-in-a-lifetime pilgrimage, then spends hard-earned money on a souvenir that has its roots *in* his village! It's a village craft, like basket weaving, but this craftsman has moved to the city to ply the pilgrim trade. So he sells his wares to his former neighbor and it hangs on a wall in the village where it all began!"

"Or it's displayed in the parlor of a most . . . discerning Englishwoman," Digby says. He turns red. The word "beautiful" floats silently.

"I do believe, Digby, that you're trying to flatter me," she says softly. She isn't displeased. A long silence follows. "I've other *kalighats*. They'd be wasted on this lot. They'd see it as an affectation." She waves gaily at someone, but the hardness regathers around her mouth. "So, are you liking Madras?"

"Yes! The surgical experience is tremendous. And the people are warm, kind."

He's thinking of Muthu, caring for him with such affection and with pride in the smallest tasks he undertakes. Muthu after some months had shyly brought over his wife and two small children to say hello. They now feel like family.

"Digby, have you been to Mahabalipuram?" she says, looking at him speculatively.

"I heard mention. Rock temples, is it?"

"Oh, it's hard to describe . . ." She looks away moodily. "It's my favorite place. I know you'd appreciate it. Would you trust me on that?"

"I would."

"Picture a beautiful, long stretch of sandy beach." Those magical hands are conjuring up images again. "And suddenly you come onto this natural rock formation. Boulders bigger than this room, and others twenty times bigger than this house. Some submerged, others strung on the beach. Ancient artisans carved temples out of them, some as small as a dollhouse and others the size of a theater, complete with seats. Hewn out of one rock, can you imagine? It's believed to have been a place to train sculptors. Mahabalipuram is a dictionary of temple imagery. Every gesture has a meaning. And all the gods are there: dancing Shiva, Durga, and Ganesha. Lions, bulls, elephants—more animals than in a zoo."

He's transported to that beach, he can already see the breeze lift the hair off her neck, and behind her the ancient temples silhouetted in the dusk; he feels salt spray on his face, the scent of ocean mingled with her perfume. He breathes in.

"I see it," he says.

"Do you?" The finger points. "Now keep your eyes glued there as the surf recedes. See that dark shape under the water? More temples, Digby! A string of them. Concealed by the sea. By time. Things have a way of coming back when we think they're gone forever."

A burst of raucous laughter brings them back to earth; sand gives way to hardwood floors and a packed living room where around the Christmas tree, the Raj makes merry, whisky glasses are topped by turbaned bearers, and no one can imagine that this party will ever end.

"That was a beautiful journey, Mrs. Arnold."

"Celeste. Please. 'Mrs. Arnold' makes me feel more ancient than an undersea temple. We must get you there soon. This crowd would never go to Mahabalipuram." She turns to him, searching his face. "I'm so pleased that you like it here. It's unfashionable to say one does, I'm not sure why. For the longest time I thought our stay here was temporary. Claude was certain he'd be transferred to Calcutta, where I grew up. Or Delhi. It delayed my settling in."

The house looks beyond settled. But he doesn't think it suits her. He sees her in a small Chettinad palace: a central courtyard and low ornamental pool edged by stone seats on which to lounge, an indoor teak swing for two, bedrooms drawing the breeze . . .

"It'll be twenty years soon, don't you know?"

"I'm sure the next posting will come soon," he stammers.

"Heaven forbid! I might have wished for that early on. But I love it here. My children call it home, even if they only come every other year. Why leave? If we do leave, Claude will still be Claude, and I'll still . . ." She turns away, studying the painting again, as though she's the guest being shown the host's collection.

He memorizes her silhouette: the brow, the nose, the ramp of her upper lip with its Cupid's bow giving way to the vermilion border of the lower lip, then gliding over her thyroid cartilage, her cricoid, to the tender hollow above her breastbone. He'd like to trace the contour with his finger.

Celeste turns in time to see his blush. Her gaze lingers on his face, her expression unreadable. Then she surveys the living room. The noise of the party swirls around them but doesn't penetrate their cocoon. They spot Claude, his face flushed, eyelids with weights on them.

"Why am I telling you all this, young Digby Kilgour?" she says, her husky voice almost inaudible. She turns back to him, waiting, eyebrows raised.

"Because," he says simply, "you knew I would care."

A brisk dilatation of her pupils. The rubies on her breastbone rise. Her eyes glisten. After a long time, she says, "You won't make my mistake, will you?" Her gaze is soft and smiling once more, her wistful expression gone.

"What mistake is that . . . Celeste?"

"The mistake, Digby, of choosing to see more in your future mate than the evidence has already suggested."

CHAPTER 17

A Race Apart

1935, Madras

Owen and Jennifer Tuttleberry are Anglo-Indian friends of Honorine's, and now of Digby's—Jennifer works as a switchboard operator, while her husband is a locomotive driver. Owen spends his days standing on the footplate of Bessie, his great hissing "dame," her plethora of dials and levers before him, a little boy whose dream has come true. His Shoranur route allows him few chances to sit. "I'll see the sun rise in the Bay of Bengal," Owen says, "then see it set over the Arabian Sea. Am I not the luckiest man alive?"

Digby has been wanting better transport. A car is too expensive, but a second-hand motorcycle may not be. Owen has sent word that he has one and at a price that Digby will like. Digby and Honorine head out by *jatka* to the Perambur Railway Colony. This Anglo-Indian walled enclave on the edge of the city is laid out like a child's toy village and dotted with small identical houses. In the central clearing, young boys play cricket using a tennis ball. Teenagers cluster around the swings under the watchful gaze of the adults. There isn't a sari or *mundu* in sight—it's all frocks, trousers, and shorts.

Outside the Tuttleberrys' house sits a car of unidentifiable make, unpainted, and with spot welds showing. While Honorine goes inside, Owen takes Digby to the backyard to meet Esmeralda, who, Owen says, can be his for a modest sum. The price *is* a bargain, though Digby worries if she really is the "cent-per-cent reliable gem!" that Owen claims. Owen has promised to expand Digby's understanding of things mechanical—a counterpoint to his knowledge of the workings of the body. Esmeralda is nominally a Triumph, but Owen admits that the fuel tank, the handlebars, the front fork, the engine mount, the chassis, the exhaust, and the wooden sidecar have all been fabricated in the Perambur Railway shed, so she is technically part locomotive. Only the single-cylinder engine is original. "She's standoffish till you know her," Owen admits. "But she'll be loyal to you like nobody's business. I love her so much that I'll be your mechanic for life. Promise." With Owen in the sidecar, instructing, Digby gets Esmeralda going and circles the enclave. By the time they return he's smitten. "She's like family, Digby. If I didn't have my car now, I'd keep her. You saw my car? A beauty, no? Need to get it painted."

They *must* stay for dinner, "no question about it." Honorine is seated next to a broad-shouldered young man in pressed black trousers and a spotless blue shirt, his cuffs rolled high enough above his elbows to display thick biceps. Jennifer introduces him as her brother Jeb. He's fairer than his sister, with light brown hair. He clasps Digby's hand in a powerful grip and says, "Doc, my brother-in-law must like you to part with Esmeralda."

Owen says, "Doc, you're shaking hands with a future Olympian, mark my words. If Jeb doesn't make our hockey team then I don't know what's bloody what."

"Don't jinx it, for Christ's sake," Jeb says.

Jennifer says, "My brother doesn't know a ticket from a brinjal but he's supposedly a ticket collector." She flashes a toothy smile framed by red lipstick. "They feed him raw eggs each morning, mutton at lunch, and he plays hockey all day. Cushy life, no?"

The contrast between the fair Jeb and his dark brother-in-law is striking. Owen, with hands that are black from sun exposure and with a permanent rim of grease outlining his fingernails, is also the simpler soul.

Jeb lives with his mother, a few houses down. Soon she joins them, together with Owen's aunt, the Tuttleberrys' two children, and a niece. The family crams around the dinner table with their honored guests. Digby is charmed by this tableau of domestic life: children seated on laps, Uncle Jeb dispensing homemade liquor whose kick is stronger than any locomotive, while Jennifer serves the one-pot meal she calls a "pish-pash": rice, mutton, potatoes, peas, and spices cooked together, a delectable dish.

Owen looks proudly at his wife. "She's a catch, isn't she, Doc? Who'd think she'd marry a darkie like me!"

Once they are outside the railway colony, Esmeralda motors past clusters of huts and shabby, makeshift dwellings. Digby is struck by the contrast: an enclave for Anglo-Indians that excludes natives, yet whose inhabitants are themselves excluded by the ruling race with whom they align. But then, he's in the same spot. Digby Kilgour: oppressed in Glasgow; oppressor here. The thought depresses him.

CHAPTER 18

Stone Temples

1935, Madras

Celeste's driver parks outside Digby's quarters. From the house next door, a quavering rich old man's voice leads young girls in singing "Suprabhatam." The devotional's parsimonious scale, melody, and syncopation feel like a part of her. Janaki, her Tamilian ayah who has been with her from the time she was a little girl in Calcutta, would sing it as she brushed Celeste's hair. That devotional is used to wake the deity, Lord Venkateswara, at the famous temple in Tirupati.

After Celeste's parents died, Janaki became the only family she had left. Years later, when Claude, despite her protests, took their young boys away to boarding school in England, Celeste felt life had flown from the house. To bring her out of her depression, Janaki took her to Tirupati. Barefoot, they joined the thousands climbing the mountain on steps polished by millions of past pilgrims, and she heard "Suprabhatam" once more. The solidarity of so many worshippers, all bearing their own troubles, gave her strength. When Janaki let the barber shave her scalp, gifting her hair to the temple, Celeste followed suit. As her tresses fell to the ground, grief lightened its grip. After hours in the queue, when she finally laid eyes on Lord Venkateswara, she felt goose bumps rise on her arms. The ten-foot-tall, bejeweled, peaceful being was no mere idol, no representation, but the incarnation of Vishnu himself, radiating so much force that she felt the mountain rumble under her feet and her life shift.

On his return, Claude could have learned of her transformation, her commitment to *seva*, if he'd asked. Instead, he stared at her shorn head and was silent. *Seva* meant erasing awareness of self through service. For her it took many forms, including volunteering every weekday at the Madras Orphanage.

Digby emerges with a cloth *sanji* over his shoulder, a bag few Britishers would choose to carry. He climbs in looking nervous and excited. Like a schoolboy ready for an outing, Celeste thinks.

A dark hand passes a tin through the car window. "Saar forgot samosas," Muthu says.

"May I?" Celeste pries open the lid. She bites into a samosa, the filling giving off steam. "Heavens," she says, leaning forward so the crumbs don't spill on her orange *kurta*, "these are the best I've ever had."

"If Missy liking, I'm making plenty," Muthu says.

As they drive away, Celeste laughs. "He called me Missy. As if I'm a schoolgirl." Digby grins, tongue-tied.

On the outskirts of Adyar, crossing the river and passing wide-open marshland, Digby stammers, "I confess, I was sleepless last night."

"Oh?"

"I worried that I've misled you into thinking I know something about art. I didn't have the kind of upbringing I imagine you had. Never saw the great museums of Europe and all that. The few months I worked in London I never left the hospital. There! I had to get that off my chest." The confession makes him blush.

"Digby, I'm going to disappoint you. No great museums in my growing up, I promise you. My parents were missionaries in

Calcutta. Ours was a two-room house. We had one ayah, not ten servants like others I knew. Don't look so worried. It was a blessing! Since they were too poor to send me to England, I was spared the heartbreak of being sent away at five years of age. That's the rule, you know. Ship the little ones across the ocean to boarding school—Claude did that to my boys. Every other year an ever-taller child gets off the boat. No *possible* way he's yours. He shakes your hand and says, 'Hello, Mother,' because his memory of 'Mummy' has already faded."

The Model T's loose suspension makes them sway in unison, a rhythm conducive to confession. "I'm fortunate they come home at all. Some children spend every summer with 'Granny' Anderson or 'Aunty' Polly in Ealing or Bayswater, who for a fee will take your role. It's unspeakably cruel."

"Then why do it?"

"Why? Because the esteemed medical opinion is that if the children stay in India they will succumb to typhoid or leprosy or smallpox. Should they survive, they'll be delicate, lazy, and mendacious. It doesn't matter that countless numbers of us survived just fine. You'll find it in the civil service handbook! 'The quality of the blood deteriorates,' according to Sir So-and-So, FRCS. Perfectly good schools here, mind you. But then my poor sons would have to be educated alongside Anglo-Indians. They'd have a chee-chee accent like their mother and be called 'fifteen annas' behind their backs, even if they were not Anglo-Indians." There were sixteen annas to a rupee, and to be a Celeste was to be one short. If her bitterness startles him, it surprises her too. He listens to her with his whole being, she thinks, offering a clean canvas for her thoughts. *God, he looks besotted. Be gentle with him.*

"I had no idea," he says. "An Englishwoman who's never set foot in England."

When Claude mentioned his new assistant surgeon, he said the man was a Catholic from Glasgow. That was all Claude needed to classify a human being. But the man beside her is much more

than that. Without thinking, she reaches out and touches the ragged
scar on his cheek. He colors as if she's exposed something grotesque
about him, though her intention was quite the opposite. She quickly
speaks to mask their surprise.

"I *did* see the motherland. A friend of my parents underwrote
my passage when I finished school. I was curious." She remembers
sailing into the cold, foggy harbor at Tilbury, and getting her first
glimpse of the great city of London. The grand buildings she had so
anticipated were gray and choked by the smoke of coal fires. In the
unyielding country towns, tiny houses shared walls and pushed up
against each other like *halwa* in a sweet shop. Even the washing on
the line was gray. "I had a scholarship to a school meant to train girls
as missionaries. Believe it or not, I aspired to go to medical school.
But then, a few months after I left India my parents died. Cholera,"
she says matter-of-factly.

She stares out at the ocean now visible on their left. A car coming toward them requires both vehicles to pull carefully to the side
so as not to get stuck in the sand.

When she turns back, she finds Digby studying her, like an
artist studying a model.

"I was orphaned too," he says shyly.

At Mahabalipuram, Celeste leads Digby through the dunes. Ahead
of them, the milky white ribbon of beach is interrupted by dark
rock shapes, like the wrecked hulls of ships. "Those five sculptures
carved out of single boulders are called *rathas*," Celeste says, "because they're in the shape of chariots. A convoy. And—" She catches
herself. "Nothing worse than a tour guide. Digby, you go explore. I'll
meet you by the fifth one, with the stone elephant beside it. You'll
see it." He takes off without hesitation. She's a bit disappointed that
he didn't protest.

Outside the first *ratha*, a pair of larger-than-life, curvaceous
female figures stand guard; a string of cloth barely conceals their
nipples, and another the pubic area. She watches Digby pull out his

sketchbook. What does this orphan child of Catholic Glasgow—how grim that sounds—make of such sensual sculptures on a sacred structure?

She sits in the shade of the fifth *ratha*, taking off her tinted glasses to examine the apsidal-shaped masterpiece. Her first visit here drove her to learn all she could about temple art. That journey led her a few years later to organize an exhibition of South Indian painters. The Hungarian dealer who bought many pieces admired her curation. He advised her to "buy what you love and what you can afford." So she became a collector. *Is that why I'm here? Am I collecting Digby?*

After a long while she spots Digby emerging from the fourth *ratha* like a rabbit out of a hat. He sees her and a flash of worry snags his smile—has he kept her waiting? They walk north through the dunes to where the driver waits with a hamper in the shade under a portia tree. She spreads out a blanket. Facing them is a massive yellow sandstone boulder, fifty feet tall and twice as long, its surface a sprawling narrative of gods, humans, and animals. Digby gazes at the panel while demolishing her tomato-and-chutney sandwiches, unselfconscious for once. "What's this, then?" he says, still chewing.

"*Descent of the Ganges.* That cleft is the Ganga, flowing down in answer to the king's prayers, but if it fell directly to earth it would shatter the world, so Shiva lets it fall through his hair—see him with the trident? Those flying pairs on the top are my favorite. *Gandharvas.* Demigods. I love how they float effortlessly. And you see laborers, dwarves, *sadhus* . . . See the cat standing on its hind legs, pretending to be a sage? And mice coming to worship? It's got humor, drama, something new each time."

Digby hurriedly finishes his sandwich, reaching for his sketchbook. "Might we stay here a bit?"

"Of course! I have my book." She rests against the tree and opens her novel.

She wakes to find Digby studying her. When did she fall asleep? She sits up. She extends a hand. "May I?" He hesitates, then yields his sketchbook. He's recorded quick impressions, three to four per page. His draftsman's eye coupled with his anatomical knowledge offers a precise shorthand of what he sees.

"My word, you've been busty!—Sorry, *busy*! I swear, I meant busy." He hasn't exaggerated the breasts any more than the sculptors have, but still, his pencil on white paper favors them. He's captured all the hand gestures, the mudras—a vocabulary for dancers. "Digby, I'm speechless. Such a talent!"

She turns to a page of a woman with tinted glasses and the tiniest gap between her lips that sip the air as she sleeps. She feels like a voyeur peering at a temple voluptuary in repose. Her image on paper alongside the rock-hewn figures has fused the centuries. She studies this other self. Flattery isn't the right word for his portrait. It's empathy—the same quality in the sculptures that surround them. The ancient artists were devotees above all else. Without love of their subject, they'd just be cutting stone; their adoration is what brings it to life. She feels her face flushing. Digby's an innocent, but he's skilled in the female form from hours of careful regard along with the macabre intimacy afforded his profession.

Digby looks on anxiously. "I like it," she says, sounding like someone she barely knows. "You have a gift . . ." Has Claude ever come close to paying her this kind of a tribute? She's overcome by a desperate urge to break free of her present life.

"Escape," she hears Digby say, as though he's reading her mind.

She blushes again. "I beg your pardon?"

"It's an escape. Not a gift. As a boy, I'd draw worlds that I imagined were happier than mine. Faces. Postures. Exactly what I'm seeing here."

Did the desire to create come with the desire to take apart? To put back together again? "Escaping what, Digby?"

His features become as still as sandstone. It's as if she touched the scar again. At last he says, in too bright a voice that deflects further probing, "They weren't shy about the body, were they? That comes across. They were comfortable in their own skin." He looks directly at her.

She nods. "Very true. I visited the Khajuraho temples up north with my ayah, Janaki. Astonishing sculptures of intimate couples, courtesans . . . well, let's say nothing is left to the imagination. The pilgrims visiting would have been scandalized to see that on a cinema poster. But on a temple wall it's sacred. The sculptures simply echo their scriptures. 'This is life' is the message."

"It wouldnae be right in the High Kirk o' Glasgow, that's for sure!" Digby says, deliberately letting his accent twist past his usual vigilance. He is rewarded by her laughter. "Seriously," he continues. "I never liked that Christianity begins by telling us we're sinners. If I had a penny for the times my Nana said to me that all boys were thieving, lying connivers, and that I'd be no exception . . . Sorry, Celeste. I hope my beliefs, or lack of them, don't offend you."

She shakes her head. After her parents' deaths, how was she to hold to their faith? She and Digby are surrounded by ghosts, and not just those of the ancient sculptors who left their mark on stone.

"Digby, how did your parents die?" Her question floats in the air like one of the *gandharvas*. Digby's features turn dark; a little boy trying to be stoic in the face of the unspeakable. "Forget I asked that, would you?" she says. "Forget it."

Digby's lips part as if to speak. But then he presses them together.

On the drive back home they are both silent. She feels the afterglow of traveling back in time, which is the gift Mahabalipuram offers its visitors. She worries about her companion. They're both cut from the fabric of loss. She steals a glance at him, at the firm chin, the wiry, strong shoulders. *He's not made of bone china, for goodness' sake. He'll be all right.*

"Celeste . . ." Digby says when they reach his quarters, his voice hoarse from the silence that piled up on the drive back.

She reaches over and takes his hand before he can say more. "Digby, thank you so much for a lovely day."

"That's what I was going to say!" he protests.

She smiles, though she's overcome by sadness and a peculiar longing. She squeezes his fingers, keeping her body reined in, upright. She looks down at their hands.

"You're a good man, Digby," she says. "Goodbye. There, I said it for both of us."

CHAPTER 19

Pulsatile

1935, Madras

Digby vows not to think of her. He thinks of her all the time. She's chiseled in his memory like a rock sculpture; his thoughts about her survive a rainy season that didn't deserve the moniker, a typhoon that did, and a "spring" that was over in a blink. He can still smell the surf, taste the chutney sandwiches, and conjure up Celeste's face as she dozed, a face that hints at what she has endured even if the scars are less obvious than his.

He has one consolation: Esmeralda. So far she has lived up to Owen's billing of being a "cent-per-cent reliable gem!" She has many idiosyncrasies, but she rewards the patient owner. On weekends she escorts him to new vistas, probing the edges of the city: Saint Thomas Mount, Adyar Beach, and even Tambaram.

Though his range has expanded from his cycling days, his circle of friends remains small: Honorine, the Tuttleberrys, and Ravichandran. Lena Mylin writes Digby chatty letters; she's recovering well and Franz sends his best. She sends an enticing photograph of their guest cottage at AllSuch estate, where she says Digby can paint and relax. He has promised to make the trip the next summer, when Madras becomes unbearable.

*   *   *

Digby and Honorine are the Tuttleberrys' guest at the Railway Institute's Fall Ball, which Jennifer says is a "not-to-be-missed" event—and it appears that no one in the Anglo-Indian community has. The gray-haired papas and nanas and the infants nod off in corners, oblivious to Denzil and the Dukes on stage playing everything from swing to polka. A sultry female crooner joins them for "April Showers" and "Stardust." Digby watches a middle-aged couple navigate the packed dance floor; they've been married for so long that their bodies have left impressions on each other.

Jennifer drags Digby to his feet, ignoring his protests. "I'll teach you, no worries," she says. "It can't be as hard as surgery." Digby would much prefer a gastrectomy. "Drive with your hips," she says encouragingly.

Her brother Jeb's arrival with a small entourage of good-looking mates creates a stir. "The Prince of Perambur honors us tonight," Jennifer says, furrowing her brows. At once, a young woman scrapes back her chair and flounces out of the hall, her parents and siblings trailing behind her, all glaring at Jeb as they exit. Jeb stands aside—humble, polite, eyes on the concrete floor. Jennifer shakes her head and says to Digby, "Mary and Jeb were an item from the time they were both in knickers. Even gave her a ring. Then this month my brother ditches her just like that. I'm still mad."

Back in his seat, Digby watches Jeb float about the room like a man running for office, offering a wave to Denzil and the Dukes, who acknowledge him like royalty. He walks past Jennifer, who snubs her brother, but then he sneaks up behind her and lifts her off the ground and onto the dance floor. Denzil and the Dukes strike up a cha-cha-cha; every eye is on brother and sister as Jeb expertly leads with just the faintest pressure on the tips of his fingers, driving with his hips. Digby is envious of a skill he knows he'll never possess. He's struck again by the contrast between Jeb's blue eyes and brown hair and Jennifer's coal-dark eyes and black bob, a finger curl on the left. With a sari, red dye in her hair-parting, and a *pottu* on her forehead, she could pass for a Tamilian lady, while Jeb could be a tanned Englishman, freshly returned from a summer in Italy.

Jeb releases his grinning sister by spinning her into her chair, only to zero in on a demure young beauty in a striking white gown with oversized red roses painted all over it and cut to show generous cleavage. But no—it's the girl's oversized mother he's after. In his high-waisted slacks and white shirt with tuxedo frill, Jeb is like a matador expertly leading Auntie across the floor, acting awed by Auntie's hidden talents as she proves that twenty years ago she was a hot number . . . and all the while Auntie's demure daughter grows nervous in her seat, because she knows what Digby only now sees: that from the moment Jeb walked in, it was all misdirection, all smoke and mirrors, because the die was cast, there was only one girl in the world for him, and it was Auntie's lovely daughter in the white, rose-decked gown, it was love-at-first-sight-my-dearest-darling, and forget the cock-and-bull you heard about me, just bloody slander by that chutney Mary and her Charley-Billy-*po-po-gunda* brothers, such up-country folks, just stories, rubbish, frogs stuck in a bucket trying to pull down the brave soul who wishes to see the world . . .

Digby is only mildly surprised to learn from Owen that Jeb's new girl is named Rose. He can't help thinking how Celeste would love the intrigue and the spectacle. But Celeste is a daydream, while flesh-and-blood women in clouds of perfume flash past him, calling him to adventure with their eyes. An hour later, when Digby and Honorine take their leave, the dance is going strong.

Digby motors at an easy pace, the only pace Esmeralda is capable of with a sidecar passenger, which is only slightly faster than a bicycle. The sea breeze is nourishing, cleansing. Digby slips his goggles up over his forehead and Honorine's hair flies about behind her as she grins.

"It's all roses for Jeb," Digby shouts over his shoulder, the image of the white swirling gown covered with red roses still vivid.

He wants to talk about Celeste, but of course he's never mentioned her, or the excursion, never uttered her name to another.

Honorine laughs, shouting back, "Roses would be annoying weeds if the blooms never withered and died. Beauty resides in the knowledge that it doesn't last."

Well, Jeb surely knows that, Digby thinks. *But does Rose? And if beauty is in the ephemeral, what about the beautiful things you can't have? Perhaps that kind of beauty does last forever.*

The arrival of the dog days of summer marks the start of another year at Longmere; Muthu notes the occasion on the kitchen calendar.

As Digby passes the operating theater anteroom, blotting away the stinging sweat with his kerchief, he recognizes a patient on a gurney. The man's blue eyes and faintly tanned skin make him appear British, a rare sight when it comes to surgical patients at Longmere.

Digby glances up at Claude's surgical list to see just one name there: Jeb's.

"It's nothing," Jeb says, embarrassed to run into Digby. "A bloody abscess." He points to an angry red bulge in his neck. "Thought I'd get it drained by Dr. Arnold. Claude's a keen sportsman, you know. Comes to every match we have in town."

"How long have you had it?" Digby says, when he really wants to say, *I wouldn't let Claude remove a tick off my backside.* He peers at it closely.

"Oh, months and months, I'd say. But now the bugger's a nuisance."

When Claude's orderly arrives to take Jeb into the theater, Jeb waves a jaunty farewell.

Months and months? It gnaws at Digby. Then it begins to alarm him.

He sends a probationer to ask Honorine to come to the theater if she can. He changes into theater garb and goes inside to take a second look. The chloroform has taken hold and Jeb's eyes are closed.

The swelling is red, angry—looking very much like an abscess. *Perhaps I was wrong*, Digby thinks. But when he puts his fingers on it, it isn't warm, as an abscess should be. It is, as Digby feared, pulsatile, lifting and spreading his fingers with each heartbeat.

"Well, if it isn't Dr. Kilgour," Claude says, coming up behind him, scrubbed and gowned, just as Honorine slips in clutching the mask to her face. It's well before noon, yet Digby thinks he can smell the metabolites of alcohol. "Aren't we working you hard enough on the native side? Come to have a look-see?" If there's a smile, it's hidden by Claude's surgical mask, and certainly not visible in the eyes.

"Oh, sorry. It's just that I know Jeb," Digby says. "A friend's brother. I happened to see him in the anteroom." He lowers his voice. "I'm wondering . . . I'm concerned, Dr. Arnold. Could this be an aneurysm and maybe not an abscess?"

Claude's eyes turn cold. The naked hatred in them shakes Digby. For a moment Digby wonders if this is about Celeste, but the only sins he's committed are in his head.

Claude recovers. "Nonsense, laddie," he says. "Surely you've been here long enough to know an abscess when you see one. It's turgid with pus. The vessels behind it are transmitting their pulsation. We're in the tropics. Pyogenic abscesses are more common than acne."

His words aren't slurred, but carefully enunciated. Claude could be right.

"It's just that it isn't warm . . ." Digby says. "Maybe a small needle first might clarify—"

"It's a pus-filled abscess," Claude says flatly. "I was opening these things when you were learning to finger-paint! Just stand back and watch."

Dr. Claude Arnold slices into the swelling with his scalpel before the antiseptic has dried. Pus wells out, thick and creamy, and Claude turns to Digby and is about to say, "You see?" but in the next instant a jet of blood, a bright arterial spray, strikes Claude in the head. He springs back, stunned, but doesn't move fast enough because on the next beat it catches him again, a surging spout, timed to every beat of Jeb's heart.

Claude knocks over a stool in his retreat. Digby steps forward, grabbing surgical towels with his ungloved hands to put pressure on the aneurysm, because that is indeed what this is: a focal weakening of the carotid artery wall. Honorine lets her mask drop and steps up to help.

Claude's cut is so long and deep that compression doesn't stanch the breach in the dyke. The pads turn red, as do Digby's fingers; blood drips off the table and pools on the floor. Digby calls for a suture on a needle holder. Already, Jeb's face has turned a ghostly white. When Digby pulls the towels away, blood is pumping less vigorously from the ragged tear. He stitches the vessel crudely, but by then Jeb's heart has stopped because there's no longer enough blood to pump. The patient has exsanguinated. Jeb's eyes are half open and Digby feels their gaze is fixed on him as if to ask, *Why did you let him do it?*

The sound of the stool crashing to the floor has summoned everyone within earshot. A small crowd stands in the theater studying the grisly tableau. "Well, I'll be damned!" Claude says from six feet back, breaking the long hush in the theater.

Claude is almost as pale as Jeb, save for the blood on one side of his face. Every eye is on Claude Arnold, a pathetic sight.

"The bloody thing would have killed him anyway," Claude says. "No harm done," he mumbles, stumbling out.

CHAPTER 20

In Glass Houses

1935, Madras

Through the church window, Digby has a view of the adjacent cemetery. *Claude, how many souls have you sent here?* The man was back at "work" the next day as if nothing had happened. Digby shudders now as an inner voice warns him: *Tread softly, Digby. No surgeon is infallible.*

The service had to be moved from Perambur to a larger venue in Vepery. The entire Anglo-Indian community has turned out, the women in hats and black veils. He can barely glimpse the altar through wreaths stacked near the coffin. A framed photograph of a strikingly handsome Jeb leaning on a hockey stick reminds Digby of Rudolph Valentino. The church is hot, the service long, the air thick with the cloying scent of gardenia.

When Jeb's teammates, a phalanx of men in blue blazers and white slacks, carry the coffin down the aisle, a woman's wail shatters the silence, and sobbing sounds fill the church.

Outside, Digby hears his name called. Owen grasps Digby's hand. He looks sleepless, hunched over. "Doc, we know what happened in the operating theater. We do. I know you tried to prevent it."

Digby hasn't said a word to anyone outside the hospital.

"I want you to know," Owen says, straightening up, "we saw the hospital superintendent. Shifty bugger! All he cared about was trying to protect Arnold. The big boss himself at the Railways petitioned the governor on the family's behalf. The governor called up the director of the Indian Medical Service. He's promised an inquiry. We won't let this go, Digby." He searches Digby's face. "I know he's your boss and all. But Doc, don't protect the bastard."

"Owen, I'll tell the truth if asked," Digby says simply.

Owen nods. He says, "Jeb was no saint. He needed more time to finish sowing his wild oats. But he didn't deserve this."

Digby asks a question that has troubled him: "Owen, why didn't Jeb go to the Railway Hospital?"

The reason, it turns out, was his new flame, Rose. "Rose is the hospital superintendent's bloody daughter. Jeb was a bit of a Romeo, you know. Anyway, Rose went all jealous-*jalebi* when she found he was putting applications with other girls here and there. And her father got into it. Worst part is the bugger lives opposite us. He came home and made a scene and then his son started yapping about how our family is like this and like that, and next thing, big bloody *gumbaloda Govinda*, with hockey sticks, stones, bones, and all. Even my mother gave a few kicks. So you see, Doc. That's why no Railway Hospital for Jeb."

•

To the Editor, The Mail:

The death of Jeb Pellingham, Olympic hockey hopeful, is a national tragedy. But the way his family is being treated is a national disgrace. Mr. Pellingham died because of the negligence of a surgeon at Longmere Hospital, but despite the promises by the Governor to hold an investigation, two months have passed and no hearing date has been set. Meanwhile, the family and delegates of the Anglo-Indian community are unable to get a copy of the coroner's report.

Mr. Pellingham's bad luck was to be in the hands of a surgeon whose reputation is so poor that he was sent away from

Government General Hospital. No Europeans seek his care. Still, he stays on at Longmere, paid well to do little, and what little he does is dangerous. The curious citizen must ask: Is it because one of his brothers is the Chief Secretary to the Viceroy, and the other a Governor of a northern presidency? Why else is this murderous man being shielded?

Once upon a time we Anglo-Indians were the proud sons and daughters of British men, with all the privileges of citizenship. No longer. If self-rule for India becomes real, no doubt we will be further disenfranchised. Yet the country relies on us for the smooth functioning of its machinery. It is time for the Anglo-Indian community to reconsider its unstinting support of the government, going back to the 1857 mutiny when the boys of La Martinière College in Lucknow held on, or to Brendish and Pilkington in the Delhi telegraph office who held on at great peril to signal the British that the mutineers had entered the city. In the Great World War, three-quarters of the eligible Anglo-Indian population served with distinction. We can hold on no longer.

India has lost a good man in Jeb Pellingham, and perhaps its best chance for another hockey gold. The indifference to his death and the absence of an inquiry is a blow to the heart of the Anglo-Indian Community. We will not let this rest.

Sincerely,

Veritas

Celeste lets *The Mail* fall to the table. Suddenly, she's in a glass house with all of Madras looking in. The Letters section of *The Mail* is more popular than the front page. In the previous month, readers were mesmerized by a debate around the hiring of qualified Indians to the Indian Civil Service. This rule change was meant to appease Indians, but the old-guard British ICS officers were livid about the dilution of their ranks by natives. "India without the 'Steel Frame' of a British ICS will collapse," said one letter, while another argued that "it is well known that Brahmins fail when admitted to the highest rank." There were so many letters from ICS officers (who signed with only one initial) that it was spoken of as the "White Mutiny," much to the viceroy's displeasure.

The letter from "Veritas" carries the stamp of truth even as it accuses her husband of little less than murder. A man who can be indifferent to his wife's pleas and who rips young children from her bosom must carry that cruel indifference into his work. The secret of the care *of* the patient, she once read, is in caring *for* the patient, and if that is true, Claude couldn't help but fail. He too was born in India, but to a military family. For the longest time she thought his wound came from being sent away to England when he was so young, torn from his ayah's arms. But so were Claude's brothers, and they grew to be caring, generous, and successful. Claude had the same promise when they first met; she was swept away by his looks, his confidence, and his determination to have her. It took time to realize that something was missing in him; this missing piece cost him a happy marriage and his professional advancement.

That evening, she's in the living room when Claude comes home in his tennis whites. His eyes fall on the *Mail* on the table before her. He doesn't look at her. At the drinks tray, he pours a small one.

"The lawn looks very dry. Would you speak to the *maali*, dear?" he says in a bright, business-as-usual voice. He heads to his study with his glass, doing a poor job of concealing with his body the whisky decanter he slipped off the tray.

The next morning at breakfast, Claude is more bleary-eyed than usual. He stops abruptly while uncapping his soft-boiled egg, then he leaves. She thinks something in the *New India* next to his plate upset him. But no, it's the telegram beneath the paper.

VERITAS LETTER PUBLISHED BOMBAY CHRONICLE STOP TOBY CONSULTED STOP DO NOT REPEAT DO NOT CONTACT TOBY OR ME AT OUR OFFICES STOP

It's from Claude's brother, Everett, the governor of Bombay Presidency. Toby, the other brother mentioned in the telegram, is chief secretary to the viceroy.

Over the subsequent days, the Letters section in the *Mail* keeps alive the issue of Jeb's death. Claude is not mentioned, but the viceroy, his chief secretary, and the governor of Bombay Presidency are, and that cannot please them.

Two weeks later, the viceroy comes to Madras for a planned visit that he will wish was not on his books. As his special carriage slides into Central Station, the partially dressed viceroy is appalled when he pulls aside the curtains in his bed-suite and sees a phalanx of hockey players in uniform, wearing black ribbons and standing silently at attention. Behind them, a crowd of nearly a hundred people hold placards bearing Jeb's name, and the words RELEASE AUTOPSY REPORT! They are as silent as ghosts.

The viceroy closes the curtain, livid. He'd been fearful of precisely this and had ordered that his carriage be decoupled at the shed, well before the platform. The locomotive driver mysteriously failed to receive that message, and miraculously during the night never encountered a red signal, thanks to every Anglo-Indian stationmaster along the way. As a result, the train arrives at six in the morning instead of at eight. The police brigade to escort the viceroy is nowhere to be seen, and in any case, they'd be waiting at the wrong place.

The crowd includes reporters and photographers from every Indian newspaper. Eventually, the red-faced viceroy, shaving cream still on the tip of one ear, appears at the carriage door, stooping so his head emerges, but not stepping out. He receives the petition from Jeb's mother graciously. He clears his throat to make a speech, but when he utters the word "hearing," a voice at the back bellows: "*Chaa!* Heard that one already, haven't we, boys?" A woman shouts, "SHAME, SHAME, SHAME," and the crowd picks up the chant. Flashbulbs pop and the viceroy ducks back inside, only to be subjected to the humiliation of hockey sticks hammering on the carriage, deafening the occupants within. The papers describe the scene in avid detail and with crisp photographs.

That night, the chief secretary to the viceroy comes home, catching Celeste unaware. Toby has the best features of the three brothers but is shorter than Claude. He ignores Claude and kisses Celeste, handing her a wrapped gift tied with a ribbon. She opens it at once. He says, "It's an ancient ivory jewel box. I picked it up in Jaipur and I knew at once I'd give it to my favorite sister-in-law."

"Your *only* sister-in-law, Toby. Oh, my word, this—"

"Celeste," Claude interrupts, "have the boy bring the drinks tray. We'll go to the study—"

"What *is* your hurry, Claude?" Toby says, annoyed. "And forget the drinks tray." Claude's smile is stuck on his face like egg yolk, but he's silent. When the siblings gather, they allow Claude to play older brother. She wonders now if that is from pity at having so exceeded him.

Toby doesn't let go of her hand. "Celeste? Give my love to Janaki, would you?"

Toby apparently has no wish to enter the study, because when she reaches the top of the stairs, she hears him speak in a tone so different than when he addressed her. "Of all the asinine things to do, Claude! Did you really think the viceroy wanted to hear your side of the story? Could you really not see how it would further embarrass him? And me?" Claude's response is inaudible. "No, *you* listen," Toby says. "No! Just the opposite. I came to tell you that by the viceroy's order there *will* be a hearing. Our hands are tied." She cannot hear Claude's mumbled reply, but Toby interrupts him. "Stop! Not another word. I want to be able to swear that I came to see Celeste and I never discussed the case with you. Neither the viceroy nor your brothers will interfere. Do not send cables or call. Get it into your head, Claude. This isn't a formality. The viceroy wants the *truth*." There is a long silence. Then, she hears him say more gently: "I'm sorry, Claude. This will throw a spotlight on you. The past *will* come up. Take a hard look at yourself. For God's sake, stay away from the drinks tray till this is over."

Toby glances back at the door and sees her frozen on the landing. His face is painfully sad.

The papers report that the viceroy authorized a hardship payment for the Pellingham family, and named a commission chaired by a former governor, two stalwarts of the Anglo-Indian community, the head of the Indian Medical Service, and two distinguished surgical professors from the Bombay and Calcutta Medical Colleges. The date is set two months hence. The commission can call witnesses; its conclusion will be binding.

For the next few days, they go about their separate lives. If Celeste feels on edge, she can only imagine how Claude feels. He spends long hours at the club despite being the subject of gossip there. Perhaps staying home and facing her feels worse; at the club he finds refuge in some dark nook, either alone or with drinking mates too anesthetized to judge him harshly.

At the end of that week when she returns home in the late afternoon, she's surprised to see Claude there. He comes to his feet graciously. Before she can pull off her bonnet, he sends for her tea. He is well into the gin.

"Darling," Claude says, "this hearing is coming up soon." She says nothing, her hands very still in her lap. "It's political, you know. Bad things happen in surgery, after all. I'm hopeful I'll prevail. I have a plan." He smiles brightly. One must have faith. One must never give up.

There are bags under his eyes that are new. The fine arbor of capillaries on his cheeks and nose are more prominent. She might pity him if he showed remorse, or didn't try so hard to conceal his fear.

"The thing is, darling, this *could* go badly. That is, if your *friend* Digby decides to malign me."

"He's *your* colleague, Claude," she says, annoyed. "I took him once to Mahabalipuram ages ago and told you I was doing so."

"Well, who do you think wrote that letter? Veritas? Had to be him."

Her eyes widen. "You're mad. Why would he pretend to be an Anglo-Indian?" This is the first they've spoken of his troubles. Perhaps for that reason she feels her anger bubbling up.

"Ah, well there it is, darling. Jealousy, what else? He wants my position. He just *happened* to be poking his nose in the theater when this . . . when there was a complication? Then, he misinterprets what he sees and the rumor mill starts spreading a false tale. That's what I'm up against. If he sticks to his story, it could sink our ship."

He waits. Celeste looks ready to laugh in his face. His courteous veneer is cracking.

"For God's sake, Celeste, how do you think I'll keep all this afloat? You have lived in comfort all these years. But the well might be shallower than you think . . ." Celeste sees the faces of her boys; she imagines them returning from England because Claude cannot pay their fees. It's a happy thought, and not what Claude intended. "If I'm dismissed from the Indian Medical Service, if I lose my pension—damn it, Celeste, it would be the end."

And once my children are back, I would have absolutely no reason to stay with you, Claude.

"The thing is, darling, I need to be certain that young Digby doesn't testify falsely."

"What do you want, Claude?" she says very quietly. "For God's sake, just say it."

"Nothing! I . . . don't want anything from you, poor darling. But I must tell you . . . I'll be getting word to Digby that I shall name him as co-respondent in divorce proceedings."

At first, the words make no sense. But then she understands.

"Claude, how dare you use me like that? As currency in your sordid little scheme!"

"But listen, it won't come to that, dear! Digby will change his tune. It's just to remind him of his place. Who'd trust the word of someone who'd stoop to going to bed with a superior's wife?"

"Going to bed with . . . with *me*?" She's surprised at her own composure. His words are so contemptible that screaming at him would be far too generous a response. Instead she stares at him for a long time, watches him squirm. She smiles, which in his present state stings him more than if she had slapped him. "Claude, I've put up with so much from you over the years. Now you want to save your hide with a lie that makes me into an adulteress? Is that the best you can do? Forget about Digby for a moment; do you care so little about slandering me? Or being a cuckold? Or dragging my sons through this muck? Is there really no honor, no decency in you once you scratch the surface? It's the missing piece. Your brothers have it and it has made all the difference for them, don't you see?"

To hold his brothers up as a standard is to incite him. It's a measure of his pathetic state that he doesn't react, doesn't flinch, but instead looks pleadingly at her.

"But I assure you, it won't come to that, Celeste. It's just a ploy," he says piteously. "Damn it all, Celeste, can you think of a better way? It's the children's future I have in mind. Our future . . ."

She regards him with disgust. "Last time you threatened to divorce me was also 'for the children.' Fool that I was, I let you bully me into taking them away. Never again."

She stands and turns to leave. He grabs her wrist. She yanks her hand away and whirls around to face him. He recoils.

In Digby's quarters, early on a Saturday evening, a wide-eyed Muthu appears in the doorway to the bedroom. Digby is propped up, reading. He has spent the afternoon painting listlessly and taking a long nap.

"*Saar*, visitor! Missy, *Saar*," Muthu says, and hurries away.

Which Missy? A puzzled Digby washes up and puts on a fresh shirt over his trousers. He sees a woman's bicycle outside on the verandah.

In the living room, when he recognizes who it is, he wishes he'd changed his paint-flecked trousers. He feels a rush of adrenaline, every little sound amplified, from the clink of dishes in the kitchen to the chirp of a bulbul outside. She has her back to him. What did she make of his décor, he wonders, the cavalry of terracotta horses on the verandah when she walked in? He'd seen giant versions of these when riding Esmeralda through villages: offerings to Aiyanar, protector from famine and pestilence. On his living room floor is a hand-loomed grass-silk mat from Pattamadai. But of course, her gaze is on the one wall that cries for windows. Instead, from floor to ceiling it is covered with *kalighat* paintings in crude wooden frames, each one no bigger than a postcard. A village of *kalighats* stares back at her. Her hands are on her chest, frozen in that first moment of surprise.

After a long while, she turns to him.

His breath catches. She's even lovelier than in memory. The orange glow of the setting sun lights the left side of her face like a figure in one of Vermeer's paintings. He remembers her goodbye in the car so many months ago, so definitive.

He speaks first, to relieve her of that burden. "I bought them in Calcutta." He walks up to stand beside her. "I was deputed to accompany the governor of Bengal's wife, who took ill here. I spent just one night there, but I went to the Kali temple on—"

"On the banks of the river," she whispers. "I grew up close by."

"The vendors were hawking these to the pilgrims. I was a pilgrim myself." *I wanted to visit the house in which you grew up, your old school, visit your parents' graves . . .*

She nods, her hands wringing her embroidered handkerchief.

To be in her presence, to smell her attar, is intoxicating. "I visited the artists' workshops," he continues. "Their repertoire goes beyond religious images. Like that one." He points. "A notorious crime involving a British soldier and his Indian lover. Or this theater-of-life series. See the curtains of a Western playhouse? But with Shiva dancing. Occident and Orient in a few brush strokes."

They've come to that threshold beyond which words lose their utility. Standing so close to her, in his own house . . . there are no more words he wants to say except her name. He has sounded it in the dark, bounced it off the ceiling and walls. *Celeste. Celeste.* Its last syllable lingers in the corners like a trapped whisper. He wants to say it aloud now. His hand moves, as though of its own volition, reaches for hers. He cannot know that hours before, her husband reached for her wrist and she yanked it away. "Celeste," he says, dragging out her name. "Celeste, there's more paintings you must see." Her fingers find refuge in his.

Hand in hand, she lets him lead her to the next room, his "studio"—formerly the dining room. The paintings, finished and unfinished, are the modest size of the *kalighats*, but the subject is unvarying: the same woman. She comes into being with an economy of line and color: chestnut eyes; the mass of brown hair; the sweep of the long neck; the slight overbite whose proof is in the pouting upper lip, which Digby thinks is the most beautiful thing on earth. Celeste had seen the template when he sketched her in the shadow of the great rock in Mahabalipuram. The artist sees in the model a grander beauty than she sees in herself.

Her hand quickens in his. He leads her to his bedroom.

In a land where parrots with clipped wings predict the future from a deck of cards, where marriages are determined by horoscopes, Celeste's foreknowledge of where this will lead—not just in the next few minutes, but in the days and weeks to come—makes her try to disengage her hand, but it is too late. He reels her in, draws her close, and with a sigh she lets herself fall into his body.

Neither of them knows that every time they seek each other out, furtively, in the heat of late afternoon, they will begin as they did today, in front of the wall of village portraits, the framed figures each sounding out a note, a *raga* that is all theirs. His tongue will run down from her lips, her chin, down the midline past her thyroid, her cricoid, to the little hollow above her sternum. Once he undresses her, he'll step back and move her like a dancer, posing her, spinning her as though on a revolving pedestal. He will take in the tall, lean figure; the small breasts; the gentle swell below her navel; the flare of her pelvic bones that are like wings hovering over the long, gazelle-like legs; the fragile instep; and finally the toes, the clever gap between the big toe and the second. He will take it all in, memorizing every detail . . .

Celeste has had one husband and one lover, the latter like her, a wayfarer in the wasteland of an unhappy marriage, and the affair didn't help either of them find their bearings. She succumbs to Digby's lack of irony or self-consciousness, an innocence and purity that gives him authority, like the bold lines he sketches. His passion for her singes her skin, enlivens her. Who would not want to be loved that way?

At this moment she can no longer bring up the purpose of her visit. She came *not* to ask for his silence, which is what Claude must have wanted, but to warn him of a perfidious and utterly false accusation that he would soon hear: that they are lovers.

If she doesn't tell him, if they don't stop . . . then the accusation will no longer be false. Why doesn't she speak? Why doesn't he ask?

She must tell him. She must.

CHAPTER 21

Forewarned

1935, Madras

Four days after they become lovers, Celeste rides to Digby's quarters once more. She crosses the railway tracks to Kilpauk, bypassing the heart of the city. She dodges a cow, overtakes a laborer struggling with a cart piled high with scrap metal. She is seeing Madras through a new lens, no longer the Celeste she was five days ago.

A group of unsmiling Indian men stare at her. They stand outside Satkar Lodge, a tall, narrow building on Miller Road. They are probably clerks or students, attired in the "modern" outfit: a white dhoti pulled through the legs, paired with a tweed jacket—an absurd choice for the weather, but no more absurd than the linen suits and ties of ICS officers. Their Gandhi side caps, the ends pointed fore and aft, symbolize the desire for self-rule. One of them calls out *"Vande Mataram"*—*Hail to thee, Motherland*—the slogan on the lips of the whole country. The sleeping giant is waking.

Vande Mataram to you, she wants to scream. *I was born here. It's my motherland too*. But is that a lie? Does it matter that she feels more Indian than British when she has all the privileges of the latter? Living with Claude is the biggest lie of all. The fear of losing her children paralyzed her, kept her from leaving. It made her something other than who she really is, and she can no longer abide that. Yet somehow, Claude's craven, despicable lie to save his skin has become true—she *is* having an affair with Digby. Why? Can the body explain? Can the mind come up with reasons after the fact? She's grateful to Digby for awakening the part of her that lay dormant, the truest part of her. He did it by adoring her in his portraits, by making her feel human again, by *loving* her. Does she need his validation, or the validation of anyone, for that matter, in order to exist? If she had to start all over again and if she were younger, Digby could well be the one she would seek. But now? Love?

She pedals faster. Racing from, or racing to? When she reaches Digby's quarters, perspiration soaks her blouse. Minutes later, sinking into his body, moving as one with him, she wonders how she survived so long in a marriage that only briefly knew this intimacy. Digby's touch is a drug; his freshness, his eagerness make it all the more potent. Their escalating need for each other is a sand sculpture that they shape together. She doesn't recognize the brazen, demanding woman who commands her young lover, rolling him this way and that, even biting him in her passion.

But in the aftermath of lovemaking the sculpture collapses. The world and its agonies recall themselves. Sooner or later, she must sit down to the meal of consequences. On rubber legs, she rises and dresses. Digby lies on the bed, watching her, his eyes begging her to never leave, to stay forever. They don't utter her husband's name. They hardly speak. He doesn't ask when he will see her again.

Soon, they become reckless. On the days she cannot come, he thinks he'll go mad. His restlessness drives him to the Adyar Club to play tennis, a recent obsession. The Madras Club is Claude's hangout. It is in the Adyar Club, after returning from the courts, that he finds the letter someone placed in the trousers he left in the locker room.

> *Kilgour: Please forgive this method of conveying certain information to you. You can make of this what you will. It is common*

knowledge that your testimony could damn Claude Arnold, and this writer will shed no tears for him. But you should know that Arnold plans to file for divorce and name you as a co-respondent. It is of course absurd. Nevertheless, by naming you, Arnold makes your testimony suspect. There is no reason to believe Mrs. Arnold is a party to this. The woman is a gem. My guess is she has no idea he is doing this. It shows you what a cad the man is. Arnold's intent is to get you to back down. If you don't, the man may be low enough to go through with it. Be warned that he's the sort who would happily manufacture evidence. If you are found guilty, the court can order you to pay substantial damages. Praemonitus, praemunitus.

One who thought you should know

Forewarned is forearmed, yes. But what is he to do with such a warning? And why an anonymous letter? Which of the casual acquaintances he's made in the club penned this note?

He folds the paper and returns it to his pocket. His indignation, his rage is gelded by the fact that Arnold's accusation is true. As he motors home, he considers the letter from every angle. For the briefest moment he wonders if Claude wrote it and had it delivered. No. That would be too farfetched.

As he nears home, he says aloud, addressing the letter writer: "I intend to testify. I have no choice. I saw what I saw. I could care less about my name or my career or what people think." *And if Claude divorces Celeste, she'll be all mine.*

CHAPTER 22

Still Life with Mangoes

1935, Madras

At four thirty, as Celeste takes her tea in the cool of the library just off the living room, she sees the Model T pull up. Claude tumbles out. He bumps into the stationary Rolls, bounces off it to knock over the potted jasmine on his way indoors. He's drinking more recklessly, starting from the moment he gets up, she suspects. When Claude sees her, he's surprised. He vainly attempts to gather himself, but his eyes are swimming.

"How was your day?" he says, enunciating too carefully, and still managing to slur. She cannot conceal her revulsion. "What the hell are you looking at?" he says at last, in an ugly voice, giving up all pretense of politeness, not waiting for the driver to withdraw.

In the past she could count on his civility, no matter what else was going on. Wasn't that the mark of an *English* education, as opposed to her chee-chee one? He might be planning to draw and quarter her, but till such time, he'll pull out the chair for her at dinner.

"Get me a drink, Celeste," he says. He looms over her.

The absence of "darling" is a relief. She rises to get away, disgusted by this proximity to him. Claude assumes she's headed to the drinks cart and says magnanimously, "Pour yourself one."

"No, it's much too early," she says. "Get a hold of yourself, Claude. You hardly need another drink."

She might as well have slapped him.

"Celeste!" he shouts, pointing a sweeping finger that seeks to find her, swaying, as he spins around. "I'll have you know—" But he loses his balance and falls, striking his head on the coffee table. He touches his forehead with his hand; his fingers come away bloody. "Oh, God!" he says, in a frightened voice, and then throws up over the coffee table.

He looks up pitifully at her, a string of saliva hanging off his lips.

She gives a bitter laugh. "Claude, your only real talent used to be that you could hold your whisky. I don't know why I stayed with you so long." And she walks out and mounts her bicycle. There is someone else she must be honest with.

It's dusk when she pushes through the door to Digby's quarters, startling him. He's in his studio, bare-chested, cleaning his brushes with turpentine. A paraffin candle throws a ghostly light on the still life he has arranged: an eccentric earthen pot and three mangoes on the wooden worktable. Next to the pot, an emerald silk sari looks casually tossed on the table, so that a part of it cascades down the leg like a waterfall, and the excess folds form a careless bouquet on the floor.

She drains a glass of drinking water. When she studies Digby's face she senses a change. *Did they get to him?* She surveys the room, a long sweeping look, as though trying to memorize it, and then turns to Digby.

Digby sees her expression, and he understands at once that she has come to say goodbye. His insides turn to stone. A pike has been shoved just under his rib cage, into his solar plexus: *Is she part of the plot?*

At long last, she says, "Digby." Her eyes glisten with tears. "I—"

"Don't! Not yet. Wait . . . don't tell me." He moves closer, breathing in her scent, seeing moisture on her brow, the circumferential groove left by her hat. In medical school he'd seen Harry the Alienist perform, dragging people out of the audience and then, finger on his temple, revealing startling personal details about them. "You've decided to stay with Claude, haven't you?" he says, unable to keep the bitterness out of his voice.

"No. Just the opposite."

He's thrown off his script. His features lighten.

"Digby, I came to tell you that Claude plans to file for divorce and will name you as—"

"I know." It's her turn to be surprised.

"What? How?"

"I got an anonymous letter warning me. At the Adyar Club. Someone with no sympathy for your husband. But what *I* want to know, Celeste, is how does Claude know?"

Her laugh sounds like the crack of a whip. "He *doesn't* know about us, Digby! It's just a stratagem. Since he can't threaten you directly, he'll sacrifice me to get at you."

"Wait . . . Is that why you came here the first time we . . . ? The day you showed up unexpectedly? Did you come on his behalf to tell me not to testify?"

"God, no! I came to *warn* you. The moment he told me what he meant to do—make me an adulteress to suit him—I was furious. I walked out on him. I rode my bicycle to get away. I ended up here. Yes, I intended to warn you." A flash of anger enters her voice. "I never got to it, if you recall."

Digby's words are loaded with venom. "Why didn't you speak up? Did you decide you might as well be hanged for a sheep as for a lamb? Did you say to yourself, 'I'll sleep with old Digs before he's silenced'? Maybe you're *still* working for him—" Digby's voice rises.

"Stop it, Digby!" She is calm, commanding . . . and wounded by his words. "If you're going to shout, I'm leaving. I've had enough of that for today." She stands tall, upright, her nail beds turning white as she clasps her purse, as though it assures her safe passage to whatever is next. In the light of the paraffin candle she's like an artist's model. The artist stares back.

"I'm sorry," he says, penitent and sheepish.

"Claude will do anything to preserve himself, including sacrificing me. *Anything* to make you look bad. But he thinks it won't come to that. He thinks if he names you then you'll buckle—I pray you don't. Maybe he thought that *I'd* buckle and come plead with you. But it won't work, not on me. I *want* the divorce . . ."

Does he dare feel jubilant? Why does her face not mirror his excitement?

"Celeste . . . Then there's nothing stopping us . . . we can be together."

She shakes her head.

"Celeste, I don't understand . . . I love you. I've never said that to another living human being but my mother. I love you."

"Digby, I'd say I love you too. But I have no idea who 'I' is. I need to know. I want a life *of* my own, and *on* my own in order to find out." His eyes are like a child's, pleading with her. She puts her hand out to his cheek, but he withdraws.

"Where will you go?"

She sighs. "I've been planning for this, even if I didn't know my leaving would take this shape. I've put away a bit of money. It isn't much, but after nearly twenty years it isn't trivial. I have jewelry he gave me in the early years. I have a warehouse full of art, and I know which pieces are worth something now and which will be worth something in the future. I'll take a room at the Theosophical Society. Janaki and I, if left to ourselves, can live very simply and happily. The only hold he had on me was the children, but they're old enough, I hope, to see through him. They're old enough to want to get to know me. Once I find out who I am."

Digby digests her words. She doesn't need him—isn't that what she's saying? He's angry with himself for allowing his dreams to sail so far ahead of her.

The door opens and Muthu enters, clearly surprised to see Celeste, to see them both standing there facing each other like combatants. He brings his palms together. "Good evening, Missy, I'm not hearing you came."

"Muthu," she says, nodding, not taking her eyes off Digby.

Muthu looks from one to the other. "Digby *Saar* . . . I'm going to my native. As before I mentioning? I gone two days only." Digby is still staring at Celeste. Muthu turns to her. "Missy is liking something to eat before I go? Shall I make samosa?"

"Muthu," she sighs, her voice sounding suddenly very tired, very husky. "Missy is liking a double whisky, please. And one for him too."

"Yes, Missy!" Muthu says automatically, but doesn't move. She finally turns to him, raising her eyebrows.

"Muthu?" she says.

"Sorry, Missy . . . Whisky we're not having."

"Gin, then?"

He shakes his head. "Doctor *Saar* not drinking—"

"Oh, for *God's* sake, Digby—" says Celeste, her voice rising in a manner that startles all of them.

"But whisky soon coming, Missy!" Muthu interjects hastily, mortified that he got Digby into trouble. He runs out the back.

The two of them stand there. They hear raised voices outside, Muthu speaking in angry tones that don't sound like him. Muthu returns, a little disheveled, bearing a tray with two glasses, an ice bucket, a soda dispenser, and a bottle of whisky that is three-quarters full, as if it had been waiting just outside the door. He sets it down, avoiding Digby's astonished stare.

"Good man, Muthu," Celeste says. She suspects that Muthu walked into the neighbor's home and grabbed their drinks tray.

"Yes, Missy," Muthu says, as he steps behind Celeste and opens the drawer where Digby keeps money, something Muthu has never done before. He counts out some bills, holds them up to Digby. "*Saar*, I am explaining after. Please just leaving tray and everything in front verandah, *Saar*. I am back in two days."

Muthu leaves by the front door and at once they hear a man shouting in Tamil, a woman's raised voice too, and Muthu placating them. The shouts subside into grumbles.

Celeste pours. She hands Digby his glass. They have been standing all this time.

Wounded, unable to meet her gaze, Digby takes his drink. Until a few minutes ago, he could not imagine a life without Celeste. Yet she can readily imagine a life without him, one in which he doesn't exist. How is a dream that involves two people to be sustained by one?

Belatedly, he touches her glass with the rim of his. He gulps it down. The whisky burns. How strange to try to drown pain with fire. Celeste's left cheek and forehead are lit by the paraffin candle, an orange glow as if filtered through layers of muslin, producing ochre and mustard tones that creep in from the side before sinking into her dark orbits. She looks as if she is about to speak. But he doesn't want to hear it. He stops her mouth with his lips.

He slowly unbuttons her dress, right there before the easel, as if he might pin her to it. In the face of her naked beauty, the sting of the message she carries is diminished. She is not just Celeste whose words grieve him, but she is also a miracle of physiology, a magnificent body housing its constellation of organs under the confines of her skin. Compared to their messy, roiling emotions, the body is always steadfast, reassuring.

He dips his index finger in the undiluted paint on his palette: Rose Madder Genuine. Celeste draws in her breath as his finger hovers over her chest. Her eyes become wide. Will he do it? She sighs when the finger touches her. Yes, he will. He will trace out her organs, working slowly to postpone the inevitable—that she will leave him. He outlines the left ventricle, peeking out from behind her breastbone and reaching her nipple. Should he have used yellow? Her traitor's heart? No, that's too harsh. Besides, for all its metaphorical freight, a heart is a singularly unimaginative organ, two pumps in a series, one pushing blood through the lungs and the other through the rest of the body. Hers is no different from his.

She could resist if she chose to, but she does not, caught up in his worship, aware of the pain she has caused him and relieved to move past words. She sips from her glass, watching him. He outlines the arch of the aorta. Now he takes the glass from her and lays her gently on the tarpaulin on the floor, smiling. He rests the pallet on her pelvis, on the mons veneris, where it wobbles precariously. The candlelight shivers across her skin. He outlines the liver, high on her right side, crossing her nipple at the fifth intercostal space. She has gooseflesh and her nipple is erect. Her breathing accelerates. Next, the spleen, the kidneys.

He gazes down at the masterpiece that is her body, which he has now adorned. Or has he defiled it? He has turned her inside out. But suddenly he feels contrite. He has gone too far. Was it the whisky? He is unaccustomed to spirits.

"Forgive me," he says. "It hurts me to think that we may not have a life together. But it doesn't stop me loving you." He tastes tears on her lips, tears that could be his too.

She raises her head to look at what he has done, the canvas of herself. She shakes her head in amazement. She whispers, "You've helped me find myself, do you know?"

Then why leave me? I'd adore your body for the rest of your life. He loves her enough not to say it. Her mind is made up. He is both aroused and resentful that she would walk away from what they have. She reads his state. She pulls him down. She pulls him in.

Afterward, they collapse, drenched in colored sweat, their release like a drug that keeps them from moving from the tarp on the unyielding floor and going to his bed. They drift off, their bodies juxtaposed, a smeared canvas.

*   *   *

Why am I leaving him? There was a reason, but sleep overtakes Celeste before she can remember. She turns to one side, feeling chilled as the sweat evaporates. She drags the emerald sari off the table—his still life be damned—and she covers herself.

When Digby wakes, his head pounds; it is a huge effort to open his eyes. The room is unusually bright, a dancing ethereal haze. Pigments riot over his naked body, the violence of it unsettling.

He smells smoke. He turns his head and the mystery is solved: they must have knocked over the paraffin candle in their sleep. He scrabbles around to find it, but then he notices, as if from afar, an optical illusion: his hand is blue and the skin hangs down, like honey pouring off a ledge. All is blue: the floor, the tarp on which he sleeps, the easel, the canvas on it. He wants to laugh at the strange sight. Laugh in disbelief. The melted paraffin has found a mound of turpentine-soaked rags, and blue flames scale the walls.

He turns to see an even stranger sight: the silk sari he uses as a backdrop is on the floor, but it is alive, writhing. It is coral and ginger and olive green, and beneath it, he registers at last, is Celeste, fighting to break free. He lunges for the sari, pulling it away even as the burning, melting silk sticks to his flesh, but he refuses to let her go. If he can only peel it off, restore the beautiful cloth to where it sat draped next to the earthen pot, next to the fruit, its folds spilling to the floor, if he can only restore it to the way it was, the way it should be—*Still Life with Mangoes*—then all will be well. He is sure of it.

Part Three

CHAPTER 23

What God Knew Before We Were Born

1913, Parambil

In the aftermath of JoJo's passing, Big Ammachi feels flung off the wheel of life, struggling to find her rhythm. The cock crows every morning before she's ready to wake; the barber walks up to the house before she remembers it is the first of the month. Were it not for her mother managing the kitchen, they'd all be foraging for food like the estate's chickens.

Parambil has lost its sole male heir, lost the child she still thinks of as her firstborn, even if he did not come from her womb. But the loss is not hers alone. The first time she goes down to the cellar, an empty pickling urn falls off a shelf above her head without any provocation. She'd seen it out of the corner of her eye and pulled her head back in time for it to shatter on the floor at her feet. She flees up the stairs, only to be met by the sight of her fearless husband looking frightened, gazing past her and down into the cellar. *So you knew she was there all this time?* The expression on his face drives her into a fury. How dare this spirit that she has treated so hospitably intimidate her husband? Big Ammachi charges back down the steep stairs and she ignores the broken shards poking at her soles. She grabs an empty urn with a strength she did not know she had and launches it toward the room's shadowy corner. "JoJo was mine too, you know?" she shouts. "I had him for longer than you! If you can make an urn fall on me, why didn't you pick JoJo up as soon as he fell in the water?" She thinks she hears faint sobs. Her anger subsides. She leaves. But it doesn't end there. A few days later she finds a syrup-soaked urn overturned, and the cellar swarms with the big red ants whose stings are excruciatingly painful. Big Ammachi wraps her feet in cloth and, lighting a torch of dried palm fronds, she drives the ants back with the flames, coming dangerously close to setting the cellar on fire before she douses the torch in a bucket. She mops the floor and then goes over it once more with kerosene. "Keep this up and I'm calling the *achen*. Is that how you want to be remembered? Not as a good mother, but as a poltergeist we had to drive out?" A truce holds in the cellar, but in the kitchen her curries taste strange in her reliable clay pots. The milk she inoculates each night for yogurt turns bad. She endures these provocations until gradually they subside. But the heartbeat of Parambil remains irregular. Neither prayers nor church nor tears restore the cadence.

In that same unsettled period, and much too soon after their loss, her husband shows up silently outside her door at night while her mother and the baby are fast asleep. She senses him and sits up, surprised. She isn't ready. JoJo's scent is still so strong in this room, and his imprint lingers on the mat beside her. Her husband too seems unsure; he doesn't extend his hand but just fills the doorway. She doesn't move. His being there feels like sacrilege. He leaves. The next day he ignores her. Then she understands: this is about Parambil needing a male heir too. Even so, she needs time.

She finds solace and sanity in her garden behind the kitchen. When she first came to Parambil, she noticed her kid goat nibbling the berries on a scraggly bush by the back steps and becoming noticeably frisky. She investigated, and the berry's scent gave it away. After careful pruning and fertilizing, the bush now towers over her, providing Parambil with coffee. The dark brew has an oily shimmer on its surface and an unexpected bite; it is a reminder that the sweetness of life comes with bitterness. But her banana trees are her real delight. She began with a tiny sucker off a *poovan* varietal from Dolly *Kochamma*. Now she has a personal grove of trees, fed by the runoff from the kitchen roof. The leaves block the afternoon sun and make a rustling, knocking sound in the wind that comforts her. She harvests the bunches while they are still green, letting them ripen in the cool of the pantry. The miniature *poovan* delights her daughter; the child's father can eat ten at one sitting. She marvels that the earth provides such a delicious bounty with nothing more than water, sunlight, and her love. For each tree, the day arrives that she must hack it down, feeding the corpse to the cows and goats. From the brood of suckers around the stump she cuts away all but one lucky one that begins the miracle all over again, carrying inside it the memory of its ancestors.

She still hasn't baptized Baby Mol. In her dialogues with God, she avoids the topic but she senses God's disapproval. One evening she addresses the issue head-on. "How do you expect me to walk past the grave of one child and then go inside to baptize another?" Besides, she has doubts about a ritual meant to confer grace, which she understands as God's inherent love, benevolence, and forgiveness. "Grace didn't save JoJo." God is silent.

One night, she awakes to see her husband once again at the foot of her mat, silent, so as not to rouse her mother or Baby Mol. How long has he been there? He holds out his hand, and this time she rises. She feels the familiar acuity of hearing and sight as he pulls her quietly to her feet. She didn't realize how much she had missed this closeness. Their task is both tender and urgent.

Fourteen months pass, and many visits to her husband's room until at last she misses her monthlies. Then she miscarries. She's stunned. That possibility hadn't occurred to her. She'd assumed another child would follow, even if it took time, but never this. It feels as though her body betrayed her. Her husband is crushed even if he doesn't speak of it. "Take nothing for granted," God reminds her, "unless you want to feel its loss." What can one do but go on? She miscarries again. When she recovers, she looks to cast blame: might this be the doing of the spirit in the cellar? Could it be that spiteful? She descends to the cellar and sits on an empty urn, sniffing the air, taking her soundings. To her surprise she feels the spirit commiserate with her. She comes away mollified. God only knows why miscarriages happen. God only knows—but doesn't choose to explain.

When Baby Mol is five, they almost lose her to whooping cough that follows on the heels of measles. As soon as she recovers, Big Ammachi arranges for the baptism, fearful for the child's soul. She asks Dolly *Kochamma* to be godmother. Dolly moves her head in assent, her face lighting up with happiness at the honor but saying nothing. In describing this exchange to her husband at dinner, Big Ammachi says, "You and Dolly are alike. Sparing with your words, and never one to gossip or speak ill of others." He grunts in response. She says, "Of course Dolly's co-sister will grumble that I didn't ask her to be godmother." In the years since her family's unannounced arrival in Parambil, Decency *Kochamma*'s prudery has more than justified her nickname; gluttony, however, is not a sin the woman recognizes, for she has now doubled in size, her face merging into her neck, and her body becoming a shapeless barrel. The big crucifix that once pointed accusingly at whomever she was addressing has risen on her expanding bosom so it faces the heavens. Dolly *Kochamma*, despite her trials with her impossible co-sister and housemate, preserves her youthful figure, her face still unlined by worry, and her friendly demeanor unchanged, all of which must feel like a violation to Decency *Kochamma*. Big Ammachi adds, "I'm sure Decency *Kochamma* thinks *she's* the saintlier of the two." Her husband mutters something she doesn't digest till he has left the table. "Only if you measure saintliness in tons." It sinks in that her husband has just made a joke!

During the baptism, Baby Mol delights in having water poured on her head, something JoJo would never have tolerated. Big Ammachi hears the *achen* intone the baptismal name she has chosen, and Dolly *Kochamma* dutifully repeats it. But that name sounds jarring to Big Ammachi's ear, while on her tongue it feels as brittle as uncooked rice.

When they return from church, her husband is waiting. He tosses his daughter into the air and the child lets out a hoarse cry of delight. "So, what's your name?" he asks.

"Baby Mol!" the little one says. He looks inquiringly at his wife.

"It's true. I left the other name in the birth register and that's where it will stay."

Five years on, she lives with the pain of JoJo's death the way one lives with vision turned cloudy from a cataract, or the ache of an arthritic hip. But the newly baptized Baby Mol is their salvation; even the little girl's father, who has long ago renounced God, must see the divine in her ready smile and generous nature. She's everyone's favorite. As an infant, she was happy to be carried, and equally happy in her little hammock. Now that she's older, she's content to sit for hours on one verandah bench that she has made her own. From there she reveals a strange ability to announce the arrival of visitors before they have come into view. "Here comes Shamuel!" she might say, and they see nobody, but three minutes later, Shamuel will arrive. Her mother finds it remarkable that Baby Mol rarely cries. The only time she recalls her crying was that one terrible day when she keened till she turned blue, the day when Big Ammachi had wished . . . It is best not to recall what she wished. She understands that violent loss begets more violence.

During the monsoon that year they all take ill with fever. The hearth fire stays cold for one whole day because there's no one to attend to it. Her mother is the last to recover: she's always tired, sleeping early, and only rising when the sun is high overhead. Rising from her mat is an effort, and her hair is unkempt because her arms fatigue in the act of combing. When her mother does eventually appear in the kitchen, she's listless, too weak to help. Most alarming is that her mother's stream of chatter is silenced. They send for the *vaidyan*, who takes her mother's pulse and examines her tongue, then prescribes his usual massage oils and tonics, but they don't help. She's getting worse. Moreover, her daughter has her hands full, trying to care for her and run the household.

Blessings come in many shapes and sizes, but the one that arrives around the Onam festival happens to be of the bow-legged variety. Baby Mol announces her arrival—"an old lady is coming"— minutes before the bow-legged Odat *Kochamma* waddles in as if she's heard a silent summons for help. This gray-haired, hook-nosed woman can stand with her feet together and Baby Mol could still pass between her knees. She's a distant cousin of "Big Appachen," as Baby Mol calls her father (a name they gradually all take to using when speaking of him in the third person). Big Ammachi finds out later that the old lady wanders among the homes of her various children, staying for a few months with one, then another before moving on. But Parambil is where she will stay.

"Where do you keep the onions?" Odat *Kochamma* says, walking into the kitchen, speaking out of the corner of her mouth so her chaw of tobacco doesn't fall out. "And hand me the knife. In all my years I keep praying for onions to cut themselves and climb into the pot, but you know what?"—and she squints at each of them while looking deadly serious—"So far it has never happened." Then her deadpan expression cracks, the face breaks into a myriad of wrinkles, and her disarming grin is followed by a cackle so unexpected and lighthearted that it banishes the dark clouds from the kitchen. Baby Mol is thrilled and claps her hands, laughing with her.

"My gracious God," Odat *Kochamma* says, spotting the rice boiling over, raising her hands up to the heavens, or trying to, but her stoop lets them get only as far as her face. "Is anyone watching over this kitchen?" The admonishment is offset by the twinkle in her eyes and the tone of her voice. "Who's in charge—the cat?" She whips her *thorthu* off her shoulder and uses it to move the pot off the fire, then pokes her head out of the back door, puts two fingers to her compressed lips, and shoots out a jet of tobacco juice. She turns back in time to spot the cat sneaking up on the fried fish. Caught in the act, the cat freezes. Odat *Kochamma's* upper lip slowly everts, then crudely carved wooden teeth emerge like muddy fangs as she pushes out a denture. It's too much for the cat, who turns tail and flees. The dentures retreat and the old lady's laugh rings out again. "By the way," she says in a stage whisper, looking around to make sure no strangers are eavesdropping, "these aren't my teeth. That *appooppan* left them on a window ledge just now."

"Which old man?" Big Ammachi asks.

"Hah! My wretched daughter-in-law's father! Who else? I was leaving that house after she called me an old goat. I saw the teeth and I thought, *Aah*, if I'm the old goat, then don't I need this more than him? If he left it there it means he mustn't want it, *illay*?" She tries to look innocent but her eyes are full of mischief. Big Ammachi cannot stop laughing. All her worries momentarily vanish.

Odat *Kochamma* is the tonic Parambil needs. The old lady is ceaseless in her toil. Within a week, Big Ammachi comes to rely on being fussed at, told to sit down and rest, or made to laugh so hard she has to pee. The only thing she doesn't like is that Odat *Kochamma* always puts on the same turmeric-spattered *mundu* after her bath, even though she hotly denies it. "But I just changed it yesterday!" In the middle of the night, Big Ammachi understands and is furious with herself: Odat *Kochamma* has only one change of clothes. The next day she presents her with two brand-new sets, saying, "I didn't see you last Onam, so these have been waiting for you."

Odat *Kochamma* acts indignant, her brow furrowed, fingering the white cloth that will never again be as white as it is just now. But her eyes betray her. "*Oho!* What's this? Are you scheming to marry me off, at my age? *Aah, aah*. If I'd known I'd never have come to visit. Send my suitor away! I won't see him. Something's wrong with him that you're not telling me. Is he blind? Does he have fits? I'm done with men. This pot has more intelligence than a man!" All the while, she keeps thrusting the clothing back at Big Ammachi yet retains a firm grip.

Baby Mol runs to her father whenever she sees him. He's more patient with her than he was with JoJo, who was in any case awed by his size and his silence; Baby Mol is not. She shows her Big Appachen her ribbons and her dolls. One rainy afternoon when he's imprisoned by the downpour, Baby Mol interrupts her father's anxious pacing on the verandah and pulls him down to what has become *her* bench. "Sit here!" He lowers himself obediently. "Why does the rain fall to the ground and not go up to the sky? Why—" He listens, befuddled, to the barrage of questions. Baby Mol doesn't wait for answers. She stands on the bench to crown her father with a hat she wove out of green coconut fronds with Odat *Kochamma*'s help. Pleased by the effect, she claps her hands. Then she wraps her stubby arms around her father's neck and presses her cheek to his, squashing both their faces. "You can go now," she says. "You'll stay dry with this hat." He wags his head in gratitude. Big Ammachi bites her lips to keep from laughing at the sight of her giant of a husband, burnished by decades of sun, crowned by a comically small, misshapen hat. Once he's out of his daughter's sight she sees him remove it and examine it.

"I never thought I'd live to see such a thing," Big Ammachi says to Odat *Kochamma*.

"*Aah*. Why not? A daughter has an open door into a father's heart."

I'll take some credit too, she thinks. *I helped to soften him. I helped unburden him of his secrets.*

The *chemachen* who comes calling for a subscription one morning is no more than a boy, the growth on his upper lip so sparse that each hair could be named after an apostle. His voice has just broken. In his white cassock, which is far too big for him, and a black cap that swallows his forehead, he looks dressed for the priest part in a school play. No doubt his family "dedicated" him to the church when he was in shorts, to be raised (and fed) by the seminary, a boon when paddy is scarce. All such boys go on to be ordained, but Big Ammachi wonders about their true conviction.

The silly *chemachen* had spent minutes observing Damo, till Unni chased him away. Now he's too busy gawking at Baby Mol to recall why he's there, until Big Ammachi asks him about the ledger. His childlike eyes turn uncomprehendingly to her.

"That thing under your sweaty armpit," she says, pointing.

He hands it over. "What's wrong with the little one?" he asks solicitously.

She jerks up, following his gaze to where Baby Mol sits on her bench, as she does for hours each day, her legs keeping time.

"What do you mean, what's wrong? Nothing's wrong with her!"

Several seconds elapse before he understands he's said something terribly stupid. He walks backward, but then remembers his ledger, reaching warily for it, worried she will clout him with it before he escapes.

A furious Big Ammachi studies her smiling daughter. What did the stupid boy see? Was it her daughter's tongue? The family is used to Baby Mol's habit of parking her tongue on her lower lip, as though there's no room in her mouth. Her face is broad, or perhaps her prominent forehead just makes it seem so. The soft diamond that babies have in the front of their heads remains visible under Baby Mol's skin, though she's going on six. Her features are blunt, that's true. Unlike her parents, she has a snub nose, and it sits on her face like a berry on a saucer.

Big Ammachi feels the *muttam* sinking beneath her and reaches for a verandah pillar for support. Baby Mol was three before she could walk without clinging to something, and four before she put words together. Big Ammachi was too relieved to have a child who didn't wish to swing from vines to make much of these things.

She seeks out Odat *Kochamma*. "Be honest—what do you think?" The old lady studies Baby Mol for a while. "Could be something isn't right. Her voice is so hoarse. And her skin is different, puffy." It pains the old lady to say this, but Big Ammachi knows she's right. "But what does it matter?" Odat *Kochamma* adds. "She's an angel!"

Big Ammachi summons the *vaidyan*, who pulls out a bottle of tonic after a cursory glance at the patient. "Give her this," he says, in his priestly manner, "three times a day, followed by warm water."

"Wait! What do you think is wrong with her?" she says, ignoring the proffered bottle.

"*Aah, aah*, this should work," he says, looking at neither of them, still holding out the bottle.

"That's the same tonic you gave her when she had whooping cough."

"Why not? Cough is gone, is it not?"

Big Ammachi dismisses him and speaks urgently to her husband. He becomes very still. After a long while he nods.

That evening, the patriarch of Parambil summons Ranjan and asks him to escort Big Ammachi and Baby Mol to Cochin; he is the better traveled of the twins and knows Cochin. Dolly reports that Decency *Kochamma* has had a fit, because of her husband's obvious pleasure in an assignment where she won't be monitoring him. She makes him kneel, prays over him, anoints him with holy oil, and threatens to skin him alive if he misbehaves.

Big Ammachi asks her mother to come with them, hoping the excursion might shake her out of her lethargy. They set out before dawn, the women dressed in their finest, carrying umbrellas and packed lunches. Baby Mol's excitement keeps them all in good spirits. A boatman takes them down the river and then weaving through canals and backwaters until they arrive at Vembanad Lake, one edge of which Big Ammachi last saw as a twelve-year-old bride on the second-saddest day of her life. A bigger boat carries them across the lake.

It's dusk when they reach Cochin and make their way through the city to a lodge. Her mother goes straight to bed, but at Ranjan's insistence, Big Ammachi and Baby Mol head out to get their first glimpse of the ocean. It laps noisily at the shore, sounding just like Caesar drinking from his bucket but with a thousand times the intensity; it dwarfs Vembanad Lake. Moored offshore is a ship so big she cannot fathom how it is afloat. The streets are thick with people and inside the grand shops it is still bright daylight because of electric lighting. In her prayers that night, Big Ammachi says, "Lord, forgive me, but sometimes I think you are the God of my little Parambil alone. I forget how vast this world is that you created, and that you watch over." After JoJo's death, she studied the book of Job intensely, searching for meaning in their senseless loss, but meaning eluded her. Now she recalls how Job, despite his suffering, praised the God, "who does great things beyond understanding, and marvelous things without number."

The next morning, with a bleary-eyed and hungover Ranjan leading the way, they visit the vast spice market, pray in the Portuguese basilica, walk in and out of shops, stroll past palaces, and spend hours by the ocean watching the fishermen operate their strange levered nets from shore. By the time they return to the lodge in the late afternoon, they've seen so many white men—*sa'ippus*—and even white women, that Baby Mol no longer wants to touch them to see if the color comes off. They bathe and then head to the clinic in Mattancherry; Big Ammachi tells Ranjan that they can find their way back; he takes off happily. Big Ammachi, her mother, and Baby Mol join the queue outside the clinic of the man who, it is said, is the most astute physician in Travancore and Cochin. Big Ammachi tries to sound out the doctor's name on the signboard, but it twists her tongue into knots.

Dr. Rune Orqvist appeared in Fort Cochin in 1910 AD, washing ashore like Ask and Embla. Like those first humans of Norse mythology, Rune quickly found his legs, and they carried him to food,

shelter, drink, women, and raucous company. With his giant girth
and his booming baritone, the first impression of the newly arrived
blond, bearded foreigner was of an oracle, the sort of man who
in apostolic robes, carrying a staff, could have stepped off a dhow
alongside that other apostle, Saint Thomas. His arrival is clouded
in almost as much myth as that of Saint Thomas. What is known is
that South India was the last stop on a journey that began in Stock-
holm. According to the good doctor, one night, full of akvavit and
"singing to myself on Stora Nygatan, I was abducted. When I woke
up I was a ship's physician on a vessel bound for Cape Town!" That
occupation took him to all the major ports of the Orient and Africa.
But, in his midthirties, he disembarked in Cochin. The beauty of
the cluster of islands forming a city at the confluence of myriad
waterways; the warmth of its people; its temples; its churches, ba-
silicas, and synagogues; and the cobblestone Dutch colonial streets
and houses led the big Swede to drop anchor for good. Soon after
settling in, he commenced the study of Malayalam with one tutor
and the study of the *Vedas*, the *Ramayana*, and the *Bhagavad Gita*
with another. His appetite for knowledge was matched by one for
toddy and female companionship, a cocktail of desires that would
sink most physicians.

For most Westerners, Malayalam's rolling "*rhha*" scrapes the
mucosa off the hard palate and cramps the tongue, but not for
Rune. He can banter with children outside his clinic who giggle at the Scandinavian lilt to his Malayalam; he even trots out
a few phrases in Judeo-Malayalam to the Paradesi ("foreign")
Jews. (After he relieved the rabbi's wife of a huge ovarian cyst, the
Paradesis—who had arrived from Iberia in the great Sephardic
diaspora—would see no one else.) The old Saint Thomas Christian ladies attend his clinic as faithfully as they attend church,
presenting him their aches and pains that are often surrogates
for chronic marital woes—he offers placebos and sympathetic
homilies, such as "*Mullu elayil vinallum, ela mullel vinallum, elakka
nashttam.*" Whether the thorn falls on the leaf, or the leaf falls on

the thorn, the leaf suffers. "*Aah, aah*, you're so right, doctor. My husband is a thorn only, what to do?"

The doctor's fortunes changed in 1912 with Mrs. Eleanor Shaw, a middle-aged woman with diverticulitis, acid reflux, and biliary colic—a constellation of unrelated disorders that he thinks of as "Orqvist's Triad" because they seem to occur together in women like her: white, perimenopausal, and overweight. Rune removed her gallbladder, treated her reflux, and regularized her bowels but Eleanor Shaw felt no relief. In a moment of divine inspiration Rune asked her a delicate question that he never had occasion to ask the poor, whose sex lives never suffered despite illness and deprivation: "Mrs. Shaw? Perchance is the marital bed less appealing after all these years? Painful, even?" His singsong Swedish intonation made it hard for her to take offense. "Eleanor—if I may—these organs are vital and they cannot rust without repercussions." Rune divined that lack of lubrication, not lack of libido, was the issue. He dispensed thirty-two ounces of an inert, oily unguent, and prescribed sixteen ounces of fresh toddy, which was to sit for eighteen hours to become eye-wateringly potent, taking pains to make clear which medicine was for which orifice. Eleanor's husband, Mr. Benedict Shaw, was advisor to the Cochin maharajah, and head of a major British trading concern. Rune's intervention with his wife was so successful that a grateful Benedict Shaw directed his trading house to refurbish an old Dutch mansion into an elegant nursing home for Rune, complete with a surgical theater, ten beds, and a clinic in the front. Mrs. Shaw's case was proof that a sound treatment has salutary effects on the family, and that a single patient can alter a doctor's fortunes.

On the evening in 1913 that Big Ammachi, her mother, and Baby Mol arrive at the clinic, the waiting bench is already full and they must stand. Rune Orqvist bustles in, clutching under his arm an impossibly large stack of newly purchased books, and grinning at the assembled patients. Rune's fees are nominal for the poor and painful for the rich. A Paradesi couple—he in a white suit with an embroidered kippah on his head, she in a high-neck buttoned chemise—sit uneasily next to two bare-chested "black Jews"; the latter community settled in Cochin at the time of Solomon, and as a group they resent the Paradesi "newcomers" for their superior attitude to their darker-skinned kinsmen. Also on the bench are a stevedore massaging a parotid swelling, a fidgety policeman, a dyspeptic Englishman, and a Brahmin lady wearing gold chains sturdy enough to moor a boat.

When at last it's their turn, Dr. Rune Orqvist welcomes them with a smile that disarms Big Ammachi. The *sa'ippu* doctor has a stethoscope around his neck. A polished stone paperweight holds down a stack of papers before him. His eyes settle on Baby Mol with a look of recognition. When he extends his enormous hand, Baby Mol, who has never shaken a hand in her life, happily gives him hers. "And who is this beautiful young lady?" he says in perfect but accented Malayalam.

"I'm Baby Mol!"

"For you I have a red sweet or a green one. Which do you want?"

"Both!" Baby Mol says. "One for Kunju *Mol* too," she says, holding out her doll.

His laughter fills the room. He hands over the treats.

He turns to Big Ammachi, who is still in shock to hear him speak Malayalam. She begins hesitantly with the Condition, JoJo's drowning, the genealogy—she's certain it's all relevant—before coming to Baby Mol. He listens attentively.

When she's done, the doctor says, "Very unusual. I don't know how to explain the drownings in the family. But," and he leans forward, touching Baby Mol's cheek, "I don't think that's the issue with this beautiful girl—"

"Thank God! My husband doesn't think so either."

"I *do* know what is going on with Baby Mol."

"You do?" Big Ammachi says, thrilled.

"Yes. You see, I recognized her at once."

"What do you mean? You've seen her before?"

"You could say that." He examines Baby Mol's hands. "I expect she has a swelling, a hernia by her belly button, am I right?" He lifts Baby Mol's shirt, and it's as he says, a bulge that Big Ammachi thought nothing of, since it never troubled her little girl. Baby Mol giggles. The doctor has her walk for him, put out her tongue.

He rests his huge forearms on the desk and leans forward. "What Baby Mol has is a well-known affliction. It's called 'cretinism'—but the name is not important." It means nothing to Big Ammachi in any case. "There's a gland here in the neck. The thyroid. You've seen it swell into a goiter in some people?" She has. "That gland produces a vital substance for the body to grow and the brain to develop. Sometimes at birth the gland doesn't work. Then children develop like Baby Mol. The tongue. The broad face. The hoarse voice. The thickened skin. She's a smart child, but she's slow to learn what others her age know." He's listed all the things about her daughter that she resisted seeing.

"You can tell all this by looking at her?" Big Ammachi asks, still doubtful.

He steps to his bookshelf and without hesitation picks out a volume. He rifles through pages just as her father could with his Bible, familiar with chapter and verse. He turns the big book around to display a photograph. It's true: Baby Mol resembles this child more than she resembles her blood relatives. Baby Mol puts her broad finger on the page and giggles in recognition.

"Is there medicine to cure this?"

He sighs and shakes his large head. "Yes and no. There's an extract of the thyroid, but it isn't available in India. Even if it were, it would have to be administered from birth. At this point, no amount of that extract will reverse what you see."

Big Ammachi looks at this man whose hair and beard are like spun gold, and whose eyes are the color of the ocean. Many Malayalis have light-colored eyes, the influence of the Arab and Persian visitors of old, but nothing like this doctor's eyes. More than the color, it's the kindness in them that is so striking; it only makes his words more painful for her to hear. The door into her daughter's future has been pushed open. The view is crushing. She wants to argue. He reads her mind. "She'll always be a child. That's what I have to tell you. She'll never grow up, I'm sorry to say." He smiles at Baby Mol. "But what a happy child! A child of God. A blessed child. I wish I had some other news for you. I wish I did," he says, his face grave, those kind eyes now full of sorrow.

Her mother looks on, her eyes wet, a hand on her daughter's shoulder. Baby Mol is her happy self, too absorbed with the doctor and his beard and the instruments on the table to be affected by the discussion.

"Bless you," Big Ammachi says, her voice choking. She has just thanked this man who gave her this terrible news, habit being so strong.

"Please understand. This happened *before* her birth. She was born this way. Nothing you or anyone else did caused it. Understand? This isn't your fault. In Jeremiah, doesn't God say, 'Before I formed thee in the belly I knew thee; and before thou camest forth out of the womb I sanctified thee'?"

"He does!" she says, shocked to hear a Bible verse from this worldly man.

He opens his hands as if to say, *God's work is a mystery to us.*

She can't help her tears. He puts his hand on hers and she clutches it, bending her head. *Nothing can absolve me*, she wants to say. After a while she looks up. "But what about the Condition, the drowning I told you about? If I have more children. Will they have it? Will they be like Baby Mol?"

Rune says, "The drownings . . . I really don't know. That is clearly something passed from generation to generation. It's just that I can't think what it is. But what happened to Baby Mol will not happen to the next child. I promise you that."

* * *

They're at the door when the doctor says, "A moment, *Kochamma*."

It's not Baby Mol but the child's grandmother who has his attention. She'd sat in the room with them, abstracted though not indifferent. "May I?" He places his fingers on her neck and probes thoughtfully. When he removes his hand, Big Ammachi sees the knot that he spotted on her mother. Is there no limit to the bad news in this room? He says, "Her eyes are a bit yellow."

"She's been weak for months," Big Ammachi says. "It's hard for her to lift her arms, and once she sits down, hard to rise."

He guides her mother to the examining table. He feels her belly. Big Ammachi notices it looks swollen, despite her weight loss. Her mother looks befuddled but doesn't protest. The doctor is noticeably subdued. "*Kochamma*," he says, addressing her mother. "I have some medicine for you. Would you take Baby Mol out to look at the garden while I get it ready? I'll give it to your daughter."

As their boat approaches the jetty, Big Ammachi sees a familiar silhouette perched high up in a coconut palm. By the time the red earth of home touches her feet, her husband is there waiting. Baby Mol regales her father with the wonders she has seen: the ocean, the electric lights, the doctor with skin painted white—a tale she will repeat for the rest of her life.

When husband and wife are alone in his room, seated on the edge of his bed, she tells him all. "Baby Mol's mind and body are fixed in time. She'll always be just as she was last year. And the year before."

The big chest heaves. He sighs, hangs his head. After a long, long while he speaks, his voice hoarse. "If you're saying she'll always be Baby Mol, a child, a happy child . . . that's not such a bad thing."

"No," she says through tears. "Not such a bad thing. An angel forever."

He puts his arm around her, pulling her close.

"There's more," she says, sobbing. She tells him of the jaundice the *sa'ippu* doctor noticed in her mother's eyes, the rock-hard lump he felt in her neck and also in her belly, her enlarged liver—it explained her lassitude. Privately, the doctor told Big Ammachi that a cancer in the stomach had spread to the liver and the glands in the neck. It was too far gone for surgery. There was no treatment other than to make her comfortable. "I felt as if the same mule that kicked me ten minutes before kicked me again," she says.

"Does she feel pain?"

"No. But he says she will. We must buy opium pills to keep her from suffering toward the end. He said, 'Some Christians think that pain confers dignity, that there's Christian redemption in pain. But I don't.' That doctor is a saint."

That night in her prayers, she says, "You knew all these things, Lord. What is there for me to tell You? Before my mother was born and before Baby Mol was born You knew what was written on their foreheads." She knows she must thank God for the few good years she's had with her mother. But not tonight. It wouldn't be heartfelt. "I pray You keep her from suffering. She has had enough of that in this life already."

She prays too for the kind doctor. How gifted he is to know in an instant what ailed Baby Mol, and then to see that something was very wrong with her mother. Yet, despite being able to name these disorders, he could offer no treatment. In that sense, the annoying *vaidyan*, with his one tonic for every malady, could argue that he was no worse. But the *vaidyan* knows nothing. "Lord, that doctor knew everything . . . but he didn't know about the Condition. I beseech You once more: If You won't heal the Condition, please send us someone who can."

CHAPTER 24

A Change of Heart

1922, Cochin

Rune locks up the clinic at midnight. He started seeing outpatients late that evening because of two back-to-back emergency operations. It has been ten years since Mrs. Eleanor Shaw changed his fortunes. On his ambling walk home along the rocky shoreline of Fort Cochin, usually with a book under his arm, it is his custom, weather permitting, to smoke one last pipe on a cement bench that looks out over the sea, and to savor the breeze. The waves celebrate their long voyage with a final splash on the rocks. The moon hangs low like a lantern, illuminating the angular scaffolding of the Chinese fishing nets, more than a dozen of them along the water's edge. The poles crane out over the water like long-necked shore birds, while the netting billows like the sails of dhows.

Rune considers himself happy. Each day is different. He lacks for nothing, has good friends and many interests outside of medicine. Why then, many a night when he sits on this bench, does he feel restive? The unsettledness comes as unfailingly as the old Musulman who appears at the end of the month, carrying his tattered rent-collection ledger and his so-sorry-to-disturb-you mien. But this restlessness isn't the kind that took him from port to port until he found a home in Cochin—it's not about geography. He is where he is meant to be. What then?

A tapping sound gets louder. Rune sees a shape shuffling along, a staff in one hand, silhouetted by moonlight. The flattened profile, the absent nose are immediately recognizable: a leprous facies. Stumps, not fingers, clutch the staff. Coins rattle in a tin cup dangling from the neck. The figure chants in a low voice, a devotional perhaps, the face tilted up to the heavens and swaying from side to side, scanning the unseen sky. The specter stops, his head ceasing its pendulum swing as though he has sensed the low-hanging moon. He's a statue, unmoving but for the rise and fall of the shoulders with each breath.

In a dizzying shift of perspective, Rune suddenly feels he has *become* the leper: it's Rune who looks out through scarred, opaque corneas; Rune who sees cloudy, smeared images with no edges; Rune who discerns light and shadow but remembers what it was like to have moonlight fall on his face; those are Rune's misshapen, ulcerated feet wrapped in bloodied gunnysack that is secured with coir rope . . . The moment passes. He has no explanation for what just happened, the sense of being momentarily embodied in another.

The figure departs, swallowed by the night, the tap of staff against stone receding. In a rush of clarity Rune sees all the things the leper could not: the distant horizon where sea meets sky, the sky that suspends the moon, and the moon with the shawl of stars draped around it . . . He feels himself disappear in the capaciousness of the universe. He has become the sagging net, the blind leper who must sleep under the stars . . . In the immensity of the cosmos, Rune feels he himself is nothing, an illusion. The difference between him and the leper is no difference at all, they are just manifestations of the universal consciousness.

In this new awareness, the restless chattering in his head abruptly ceases. Just as the ocean manifests as a wave or surf, but neither wave nor surf *is* the ocean, so also the Creator—God or

Brahma—generates an impression of a universe that takes the form of a Swedish doctor, or a blind leper. Rune is real. The leper is real. The fishing net is real. Yet it is all *maya*, their separateness an illusion. All is one. The universe is nothing but a speck of foam on a limitless ocean that is the Creator. He feels euphoric and unburdened—*the peace of God, which passeth all understanding.*

In the early hours of morning, his worried watchman comes looking for him. In times past he has pulled his master out of the toddy shop, where the good doctor is slumped over the table. But on this night he finds the doctor rapt as a *sadhu*, gazing out through unfocused eyes. The watchman shakes him gently. Rune, smiling, reenters the illusion that is the world.

By the end of that week, he has given away all his furniture and stored his instruments and sterilizer in the godown of Salomon Halevi, the Jewish merchant and banker. Cochin now has many doctors, fresh graduates of the medical schools in Madras or Hyderabad, and it has an expanded public hospital system. He will miss his patients, but they'll manage without him.

Two weeks later, without formal goodbyes, he heads to Bethel Ashram in Travancore. This monastic retreat was founded by a priest, BeeYay *Achen*, who is guided by the writings of Saint Basil on the pursuit of manual labor, silence, and prayer in order to become closer to the Creator. He was one of the first priests to get a BA, and no one knows him by any other name than BeeYay *Achen*. He encourages Rune by quiet example: service, prayer, and silence. After seven months, a leaner, almost unrecognizable Rune emerges like a butterfly from its chrysalis, sure of its destination, even if its flight is erratic. The beard, the joy, and the belly laugh are intact, but he is burning with a mystical sense of purpose. BeeYay blesses Rune when he leaves. "I believe God brought you here and revealed to you your life mission. But the important thing is you accepted. Remember,

God didn't speak just to Isaiah, but to *everyone*, when he said, 'Whom shall I send? Who will go for us?' Isaiah said, 'Here I am. Send me!'"

Rune cajoles the enterprising boatman who supplies the monastery with fish, kerosene, candles, and other provisions to take him to his journey's end. "Where? There? What! Why?" the boatman says, incredulous. "Did you forget something at that place?" When he realizes Rune is serious, he says, "Who knows if my boat can pass? Who knows if the canals are dry? Who knows if anything remains there anymore?"

The two of them set off at dawn into the backwaters, the white man dwarfing his dark companion. The canoe slides through a succession of canals whose sides are built with rock and mud. In the afternoon they cross a vast lake and pass into another narrow channel, which should lead to their destination. They call out to a toddy tapper aloft in a palm tree, who gives them final directions. "Go straight—don't look left or right! In a furlong a canal will join. Cut in there. Then you'll see ten or a hundred steps up."

The "ten or a hundred steps" are fourteen, and so overgrown with moss that they nearly miss them. The boatman helps carry Rune's sacks to a back gate that has rusted off its hinge, but he declines to go in further. "One more favor," Rune says, counting out more notes than the boatman has seen at one time. "Sell me this boat."

His first night alone is spent in the only one of the six crumbling redbrick buildings that has two intact walls and a sliver of thatch overhead. As the sun goes down, he sees a stone move—a snake was sunning itself there. Flat on his back, listening to the scurrying of mice, he looks up at the starscape and questions his sanity. The word "lazaretto" used to refer to a quarantine station where infectious patients could be isolated, but over time it came to mean a leprosy hospital. This lazaretto is tucked away on the furthest inland reach of the backwaters. It was built and abandoned by the Portuguese, rebuilt and abandoned by the Dutch, rebuilt again by a Scottish Protestant mission. The stigma of the unfortunates once housed here is so strong that in the decades since the last mission pulled out, no squatter has claimed the land.

The next morning, a stout staff in hand, Rune explores the large property. He charts the perimeter, explores each ruined building, sounds the well, and examines the intact but rusted front gate. Stepping outside, he finds a well-maintained gravel road that passes directly in front of the lazaretto; in one direction it leads back to the huts and houses of a small village whose canal side he traveled the previous day when they encountered the tapper. In the other direction the road runs as straight as a hair-parting through the vast dusty plain, before rising slightly, then abruptly snaking back and forth to become a ghat road, looking like a sinuous scar at the base of the ghostly, distant, mammoth, mist-shrouded mountains: the Western Ghats.

Rune's spirits sink as he comes back into the compound and digests the task ahead. "Reality is always messy, Rune," he says aloud. "Once you open the belly, it's never as neat as the textbook suggested."

Near the front gate, a flash of white catches his eye. Hidden by tall grass are the bleached bones of a human skeleton, strewn around by animals. The skull and pelvis are relatively intact, sutured to the ground by creepers. A woman, judging by the pelvis, and clearly a leper, based on the erosions over the cheekbones. He has a vision of her coming to this place, weak, perhaps feverish, hoping for relief and instead finding rubble. She lay down unattended, without food or water. She died. The shiny bones make him terribly sad. "This is a sign, isn't it, Lord?"

That night he dreams of Sister Birgitta at the orphanage in Malmö, where he was raised. He used to feel sorry for her, dedicating her life to a place that he couldn't wait to leave. Now he understands. In the dream Sister Birgitta is knitting, seated close to the lamp, which gets brighter and brighter, blinding his eyes.

He awakes to see two terrifying faces, inches from his, their features exaggerated by the candle flame held under their chins. He screams. They pull back, yelling. The two frightened shapes retreat to a corner. Rune lights his lamp. "I didn't mean to scare you," Rune says in Malayalam, compounding their shock.

"We thought you were dead," says a man with a hole for a nose. His name is Sankar, and the woman's is Bhava. They are returning from a temple festival. Such events are where they seek alms. "It's a long walk here," Sankar says, "but there are walls and a roof under which to sleep."

"Just two walls and not much of a roof," Rune says.

"Better than out in the open, where wild dogs come at us," Bhava says, making a sibilant sound as she takes her next breath. Rune guesses that her larynx is riddled with leprous lesions. "People won't even let us lean against a cattle shed."

"You don't have leprosy," Sankar observes. "Why are you here?"

"The well is silted up," Rune says. "We must fix that first. Then we will restore the rest, bit by bit." He gestures at the untended land, the rubble heaps that once were buildings.

"You and who else?" Sankar inquires.

Rune points up to the star-blazing sky.

The next morning, the two lepers wish Rune well and shuffle away in the cool of dawn. The battered tin vessels dangling from their necks that are to hold food or coins are filled with the coffee Rune brewed for them.

An hour later, as Rune stacks usable bricks from the rubble, he sees them hobbling back.

"We decided you could use help," Sankar says. He shows Rune his hands and laughs. "I used to be a carpenter." He is short two fingers on the right and the rest are clawed. The flesh of the palm is wasted, giving the hand a simian appearance. The left has all its fingers, but the index and middle stick out in a gesture of papal benediction. Still, he scoops up and squeezes a brick to his body. Bhava, whose hands are in only slightly better shape, does the same. These two, Rune realizes, are angels sent his way. *Thus the heavens and the earth were completed in all their vast array.*

That evening, Rune cooks rice and lentils for them and hears their tales. Sankar was a new father when he noticed a welt on his face, then more over the ensuing months. His hands turned numb. "I couldn't hold my carpenter's pencil. My wife's brother threw me out. The whole village threw stones at me. My wife watched." The emotion in Sankar's voice belies his face, frozen forever into a snarl. Bhava's face became gradually thickened, unnaturally smooth, and she lost her eyebrows. Her husband made her stay indoors. "'Even the dogs run away from you,' my husband said. *Aah*, but it didn't stop him climbing on me at night. 'You're still pretty in the dark,' he said." When her fingers curled to her palm, her husband chased her out before she could say goodbye to her children. She cackles at this memory, a solitary tooth flashing in her mouth like a lone tree in a cemetery. Sankar joins in.

Rune puzzles over their strange laughter. The mind must get scarred from being rejected in this manner. These two have died to their loved ones and to society, and that wound is greater than the collapsing nose, the hideous face, or the loss of fingers. Leprosy deadens the nerves and is therefore painless; the real wound of leprosy, and the only pain they feel, is that of exile.

That's the purpose of a lazaretto, Rune thinks. *A home at the end of the world. A place where the dead can live with their own kind and where the spirit might rise.* He stares at his blistered hands. The thumb alone would prove the existence of God. A working hand is a miracle; his are capable of removing a kidney or stacking bricks. *Lord, what if I lose my use of them?* Rune was taught that leprosy is rarely contagious. The causative bacterium lives in the environment, more so in unclean settings, but only those with unique susceptibility get the disease. He recalls Professor Mehr in Malmö dressing leprous wounds with impunity, saying, "Worry about other diseases you might get from your patients, not leprosy." Indeed, Rune lost one classmate to tuberculosis, and another to sepsis from a scalpel cut.

In his head Rune now debates Professor Mehr. *What about Father Damien, serving all those years with lepers on Molokai? He caught it and died from it!* He imagines Mehr's response: *But think of Sister Marianne, who nursed Father Damien. Think of all the other nuns who served on Molokai—they were fine.* Rune decides he will simply not worry about contagion. *Lean not on your own understanding.* Let God worry.

In a month, there is a signboard in two languages on the gate: SAINT BRIDGET'S LEPROSARIUM. The name honors his beloved Sister Birgitta of his Malmö orphanage. It happens to be the name of Sweden's patron saint, and perhaps it will help in getting support from a Swedish mission. They restore two buildings and desilt the well. Rune buys provisions from the Mudalali's store in the village. Mathachen, the toddy tapper who gave his boatman directions, is an efficient middleman, dropping off other purchases—thatch, lumber, tools, coir—outside the front gate or on the steps on the canal side. If the villagers have qualms about Rune's work, they have no objections to his money. He soon has a bicycle in addition to the boat. Thambi, Esau, Mohan, Rahel, Ahmed, Nambiar, Nair, and Pathros join his two angels. Like a teak forest with underground roots, the lepers have a network; word of the lazaretto's resurrection travels fast.

Half a mile down the road from Saint Bridget's is a walled property where a traditional thatch house with carved gables and wooden walls has been tastefully fused onto a larger, modern house with whitewashed walls, a red tile roof, tall windows, a broad wraparound verandah, a porte cochere extending well out from the front entrance with a car sitting under it, and a brick-lined gravel driveway. The inset on the stone pillar of the gate reads THETANATT—the house name—and below that, the owner's name, T. CHANDY. Once, when riding past on his bicycle, Rune caught a glimpse of a heavy-lidded man smoking on a verandah bench-swing, a gold watch on his wrist. On another occasion he saw him drive past Saint Bridget's gates, a woman at his side, just as Rune emerged. Rune waved, and the couple smiled and waved back. Each time he rode past the house, he wanted to drop in, but for the first time in his career, his kind of doctoring could make people uneasy. Mathachen, the tapper, tells him that Chandy had been a contractor for the British Army in Aden—"minting money." When he returned, Chandy purchased an estate of several thousand acres up in the distant mountains that Rune can see from Saint Bridget's. During the week, Chandy stays up in the estate bungalow, overseeing the planting and harvesting; on weekends he drives back down, a three-hour journey, to his ancestral home, where his wife and her aging mother live.

Three months after Rune's arrival at the lazaretto, there is a commotion at the gate—someone yelling, "Doctor-ay! Doctor-ay!" The agitated servant from the Thetanatt house stands ten feet from the gate with a message: Chandy's wife begs him to come at once because Mr. Chandy has collapsed. Rune races over on his bicycle. On the verandah, a pair of men's slippers sits askew. Smoke curls lazily from an ashtray beside a tin of State Express 555s. From inside, he hears the clattering of furniture. He sees Chandy thrashing on the floor, his *mundu* askew, his large feet kicking. The terrified wife leans over the prone figure. She's in a sari, with glittering earrings and bangles on both hands—the couple looks dressed to go out.

Rune kneels, checking Chandy's airway and feeling his pulse, which is strong and bounding. "What happened? Tell me."

"Thank you, Doctor," the tearful woman says in English. "He was behaving different today. He wouldn't permit me to take him to hospital. Then just now he gave a cry, then he fell like that on the floor. Then he was stiff—very stiff—and unconscious. Driver is not here. I didn't know what to do. I sent our boy to you. Just now he started shaking, shaking."

Out of the corner of his eye, Rune sees an old woman in *chatta* and *mundu*, and enormous gold spikes in her ears, looking pale, her hands bloodless as she stands gripping the doorframe, her lower lip trembling. He calls out to her in Malayalam. "*Ammachi*, don't be afraid, it's just a fit and he'll recover momentarily." Even as he speaks, the thrashing subsides. "But I want you to sit down because if you faint it won't help." She obeys.

Rune registers Chandy's swollen parotid glands, his red palms, his womanly chest, and the burst of new blood vessels on chest and cheeks. He has a feeling that Chandy has spilled more liquor than most men will ever drink. An ammoniacal odor of urine precedes the yellow stain that blossoms on the pristine white *mundu*.

"Has this happened before?" he asks.

"Never! He was as usual when he came back from the estate last night. Tired from driving from our estate." She has switched to Malayalam.

"No, he wasn't *as usual*," the old lady says, finding her voice. "It was like an ant was biting him. *Aah*, fighting with everyone." The embarrassed wife glares at her but she holds her ground. "*Molay*, it's the truth and doctor must know."

"He always gets irritable at the start of Lent," the wife acknowledges.

"Ah," Rune says. "He gives up his whisky for forty days?"

"Fifty days. Yes. Gives up his brandy. He does it for me," she says, shyly. "He took a vow, the first year after we married."

Lent began the previous day. Chandy's sudden abstention probably precipitated a "rum fit," an alcohol-withdrawal seizure. Rune stands. "Don't worry." Chandy is breathing noisily but regularly. "He'll wake up shortly, but he will be very confused. I'll be back right away with medicine."

Mathachen, the tapper, also brews illicit *arrack*—not the anise-flavored *arak* of North Africa that Rune knows, but a tasteless distillate that Rune uses as an antiseptic. Back at Saint Bridget's, Rune compounds a tincture of opium, *arrack*, lemon, and sugar into an apothecary bottle and heads back.

Chandy is on the floor, but awake, a pillow under his head, the soiled *mundu* replaced. He's confused, but like a child he obediently swallows the medicine.

"Give him a tablespoon four more times before midnight," Rune says to Leelamma—that is Mrs. Chandy's name. "Tomorrow, three times a day. Then the day after, two times a day, and then once a day. I wrote it down."

He calls again in the evening, by which time Chandy has come to his senses, though he is sleepy. Rune tells them that in the future, Chandy will need to taper his brandy consumption heading into Ash Wednesday.

A week later, a car honks at the gate. Chandy drives in. Other than Rune himself, he is the first non-leper to enter the property in Rune's time there. Chandy, now that he is upright and recovered, proves to be a stocky man with a barrel chest and powerful forearms, and carrying excess weight around his waist. He is the rare Malayali without a mustache, his hair parted in the middle and slicked back. In his yellow silk juba and off-white *mundu*, he looks like a man at ease anywhere, even Saint Bridget's. His gratitude takes the form of a bottle of Johnnie Walker whisky. He says, "We would be honored if you join us on Easter Sunday for a late lunch. We'd invite you sooner, but Leelamma doesn't want to serve you rice and green beans. And I'd like to be able to offer you a drink." Rune accepts.

Chandy's gaze takes in what he sees with interest; he is unruffled by the curious residents who emerge. Rune offers a tour and Chandy readily accepts. They walk through the buildings that are being restored. Rune had hoped to reuse wooden beams from one of the old buildings, but Sankar thinks there's termite damage. Chandy squats to carefully examine the beam, then says, "I agree with your man. Termites and also flood damage. See how the color is different halfway up?" Chandy is knowledgeable about concrete and varieties of roof tile. In the fields, Chandy stoops down several times to gather soil and crumble it in his fingers. "I hope one day we can make the place self-sufficient," Rune says. Chandy makes no comment, but a few days later he's back with his driver in a car whose back seats have been removed; it also has a platform welded to the rear. The driver unloads pots of mango, plum, and plantain seedlings, as well as gunnysacks of bone and manure mix. Chandy unfolds a hand-drawn schematic of the grounds, on which he has marked his recommendations for the best spot to clear for an orchard. A low-lying, damper area near the canal is ideal for plantain. "This fertilizer, by the way, is for your existing coconut and date palms. Doesn't look like anyone has done that for years. This land in between these coconut palms keep free for grazing; it will support two cows. A chicken coop would be good too."

Easter at the Thetanatt house marks the beginning of a lasting friendship. Rune becomes a regular dinner guest at the Thetanatt home on Sundays, enjoying Leelamma's lavish spreads and Chandy's brandy. In summer, when the heat is oppressive, the family decamps to the estate bungalow for two months. They invite Rune to visit the mountains and stay with them in the bungalow some weekends.

Salomon Halevi ships Rune his stored surgical instruments, and now he has a clinic and a rudimentary theater. He can do more than dress wounds and drain abscesses. He operates selectively on hands, trying to preserve function or to restore it by releasing contractures. To raise money, Rune writes many letters. The Paradesi Jews fund the brick kiln, while a Lutheran mission in Malmö pays for the sawmill and a small carpentry workshop. At Christmas, the same Lutheran mission commits to an annuity for the leprosarium; Rune's chatty letters in Swedish are printed in their newsletter. Mr. Shaw, whose wife Eleanor was Rune's patient, arranges the gift of two dairy cows and a stack of lumber.

Fifty years after Armauer Hansen discovered, under the microscope, the rodlike bacilli in the tissue of lepers—*mycobacterium leprae*—there is still no medicine to cure leprosy. Rune provides a home and meaningful work, but he's frustrated that he can do little to prevent the progressive damage to the hands and feet. The day after they open the sawmill, he discovers a severed finger in the shavings. The owner, still working, doesn't notice the missing digit until Rune points out the bleeding stump. That leads Rune to hold a weekly catechism on preventing injuries. He pairs the residents off for daily inspections of their partners' hands and feet; he dresses fresh injuries. He is quick to put a finger or a foot into a cast to prevent further damage and to allow the wound to heal. Every tool at Saint Bridget's carries a padded strap, to make up for fingers that can't grip, and to protect the skin. Buckets and wheelbarrows have harnesses that go around the neck.

In the lazaretto's first year, a grinning newcomer walks in, blissfully unaware that his ankle is grotesquely dislocated, with bone sticking through skin. Anyone but a leper would be shrieking in pain, while this garrulous fellow is proud to have walked all day to the new lazaretto. Rune has noted in his residents this same perverse pride: their "advantage" over those who rejected them is that they can walk forever; and they can also stand like statues for hours, having no need to shift weight from one foot to the other because they have no discomfort. The cumulative trauma of walking on injured feet, and of prolonged standing, inflames, stretches, and ultimately ruptures the ligaments that hold the bones of the foot together. When the talus—the saddle-shaped bone under the tibia that transfers body weight to the heel—finally collapses, the arch of the foot becomes as flat as an *appam*, then convex, like the bottom of a rocking chair. The body weight is no longer spread over the entire foot but concentrated on one spot, and a pressure-ulcer results. If neglected, the ulcer grows and turns gangrenous, forcing Rune to amputate. But it never hurts.

CHAPTER 25

A Stranger in the House

1923, Parambil

When she is thirty-five, in the year of our Lord 1923, she's pregnant again. It feels like a miracle. Her first clue is a metallic taste in her mouth, followed by her appetite walking away. When she tells her husband, he seems startled. She's tempted to say, *Don't tell me you have no idea how it happened!* But his worried expression stops her; there've been three miscarriages in the long years since Baby Mol was born, each bringing crushing sadness, a sense that she's being punished for JoJo. Her husband's fears are never spoken, but she knows how badly he wants a son to whom he can pass on the Parambil he created; a son who will care for his parents in their old age. If he is anxious, she's at peace, confident this pregnancy will come to term. Her certainty must come from God. Has it really been fifteen years since she brought a child into the world? Her only sadness is that her mother isn't with her. The cancer took her within two months of their visit to the doctor in Cochin.

* * *

When she's in her seventh month, her center of gravity lowered, her feet spreading out as she walks, she finds her husband seated on the verandah after dinner, staring at the moonlit yard. His expression is dreamy, a rare sight. In profile he's ageless, though his hair is receding and mostly gray and he hears poorly. At sixty-three, he still pitches in to repair a bund, or dig an irrigation channel. He makes room for her, smiling. Of late, he's often troubled by headache, though he never complains; she knows only from the set of his jaw, his furrowed brow, and because he'll quietly take to bed with a wet cloth over his eyes.

She eases down beside him, her back aching, the baby pressing down on her. She remarks on her swollen feet, and that she can't imagine how Odat *Kochamma* had ten children . . . She has hungrily watched Shamuel and his wife Sara in their unguarded moments, seen their back-and-forth, their talking over each other—even their arguing feels intimate. But she must carry speech for both herself and her husband.

He watches her lips so as not to miss a word. His feet swing almost imperceptibly in time with his heartbeat. "Why do you speak so little, my husband?" she says after a while. He answers wordlessly by lifting and slowly lowering both his eyebrows and shoulders. *Who knows?* She shakes him in annoyance. It's like trying to shake the trunk of a banyan tree.

He says, "Since you fill the spaces where I might drop in some words . . . I keep quiet."

She makes to rise, offended, but laughing silently, he pulls her into him. His laughter, silent or otherwise, is even rarer than his speech, and she especially loves it when it leaves his body, unguarded and booming. His arms encircle her. She laughs with him. Why should she be self-conscious about anyone seeing them embrace? His nephews—the twins—walk together holding hands (even if their spouses are at each other's throats); heading to church, she sees women hold hands. But married couples stay conspicuously apart, as if to deny that in the dark they touch and more.

He releases her, but his shoulder still presses against hers. She waits. It's too easy to snuff out what he might say by speaking first. "I never learned to read," he says at last. "But I learned that ignorance is never revealed if one holds one's tongue. To speak is what removes all doubts." *You aren't ignorant! You're wise, my husband.* His confession sits between them in the friendly twilight. She puts her arms around him as if to enfold him, but she can no more do this than wrap her arms around Damodaran.

In the throes of labor, she screams her resentment that men should be spared what they brought about, just as she resents this thankless infant she's grown within her who now wants to split her in two. But then, when that minuscule mouth latches onto her nipple, she feels a rush of both colostrum and forgiveness, the latter bringing a kind of amnesia. Why else consent to sleep once more with the man who caused such pain?

After his first squawking breath, her baby boy looks around at the world of Parambil with an alert, serious expression, frowning in concentration. She'd already decided (with her husband's blessing) that she'd name him after her father, Philip. But her newborn's scholarly expression makes her record his baptismal name as Philipose. She could have chosen "Peelipose," "Pothen," "Poonan"—all local variants of "Philip." But she likes "Philipose" for its echo of ancient Galilee, its soothing last syllable that sounds like flowing water. She prays he will know the pleasure of being carried by a current, then striking back to shore.

His baptismal name will be used in school and in anything official. She prays it won't be altered into some diminutive before then. Too many children get a pet name early that they can never shake: "Reji," "Biju," "Sajan," "Renju," "Tara," or "Libni," to which a tail might be affixed: "*mon*" (little boy) or "*mol*" (little girl) or the genderless "baby" or "*kutty*" (child). Baby Mol has two tails in lieu of her Christian name, which sits abandoned in the birth register. When Philipose is middle-aged, younger people will address him with a respectful suffix: Philipose *Achayen* or *Philipochayen* (and for a woman it might be *Kochamma* or *Chechi* or *Chedethi*). When he's a father, he'll be *Appachen*, or *Appa* to his children, just as he'll soon call his mother *Ammachi* or *Amma*. Confusion is inevitable. She heard of a man known to his family as Baby *Kutty* and to his adult friends as Goodyear Baby, though he'd left that company after his marriage and now worked for the tax office in Jaipur. His wife's relatives knew him as Jaipur Baby. His wife's portly uncle arrived in Jaipur after a long journey and went seeking him in the tax office and became enraged when the staff said no Jaipur Baby worked there; the police were called. When George Cherian Kurian (aka Jaipur Baby) heard of this and went to post bond, he couldn't find the uncle because he only knew him as *Thadiyan* Baby (fat baby) and not by the name he was booked under, Joseph Chirayaparamb George.

A few weeks after she gives birth to Philipose, her husband takes to bed for five days with a crippling headache, along with alarming projectile vomiting. She's beside herself with worry, trying to nurse the child while rubbing oil on her husband's brow, and reassuring Baby Mol, who is upset by her father's state. Shamuel camps outside the *thamb'ran*'s room, refusing to go home. The *vaidyan*'s pills and poultices make no difference. She wants to take her husband to Cochin, to the *sa'ippu* doctor Rune, but he refuses to travel by boat. Then, as mysteriously as it began, the headache eases, but in its wake he has a droop on the left side of his face; he cannot quite close the left eye, and water dribbles out of that corner of his mouth. It bothers her more than it bothers him. He takes off to the fields. Shamuel reports the *thamb'ran* is working as hard as ever, though he's now stone deaf in his left ear.

Her husband's face lights up every time he sees his newborn son, but his smile is lopsided; she learns to look at the right side for his true expression. There's something new in his eyes; at first, she thinks it's sadness. Is he recalling the fate of his first son? No, it's anxiety, not sadness; anxiety untethered to anything she can put her finger on, and it troubles her. Baby Mol too is worried, abandoning her bench to trail after her father when he's in the house, or to perch on his bed, silent, staying there until her mother takes her to bed.

When Philipose is a year old, Big Ammachi cannot deny the truth about her little boy: he bathes willingly, but alarms her whenever she empties the pail over his head: his eyes close but then open to reveal his rolling eyeballs, and often his limbs turn floppy. Despite this, and unlike JoJo, he laughs, as though he welcomes the disorientation. He thinks it's a game. His swimmy eyes urge her to do it again. When he's big enough for her to put him in the shallow *uruli*, the giant unused vessel meant for cooking *payasam* on festive occasions, he splashes with pleasure, laughing as the vertigo tumbles him out of the *uruli* onto the *muttam*. Like a drunken sailor, he gathers himself and crawls back in. His shocked parents watch in disbelief.

Big Ammachi says to her husband, "I cannot lose this beautiful child."

"Then let him live. Don't imprison him," he says vehemently. "That's how my older brother could take advantage of me. Because my mother never let me go anywhere. Did I tell you that story?" *Has he truly forgotten?* "What I don't understand is why my son seeks out water when it is no friend of his," he concludes.

A few months later, in the evening, while Odat *Kochamma* looks after Philipose, Big Ammachi escapes to plunge into the river. Unlike her husband and son, nothing restores or renews her more than this. Nearing the house on her way back, she hears a repetitive scraping sound. She finds her husband squatting and digging half-heartedly with a stick at the edge of the *muttam*. For a moment, she feels she's watching a child at play, but his face is serious.

"Why are you digging? That too *after* your bath!" He looks up. For the briefest moment it's as though he has no idea who she is.

He rises and staggers. But for a few stuttering steps he'd fall to the ground. Her heart rises to her mouth. She's peering into the future.

In the ensuing weeks, it happens again: she finds him scraping at the soil, but he doesn't say why. It prompts her to say to Shamuel, "Keep a close eye on your *thamb'ran*."

He's startled. "What's happened? Why do you say that?" She doesn't answer, just looks at him. "There's nothing wrong with him," Shamuel says vehemently. "His face is tired on one side, but who needs two sides? That's what I tell him. One is enough."

"Well, he's not a young man. How old are you, Shamuel?" Shamuel's hair is gray, and his mustache, where it's not yellow from the *beedi*, is white. The wrinkles around his eyes are as plentiful as Damodaran's.

Shamuel makes a twisting motion with his wrist. "At least thirty years, maybe more," he says. She bursts out laughing, and then he does too—a rare sound for both of them these days.

She decides to tell Shamuel about the digging. It's as though she struck him.

When he finds his tongue he says, "Maybe *thamb'ran* is looking for coins that he buried. Before we built the *ara* we did that. There may be one, or one hundred coins. Gold, silver, brass," he says, taking refuge in nouns, which he prefers to numbers.

"You really think there's buried treasure?" she asks.

He avoids her gaze and his voice trembles. "Why ask what I think? I think only whatever the *thamb'ran* thinks."

His fear is palpable. For his forefathers there was never certainty of shelter or of food. They were indentured laborers to a household, forever paying off ancestral debts, but that practice is now illegal. Shamuel gets paid for his labor and he owns the plot his house sits on. He could work anywhere. But he can't imagine working for anyone else. Her heart breaks for this man who for all his years has been at her husband's side, his shadow. She senses

Shamuel's enormous love for her husband. Without the *thamb'ran*, what happens to the shadow? If he can't depend on the *thamb'ran*, he must depend on her.

A few days later, she stands holding Philipose on the verandah in the late afternoon while they watch Damo. Suddenly the hairs on the nape of her neck rise and she senses a hulking presence behind her. It can't be Damo and yet it is the same sensation of an immense form throwing a shadow over her. She turns to see her husband. He looks over her shoulder to where Damodaran feeds noisily, kicking his leaf pile around. Standing beside her father is Baby Mol, dabbing at her face with both hands. Baby Mol, who never cries, doesn't understand the nature of tears, or why they are salty, and why they won't cease.

Damo becomes very still, eyeing the *thamb'ran*. The two old giants face off, expressionless, and for a moment Big Ammachi imagines they'll charge and lock tusks. Her husband puts a hand on her—not for support, but to indicate possession.

"What's he want?" he says in a low voice, saliva glinting at one corner of his mouth.

"What do you mean 'want'? It's our Damodaran!"

"No, it isn't. It's some other elephant. Send him away." He walks off, meandering a bit before finding his way to his room, thanks to Baby Mol.

At dinner time, Damodaran lumbers up to the house, ignoring the fresh coconut fronds Unni gathered for him. He seems to be waiting for the *thamb'ran* to emerge, perhaps to complain about being called an impostor. Big Ammachi takes a bucket of rice and ghee to Damo. He ignores it.

She makes her husband's favorite dish, *erechi olarthiyathu*. When he sits down at the table for dinner, on the verandah of the old section of the house, he doesn't seem to notice that Damo has made his way there, though Damo is impossible to ignore. As usual, as soon as the sizzling meat touches the banana leaf, her husband can't resist sampling it before she can serve rice. But then, to her utter astonishment, he spits it out. Since his lips don't seal well, he has a mess on his chin. He flings what's on the leaf to the *muttam*.

"This isn't fit for dogs!"

Caesar, their newest pye-dog, disagrees, racing up to lick the meat cubes off the pebbles. Damodaran steps closer.

"*Ayo!* Why did you do that?" She's never before raised her voice to her husband. She tastes the meat. "For goodness' sake, there's nothing wrong with this! What got into you? I've been frying this dish just this way for nearly a quarter century!"

"*Aah*, isn't that my point? You've been making this dish for so long. You think by now you wouldn't make a careless mistake. So it must be deliberate."

She looks at him in disbelief. This man who hardly speaks, and never harshly, now lances her with his words. "All these years I wanted you to talk more! I should've been grateful for your silence." She turns her back and walks away seething, another first. She finds Damo looking right at her, his trunk held curled in his mouth. *Forgive your husband, he knows not what he does.* She hears it as clearly as if she'd heard a human voice.

Heeding this, she returns from the kitchen with vegetable, and pickle. He hardly eats. She holds the *kindi* for him, directing the spout over his fingers as he rinses off. He walks stiffly to his room, passing Baby Mol as he does so. Big Ammachi realizes that for once, Baby Mol wasn't by her father's side at dinner. Instead, she'd retreated to her bench. Her tears are gone and she's happy, chattering to her dolls instead of obsessively tailing her father. He pauses, looking down at Baby Mol, expecting his daughter to latch onto him as she's done for days now. But Baby Mol looks right through him.

Big Ammachi checks on her husband after covering the embers in the kitchen. She's still smarting from earlier. He's in bed, staring at the ceiling. She sits by him. He looks at her and asks if he can have some water. The glass is by his side. She holds it out to him. He rises up and, in the manner of a child, he covers her fingers on the glass with both his hands. His hands are powerful, but gnarled and weathered by age, callused from the trees he has climbed, and the ropes, axes, and shovels he has wielded. Together they raise the glass to his mouth, and he drinks. Her hand, dwarfed by his, is no longer that of the girl who came to Parambil a lifetime ago; it bears scars from the sparks of countless wood fires, and from splattering oil. Her knobby fingers show the wear and tear of endless chopping, grinding, peeling, mincing, pickling . . . Their overlapping hands bracket their many years together as husband and wife. When not a drop remains, he releases his grip, lies back down, sighs, and closes his eyes.

She leaves him after a while. She'll check on him after putting Baby Mol and Philipose to bed. But despite her best intentions she falls asleep with her children. She wakes up in the middle of the night and gets up to look in on her husband as has been her habit for some months now. His dark form is very still. When she touches him, his skin is cold. Even before she lights the lamp, she knows he's gone.

His face is still, his expression troubled and penitent. In the silence, she feels her heart beating furiously, feels it strain at its moorings, trying to tear free of her chest and beat for him, because the heart of Parambil that toiled for so many years cannot do it any longer.

Weeping quietly, she climbs onto the bed and lies next to her husband, gazing at the face she'd first glimpsed at the altar and had been terrified of, and then loved so fiercely, her silent husband who'd been so steadfast in his love for her. All around her, the sounds of the land he made his and where he lived his life feel sharper and exaggerated: the chirp of crickets, the croaking of frogs, the rustle of foliage. Then she hears a prolonged trumpet, a lament from Damo for the man who rescued him when he was wounded, for a good man who is no more.

Her husband would be pleased that he didn't have to receive or converse with the many mourners who stream into the house, all the relatives and the craftsmen whose lives and fortunes he altered so profoundly. The Nairs from the *tharavad* on the edge of Parambil come to pay their respects. All the *pulayar* are there too, from every house, standing silent on the *muttam*, their faces dark with sadness. Shamuel is chief among them, shattered and weeping—Shamuel whom she'd led inside to the bedroom despite his protests, so he could take his final leave of the *thamb'ran* he worshipped. Her husband would have been impatient with the funeral, wanting nothing more than to be in the earth he so loved, to lie beside his first wife and his firstborn son.

A few weeks after they bury him, as life at Parambil struggles to find its new normal, she hears the sounds of digging and scratching in the courtyard just as she's about to fall asleep. It stops. The next night, she hears it once more. She goes out to sit on the verandah, facing the sound. "Listen," she says, "you must forgive me. I chastise myself for not coming to you after putting the children to bed. I fell asleep. I'm sorry we argued at dinner. I overreacted. Yes, I too wish it had been different. But it was just one night out of so many that were perfect, was it not? I hoped for many more perfect nights but each was a blessing. And listen: I forgive you. After a lifetime of goodness together, you were more than entitled to a tantrum. So be at peace!"

She listens. She knows he has heard her. Because, as was always his way, he expresses his love for her the only way he knows how: through his silence.

CHAPTER 26

Invisible Walls

1926, Parambil

When her son is nearly three, she takes him by boat to Parumala Church, where Mar Gregorios, the only saint of the Saint Thomas Christians, is entombed. Philipose is delighted by his first boat ride, but she keeps a close eye on him. Neither her husband nor JoJo could ever be persuaded to get on a boat, whereas this one cannot see water without wanting to challenge it. His friends dart around the pond like fish. He doesn't understand why he is unable to do the same. It makes him fiercely determined like a fire ant to overcome the obstacle. His many attempts at "swimming" terrify his mother; his failures are pathetic to watch.

The saint's tomb is to one side of the nave of Parumala Church. Above it is a life-size photograph of Mar Gregorios; this image (or else the widely reproduced portrait by the artist Raja Ravi Varma) is on calendars and framed posters in every Saint Thomas Christian household. Mar Gregorios's beard outlines delicate lips, and his white sidelocks frame a handsome, kindly face with eyes that look surprisingly youthful. He alone had advocated for the *pulayar* to be converted and welcomed into their churches, but it didn't happen in his lifetime. She doesn't think it will happen in hers.

Her little boy is awestruck by the church, and more so by the saint's tomb with the hundreds of candles before it. He tugs at his mother's *mundu*. "Ammachi, ask him to help me swim." His mother doesn't hear him; she stands with her head covered, gazing up into the saint's face. She's in a trance.

Mar Gregorios looks directly at her, smiling. *Really? You came all this way for me to put a spell on the boy?*

She's stunned. She heard his voice, but when she looks around, she sees that clearly no one else did.

Mar Gregorios has seen right through her. She cannot hold the saint's gaze. "Yes," she says. "It's true. You heard what the boy said. He's so determined. What am I to do? The boy has lost his father. I'm desperate!"

One of the legends about Mar Gregorios is that he had wanted to cross the river flowing past this very church to visit a parishioner on the other bank. But near the jetty, three high-spirited women were bathing in the shallows, their wet clothes clinging to them, their shrieks and laughter floating in the air like festive ribbons. Out of modesty he retreated to the church. Half an hour later, they were still there. He gave up, muttering to himself, "Stay in the water then. I'll go tomorrow." That night his deacon reported that three women seemed unable to get out of the river. Mar Gregorios felt remorse for his casual words. He fell to his knees and prayed, then said to the deacon, "Tell them they can come out now." And they did.

Big Ammachi is there to shamelessly ask for the inverse: that Mar Gregorios prevent her only son from stepping into the river. "I'm a widow with two young ones to raise. On top of that I must worry about this boy, who, just like his father, is in danger around water. It's a Condition they were born with. I already lost one son to water. But this one is determined to swim. Please, I beg you. What if five words from you, 'Stay *out* of the water,' mean he'll live long and glorify God?"

She hears no answer.

Philipose is frightened to see his mother, her face ghost-lit by the rows of candles before the tomb, talking to the saint's photograph.

On their way home she tells Philipose, "Mar Gregorios watches over you every day, *monay*. You heard me make a vow before his tomb, didn't you? I vowed that I would never let you get into water without someone by your side. If you do then harm will come to your mother." That part is true. She would die if something happened to him. "Will you help me keep my vow? Never go alone?"

"Even after I learn to swim?"

"Yes, even then. Forever. Never swim alone. A vow cannot be broken."

He's shaken by the thought of harm coming to his mother. "I promise, Ammachi," he says earnestly. She will often remind him of their visit and of her vow and his.

When he turns five, her little boy goes to their new "school" for three hours a day; it's just a shed with a thatched roof, open on three sides. On their first day, Philipose and the five other new students bring betel leaves, areca nut, and a coin for the *kaniyan*, who receives the gift and then takes each child's right index finger and traces the first letter of the alphabet in a *thali* filled with rice grains. This school is her creation, a place to keep the children out of trouble for a few hours, teach them their letters. The pupils—the children and grandchildren of the Parambil families, as well as those of the ashari, the potter, the blacksmith, and the goldsmith—will learn their alphabet.

The *kaniyan* is a small, fussy, bald man with a shiny wen, or cyst, on top of his dome that Baby Mol labels a "Baby God." The *kaniyan* scrapes by reading horoscopes for prospective brides and grooms. Teaching gives him some welcome additional income. Some Brahmins think of the *kaniyan* caste of astrologers and teachers as pretenders or pseudo-Brahmins, but this *kaniyan* doesn't let such prejudice bother him.

* * *

As soon as Big Ammachi is out of sight, Joppan, the son of Shamuel *pulayan*, emerges from the plantain grove where he's been hiding. He winks at Philipose and walks into the classroom. The two are playmates and best friends. Since Joppan is four years older, he's also Philipose's official minder. Whenever they march about with arms around each other's shoulders they look like twins, especially from a distance, because Joppan is short for his age.

Joppan carries a leaf that isn't really a betel leaf, a stone that's meant to stand in for an areca nut, and a coin he carved out of wood. He steps inside the classroom, bare-chested, holding out his gifts, displaying his strong teeth, his hair slicked back with water but already springing up like trampled grass.

The *kaniyan* says, "*Ah ha!* So *you* want to study, is it?" The *kaniyan*'s smile is unnatural, the wen on his scalp getting turgid. "I'll teach you. Stand there behind the threshold. *Aah*, good." The *kaniyan* turns away then whirls back to crack his bamboo cane across Joppan's thighs. Philipose's cries of protest are drowned out by the *kaniyan*'s screams of "Upstart *pulayan*! Filth! Polluting dog! Don't you know your place? What's next? Would you like to bathe in the temple tank?" Joppan races out of reach, but turns around, disbelieving, his expression one of hurt, and shame. The others cringe to witness this. Joppan is their hero. No other boy has his self-confidence, or can swim across the river and back, or fearlessly kill a cobra. Some of the children (being little adults in the making) are secretly pleased by Joppan's humiliation.

Joppan's chest expands, and he bellows out in the loudspeaker voice of his for which he's notorious: "TAKE THAT EGG ON YOUR HEAD AND EAT IT! WHO WANTS TO LEARN FROM AN IDIOT LIKE YOU?" This blasphemy carries to the paddy field and Shamuel raises his head. The *kaniyan* lunges, swinging his cane. Joppan feints one way and jumps in the other and the *kaniyan* stumbles. Joppan's amplified guffaws as he struts off have the other children grinning. The teacher has a moment of doubt: Could Big Ammachi have sent the *pulayan* child? Parambil is known to give land to its *pulayar*, but does such eccentricity extend to educating them? *She may pay my wages, but I'll starve before I raise up children of the mud.*

At home Philipose spills angry tears and tells his mother all. The world's hypocrisy burns on his face. Big Ammachi holds her little boy and rocks him. She's ashamed. The injustice he witnessed isn't the *kaniyan*'s fault alone. Its roots are deep and so ancient that it feels like a law of nature, like rivers going to the sea. But the pain in those innocent eyes reminds her of what is so easy to forget: the caste system is an abomination. It is against everything in the Bible. Jesus chose poor fishermen and a tax collector as his disciples. And Paul said, "There is neither Jew nor Gentile, neither slave nor free, nor is there male and female, for you are all one in Christ Jesus." They are far from being all one.

She tries to explain the caste structure simply to Philipose, conscious of how absurd it must sound: The Brahmins—or Nambudiris, as they are called in Travancore—are the highest caste, the priestly caste, and like European monarchs they owned much of the land by divine justification. The maharajah is of course a Brahmin. A Nambudiri has the privilege of free meals at any temple because there's honor in feeding a Brahmin; they stay free at guest houses maintained at state expense. Only the oldest son in a Nambudiri joint house, or *illam*, can marry and inherit the property; he alone can take multiple wives and often does, well into his dotage. Sons who are *not* firstborn are only allowed informal unions with Nairs, the warrior caste who are just below the Nambudiris. Children of such unions are Nairs. The Nairs are upper-caste, and like the Nambudiris consider themselves polluted by contact with lower castes; they are the overseers for the vast Nambudiri holdings, but these days they are landowners themselves. On a lower rung than the Nambudiris and Nairs come the Ezhava—the craftsmen who were traditionally toddy tappers but increasingly are in the coir business, or are landowners. The lowest caste are the landless laborers: the *pulayar* and the *cheruman* (also called *adivasis*, *parayar*, or "untouchables"). The "tribals" in the hills are outside all caste hierarchy; their traditional bond with the land on which they lived, hunted, and farmed was never recorded on paper, a fact that newcomers from the plains easily took advantage of.

"As for us Christians, *monay*," Big Ammachi says before he asks, "we slide between these layers." Legend has it that the original families converted by Saint Thomas were Brahmins. Hindu rituals remain embedded in the Christian ones, as in the tiny gold *minnu*, shaped like a tulsi leaf, that her husband tied around her neck at her wedding; or the *Vastu* principles followed in building their houses. Christians haven't rid themselves of casteism. In Parambil, just as in every other Christian household, a *pulayan* never enters the home; Big Ammachi serves Shamuel in a separate set of vessels—but surely, Philipose has already observed this.

What she doesn't tell him is that the Saint Thomas Christians never tried to convert their *pulayar*. The English missionaries who arrived centuries after Saint Thomas knew only one caste in India—the heathen who had to be saved from damnation. The *pulayar* converted willingly, perhaps hoping that by embracing Christ they'd become equals with households like Parambil where they were employed or bonded. That never happened. They had to build their own churches with Anglican, or Church of South India (CSI), rites. "Ideas about caste are centuries old, so hard to change," she says.

Her son's face shows his disappointment in his mother, his disillusionment with his world. He walks away. She wants to call after him. *You can't walk across a lake just because you change its name to "land." Labels matter.* But he's too young to understand. She thinks her heart will break.

The *ashari*, the potter, and the goldsmith call Shamuel out of his hut. "Your son needs a thrashing," the potter says. "What made him think he can go to school? Don't you teach him anything?" Shamuel stands there, mortified. He begs forgiveness, crossing his hands to tug at both his earlobes while bending his knees, a gesture of obeisance to make the Baby Ganesh smile. Later, Shamuel canes Joppan harder than the *kaniyan* did, shouting that Joppan has brought shame on the family—he wants those living upstream to hear. The only crying heard is that of the boy's mother; the nine-year-old takes the hiding silently, and isn't the least penitent. He retreats just like a wounded tiger slipping into the overgrowth. Joppan's resentful eyes make Shamuel fearful. He isn't afraid *of* his son, but afraid *for* him.

Big Ammachi could insist the *kaniyan* take Joppan as a pupil. But she knows he will quit, and even if he agreed, the parents of the other children would pull them out. The next day the *kaniyan*'s lessons begin in earnest, using the sandy ground as a blackboard. Big Ammachi sends for Joppan, but Shamuel says the boy is probably swimming somewhere. When Philipose comes home, he shows his mother the palm-leaf "book" in which the teacher wrote the first letters—*a* and *aa*, *e* and *ee* (അ and ആ, and എ and ഏ)—with a sharp nail. The next day another leaf will be bound to the previous ones with a string.

Later, she spots Philipose with Joppan, threading leaves to make Joppan his own book, and tracing letters in the sand for him to copy. Her joy vanishes when she sees the welts on Joppan's back that are Shamuel's doing. Why punish Joppan for a system he didn't create? She tells Joppan she will be teaching him herself while the others are in school. She can't undo the evils of casteism, but she can do this. In a year, the children will be ready to go on to the new government primary school near the church, where *all* will be allowed. A high school is going up behind it, and it will serve several surrounding towns and villages in the district.

Joppan is punctual, a quick learner and a grateful one. His swashbuckling demeanor is unchanged despite his beatings. But she can tell he yearns to be in class with his playmates. The day will come for both her son and Joppan when their studies end, and they will have to face the world, with all its duplicities.

CHAPTER 27

Up Is Good

1932, Parambil

Six years after tracing his first letters with the *kaniyan*, Philipose has yet to master a skill more vital to him: swimming. He refuses to concede defeat. Every year when the flood waters recede, he tries again. Joppan, who is more comfortable in water than out, perseveres the longest in trying to teach him. But the day comes when Joppan refuses to accompany him to the river, and not just because he works all day. It's the first falling-out between the two friends. Philipose persuades Shamuel to go with him because he has vowed not to go alone.

When Philipose went off to primary school, Joppan enrolled with him. Shamuel didn't approve but couldn't say so to Big Ammachi. What did a *pulayan* boy need with letters? Then, after third standard, Joppan witnessed a barge adrift in the new canal near Parambil. It got wedged and took on water. The boatman was unconscious from drink. Somehow Joppan pried it free and then, by himself, poled it down to join the river and on from there steered it to the jetty in front of the godown of its owner, Iqbal. The grateful proprietor offered Joppan a job and he took it. Big Ammachi was furious with Shamuel, as though it were his fault! The job is a good one. Still, Shamuel wishes the boy would just work at Parambil instead. After Shamuel's time, Joppan could take over from him. Wouldn't that be the natural thing to do?

"Do you think this is the year I master it, Shamuel?" Philipose says as the two of them head to the river, while the nine-year-old windmills his arms, rehearsing a new stroke that he's convinced will keep him afloat. Shamuel doesn't reply, hurrying after the "little *thamb'ran*" just as he once scrambled to keep up with the boy's father.

At the dock, the two boatmen are counting flies. One fellow's front incisors jut out like the bow of his canoe, his upper lip draped around them. The sight of Philipose pulling off his shirt rouses the men from their lethargy. "*Adada!* Look who's back!" the toothy one says, his gestures as languid as the slow river. "The Swimming Master!" Philipose doesn't hear them. With his eyes wide open, pinching his nose, he takes a deep breath and jumps in. That much he has mastered: with his lungs full he will always pop up, though he only tries this in the shallows. And he does pop up, his glistening hair sheeting over his eyes like a black cloth. Now, his arms thrash wildly: his attempt at "swimming."

"Eyes open!" Shamuel shouts, because he knows from his years with the *thamb'ran* that this confusion with water is always worse with eyes closed. But the boy doesn't hear him. Joppan believes Philipose is hard of hearing, but Shamuel thinks the little *thamb'ran*, unlike the big one, hears only what he wants to hear.

"It's shallow, *monay*," the toothy boatman calls. "Just stand up!" The frenzied flailing stirs up mud and spins Philipose in circles, first on his belly, then on his back, then he heads down, white soles flashing. Shamuel has seen enough and jumps in and rights him like a jug that's been knocked over.

The boatmen clap, which pleases Philipose. Despite his eyeballs parting ways from each other, he grins victoriously, pausing the celebration to retch and disgorge the mud he borrowed from the river. "I think I was nearly almost halfway across this time, wasn't I?" he sputters.

"*Ooh, aah,* more than halfway!" the toothy one says. The other boatman laughs so hard he loses his *beedi.*

Philipose's face falls. Shamuel leads him home, shouting over his shoulder, "Why you fellows need oars when your tongues can do the job?" He looks nervously at the boy, who is unusually silent. He did not inherit his father's taciturn nature. Could it be the little *thamb'ran* is discouraged?

"I'm doing something wrong, Shamuel."

"What you're doing wrong is getting into the water, *monay,*" he says sternly. He'll be firm even if Big Ammachi isn't. "Your father doesn't like to swim. Do you see him near the water? Be like he is."

Without being aware of it, Shamuel speaks of the big *thamb'ran* as if he's working in the next field over. After all, the artifacts of his master's life are all there and call out to him: the trestle, the pickaxe, the plow, the fences their hands dug together, every field they plowed, every tree . . . How could the *thamb'ran* not be around?

Philipose peels away to desultorily kick an *ola* ball. Shamuel heads to the kitchen.

"Did he get any farther this time?" Big Ammachi says.

"Farther down in the mud. He buried his head in the riverbed like a *karimeen.* I dug mud out of his ears and nose."

Big Ammachi sighs. "Do you know how hard it is for me to let him go to the river?"

"Then forbid him!"

"I can't. My husband made me promise. All I can do is hold him to his vow not to go alone."

Later she finds Philipose sitting with his ball in the shade of their oldest coconut tree, poking at an abandoned anthill with a twig. He is downcast. She sits with him, ruffles his hair.

"Maybe I should try to go *up,*" he says softly, pointing to the top of the tree, "instead of . . ."

What is it with men needing to go up or down, turn bird or fish? Why not just stay on the ground? He looks at her so intensely it makes her shudder. *He believes I have all the answers. That I can protect him from the disappointments of this life.* "Up is good," she says.

After a while, the boy speaks. "Did you know my father climbed this tree the week before he died? Shamuel says he cut down tender coconuts for all to drink that day!" The animation in his voice is returning, like a parched shrub uncurling after the rain. *Thank God he didn't inherit his father's silence.*

"*Aah.* Well . . . he almost fell—"

"Still, he managed to go all the way to the sky," the boy says, standing and putting one foot into the wedge cut on this side of the bark, gazing up as he visualizes this feat, looking to where the tree ends, and where the firmament begins.

"*Aah*, that's true . . ." she says.

But it isn't true. Evidently Shamuel hasn't told Philipose what really happened. Her husband had stopped climbing in the last year of his life. But a week before he died, some impulse sent him aloft. The tree was as familiar to him as the bodies of the two women who bore him children. Decades ago he'd cut the wedges that serve as footholds. It wasn't the tree but his strength that betrayed him and he was stuck a quarter of the way up. Shamuel climbed after him, a loop of coir strung between his feet, jackknifing himself up till he reached the *thamb'ran*. Shamuel touched the *thamb'ran*'s foot and got him to slide it down to the next toehold. "*Aah, aah*, that's it. It's nothing for you, isn't it? Now the other . . . and slide the hands down." She could only breathe when he was back on earth, the only place those feet belonged now. "I cut down tender coconuts for you," her husband said to her, pointing vaguely behind him, but there were no coconuts. "*Aah.* I'm very happy for that," she replied. They walked back into the house hand in hand, not worrying about who was watching.

Philipose brings her back to earth. "I may not want to climb that tree just yet. It's a bit high for me, isn't it?" She detects the rare note of caution in her son's voice.

"For now, it is."

"Ammachi, if he was strong enough to climb this tree . . . then why did he die?"

He catches her off guard. By her feet, red ants carry off a leaf, absorbed in their labor. If she dropped a pebble on them, would they see it as a natural calamity? Did they talk to God, or answer impossible questions from their children?

"The Bible says we live three score and ten if we're lucky. Seventy years, that is. Your father was close. Sixty-five. I'm much younger than him. I was thirty-six when he died." She sees worry in his face and knows he's doing the arithmetic. "I'm forty-five now, *monay*."

Her son puts a thin arm around her and hugs her. They stay that way for a long while.

Abruptly he turns to her and says, "I'll never be able to swim for a reason, isn't that so? My father also couldn't swim for a reason." The expression on his face is no longer that of her nine-year-old. In admitting defeat he looks older, wiser. "What is the reason, Ammachi?"

She sighs. She doesn't *know* the reason. Perhaps *he* might be the one to discover the reason. How wonderful if his stubborn determination turned into a quest to cure the Condition! He could be the savior of future generations. He could spare *his* children from what he suffers. For now she can only name it for him, describe the havoc it has caused this family since ancient times. Perhaps she will hold off on showing him the genealogy—the Water Tree—so as not to frighten him with visions of an early death. She takes a deep breath. "I will tell you what I know."

CHAPTER 28

The Great Lie

1933, Parambil

A ten-year-old boy who cannot claim the waters turns fiercely to the land. The potter lusts for blue alluvial clay on riverbanks, while the brickmaker submerges himself in shallow tributaries, basket in hand, filling his boat with river mud, not caring for any other kind. Philipose's tastes are eclectic; with his prehensile toes he gauges the proportions of sand, clay, and silt. For feel underfoot, the pillowy sandy soil by the church is unsurpassed, a contrast to the unyielding red laterite near Parambil's well. The granite-rich sod by his school is the color of altered blood and as cold as the headmaster's handshake; yet this varietal, when ground and filtered and dried on paper, leaves vivid, chromatic stains. Tinkering like an alchemist, he arrives at a formula for ink that glitters on the page like no commercial brand and makes writing a pleasure. The final recipe includes crushed beetle shell, gooseberries, and a few drops from a bottle in which copper wire is suspended in human urine (his own).

Like his late father, he has become a prodigious walker. Let others be poled, rowed, or ferried to school. He will walk. Yes, call it a feud with water. He hasn't lost his hunger to see the world. But he'll skip the seven seas. A walker sees more and knows more, so he tells himself. Only a walker could befriend the legendary "Sultan" *Pattar* who is always seated on a culvert outside the large Nair *tharavad*. *Pattar* is the term for Tamil Brahmins who migrated to Kerala from Madras. His nickname "Sultan" comes from his signature style of wrapping his *thorthu* around his head, leaving a little peacock tail sticking up. What makes him a legend is his *jalebi*. Wedding guests soon forget if the bride was fair, or the groom ugly, but none forget Sultan *Pattar*'s dessert that caps the feast. Some mornings *Pattar* gives the young walker a piece of *jalebi* left over from the previous night's festivities. For over a year, Philipose begged *Pattar* for the secret recipe. One day, without warning, before Philipose could write it down or memorize it, *Pattar* rattled off the formula like a priest reciting a Sanskrit *shloka*. It was hopeless, because *Pattar*'s measures for chickpea flour, cardamom, sugar, and ghee and whatnot were in buckets, barrels, and oxcart loads.

One afternoon, as the walker returns from school, a panicked voice behind him cries, "Out of the way!" A bicycle clatters by, bouncing off the ruts carved in the mud by cartwheels and now baked solid. The white-haired rider bails out moments before the machine flies into an immoveable object: the embankment. Philipose helps the old man up. His glasses are askew and his *mundu* is mud-streaked, but he's comforted to find his pen still in his shirt pocket. This cyclist's bushy gray mustache reaches his lower lip. "No brakes!" he says. Alcohol fumes accompany that pronouncement. He collects himself and his bicycle and straightens the handlebars. He taps the pen clipped to Philipose's pocket and asks, but in English, "What model is that? Sheaffer? Parker?"

Philipose replies in Malayalam, "Nothing that fancy. But in any case, what matters is the ink, and this I call Parambil Copper River. It is handmade by me from a filtrate of laterite soil, copper, and urea." He doesn't volunteer the urea source. He draws on his notebook to demonstrate. The old man's eyebrows, which match his mustache, shoot up. "Hrmphh!" he says, fluttering all three.

Half a mile later, Philipose sees the old man again, now shirtless, standing at the top of steep steps leading up from the road
to a ramshackle house. He's holding forth in a loud voice in English, as if addressing multitudes, though no one but Philipose is
around. "Cannon to left of them, cannon behind them—" is all Philipose makes out. But to the boy's ear this English is melodious and
rings true, unlike Kuruvilla Master's English, which is suspiciously
similar to Kuruvilla Master's Malayalam, with the words stepping on each other's tails—"ThedogisalwaysfollowingtheMaster"
or "Napoleon'sdefeatatWaterloo"—and interspersed with "*nayinte
mone*" (son of a bitch) and other Malayalam phrases that suggest his
pupils have coconut shells for brains. Philipose thinks the old man's
English is the genuine article, the language of progress, of higher
education, even if it is the language of the colonizers.

"Ink-Boy!" the man calls down in English, while retying his
mundu just below his nipples. "Good Samaritan! I say, identify yourself, my good fellow."

"Is it me *Saar* is speaking to?" Philipose says in Malayalam.

"ENGLISH!" the old man roars. "We shall converse only in English. What is your good name?"

"MynameisPhilipose, *Saar*." He hopes it's the same as his good
name.

"*Sir!* Not *Saaaaar*."

Philipose repeats. The mustache flutters. "Good, come up,
then. Let's begin."

"Ammachi!" Philipose says, bursting excitedly into the kitchen.
"Koshy *Saar* has shelves on every wall that are full of books. And
stacks of books this high on the floor!"

Big Ammachi digests this. Her "library" is two Bibles, a prayer
book, and piles of old *Manoramas*. She knows of Koshy *Saar* because
the fishmonger's fresh catch includes the latest gossip. Koshy finished his pre-degree in Calcutta, then worked as a clerk for many
years. But during the Great War, tempted by the sign-on bonus and

pay, he enlisted. He returned a changed man. Then he attended Madras Christian College and stayed on as a lecturer. Now he's back with a small pension and living in his ancestral home on a tiny fringe of property, enough for a patch of tapioca, and little else.

"Did you see the wife, *monay*?" Odat *Kochamma* pipes in, standing behind him. Philipose doesn't hear the old lady, so she must tap him on the shoulder and repeat herself.

"*Ooh-aah*. Saw her. *Saar* sent me to get us tea. She asked where I'm from, what family, all that. *Saar* shouted from his room in English: 'Is *that woman* holding you prisoner?' She shouted back in Malayalam"—and Philipose imitates her—"You old bandicoot, if you speak English to me, you can make your own tea!"

"The old bandicoot!" Baby Mol says, bursting into laughter.

"The poor woman," Big Ammachi says.

"You have it wrong," Odat *Kochamma* interjects. "I knew Koshy when we were young. So bright . . . *Ayo*, and so good-looking too in uniform before he went overseas. Shiny boots and belt and *athum ithuk okke*," she says, her hands fluttering over her body to suggest the this-and-that scattering of buttons, medals, and epaulets. She throws out her chest like a pigeon and stands at attention, but her bowlegs and dowager's hump make it comical. Baby Mol imitates her, and they salute together. Odat *Kochamma* sighs. "When he was young there were better proposals for him . . . Why on earth he married her is beyond me." A crow squawks on the roof. "Maybe God understands, I don't."

Noticing their stares, she snaps, "What? . . . I'm saying, if brains were oil, that one didn't have enough to prime the tiniest lamp."

"Have you met her?" Philipose says, puzzled.

"*Aah, aah*. No need to meet and all. Some things I know."

Philipose says, "The British Army let him keep the bicycle. He says it's worth more than a dowry. He fought in Flanders. He was annoyed that I'd never heard of it. Oh, and he lent me this book. He said all of life was summed up in it."

Baby Mol, Odat *Kochamma*, and Big Ammachi all peer at it. "It doesn't look like a Bible," Big Ammachi says suspiciously. The text is dense and has illustrations, but its verses are unnumbered.

"It's a story about a giant fish. I have to read ten pages by next week. I must write down all the words I don't know. He loaned me this dictionary. *Saar* says it will improve my English and teach me everything about the world. Next time I must be ready to discuss what I read."

Big Ammachi can't help feeling jealous. Once her son abandoned his efforts to swim, he'd turned his curiosity with a vengeance to learning about everything else in the world. His hunger for knowledge long ago eclipsed what Parambil could offer. School hardly sufficed. Koshy *Saar* is no doubt more learned, more worldly than Philipose's schoolteachers. She's watching her starving son being fed, though not from her hands.

"Is he expecting to be paid?"

"With a regular supply of my Parambil Copper River ink," he says proudly.

Odat *Kochamma* says, "*Aah.* Just don't tell him what all you put in that ink, that's all I'll say."

The following week, Philipose returns even more animated. "Ammachi, he can recite pages of that book from memory! 'Think not, is my eleventh commandment; and sleep when you can, is my twelfth.'"

She worries about such knowledge. "So what if he can remember that book. Odat *Kochamma* can recite the whole Gospel of John, even if she doesn't read. That's how they taught in days past, isn't that right?" she says, turning to the old lady, and trying to defend the one book Philipose should be trying to memorize. But the old lady is too focused on what else the boy might report.

"*Saar* only asked me one question. 'Who is telling the story?' The answer is Ishmael! It says so in the first line. Ishmael is the 'narrator.' I know my English will improve because he won't let me use a word of Malayalam."

* * *

For many weeks to come, the family gathers to hear Philipose translate, or else summarize, the assigned pages of this *Moby-Dick*. When he says, "Better to sleep with a sober cannibal than a drunk Christian," they burst out laughing. Big Ammachi is scandalized by the tale but also enthralled. One morning, as soon as Philipose leaves for school, she decides she must examine again the illustration of the tattooed savage, Queequeg. She goes to his room only to find Odat *Kochamma* and Baby Mol huddled over the book.

"He's a *pulayan*, that Kweek-*achine*!" Odat *Kochamma* says. "Who else sees his fate in dice? Who else will build their own coffin? Remember when Paulos *pulayan* was convinced a devil clung to his back? He could do nothing to get free. Finally he crawled into a slit in the rocks, a space so narrow the devil couldn't follow—"

"And lost half his skin and almost died from ant bites," Big Ammachi says.

"*Aah*, but he came out smiling! Devil was gone."

Until now, the measure of the years at Parambil has been Easter and Christmas, births and deaths, floods and drought. But 1933 is the year of *Moby-Dick*. Halfway through the book, Big Ammachi wants Philipose to ask Koshy *Saar* if this *Moby-Dick* isn't all made up. "It's entertaining. But isn't it one big lie? Ask him."

Koshy *Saar*'s response is indignant. "It's fiction! Fiction is the great lie that tells the truth about how the world lives!"

Fittingly, the monsoon comes to Travancore just as the *Pequod* sinks. In Parambil they don't notice the rain hammering down because Queequeg's coffin has become a life buoy for Ishmael, while Queequeg is last seen clinging to the mast. Four heads huddle under the lamp and over a book that only one of them can read. "God keep their souls," Odat *Kochamma* says when it is over; Baby Mol is despondent, and Big Ammachi crosses herself. She's come to love Queequeg. She thinks of Shamuel, and how that word, "*pulayan*," diminishes him when, like Queequeg, he's superior to nearly every man she knows. The goodness in Shamuel's heart, his industry and dedication to doing things well, would be fine qualities for the twins—Georgie and Ranjan—to have, for example. She's past feeling guilty about being in the thrall of this lie-that-tells-the-truth that is *Moby-Dick*.

"Koshy *Saar* doesn't believe in God," Philipose confesses the night he returns from his lesson with a new book. Clearly he has been keeping his mentor's atheism a secret till they finished *Moby-Dick*. He looks guilty, fearful his mother will put an end to his visits, but eased of his troubled conscience.

She hungrily eyes the new book in his hand—*Great Expectations*—the novel that will define 1934 just as *Moby-Dick* has defined 1933. "Well, Koshy *Saar* may not believe in God, but it's a good thing that God believes in that old man. Why else did he send him into your life?"

CHAPTER 29

Morning Miracles

1936, Parambil

On a stormy weekday, Big Ammachi is full of misgivings as her teenager slouches to school and into the early-morning darkness. In his sleepy shoulders, she sees no hint of his father. The son is more delicate—more sapling than tree trunk. She stifles an urge to call him back because he stepped over the threshold with his *left* foot as he departed—why invite bad luck? But then to summon a person back once they have embarked on a journey is worse luck.

"Ammachi?" she hears from behind her, as her daughter stirs. She waits anxiously for what Baby Mol says next. Her daughter's gift of announcing visitors ahead of their arrival extends to predicting bad weather, disaster, and death. "Ammachi, the sun is coming up!" Big Ammachi lets out her breath in relief. For twenty-eight years of Baby Mol's life, the sun has never failed to come up, yet every morning she's ecstatic at its return. To see the miraculous in the ordinary is a more precious gift than prophecy.

After breakfast Baby Mol holds up her broad palm and Big Ammachi counts out three *beedis*. No self-respecting Christian woman smokes, though some chew tobacco and old women treasure their little opium boxes. No one knows who got Baby Mol into the *beedi* habit and Baby Mol won't say. But the joy it gives her makes it hard to object to her daily three-*beedi* allotment. Her mother can't imagine a world where her daughter isn't on her bench, her wizened face smiling as she sings to her rag dolls. The *muttam* is the stage that entertains her. When parboiled rice is left out to dry, no scarecrow can match Baby Mol's vigilance.

"Where's my pretty baby?" Baby Mol asks. Her mother reminds her that he's gone to school. "What a pretty baby he is!" Baby Mol says, giggling.

"True. But not as pretty as you."

Baby Mol laughs aloud, a hoarse sound of delight. "I know," she says modestly.

But then, out of nowhere, a shadow falls across Baby Mol's face. She says, "Something has happened to our baby!"

The sky is low and as heavy as wet sheets on a sagging clothesline as Philipose walks to school. The high, mossy embankments on either flank form a dark tunnel. A lightning flash outlines a sinuous, rope-like object on the ground ahead. He freezes until he's satisfied it isn't alive. Just a stick.

His thirteen-year-old brain still carries the memory of being seven and running with Caesar through the rubber trees. ("Caesar" and "Jimmy" are the only dog names in Travancore, no matter the dog's gender.) The little pye-dog spun around, crouching on his front paws, grinning and daring Philipose to catch up, his tail wagging so vigorously that his hind end was in danger of coming loose, before he took off again, delirious with joy. Suddenly, the little fellow shot up in the air, as if he'd stepped on a spring; Eden was no more. Philipose caught a glimpse of a hood and heard a rustle in the undergrowth. It was an *ettadi moorkhan*, or "eight steps serpent." Eight was all you had once bitten, but only if you didn't dawdle. Caesar managed four. "Dogs have names," he says bitterly, feeling the pain of Caesar's death just as if it happened yesterday, and continuing an earlier dialogue with the cat who'd wandered into the kitchen and eyed the *karimeen* his mother packed for his lunch. "A dog lives *for* you. A cat just lives with you."

His collar is damp, and his shirt sticks as he walks parallel to the swollen waterway. He feels a presence behind him; a wave of gooseflesh spreads up his arms. *Don't let Satan mount your will because he will ride you to perdition.* He says aloud what his mother has taught him: "God is in charge!" He turns to see a sinister shape in the water, blocking out the sky. A hulking rice barge, slowing to a stop. It is mooring. According to Joppan, the debauched barge-men he oversees have secret mooring spots where women sell them companionship and country liquor, relieve them of their wages, and pilfer from the load. He's envious of Joppan, who instead of the drudgery of school enjoys sunsets on Lake Vembanad and mov-ies in Cochin and Quilon. Joppan has dreams of motorizing these barges and revolutionizing the transport of goods; he says no one has considered this because the canals are shallow and the barges ancient, but Joppan has detailed drawings on how an engine could be mounted.

The waterway broadens and forks around a small island, the water reaching the steps of the two new churches built on it. What had been one Pentecostal congregation split into two when tempers suddenly flared like flames on thatch. After fisticuffs the splinter group built their church on their share of the land. The churches are so close together that the Sunday sermon in one tries to drown out the other.

Now he hears the roar of the main river ahead into which this canal feeds, much louder than usual; he feels a rumble underfoot. He recalls Shamuel saying that flash floods have chewed up the river banks. It explains why the barge chose to tie down. Fat rain-drops kick up bullet-craters in the red soil and beat a tattoo on his umbrella, while the wind tries to claw it away. He shelters under a cluster of palms. He will be late for school. He has two choices: he can stay dry and be caned for tardiness, or be punctual but wet to the marrow. Either way he will get his knuckles rapped by Saaji *Saar*, who is mathematics teacher and football coach at St. George's Boys High School. *Saar*'s athleticism shows in the force and accuracy with which he flings chalk or smacks a head. As Philipose can testify, having borne the brunt of it, one doesn't see it coming. "I *wasn't* inattentive," he says to Big Ammachi. "*Saar* mumbles! When he's facing the blackboard, who can tell what he says?" Big Ammachi visited *Saar* and insisted that Philipose be seated in the front, because he struggles to hear from the back. His grades soared, even topping Kurup, who usually tops everything, but now he is an easy target for spitballs from the rear and *Saar*'s frontal assaults. He is getting known in school, but not for the best reasons.

There is a third choice. "Fill your stomach, then decide!" He unwraps his lunch packet. "I was led into temptation," he says aloud to his mother. He meditates on the delicious blackened crust and the flavors of pepper, ginger, garlic, and red chili. His tongue probes for the *karimeen*'s fine bones that are nature's way of saying, *Slow down and savor*.

A terrifying but human sound assaults his ears. The morsel on his tongue turns to clay. His hairs stand on end. It's a man's voice, a keening.

A figure in a loincloth is beating its chest, crying out to the heavens. Philipose recognizes the scissored front incisors that raise the upper lip like a tentpole. It's the boatman from the jetty, a man who still teases Philipose, calling him "Swimming Master." He hesitantly walks in the man's direction. The boatman's dugout, a hollowed-out matchstick, sits dragged up to the bank. On it he ekes out a living, transporting only solitary passengers like the fishmonger and her basket. But when the river is like this, the man must be hard-pressed to fill his belly— Wait, what is the bundle of rags at the man's feet? A baby! Philipose sees the tiny, bloated, immobile face and eyes just like those of the dying Caesar. Was the baby bitten by an *ettadi*?

The shrieking boatman pounds his head on the palm tree until Philipose restrains him. He spins around, his black face staring up in fear, his crazed eyes bloodred like a mongoose's, as he looks at the figure who towers over him, a boy who is half his age. Recognition dawns.

"A snake, was it?" Philipose says gently.

The boatman shakes his head and resumes wailing. "*Monay* . . . please do something! You have education . . . save him!"

Philipose squats down to get a better look, wishing the man would stop screaming. Education? What good will anything he learned in school do here? He gingerly touches the baby's chest. He's shocked when it heaves effortfully. Despite that, no air seems to get past the lips. The baby's neck is strangely swollen. Something white, like the coagulated latex from a rubber tree, peeks out behind the froth of saliva.

"Stop it! Please!" he commands the keening boatman. Overcoming his revulsion, Philipose probes the baby's mouth with his index finger. The white rubbery peel is bloody at the edges. He tugs and it comes easily at first; he must rip the last bit free. The tiny chest heaves and now there's a rattle of air—the sound of life! That was common sense, not education. Just a matter of removing what clogged the mouth. But after a few breaths, the baby makes a strangling sound, the chest heaves hugely, the mouth opens and shuts like a fish's, but air isn't going in. The sight is agonizing, distressing— Philipose's own breathing feels painful. He reaches in deeper this time and pulls free a big, chunky, bloody rubber peel. Air enters with a honk, like the cry of a gander, rattling in its passage, as if pebbles are loose in the windpipe.

"*Saar*! I knew it! I knew you could save my child!"

No more "Swimming Master"? I'm Saar now? He says to the boatman, "Listen. We must take the baby to some clinic."

"How, with the river like this?" the boatman wails once more. "And with no money and—"

"Stop!" Philipose interrupts, shouting. "I can't think with you screaming." But the boatman doesn't stop. That maddening sound and the baby's desperate battle for air drive Philipose into a frenzy. In the next instant, forgetting his feud with the river, Philipose snatches the baby in his arms, then shoves the boatman so hard that the man topples back into his dugout. Before he can rise, Philipose tosses the baby into its father's lap, then shoves the boat into the river. He jumps in at the last moment. "Come on!" Philipose cries. "Paddle!"

"My God! What have you done?" the boatman yells. Philipose relieves him of the baby, and the boatman automatically scrabbles in the canoe's bottom for his paddle as the powerful current rocks the dugout and threatens to capsize them. The boatman reflexively does the only thing that he can to keep them afloat: he points the prow into the current. Just like that they're in the clutches of the river, sailing down the center at breakneck speed. Glancing to the side, Philipose sees the river churn white on the shore, tearing out a new bank. "We're doomed!" the boatman wails.

Philipose screams, "Paddle! Paddle!" Water hammers down from the sky. The river's roar is impossibly loud and it makes human groans. The canoe rises and drops, and Philipose feels his stomach fly to his mouth and he must clutch the baby tight to keep it from being flung free. Is it really possible to travel at this speed? A broad wall of water rises up on one side of them and the swell casually pours into the canoe. What was a roar has turned into an even louder hiss, as though she laughs at their folly. Philipose is experiencing true terror for the first time in his life.

"Shiva, Shiva!" shrieks the boatman. "We are going to die!"

Ammachi, I broke my promise. True, he didn't enter the water alone, but a useless boatman doesn't count. *But I'm not* in *the water, just* on *it.* The useless boatman is beyond paddling, letting the boat twist and turn and be carried wherever the river chooses. The sight of the man infuriates Philipose. He is too proud to confess his fear, or acknowledge his mistake. He reaches forward and slaps the boatman's face as hard as he can. "Show some real courage, idiot! Keep us straight! Are you only good for making fun of my swimming? Don't you want to save your child? Paddle."

The boatman digs his oar into water that is as thick and angry as boiling paddy. Philipose bails frantically with one hand. He glances down and the baby has stopped breathing again. Blindly he shoves two fingers down the small throat, feeling milk teeth scrape on his knuckles. He claws at rubbery material until he feels air fluting past his fingers. The chest moves again.

It should end any second, yet somehow, second after second, they race on. They are flying past the stationary trees, moving faster than a speeding train. He bails for his life. How long can this go on? How long have they been in the river? How soon before they capsize?

The nightmare feels like it cannot end, then, suddenly, at a sharp curve in the river, the dugout is spun away from the center and shoots backward into a churning, flooded canal. With a splintering of wood, they slam into a hidden obstacle—a submerged boat jetty—sitting under stone steps. Philipose leaps out, holding the gasping baby aloft. At the last second, the dazed boatman jumps to shore, the recoil of his leap propelling the canoe out like a dart into the waterway and then into the boiling confluence, where it is immediately pulled under. On seeing this, Philipose shakes uncontrollably. Not from cold, but from anger at his own stupidity. He could have died! He recalls Queequeg's floating casket: it buoyed life. Just not Queequeg's.

Clutching the baby, his legs wobbly, Philipose scrambles up the steep, slippery laterite stairs cut into the bank, the boatman breathing heavily behind him. The steps end at a wooden gate.

Part Four

CHAPTER 30

Dinosaurs and Hill Stations

1936, AllSuch Estates, Travancore-Cochin

Digby's memory of the inferno, of Celeste twirling in the flaming silk sari like a child playing dress-up, of the smoke searing his windpipe as he screamed out to her, of the shattering sound of doors kicked down and hands pulling him out, melts into the agony of his hospitalization. He's bandaged and sedated, but through the haze of morphia, the fire rages on; for five more days it burns. He sees Celeste's face, masked in melting fabric, contorted with fear, as he battles to get to her. His nostrils are filled with the stink of a butcher shop, of hair singed off an animal's carcass. When he coughs, he hacks up particles of soot; the hoarse voice that screams out her name is no longer his. Mind and body have parted ways. The terrible pain is still less than what he deserves. He has no clue to the extent of his burns. The savage, life-threatening injury is to his mind, strewn around like shattered china, no longer recognizable as Digby from Glasgow, Digby the faithful son, Digby the single-minded medical student, Digby the surgeon with the good hands.

Every face that hovers over his bed—Honorine's, Ravi's, Muthu's, and the probationer's whose harelip he repaired in a previous life—pierces him with shame. Shame for disappointing them. Shame because he is Digby the adulterer, Digby the murderer. Shame hounds his waking. He wants to crawl to a cave where light cannot penetrate, where he might be spared the gaze of others, especially that of his forgiving friends. If only he could leave the human race and become the earthworm he deserves to be. His friends despair at his mental state.

On the sixth day after the fire, while it is still dark outside, he rises. Wincing with pain, he takes off the bandages. Under the glow of a bulb that stays on all night, he catalogs his wounds. The back of his right hand frightens him: from the wrist down to the knuckles the anatomy is laid bare, the shiny ribbons of the tendons are displayed, framed by blackened flesh. Were it not for the dark eschar forming on the surface, it would look just like an illustration in his *Gray's Anatomy*. It is painless, and therefore must be a third-degree burn—the deepest kind—taking the cutaneous nerves with it. During the fire he must have reflexively made a fist, exposing the dorsum of his hand and sparing his palm and fingers. On his left, he has burns of both palmar and dorsal surfaces, the skin a fire-engine red, oozing and blistered, and the fingers like sausages, twice their usual size. These must be first- and second-degree burns, the nerves intact, and thus excruciatingly painful. The skin here will one day regenerate, albeit with scarring. The same cannot be said of the right.

He is naked. His back hurts. He must be burned there too. He moves haltingly to the mirror, the room spinning, trying not to scream from the pain. Who is this singed creature without eyelashes, eyebrows, or hair, and with ears swollen like the cauliflower appendages of a pugilist? A half-human, half-stegosaurus bald-eyed creature stares back at him. It speaks: *Y'er half-broiled already, might as well finish yirsel off. No righteous testimony for you, not with her blood on your hands. No pity, ye laughable fool. Hearts will bleed for the poor widowed Claude, but not for you. Get away! Run!*

The sky lightens. He eyes the prone figure on the mat in the corner. "Muthu," Digby whispers, and Muthu rises at once. "Muthu, please, I beg you. I can't stay here."

In bare feet, and wrapped in one sheet in lieu of all the bandages, he slips out with Muthu. The rickshaw ride is excruciatingly painful. At a travelers' lodge near Central Station, the fellow at the desk gawks at the ghostlike guest who might possibly be white. Muthu hurries out on Digby's errands.

By evening, Digby, in fresh bandages, and a loose shirt and *mundu*, is stretched out in the baggage car of the Shoranur Express. On this run, Owen Tuttleberry isn't locomotive driver but escort, swallowing his disquiet. A tearful Muthu stands forlorn on the platform. Owen says, "If my missus knows I fibbed to her, she'll give me a great big *jhaap* across my cheek. No doubt she thinks I've got a dame on the side." Owen hides his disappointment; Claude Arnold, who killed Jeb, will get away because the blessed star witness was shacking up with the butcher's wife.

Franz and Lena Mylin, and Cromwell, their driver, meet the train at dawn, having motored down from AllSuch in darkness. They lay the drugged, senseless fugitive out on the back seat, and place his carry bag of bandages, salves, and opium on the floor. He moans but doesn't speak on the three-hour drive up the winding ghat road. AllSuch has a separate guest cottage. They ease Digby into the bed. He sleeps all day.

In the late afternoon, Lena and Franz knock. Digby opens the door, a bedsheet draped over his head and body as he stares with pinpoint pupils at the man in khaki shorts, shirt, and slippers standing behind the couple.

"This is Cromwell," Lena says. "He'll be here to help you with whatever you—"

"I'll manage!" Digby snaps. Recognizing his rudeness, he says, "Forgive me," and hangs his head. He owes them an explanation. The shame, he says simply, was more painful than the burns. He had to escape Madras. Their hospitality is a godsend. He begs them

to tell no one he is here. "One day I'll repay you. I need some supplies. Tweezers—finest you can find. And fine scissors. Spirit for
disinfection. Whisky for the spirit. More rolled bandages like this.
Petrolatum. And razor blades."

Up in the mountains, without faces to reflect his shame, he can think.
Already a thick black crust has formed on the back of his right hand.
If he doesn't remove this eschar it will become rock hard before
eventually falling off, and the body will fill the hole with granulation
tissue, turning it into a thick, leathery scar that forever imprisons
the tendons. He begins as soon as the tweezers arrive, picking at the
eschar, using the razor blade when needed, until the tendons and
muscles show cleanly. The deadened nerves make it painless only to
a point: at the edges, the tissue bleeds and the pain is intense.

   He moves furniture for what he must do next if he is to have
some hope of retaining function of his right hand. He omits his dose
of opium to stay sharp; his left hand must do his bidding. Wedg-
ing the front of his right thigh between the dresser and the table's
edge, he pushes up a ridge of skin—his "donor site." After cleaning with spirit, he shaves off a gossamer-thin piece of skin, the size
of a button. He screams as the blade slices. The pain is exquisite,
unbearable. He downs a slug of whisky. The tweezers shake in his
fingers as he picks up the wafer of skin then lays it on the raw surface of the back of his right hand, teasing it out flat. Over the next
hour, his hosts hear his periodic screams, as though a slow revolving
torture wheel cuts him on its every turn. He declines help when
they call out. They leave food outside his door and Cromwell keeps
vigil. Digby's hope is that these "pinch" skin grafts, like a cluster of
tiny islands, will take root, grow out, and fill the space. It's hardly a
standard operation. A surgeon should never be his own patient, nor
substitute whisky for ether.

   The next day Digby limps out of the cottage. Cromwell materializes like a shadow behind him. "I must walk," Digby says. Each
day he increases the length of the walk, sticking to level footpaths

through shaded forests of rubber trees; nature soothes Digby. He keeps Franz and Lena at bay, ashamed to converse with them beyond that first confession. He tolerates Cromwell. With him he has no history, nothing to live up to. Subtly, Cromwell directs the twice-a-day walks, leading Digby to different parts of the estate each time.

Three weeks after Digby's arrival, Cromwell tells Lena, "Doctor much sad. Not moving." Lena finds Digby shirtless, seated on the steps outside the guest cottage. His expression of utter despair makes her shiver. Silently he displays the back of his right hand: a dark, blotchy lava pit. She doesn't know what to make of it, other than the owner looks ready to cut it off.

"Lena," he says after a while. "I've accomplished nothing. My tendons are still imprisoned." She cannot help herself; she needs to touch him. She selects his shoulder, where the skin looks normal. He shudders but doesn't pull away. "Oh, Lena, what's become of my life?"

She stays with him, holding him to her, offering him her presence, conveying to him that he isn't alone. At last, she says, "Digby, look at me. You said no visitors. That you'd leave if anyone came to see you. Please, I must tell you of a friend who comes up from the plains to the mountains on weekends. He's a surgeon. He specializes in hands."

CHAPTER 31

The Greater Wound

1936, Saint Bridget's

Saint Bridget's suffers through the last days of summer, the water in the well hovering inches above the silt bed. Rune motors up the ghat road to Chandy's estate in the mountains, trailing a plume of dust. In the fourteen years since he arrived at Saint Bridget's he has become part of their family. When they decamp from the Thetanatt house to the spacious estate bungalow for the summer, Rune often goes for the weekend. In the space of three years, Chandy and Leelamma had a son, then a daughter. The boy was born temperamental, and at twelve, to Rune he still seems that way. The little girl, Elsie, is the opposite, and she adopted her bearded "Uncle Rune" right away. Life drastically changed for the children just five months ago, when Leelamma contracted typhoid. She seemed to be defervescing, but then she suddenly collapsed with severe abdominal pain. Chandy rushed her to Cochin, where surgeons discovered that a typhoid ulcer of her intestine had perforated; she died on the table. For the children it was as though the scythe that swung through their house the month prior, taking away their beloved grandmother, had, on its backswing, cut down their mother. Rune swore to make the three-hour drive every weekend in the summer to keep a close eye on the family. They are barely coping.

By comparison, the years have been kinder to Rune. He built himself a small bungalow near the front wall, on the edge of the property, with its own entrance, separate enough from the leprosarium so his outside friends can visit easily. Saint Bridget's has an official car, gifted by the Swedish Mission, to complement the ancient Humber that Rune drives. Thanks to their poultry, the small dairy, the vegetable garden, and the orchard—all run by the flock—they are self-sufficient with excess to sell or give away. But not even a starving beggar will let his lips touch what comes from a leprosarium. The exception is Saint Bridget's plum wine, thanks to Chandy. On the first day of Lent, Chandy, alone in the estate, found himself tremulous once more, at risk of a convulsion. To reduce temptation Leelamma had removed all liquor from the bungalow. But a few dusty bottles of Saint Bridget's plum wine escaped her notice; one glass cured Chandy's tremulousness. Chandy decided that, given its saintly origins, it could be consumed through Lent. He bought it by the case now. It caught on with the estate crowd, especially the ladies, because it was mild, delicious, and (so Chandy swore) "medicinal." Rune carries four cases in the car on this drive.

The children are asleep when Rune arrives at the Thetanatt bungalow, but Chandy waits for him. Chandy says Lena Mylin left a message for him; she and Franz want to see Rune the next evening— it is urgent. The planters and their families in the region—Chandy's friends—are now Rune's friends too.

Before retiring, Rune smokes a last pipe on the verandah, taking in the night sounds. The misty veil above him parts to reveal stars, the sky so low he feels he can extend a hand and touch the robe of God. He's at peace. The chest pains that trouble him he is quite sure are angina, but he accepts this with equanimity. He's living his faith, his amalgam of Christianity and Hindu philosophy. Medicine is his true priesthood, a ministry of healing the body and the soul of his flock. He will go on as long as he's able.

* * *

After a full morning with the children, and bridge in the afternoon, Rune heads to AllSuch at sunset. As he turns in to the Mylins' mile-long driveway, he glimpses an apparition: a white man in a check-ered lungi walking rapidly, bandages on his hands. Rune is startled: it's like sighting a leopard that has strayed into a human enclave.

In their living room, Lena recounts a story that begins with a surgeon saving her life with an emergency operation in Madras and ends with her and Franz sheltering the surgeon in their guest cot-tage. They had sworn to keep his presence a secret—till now. Franz sits silent.

Rune walks over to the guest cottage with a bottle of plum wine. He finds its occupant—the apparition from earlier—in the screened-in sunroom, a cashmere shawl over his head and shoulders, his hands exposed. The sight of the young surgeon, perhaps in his late twen-ties, moves Rune. He feels he is encountering a comrade in arms, a fellow soldier, fallen on the battlefield. Whatever Rune had planned to say has evaporated. Wordlessly, Rune finds two glasses inside, pours, and sits next to the silent stranger. The verandah cantilevers out over a steep slope. As he gazes down, Rune feels a disequilib-rium, the sense of standing on a precipice. Below him the tea bushes run in neat, parallel rows, as though a giant comb has been dragged across the hillsides.

After a time, Rune moves the lamp over, turns his chair to face this stranger, and puts on his spectacles. He supports the younger man's forearms in his hands. The spectacle of these ruined tools of a surgeon's livelihood fills Rune with sorrow. This is, after all, his own nightmare, though in his dream the culprit is always leprosy. He is overcome. He takes a deep breath. The journey the two of them embark on together must begin with love, Rune thinks. To love the sick—isn't that always the first step?

He gives Digby's forearms a meaningful and sustained squeeze while looking him in the eye. The young man is startled. He's like a wild animal, Rune thinks; his instinct is to snarl, to pull back . . . but

Rune holds his gaze and his forearms. He hopes this man will see in Rune's eyes not pity but recognition, warriors fighting shoulder to shoulder against a common foe. The seconds pass. The young man blinks furiously, then is forced to look away. The normally voluble Rune has managed—by his silence, by his touch, by his presence—to convey a message: *Before we treat the flesh, we must acknowledge the greater wound, the one to the spirit.*

Rune tries to digest what he sees. The back of the right hand is a mosaic, with islands of paper-thin, crinkly skin dotting a thick scar that has contracted, cocking the wrist back. Rune pushes, but there's little give. The fingers are curled, imprisoned talons because the tendons are frozen. Gently, Rune slides Digby's lungi up from the shin to expose the right thigh, revealing coin-sized scabs—a good guess. They testify to a desperate surgeon trying to treat himself. What but shame would drive him to try such a stunt?

The left hand is in better shape, the damage confined to the palm, where a thick, leathery scar runs across the palm like a stripe; it has ruler-like edges—clearly Digby had grabbed some kind of superheated object. The contracting scar puckers the palm, drawing the fingers down into a beak. Digby's ears and cheeks have flaking, discolored skin from superficial burns. The linear scar at the corner of the mouth must be an old story, unrelated to this one.

Rune hands Digby his wine, then, meditatively, he loads and lights his pipe.

"Will I ever operate again?" The voice is like dry twigs cracking underfoot.

So, Rune thinks, *we can speak*. Rune's eyes narrow. He considers his answer, puffing away. "Your left, I will do right away. I have a trick to release the scar on your palm. It will be functional. Your right . . . ? Well, it was a good try, covering it with those grafts."

"And . . . ?"

"And, my friend . . ." Rune refills his glass, gesturing to Digby to taste his. He does. "Digby—may I call you that? Have you heard of Cowasjee's nose?"

Digby stares at Rune as if at a madman. Then he nods. "Yes."

Rune is impressed. Cowasjee was a cart driver for the British. He was captured by Tipu Sultan's army in a battle with the British in the eighteenth century. Tipu's men cut off Cowasjee's hand and his nose and set him free. One can live without a hand, but nothing is more disfiguring or shameful than a hole in the face. Since the British surgeons could do nothing about his appearance, Cowasjee vanished, only to return a few months later displaying his new nose. He'd been operated on by the bricklayers in Poona, who practiced a seventh-century technique passed down from Sushruta, the "father of surgery." The bricklayers made a wax nose—a hollow pyramid— to fit over the hole in Cowasjee's face. They removed this mold, flattened it out, and put it upside down at the center of Cowasjee's forehead to serve as a template. With a scalpel they traced an incision on the forehead around this template, save for the bottom, where the eyebrows met. Dispensing with the template, they undermined and lifted the forehead skin into a flap, hinged between the eyebrows. Swinging it down, they sewed it to the edges of the nose hole, with small sticks to keep the nostril holes patent. It healed well, since it had an intact blood supply from its attachment near the eyebrows. True, it was a bit floppy from no cartilage, but air could pass, and more importantly, his looks were restored. A British surgeon reported this technique in a journal.

"Is that what you have in mind for me? A flap?" Digby says.

Rune parries with his own questions. "Why did it take us in the West centuries to learn a technique that was right under our nose? What else don't we know, eh, Digby? What else?"

"Dr. Orqvist. Please. What do you propose?"

"Call me Rune, please. *Homo proponit, sed Deus disponit*," Rune says, pointing heavenward. "I propose that you come to Saint Bridget's. We'll leave in the morning. But it's contingent on one thing."

Digby looks anxious. "What?"

"Tell me you like our plum wine."

CHAPTER 32

The Wounded Warrior

1936, Saint Bridget's

Digby has landed on an alien planet. After weeks living at high altitude at AllSuch, the heat and humidity of the lowlands add to his dislocation. He is a guest in Rune's cozy bungalow. On his first day, Rune leads him through well-tended gardens to his clinic, chatting in Malayalam with residents they meet. Digby brings his hands together stiffly to return their greeting. His experience with leprosy is limited to seeing street beggars in Madras. He has too many other worries to worry about contracting leprosy; it helps that Rune seems unconcerned.

In what looks like an orthopedic cast room, the big Swede vigorously massages and stretches Digby's hands, gauging the degree of contracture. The inhabitants of Saint Bridget's crowd around the open windows like gawkers at a carnival's freak show, intrigued by this sight. When Digby yells with pain, the audience breaks into excited murmurs. "Well, you've convinced them you don't have leprosy," Rune says. "They scream for many reasons, but never from pain." Rune readies a syringe. "Your right needs a lot more flexibility in the wrist before I think of operating. But the left? That we make right today, okay?" He is like an overgrown child, Digby thinks, laughing uproariously at his own pun. Rune sketches for Digby on a paper what he plans to do. "I thought *I* invented this. But a French-man claimed it before me. He called it the *'mèthode de pivotement.'* I call it the mark of Zorro. It makes this horizontal scar into a vertical one and creates space. Yes?"

Not waiting for an answer, Rune injects local anesthetic over the nerves in two spots at Digby's wrist as well as directly into the thick horizontal scar. He scrubs the palm with antiseptic, and then draws on it with a surgical pen, making use of a protractor and ruler. By the time Rune walks Digby down a hallway to the small operating theater, all sensation in his palm is gone. Rune puts on gloves and a mask and makes the long, horizontal incision along his pen mark, right through the middle of the scar. From the ends of this long cut, he makes two smaller cuts at sixty degrees, resulting in a ⌄. Digby observes as if from outside of his own body. Rune, using forceps and scalpel, raises triangular flaps from the two corners by undermining the skin. Then he transposes them, swinging the bottom wedge up and the top one down, suturing them in place. The ⌄ has now become a *Z*, creating slack in the scar. Digby sees his fingers already straightening out.

"Voilà!" Rune says, stripping off his gloves. "The mark of Zorro!"

Every morning and evening Rune works to loosen Digby's right wrist, torture sessions that leave Digby sweating. The Swede seems to enjoy having a houseguest to talk to, even if the conversations are one-sided. One evening, as Rune comes into the house, his face looks ashen, his right hand on his chest while he leans on the door-frame. Digby rises automatically to go to him but Rune waves him off. "I just need to catch my breath . . . I get this . . . nuisance some-times in my chest. When it is hot and I walk uphill from the clinic to the house. It passes." And it does.

Ten days after Digby's arrival, Rune says, "No dinner for you tonight, Digby. We operate tomorrow on your right hand. This time we put you to sleep." Digby is astonished when Rune describes what he has in mind.

Once the ether takes hold, Rune preps and cleans Digby's right hand and does the same for the skin over Digby's left breast. Using scalpel and forceps, he laboriously picks away at the back of Digby's right hand, removing Digby's pinch grafts as well as the intervening scar. "Don't feel bad, my friend," Rune mutters. "Your grafts helped a little. Without them, your tendons would be fixed in cement. Now they are just being strangled by weeds." It takes over an hour before the back of the hand from the wrist to the knuckles is exposed, raw, and bleeding, with the tendons laid bare but moving freely. The cocked wrist flattens out when Rune presses down.

Rune positions Digby's right hand, palm facing down, on the left side of his chest. Then he traces its outline on the chest with a surgical pen, the tip dipping down in between the spread fingers.

Putting the hand aside, covered with sterile towels, he makes a vertical incision just to the left of Digby's breastbone, corresponding to the wrist of the tracing of the hand. He tunnels under the skin through this incision by inserting and spreading the blades of closed scissors till he has created a pocket wide enough to admit Digby's hand. Then, with the inked handprint as his guide, he makes five stab incisions on the chest corresponding to the base of each finger. Now he feeds Digby's denuded hand into the skin pocket he just created, pulling each finger out through its stab incision. When he's done, Digby's hand sits tucked under a skin pouch on his chest, only the intact fingers peeking out, as though from a fingerless glove. *My young Bonaparte*, Rune thinks. He applies a plaster of Paris cast from above the shoulder to the elbow, and extending round the trunk, ensuring there can be no movement.

The next day, a groggy Digby walks the grounds, his hand imprisoned in his own marsupial pocket, his elbow, encased in plaster, winging out. As he passes the woodshop all work stops when the residents spot him. They emerge, and their lopsided smiles and headshakes say, *We've seen this trick before*. But Digby hasn't. It's not in any textbook. They invite him inside, and chattering away in

Malayalam, his hobbling escorts show him the lathe, the drill, the saw, and the unvarnished chair and table that their carpentry has produced; they hold up hands and feet to display Rune's carpentry on their flesh. He's struck by the generous reception. It isn't deference to his profession, since he no longer has one. Is it because he's Rune's guest? Because he's white? No, it's because he's one of them, wounded, winged, and disfigured. And they want him to witness their usefulness, even if the world has no use for them. He expresses with facial and left-handed gestures his awe, his admiration. He is overwhelmed by their scarred, skewed faces, their stiff, deformed limbs; he ponders his own situation. He wonders if he's avoided his fate or found it.

Over the next few days, he tackles a task he couldn't face before: he writes to Honorine, with messages for Muthu and Ravi. The act of printing with his left hand is nowhere near as hard as expressing his contrition.

Twenty days after the first surgery, Rune decides that the blood vessels in the skin of Digby's chest have had enough time to put down roots in the garden that is his denuded hand. With his patient under ether anesthesia, Rune cuts the skin all around the entrapped hand until it comes free, but now sporting its new, puffy, living skin-coat. He covers the raw wound left on Digby's chest with thin, shaved rectangles of skin from his flank. Unlike the pinch grafts that Digby attempted, these longer strips won't shrink as much as they fill in the shield-shaped defect on the chest.

Digby wakes retching from the anesthetic. A face hovers over him, a warm hand supporting his head, the voice familiar. He thinks he's dreaming. He has searing pain in his flank, but senses the liberation of his right hand from its prison. He drifts off. When he is fully awake it is dusk. Honorine looks down tenderly. With his left hand he touches her face to see if she's real. Then, tears he didn't know he could make trickle into his ears. He closes his eyes, too ashamed to look at her.

"There, there. Shhh, stop. Look at me! It's all right, pet. It's all right." She holds his head to her bosom until he calms down. "Digby, we're going to walk you back to Rune's; nothing wrong with your legs. Then you can sleep. We have plenty of time to catch up."

In the morning, he feels groggy but restored. He's thrilled by the sight of his right hand with its new skin cover; it makes the stinging pain on both his chest and flank bearable.

"Ah, we're awake, are we?" Honorine says, coming in with a tray. "Feel all right, then, pet?" He tries to stammer out an apology. "Oh hush, would you? Yes, you had us worried sick. Thought you might do something silly to yourself. Good thing yer Muthu couldn't keep secrets from me. I knew you'd reach out when you were ready. Now eat something."

He wolfs down the omelet and has two pieces of Rune's home-made buttered bread and jam. Honorine sits by his bed and brushes back his stubby hair with her fingers.

"Dear Digby. What a job you had to write that letter! Had me in tears, you did. I had to come have a see me'self. I had no idea about your surgery."

"I'm such a fool, Honorine—no, please, hear me out. It'll do me good. Celeste and I only became lovers after Jeb died. That's the truth. I'd met her twice before, socially. I fell for her the first time I met her. Maybe because I knew nothing would come of it." He laughs bitterly. "And nothing *would* have come of it, except she came to warn me that Claude planned to name me in a divorce suit. He didn't care that it was untrue, or that it besmirched her name!" The hypocrisy of his indignant tone sinks in. He flushes. "Well, on that visit, Claude's lie became the truth."

Honorine has been fidgeting, and she interrupts. "Digby, why dredge it all up? Yes, you made a terrible mistake. With tragic consequences. Yes, us was mad at you. Disappointed. I won't make any bones about it. But I got over it long before I got your letter. Yer human! Flawed. Ya' think you're alone. You deserve to be forgiven.

We all do. I don't know if you will ever forgive yourself, but you must try. I wanted you to hear that from me."

Digby is anxious to know about Celeste's children, but Honorine has heard little. There wasn't time for them to come for the funeral. Digby wonders what it was he hoped to hear. That they'd sworn to avenge her death? Did they know of their mother's misery in the marriage? Would they judge her only in light of her affair with him? Celeste's ghost is always with him, but never more so than now.

Honorine is surprised that he hasn't heard about the inquiry concerning Jeb's death. But Digby has been hiding from the world.

"I thought it'd be a sham, given everything," Honorine says. "Claude looked terrible, more the drink than grieving— Aye, it's not charitable of us. He lied, Digs. It wasn't pretty. He blamed you. Said you were betraying him with her from the moment you arrived. And the Jeb thing was you trying to sabotage him professionally, despite the hours he'd labored to teach you surgery! Yes." Digby laughs bitterly. "Said Jeb's death was unfortunate, but a known complication of an abscess that can weaken the artery. The outside pathologist shot it down, saying there was no abscess, just necrosis above the aneurysm. Said that Claude's cutting into the aneurysm killed Jeb. The aneurysm might have ruptured without treatment, but not on that day." Her voice tightens. "Then it was my turn. I says you summoned us to the theater because we knew Jeb and also you didn't think it was an abscess and that Arnold wouldn't take kindly to your opinion. I described what I saw. And that far from learning from Claude, who hardly ever operated, you'd been learning from Ravichandran at General Hospital. Ravi was there and everyone looked his way. Ravi stands up uninvited and says it was true, and he'd have trusted you to operate on him or anyone in his family, you are that good. Yes, you are, Digby."

The damning part of Honorine's testimony was Claude's paralysis in the face of the torrential bleeding. Digby and she stepped in and did their best.

"The hospital superintendent had to bring in the theater and ward registers for Claude. You and I knew. But it was still shocking to see them blank pages. The committee has yet to issue its final judgment. God knows why it should take so long. But they did recommend Claude's suspension at once. Not medical leave, but suspension. You're on indefinite medical leave too, by the way. That was automatic when you were admitted with burns."

Honorine departs the next evening. In the ensuing days, Digby's hands aren't ready for anything but the gentlest massage and stretching. He must bide his time, the one thing he has in abundance.

Digby has been living with Rune for over a month. He worries about the Swede, a man more than twice his age. More than once he has seen him come to a stop while walking, waiting for a "catch" in his chest to pass. As the two men sit together in the living room one evening, Digby broaches the subject but Rune deflects him. So Digby keeps silent, watching Rune work the pipe cleaner, fill and tamp down the tobacco, and finally circle the two matches around the bowl. The ease of the coordinated, complex, and largely automatic movements Digby thinks might be forever beyond his abilities. Sweet-scented tobacco plumes fill the air.

Rune studies his young colleague, a man soon to turn thirty, born just before the Great War. Rune was already in his late thirties when he landed in India. He feels paternal toward the young Scot who was walled in by silence when they first met. Gradually, the walls have come down. One can witness a spirit heal, Rune thinks, just as much as one can see a wound heal.

"So, Digby. You like our Saint Bridget's?"

"I do." Digby had thought of Saint Bridget's as a way station on his journey, but not the destination. Inexplicably, in the time he has been here, enduring his surgeries and the subsequent pain, and waiting to heal, it has begun to feel like home. He's a pariah in a community of pariahs. "I feel I'm with my tribe here, Rune."

"What! You're Swedish and never said?"

Digby's laugh sounds more human.

"I'm Glaswegian. From the wrong side of the tracks."

"I've been to Glasgow. Is there a right side?"

Digby refills their glasses using both hands. "You understand what I mean. Every hand I see here is related to mine. The 'flock,' as you call them, they are . . . my brothers and sisters." He stops, embarrassed.

"They are, Digby. Mine too." Rune drains his glass and smacks his lips. "Hands are a manifestation of the divine," Rune says. "But you must use them. You can't let them sit idle like a clerk in the land registrar's office, God help us. Our hands have thirty-four individual muscles—I've counted. But the movements are never isolated. It's always collective action. The hand knows before the mind knows. We need to free your hands, Digby, by getting you started on natural, everyday movements—especially the right hand. So, what do you enjoy doing with your hands?"

"Operating." Digby cannot help the bitterness in his voice.

"Yes. And what else? Needlepoint?"

"Well . . . a lifetime ago, I liked drawing, painting."

"Excellent! God knows these walls and doors need some freshening up."

"Watercolors. Charcoal."

"Ah, wonderful! That's what we will do. The best rehabilitation is doing what the brain and the hand are familiar with; it's good for both. And I have just the teacher for you."

CHAPTER 33

Hands Writing

1936, Saint Bridget's

Digby's new therapist walks over in the afternoon from the Thetanatt house, her ink-black pigtails bouncing off her shoulders, art supplies in her schoolbag. The maid accompanying the nine-year-old squats on Rune's verandah, keeping her *thorthu* over her nose, her gaze darting around like a sentry's. Rune introduces the young surgeon to his even younger therapist; he's amused to find Digby the shyer of the two.

Rune fusses over Elsie, with hot chocolate and toast and plum jam. Leelamma's death had stripped the playful, outgoing girl of the innocence she should have enjoyed for a few more years, Rune thought. She was lost, like a flower whose petals turned inward. In her grief she discovered a solace and a gift, all thanks to Rune's present of a sketchbook, charcoal, and watercolors. Elsie felt no need to proclaim it, but she was going to be an artist.

Elsie sets out paper, hands Digby a charcoal stick, and sits beside him to do her own work. Soon figures populate her paper. Watching her, Digby is reminded of his compulsive sketching in the days when he kept vigil over his depressed mother. Elsie has captured Rune in mid-stride, leading with his beard, his *juba*'s baggy tail like a sail behind him as he sallies out. The sketch is astonishing for its speed and accuracy. His paper remains blank.

Elsie sets out a new sheet for herself. She pulls down a squat book from Rune's shelf. Digby recognizes Henry Vandyke Carter's distinctive illustrations that made *Gray's Anatomy* such a classic, by coupling clarity with artistic skill. The text has faded in Digby's memory, but the figures remain. Does Elsie know that the Londoner, Henry Gray, cheated Henry Vandyke Carter of royalties and acknowledgment? Embittered, Vandyke Carter joined the Indian Medical Service, where he spent the rest of his career, seeing his name vanish from subsequent editions of the iconic textbook, though his illustrations remained. Henry Gray died at thirty-four of smallpox, his name immortalized by his eponymous book. Which Henry's fate was worse, Digby wonders: Dying young but famous? Or living a full life with one's best work unacknowledged?

By the time Elsie leaves, Digby's paper has a few lines and many divots where the charcoal stick, grasped clumsily in his right hand, dug in too far. The image he had in mind, a Vandyke Carter–inspired profile of the muscles of the head and neck, met a roadblock on its journey from his brain to his fingers.

Digby picks up the sketch Elsie left behind. At first he thinks she's drawn a leper's hand. But those square nails, the puffy, discolored skin on the back, the suture marks—it's *his* hand. He stares in horrified fascination. The stiff, leaden, and bony appendage grasping a charcoal stick is the inverse of the hands in Michelangelo's *Creation of Adam*. The gift Elsie possesses is breathtaking. The young artist shows no revulsion, no recoiling from the subject—quite the opposite. With devastating accuracy and without judgment she has rendered Digby's hand the way it appears, and accepted it for what it is. He has yet to.

That evening, a letter comes from Honorine; his clumsy efforts with the letter opener wind up tearing it down the middle. The commission ruled that Claude Arnold be dismissed from the Indian Medical

Service. Jeb's family will be compensated generously for his wrong-ful death. "God knows what Claude will do next," she writes.

It is little solace. Claude could operate again in private practice anywhere in the world. A murderously incompetent surgeon lives to kill again. *And what are you, Digby? Something less than a murderer?* The torn halves of the letter remind him that his own hands are bet-ter at destroying than anything else. Thoughts of Celeste, never far away, engulf him. If she hadn't come that day, if . . . So many ifs. His guilt is carved on him as permanently as his Glasgow smile.

The next day, when Elsie arrives, Digby points to her sketch. "That is so very good!"

"Thank you kindly," she says in formal schoolgirl English, smiling ever so slightly. Digby senses that he has merely articulated what she already knows. She sets fresh paper out for Digby, but then says, "May I please . . . ?" She wedges the charcoal between his stiff thumb and fingers, where it wobbles. He struggles to find the right amount of pressure that won't snap the stick and yet will keep it firm on the page, something that was once effortless and unconscious. Removing a ribbon from her plait, and biting her lips in concentra-tion, Elsie secures the stick with a few turns. She carefully lowers his hand to the paper like a gramophone needle meeting vinyl. "Now please try?" A dark, jerky line emerges. The movement originates in his shoulders, it seems. The point catches and stops. She nudges his forearm, hoping to jump-start it. Another stuttering line emerges but the charcoal swivels—the gramophone needle is bent. He looks up and meets her gray eyes, slanting at the corners, the irises paler than those of most Indians he has met. There's compassion in them, but no pity. She won't give up.

She unwraps the ribbon, hesitates, then places her hand on top of his and binds their hands together, her fingers buttressing the charcoal stick. She makes a "try it now" gesture, her chin leading the head shake. He doesn't understand Malayalam, but he's getting better at this shorthand.

The movement of his hand (or is it hers?) over the paper feels smoother, the machinery gliding on new bearings. His hand carries hers on piggyback as it zooms around the paper, making big, liberating circles—a warmup, a reckless frolic. She slips in a fresh paper and they race effortlessly around the new sheet, the tires warm, turning the sheet dark with loops and sinuous *S*'s, then, on a fresh sheet, triangles, squares, cubes, and shaded pyramids.

He's mesmerized by the sight of his hand carousing on the page, by the fluid movements that it now seems capable of. Seeing it this way rouses his brain, pushing out images, memories, sounds: a kali pod bursting in the forest at the Mylins' estate, a flock of mynah birds startled and scattering, the sound of surf on wet sand, skin parting under an eleven-blade scalpel.

A shaft of light from the window falls onto the paper. Has it been there all this time? Dust motes twirl inside like acrobats in a spotlight, freed from gravity, a sight so beautiful he feels a catch in his chest. Fresh papers replace used ones, as if Elsie recognizes that movement is salutary and must not cease, and indeed, the flowing charcoal lines are overcoming the spasm in his wrist and palm, thawing a frozen part of his brain, generating a rush of ideas that travel down his arm to the paper. He laughs, a sound that surprises him, as his hand—*their* hands—now moves with deliberation, finesse, and purpose.

A woman's face inexplicably emerges on the paper. It's not Celeste—he has drawn her face hundreds of times. No, it's his mother, her beautiful features evolving: the sleepy eyes, the long nose, the pert and pouting lips—a triad that was her signature. To signal the hairline, the charcoal produces a puff, a smoke plume at the top of her forehead, and then long, wavy tresses framing her cheekbones.

This is his mother in happier times, his maw on Wednesdays when they had tea at Gallowgate. She'd have loved this drawing. She'd have said, "Weel done, Digs. That's a fair braw giftie ye've got there!" The alchemy of shared hands, this pas de deux, has reached back through his fingers, up through his nerves, to liberate a portrait from his occipital cortex, pry it out of memory, tagging it with love and laughter.

In medical school he memorized the diagnostic facial expressions, or facies, of disease: the masklike facies of Parkinson's; the Hippocratic facies of terminal cancer, with its gaunt, hollowed-out cheeks and temples; the *risus sardonicus*—sardonic smile—of tetanus. Bound to this young girl, his hand has produced function and form, spun out a loving portrait. He glances up at his partner. *Elsie, little fawn who has also suffered the loss of a mother, do you know that somehow we managed to do what time could not? For all these years, the only image I carried of my mother, the facies that superseded any other, was of her obscene, monstrous death mask.*

His mother rises off the paper. He smells the lavender she placed in her folded cardigans; he feels he is in her arms again. *Forgive her*, he hears a voice say. "I do," he says aloud. "I do." Helpless tears trickle down his cheeks. Elsie presses her lips together in alarm . . . the living, moving sculpture of their two hands stutters and then stops. With his awkward left hand, Digby tugs the ribbon loose and sets her free; he tries to give her a reassuring smile.

On a day that none of them at Saint Bridget's will forget, Rune's voice rises over the compound as it does each morning, coming from the outdoor bathing platform behind his bungalow, where the big man booms out "Helan Går," a rousing Swedish drinking song, Rune had said. Digby, in the orchard, is astonished to hear his three workmates sing along. They don't know the meaning but they recognize the emotion: a call to the day's labor. The tune is accompanied by the slosh of water as Rune dips his bucket into the tank and dumps it on his head.

But the song breaks off suddenly in mid-verse, followed by a metallic crash. All over the compound the flock pauses. Digby drops his hoe and runs. The bathing platform is screened on three sides with thatch panels. He finds Rune on his back, unmoving against the concrete, a hand clutched to his chest, a bar of Saint Bridget's homemade soap still in his fingers. The heart of the beached Goliath, the great Nordic heart is still. Despite Digby's ministrations it will not restart.

The leprosarium is usually a dark and quiet place once the sun sets, but that evening it is ablaze in lamplights, the gates wide open. The tapper, the Mudalali, and others from the village who knew and loved the giant Swede come to pay their respects, even if it means crossing the threshold of the leprosarium for the first time. Cars drive in from the estates: Franz and Lena Mylin, the Thatchers, the Kariappas, the entire Forbes crew, the club secretary and the club's cook and two bearers—all friends of Rune—drove for hours to be there. The visitors stand respectfully outside the tiny chapel while the weeping flock fill the hand-hewn benches, one of their own conducting a service. The chapel air is redolent with the scent of fresh-cut jackwood, shaped in their own sawmill for the casket.

Rune's pallbearers are his flock, Sankar and Bhava at the head, limping, on crutches, swaying, shuffling forward in ungainly procession as they carry him to the cemetery in the clearing just within the front wall. Hands that are missing fingers, hands curled into claws, and hands that are not hands but clubs of flesh ease out the ropes so as to inter the mortal remains of the saint who dedicated his life to making theirs better. The laments of the flock tear at the firmament and break the hearts of the onlookers who, for the first time, can see past the grotesque disfigured faces and recognize themselves.

In the ensuing days, the shell-shocked residents turn to Digby as they once did to Rune, while he leans on Sankar and Bhava. Digby, using Basu, who has some English, as his translator, encourages them to go on as they did before, tending the crops, the orchard, and the livestock. At night, in the privacy of the bungalow, Digby's grief spills out. Rune was not just his surgeon, but his savior, his confessor, and the closest he'd ever had to a father.

Perhaps Rune had a premonition of his end. He must have known better than anyone that he had angina because his will is recent. The sizable sum in his savings account goes to the Swedish Mission, with instructions that the principal be maintained, while the interest be used to support the leprosarium.

Digby informs the India Swedish Mission by telegram. The reply comes promptly.

DEEPEST SORROW STOP A BETTER MAN NEVER LIVED STOP OUR PRAYERS CONTINUE STOP AWAITING INSTRUCTIONS FROM UPPSALA

He follows up with a letter to the India bishop in Trichinopoly who heads the mission, copying out the relevant part of Rune's will. He ends with:

I am a surgeon presently on indefinite medical leave from the IMS because of hand injuries that are not leprosy related. Dr. Orqvist completed two surgeries on me. I cared deeply for him and I care for the residents here. I am doing my best to keep St. Bridget's running and to provide basic medical care. If it meets your requirements, I can continue here. However, my hands won't ever be capable of the kind of surgery Rune carried out.

His answer comes in ten days. The Mission is sending two nuns to run Saint Bridget's; they hope to recruit a doctor in the future. Digby gives a wry laugh and crumples the letter. "You made enquiries, didn't you?"

For now, Digby's medical leave remains indefinite. What will the Indian Medical Service do when that period concludes? Press him back into some sort of medical duty? Dismiss him without pay?

Is there no home for him in this world? Not even in a leprosarium?

CHAPTER 34

Hand in Hand

1936, Saint Bridget's

Philipose, baby in his arms, drenched through and through, stands staring at the sign, wondering if in fact he really has drowned. Did the river swallow them after all? The sign reads:

സെന്റ് ബ്റിജിറ്റ് കുഷ്ഠരോഗ
ചികിത്സാ പരിരക്ഷാ കേന്ദ്രം.

In his mind that translates to *Saint Bridget's Treatment Center / Asylum for Those Suffering from Leprosy*, even though the English words below are more concise: SAINT BRIDGET'S LEPROSARIUM. Is this really the gate to a leprosarium or the gate to hell? Are the two different?

His lungs are burning, but at least it is air, not river water, he is sucking in. The baby is as heavy as a burden stone, its purple face just as still. Won't a leprosarium have a doctor or nurse? It'll have lepers, that he knows. To step inside feels as reckless as pushing the dugout into the river. How would he explain to Big Ammachi why he risked his life for the boatman's baby? *Ammachi, I felt the baby was me. I felt I was drowning, fighting for air, trying to surface, struggling to survive. I had no choice!*

He still has no choice. He pushes through the gate and runs with his burden. The boatman has no idea where they are. The sky is dark, but here and there light burns through rents in the celestial fabric. Up ahead is a tile-roofed central building, with smaller ones all around it, like offshoots, all whitewashed, though stained a muddy red where they meet the earth. If this is hell, then hell is neat and orderly. He heads to the main structure.

"What's going on? No children here! Why have you come?" A thin man in a blue shirt and *mundu* bars their way. To Philipose he looks like an egg with his smooth and expressionless face, lacking eyebrows and hair. One eye is white, and the nose flattened. The boatman recoils.

"This child is dying," Philipose says. "Summon your doctor."

"*Ayo!* Our doctor died!" the man shouts. "Didn't you know? He can't help you."

A white man enters from the room beyond, hearing the commotion. He's perhaps thirty, tall, a handsome man. But the scarred hands that fumble with his buttons seem to belong to an old man; his eyes sit in dark hollows.

The boatman shouts, "If he died, then who's this white man? Tell him to help us, for the love of God!"

"I'm not talking about this doctor. The other one, the big doctor. Now get out! No children, I told you."

The white man winces at the raised voices. He takes in the bedraggled and winded strangers: one dark, short, shirtless, and thin; the other a boy in a soaked school uniform, his hair streaked down over his forehead. The boy holds a moribund baby with the glassy eyes of a mackerel on a fish stall.

"Gowon, give us peace!" the white man says sternly in English to the shouting men, as he beckons Philipose to the light. His meaning is clear in any language. "What in the world have we got here?" the doctor says to himself, bending over the baby.

"The baby ceased its breathing," Philipose says. He colors as the doctor looks up, surprised. Philipose has never been this close to a white person, never conversed in English with a native speaker. He's even harbored doubts that there really is a world where people speak the language of *Moby-Dick*. "Baby having much white . . . barnacles in his mouth and throat. Like whale blubber. But tough . . . like leather. I harpooned some and he breathed a little. Then presently it ceased again, sir."

The doctor stares at the boy, baffled by the strange diction. *Harpooned?* He pries open the baby's mouth with clumsy hands and stiff, awkward movements, driven by the elbow more than by the wrist. He gestures for Philipose to put the baby on the table, while he turns an instrument tray upside down with a great clatter, scrabbling for something.

"Rune, really, no tracheal tubes?" the white man mutters. The doctor's strangeness fits this place, as if he, like the white buildings with their mud-red skirts, pushed himself up from the earth, his hands not yet fully formed, the soil still clinging to them.

"You! My harpooner! I'll need your help," the doctor says. He swipes the baby's neck with a dab of pungent liquid. "Are you and he kin, then?" he asks, nodding in the direction of the boatman.

"Not kin, sir. I was pacing straightly for the school, and seemingly bounded for that destination." He cannot help this voice of recitation, even if it's not truly his, but Ishmael's. Melville is musical, Dickens less so, and Philipose's English leans heavily on great swaths of their prose committed to memory. "The needle of the compass allowed me to hark the cry and I saw his child. This father he feared the river . . . but I, it swayed me to purpose, and hither thither we boatingly floated."

"Why here?"

The boy looks flummoxed. "God's grace?"

The doctor grimaces. He pulls a lamp down close to the baby's neck. He tries to pick up an instrument but cannot. He points and Philipose picks up and hands over the scalpel.

"What's your name?"

"Call me Philipose."

The doctor's lips move, as though practicing the sound. "Listen, you're going to be the one to do this," he says, thrusting the knife back at him, handle first.

"No!" It comes out louder than he intended.

"The baby's as good as dead," the doctor hisses. "Do you understand? You have nothing to lose. Even now, its brain is beginning to die. Come on. You saved its life once already."

"But I'm a schoolboy, not a—"

"Look, I can't do it with my hands. I had surgery. I am still recovering their use. And no, I don't have leprosy. I will tell you exactly what to do."

The blue eyes give him no choice. With a finger seized up in a stiff curve, the doctor traces the vertical path where Philipose should cut, at the lowest part of the neck just where it meets the breastbone. "The windpipe. That's where we're headed. Quick! Cut!"

He's seen Shamuel cut a chicken's neck, but never to save the chicken. He drags the scalpel down the imaginary line and steps back, terrified, expecting a blood spurt, expecting the baby to flap its arms and take off around the room. It doesn't flinch.

"Too shallow. Hold it like a pencil. Push harder. Until you see the skin part. Go on!"

He does, and now a pale line appears where the knife ran, and dark blood blossoms in its wake, pushing out like a river overflowing its banks. He feels the room spin and his stomach turn. The doctor ignores the blood and with gauze on his fingertip pushes the skin away on either side of the cut, revealing a cobweb of pale tissue.

He hands Philipose a blunt-tipped instrument like scissors, but without cutting edges. "Stick this under there and spread," he says, miming the movement with two fingers. Philipose slides the closed instrument under the wound edge, then opens it. He's too tentative because the doctor's stiff claw clamps over his, guiding him to the right plane. "Spread. All the way." He feels tissue rip. More blood wells up, dark and menacing.

"What about the bleeding?"

"Means he's still alive, lad," he says, pawing with the gauze like an anteater, until he reveals a pale, corrugated cylinder no bigger than a drinking straw.

"That's the trachea. Now we make a small vertical cut into its front wall with just the scalpel tip." Seeing Philipose balk, he says, "There's only air in the windpipe, not blood. But don't cut deep. We just want to make a small opening." When Philipose hesitates, the paw closes over his thin hand, steadying it. Together, they access some grace as they press the scalpel tip into the trachea, where it lodges like an axe in a tree. The boatman creeps up to peer in horror at the wound in his son's neck.

"Stop. No deeper," the doctor says. "Now we saw very gently down."

The blade tip slices as if through balsa wood. The bile rises in Philipose's throat. He looks up to ask, *Now what?*

Just then there's a wet, sucking sound whose origins are not in the mouth, nor in the nose, but in the bloody neck, a bubbly intake of air around the knife tip. The toddler's chest balloons out. As it exhales, a fine spray shoots out of the wound, and before Philipose can move, it lands on his cheeks.

The doctor removes the scalpel, inverts it, then slips the blunt end into the slit they made, turning it ninety degrees to splay open the slit. Inside the hollow windpipe, jockeying for space with the bubbling air, is a thick curd. The doctor pulls out a long, rubbery piece, like a strip of linen. At once breath rasps in and out of the small opening, a coarse, ravenous sound.

"That's the membrane of diphtheria. Greek for 'leather.' You used that word, didn't you? 'Leather'? You made the diagnosis when you said that. It's the dead lining of the throat that sloughs off, all tangled with pus cells. You've heard of diphtheria? Well, it's common. There's a vaccine now. It's the young'uns who die of it."

He sees flecks of blood on the doctor's face, just as there must be on his.

"Can we get it?"

"We probably had it as children, whether we knew it or not, so we are immune. This baby is malnourished, couldn't fight it well. As adults if we get it, because of our bigger airways, it's not this severe."

The doctor picks up a metal straw and eases it into the slit of the windpipe in the direction of the feet. Breath flutes through the tube, harsh aspirations. Color washes into the baby's face. Then it moves its limbs.

Philipose is stunned to witness this resurrection. His hands are badged with the blood of a stranger, and the sight brings another wave of nausea. The moment is both transcendent and revolting; he feels lifted above this room with its pungent antiseptic smell, looking down at the child, the father, the doctor, and his hands. Metal, blood, water, soil, flesh, sinew, white and brown skin are all one. He feels no triumph, just a desire to run away. But the doctor hands him pliers with a curved needle and a thread affixed to it, and the white paw clamps over his fingers. The movements don't originate with Philipose, but he executes them all the same, as they stitch the tube to the skin and close the wound. "You're my amanuensis," the doctor says to his assistant, who has no idea what he means.

The baby's eyes focus on them, alert and looking ready to speak. Then, as it spots its father's face, its hands reach up and the corners of its mouth turn down. It takes a lungful of air and its face contorts for a mighty wail . . . but no sound emerges, just air through the tube. The baby is surprised.

"Your vocal cords were bypassed, little one," the doctor says. "Welcome back to the bloody world. Maybe you can do something to change it."

CHAPTER 35

The Cure for What Ails You

1936, Saint Bridget's

Philipose rushes out to the verandah as his stomach rejects its contents. The spices and acid burn his throat. He washes his hands and rinses his mouth under a downspout from the roof. His nails have black outlines of blood. He cleans in a frenzy.

When he looks up, a monstrous face is inches from his, leering at him. The apparition has holes for nostrils, and unseeing eyes, though it cocks its head as if it hears his breathing. Philipose's scream emerges as a choked gurgle. The ghoul stumbles back at the sound, more frightened than he is.

He must get out of this place. He must get back home. But where exactly is he?

The leper or watchman they first met, and who tried to turn them away, gives him the answer, but Philipose can't believe it—surely not. Another leper, coming up beside them, confirms it. They notice his surprise at how well they know the roads. "There's nowhere we haven't walked! Did you think we go by bus? Or ferry?" Their laughter is macabre. His only interactions with lepers have been to drop coins into tin cups; who knew they were intelligent, capable of speech? His walk home will be circuitous because the main Pulath bridge is washed out. It's a five-mile detour in the wrong direction, and then he must backtrack for perhaps ten more. No buses come by the leprosarium. His heart sinks. To think he was worried about being late for school! It could be very late before he gets home.

The doctor comes looking for him. "Philipose, yes? My name is Digby Kilgour, by the way. Can you translate for me?" They go back inside to the boatman, who stands soothing his silent yet crying baby. "Tell him that I'm hopeful we can take that tube out in twenty-four hours. It's best he stays here till then."

The boatman says, "What choice do I have? I've lost my boat. Lost my livelihood. But so what? I have my son, don't I?"

Dr. Kilgour notices Philipose's restlessness, his anxiety. When Phili-pose explains, Digby says, "We'll get you home. You saved a life today." He says he expects a friend named Chandy to return in the afternoon from his estate in the mountains—by car. The doctor reassures him that Chandy's driver will get him back.

It's a long wait, more so because he declines Digby's offer of food or drink, fearing contagion. The sun is out, the sky cloudless, as though the morning downpour was a bad joke. He finds a shady spot in the orchard, and when he can't hold out any longer, he draws water from the well and scoops mouthfuls from the bucket, trying not to touch the edges. The heat bakes the whirls and ridges of mud on the driveway into a hard crust.

It is midafternoon when a car pulls in. The large, well-to-do man driving it steps out and goes to the bungalow where Digby disappeared. Philipose sounds out the name on the badge on the car: "Chev-Ro-Lett." The word is familiar. It has a sense of motion, a snap at the end. It sounds the way he imagines America to be: a land of hard-working, ambitious people like the inhabitants of Tisbury or the Vineyard of Martha. This car is like a wealthy man who shed his finery to work alongside his *pulayar* in the mud. The fenders are gone, exposing its wheels and its innards, and it is as mud-caked as Coconut Kurian's bullock cart. A hook juts out from the prow. The front passenger seat is being used to haul some kind of motor sitting on a tarpaulin. A metal platform is welded to the rear of the car, holding petrol cans, rope, a block and tackle . . . and a dark, squatting figure who regards him indifferently. Philipose would have missed the man but for the whites of his eyes flashing when he blinked.

Digby emerges with Chandy, who speaks to Philipose in Malayalam and asks him where he lives. "All right, don't worry, *monay*. We'll get you home. Wait here. I'll be back."

But it's five by the time Chandy finally returns, freshly bathed, his beige silk *juba* shimmering, his starched *mundu* a blinding white. A gold watch slides loosely on his wrist, its color matching the State Express 555 cigarettes in his paw. Philipose sits in the back next to a girl in a white-and-blue school uniform. She has shiny black hair parted in the center and pigtails hanging over her ears. Chandy's daughter, no doubt. She smiles at Dr. Kilgour, who waves at her. She's a few years younger than Philipose, but her direct manner and the frank way she studies him make her seem older. It makes him even more self-conscious: he has never had occasion to sit this close to a girl other than Baby Mol.

The rumble of the engine reminds Philipose of the roar of the river. Once they are moving, windows wide open, he leans his head out. The wind blows his hair off his forehead and pulls his cheeks back into a smile. This is his first-ever car ride.

Chandy's voice is equal to the engine. "So, *monay*," he says over his shoulder. "Doctor said you saved that *kutty*'s life. Are you some sort of saint in disguise?" He turns to grin at Philipose, a gold tooth flashing under a bushy mustache.

"Doctor's hands on top of mine showed me what to do."

The daughter's fingers glide over the expanse of seat between them. Philipose watches in disbelief as they approach. Then her fingers are on top of his, pushing down his digits one after another, as though she's playing the harmonium. Before he can react, she takes her hand back, the experiment having concluded. She picks up a notebook.

"*Monay?*" Chandy says. Philipose freezes. Did Chandy think he reached for his daughter's hand? "Is the baby cured?"

"Not yet. Doctor said the diphtheria makes a poison that affects the nerves and the heart. But he said with any luck baby will recover."

"Elsie had diphtheria. You remember, *molay?*" She looks up, interested. "You were six. Just a sore throat. We didn't even know it was diphtheria till the following week, when we took you to the doctor because every time you drank water it came up through your nose." He laughs, a big brassy sound, and Elsie smiles at Philipose. "Turned out that your palate couldn't close. The nerve was damaged temporarily. Like a stuck valve."

Philipose is acutely aware of Elsie. He has the urge to touch her thick, glossy hair. The thought makes him flush. He feels her studying him, which makes him even more self-conscious. He focuses on the houses flying by, and on the sense of speed that feels more immediate than in a bus. *Chev-Ro-LETT.*

When the familiar roofline of Parambil comes into view, he fights to keep his composure, because the sight unexpectedly moves him. For the last two years he has itched for adventure, wanting to roam like Joppan, except farther afield. But this morning had almost been his last on earth. By all rights he should have drowned. Not even leprosy or diphtheria compares to the danger of riding the swollen river. The moment he jumped clear of the dugout, the moment his feet touched solid ground, he knew he'd cheated death. But he hadn't felt *safe* till this moment of seeing Parambil. He'd always imagined that as an adult he'd live in a bustling city far away from here, a place full of life. Only now has he grasped just how vital Parambil is to him, as necessary as his heart or his lungs. One leaves home at one's own peril.

Bullock carts, horse-drawn wagons, handcarts, and an elephant
have come up this driveway, but never a motorized vehicle. Philipose sees many figures on the verandah. The extended family must
have gathered because they feared the worst. On seeing the car, they
freeze, like a family of sloth bears surprised in the forest. He sees
the silhouettes of the twins, Georgie and Ranjan, holding hands, and
the slim figure of Dolly *Kochamma* next to the shorter figure of his
mother and the much shorter Baby Mol. Off by itself is the larger,
lumpier outline of Decency *Kochamma*. A solitary figure holds vigil
in the *muttam*. Shamuel.

Big Ammachi watches her son descend from the running board, but
she cannot move. Only when he runs to her can she break her paralysis. She hugs him, feels his flesh. "*Monay, monay*. Is it really you?
Are you hurt? What happened?" She clutches her throat to express
her agony, saying, "Ammachi *thee thinnu poyi!*" *I swallowed fire!*

Baby Mol, hands on her hips, looks cross and smacks him on
his leg. But then she leaps into his arms, her tongue out, laughing.
Even Decency *Kochamma* crushes him against her bosom, where
he feels smothered in Cuticura powder mingled with sweat as her
crucifix pokes his cheek. Shamuel stands there, happy tears running
down his face. Philipose puts an arm around him. "Shamuel, I'm all
right."

He learns that they retraced his route to school; Shamuel
found the umbrella and the discarded banana-leaf wrapper. They
searched the banks of the waterway, fearing the worst. His mother
says, "Tomorrow we will go to Parumala church. I made a vow to
visit and give thanks there if God brought you back."

Philipose worries that Parambil must look shabby to someone like
Chandy, who drives a Chevrolet. But Chandy makes himself at
home as though he's a long-lost cousin and not the messenger of
God who brought back the missing son. "*Ayo, kochamma*," he says
in his booming voice, addressing Big Ammachi, "this boy of yours

is a real hero, did you know?" He regales the assembled family with a much-embellished story, speaking with such authority that even Philipose, who was there, starts to believe his version. But Chandy's true genius is that he manages to leave the lepers out of the tale. He ends with "*Kochamma*, this is a sign from the Almighty that your son must become a doctor, is it not? What a gift."

Philipose feels every eye on him. He forces a polite smile to his face but inwardly he shudders. He has never had the least desire to be a doctor. If he had, the morning's events would have cured him of such a notion.

The women help Big Ammachi organize refreshments in the kitchen. In their absence, Georgie makes the "little" gesture with thumb and index finger, and inclines his head, which Chandy reciprocates with his own minute head tilt and eyebrow twitch. The twins vanish and return with morning toddy, which, by this late hour, has fermented sufficiently to give it a kick like a goat. Philipose is surprised by the feast that emerges from the kitchen: *appam* fresh off the griddle, meat stew, freshly fried *ooperi*—plantain chips—mango *thera*, fish fry, and roast chicken. He understands that the food came from the surrounding houses in anticipation of a long vigil and the possibility of terrible news.

When it's time for the visitors to leave, Chandy calls out, "Elsie, where are you?" Baby Mol responds from the verandah, "She's with me!"

They find Elsie on Baby Mol's bench, her legs tucked under her pleated blue skirt, sketching away, while Baby Mol stands behind her on the bench, her pudgy hands adding Baby Mol ribbons to Elsie's pigtails. Strewn around them are sketches that Baby Mol asked for: a *beedi* maker, an elephant, one of her dolls . . . the figures are skillfully rendered. Elsie rolls all the sketches into a scroll and secures it with one of Baby Mol's ribbons.

"*Chechi*," Baby Mol says, as if Elsie is the older sister, though Baby Mol is old enough to be her mother, "*Povu aano?*"

"Yes," Elsie says. "I must go."

"Will you come back soon?"

Elsie's side-to-side head gesture says she will.

Baby Mol reciprocates with the same, saying, "*Poyeete vah*." *Then go-and-come-back*.

Later, at Baby Mol's request, Philipose unties the scroll. The first sheet is a portrait of someone familiar: a boy in profile, his face to the wind, eyes half-closed, hair swept off his forehead and sailing behind him. He's never seen himself through the eyes of another; it's so unlike the person he greets in his mirror. He marvels at the economy of the lines around his nostrils and lips, allowing the viewer's imagination to complete the shading. Elsie has captured the sense of movement, of speed. In the way she rendered his eyes, the tilt of his eyebrow, the anxious crease in his brow, she's recorded for posterity the madness and terror of a day like no other, a day that could have been his last. And though she doesn't know it, she's captured his burning and naked need to be home.

CHAPTER 36

No Wisdom in the Grave

1936, Saint Bridget's

When the nuns from the Swedish Mission arrive, Digby takes his leave of Bhava and Sankar. He seeks the others out in the distillery, in the grain shed, in the orchard, and in the vegetable patches. When he first came to Saint Bridget's, the residents appeared almost indistinguishable, too much alike in their disfigurement. But now he knows them individually, and also recognizes each one's unique character: the jester, the peacemaker, the stoic, the curmudgeon—every personality type is represented. Collectively, though, they share a mischievous, playful quality. Or they did when Rune was alive.

He thanks each of them for welcoming him into their midst; he conveys this message and his sorrow at parting by bringing his palms together, looking them in the eye. In this upside-down world, snarls are smiles, ugly is beautiful, and the crippled outwork the able-bodied, but tears are the same. In response, they drop their tools to appose their hands as best they can. He's moved by the asymmetric "namastes" of clawed or absent fingers, or absent hands. *Imperfection is the mark of our tribe, our secret sign.* Rune said the divine was never more visible to him than at Saint Bridget's, *because* of the imperfections. "God says, 'My grace is sufficient. My strength is made perfect in weakness.'" It'd be a comforting thought to Digby if he believed.

Digby came to Saint Bridget's with nothing. Alone in Rune's bungalow, he recalls their evenings, mellowed by plum wine and the haze of rich, woodsy-scented tobacco. On just such an evening a few days before Rune's death, Digby had asked him the question he'd first asked when they'd met at the Mylins' estate. "Will I operate again?" Rune had deliberated, the plumes of smoke rising like cartoon bubbles as yet unlettered. Then he tapped his skull with the stem of his pipe. "Digby, what differentiates us from other animals isn't the opposable thumb. It's our brains. *That's* what made us the dominant species. Not hands, but what we think to do with our hands. You know our motto at Saint Bridget's? It's from Ecclesiastes. 'Whatsoever thy hand findeth to do, do it with thy might; for there is no work, nor device, nor knowledge, nor wisdom, in the grave, whither thou goest.'"

He has one last bit of leave-taking. Chandy and his son are away on an errand; only Elsie and the maid are at the Thetanatt home. He sits opposite Elsie on the verandah, surprised how tongue-tied he is around her, as if *he* is the nine-year-old, and she twenty-eight. She waits calmly, a maturity in her eyes, a wisdom and equanimity far beyond her years.

"I came to say goodbye. I . . . You know Rune's surgeries rebuilt my hands. But Elsie, it was you who brought life back to this one." He holds out his right. Her inspired act of coupling their hands together, her palm atop the new skin of his hand, reignited his seized fingers, smashed through barriers of rust and disuse to reconnect his brain to his hand. He wants her to know that in seeing his mother's beautiful face on the paper, he'd erased the grotesque death mask etched in his memory, an image that had been blocking every other memory of her. But now, blood rising to his face, he finds he's too self-conscious to make this intimate confession. Perhaps when Elsie is older. If their paths ever cross. He hands over the gift he brought his young therapist.

Elsie unwraps the parcel. Her eyes widen with pleasure when she recognizes Rune's copy of *Gray's Anatomy*. Digby believes she has Henry Vandyke Carter's particular gift: to render an object as it is; to let it then speak for itself.

Elsie's lips silently mouth the inscription over which Digby labored. The first line is from that great Scot Robert Burns; the lines that follow are by a Scot who'll leave no mark in history.

> *"Some books are lies from end to end, and some great lies were never penned."*
>
> *But you have my word this book is true, as I know it through and through.*
>
> *For Elsie, who helped me understand, that past and present go hand in hand.*
>
> *With eternal gratitude,*
> *Digby Kilgour*
> *1936. St. Bridget's Leprosarium*

She hugs the tome to her chest, dropping her head over it, the way a child might embrace a doll. When she looks up, her expression takes the place of words of thanks.

He rises to leave. She sets the book down and walks out with him. She slips her hand into his, as though that's the most natural thing in the world. Once outside, she releases him.

He feels his soul slipping off its mooring, leaving him adrift without sail or map.

CHAPTER 37

Auspicious Sign

1937, AllSuch

Franz and Lena host a New Year's Eve dinner for their closest circle; the occasion is bittersweet, as it is also Rune's birthday. Chandy is detained in the plains, but the regulars—the Kariappas, the Cherians, Gracie Cartwright (but not Llewellyn), Bee and Roger Dutton, the Isaacs, the Singhs—are seated around Lena's dining table, forearms resting on the damask cloth, the candelabra lighting their faces as in a Rembrandt painting. They toast Rune with plum wine and remember him with tears and laughter.

Digby is there too, having come three weeks earlier to occupy the guest cottage at AllSuch once more. He bears no resemblance to the shrouded, charred creature who sequestered himself in the Mylins' guest cottage from all but Cromwell until Rune took him away. This time he is with Franz and Lena for every meal; he has driven with Franz all over the estate, observed him in the tea-tasting room, and accompanied him to the weekly tea auction. At other times he has ridden with Cromwell on horseback, learning the intricacies of tea plucking, of harvesting cardamom and coffee. Early every morning he sketches in a disciplined way for an hour, seeking to restore fluidity, if not grace, to his fingers. His plan is to return to Madras and stay with Honorine—but the Mylins insisted he stay till Rune's birthday. Once his medical leave expires, he has no idea what will happen next.

Now, at the New Year's Eve dinner, a shy Digby, encouraged by the pleas of the guests, and with his inhibitions loosened by wine, conjures up the aspect of Rune only he knew. He speaks of Rune's surgical genius, Digby's gesturing hands themselves a testament to the Swede's skill. He even bashfully opens his shirt so they might see the glowing, shield-shaped scar on his left breast. ("The sacred heart of Jesus!" exclaims Gracie, pressing her hands to her bosom.) "He died singing," Digby says, "as alive in that moment as he was in every moment . . ." He swallows, unable to go on.

The hush that follows is unbroken even as Franz pours a round of brandy, and they wordlessly raise their glasses once more to Rune. The silence of the night pulses around them. Betty Kariappa lowers a match to the golden remnant in her glass. A blue flame, a ghost, runs across the brandy's surface and up and down the sidewalls before it vanishes.

In the first hours of the new year, 1937, they are still at the table, the mood shifting from nostalgic to celebratory and then to numinous, as though their blood alcohol levels have crossed the threshold that unlocks their mystical natures. That is when, in the wee hours, these planters arrive at the subject they know best: the mountain slopes on which they live their lives; the fecund soil and its munificence. Sanjay brings up Müller's Madness and the golden opportunity the sale of that distant estate presents—but only if the price is right. Then, in a sequence of steps that neither Digby nor the others later recall, they've formed a consortium, sketched out its charter on a napkin, and passed its first resolution unanimously: Digby and Cromwell are to go forth like Lewis and Clark, as delegates of the consortium, to meet Müller and explore Müller's Madness.

Two days into the new year, Cromwell and Digby set out in the Mylins' Chevy, carrying spare tires, petrol, and camping equipment. The Western Ghats run parallel to the coastline for four hundred miles, most of it unspoiled, lush forest, save for a dozen discrete estate regions established in the previous century by daring adventurers. Those pioneers found their way up on old elephant trails known only to the indigenous people, the "tribals," and staked out choice land on the fertile slopes. But if they didn't soon carve out a ghat road by blasting through rock, building tunnels and switchbacks, their claim was worthless—they had to have a way to bring laborers from the plains to estates sitting at five thousand feet or higher, and to take the tea, coffee, or spices down to market. The first owners sold land at a nominal price or just gave away great swaths so as to have partners to share the expense of building and maintaining the ghat road. The largest established estate regions are Wayanad, the Highwavys, Anaimalais, Nilgiris, and the Cinnamon Hills—the last being where the Mylins and their friends have estates.

Their start is inauspicious, with early engine trouble, but Cromwell fixes it by taking the carburetor apart under a tree, cleaning and reassembling it. Cromwell is a member of the Badagas—an indigenous tribe in the Nilgiri mountains who live in tight-knit communities, farm collectively, and are proud to never have been in bondage. Those Badagas who migrated out are known for being skilled welders, carpenters, mechanics, and shop owners. Digby finds Cromwell easy to be around. A former employer dubbed him a "regular Cromwell" for bravely and cleverly defusing a volatile situation involving the employer's son, a married woman, and an aggrieved husband—Digby heard this tale from Lena. Kariabetta, once he understood the nature of the comparison, decided he preferred "Cromwell" to his given name. Now even his mother calls him Cromwell.

They camp overnight by a stream. At noon the next day they arrive at the base of a highland range whose jagged contours remind Digby of the craggy peaks of Càrn Mòr Dearg or Lochnagar. Somewhere in the clouds is Müller's Madness. Gerhard Müller was an early pioneer who never put in a ghat road. Sitting on a vast estate that he could never develop—hence the madness—he and his wife preached the gospel to tribals and scratched out an existence. His son, Bernard, did only marginally better, seeking but then scaring away potential partners by his asking price for land. He built a poor excuse for a ghat road that washed out every rainy season. Now, suddenly, Bernard Müller is selling it all and heading to Berlin, to a homeland that he's never seen. His asking price has dropped three times in as many months, a sign of his desperation.

Getting to Müller's property proves extremely tricky, and after one flat tire they hike the rest of the way in the mist. *What am I doing here?* Digby wonders. He knows he can't be a surgeon anymore. He has been so focused on surgery for so long that he simply cannot imagine doing anything else in medicine. Being a planter is more appealing than the thought of being a general practitioner, dispensing unguents and digitalis, and seeing a hundred people a day. If he's running from his past, these mountains are as good a place to hide as any other. He slogs on, following Cromwell, his breath short. Should Müller take the consortium's offer, the plan is for Digby, with Cromwell as manager, to run the estate, and in time be given a piece of it for his effort. If Müller accepts the offer, Digby will take it as a sign that this is precisely what he is destined to do. *Rune would approve. Whatsoever thy hand findeth to do, do it with thy might.*

The valley below, the rock underfoot, and the mountain before him will outlast him. On the scale of this land, he is nothing; words like "shame" and "guilt" mean little here; and a reputation is no more than a fleeting blue flame, an evanescent spirit in a brandy glass.

Part Five

CHAPTER 38

Parambil P.O.

1938–1941, Parambil

The arrival in Parambil of the man who would be known as Uplift Master, along with his wife, Shoshamma, goes unheralded. Could anyone have predicted that one person would so uplift their community? Soon no one can recall his baptismal name. The couple were happily settled in Madras when Shoshamma's brother died suddenly—of drink. He was unmarried, without children, and so, quite unexpectedly, Shoshamma inherited the property. That house plot and surrounding two acres is on the far west edge of Parambil, well away from the river, one of a dozen that Philipose's father sold or gave away to relatives in the last decade of his life.

In Big Ammachi's opinion, Shoshamma's deceased brother had less initiative than a washing stone. The house he leaves behind is in bad shape, but the timber and coconut palms on the land are good. When the couple first call on Big Ammachi, she's impressed by their two well-behaved young children, a boy and a girl, of seven and nine. Shoshamma has a pleasing face, a ready laugh, and seems full of energy. Her husband, despite his years working in a prestigious British company, is modest and unassuming. Big Ammachi introduces Philipose, saying her dream is that he will study medicine in Madras. Uplift Master speaks up: "That's wonderful! Madras Medical College is the oldest in the country. I visited once. I saw a British professor and all the student doctors around a bed . . ." He trails off, because something about the boy's forced smile tells him that Philipose has no desire to study medicine but is too polite to contradict his mother.

Soon after they move back, Uplift Master gets a loan from the Government Development Office—who knew such a thing was even possible? He purchases a cow, puts in a new approach road, and rebuilds the house. His invitation to his neighbors to join his appeal of the property tax assessment is met with ridicule; Decency *Kochamma* says, "What nerve! The fellow returns from Madras and thinks the government should tax him less!" Only Big Ammachi joins his petition, sharing the cost of the survey and stamp paper. The appeal succeeds. When the naysayers understand just how much money they could have saved, they clamor for Uplift Master's help. "With pleasure," he says. "Next assessment in two years, so we have plenty of time."

Uplift Master and Shoshamma's arrival coincides with a change in the entrenched attitudes of the good people of Travancore. There are more newspapers to choose from and more readers. The illiterate can always find a tea shop where the paper is read aloud. News of the mounting opposition to British rule, and of a world on the brink of war, filters into the smallest village. Literacy alters patterns of life that have gone undisturbed for generations. The proof of this, as Uplift Master recounts to Shoshamma, is his encounter in the tea shop. "This shirtless fellow on the bench says, just to impress me, I think, 'The maharajah is a British stooge. I'm with Gandhi! Last week when Gandhi marched to the sea, why no one told me? I'd have gone with him! Why pay tax for salt when it's there for the taking?' Poor fellow. I didn't have the heart to tell him Gandhi's Salt March was eight years ago. But the fact that he *knows* of the march is progress!"

When Uplift Master discovers Philipose is a voracious reader, he congratulates him and explains to him his own passion for literacy: "Reading is the door to knowledge. Knowledge raises the yield of paddy. Knowledge combats poverty. Knowledge saves lives. Is there a family around here that hasn't lost a loved one to jaundice or typhoid? Sadly, few understand that contamination of food and water is the cause, and better sanitation might prevent it!"

Master's enthusiasm for such social causes makes him a magnet for Philipose and his peers. The teens adopt Uplift Master's motto as their own: *Each one must teach one*. The newcomer encourages them to organize a YMCA and a YWCA, and the Parambil Lending Library and Reading Room, all of which meet in one half of a shed on his property, which sports a signboard proclaiming the existence of all three. Philipose, now thirteen, leads his YMCA mates in drilling borehole latrines for every dwelling, aiming to eliminate night soil and, thereby, hookworm infestation. The YWCA girls give lessons on food handling and storage.

The other half of the shed is Uplift Master's office. Next to a tall filing cabinet is a small table on which sits, like a deity, his precious typewriter. With this instrument he peppers the branches of government with petitions for roads, sanitation, health educators, a bus stop, and other improvements, all in the most officious Raj English. "*Monay*," Uplift Master says, explaining his philosophy to his most devoted acolyte, Philipose, "to bring about social change, you must understand the first principle about money: no one wants to part with it. Be it husband giving to wife, or you paying the barber, or the maharajah paying his tithe to the British, or his government giving money to us—who gives willingly? My word for this is 'resistance.' Our villagers don't understand that our government is *supposed* to fund civic projects to better our lives. Why else pay taxes? The money is in the budget! But the clerk in the Secretariat has resistance when he sees our grant application. The fellow thinks, '*Aah*, those Parambil families survived all this time without a bridge. If my cousin gets the grant and the bridge comes to my village, won't *our* property value increase?' *Monay*, that's why I type 'c.c. His Excellency the Maharajah' in all my correspondence. And 'c.c.'

to any other functionary who sits above the person the letter is addressed to. Makes the fellow think twice, does it not?" Philipose is intrigued and asks Master if he files the carbon copies. "*Aah*," Master says, with a glint in his eyes, "actually, there are no copies. But *they* don't know that."

When Uplift Master invites the maharajah (this time sending genuine carbon copies to a legion of officials) to inaugurate the "First Annual Parambil Exhibition of New Advances in Fertilizing, Irrigation, and Animal Husbandry," even Big Ammachi wonders if he's gone too far. Master assures her that he doesn't imagine for a moment that the maharajah will come—he's only seeking the cooperation of the officials he carbon copied to bring about the exhibition.

No one is more astonished than Uplift Master when the maharajah accepts! On that unforgettable day, people come from all around, dressed in their finest; invalids crawl out of bed to witness this once-in-a-lifetime royal visit by His Excellency Sree Chithira Thirunal. They all expect the maharajah to look exactly like the ubiquitous tinted photograph displayed in schools, stores, and government offices: a placid face with ghee-fed cheeks, the head dwarfed by a bejeweled turban, and the chest full of medals and crossed by a sash. They're shocked instead to see a smart, self-confident, turbanless young man in his twenties spring out of the royal car, dressed in a spotless black jacket with a band collar, khaki jodhpurs, and polished brown shoes. His genuine curiosity and interest in every detail of each exhibit shames the audience into actually paying attention to what is displayed. The maharajah's affection for his people shows in those soft, friendly eyes and his shy smile. This same maharajah, just two years before, defied his relatives and advisors by bravely enacting the Temple Entry Proclamation, allowing *all* Hindus of *all* castes to enter temples. This revolutionary act angered the Brahmins; it moved Gandhi to say it was the maharajah, not he, who deserved the title "Mahatma," or Great Soul.

The young maharajah ensures that Uplift Master is by his side the entire visit, leaving the district functionaries to jockey with

sharp elbows to get closer; His Excellency in his speech acknowledges Master by name, and hails Parambil's progressive spirit of
village uplift as a "model for Travancore." The photograph of His
Excellency with Uplift Master that runs in the paper is framed in the
lending library/clubhouse. That is the day when the man who had
the idea, did all the hard work, and brought the maharajah to their
little corner of the world gets the name Uplift Master. Now, no one
can recall his baptismal name.

Four years after his arrival in Parambil, three years after the maharajah's historic visit, Uplift Master presents Big Ammachi with his
boldest idea: if they take a head count of all the families, including
the *pulayar* and the craftsmen, and if they list the rice mill, sawmill,
one-room pre-primary schoolhouse, the tea shops, tailors, and other
establishments; and if they count the total number of livestock, then
Parambil might just qualify as a "district village." He explains to her
the advantages of that designation. Big Ammachi gives her blessing
at once. She sees Uplift Master as the one person carrying forward
her husband's vision for the land he settled. Master gets the required
signatures from all the families, invoking Big Ammachi's name if
they balk. The skeptics say, "What for? Will being a district village
make the rooster crow on time? Will the paddy harvest itself?"
     It takes a forest's worth of paper, many bus trips by Master
to the Secretariat in Trivandrum, and seven months and six days
before Parambil achieves the "district village" designation, and with
it an infusion of funds from the maharajah's coffers for "Village
Uplift." The doubters are silenced. Government-paid laborers build
culverts and drains so the new roadbeds will not wash away. The
nearby canal is extended, widened, desilted, and shored up with new
masonry walls, increasing barge traffic. The new designation brings
an Anchal post office and a postmaster on government payroll. For
generations, the Travancore maharajahs sent their mail through the
Anchal system: the runner, carrying a staff with bells on it, has the
right of way by royal decree, though these days the runners use bus,

rail, and ferry too. An Anchal P.O. also connects them to the British Indian Postal Service; a Parambil resident can send letters anywhere in India or overseas—no need to trouble *Achen* to carry letters back and forth from the Kottayam diocese.

The day arrives to inaugurate the one-room office building, whose board reads, PARAMBIL P.O. Uplift Master insists that Big Ammachi, as the matriarch of Parambil, cut the ribbon. The only photograph ever taken of Big Ammachi appears in the paper the next day. At first glance, there appears to be a smiling girl standing in the center of the photograph, holding scissors, and dwarfed by taller adults clustered behind her. But it's none other than Big Ammachi, and there's no mistaking the pride that illuminates her face.

The night the photograph appears, she clutches it in her hand when she converses with God. "My late husband couldn't read or write, but he had a vision, didn't he? And it has come to fruition in ways that he never imagined." She tears up. "I so wish he could see it."

Generally, God is silent, but on this night she hears God speak to her as clearly as he did to Paul on the road to Damascus. *Your husband* does *see it. He sees you. He's smiling.*

CHAPTER 39

Geography and Marital Destiny

1943, Cochin

The war effort has every tailor in Cochin stitching uniforms, and they turn away Uplift Master and Philipose as the two of them scramble to outfit Philipose for college. One tailor suggests they try Jew Town. So they walk past the spice market, gawking at the mountains of pepper, cloves, and cardamom inside the high-ceilinged godowns. They stop to watch an ancient ritual: a buyer squats before a seller and grasps his hand; the seller throws his *thorthu* over their hands. With silent finger signals that are centuries old and don't require a shared language, offer and counteroffer fly back and forth under the wiggling *thorthu*, hidden from the other buyers.

A tailor in Jew Town has the ready-made clothes they want, while from a dry goods store they purchase a metal trunk, bedroll and bedding, leather sandals, blue laundry soap, white body soap, and toothpaste. "No more green-gram shampoo or powdered-charcoal toothpaste, my friend!" Uplift Master says cheerfully, trying his best to buoy the younger man's spirits.

Big Ammachi's fervent wish had been that her son would study medicine; his saving the life of the boatman's baby was God showing him his calling. But Philipose felt God was showing him quite the opposite: that he had no stomach for sickness or for disease. He'd been squeamish before that event, but ever since he would faint at the sight of blood if he didn't quickly sit down. It didn't help Big Ammachi's argument that the boatman's baby died six months later from a diarrheal illness. If her son had a calling, had one passion, it was for words on a page, and the magical way they could transport him and his listeners to faraway lands. "Ammachi, when I come to the end of a book and I look up, just four days have passed. But in that time I've lived through three generations and learned more about the world and about myself than I do during a year in school. Ahab, Queequeg, Ophelia, and other characters die on the page so that we might live better lives." It bordered on blasphemy, but he had her blessing to study literature. He had applied to the prestigious Madras Christian College—the place Koshy *Saar* studied and taught—and he had the old man's letters of support. He was ecstatic when he was admitted. But in the two weeks preceding his departure, Big Ammachi and Uplift Master noticed that Philipose's excitement gave way to apprehension; he seemed withdrawn. Uplift Master had tried his best to reassure him.

At three in the afternoon Uplift Master and Philipose take a rickshaw from their lodge to the train station. The Cochin heat and humidity are so stultifying that houseflies lose altitude and tumble to the floor. Shop boys sit heavy-lidded after lunch, as unmoving as the cement barriers in the harbor. The city will come to life again only in the evening, when it is cooler.

But on the platform of the new Ernakulam South station, the imminent departure of *The Mail* creates its own whirlwind. Porters wobble down the platform with headloads of luggage, their faces strained. A Romeo, garland in hand, hurdles over a cart, sprinting to say his goodbye. The Anglo-Indian engineer, a toe on the footplate, leans out to examine his smoke plume with the eye of an artist mixing colors, and in anticipation of pulling the release chain.

"First whistle," says a cheerful Uplift Master. He stands on the platform outside the bogie, looking wistfully through the bars into the third-class sleeper. Philipose, seated inside by the window, was first in his compartment; the seven other passengers are settling in.

Uplift Master whispers, "By the time you reach Madras tomorrow morning, you'll be one big happy family, I tell you." Philipose doesn't hear him and raises his eyebrows quizzically. Master speaks louder. "I said, I'd give a lot to come with you the whole way. Big Ammachi offered . . . but Shoshamma . . ." He pushes aside the memory of her frown. "You'll have so much fun!" He thumps the side of the carriage as if it were a beloved bullock. "You know I never slept better than on a train."

Uplift Master is in pants and a collared shirt—Philipose has never seen him in this formal garb—with a handkerchief folded into a rectangle and parked inside his collar to protect it from sweat. "Second whistle is late," the older man says, checking his watch. Just then, they hear the crunch of hundreds of boots, and the platform is soon thick with Indian soldiers marching past, rifles and kit in hand. The silent, tanned, fierce-looking men barely register their surroundings. A third of them are bearded, turbaned Sikhs. The Fourth Infantry's Red Eagle insignia is stenciled on the trunks in the carts that follow. "*Aah*, no wonder," Uplift Master says. These men were rushed to British Sudan and fought for the liberation of Abyssinia from the Italians; they have seen death and brought it about. The Fourth is headed to Burma, where the Japanese are advancing. The war that seemed so abstract in Parambil is suddenly all too real, etched on the faces of these brave men.

Uplift Master strokes his mustache with his thumbnail. He sees Philipose unconsciously imitate him, though in his opinion the nineteen-year-old's downy shadow is better off shaved than shaped. But who can blame him? A man without a mustache is exposed and vulnerable, like an unbaptized child, the soul still in jeopardy.

"By the way," Uplift Master says, "keep this letter just in case. It's to my friend Mohan Nair. He's the man to see in a pinch. He runs Satkar Lodge, near Egmore Station." Philipose puts it away. Uplift Master sighs. "Oh Madras . . . how I miss it! Marina Beach, Moore Market . . ."

Philipose has never heard this note of regret before. "Why did you leave?"

"Why indeed, eh? I had a good job, pension fund . . . But doesn't every Malayali dream of coming home? My father had no land to give me. When Shoshamma inherited the Parambil property, it was our dream come true. A blessing."

"For us too," Philipose says quietly. "My mother always says so."

Uplift Master waves this off, but he's pleased. The carriage jerks. Master reaches in and squeezes Philipose's shoulder. "We're all so proud! Someone from Parambil going to Madras Christian College. You'll be the very first in our family to get a degree! It's as if we're all going with you on this train. God bless you, *monay*!"

Master walks alongside; the carriage is moving at a snail's pace; he's chagrined by the look of dread on Philipose's face. "Don't worry, *monay*. All will be well, I promise!" He waves long after his ward's hand is no longer visible.

Uplift Master wants to weep, wants to run after the train. His being feels fractured in two and it has nothing to do with Philipose. One half, the better half, pines to jump on that train and resume his life as a clerk in What-Was-Once-The-Old-East-India-Company. The other half, a solitary figure with slumped shoulders and pants that he can no longer button, stands despondent on the deserted platform, only a stray dog to keep him company, unable to imagine going home.

When he closes his eyes, he can smell the leather binding on the ledgers of What-Was-Once-The-Old-East-India-Company (a name he prefers to "Postlethwaite & Sons," which knots his tongue). For a poor fisherman's son, educated only to high school, to have been a clerk there was a towering achievement. He and Shoshamma were happy in Madras. Like all Malayalis, they fantasized about buying a property back in God's Own Country one day, returning to the lush green land of their birth, with a backyard bursting with plantain and *kappa*. On Fridays he and Shoshamma would go to Marina Beach, sit on the sand, lean on each other, and even hold hands. When the lottery vendor's cart came by, they bought a ticket and said a prayer. Inevitably, once they got home, they'd make love, Shoshamma's hair smelling of the salt breeze and jasmine.

When Shoshamma inherited the property, there was no debating what they should do. They had won the lottery. He resigned, they took leave of their friends, and they moved to Parambil. Village Uplift keeps him busy, but he misses the bustle of the Madras office, misses the brokers and agents—British and native—who came and went. He was a cog in the engine of global commerce, and he'd recount to a rapt Shoshamma the stories of the day. Of course, he never mentioned Blossom, the Anglo-Indian stenographer with the flowery frocks with tight bodices who had a special smile for him. Blossom unlocked a door in his imagination. Oh, the things his mind conjured up! When he was intimate with Shoshamma, he sometimes imagined Blossom saying naughty things in his ear, because with Shoshamma their intimacies took place in sepulchral silence. Now, at Parambil, even Blossom has faded. A fantasy far from its source is hard to sustain, just as winning the lottery doesn't bring happiness forever.

"Geography is destiny," his boss, J. J. Gilbert, loved to say. Uplift Master thinks it should be "Geography is personality." Because the Madras Shoshamma who bathed, chewed a clove, put on a fresh sari and jasmine in her hair before he returned from office, gave way to the Parambil Shoshamma, who wore the shapeless *chatta* and *mundu*. Gone was the sight of her bare midriff peeking between sari and blouse, or the way those garments accentuated her breasts and buttocks. In Madras they were occasional churchgoers but now Shoshamma insisted they attend every Sunday and she instituted evening prayers. She was as loving and playful as ever, but she began meddling in affairs of business that she had always left to him. It was small things at first, like countermanding his orders to their *pulayan*. Then, not long ago, he returned from Trivandrum to find Shoshamma had sold their entire coconut harvest to the trader Coconut Kurian. Uplift Master was stunned, hurt, and angry, but held his tongue. He decided to punish her with silence. The very next day, an anti-hoarding edict passed, and coconut prices plummeted, catching Coconut Kurian and others flat-footed, while thanks to Shoshamma, they made off extremely well. That was luck and it didn't excuse her actions. That night in bed, maintaining his silence, he reached for her out of habit. Many nights, indeed, most nights, and certainly on Saturday and Sunday, they were intimate. She had always taken up the customary position and he'd assumed that meant willingness, if not eagerness on her part. But that night when he tugged gently at her hip, she didn't roll over. He tugged again. "Is that all that's on your mind?" she said, in her playful, sleepy voice, her back to him. "After two children, surely we can be done with this."

He sat up, stung by words that were not foreplay, but no-play! Did she mean she'd suffered his lovemaking all these years? Breaking his silence, he addressed her backside indignantly. "What? All these years I take the initiative to fulfill my conjugal duties as it says in Corinthians, and now my reward is to be characterized as a lascivious man?" She didn't stir, which infuriated him. "If that's how you feel then mark my words, Shoshamma, I will henceforth not initiate intimacy!" She turned slowly to study him, alarmed by this threat—or so he imagined. "Yes, I vow before Mar Gregorios that I will never initiate. From now on, Shoshamma, you must initiate." She looked astonished, then she smiled sweetly and said, "*Aah. Valare, valare* thanks." *Many, many thanks*. Her using the English word "thanks" only made her sarcasm more wounding. She turned back and went to sleep.

At once he knew he'd made a horrible mistake: Shoshamma had never initiated. With her new Christian propriety, she never would! He hardly slept, while she slept the sleep of the sinless. In the morning she brought him coffee and smiled. If she felt remorse, he saw no sign of it. His self-inflicted celibacy now extending over a year is like a preview of death. With time his feelings for her harden, but his desire is intact. In sleep he's led down carnal paths. In his waking hours all his energy goes to Village Uplift.

Now, as the train carrying one part of him pulls away, Uplift Master feels himself unraveling, and his heart is so heavy. Can Village Uplift alone sustain his spirits? Even if the maharajah one day bestows on him a formal title, will it ease the pain? Is the best part of his life already over?

Outside the station, his eye is caught by a sign nailed to a palm tree by a canal. A crude arrow sits beneath the hand-drawn letters: കള്ള്. *Kall-uh.* Toddy. He walks along the canal in the arrow's direction, the water shimmering green, until he sees the shack slouching in tall reeds, with the same sign, like a *pottu* on its forehead. In the dark interior, he drinks alone, a first. A man fulfilled at home has no reason to be in a toddy shop. He takes a long pull from the bamboo gourd. There's nothing new about toddy. But on this afternoon, to his astonishment, the cloudy white liquid turns into a magical elixir that restores his equilibrium, eases his distress. It's as if a rock the size of an elephant has been sitting on his chest, ever since that regrettable night with Shoshamma. Now, in the gloomy shop, through the medium of toddy, the stone slides off. He realizes at that moment that he has fallen in love, and that not every love affair requires a second person.

CHAPTER 40

Labels That Take Away

1943, Madras

When Philipose opens his eyes, it is morning and they're tearing noisily past busy railway crossings on the out-skirts of Madras, passing paved roadways and low-slung houses. The sky and the horizon are visible in every direction with not a coconut palm in sight. The palette of Madras is a single shade: the soil is brown, the tar roads are coated dusty brown, and the whitewashed buildings have a brown tinge. There appear to be no streams or rivers at all. The locomotive thunders through an urban tunnel, its whistle amplified, and then they crawl into the hangar-like space of Central Station, a city unto itself. Red-turbaned porters squat on the edge of the platform, their noses inches from the passing carriages, motionless. At the sound of a whistle, they leap like monkeys into the compartments, ignoring the passengers, attacking the luggage, and baring fangs at each other.

His porter's white mustache pushes out like the cowcatcher of a locomotive as he weaves through the crowds on the platform with Philipose's trunk and bedroll on his head. Noise batters Philipose's eardrums: the shriek of metal-wheeled trolleys whose axles cry for oil; whistle blasts; vendors yelling; children squalling; brazen over-sized crows squawking over remnants of rice on discarded banana leaves; the porters' incessant cries of "*Vazhi, vazhi!*"—*Give way, give way!*—all of these drowned out by a thunderous voice from over-head speakers announcing an arrival on Platform something-or-other. Philipose's head reels from the sensory assault.

The platforms converge on a cement-floored lobby bigger than three football fields and shaded by a five-story-high metal roof on steel girders. There are more soldiers here than there were at the platform in Cochin. The seething humanity swarms like ants on a corpse, moving in streams and eddies that curl around station-ary islands of travelers camped atop their luggage. One such island is a family with shaved heads, sitting like eggs cosseted in saffron cloth—pilgrims from Tirupati, or Rameswaram. His porter detours around another static cluster of colorful gypsies, one of whom, a woman in a fiery-red sari, studies Philipose with her dark, kohl-lined eyes. She sits atop a crate, knees up, legs apart, as though seated on plush cushions, a slovenly maharani. He cannot look away. She deliberately hikes her red sari and flicks her tongue out at him, the beefy wet organ sliding over very white teeth, then she laughs at his shocked expression. *This is just the station, country boy. Wait till you see what's outside.* In her gaze, his ambition to be a literary man feels like a joke. What his nose, eyes, ears, and body are experiencing is not something words can capture. If he could turn back, get on a returning train at this instant, he would.

"OY! OY! OY!" someone yells, and he turns to see a red-faced, stocky white man, a straw hat on his head, his face showing great alarm. The man points, still shouting. The buttons of his linen suit strain against his barrel-like torso. Philipose wonders if white people are cold-blooded creatures—how can he wear that many layers? The man yanks Philipose aside just as a cart loaded with metal boxes brushes past, a sharp edge ripping his shirt. The porters pushing it scream at Philipose in Tamil, which is close enough to Malayalam for him to gather they want him to take his head out of his anus so sound can reach his ears. They must have been yelling at him for some time, but with noise crushing him from every direction, how was he to know?

The white man points emphatically to his ears in a gesture that says, *Use them!*

A flustered Philipose trots behind the porter, through a gap in a three-story mountain of parcels stitched in jute cloth with purple writing on the sides. The sweat of machinery, the exhalation of locomotives, the steam of packed humanity violates his lungs. Outside at last, he looks back at the redbrick furnace of a building from which he emerged. The clock tower of Central Station is the tallest manmade object he has ever seen. He would rather walk home than step in there again.

He makes his way by rickshaw and electric train to the suburb of Tambaram, to Madras Christian College, and joins new students outside the bursar's office to pay his fees. The other students are dreading something he hasn't thought about: the monthlong hazing, or "ragging," by the senior students. Uplift Master told him to expect it. He had forgotten about it.

Sure enough, at his assigned hostel, Saint Thomas Hall, a phalanx of seniors leads the freshies to the "bogs"—the common bathrooms—and has them shave their mustaches and raise their sideburns an inch above the top of the earlobe, a plucked-chicken look that serves to easily identify them. Then, while screaming at them like drill sergeants, they teach them to execute the freshie salute, necessary for greeting a senior: it involves clutching one's testicles while jumping high. Philipose finds the whole thing shocking, and a bit comical. Some of his classmates are quaking in fear; one of them faints. Hours after moving into the hostel, he's busy on errands for the seniors on his wing: he buys cigarettes for Thangavelu and washes the underwear of Richard Baptist D'Lima III.

On Sunday morning, the freshies shave the seniors, who are lined up in chairs on the verandah. Philipose wields the razor, a delicate task, since Richard D'Lima III is never quiet, his Adam's apple bobbing up and down as he shouts greetings to seniors passing by. Philipose and the other freshies are like the lowest caste, invisible as they conduct their masters' menial tasks.

"I say, brothers, who's coming to Madam Florie's in Saint Thomas Mount?" D'Lima says. "Discount for virgins. You, Thambi, come start the year right!" Thambi and the other seniors ignore him. Philipose struggles to hold the razor steady. D'Lima notices and laughs. "Hey, Philipose. What use is education if you don't know practical things?"

"Sir, yes sir," Philipose stammers. He can feel his face getting flushed.

D'Lima gazes at him with something like compassion. He lowers his voice. "Listen, bugger, you haven't lived till you go to Florie's. If nothing else, you'll know what to do on your wedding night. Ragging aside, I'm serious. I'll take you. My treat. What d'you say?" Philipose is too tongue-tied to answer. D'Lima waits, then stands up, insulted at being rebuffed. "A Japanese plane bombed Ceylon two weeks ago, did you know that, Philipose? Just to show us they can come this far. If they bomb us tonight, you'll die a virgin with your prick in one hand and your shag book in the other, shagging your way into the afterlife. Bloody idiot, you are passing on your chance."

Philipose glimpses his face in the shaving mirror. He sees what the gypsy woman seated on the crate in the railway station saw when she stuck her tongue out at him: a flustered boy, now with a naked upper lip and shorn temples; a boy destined to die a virgin.

Their first class, "English Grammar and Rhetoric," is for all first years, whether in the sciences or the arts. It is held in an old, dark auditorium, with rows of semicircular wooden seats sloping up to the rafters. The schedule says the lecturer is A. J. Gopal, but there is to be a short welcome by Professor Brattlestone, the principal. A handful of women fill the first row; the men leave one row empty behind the women, as though they were contagious, and they occupy the rows beyond. Philipose winds up in the last row at the very top. Two men walk in—one a tall, lean Indian, who must be Gopal, and the other a white man. Philipose recognizes him at once: it's the man who saved him from being run over in Central Station. The man who told him to use his ears. He, like Gopal, now wears a black don's cape over his suit! Philipose tries to make himself invisible.

His classmates are all writing down something that Gopal must have said. But what? He peeks at his seatmate's notebook. "First review session, Friday 2 p.m." As he's writing this down, the same student nudges him, and points. "Hey! Isn't that you? You're Philipose?" Philipose looks up to find every single eye in the room on him. Gopal must have called his name. Philipose jumps up and says, "Yes, sir?"

"Just say, 'Present,'" Gopal says in a stern voice. "Can you do that?"

"Present, sir."

Professor Brattlestone looks at Philipose, for a long time. Once the man's gaze moves elsewhere, a flushed Philipose whispers to his seatmate, "I didn't hear Gopal!"

"It's a small thing, not to worry," the fellow replies, even though his expression, one of pity and slight amusement, suggests the opposite. It wasn't a small thing. When everyone had turned to stare at him—Brattlestone too—Philipose had wished for a trapdoor to open under his chair. The class hasn't really begun, and yet he feels marked, like a man with crow shit on his head.

Brattlestone's welcome speech is lengthy. It must be funny because the audience titters at several points. Philipose can hear him, but curiously he can't quite make out what he says except for occasional words here and there. Once Brattlestone leaves, Gopal pulls up his chair, takes out his lecture notes, and says, "Take down!" They sit poised, waiting. Then Gopal looks down at his notes, so from above Philipose sees only his bald spot. He begins to read his lecture notes, looking up occasionally to wag his head or emphasize a point. All around Philipose, pens scribble away; his doesn't move. The next class, "Introduction to Poetry," is in the same auditorium. He moves discreetly down to the first row of men, which is still three rows back. The lecturer, K. F. Kurian, seems to enjoy his subject, pacing up and down before them, cracking jokes. Philipose hears him very well, but only when Kurian faces him.

He survives the ragging in the hostel through the course of the week; it doesn't bother him as much as his sense of dislocation in the classroom. He walks around with the feeling of being in a country where people speak a different language. He borrows class notes and copies them out. The textbooks he purchased from Moore Market—*Elizabethan Poets* and *Medieval English Literature* the fattest ones—are uninspiring. Other than *Shakespeare: An Introduction*, there isn't a single book he would read for pleasure.

In his third week, a peon seeks him out. Professor Brattlestone wants to see him. Philipose waits in the reception area till Brattlestone beckons him in. He points Philipose to a chair. "How are things going in your classes?" Brattlestone says, still standing, and walking slowly to his desk.

"Very good, sir."

"Forgive me for asking, but are you . . . struggling to hear the lecturer?"

Philipose pauses, surprised. "No, sir!" he says automatically. A shiver runs through his body. An ancient part of him recognizes that it is in danger and being cornered; it blinks out at its interrogator. Brattlestone studies him with clinical curiosity, if not empathy.

Brattlestone turns away and nudges a book on the shelf to line it up with the others. He turns back and looks at Philipose expectantly. "Did you hear what I just said?"

He feels himself sinking. He's the boy who keeps trying to swim but invariably sinks to the bottom and has to be fished out, spitting mud, while boatmen fold over in laughter. "No," he says quietly. "No, I did not."

"Mr. Philipose, I witnessed you in some danger at Central Station. I trust you remember. A few, but not all, of your lecturers have noticed that you are struggling. That when a question is asked of you, either you fail to hear the question, or your answer falls short because you misunderstood what was asked. I'm afraid your deafness may be severe enough to preclude your continuing."

"Deafness." That word feels like a cudgel blow to the back of his head. Call him inattentive, say he's unfit, unmotivated, but not that. *I'm not deaf.* The issue is volume. People choose to mumble, to speak in half sentences or whispers. He's kept that terrible word at bay. He despises labels that take away. *Can't swim. Can't hear. Can't . . .*

In the silence that follows there's so much he can hear: the ticking of the big clock, the creaking of a chair as the principal takes a seat. This must be uncomfortable for him too.

At last, Brattlestone says, "I'm sorry. I will refer you to the college doctor. He might arrange for you to see a specialist. I don't see how you can continue unless your hearing improves. Be prepared."

CHAPTER 41

Advantage of the Disadvantage

1943, Madras

B ut he isn't prepared. He isn't prepared for the relief that washes over him—relief mingled with humiliation. Relief, because his body must have known that college would be a struggle, and meanwhile his soul pines for Parambil. His romantic notion of the study of English literature has been cruelly dashed by the dry texts, and even drier lectures—judging by his fellow students' notes that he borrows. He had secretly wished for a miracle to spring him free, but he isn't prepared for this kind of degrading exit.

Nor is he prepared for the line that snakes out from the Ear, Nose, and Throat Clinic at General Hospital, just opposite Central Station. One patient breathes down the neck of the next, right up to the examining stool beside Dr. Seshaya, and no patient is on the stool more than a minute. Dr. Seshaya has a bulldog's jowls, growl, and breath. He spins Philipose sideways on the revolving stool, grabbing his earlobe in a mastiff's clamp, then swivels his head-mirror down, to peer and poke in his ear canal, before spinning him the other way to manhandle the other ear.

Seshaya holds his fist by Philipose's ear and says, "Tell me what you hear." *Hear what?* "Never mind." He repeats on the other ear. Seshaya unclenches his fist and restores his watch to his wrist. Now he presses a tuning fork here and then there, saying wearily, "Tell me when the sound stops," and "You hear it the same on both sides?" while ignoring Philipose's answers. Exam over, Seshaya scribbles on a piece of paper. "Your tympanic membranes are fine. Middle ear is fine. Show the peon this chit. He'll take you to Gurumurthy for formal audiology tests."

"So am I all right, sir?"

"No," Seshaya says, without looking up. "I'm saying that it's not a problem in your eardrum, or your ossicles—your ear bones. Things we might fix. The problem is in the nerve that takes sound to the brain. You have nerve deafness. Very common. Runs in families. You're young, but it happens."

"Sir, is there treatment for the nerve—"

"Next!"

The next patient, a woman with a red, mushroom-like growth pushing out of her nostril, bumps Philipose off the stool with her hip and the peon leads him away.

Vadivel Kanakaraj Gurumurthy, BA (Failed), doesn't hear them knock or enter or call his name, and is busy scribbling with ink-stained fingers, papers spread out before him and thick with his writing. The peon finally shouts, "GURUMURTHY *SAAR*!"

"Yes? . . . Yes, welcome, yes!" He hastily puts his papers away and studies the chit. "College student, *aah*? Oh . . . So sorry." And he truly *is* sorry, unlike Seshaya, who hardly registered his existence. Gurumurthy's patients must be very deaf because his voice is unnaturally loud. "Not to worry! We shall tesht! Auditory and vestibular. Fully teshting will be there!"

Gurumurthy's tests are more sophisticated than Seshaya's. With the tone generator, Philipose hears tones that Gurumurthy does not—the audiologist's hearing is worse than the patient's. He deploys two different tuning forks, does tests of balance, and finally injects cold water into each ear while studying Philipose's eye movements. The last causes shocking dizziness.

"Doctor Seshaya is miserably correct," Gurumurthy says at last. "I'm sorry, my friend. It's nerve deafness. Me also! Not canal, not ear bones, but nerve only."

"Is there nothing to be done?" Philipose hears his mouth reflexively sound this question. His brain is still in shock.

"*Everything* can be done! You're doing it, only you are not knowing! Face-reading, is it not? Preferable term to lip-reading because we must learn to read whole face. I will show you how to read the world, my friend, not to worry! I will give you tips and some personal observations in a booklet. See, I may not be medical doctor, but I am audiologist. And also physicist. BA only! Madras University!"

"Yes, I saw on the door."

"*Aah*, yes. 'Failed,' but one day it *will* be 'Honors.'" His smile is that of a man who must give himself frequent motivational talks. "See, I am always clearing the written exams!" he says, as if Philipose had asked. The bright smile crumbles at the edges. "But every year in viva only, Professor Venkatacharya is failing me. He is whispering— who can hear his questions? Anyway, if not before he dies, most certainly after, I shall pass viva."

Philipose spends the next two hours with Gurumurthy. Seshaya does not seem to send him many patients at all, and so Gurumurthy has plenty of time and is eager to share what he knows.

Back in the college hostel, Philipose repacks his trunk, ties his bedroll, and takes down the "picture" that Baby Mol gave him. Her self-portrait captures the essentials: a smile stretching to the edge of the disc that is her face, and a red ribbon poking out of her hair. He waits till there are no voices in the corridor; everyone is now off to class. He pulls out the letter Uplift Master gave him at the railway station.

Satkar Lodge turns out to be a narrow five-story structure in a warren of such buildings, each one just inches from its neighbors.

Mohan Nair, the "man to see in a pinch," is not to be seen. Philipose
hears a radio crackling. He calls out. A face creased like an old map
peeks out from a curtained area behind the counter. Mohan Nair's
eyes are bleary and bloodshot, but he has an innkeeper's easy smile.
"How is that old goat?" he says after studying Master's letter of
introduction. "Does he wear that Favre-Leuba watch? Don't ask
how I got it for him. And at that price!"

Philipose says he needs a room for two nights, "and a train
ticket to Cochin in three days if you can, please." He tries to sound
like someone who's sure of what he wants, instead of one whose legs
have been chopped off.

"*Aah, aah!*" Nair says. "Ticket in three days? What else? A flying carpet? *Monay*, if you get in queue at Central Station, you won't
find a ticket for at least two months." Philipose's heart sinks. Nair
rings a bell. "But . . . let's see what I can do." He winks and flashes
the smile that says, *In a crooked house, there's no point using the front
door.*

That next day, carrying the textbooks he recently purchased,
he heads out. Moore Market is a vast quadrangular hall made of
red brick and closely resembling a mosque, but with a labyrinth of
lanes inside that are lined with stalls. A shrill voice screams in his ear,
"Come, madam, best price!" Two mynah birds in a cage dare him
to guess which of them spoke. He averts his eyes from the puppies,
kittens, rabbits, hares, tortoises, and even baby jackals for sale. This
pungent, ammonia-scented area gives way to a section that has the
fragrance of newsprint and book bindings. It's like coming home.

The shelves and the stacked tables in JANAKIRAM BOOKS USED
AND NEW are in sections for law, medicine, science, accounting, and
humanities. Janakiram presides atop a dais, the ceiling fan inches
from his scalp. His half-moon glasses lack temples but find purchase
on a bump halfway down his nose. "J. B. Thorpe is the Gita and Veda
for cost-accounting," he says to a young man. "Why pay for Priest-
ley when Thorpe will get you through the exam?" His gaze falls
on Philipose, then on the books he carries. He descends from his

platform; his spidery fingers gently touch the textbooks that Philipose so recently covered in brown paper. He sends a boy to bring
tea and ushers Philipose to an alcove—his *puja* room. "*Thambi*, I
am refunding money fully, not to worry. But, *Ayo*, tell me what happened?" he says, once they sit cross-legged facing each other.

Philipose had not planned to tell him the story, but the kindness of this legendary bookseller, a friend to every college student
in Madras, persuades him. Jana's expression goes from concern to
indignation, then sadness. To be listened to is healing, as is the brick-
red tea, thick with milk, strongly sweetened and with fat cardamom
pods floating on top.

"Good tea, that much I will say," Jana exclaims at last, smacking his lips. "Life is like this. Crushing is there, and success is there.
Never *only* success." He pauses for emphasis. "I wanted to study.
Father died. Crushing! What to do? I work! Buying old newspapers
firstly and reselling, then secondly old books. Now? I'm sitting on
knowledge! I read anything and everything. *Better* than education. I
am saying you *will* succeed! Never to give up!"

Crushing, Philipose has had aplenty. He'd wanted to sail
the seas like Ishmael, but the Condition dashed that dream early.
He told himself he'd explore the world by land, but here he is in
Madras and already eager to return. He's had the crushing. What
can success look like now? Janakiram has the answer. "Success is not
money! Success is you are fully loving what you are doing. That only
is success!"

Back at the lodge, Mohan Nair has a train ticket for a little over a
week from that day. "It's a miracle. All are worried about Japanese
bombing in Ceylon. All trains overbooked only. Speaking of that, let
me show you something." He takes him back into the curtained-off
area behind the front desk, where Philipose is surprised to see not
one but more than a dozen radios. "I'm selling without any license.
Nobody bothered with license till last week, till all this fear of Japanese. Everyone is wary. Oh, and no licenses to be had." With a twist

of the dial, Nair brings in an Englishman's voice. Philipose instinctively puts his hands on the radio. At once he's *in* the place where the sound originates, hearing it with his whole body. The dial turns to orchestral music. "With a radio," Nair says, "the world comes to your doorstep. You'll never get one cheaper."

The next day, it pours, a strange and welcome sight. Roads are flooded. By evening the power is out all over Madras. Moore Market's dim interior is lit only by candles and lamps because there's no electricity in the entire city. Philipose is there because of an idea triggered by Nair's "the world comes to your doorstep." *I may be headed home, but I'll not be exiled. As long as I have my eyes, then novels, the great lies that tell the truth, the world in its most heroic and salacious forms can always be mine.* Even after paying for the radio, he has money left over from the tuition refund. It's money his mother saved for his education; he hopes she'll appreciate that he will spend it for just that purpose.

"Brilliant, my friend!" Janakiram says, after hearing him out. "But you're not the first with same idea!" He leads Philipose to a set of bound, blue volumes with embossed gold lettering, packaged neatly inside their own matching, three-tiered cardboard shelf—a beautiful sight. The spine of each volume is stamped with THE HARVARD CLASSICS. Jana reads from the introductory volume. "A five-foot shelf would hold books enough to afford a good substitute for a liberal education to anyone who would read them with devotion, even if he could spare but fifteen minutes a day."

Philipose recoils at the price. "Not to worry," Jana assures him. "I have same authors, used only. However, I am protesting Harvard choices. Not enough Russians! Too much Emerson . . . Will you trust Jana to suggest *true* classics?" Philipose does.

He buys another trunk to hold his treasures: Thackeray, but not Darwin; Cervantes and Dickens, but no Emerson. Hardy, Flaubert, Fielding, Gibbons, Dostoevsky, Tolstoy, Gogol . . . Though he's read *Moby-Dick* and *The History of Tom Jones, A Foundling*, he wants his own copies. *Tom Jones* is the raciest thing he has ever read in his life. As a parting gift, Jana throws in volumes 14, 17, and 19 of the *Encyclopædia Britannica*: HUS to ITA, LOR to MEC, and MUN to ODD. The used volumes carry the scent of white people, mildew, and cats.

Two trunks of books and a roped carton holding the polished, faux-ivory-knobbed, mahogany radio now occupy the floor of his room. His purchases are the only thing that allows him to return home with a sense of purpose, instead of abject defeat. He isn't retreating to Parambil P.O. or fleeing the larger world. He's bringing it to his doorstep.

CHAPTER 42

All Getting Along

1943, Madras to Parambil

The other passengers in the cubicle have long ago settled in, stored their luggage, and pulled out their cushions and playing cards, by the time a soaked, bedraggled Philipose boards. His porters shove around the other passengers' bags, trying to make room under the two benches for both his trunks and the carton with the radio. A large woman in a yellow sari, baby on her lap, is incensed when one porter topples her suitcase, and she scolds him in choice Tamil; the porter responds in spades. A young woman in dark glasses and with a scarf over her hair defuses the situation by telling the porter to put the carton and one trunk on the uppermost berth—hers—just as the train jerks into motion.

Ten cubicles in a carriage, six passengers to a cubicle, three seated on each facing bench. At night, two berths above each bench fold down, and the benches become berths as well. From adjacent cubicles Philipose hears laughter and happy voices. But in his, the fellowship of a shared journey eludes them; he is responsible.

He pulls out his notebook. On the first page he's written axioms from Gurumurthy. "One writes to know what one is thinking." "If hearing is impaired ensure that olfaction and vision become hyperacute."

In the periphery of Philipose's vision he is conscious of the bobbling Adam's apple of the thin chap next to him; the man's fluttering fingers that adjust his spectacles are sure signs of incipient speech. He gives off a mysterious scent of camphor, menthol, and tobacco.

"Next station is Jolarpet," the man blurts out. "The busiest *alleged* junction in Asia!" Philipose finds his hearing is enhanced on the train, just as Gurumurthy predicted, because in noisy places, people turn up the volume and pitch.

"Is it really?" Philipose caps his pen, grateful to be spoken to.

"Indubitably! Technically, it's not a junction. Junction means four ways, is it not? But Jolarpet is only three ways! Salem, Bangalore, and Madras!"

Philipose indicates he's impressed. His seatmate beams and proffers a bony hand. "Arjun-Kumar-Railways." He opens a tiny, engraved metal box that explains the strange scents, takes a pinch, and sniffs, expertly absorbing the instantaneous double-sneeze. He settles back, noticeably calmer.

The young lady with the scarf sitting next to Arjun who had allowed the porters to store his baggage on her berth removes her sunglasses and leans over. "May I see?" she says politely. Her fingernail traces the etched leaf-and-bud-pattern engraving. It's unusual for a single woman to initiate conversation. Philipose is struck by the delicate vein arching over the back of her hand, tributaries gathering from between her knuckles. Her hands look capable, like those of a tailor or a watchmaker.

"This is such fine engraving!" Her voice is striking for its low timbre. She turns the box over and squints at the lettering, worn away by use. "Do you know what it says?"

"Yes, I am knowing, Young Miss!" Arjun-Kumar-Railways giggles and swallows, his eyeballs magnified by his spectacles. She waits.

"And . . . can you tell me?"

"Indubitably I can!"

She and Philipose exchange glances and come to the same realization: for Arjun-Kumar-Railways, anything but a literal answer is as egregious as calling something a "junction" when it isn't. She smiles. Her scent is fresh, a faint hint of a perfumed soap that Gurumurthy wouldn't approve of (because perfumes overpower olfaction) but Philipose finds delightful.

"Then *would* you please tell me what it says?"

"Certainly! It is saying, 'Don't swear, here it is.'"

There's a pause before she laughs, a bright, delightful sound.

Arjun Railways is beyond pleased. "You see, Young Miss, snuffing is very impatience! Supposing it is time, and supposing you are wanting your pinch, then if you are not having, swearing will be there, is it not?" His excitable, high-pitched voice is a contrast to hers. "I am having collection of snuffboxes at home," Arjun Railways says proudly. "My hobby. This one is for travel only. However, just now in Madras I purchased new one. One moment, Young Miss."

As he searches, Young Miss tears a sheet from her notebook, places it on the snuffbox, then rubs with her pencil to reveal the exquisite foliate pattern. Arjun hands her his newest acquisition, a jeweled box, hand-painted with a fine brush, showing turbaned horsemen riding through a mother-of-pearl desert.

"Art on a snuffbox!" Young Miss says, almost to herself, completely absorbed, tracing the outline with her fingernail.

"Correctly you told, Miss! Every human bad habit generates art! Cigarette cases, whisky bottles, opium pipes, is it not?"

"I read that this is called the 'anatomical snuffbox,'" says Young Miss, arching her thumb back to exaggerate the shallow, triangular depression on the back of her hand between the two tendons that run from the thumb base to the wrist. Philipose is mesmerized by the elegance of that bowed digit resembling a swan's neck, and by the fine, translucent hairs on her forearm. She looks up at the two men inquiringly. Her close-set eyes slope up at the outer edges, an angle echoed by her eyebrows, giving her an exotic look, like an Egyptian queen. Her nose is sharp, in keeping with her slender face.

Young Miss is erasing every woman on earth from Philipose's head, just as in Shakespeare's play Juliet displaces Rosaline.

Arjun frowns. "Indubitably, some are putting *podi* there only and snuffing-sniffing! Pinching is preferable."

Young Miss looks tall even while seated, with a dancer's elongated posture. Her scarf has slipped to reveal thick black hair gathered in a simple plait, which she now draws over her left shoulder, an unconscious movement, its tapered end snapping like a whip and reaching her waist. Hers is not a beauty that is easy to grasp, Philipose thinks. (Later, in his notebook he will write, "A woman with unconventional beauty raises the hope that the viewer might be the only one to see it, that in recognizing and appreciating it, he alone has created her beauty.")

Young Miss says, "Well, now I think we must try it." Her lips curve up. Her eyes show mischief. She looks directly at Philipose. "What say you?"

If it pleases Young Miss, yours truly will snuff-and-sniff baby scorpions. Young Miss and Philipose each take a pinch, heeding Arjun's caution to "sniff only! No breath inhaling. Sniiii-fffff-ing gently only to front of nostril! Kindly avoid going to backward compartment. Kindly observe." Arjun demonstrates and at once, like the recoil of a rifle, he sneezes twice, after which his face relaxes. "*Precisely* two sneezes will be there. Unless there are more."

Young Miss and Philipose sniffffff . . . then sneeze in unison, twice. Their mouths are agape as another sneeze hangs there. They sneeze four more times. A duet. Mrs. Yellow Sari bursts into loud peals of laughter and the others join in. The ice has melted.

After Jolarpet, Philipose rocks the infant to sleep as Meena—Mrs. Yellow Sari—repairs to the toilet and her husband readies their berths. Arjun deals cards, teaching Young Miss to play Twenty-Eight. When the sun sets, the tiffin carriers and dinner packets emerge. All class distinctions have vanished in Third Class, C Cubicle. Philipose has food thrust at him from every direction; he's grateful because he brought nothing. The taciturn Brahmin with winking ear-diamonds and shabby slippers is of course vegetarian and he offers his *thayir sadam* (rice soaked in yogurt and salt) in exchange for a taste of Meena's chicken roast. "Not telling wife. Why to simply worry her?" Meena's eight-tiered tiffin carrier is the size of an artillery shell. Young Miss's contribution is a tin of delectable Spencer's biscuits, packed in pink tissue.

By ten o'clock, Meena's husband and baby are asleep on the middle bunk and the Brahmin snores above. Meena, her mouth red with *paan*, leans forward to confide to Young Miss (and therefore to Arjun and Philipose) that the man snoring on the middle bunk "is my cousin only." They've lived as husband and wife in Madras for three years. "How it happened, you ask?" Young Miss had not. "We studied together till fifth standard. I liking him and he too liking same. But cousins, no? What to do? My parents married me off. On wedding day only I'm first seeing my husband. Good-looking, fair complexion, like you. But after marriage I find he is child only. Outside, looking normal. Inside, he is ten-year-old. After two years, I'm still remaining innocent. He didn't know how!" Her in-laws blamed Meena. When her cousin, who had prospered in Madras, came to visit, they fell in love and eloped.

The anonymity of a train journey, Philipose thinks, gives strangers license for such intimate revelations. Or the freedom to invent. *If I'm asked who, where, and why, I'll make something up. If they want a story, they shall have just that. But what* is *my story?*

"Me? I've run away too, I suppose," says Young Miss when Meena asks. This startles her listeners. It's not surprising that a college-aged girl is traveling unaccompanied. The communal atmosphere of the third-class sleeper is safer than first class (there is no second class), where the individual private cabins have doors that lock, rendering a woman vulnerable to whoever gains entry. "The nuns at college didn't care for me," she says. "Perhaps because I didn't care for them."

"And your good father and mother?"

"My mother is no more. My father won't be too happy."

Philipose is thrilled to realize they are in a similar predicament. Her confession diminishes the sting of his retreat to Parambil. But Young Miss is weathering her return better. He notices the cross on her necklace; she must be a Saint Thomas Christian, though all conversation in this cubicle with passengers from Madras, Mangalore, Vijayawada, Bombay, and Travancore has been in English thus far.

Meena clucks sympathetically. "Why college anyway? A waste. After wedding it won't matter."

"I hope my father sees it that way. But I'm not ready for marriage, Meena. Not yet."

Soon Meena stretches out and just the three snuff-sniffers are awake. Philipose's berth is the bench on which they sit; he can retire only when they do. Young Miss's pencil flies across the creamy pages of a notebook twice the size of his. Philipose wishes Arjun would go to his berth, but he is making calculations on a racing form. Of course, if Arjun retired, Philipose would have to find the courage to talk to Young Miss. His pen flows with his glittering ink, giving voice to an inner dialogue that has perhaps always been there. It's exciting. Why did "Ink-Boy," as Koshy *Saar* calls him, come to this discovery so late? How many insights vanished in the ether because they weren't written down?

A loose, folded foolscap paper falls out of his notebook. It is a scribbled list of possible careers he'd considered, careers that didn't require a classroom or normal hearing. A painful memory emerges of his new classmates turning to look at him: *Wake up! Isn't that your name they're calling?* Discouraged, he puts the paper away. Besides, every career he listed there he crossed out. Yes, he'd been aware that his hearing wasn't as acute as others' before this, but in the insulated world of secondary school, sitting in the front and so close to the teachers that he could feel their saliva spray, he'd managed. He'd always felt the burden was on others to make sure he heard them. All his life to this point, it has been his feud with water—the Condition—that has felt like the real handicap. Never his hearing.

* * *

Young Miss leaves to wash up. Arjun climbs to the middle bunk and is soon snoring. Philipose must get his luggage off Young Miss's bunk if she is to lie down. He removes the bulky cardboard box with the radio, setting it on his bench. Next, he grapples with the trunk full of books, sliding it to the edge, but then, when it tilts onto his hands, it threatens to topple him. A pair of strong hands—Young Miss!—comes to his aid and together they lower it to the bench. She grins, as though they've pulled off a superhuman feat together. She waits.

"Don't mention," she says, looking directly at him.

He failed to say thank you! It was because of her presence so close to him. He was caught up in the scent of her minty toothpaste, forgetting his manners, forgetting everything.

"Sorry!—I mean, thank you. And thank you for letting the porter . . ." It feels intimate to be staring into her pupils. He has never made eye contact for this long with a woman who wasn't family. The train feels suspended in space.

"That trunk feels full of bricks," she says matter-of-factly.

"Yes, as many books as I could afford." *Did she say books or bricks?* "And more in that trunk too," he says, pointing to the one under the seat that toppled Meena's suitcase.

She ponders this information. "And that carton? Also books?"

"A radio. You see, I'm heading home. For reasons similar to yours," he blurts. What happened to his plan to spin a tale? "Not nuns, but I too was sent away from college. Issues with my hearing . . . they claim. But it's all right. It's probably a blessing." He's shocked by his own confession.

She nods. "Me too. I was studying home economics." She makes a wry face and laughs. "Which one can surely study at home. Still, I would have stayed in college. But it wasn't up to me."

"I'm sorry."

"Don't be. As you said, it's a blessing."

"Well . . . For what I wanted to learn—literature—I didn't need to be in Madras. I won't let it stop me. One thing I know, I love to learn. I love literature. With these books I can sail the seven seas, chase a white whale . . ."

She glances down. "Unlike Ahab you have both legs."

She knows his favorite book! He follows her gaze helplessly, as though to confirm that he does indeed have both legs. He laughs. "Yes," he says, with some feeling. "I'm luckier than Ahab. I have been bent and broken but I hope into better shape."

She digests that. "Good for you," she says finally. "And with a radio, the world comes to you, doesn't it?"

These are the most words he's ever exchanged with a woman his age. His eyes are on her lips. She asked a question. He's already invoked Ahab. And Dickens. He worries he's sounding pompous. He should crack a joke. But what if it sounds stupid? Besides, he can't think of one. He opens his mouth to speak, to say something . . . but God help him, she's so beautiful, her eyes such a pale gray . . . She can see every thought of his as it bounces around his skull. His brain is overheating and seizes, when all he has to say is yes.

"Well, goodnight then," she says softly. She moves to the ladder, one foot on the first rung, then pauses. "Was that *Great Expectations?*"

"Yes! Yes, it was. Estella!"

"Please can you say it again?"

"Indubitably I can."

After a beat, she bursts out laughing. They glance guiltily at the sleeping Arjun, and she leans forward, lowering her voice. "Well, *would* you please say it again?"

"I have been bent and broken but I hope into better shape."

She smiles her thanks. She nods slowly. Then her face disappears.

He watches her pale soles, so creamy and soft, float up the ladder, trailed by the hem of her cotton sari and the shimmery slip beneath. She vanishes but the image lingers—the fleeting glimpse of the ball of her foot, of the underside of her big toe, the other toes winging out in its wake, babies trailing the mother. A slow heat starts in his belly and spreads to his limbs. He slumps heavily on the bench, then raps his head on the window bars—but softly. *Idiot! Why didn't you converse more? Did you even ask her name? I didn't want to be inquisitive. What do you mean "inquisitive"? It's called making conversation!* Belatedly he remembers a joke: What do you call a Malayali who doesn't ask for your family name, where you live, your income, and what's in the bag you carry? A deaf-mute. *That's you.*

He settles in as best he can against his luggage, unable to stretch out. He sets aside the loose foolscap paper with its list of careers crossed out, and now his pen races back and forth in the bound journal.

She must think I'm the sort who sniffs when others sniff, eats when they eat, and speaks only when spoken to. But I'm not! Please don't judge me, Young Miss, from my hesitation. And was it fair for him to judge her as he had, sure of herself, willing to ask about things that interested her but content also to keep her peace when someone doesn't reply? He's acutely aware of her lying above him, only Arjun Railways between them.

He wakes to blinding light and a shockingly verdant landscape: flooded paddy fields with narrow mud bunds snaking between them, barely containing the water whose still surface mirrors the sky; coconut palms that are as abundant as leaves of grass; tangled cucumber vines on the side of a canal; a lake crowded with canoes; and a stately barge parting the smaller vessels like a processional down a church aisle. His nostrils register jackfruit, dried fish, mango, and water.

Even before his brain digests these sights, his body—skin, nerve endings, lungs, heart—recognizes the geography of his birth. He never understood how much it mattered. Every bit of this lush landscape is his; its every atom contains him. On this blessed strip of coast where Malayalam is spoken, the flesh and bones of his ancestors have leached into the soil, made their way into the trees, into the iridescent plumage of the parrots on swaying branches, and dispersed themselves into the breeze. He knows the names of the forty-two rivers running down from the mountains, one thousand two hundred miles of waterways, feeding the rich soil in between, and he is one with every atom of it. *I'm the seedling in your hand*, he thinks, as he gazes on Muslim women in colorful long-sleeved blouses and *mundus*, with cloths loosely covering their hair, bent over at the waist like paper creased down the middle, moving as one line through the paddy fields, poking new life into the soil. *Whatever is next for me, whatever the story of my life, the roots that must nourish it are here.* He feels transformed as though by a religious experience, but it has nothing to do with religion.

Young Miss returns from the washroom and stops Philipose when he makes to move his trunk and carton from the bench; she squeezes in beside him and Arjun. She dons her sunglasses with their cat's-eye corners and wraps her scarf round her neck, as though steeling herself for what's ahead. Arjun, he sees, is freshly shaved and sports a crisp shirt and a Vishnu *namam*, its three-pronged pitchfork a contrast to the elderly Brahmin's *namam*, which is a horizontal brushstroke, indicating his allegiance to Shiva. Lines are drawn—Shaivites versus Vaishnavites—but both men smile. Arjun confides to Philipose, "Half my life is spent on trains. Strangers of all religions, all castes getting on so well in a compartment. Why not same outside train? Why not simply all getting along?" Arjun looks out of the window and swallows hard.

Philipose hasn't time to respond because they're in Cochin. A porter grabs one of his trunks, while Meena's porter threatens to take off with his radio. In the confusion, Young Miss taps his shoulder and hands him his folded sheet of foolscap paper. It must have slipped out of his notebook. She says farewell wordlessly with a brief tilt of her head and a smile. *Good luck*, her eyes say. Then she's gone.

Once he's on the bus to Changanacherry, with all his luggage accounted for, he can relax. But he's furious with himself for not asking for Young Miss's name. "Idiot! Idiot!" He smacks his forehead on the seat in front of him. Its occupant turns and glares at him. He digs out his foolscap, embarrassed at the thought of Young Miss reading his list of careers. But there's an additional sheet folded in. It's one of hers—a portrait. It shows him asleep, his head resting against the window of the train, his body bent sideways, the carton with the radio pushing at his ribs. His lips are set together, the philtrum a dugout in the flesh above the vermilion border of his upper lip.

We have no practice, he thinks, of seeing our real selves. Even before a mirror we compose our faces to meet our own expectations. But Young Miss has captured him completely: his thwarted ambition, his anxiety about what comes next. She has also caught his determination. He's heartened by this, and even more thrilled to see the way she depicts his hands, one resting on the radio, the other on the trunk full of books. Their resting posture speaks to his old courage, his confidence, the hands of a determined man. *My father cleared a jungle; he did what others thought impossible. I'll do no less.*

How is it that in just a few pencil strokes she captured all this, even the cool breeze that blew in during the early morning, numbing one side of his face? Thank goodness he didn't invent some story for her and just told her the truth. Because she'd have seen through everything.

At the bottom of the paper, she's written:

Bent and broken, but in better shape. Good luck.
   Always,
   E.

A lifetime ago, a schoolgirl named Elsie had sketched him as he took his first-ever ride in her father's Chevrolet. He'd been so preoccupied then, so sick with worry, knowing that given the flash flooding, his mother would be fearing the worst. A much younger Young Miss had sat in the back seat with him and slid her fingers over to touch the hand that had somehow helped a baby live. He'd affixed that early portrait of him to the inside of his wardrobe: it was a more accurate reflection than the mirror image on the outside.

If Young Miss is none other than Chandy's daughter, grown up and even more skilled with her pencils, then surely fate brought them together. He revisits their exchange on the train, and the way she looked . . . her wordless goodbye, her parting smile indelible in his memory.

The bus lurches to a stop and the driver streaks out behind some bushes. "Had to go, is it?" a woman grumbles. "If men only knew how women suffer! 'Had to go' means you wait!" The scent of his fellow passengers—coconut oil, wood smoke, sweat, betel leaf, and tobacco plugs—smothers him and brings him back to reality. Saint Thomas Christians are a relatively small community and rarely marry outside. Even so, Chandy, with his Chevrolet and his vast tea estate and his State Express 555 lifestyle, has many, many candidates to consider for his only daughter, all of whom will be boys who are extremely rich and incredibly accomplished, or at least extremely rich. At Parambil, they are very well off, but it doesn't compare to the likes of the Thetanatts.

The bus starts again, and the motion jump-starts a change in his attitude, a new resolve taking hold. *I won't give her up.* Elsie is beautiful, talented, willful. Surely she felt their connection, felt that they shared more than just snuff. She must have recognized him at once, though she only revealed herself to him at journey's end. *Elsie, I'll make a name for myself. I'll be worthy of you,* he thinks. *And then I'll have Big Ammachi approach Broker* Aniyan *to propose an alliance. The worst that can happen is your side says no. But at least I'll have tried, and you'll know I did.* "But, oh, Elsie, please wait. Give me at least a few years." The couple in the seat in front turns to glare at him—he must have spoken aloud. The man says to his wife, "*Avaneu vatta.*"

Yes, I am *mad. You can't set out to achieve your goals without a little madness.*

CHAPTER 43

To Thine Own House

1943, Parambil

In Philipose's absence, Parambil tilts into disorder. Shamuel falls while climbing a palm that he has no business climbing; his ankle is the size of a coconut. The graying ghost in the cellar knocks over an urn and makes groaning noises. Big Ammachi, already in an irritable mood, goes down prepared to do battle if needed. But now, in that airless space full of cobwebs, she sees no damage done: the urn was empty, and it remains intact. It comes to her strongly that the spirit is simply lonely. She sits down on the inverted urn and chats, sounding like the fishmonger as she describes the rash of recent calamities. "Ever since he came back from Cochin, Uplift Master is his reliable self in the daytime, but when the sun sets he drinks himself into a stupor. And our Decency *Kochamma* slipped in the kitchen and broke her wrist, blaming Dolly *Kochamma* for grease on their shared floor. Dolly said in her calm, peaceful way, 'Next time, God willing, you might break your neck.'" Big Ammachi leaves, but not before promising to visit more often.

In the afternoons, out of habit, she finds herself expecting to hear Philipose shout out "Ammachio!" as he returns from school. "Ammachio!" means new ideas swim in his head like tadpoles in puddles. How much she's learned of the world from her son! His hand-drawn map covers a wall of his room, charting where Indian forces are fighting and dying. Tripoli, El Alamein—even the names are fascinating. She, Baby Mol, and Odat *Kochamma* miss his nightly reading as the three of them sat on the rope cot like mynah birds on a clothesline, eyes glued on him as he paced. That year he performed two Malayalam short stories by M. R. Bhattathiripad. And an unforgettable English drama, taking on every part: the murdered king, his brother who married the king's wife, the late king's ghost. When the beautiful Ophelia went mad, making wreaths to hang on branches, then falling into the stream, the Parambil women clutched each other. Her dress, spread out over the water like a sari, trapping air, keeping her afloat for a while. Then, despite desperate prayers from Parambil, she drowned. After Philipose left, Odat *Kochamma* announced, "I'm going to visit my son's house. It's dull here without our boy." She doesn't last more than a week.

On a bright, sunny morning, not even a month after Philipose's departure, she sits down with the *Manorama*.

JAPANESE PLANE BOMBS MADRAS. MASS EXODUS FROM CITY.

The headline scratches at her eyes; her throat suddenly feels as if she's swallowed lye. She stands, wanting to run to her son.

Baby Mol stands too, saying, "Our baby is coming!"

The paper says the bombing happened three days ago. A lone Japanese "scout" plane flew over a city already darkened by a power outage, the result of rains. It dropped three bombs near the beach. Air raid sirens never sounded, and the explosions were unexplained: for two days, the citizens didn't know of the bombing because radio stations had no electricity, and the military didn't want to provoke panic. When word got out, fear of a Japanese invasion caused a frenzied exodus from the city.

God help me, how do I find my son?

Baby Mol bounces up and down excitedly, distracting and annoying Big Ammachi. To add to that, a bullock cart rattles up to the house.
What now? The beaten expression of the animals mirrors that of the
lone passenger who steps out and says a subdued "Ammachio . . ."

She presses the heels of her hands to her eyes. Is she hallucinating? Then she and Baby Mol run out and cling to him as if to
keep him from leaving again. He has lost weight and looks gaunt.

Philipose is relieved but bewildered. "Aren't you going to ask
me why I'm back?"

Big Ammachi, newspaper still in her hand, slaps it against his
chest, as though to measure reality against the newsprint. "I saw this
and I almost died. God brought you home to save you and to spare
me." He reads. He had no idea.

That night, after Baby Mol and Odat *Kochamma* are asleep, Big Ammachi carries hot *jeera* water in two glasses to his room. They sit on
his bed as was their custom. Without any preamble he tells her that
he was dismissed from college. It all comes out: his encounter with
his professor in Central Station—an omen. Then failing to hear his
name in class. She bleeds for him, wishes she could have spared him
such misery. "Ammachi," he says. "I'm sorry to disappoint you."

"*Monay*, you can never disappoint me. I am so glad you are
home. God heard you. You weren't meant to be there."

Hesitantly, he shows her the contents of his two trunks full of
books, unable to conceal his excitement. And then the radio, now
unpacked and sitting in the corner. He is anxious to justify the purchases. "Radio waves are all around, Ammachi, and now we have the
machine to catch them, to bring the world right to us. We just need
electricity."

"It's all right, *monay*. You put the money to good use."

They sit quietly in the soft glow of the lamp. She holds his
hand, a hand so different from her husband's, his fingers elongated,
more like hers. It's as though he never left.

"Ammachi, there's something else."

My God, what now? But his expression is of wondrous excitement, just like the day he came home with *Moby-Dick*, calling out, "Ammachio!"

He tells her of the young woman traveling in his cubicle.

"Chandy's daughter?" she says. "My goodness! I remember her as a little girl, drawing with Baby Mol. What a coincidence. How is she?"

"Ammachi, she's beautiful!" he says with great feeling, looking directly at his mother, his pupils widening. He recounts every detail of their meeting as though he's reciting a mythical tale, from the time he boarded to when she put that drawing in his hand. He shows her the portrait. It breaks her heart: her son retreating home, full of worry, his boxes around him.

"Ammachi, I'm going to marry her one day," he says quietly. "God willing. Yes, I know. Now that I won't be a college graduate my prospects are not great. Not to mention my hearing, and the Condition." He waves off her protests. "But I'll make something of myself. I won't fail. I just pray she's not married off before I have that chance."

Her heart is full of worry. "You didn't say any such thing to her, did you? About marriage?"

He shakes his head.

After his mother goes to bed, Philipose is wide awake. He had had no idea who the beguiling Young Miss was and had missed his chance to ask. It could have all ended there. But Elsie ensured he knew. His fantasy, his hope, his prayer is that he lingers in her consciousness tonight as she lives in his.

Perhaps she's thinking of him now, wondering what his return home was like, just as he's trying to picture how her father received her. If two people at the very same moment hold visions of each other, perhaps atoms coalesce into invisible forms, like radio waves, and connect them. Her beautiful face is before him as he falls into a peaceful slumber, the kind of sleep that can only happen in his own bed, in his house, on Parambil soil and in God's Own Country.

CHAPTER 44

In a Land of Plenty

1943, Parambil

Philipose was lucky to get out of Madras when he did. The papers say that bus and train stations are jammed with people decamping. He wonders if his classmates are gone too. Everything in Madras is on hold. *He* is on hold.

He had dreaded having to explain to everyone why he's back but for now no explanation is needed. Fears of a Japanese invasion grip Travancore. Overnight, the price of paddy skyrockets. South Indian rice is so prized that it all usually goes for export; what is available for consumers in India is cheap imported Burmese rice. But with the fall of Rangoon, imports of rice cease and meanwhile the British have seized and stockpiled locally grown rice, saving it for the troops. This is how one triggers a famine.

Soon, the war slides off the pages of the *Manorama* and limps up to the house; it takes the form of a decently dressed man with a sardonic smile, a consequence of cheeks so lacking fat that they are glued to the bone. The points of the man's shoulders jut out like areca nuts, and deep hollows sit above his collarbones. His wife waits with her baby in the shade. The man's voice quavers. Displaced from Singapore by the Japanese, he came home with nothing. "Forgive me. This morning I said, 'Should my baby die because pride won't let me beg?'

So I beg, not for money. Just a morsel of rice, or the water left over from its boiling. We've been living on chaff and now that's gone. My wife's breasts are shriveled like an ancient's. She's just twenty-two."

Another day, it's a gaunt man speaking on behalf of his silent brother. The brother's wife threw herself and their children into a well, seeing that as a kinder fate than slow starvation. One girl managed to pull away, and she stands there now, imprisoning her father's hand, while her uncle tells this story and begs for food. Philipose identifies a new scent: the fruity, acetone odor of a body consuming itself, the scent of starvation.

Tormented by these sights, Philipose drags out to the *muttam* the great brass vessel used for Onam and Christmas and sets it on bricks. With Shamuel's help, he cooks a rice and *kappa* gruel, mashing in bananas and with coconut oil in place of ghee. He readies banana leaf packets that can be handed out discreetly to select supplicants. If word gets out, there'll be a stampede.

A few weeks after Philipose's return, glum relatives gather at Parambil after church, drinking tea. Philipose listens and lip-reads, following the gloomy conversations. The visitors, who don't really lack for food, talk only about how the current hardship affects them. Surely, they have also had starving people coming to their houses to beg.

"Did you hear about our own Philipose?" Manager Kora says in his usual jocular tone, as though to cheer everyone up. He wheezes chronically and chops up his sentences to take a breath. He speaks as though Philipose isn't there, while grinning at him. "Philipose came back with a radio! But problem is radio needs electricity. *Aah!* If there's no electricity in Travancore, how can it come to Parambil?"

His words get under Philipose's skin. Kora's father had the honorific "Manager" bestowed on him by the maharajah for his volunteer work when he lived in Trivandrum. The father deserved the title even if its only privilege was to be addressed as "Manager." The title isn't hereditary, though Kora insists it is. The poor father cosigned a loan Kora took out for a business that then failed, and the father lost his Trivandrum property. He would have been homeless had his third cousin—Philipose's father—not gifted him a house plot at Parambil. After Kora's father died, Kora showed up at once with his bride to claim his inheritance. It was in the same year that Uplift Master and Shoshamma moved back. Kora was younger and seemed the more outgoing of the two men; Philipose would have guessed Kora was more likely to succeed. He was utterly mistaken. Kora is full of schemes, but nothing comes to fruition.

Everyone adores Kora's wife, Lizziamma, or Lizzi, as she is called by most. Lizzi is an orphan, convent-educated through pre-degree. She's good-natured, beautiful, and the spitting image of the goddess Lakshmi in the Raja Ravi Varma painting found on so many calendars. Varma was from the Travancore Royal Family. His foresight in having his own printing press allowed him to widely distribute prints of his paintings. He portrayed his Lakshmi with distinctive Malayali features: a wide cherub's face, thick, dark eyebrows framing doe eyes, and long wavy hair that reached beyond her hips. Given Varma's popularity and shrewd business sense, his Malayali Lakshmi is the Lakshmi embedded in the consciousness of Hindus all over India. Philipose thinks Lizzi has no idea how pretty she is; she is humble and quite the opposite of her boastful husband. Big Ammachi adores Lizzi and treats her like a daughter. Lizzi spends a lot of time in Big Ammachi's kitchen, and when Kora is gone overnight on some new "business" of his, Lizzi sleeps with Big Ammachi and Baby Mol. The only good thing one can say about Kora is that he adores his wife; for all his failings, one must grudgingly admire his devotion to her.

"Kora," Uplift Master says, "with your maharajah connections didn't you know that Trivandrum *has* electricity? The diwan has a campaign to electrify all of Travancore." The diwan is the chief executive of the maharajah's government.

"Who said?" Kora's tone is challenging, but it's clearly news to him.

"*Chaa!* There are thermal generators already at Kollam and

Kottayam! And here I thought you had your fingers on the pulse of Trivandrum."

Georgie, sitting next to his twin, says, "Kora's fingers were in Trivandrum's pockets, not on the pulse."

Kora's smile won't stay on his face. He makes his excuses and leaves. Philipose doesn't know whether to feel pleased that Kora was put in his place or to feel sorry for the man. But Kora's "joke" still bothers him because he knows that what he spent on the radio that sits gathering dust could have fed so many.

He's haunted by the faces of the starving who show up every day. The packets of gruel he dispenses are just a salve. *We must do more. But what?* He comes up with a plan and enlists Uplift Master to help him with the execution.

They put up a thatch-roof shed by the boat jetty, then borrow large cauldrons from the Parambil houses, the sort everyone keeps for weddings. They seek out old Sultan *Pattar*, the legendary wedding cook, who is reluctant until he sees the shed, the stacked wood, the four firepits, and the polished cauldrons. The old man's blood stirs. *Pattar* concocts a cheap, nutritious meal with *kappa* as its base, because every household can donate a few tapioca tubers.

Soon the "Feeding Center" opens. Each person gets a mound of *kappa*, one dollop of a *thoren* of moong beans, a dab of a lime pickle, and a teaspoon of salt on their banana leaf. An animated Sultan *Pattar* is unrecognizable: clean-shaven, shirtless, bouncing on his toes, and barking orders at *Pattar's* Army—the enthusiastic Parambil children who are pressed into service to chop, scrape, ladle, and clean. *Pattar* entertains them, dancing with mincing steps, his breasts jiggling while he belts out songs with sly meanings.

On the first day, they feed nearly two hundred before they run out. After two weeks a reporter visits. He describes *Pattar's* simple meal as one of the best in memory and gives Philipose credit for the Feeding Center, describing him as a young man who found it hard to witness so much suffering and not act. Philipose quotes Gandhi:

"There are people in the world so hungry, that God cannot appear to them except in the form of food." The accompanying photograph shows Sultan *Pattar*, Uplift Master, and Philipose standing behind *Pattar*'s Army, the youngest of whom is only five, the oldest fifteen. The article triggers donations, volunteers . . . and more hungry people. Inspired by their example, other Feeding Centers open up across Travancore.

At the end of each day, Philipose writes in his notebooks, trying to capture the conversations he overhears at the Feeding Center, the tales of misery and sacrifice, but also of heroism and generosity. He's surprised by people's capacity for humor in the face of suffering. The writing is an exercise, not a journalist's report, and so he can conflate characters, invent elements that weren't in the original telling, and make his own endings—"Unfictions" is how he thinks of this genre. He thinks often of Elsie as he writes; is she doing just this with her charcoal stick, trying to make sense of these uncertain times? He closely studies the stories and essays he admires in the *Manorama*'s weekly magazine. What he's writing feels different. He decides to submit one of his Unfictions to a short story competition in the *Manorama*.

SATURDAY COLUMN: THE PLAVU MAN
by V. Philipose

Is it possible to confuse a man with a jackfruit tree—a plavu? *Yes. It happened to me. I'm an ordinary man, not a storyteller, so I give you the ending at the beginning. (Why not every story begin with the ending? Why Genesis, Zephaniah, and whatnot when we can begin with the Gospels?) Anyway, this story begins at our Feeding Center. Don't call it Famine Center because the Government says there's no famine, no matter what your eyes tell you. After everyone left, a pencil-thin old man came carrying a giant* chakka *bigger than him. This is for you to feed the children tomorrow, he said. If you have a decent cook you can make a good* puzhukku. *Brother, I said, forgive me, but you look like you are starving, so why give away your* chakka? *Ha, I don't give it, he said. The* plavu *gives it! Nature is generous. I wanted to say, In that case let the* plavu *send pickle and rice too. Next day he brought an even bigger* chakka. *From afar he looked like an ant carrying a coconut. I said, brother, eat* puzhukku *before you go. He refused. Who refuses a meal in these times? I said, brother, how is it a thin old man can carry such heavy things? What's the secret? He said: Secrets are hidden in the most obvious places.*

That day I passed our famous Ammachi plavu—*the mother of all jackfruit trees—the very one in whose hollow our Maharajah Marthanda Varma hid from enemies, centuries ago. Yes, your village claims it has the legendary tree, but you're wrong. It's here, so let's not argue. Anyway, I heard a voice say, Have you come to find my secret? I recognized that old man's voice. But I saw no one. Show yourself, I said. He said, You're looking right at me.*

If I tell you he leaned on the tree, you'd misunderstand. No, he leaned into the tree. His skin was bark and his eyes were knots in the wood. He said, When the famine started, I had no more paddy. I sat against this plavu *and awaited death. The bark was rough, but I thought, why complain? I'm soon leaving this world. After a few hours I sank into the tree. It was comfortable, as if I was resting against my Ammachi's bosom. I said, Oh mighty* plavu, *if you can make giant fruit even in drought, can you not nourish me? The* plavu *said, Why not? So that's how I am here. The* plavu *provides me everything. Nature is generous. I said, Old man, if nature is generous, why this famine? He said, Blame human nature that makes merchants hoard and Churchill take our rice for his troops while we starve. I said, Don't you miss company, living alone like this? He smiled. Who says I'm alone? Look there on that small* plavu—*do you see Kochu Cherian?*

And here next to me you see Ponnamma? Why not you come sit on my other side? Nature provides.

    Friends, I ran for my life. What's the shame in saying so? Dear Reader, the moral is give as generously as nature gives. And take a good look at your plavu *because secrets are hidden in the most obvious places.*

"The Plavu Man" wins first prize and is the only story of the three winners to get published. Philipose takes it as a sign. In the space of a few months, he's been mentioned in the *Manorama* for starting the Feeding Center, and now his writing appears there. Perhaps newspaper writing is his true vocation. His success doesn't silence the snide remarks of the likes of Manager Kora over his not returning to Madras, nor does everyone care for "The Plavu Man"—Decency *Kochamma* thinks it's blasphemy. But there's only one reader whose opinion Philipose cares about, the one reader he writes for. He prays Elsie has seen it; he hopes she can tell that he is bent but not broken.

It is now over a year since his return from Madras, even if the wound of that brief sojourn is still raw. After his first published story, the *Manorama* editor is willing to see more, but he turns down three stories in a row before publishing the fourth under the heading "The Ordinary Man Column." It suggests to Philipose that he might get to be a regular contributor, though he doesn't care for the title the editor chose—who wants to be called ordinary?

    In that year and the next Philipose has a few more of his Unfictions published. His writing is well received judging by readers' letters, though Malayalis can always find fault, and do. Still, nothing prepares him or the newspaper for the uproar that follows the publication of a piece entitled "Why No Self-Respecting Rat Works at the Secretariat." The narrator is an injured rat who drags himself into a grand government building at night and is delighted to find none of his kind there to compete with. The next morning, the employees of the Secretariat arrive:

This huge open space must be a place of worship, I concluded. God is on high, invisible. The ceiling fans are the manifestation of God because they sit directly over the high priests (who are called Head Clerks). The lower your caste, the further away you sit from the fan. What is the work? Aah, it took me hours to understand though it was staring me in the face: the work is to sit. You come in the morning, you sit and stare at the files in front of you, and you make a long face. Eventually you take out your pen. When the high priest looks your way, you take the first file and untie the laces holding papers down. But whenever the high priest steps out, you and the others jump up and stand near his desk, under the fan, telling jokes. That's the work.

The Clerical Workers' Union takes strong exception to Philipose's piece and calls for the Ordinary Man's head; the uproar only brings more readers to his column. Public sentiment (along with the Union for Journalists and Reporters) is on the writer's side, because every citizen of Travancore has had the experience of getting tangled in red tape and leaving the Secretariat disheartened. Uplift Master is the rare individual with the patience and skill to take on bureaucracy; he even relishes the battle.

One reader announces himself late at night with a laughing-dove call, a crescendo, a chuckling sound like a woman being tickled. Philipose emerges and greets Joppan by punching him hard on the shoulder. "That's for not coming by to see me for so long."

"*Aah*, did that make you feel better?" Joppan is as sturdy as ever, his compact frame low to the ground, and shoulders as broad as his smile. He has a bottle of toddy in one hand and with the other he punches Philipose back. "And *that's* for me being the last person to know that you were a Communist all this time."

"Is that what I am?" Philipose rubs his stinging shoulder.

"Didn't you start the Feeding Center? You care enough to do something. I'm proud of you. Vladimir Lenin said, 'The press should be not only a collective agitator, but also a collective organizer of the masses.' So you see, your actions, your words—you're a revolutionary!"

"*Aah*, alright. Now I can sleep better. So, how are you, Joppan?"

Joppan shrugs. Iqbal's barge business, just like every business around, has ground to a halt. Iqbal can't pay him, but since Joppan is like a son to him, he feeds him. Joppan says, "Look at me. I speak and write Malayalam and can read English. I can keep accounts. I know the backwaters inside out. But now I'm lucky to work as a day laborer now and then. In the evenings I attend Party meetings. It feeds my brain if not my belly. I sleep on the barge because if I come home all I do is argue with my father."

Philipose says, "You can't expect him to change."

Joppan sighs. "He and Amma want me to marry, can you believe? I barely support myself!" He laughs. "I may do it to make them happy. Nothing else I do pleases them."

They talk just like old times till past midnight when Joppan rises to leave, glowing from the toddy of which he's had the lion's share. "About the Feeding Center. I meant it, Philipose—I'm proud of you. You're saving lives. But think about this, Philipose: if nothing changes, if the people have no way to escape poverty, if the *pulayar* can never own land or pass on wealth to their children, then the next time there's a famine, it'll be the same people standing in line. And it will take people like you to feed them."

That thought makes it harder for Philipose to fall asleep.

A few weeks later, Big Ammachi announces that Joppan is to be married the next day.

"What? It can't be! He never told me. Did he invite us?"

"It's not for Joppan to invite. Shamuel invited us today. And now I'm telling you." Seeing his crestfallen face she says, "Look, it's not some alliance they spent months planning. It must have just happened."

"Where's the wedding? At their CSI church? I'm going."

"Don't be silly. It doesn't work that way."

"I'm going anyway," he says peevishly. "Joppan will be glad to see me."

"No, you are not," his mother says firmly. "That family means too much to us. Don't embarrass them just because you don't understand your place."

After the wedding, the new couple and the groom's parents come calling, bearing jaggery sweets. Joppan grins sheepishly as he squeezes Philipose's hand. He murmurs, "I told you I would."

"You said you might!"

His bride, Ammini, is shy, and keeps her head covered so Philipose never gets a good look at her. Shamuel beams as if all his worries are over and he holds his son's hand affectionately. Big Ammachi presents the couple with three bolts of cotton, a shiny new set of brass vessels, and a fat envelope. Joppan brings his palms together and bends to touch her feet, but she stops him. Shamuel and Sara run their hands over the gifts like excited children. Philipose marvels at his mother's foresight. After they leave, she tells him that she's given Shamuel a rectangular house plot behind his own for him to build a separate dwelling for Joppan and his new daughter-in-law if he wants to, or to give to the couple outright.

One year and four months from the time Uplift Master first began his petition campaign, electricity comes to Parambil P.O. from a substation two miles away. Only four families were willing to share the cost for the extension. Uplift Master says, "When the others decide they want electricity, they'll have to pay a share of our initial costs adjusted for price increases. We might even get our investment back."

In the glow of twenty-watt bulbs, the electrified households celebrate while their neighbors grumble. For Philipose, the expression on Baby Mol's face as she switches on the "small sun" makes it all worthwhile. Insects swoop in from the dark and swarm around the bulb as though the invertebrate Messiah has arrived. Philipose fires up the radio that has sat idle for so long. A man's voice fills

the room, reading the news in English, and at that moment, Philipose, his hand on the cabinet, feels vindicated. He has brought the
world to his doorstep. Odat *Kochamma*, hearing the disembodied
foreign voice, comes at once, grabbing the first thing she finds on
the clothesline to cover her head—it happens to be Baby Mol's
underwear. Philipose sees her in the doorway, making the sign of
the cross, with the strange cloth hanging over her forehead. "Stand
up, *monay*!" she says sternly. "A voice from nowhere is the voice of
God!" She's not entirely convinced by his explanations. He dials in
music, and Baby Mol dances till she has to go to bed. Hours later,
he's still bent over the radio, feeling like he is Odysseus steering his
galley over crackly shortwave oceans. He stumbles onto a theater
performance and is transported from Parambil to a distant stage,
echoing words he has by-hearted. "If it be now, 'tis not to come: if it
be not to come, it will be now: if it be not now, yet it will come: the
readiness is all."

Big Ammachi declines an electric bulb in her bedroom, or in
the kitchen. Her oil lamp, her old, faithful friend, its base worn and
shaped to her palm and fingers, suffices; she takes comfort in its
golden halo, the liquid shadows it throws on the floors and walls,
and the smell of the burning wick. These swimming elements of her
night she'd rather leave just as they are.

Before she goes to bed, Big Ammachi brings hot *jeera* water to
her son. The ethereal glow from the dial illuminates his face. The
world deserves his curiosity, his good heart, and his writing, she
thinks. He once sought a larger world than she could ever imagine.
Instead, he has settled for his books and his radio. She hopes it suffices. *Lord*, she prays, *tell me this was where my son was meant to be.*

Philipose senses her, turns, and says, "Ammachio!" He waves
her in and turns off the radio for the first time in many hours. His
face is flushed with excitement, and he looks a little nervous. She
braces herself for what his new passion might be.

"Ammachi," he says. "I want you to send for Broker *Aniyan*.
I'm ready."

CHAPTER 45

The Engagement

1944, Parambil

Broker *Aniyan* is a dignified man, his steel-black hair shooting back at the temples, giving him a sleek, aerodynamic look, his manner unhurried. *Aniyan* means "younger brother"; the pet or baptismal names he carried have long vanished. He neither smiles nor acts surprised when Philipose recounts the story of meeting Elsie on the train, though he does look over at Big Ammachi.

To Philipose's surprise, *Aniyan* knows exactly who Elsie is, and that she isn't married, "as of day before yesterday." The Saint Thomas community is tiny by comparison with the Hindus or Muslims in Travancore and Cochin, but it's still in the hundreds of thousands and scattered over the world. Brokers like *Aniyan* must be walking repositories of house names and family trees, dating back to the original converts.

"Well," *Aniyan* says, "I'll approach the Thetanatt side—Chandy, that is. If he's interested, and since you've seen the girl already, no need for *pennu kaanal*." He's referring to the "viewing of the girl" by the prospective in-laws, an event the boy doesn't always attend.

"I still want a *pennu kaanal*," Philipose says.

Aniyan's expression doesn't change. In his line of work his face must reveal nothing, no matter the provocation.

"If Chandy is under the impression that you are yet to see her, then . . . it's possible."

"And I wish to talk to her," Philipose adds.

"Not possible."

"I insist."

There's a slight distention of the serpentine veins on *Aniyan*'s temples. He smiles faintly, rising. "Let me present the proposal to Chandy. That's the first step."

"Look, *Anichayan*. I'm going to marry her. Think of it as being both the *pennu kaanal* plus the engagement. Then surely it's all right to say a few words."

"The engagement is to fix the marriage. Not for talking with the girl."

Aniyan reports back by the end of the week: Chandy is interested. They can proceed to the *pennu kaanal*.

But Big Ammachi has a question. "Did they ask about JoJo? Or Baby Mol? About water—"

Aniyan raises an eyebrow. "What's to ask? A tragic accident causing a drowning. That's not like lunacy in the family. Or fits. That I'll never hide. And Ammachi, believe it or not, there are more Baby Mols in our community than you might imagine. It's not an impediment to a matrimonial alliance."

Big Ammachi turns to Philipose. "If this marriage comes about, you're to tell Elsie everything, you hear? No secrets."

Aniyan watches this exchange, waiting. He says, "So . . . Ammachi, you and one or two senior relatives will come to the Thetanatt house. *Aah*, and you may come too, *monay*," he adds as an afterthought. "Barring any obstacles, that day can be the engagement, and we'll fix wedding date and dowry—"

"I want some time to talk privately with Elsie," Philipose says.

Aniyan looks to Big Ammachi but sees he'll get no help there. "Well, maybe after prayers and tea . . ."

"Privately?"

"*Aah*, *aah*, privately, certainly. But with everyone there."

Big Ammachi sits on an impossibly long, white sofa in the Thetanatt house, clutching the gold-trimmed cup and saucer. Framed photographs of the deceased hang side by side, high on the wall and angled down. It's a trend that she finds ghoulish. Chandy's late wife looks down. Beside her is the reassuring portrait of Mar Gregorios by Ravi Varma. She addresses the saint: *Tell me it's the right thing we're doing.*

"*Ena-di?* What you muttering?" Odat *Kochamma* says crossly. "Drink your tea." The old lady is thrilled to be invited as one of the elders, along with Uplift Master. She's not in the least cowed by the house or the occasion; she pours the steaming tea into the porcelain saucer ("What else is this for?") and blows on it. "*Aah*, good tea, that much I will say!"

Broker *Aniyan* neither eats nor drinks, his face as still as standing water, while his eyes sweep the room, cataloging future prospects, even if they are presently infants.

Big Ammachi eyes Chandy, their gregarious host, talking to Uplift Master. *Why my Philipose?* Her son is a gem, of course, a most eligible groom, and he'll inherit Parambil, which at one time was nearly five hundred acres. But it doesn't compare to Chandy's estate, which she's told is some hours away and is reported to be several thousand acres of tea and rubber, in addition to this, the ancestral house, and other properties he has elsewhere. His wealth shows in the furnishings of the house, and in the two cars outside, one of which is sleek, with a long prow and a finned tail, glowing like a sapphire under the portico, while the other, which is parked on the side, is the one that brought Philipose home years ago, a vehicle stripped to its skeleton and with a platform jutting from the back. Chandy could have sought the scion of another estate owner for Elsie, or a doctor, or a district collector. Perhaps he just took to the schoolboy Philipose he first met—he called him a hero then. The schoolboy has made a name for himself with his writing. Or else Elsie (who has yet to emerge) was just as insistent as Philipose on this match. She sighs, gazing at her son, looking so handsome despite his nerves, sitting tall, his thick hair forming waves off its center part, the white *juba* highlighting his fair complexion.

After prayers, more tea and *palaharam* are brought around by a young girl in a sari, Elsie's cousin, who then ushers Philipose out to one of two benches on the broad verandah, leaving him in view of all the guests through the open French doors. At once, three ancient *ammachis* from the Thetanatt side, their ears sagging with gold, rise and follow. Every pleat of their *mundus*' fantails is ironed to a knife-edge, belying the curve of their spines, and their *chattas* are so stiff with starch from being soaked in rice-water that they might splinter as the ancients heave themselves onto the second bench. They adjust their gold-brocaded *kavanis* to doubly conceal their bosoms.

A frowning Odat *Kochamma* sets down her saucer with a clatter and heads out, her bowlegged gait making her trunk sway side to side. The *ammachis* eye her advance with alarm. She squeezes onto their bench, making good use of her elbow, saying, "Plenty of room. Move over." Odat *Kochamma* picks up a *halwa* from the plate the young girl brings around, sniffs, then wrinkles her nose, dropping the *halwa* back and waving the girl off emphatically, rejecting it for the others as well. The *ammachis*' mouths gape in protest, but Odat *Kochamma* ignores them and loudly clicks her wooden teeth. The *ammachis* must peer past their cataracts and past Odat *Kochamma* to see Philipose. Their voices are unnaturally loud because they're hard of hearing.

"Speak to the girl, is it? What for? Just show up at the wedding—that's all he needs to do!"

"*Aah, aah!* Whatever he wants to say, there's a lifetime to say it, isn't there?"

"*Ooh-aah.* Why not he saves some words for when he's old? Words at least he'll still have when all else stops functioning!"

Their shoulders shake with laughter; gnarled hands cover their toothless grins. Odat *Kochamma* pretends she doesn't hear them. She winks at Philipose before she lets out a fart, then glares accusingly at her seatmates.

Philipose feels every eye on him. The air is so thick he can trace letters in it with his finger. Indoors, his mother looks ill at ease, dwarfed by the long sofa that doesn't allow her feet to reach the floor. He notices heads and eyes turning, voices faltering: Elsie must have emerged. He rises, wiping his face one last time with the kerchief. His heart pounds so loud that Elsie can follow the sound to its source.

She's even more beautiful than the woman he remembers from the train cubicle. He's struck dumb, unable even to say hello. They sit side by side. Her coral-and-blue sari forms a serene backdrop for her hands, which are unadorned, not even a bangle. Her fingers sweep off her knuckles in long lines, like the brushes and pencils they wield. He's intoxicated by the scent of the gardenia in her hair.

He clears his throat to speak, but then sees her toes peek out from under the sari's edge and his words vanish. He's back on the train, her soles flashing before him as she climbs to her bunk.

His vocal cords seem frozen. *Oh, Lord, is this what it means to have apoplexy?* He reaches for his hankie, but dips into the wrong pocket; his fingers emerge with a one-chakram coin, the image of Bala Rama Varma on top. He holds it out to her, and then the coin vanishes. He displays his hands, front and back. *Please examine carefully, ladies and gentlemen; satisfy yourself that nothing is concealed.* He reaches for her ear, producing the coin and putting it in her palm.

One of the ancient *ammachis* brings a hand to her mouth, as if she's just witnessed a rape. "Did you see that?" The others did not.

"*Aah*, he did something! Putting this here-there!"

"It was magic," Philipose says at last, conquering speech. His words come out in English, not a deliberate choice, but a good one, as it turns out, if they want privacy. Elsie takes Philipose's hand and turns it over.

"You have nice hands. Hands interest me," she says in English. It was English they had spoken on the train too. He remembers her voice. Its slow, seductive timbre requires him to watch her lips carefully. "I noticed yours the first time I saw you."

"And I yours when you traced that snuffbox," he says.

He notices a fleck of green paint on her palm. His skin tingles where she touched him.

"I have notebooks filled with drawings of hands," Elsie says. He asks why. "I suppose because anything I draw or paint begins with my hands. Sometimes I feel my hand leads and my mind follows. Without a hand I'd have nothing."

"I have a notebook on feet," he says. "Feet reveal character. You could be a king or bishop and adorn your hands with jewels. But feet are your unadorned self, regardless of who you proclaim yourself to be."

She leans forward to look down at their bare feet. She slides a foot alongside his. Her second toe, reaching just beyond her great toe; her clear, luminous nails; and the wavy undulations of the joints all speak to her artistic nature, he thinks. His foot dwarfs hers. Her skin brushes his.

The watching *ammachis* are close to being apoplectic. If they possessed a whistle, they'd have blown it now. "*Ayo!* First putting hands. Now touching feet! Can't this wait?"

Elsie suppresses a giggle. "You hear them?"

He hesitates. "I can't quite make out every word. But I have a good idea." English was a brilliant idea.

"Philipose?" she says, as though trying his name out, and looking directly at him. The sound thrills him. "You asked to talk to me?" She's smiling.

He's lost in her smile and late to respond. "Yes, yes, I did! I broke all kinds of rules by asking. Yes, I wanted to talk. Honestly, may I tell you why?"

"Honestly is better than not-honestly."

"After we . . . After the train . . . I hoped. I mean, it felt like fate that after all those years we were on the same train, the same cubicle, same bench, same . . . We parted too soon. Ever since, I . . . daydreamed about marrying you. But I was someone who wasn't going to finish college. Bent and broken. I worked hard and I'm not bent or broken anymore, and that's when I asked for Broker *Aniyan*. The thing is I remember on the train you said to Meena you weren't ready for marriage. Elsie, *I* want this. I wanted to be sure that . . . that *you* want it too. That it's not being forced on you."

She considers this. Then she turns and smiles, wordlessly conveying, *Yes, I want this*.

"Oh, thank God! I feared your father would want someone like . . . someone more—"

"*I* wanted this. You." It's as though she just kissed him. He feels himself tumbling into her gaze, into the explosion of browns, grays, and even blues of her iris. He wants to leap up in celebration. He grins at Odat *Kochamma*, who winks back at him. She slips off the bench, tossing the tail of her *kavani* over her shoulder and into the faces of the *ammachis*. With her nose held high, she rejoins Big Ammachi, grabbing a piece of *halwa* on her way.

He says, "I'm so lucky. Why me?" Now she's the mute one, uncharacteristically reticent. "Is it a secret?"

She says, "Secrets tend to be hidden in the most obvious place." He's flattered. It's the last line from his first Unfiction, "The Plavu Man." "You really want to know, Philipose? Shall I tell you, *honestly*?" She's teasing, but then she turns serious. "It's because I'm an artist," she says simply. He doesn't quite understand.

"You mean like Michelangelo? Or Ravi Varma?"

"Well, yes, I suppose . . . But also not like Ravi Varma."

"Then like who?"

"Like me." She's unsmiling. "If Ravi Varma had been born a girl, do you think he'd have been free after marriage to study with a Dutch tutor? Or to exhibit in Vienna? Or to travel all over India?

He bought a press in Bombay. A smart move. That's why his prints are everywhere. He met and painted all the famous beauties of his day, the maharanis and mistresses. Got close to one or two of them." *Is there nothing she won't say?* thinks Philipose with admiration. "Philipose, what I mean is that if Ravi Varma had been a woman, there'd be no Ravi Varma."

He understands her point, but not how it relates to him.

"Philipose, you're an artist too." It's flattering to hear this. "You can spend most of your day on your art. There's no one to tell you not to write, or when to write. Marriage won't change that."

He can't argue with that.

"My father had others in mind from the moment I got back. A boy in the estates … another who owns textile mills in Coimbatore. I refused. I thought that of all the men I might marry, you would take my art, my ambition seriously." Her expression is grave as she recounts this. "I'm well provided for. My father isn't pushing me out. But if something happens to him, everything except my dowry, I mean *everything* goes to my brother. That's how it is with our community, isn't it? It's unfair but that's how it is. If I were unmarried, I'd have no home to belong to after his time. That's why he was so anxious to have me married. For my future."

"Men are under pressure to marry too. To please family." He's thinking of Joppan.

"Yes, but after marriage, no one will say, 'Philipose, put aside your writing. Your duty is to serve your spouse and her parents for the rest of your life. Manage the kitchen, raise the children.'" She adds, with a hint of bitterness, "My brother will have the life I should have had. I hope he makes good use of it."

They glance in the brother's direction. His belly swells under a fine double *mundu*; his face is puffy, with dark circles that will soon be permanent under his eyes. He could pass as his father's gluttonous understudy, and for the same reasons, but only at a younger age: cigarettes, and too much brandy. But the face lacks Chandy's humor, his humanity and vitality. Feeling their gaze, the brother looks over with flat, soulless, eyes. *There's no love lost between the siblings*, Philipose thinks.

Elsie moves her head closer to him. "I'm only telling you because you asked. It's hard to explain how much a girl loves her father. Getting married is the best gift I can give him. Then I become your worry. I thought, if I must marry, who will respect me as an artist and allow me to be what I think I was meant to be? I thought you would."

He's flattered. But her words are also a little deflating. Where is *love*? Where is desire in this explanation? She reads his thoughts. "Listen, if what I said disappoints you, I'm sorry. This is just the *pennu kaanal*. You can say you came, you saw, and it's not for you. You can call it off. Or I can. You did ask. So I'm telling you honestly."

Such brutal honesty! Would he ever have had the courage to say what she has said?

"Elsie, the last thing I want to do is call it off—"

"When I drew you that morning on the train, I thought I saw into your heart. I was no longer the schoolgirl who rode in that car with you. And you were no more the brave boy who saved that child. I saw a man struggling to find his way. You've found your way—I see it in your stories. When the proposal came, I was happy. I thought, here's someone who sees the world the way I do. Who hungers to interpret it as I try to do. Tell me I didn't get that part wrong."

"No. You got that right. Just so you know, I don't want to get married for the sake of being married. I want to get married to *you*. And when we are married, I'll do everything to support your art. How could I not?"

She's pleased. "You're sure? Your dear mother is hoping that I'll take over the kitchen, keep the keys to the *ara*, make a good fish curry. She'll be scandalized when the fishmonger comes and I don't know *mathi* from *vaala*—"

"Wait, you don't? In that case—" He pretends to stand. Her wing-like eyebrows shoot up and then she bursts out laughing, a lovely bell-like sound. The perfect line of her teeth, the sight of her tongue, the back of her throat make him dizzy. "Elsie, as long as you laugh like that, I won't care. I promise you. You'll have the same time and opportunity to pursue your art as I have to write. You don't know my mother yet, but she's a gem. She'll understand."

"Philipose . . ." she says softly, grateful, dropping her head, and sagging against him. He leans back against her, supporting her weight, the ancient *ammachis* be damned. His arm where it touches her is on fire. His heart leaps, his pulse pounds, not in fear or panic but in recognition of having found what it sought. He's proud of himself. The Ordinary Man has managed something extraordinary.

CHAPTER 46

Wedding Night

1945, Parambil

After six years of war, it is just about over. Two and a half million Indian soldiers will be demobilized, including, for the first time, hundreds of Indian officers. During the Great War, the British never appointed any Indian officers, worried that they'd be training future rebel leaders. They were right. Now the returning Indian officers are men decorated for their valor; men who witnessed soldiers under their command die to free Abyssinians, to free the French, to free Europe of Hitler's yoke. They won't abide anything less than freedom for India. The British stupidly announce that those Indian soldiers captured by the Japanese and then forced to join Subhas Chandra Bose's Indian National Army or else have their heads cut off are to be tried as "traitors." The fury of every Indian soldier and the Indian public terrifies the British. If a single garrison mutinies, nothing will stop the dominoes from falling. Two hundred thousand British civilians in India could be slaughtered overnight by three hundred million natives.

In Travancore, a groom-to-be rides the airwaves night after night, witnessing from Parambil P.O. the liberations of Leningrad and Rome, of Rangoon and Paris. He adds fresh sheets to extend his wall map, but the Pacific war is impossible to draw on any kind of scale. He prints the names next to dots: Guadalcanal, Makin Atoll, Morotai, Peleliu. Men have died in droves on those tiny islands. It's all senseless. And personal: one of the potter's grandsons enlisted for no other reason than for the sign-on bonus and the salary. The poor fellow died in North Africa.

He and Uplift Master decide to close the Feeding Center because the food supply has steadily improved. Philipose can't help feeling that the changing tide of war, the optimism in India about imminent freedom, is linked to the change in his own fortunes.

They wed in the church where Big Ammachi was married and where Philipose was baptized. When Elsie enters, she draws the *pallu* of her sari over her hair, her eyes down as prescribed, right foot first over the threshold. There's a collective gasp at the beautiful bride, perhaps the first to marry in a sari in this church. Philipose thinks a golden aura surrounds her like a dusting of cinnamon. Instead of weighing herself down with her mother's jewelry, she has a solitary bangle on each wrist, a thin gold chain with a pendant, and gold earrings. At nineteen she has the poise, the sureness, of a woman who has lived twice as long. When Philipose studied himself in the mirror one last time before church, he had the opposite impression of himself: a twelve-year-old boy trying to pass for twenty-two.

Joppan, in his finest *mundu* and *juba*, stands proudly with Uplift Master and the Parambil relatives on the men's side at the very front. But despite all Philipose's entreaties, Shamuel refuses to step into the church. He watches through a window.

Chandy's long, sleek, finned Ford, decked with roses, carries the couple home. They approach Parambil on the newly widened driveway, on one side of which the huge white *pandal* is filled with seated guests. On the other side is the hulking form of Damodaran, who understands the significance of the occasion. When they emerge from the car, Damo nuzzles Big Ammachi, who reaches up to stroke him. Then Damo hooks Philipose roughly to him and musses his hair as the Thetanatt party gasp. Damo places the jasmine garland that Unni hands him over the bride's head. His trunk lingers, sniffing her cheeks and neck as Elsie laughs in delight. She reciprocates with the bucket of jaggery-sweetened rice that Big Ammachi hands her.

Bearers tear around the tent with steaming platters of Sultan *Pattar*'s delectable mutton biryani. There's the shocking sound of Decency *Kochamma*'s uninhibited laughter, a beautiful high-pitched peal that no one knew she possessed. Chandy's "estate punch," a plum wine named for a saint, is a hit on the women's side.

On the elevated platform, Philipose and Elsie receive a dizzying line of guests, including Chandy's estate friends, several white couples among them. Philipose spots Shamuel outside the *pandal*, looking regal in the bright, mustard-colored silk *juba* that Philipose bought for him and a dazzling white *mundu*. He scowls and doesn't budge when Philipose waves him over. His expression says the *thamb'ran* ought to know better. So Philipose drags Elsie outside, putting his arm around Shamuel to hug the old man, not just out of love, but because he was about to flee.

"Elsie, this is Shamuel, the only father I've really known." Shamuel's shock at their approach changes to consternation at the little *thamb'ran*'s blasphemy. He can hardly look Elsie in the eyes, as his palms come together by his chin. She reciprocates, then bends to touch his feet. With a shriek, Shamuel is forced to grab her hands to stop her. She holds onto his hands, bows her head, and murmurs, "Give us your blessing." Wordlessly, unable to deny her, his lips quivering, his trembling weathered hands hover over both their heads. Philipose tries to hug him, but Shamuel pushes him away roughly, feigning anger. He points to the dais to say they must go back, turning his head so they might not see his tears.

It's nearly midnight before the two of them are finally alone in Philipose's room. In the letters they'd exchanged before the wedding, he mentioned Odat *Kochamma*'s edict that his map must come down to ready the room for his new bride. That triggered a cable from Elsie, a first at Parambil P.O.

KEEP MAPS STOP DONT CHANGE ANYTHING STOP WANT TO
SEE YOU AS YOU ARE STOP

Elsie smiles when she sees her cable pinned to and now part of
the rich annotated tapestry of nations, armies, navies, and mankind's
folly. With Elsie's trunks in the room, it feels smaller. There's a
newly built bathroom adjoining their bedroom; a large tank of water
outside must be filled from the well every morning for it to pour
out of the faucets, though Philipose plans to get an electric pump
soon. Elsie heads off with her toiletries as if she's been doing this at
Parambil for years. Thank goodness she doesn't have to walk to the
outhouse or the bathing enclosure; Philipose bathes in the latter and
hurries back.

He has the oil lamp lit when she returns, its soft glow less
jarring than the naked bulb on the wall. Elsie has changed into
a white nightdress dotted with faint pink roses, while he's in just
his *mundu*, his chest bare. They lie next to each other, looking up
at the ceiling. All through the ceremony, every time their hands
brushed together, he felt a shock up his arm. As they were driven
home, they'd leaned against each other and grinned like little children, as if to say, *We did it!*

He lowers the wick. They lie still for a long time, listening to
the wind stir the palm canopy, a pigeon cooing, the distant clink
of the chain on Damo's leg. The room is dark, but gradually two
pale rectangles of the window emerge on the far wall, the curtain
covering only the bottom half, while the high branches of the *plavu*
outside are silhouetted against the sky. The three developing fruits
dangling at the forks look like young children playing in the tree.

He turns to her, and she rolls to him, as if she had been waiting. Their knees bump awkwardly. He puts his leg over hers, and
she slides hers between his; their feet find each other. He can
just see her face, feel her breath on his cheeks, and register the
scents of toothpaste and soap, and the natural smell of her skin.

Gingerly, her fingers trace his temple, his jaw, his neck—a sculptor measuring. His fingers run through her hair. Their bodies are pressed together, her chest soft against his. She cannot suppress a yawn, and he yawns before she finishes hers. They suppress their laughter. She sighs and burrows toward him. Her head rests in the cove formed by his shoulder and trunk while her long fingers are splayed out over his chest.

His shameful retreat from Madras left him feeling incomplete, the threads of his being tangled and with sections missing. But now, with Elsie docked next to him, he is whole. Her stomach pushes against him, then retreats with each breath, her breathing slowing. He observes this miracle. Then, despite the heart-pounding excitement of holding this beautiful woman—his wife—against his body, he falls asleep too.

When he awakes past midnight, they're still entwined at the legs, but her nightgown and his *mundu* have shifted so that the bare skin of her thigh is against his. He's suddenly as alert as if he'd been splashed with water. The places where his skin touches hers burn. He presses gently against her and, astonishingly, she responds. Her eyes open. He's uncertain as to how, precisely, to proceed. His head drifts closer. She presses against this new hardness of his that wasn't there in the tender embrace before sleep.

Their lips meet, an awkward brushing—exciting, but dry. Not what he had imagined. They try again, a more determined exploration, and now their tongues touch, an electric sensation, and an intimacy so profound that his body tingles. He fumbles with her gown, and suddenly her breasts are exposed. Nothing, but nothing in his life will surpass that first moment of seeing them, of touching them, of feeling her respond. His hand moves diffidently down, while the back of her hand and then her fingers gingerly touch that part of him that cannot be ignored. Their shared uncertainty and clumsiness are as erotic as all that preceded it. He props himself up and over her. He is like a blind man who has stumbled into a corner and probes with his cane, but she guides him with one hand, the other on his chest as a brake. Ever so slowly, she eases him in. She winces, but still holds him. Only when he feels her relax does he move very gently. *Lord*, he thinks, *once you discover this, how is it possible to do anything else?* He has melted into the body of his new bride, their breath, their sap and sinew all one. No self-experimentation and nothing in *Fanny Hill* or *Tom Jones* prepared him for the thrill and the tenderness of what has just happened.

They succumb to a mysterious anesthetic veil that settles over them, thick with their mingled scents. He wakes, remembering what just transpired, and the memory leaves him fully aroused once more, achingly so, wanting it all over again. He wills her to open her eyes, and out of the fog of sleep soon she does, momentarily trying to figure out where she is. She looks suddenly vulnerable, waking up in this new house. Recognizing her state, he gently gathers her in his arms and holds her. He wonders if she is in pain. The way she snuggles against him makes him think that he did the right thing to hold her. After a long while, she pulls her head back, looks at him, and kisses him, her breath tasting of him and of sleep. She whispers something, but he can't quite make out her lips. "Elsie, I struggle hearing the whispered voice. I'm sorry." She brings her lips close to his ear. "I said, 'I don't think if I had married anyone else, I would feel as safe as I do with you.' That's what I said." She nestles back against him, and they fall asleep once more.

They wake in unison. Light streams in through the cruciate vents and windows. The lazy rooster crows, *The-Sun-Has-Risen-Before-Me-Ayo-ayo-adoo.* A distant clang of a bucket against the side of a well, the creak and whirr of rope and pulley. The household rousing itself.

Sweat glistens in the hollow behind her collarbone. Their mingled scent is so rich, so carnal. He wants to tell her how stunning last night's congress was, how . . . But words might only diminish it. Instead, he kisses her eyelids, her brow, and every inch of her face. "I want you to be happy here, Elsie," he whispers. "Any wish that I can fulfill, just say . . . Anything."

The words sound grand even to him. They ennoble him. Benevolent, besotted sovereign, he gazes lovingly at his queen, her straight nose, the eyes so long and narrow, echoing the shape of her face. In the many months after their train ride, he remembered her eyes as close-set, but that was because of the way they sloped down to her nose, his Nefertiti. And memory never sufficiently recorded the delicate Cupid's bow of her upper lip. He's drunk, so drunk on his beautiful bride, his being bursting with generosity, like Emperor Shah Jahan offering to build a palace for his beloved.

"Anything?" she says dreamily, her arms stretched out beside her like wings, her lips barely moving, her eyes half open. "Like the genie in Aladdin's lamp? Are you sure?"

"Yes, anything," he says.

She raises up on one hand, turning to him, her breasts on his chest, a sight so astonishing in daylight that if she asked him to cut off his head in order to keep feasting on the sight, he'd agree. She's amused and pleased by his attention, not self-conscious, remaining just as she is so he may keep gazing. The skin is unnaturally smooth, creamy, and paler than the rest of her before abruptly transitioning to the darker areola. Their passion for each other's bodies, so recently discovered, overtakes shyness. The schoolgirl in the car, the Young Miss who took snuff with him on a train, is now his bride, and her eyes say, *Go ahead, look, kiss, touch* . . .

"Anything," he says, his words slurring with love and sated lust. "And I don't mean building a studio. That, we'll do. I've drawn a plan—extend that south verandah, put a roof over it. It'll have good light, but it's for you to decide. No, I mean anything else. Recapture the Holy Land? Slay the dragon?" He strokes her face.

She studies him, smiling, hesitating. Then she looks to the window—no hesitation there. He follows her gaze, trying to see his familiar world through her eyes.

"I love morning light. That *plavu*," she says, pointing to the tree where the closest jackfruit, the size of a child's head, stares back at them. "It keeps this room dark. You can cut it down. That's my wish."

Cut down the *plavu*? The tree that has watched over him in his sleep ever since he was a boy?

She says, "Beyond it there must be a lovely view."

CHAPTER 47

Fear the Tree

1945, Parambil

*I*t'll be gone by evening, darling! That's what he should say. Instead, he hesitates long enough for the rooster to crow again. "That tree?" he says. The false note in his voice sickens him.

Her gaze retreats. Her smile crumples like that of a child offered sweets only to have them snatched away. In a planet divided into those who keep their word and those who just speak words, she's given her body to one of the latter.

"It's all right, Philipose—"

"No, no, please, dear Elsie, let me explain. I'll cut it down. I will. I promise, yes. But will you give me some time?"

"Of course," she says. But already he feels the fissure, the seam in their union. If only he could step back. Or if only she'd made another wish.

"Thank you, dear Elsie. Here's the thing . . ."

His story "The Plavu Man" struck a peculiar chord with some readers. A few people make pilgrimages to see this *plavu*, believing that his story is real and that this is the very tree described, and nothing Philipose says will change their minds. Others write to him, care of the newspaper, requesting their letters be placed in the tree, tucked into its hollow—their words are addressed to the departed soul they are trying to track down. All this prompted his editor to commission a photo of Philipose in front of the tree.

"The photographer comes soon. Meanwhile, I will also get Shamuel's blessing. You see, he's often told me the story of his father and my father planting this tree when they cleared the land. This was the first. When I was a boy, Shamuel showed me how. We dug a hole, put one giant *chakka* inside, intact. From the hundred seeds inside that crocodile skin, twenty sprouts pushed up. Any one of them could have been its own tree. But we weaved them all together, forced them to be one mighty *plavu*." He has said too much, he knows.

From the kitchen, he hears pots rattling. A raucous crow calls to its mate, *Look at our idiot friend, opening his mouth when it should have stayed shut.*

"Don't worry. Don't ask Shamuel. You don't need to—"

"Elsie, no! Pretend it's gone. Consider your wish fulfilled. Ask me something that I can do right now, ask me—"

"It's all right," she says more gently than he deserves, hunching her shoulders into her nightgown, corralling her breasts. "I don't need anything else." She rises, tall and proud, fastening the buttons from top down until the dark triangle of her womanhood and the gleam of her thighs are just a memory.

She pauses at the doorway. Filtered by the *plavu* leaves, the light through the window illuminates those gray-blue irises that glint like graphite.

"But Philipose? Please . . . please keep your word about my art?"

He hears her faintly outside chatting with Baby Mol, and then with Big Ammachi and Lizzi, their voices bright, happy, hers low-pitched, easier to discern than theirs.

The photographer has come and gone, and weeks and months pass. Every night in the sleepy aftermath of their lovemaking, Philipose tells himself he'll make secret arrangements with Shamuel so his beautiful wife might wake in a pool of light and find that her husband is a man of his word. Elsie doesn't seem to ever think about the tree. It never comes up. But Philipose can't get it out of his head.

The radio spills jazz by a duke from America named Ellington. Philipose sits up close to it, Elsie sketching beside him. He peeks to see what's being born on the page: it's him, bent over the radio, his hair falling into his eyes. A shiver runs through him—pride in her, but also a disquiet that he struggles to name. The sketch flatters him—strong lines for his jaw and delicate ones for lips that are full and sensuous. But whether she knows it or not, she's captured his confusion, his secret fears. He, a flawed mortal—not Emperor Shah Jahan or a genie after all—is dwarfed by her talent; he's no longer sure of himself, searching for the right way to be with her, to be worthy of her.

Inspired by her, Philipose works harder than ever. But work is her resting state, as unconscious as breathing, while he, by comparison, wields his pen too selectively, even though his subject—life—is always there. His art, so he tells himself, is to give voice to the ordinary, in memorable ways. And by so doing, to throw light on human behavior, on injustice. But he simply can't produce in the way she does.

In their lovemaking she sometimes surprises him by rearranging his limbs, asserting herself so completely that he feels like one of Baby Mol's dolls. It's thoroughly arousing. Once sated, she's gone from the world, present only in breathing flesh as he untangles himself. Observing her unconscious form, the disquiet surfaces again: was he the paper, the stone, the charcoal stick, which satisfied her vision of that night's desire? When he takes charge, she gives herself so completely that his doubts vanish . . . only to surface later, a nagging suspicion that a part of her is hidden from view, a locked *ara* whose key he's not entrusted with. Is he imagining this? If he isn't, then only he is to blame: his impulsive promise about that stupid tree is the cause. He cringes whenever he thinks about this, and it festers within. He should take an axe to the tree.

*   *   *

Big Ammachi is smitten with her daughter-in-law. It delights her
to see the couple so happy, her son so preoccupied with his bride.
Before the marriage, he had conveyed to his mother what is now
self-evident: Elsie wouldn't be taking over the household. She was
a serious artist. Big Ammachi had acted annoyed. "Who said I need
anyone to take over? What am I supposed to do if I hand over everything? How many times can I read your column without burning
a hole into the paper?" She's quite content for Elsie to do whatever
she chooses. Elsie chooses to be in the kitchen often, seated on
the low stool, happy to sift through the rice for stones, laughing at
Odat *Kochamma*'s chatter and listening intently to Big Ammachi's
tales. Big Ammachi's affection for Elsie grows each day. Since Elsie's
mother died young, who was there to tell her these stories, call her
molay, comb her hair, or send her for her oil bath? Big Ammachi does
all that and more. Wherever Elsie goes, her tail, Baby Mol, accom-
panies her. Lizzi, Manager Kora's wife, is there a lot; she and Elsie
quickly bond like sisters.

Elsie approves the *ashari*'s plans. Construction begins. Their bedroom (once his father's bedroom) is enlarged to thrice its size. A
third of it becomes Philipose's study, with bookshelves on two walls
and an alcove for the radio at the back, while the remaining two-
thirds is an enlarged bedroom. For Elsie's studio, they pour cement
to make a patio that stretches out twenty-five feet from the back of
the extended bedroom. A peaked roof, tiled and not thatched, covers bedroom, study, and patio. A knee-high brick-and-cement wall
encloses the patio; it will keep out cows and goats but allow lots of
light. It has a broad hinged gate at the back. Rollup coir shades on
all three sides of the patio can be lowered to block the sun or to
keep out rain. The driver from the Thetanatt house delivers Elsie's
supplies: stretched linen; stacks of half-finished paintings; contain-
ers of brushes, pencils, and pens; wooden boxes with paint in tubes

and in tubs; easels; carpentry tools; and barrels of turpentine, linseed oil, and varnish. The scents of paint and turpentine soon become as familiar in Parambil as the aroma of frying mustard seeds.

Big Ammachi overhears Decency *Kochamma* request Elsie to paint her portrait ("in oils, like Raja Ravi Varma"). Elsie demurs. Perhaps in the future. She adds politely that she trusts Decency *Kochamma* understands three things: the artist is free to depict her the way she chooses; the model never sees the work until it's finished; and the portrait belongs to Elsie unless it is being commissioned. With every word, Decency *Kochamma*'s mouth sags further. Only Big Ammachi's presence keeps the woman from saying something cutting. She stalks off, red-faced.

The long chats between Lizzi and Elsie evolve either by design or by accident into Lizzi being the first model. Philipose only wishes he could overhear their extended conversations. He has noticed that Lizzi has been sleeping at Parambil for two weeks now, but he didn't think anything of it until Uplift Master tells him that Kora has absconded. A creditor discovered that Kora had forged land documents he used for a loan; the originals are with another lender and that loan is also in arrears. "Maybe running away was the best plan," Master says. Philipose marvels that Lizzi's face gives away nothing. She's not said a word of this to anyone and no one brings it up with her. Just as news of Kora's vanishing gets out, Philipose gets a special preview of *Portrait of Lizzi*; Lizzi's poise comes across in it; her comfort, her sense of belonging to Parambil are also evident. He's startled to read in the portrait what he missed on the live model: Lizzi's anger, undoubtedly related to the mess Kora is in. Philipose is there when Lizzi gets to see the finished work; she doesn't move for so long that Philipose worries. He and Elsie withdraw. When Lizzi finally emerges, her face shows a new resolve. Silently, she gives Elsie an affectionate hug, nods to Philipose, then heads home.

The family will never see her again. They learn the next morning that Lizzi vanished in the night. Big Ammachi is distraught; she has lost a daughter. "I had told her she could stay with us forever.

This is her home. She didn't say goodbye to me because she couldn't lie to me about where she was going. I suppose she felt it was her duty to go to wherever he is hiding."

Elsie is in tears, feeling that the portrait somehow triggered Lizzi's departure. Philipose says, "If it did, it was for the best of reasons. I think Lizzi saw herself for the first time in your work, saw her own strength. She has known for some time that Kora can't make his life work or provide reliably for her. Yes, she could have stayed here. But she *chose* to go to Kora for one reason only: not to be the dutiful wife, but because Lizzi has decided to take over the reins, be head of the house. Kora will be so grateful, and he'll agree to her terms or be lost forever All thanks to your portrait."

Elsie listens, wide-eyed. "Is this one of your Unfictions?"

"No. It's simply the truth that you captured. Don't you see it? Well, I do. You forget that I've had the experience of being sketched by you. Believe me, it gives the model a profound insight into who they really are."

In the wake of her departure, the relatives come to see *Portrait of Lizzi*. Philipose watches them do just what Big Ammachi did: stare for a long time, drawn into a silent dialogue with themselves as much as with the subject, and emerge subdued. The portrait perhaps helps each viewer come to terms with Lizzi's disappearance. But it also makes them understand something Philipose already knows: Elsie is an artist of the highest rank. Not *like* Raja Ravi Varma, but so much better, a painter with her own vision. Elsie's portraits make Ravi Varma's work look flat and lifeless, despite the theatricality of his compositions.

In June of that year, Philipose ruptures the evening quiet with a cheer that brings everyone to the radio. "Nehru is free! After nine hundred and sixty-three days in prison! It's the acknowledgment by the British that it's over."

Philipose stays glued to the radio late into the night. America, Ireland, and New Zealand broke free from Britain in the past. He pictures Brits in the remaining colonies—Nigeria, Burma, Kenya, Ghana, Sudan, Malaya, Jamaica—sitting by their radios, nervous, because Britain is soon to lose the jewel in the crown, and the sun that never sets on the British Empire is about to do so. Negotiations for a free India are already underway. The road ahead is treacherous because Jinnah and the Muslim League want a separate homeland for Muslims, who make up almost one third of India's population. Jinnah doesn't trust the Hindu-dominated Congress Party.

Elsie is reading when he climbs into bed. He says, "How did a small island wind up ruling half the globe? That's what I want to know."

She puts down his dog-eared copy of *The History of Tom Jones, A Foundling*. It has consumed her at bedtime for days. "What *I* want to know," she says, "is the effect this rascal Tom had on the young boy who read this book."

"Well," says Philipose, "as a matter of fact—" but she silences him by covering his lips with hers. He fumbles for the light switch.

In August, in the space of three days, atomic bombs level Hiroshima and Nagasaki. A hundred thousand people die in an instant. The Parambil family gathers to stare at the paper's montage of photographs from both cities. Of all the grisly war images seen at Parambil, nothing compares to this.

Later Philipose finds Odat *Kochamma* staring at the newspaper by herself, tears trickling down her cheeks. He puts his arm around her. She pretends to push him away while leaning wearily against him. "I may not read, but I understand more than you think, *monay*. You think I'm sad? Wrong! These are tears of joy. I'm happy that I'm old, so I'll be spared what's coming. If we can kill each other so easily, then that's the end of the world, isn't it?"

He takes down the map montage that covers one wall. War had become a guilty hobby, but he can no longer bear the human suffering cataloged on that map. Elsie watches him, silent. "There are better things I want to remember about the last few years," he says. "I came home to Parambil where I belong. I became a writer. But most of all, you came into my life. Those are the things to memorialize."

A letter arrives from Chandy saying that he's moving up from the Thetanatt house in the plains to the bungalow for the summer; he invites them to visit. Elsie is excited. "It will be so humid here, while there we will have morning mists over the garden . . . You can write. I can paint. We can go for walks, play tennis or badminton. Horse racing too on weekends, if you care to go. You have to see the estate. Everyone is dying to meet you."

"Well . . . that sounds wonderful." But the truth is her every word is making him anxious. He feels giddy and breaks out into a sweat.

"We'll pick a date, and I'll ask my father to send the car, and—"

"No!" he says. Elsie's shocked expression embarrasses him. "I mean, let's think about it. Yes?"

Traces of her earlier smile cling to her lips, unwilling to give up hope. Surely someone who takes fervent notes while listening to the radio, who reads even at the dinner table, who orders more books than the shelves can hold, surely such a man would be eager to explore new territory, experience new things.

"Philipose . . . It's good for us to leave Parambil now and then. See a bit of the world." As an afterthought, she adds, "Good for our art."

"I know." But if he knows, then why is his heart pounding, and why this terrible feeling of dread, as though he cannot breathe? Going to Madras, brief as his stay there was, gutted him. He had to come home to reclaim himself, to reconstruct his being. But not until this moment when Elsie spoke about leaving did he discover that the very thought of it would evoke a terror akin to drowning. Parambil is his solid ground, his equilibrium, and all else feels like water. And it isn't just the going away to far mountains; the rituals of clubs, parties, races will mightily challenge his hearing. People who've known Elsie since she was young will be judging him, which only compounds his fears.

Elsie stands there waiting for an explanation. His fears are irrational, and he's ashamed. He simply cannot admit them to her without diminishing himself, without sounding like a weakling, a complete failure as a man and husband. His thoughts are bouncing around his brain, hurting his head.

"Let the world come to us," he hears himself say at last, and it sounds haughty and harsh. Elsie flinches. It was a silly thing to say, and he knows it. But having said it, he's cornered. There is no retreat. "I have everything I need here. Don't you? I visit every place in the wide world through the radio."

The woman he adores stares at him as though she doesn't recognize him.

"Philipose," she says after a while, her voice quiet, so he has to focus on her lips. Her hand reaches out tentatively, like a child about to pet a beloved dog who is behaving strangely. "Philipose, it's all right. We'd be going by car. No boat, no rivers to—"

This allusion to his other handicap further shames his shrinking, retreating, anxious self, and an ugly defensive and reflexive response bubbles out before he can pull it back. "Elsie, I forbid it," says someone he doesn't recognize, someone using his lips and his voice. The words sound awful as they leave his tongue. "I forbid you to go." There. He's done it.

Her hand recoils. Her features become still. He watches her retreat to that place that's closed to him. She turns away while saying something he misses. "Elsie, what was that?"

She squares herself to him, her head held high. The words he reads off her lips and that also arrive at his ear are without malice, without rancor, with nothing except sadness. "I said that I'm going to see my father."

That night, his wife doesn't come to bed. When he looks for her, he finds her sleeping on the mats with the three others, something she has done only when Baby Mol is unwell and pleads for it. His pride won't let him wake her or risk waking his mother. At dinner, when Big Ammachi asks him what is going on, he pretends not to hear.

The days that follow feel awkward. But silence still feels better than confessing. Besides, how does one rationally explain irrational fears? He tries on a new persona each time he's around her, the way a man might try on a new shirt or grow a mustache, hoping the world (and his wife) will perceive him differently. Nothing works, though. It's on the tip of his tongue every moment they are together to say, "Forgive me, I've been an idiot." But a belligerent voice inside him warns against it, or else he'll be making concessions for the rest of his married life. How long can this feud go on?

Not much longer, as it turns out, because Baby Mol, sitting on her bench, announces that a car is coming. A half hour later, the estate car and driver pull up. Elsie must have written home. She hands a stack of canvases to the driver and returns to their room for more. Philipose follows, furious, disbelieving, conflicted, the blood pounding in his ears. She's putting a hairpin in her locks while gazing out of the window at the *plavu*—

He seizes on it. "Look here," he says. "This is all because of that damn tree, isn't it? I'll take care of it, I told you. But in case you forgot, I forbade you to leave." She turns calmly to regard him, but she doesn't seem surprised or affected by his words. He waits. She's silent, gathering her brushes and combs. Her reaction deflates him. He stands there, feeling sillier by the second.

"Stay in this room then until you change your mind," he says, in too loud a voice, and storms out, slamming the lower half of the split door, but since the bolt is on the inside, he must reach over and slide it into place. He's only looking more stupid: the jailer leaving the keys on the inside. He stands there, breathing heavily, and turns around to find his mother in his face. She came running at the sound of slamming doors and his raised voice. He tries to step around her, but Big Ammachi won't budge till he explains. He mumbles disjointedly about the tree . . .

"What nonsense! Cut the stupid tree down. It's an eyesore," she says. She shoves him aside, reaching over and opening the door. Before she steps inside, she turns to him, lowering her voice. "And don't you see she's pregnant? How silly of you not to go with her!"

He watches helplessly as his wife is driven away.

Over the next week he has time to get accustomed to the shock of Elsie being pregnant, of her absence, of his idiocy. Baby Mol refuses to talk to him. Big Ammachi's anger fades as she sees him moping around the house. "It's good for her to see her family. I wish I'd had that chance as a young bride. If Elsie's mother were alive, Elsie would have gone there to deliver anyway. As much as you like home, you need to get out more, for her sake."

He wants to go to his wife, but he has no idea whether she's in the Thetanatt home or up in the bungalow in the estate—a place he has never been. He writes long penitent letters to both places and waits. A fortnight later, Elsie writes him a short, formal note, making no reference to his letters. She lets him know that she's in the estate bungalow in the hills and plans to stay there another week before returning with her father to the Thetanatt house in the plains. Nothing else.

A week and a day later, he travels to the Thetanatt house for the first time since the engagement. Mercifully, the servant says Chandy and his son are away. He sits in the airy living room on a small sofa, facing that too-long white settee that has more legs than a centipede. One of the framed photos high on the wall is a *memento mori*: the family posed around an open coffin. A six- or seven-year-old Elsie, eyes glazed, stands next to her brother—how did he miss this? It compounds his remorse.

When Elsie emerges, her beauty, the sight of her takes his breath away. She sits across from him on the sofa. If he's been sleepless and fraught during this brief separation, she looks rested, as though being apart has suited her. Pregnancy brings a ripeness to her face, and a deep tan to her cheekbones and the bridge of her nose. She's wearing the same coral-and-blue sari she wore at her engagement—is that a good sign? She looks at him without anger, without anything, the way she would look at a gecko on the wall, wondering what it will do next.

"Elsie, I'm sorry." She says nothing. He's mortified to recall sitting on the verandah with her at their engagement and promising he understood and would support her desire to be an artist. And he did! He has. He does. Yet here he is.

He tries again. "And we're going to have a baby! If I'd only known!" She doesn't reply. He sighs. "Elsie, I was wrong to behave as I did. Like a bullock kicking over the loaded cart." His words seem to sadden her, and perhaps to soften her expression. "Elsie, are you feeling well?"

She shrugs and presses her lips together. He wants to rush over and hold her.

She glances down at her waist. Nothing shows. "My stomach twists . . . I can't stand the smell of paint. I'm doing charcoals. But it did me good to be with my father in the bungalow. To see old friends."

"Elsie, you should see the studio. The *ashari* finished the beautiful teak cabinets for your supplies. I put them all away. It looks so nice."

He doesn't say that in the process he'd understood just how prolific she's been. It made him feel like a pretender. His few inches of musings are published in a regional newspaper in a regional language, even if it has a huge circulation. "Elsie, please understand, after Madras . . . things that take me out of my routine make me feel unsettled, anxious, especially meeting a lot of new people, worrying if I'll hear what they say. When you told me about your father's invitation, at that moment, my heart was racing, I felt faint. But the worst thing is I was so ashamed, too ashamed to tell you the truth, so—"

"It's all right, Philipose," she says. She looks at him with pity and perhaps even affection. He's exposed himself before her. His turmoil, his confusion are the most real things about him. He'd imagined that once he explained, she might come home to Parambil. But now he sees that if he loves her, he must accept anything she decides to do. Still, if only she'd let him sit by her, hold her hand.

The maid brings two glasses of lime juice on a tray that she sets before Elsie. The woman steals a curious glance at Philipose. Elsie brings the two glasses over and sits by him. He sighs, his relief so evident that it must move her. Whenever they sat this close there was a magnetic pull that made them touch, they couldn't help it. Perhaps she feels it because she leans against him and smiles. He reaches for her hand, and their fingers intertwine. A groan escapes him as the agonies of the last month ease.

"Elsie, forgive me," he says. "I love you so much. What am I to do?"

She looks at him with affection, but still wary, still with some distance. "Philipose . . . You can love me just a little less."

CHAPTER 48

Rain Gods

1946–1949, Parambil

Baby Ninan arrives in the year of our Lord 1946, like a summer squall out of a cloudless sky, neither rustle of leaves nor ripple of clothes on the line to offer a warning.

That day, Big Ammachi and Odat *Kochamma* are in the kitchen, the palm spathe and dried coconut husks crackling on the red embers, and smoke seeping out from under the thatch roof as though emerging from hairy nostrils. "*Yeshu maha magenay nennaku,*" *For you, Lord Jesus, son of God*, Odat *Kochamma* sings as she stirs the pot. Philipose is gone to the post office.

"AMMACHI!"

The peace of that blessed morning is shattered. The terror in Elsie's voice that is coming from the main house stops everything. They find her in the doorway to her room, as though trying to prop it up, her hands white as she clutches the frame. Her hair is uncorralled and spilling down to frame a face that is deathly pale. The light illuminating the house is so beautiful that day, so substantial, that one could lean into it, something Big Ammachi will forever remember.

Through gritted teeth, Elsie says, "*Ammay!* But it's much too soon!" She reaches for Big Ammachi as a wave of pain folds her over.

Big Ammachi feels something wet underfoot and sees a clear, reflective puddle: Elsie's water has broken.

In a preternaturally calm voice, Big Ammachi says, "*Saaram illa, molay. Veshamikanda.*" *It's all right. Don't worry.* But it isn't all right. A glance passes between Big Ammachi and Odat *Kochamma*, and without a word the old lady waddles back to find thread and needle, and thank goodness, water is always boiling in some pot in the kitchen. Big Ammachi walks Elsie to the bed, as though escorting a sleepy little girl and not the grown woman who towers over her.

As Big Ammachi washes her hands, she hears Elsie call out from the bed, "*Ammay!*" Not "Ammachi" but "*Ammay*" for a second time. Big Ammachi's heart melts. *Yes, I am her mother now. Who else is there?* She rushes over in time to see a tiny head crown. Odat *Kochamma* returns, lugging the pot of water.

Just then, with hardly any effort, the smallest baby either woman has ever seen lands in Big Ammachi's palm, a wet, blue, limp mound.

The two older women stare in disbelief at this tiny form, this beautiful miniature boy, his life story still unwritten . . . Except, he's too soon for the world. The baby is like a wax doll, chest unmoving. Once more, Big Ammachi and Odat *Kochamma* exchange glances, and the latter leans forward stiffly at the waist, her hands straight back behind her for ballast, her bowlegs planted wider than usual, and directs a hoarse whisper to the tiny curl that stands in for an ear: "*Maron Yesu Mishiha.*" *Jesus is Lord.*

With a start, arms flinging out, the baby cries. Oh, that sweet, sweet, precious, shrill mewl of the newborn, the sound that says there is a God, and yes, He still performs miracles. But it is the faintest of cries, barely audible. His color hardly improves.

Odat *Kochamma* ties and cuts the cord. The placenta slips out. Seeing Elsie propped on her elbows, peering down anxiously at the baby, Odat *Kochamma* says crossly, "Boys! Always in such a hurry!" Big Ammachi gently wipes off the baby—no time for the ritual bath. He weighs less than a small coconut. Husked. She eases Elsie's blouse aside and places the naked child on her bare chest, up high, where he's no bigger than a large pendant; she covers mother and child with a sheet. Elsie gingerly clutches her son and looks down with wonder, with fear, tears trailing down her face. "Oh, *Ammay*! How can he survive? His body is so cold!"

"He'll warm up against you, *molay*, don't worry," Big Ammachi says, though she's besieged with worry. She spots Baby Mol on her bench, unconcerned, chattering away by herself—or to the unseen spirits who let her peek into what is to come. Baby Mol's calmness is either a good sign or a terrible one.

Baby Ninan—that was the name Elsie planned for a boy— looks like a newborn rabbit, his nails barely formed and blue, his eyes squeezed shut, his skin pale against his mother's bare skin. It's all wrong, Big Ammachi thinks. Too early, too small, too blue, too cold, and the father isn't here. The words *"Maron Yesu Mishiha"* are meant to be spoken in the infant's ear by a male relative or priest. She marvels at Odat *Kochamma*'s quick thinking: time was of the essence, and they had both been sure this one would be on his way back to his heavenly father before his earthly one came back from the post office.

Elsie's lip trembles and she looks anxiously to the older women for some sign of what comes next. Big Ammachi says, "He'll hear your heartbeat, *molay*. He'll warm up." Odat *Kochamma* wordlessly removes Elsie's wedding ring, scrapes a fleck of gold from the inside, puts it in a drop of honey, and with her fingertip dabs it onto the child's lip, for every child in the Saint Thomas Christian fold must have his taste of good fortune, if only briefly.

Odat *Kochamma* intercepts Philipose before he enters the house. He listens carefully then says, "Does Elsie know that the child might die?" Odat *Kochamma* pretends not to hear.

Elsie knows. He sees it in the way her face collapses when he enters. He presses his cheek to hers. He peeks at their son. The strength in his legs vanishes.

* * *

Three hours later, Baby Ninan is still of this world, his fingertips less blue and his breathing regular but rapid against Elsie's body. She tries him at her breast, but her areola dwarfs the tiny face, and her nipple is too much for the slit of the mouth. Big Ammachi helps Elsie express first milk, thick and golden, into a cup. "It's the concentrated essence of you. So good for him." Elsie dips the pulp of her finger in, then rests it on Ninan's mouth; a drop dribbles in.

Big Ammachi offers to relieve Elsie. "No!" Elsie says sharply. "No. He knows my heartbeat all these months. He'll stay here hearing it." Carrying him is effortless, like holding a mango to her breast. Still, a sling of soft muslin around Elsie and under the child helps. Big Ammachi caps the baby's head with the same muslin.

That night, three of them hold vigil, Elsie propped up on the bed, Big Ammachi next to her, and Philipose on a mat on the ground. Elsie stares down at her son endlessly. "My body keeps him warm just as when he was inside me. His temperature is my temperature. He hears my voice, my heartbeat, my breathing, just as he did all this time. If he's going to make it, this will be his best chance." The oil lamp illuminates the nascent life in its womb-outside-a-womb.

Elsie sequesters herself from visitors for the next two months. She takes walks on the verandah, Philipose shadowing her. She does not care to read or be read to, or draw, instead bringing every bit of her concentration to bear on their fragile masterpiece. If a newborn normally pushes the father to the edge of the household orbit, this one draws Philipose into the heart of the family.

One night when mother and grandmother are feeding him by the laborious fingertip method, Ninan opens his eyes, the lids separating enough for him to look out and for them to see him for the first time. Big Ammachi thinks her grandson's eyes are so clear, so luminous.

*   *   *

In ten weeks Baby Ninan signals that he has outgrown his nest by stirring his limbs, kicking his feet; when he's awake, his eyes are now more open than closed. He can even suck on the nipple, albeit only for short periods. One day, Baby Ninan snuggles for the first time on a body that isn't his mother's but instead his father's, with its comfortingly furry chest. They quickly oil and massage Elsie and scrub her down with coconut husk before she submerges herself in the stream, luxuriating in the flowing water. She hurries back, restored and renewed after weeks of washing her body in parts.

Big Ammachi gives Baby Ninan his first bath, then they dry him off, swaddle him, and put him down for the first time on the bed. He sleeps. Father and mother lie on either side of their son, getting used to the sight of him separate from his mother's body. The baby suddenly extends his arms, as though he's dreaming that he's falling. Then, the index fingers stay extended, a benediction to his parents. They grin happily at each other.

Falling unabashedly in love with Baby Ninan allows the parents to renew their love. It thrills Philipose that Elsie has a special look for her child's father every time he walks in. Their hands seek each other's, and if no one's around, he kisses her. The brushing of lips used to drive them both mad, but now it signals a new bond, and the patience to defer the other kind.

Whenever he recalls his churlish behavior over Elsie's desire to visit her father's estate, he cringes. "That wasn't me," he says one day and for no reason when Ninan is in his grandmother's arms and the two of them are alone. He smacks the side of his head. "That was someone else, Elsie. A stupid, fearful child who took dominion of my body and my senses. That's the only explanation I have." She regards him indulgently.

Every now and then Philipose looks out the bedroom window and is reminded of his failed promise. The photographer came and went, and the Ordinary Man column is now graced by a grainy photograph of Philipose in front of the tree; Shamuel had no objection at all to the tree coming down. Yet somehow the *plavu* still stands. Thankfully, Elsie seems to have forgotten.

The lump of blue clay that came into the world so precipitously makes up for lost time. His incessant movements and precocious Malayali inquisitiveness leave them all convinced that he instigated his premature arrival; he must have scaled the walls of his confined watery jail, looking for the exit. Now on the outside, he resumes his exploration. Baby Ninan's life mission is very simple: UP! When in their arms, he wants to climb onto shoulder or neck, using their ears, hair, lips, or nose for a handhold. He jumps readily into the hands of any suitor, but what he really wants is locomotion and height. His mother's chest is home, but even the succor of the nipple is trumped by the thrill of being bounced, swung, or tossed up high, even if it makes him gasp and hold his breath. He laughs and kicks his legs to signal, "Again!"

One day, without fanfare, Elsie enters her studio and she's back at her easel whenever the baby allows. Philipose notices her last landscape losing its connection to reality: How can the water in the paddy field be ginger colored, or the sky lime green? Toy clouds line up like boxcars. This exaggerated primitive style is somehow pleasing. Also, giving in to Decency *Kochamma's* pleadings and her promises she will abide by the artist's condition, Elsie embarks on her portrait. Whenever Philipose sees the formidable lady seated and posing, he is convinced she sees herself as a Mar Gregorios, missing only crosier, vestments, and sainthood.

Ninan is uninterested in walking except as a means to climb. *Why use two limbs when we have four?* is his philosophy. Four allow one to ascend. Soon, the dull thud of a tiny body landing on an unyielding floor is an all-too-common sound. A brief silence is followed by a short-lived wail, more indignation than pain, then the climber starts up again. Shamuel says, "He's like his grandfather, part leopard."

Big Ammachi knows that he's like his grandfather and his father in another way: water poured over his head disorients Ninan, sends his eyes bobbing to one side then drifting back to the midline only to hammer sideways again. He has the Condition.

Big Ammachi summons both parents to her room and, mirroring the motions of her late husband, uncovers and spreads out the "Water Tree"—her name for the genealogy. At the time of their marriage, Philipose had told Elsie about the Condition. She hadn't been concerned and besides, she'd heard a little bit about it already. "Every family has something," Elsie had said. What was it in her family? "Drink. My grandfather. My father. His brothers. Even my brother."

Now Big Ammachi guides Elsie through the genealogy. "You'll just have to be careful with Ninan around water. You won't have to teach him to avoid it. He won't want anything to do with water. Unless he's like your husband who kept trying to swim—thank goodness at some point he gave up." Philipose says nothing. He worries about his son's safety in a way he never worried about his own.

Nearing midnight on August 14, 1947, Prime Minister Jawaharlal Nehru's voice comes through the radio, the most exciting words to emerge from it in its existence to date. Earlier that day, Pakistan was born. "Long years ago," Nehru says in an Englishman's English, "we made a tryst with destiny. At the stroke of the midnight hour, when the world sleeps, India will awake to life and freedom."

But India's awakening proves bloody. Twenty million Hindus, Muslims, and Sikhs are forced to uproot themselves from the lands where their families have lived for generations. Muslims stream to the newly formed nation of Pakistan, while Hindus and Sikhs who find themselves no longer in India, head there. Trains packed with refugees are set upon by gangs of the opposite religion. Bloodthirsty mobs crush infants' skulls, rape women, and mutilate men before killing them. Life or death for a man and his family teeters on the presence or absence of a foreskin. Philipose remembers his train journey back from Madras and Arjun-Kumar-Railways, the snuff-sniffer, marveling at how all religions, all castes got on so well inside a railway compartment. "Why not same outside train? Why not simply all getting along?"

In South India, particularly in Travancore, Cochin, and Malabar, they *do* get along. The violence to their north feels as though it's happening on another continent. Malayali Muslims, whose blood-lines reach back to merchants from Arabia who scudded to the Spice Coast in their dhows, have nothing to fear from their non-Muslim neighbors. Geography is destiny, and the shared geography of the Spice Coast, and the Malayalam language, unites all faiths. Once again, the fortress of the Western Ghats, which has kept invaders and false prophets at bay for centuries, spares them the sort of madness that leads to genocide. In his notebook Philipose writes, "Being a Malayali is a religion unto itself."

Just before Baby Ninan is two, a wax-sealed envelope arrives for Elsie, forwarded from the Thetanatt residence. *Portrait of Lizzi* has been accepted for a National Trust exhibition in Madras. Her eyes light up with pride.

Philipose says, "I didn't know you were competing!"

"There wasn't any point to mentioning it. I've submitted since I was fourteen. My father's tea broker and friend in Madras submits for me—he likes my work. But it's always been rejected, till now." She looks at him mischievously. "This year, instead of 'T. Elsiamma' I asked him to submit it as 'E. Thetanatt.'"

"That made the difference?"

She shrugs. "The judges are all men. They think I'm a man. In any case I have to send more pieces to accompany the *Portrait of Lizzi*. I don't have much time."

"Well . . . Elsie, that's wonderful. I'm so proud," Philipose manages to say.

She hugs him, squeezing him so hard that it takes his breath away. Belatedly, he realizes that he should have hugged her first.

He's happy for her, but ashamed to recognize that this news rattles him. Is it that she's used her maiden name? But it's not that. He thinks of all the rejected manuscripts he's grumbled to her about, and the way he would mope around for a few days. Meanwhile Elsie doesn't think her rejections are worth mentioning.

He sees her still gazing dreamily at him, her thoughts far away. Uncharitably, he tells himself that she's picturing her work in the show and getting first prize. But he's wrong.

"Philipose, there's no requirement for the exhibitors to be there. But what if we go to Madras together for the opening. Spend some time, just the two of us. Big Ammachi can care for Ninan. Won't it be exciting to take the train again in the other direction?"

He turns visibly pale, unable to conceal his distress. Sweat beads on his brow. She notices. He comes clean. "Elsie, I promised to come with you to the estate. Any time. Or any other city. Just say so. But Madras? My heart is racing just to hear the word. It affects me bodily. It's the city where I was defeated, humiliated, sent packing."

"Me too, Philipose. That's why I was on that train. But this time we'll be together."

"My darling," Philipose says. He wants to please her, but his throat feels as though it is closing, and sweat is pouring down his face. "I'm so proud of you. Please understand, I'll go anywhere else with you. Kanpur, Jabalpur, Any-pur. Just not Madras."

"It was just a thought," she says. But the sad note in that husky voice catches in him like a fishhook, shaming him. The antidote to shame is indignation, righteous anger. Fortunately, this time he pushes it down; he knows those emotions aren't justified. He's fearful of returning to Madras, and he can't hide it. But he's more fearful of losing her, fearful that she'll outgrow him.

That night, atypically, Ninan climbs onto his mother's chest and stays put, glued there, his legs curled up till he falls asleep, reminding his parents of the time he lived bound to that spot. Elsie says, "It would have been a shock for him if I was away even for a night. I would have missed him too." She looks up at Philipose mischievously. "Would you have missed me if I had gone alone?"

"Terribly! And I would have tortured myself with jealousy imagining you sniffing snuff with a stranger. I would probably have jumped on the next train to join you."

She smiles. She looks down at Ninan. "Well, if we'd gone, at least we'd have missed him together. And we could have replaced painful memories in that city with new ones."

Philipose says, "I know. But let's visit some other city first. Save Madras for when I feel more resilient."

Six weeks later, when he comes to bed and turns out the light, Elsie says, "My father's driver brought a letter today when you went out with Uplift Master. The *Portrait of Lizzi* won the gold medal at the Madras exhibition. And the Decency *Kochamma* portrait got Honorable Mention."

He sits bolt upright. "What? Only now you tell me? I must wake Ammachi, I must—" She puts a finger on his lips. She insists it can wait till morning.

The news is in the *Indian Express* the next day. The *Express* reporter asks why it has taken so long to recognize this artist's skill. By using a name that didn't reveal her gender, she won the gold medal. But was this not the same Elsiamma, and some of the same works that were rejected the previous year by the same judges? (The reporter's source is Chandy's friend and Elsie's ardent champion: the head of the tea brokerage in Madras and the man who submitted her work.) Three of Elsie's paintings sold on opening day. *Portrait of Lizzi* commanded the best price at the auction. The following day, the Malayalam papers quote the *Express* story.

When Ninan is three, Uplift Master speculates that the boy is a budding Congress Party politician because he regularly visits every house in Parambil. He loves pickled tender-mango preserves but eats whatever is proffered, his appetite so astonishing that others wonder if they starve him at home. Fortunately, he has no desire to swim. His eyes are on the heights: the top of the wardrobe, the top of the haystack, the center pole of the roof. His highest ascent to date is Damodaran's back, lifted there by Damodaran, who handed him to a waiting Unni. The holy grail of all ascents is off limits for the prince: the fruiting top of the palm where the tapper makes his living. Emulating his heroes, he sports a cloth belt, tucked into which is a desiccated bone and a twig that stands in for a knife. He has a young *pulayi* in tow; her only job is to keep him as close to sea level as she can. On a memorable evening the family sits on the verandah and watches in astonishment as Ninan scales the verandah pillar, his soles flat against the smooth surface like a lizard's feet, while his hands gripping the back of the pillar provide counterpressure. Before they can react, he's grinning down at them from the rafters.

One morning, when Philipose returns from the post office, he finds Elsie in bed, an anxious look on her face, and her skin burning to the touch. He sponges her with cool cloths to bring the temperature down. For the next few days, the high fever doesn't abate, which suggests to the family that it is typhoid. At some expense, Philipose hires a car and brings a doctor to Parambil from an hour away; he confirms that it is typhoid. There's no specific treatment, he says, and reassures them that Elsie should get better.

Philipose alone nurses his wife, waving off help. He discovers that he's at his best—*they* are at their best—when she depends on him as she does now. Shouldn't love always be this way, like the two limbs of the letter *A*? When she's absorbed in her work, and isn't leaning against him, he feels off-balance, unstable.

By the third week of the illness, she rallies. Philipose helps her with a proper bath, after which she's so weak that he carries her back to bed. She clutches his hand, doesn't let go. Her finger runs into the depression at the back of his thumb between the wrist tendons. Her face breaks into a silly grin. "Sn*iiiiiffff*ing only," she says, stroking the hollow of the "anatomical snuffbox."

"Exactly two sneezings will be there," he says. "Unless it is more." She laughs silently. He kisses her forehead. He feels a surge of tenderness and a strong urge to articulate his inchoate emotions. But that, he knows, is when he is most dangerous to himself.

She asks about Ninan, whom they have kept away from her for the child's safety. "He climbed on top of Decency *Kochamma*'s goat shed and plucked her mangoes," Philipose reports. "She was not happy. She said he was goat above the waist and monkey below. Not flattering to either of us." Elsie laughs, then winces. Her belly is tender. She opens her eyes to look at him. He leans his head against hers so that they're looking cross-eyed at each other, grinning like silly children.

What name can he give to this energy swirling in the room, binding them together. If only he could bottle this elixir that illness has made so potent. Is it possible to love her more? Or to feel as valued as he feels now? What to call it but love? A little later, tears well up in her eyes. Is she thinking of her mother, claimed by this same illness when Elsie was not much older than Ninan? He has a frantic need to comfort her.

"What is it? What can I do for you, Elsiamma? Tell me. Anything—"

Idiot! You did it again! He's embarrassed. On the verge of speech, she gives up. He waits. The vitality that was in the room vanishes, leaving sadness in its wake.

She looks out the window.

"Okay." He sighs, theatrically. "I promise. The tree will go. No more excuses." Her eyes close. Was that what her gaze through the window had meant? In any case, he has made a promise. Again. He won't let her down.

On the first of June that year, 1949, the household is tetchy. Raw, exposed nerves are a pre-monsoon symptom afflicting all on India's west coast. Columnists write crotchety pieces that rework prior crotchety pieces about this irritability, whose only cure is rain. The monsoon always arrives on June 1, and here it is the fifth already. Farmers clamor for the government to act. Mass prayers are organized. In Mavelikara a woman cuts off the head of her husband of twenty-five years. She said that she found her husband's cheeriness and talkativeness unbearable, that something in her snapped.

During this period, with little work for the *pulayar*, Philipose gives Shamuel the order to cut down the tree. The old man listens to the instructions and walks away puzzled.

Philipose sees Shamuel return with a *pulayar* crew, including a rare sighting of Joppan. Philipose often sees Joppan's wife, Ammini, working alongside Sara, but little of Joppan. He heard that Joppan has remodeled his dwelling, bringing in timber to replace the thatch walls and putting in a cement floor that extends out to make a porch. The barge business is thriving again. Ammini works alongside her mother-in-law, weaving thatch panels, and she has taken over the *muttam*-sweeping and gets paid for it.

"First, remove the fruits. Each of you can have one," Shamuel says to the crew. He squats to watch. Sara appears and hunkers beside him. The men lower the heavy, prickly orbs down. "Good thing these fruits grow close to the trunk," Shamuel says to his wife after a while. "They're like boulders! Falling coconuts are dangerous enough, but a falling *chakka* will kill you. Look at my toe if you think I'm joking! You know, don't you?"

Sara acts as if she doesn't hear him and leaves without a word. Shamuel was urinating behind a jackfruit tree, needing privacy as there were women around. He'd fished out his penis—his "Little-Thoma"—and looked down. At Shamuel's age, to get flow going, he had to cough, spit, imagine a waterfall, lean a hand on something, or look up. His tale always finishes with "If I'd been looking down at my Little-Thoma, that would have been the end. If I hadn't looked up, I wouldn't be talking to you now!" He had time to pull his head back before the jackfruit landed on his toe.

As Sara walks away, she thinks, *Why do men look down? Isn't it always there? It won't walk off. Just point and shoot!* She rejoins Ammini to finish a thatch panel. She says to her daughter-in-law, "That man is my life. But if he repeated his *chakka*-landing-on-foot story today, I'd have finished off what the *chakka* left undone."

Once the fruits are down, Shamuel directs the men to amputate every branch near its origins, "just beyond the shoulders." They look puzzled. His nephew, Yohannan, asks, "Why not cut the whole tree down?"

"*Eda Vayinokki!*" Shamuel says. *Busybody!* "Who are you to ask? 'Why' is because the *thamb'ran* asked. Isn't that enough?!"

What's wrong with Yohannan? Shamuel thinks, annoyed. *Did he wake up and forget what it means to be one of us?* The truth is he himself doesn't understand why the tree should be cut this way. So what? How many things has he done because the *thamb'ran* said so? What else matters?

The men chop off each branch with their sharp *vakkathis* by cutting a wedge on two sides until it weakens and crashes down, leaving behind a pointed spear, a sharp stump. Sap pours out at these cuts, and the men quickly collect it in gourds. Children use the sap as birdlime, a cruel practice as far as Shamuel is concerned. But it makes an excellent glue that he'll use to caulk his old canoe. Who would think one could caulk a canoe this late in June? Flecks of white sap dot the men's skin and stick to their *vakkathis*. It'll take oil and scraping with coconut husk to get it off the blades and handles of these machetes.

"That's good wood," Shamuel calls out. "Just keep one branch for me to make an oar. It isn't easy wood, but if you do it right it has a beautiful shine. Take what you want to make whatever you like. Sell it to the *ashari* if you're too lazy, what do I care?"

Soon the air is thick with the sick, cloying smell of ripe jack-fruit. Once the others are gone, Shamuel and Joppan stare at what's

left: a thick, tall trunk with dagger-like arms and fingers. A malevo-
lent goddess. Joppan says bitterly, "This is stupid. People who don't
know what to do with the land shouldn't be allowed to keep it." He
walks off before his astonished father can respond.

From the bedroom, Philipose watches the men as they finish up.
Perhaps Elsie will consider what's left to be a sculpture, a candelabra with a dozen pointy upturned limbs. But he's deceiving himself
and knows it. What's left is an unsightly scarecrow clawing at the
sky. This compromise was meant to give her a well-lit room while
preserving his talisman, but the result is ugly and embarrassing, like
an old man's nakedness. They should just fell this tree. Shamuel is
there alone and Philipose is about to call out, "*O'Shamuel'O!* Have
them just chop the whole thing down," when he spots Joppan next
to his father. Pride stops the words from leaving his mouth. It will
only make him look sillier.

The bedroom *is* brighter, the light revealing a cobweb in a corner. Elsie was right: the tree obstructed the view. And what's this he
sees? He leans to get a better look. A change in the sky? No clouds,
but the blue fabric has a different texture. Also a new scent in the
air. Could it be?

Philipose heads outside. Caesar barks. A gust blows his *mundu*
back between his legs. A flock of birds wheels around, confused. If
he were on the beach at Kanyakumari, he might have seen the great
southwest monsoon rolling in the previous day retracing a path that
brought the ancient Romans, Egyptians, the Syrians to these shores.

He averts his eyes as he skirts the amputated *plavu*. He crosses
the pasture, until he comes to the high bund on the edge of the
paddy fields that extends into the distance, offering an unobstructed
view of sky and a palm-fringed horizon. Others join him from the
nearby huts, their faces taut with anticipation. They've forgotten
that the monsoon will confine them for weeks, drown these parched
paddy fields, leak through thatch, and deplete their grain stores; all
they know is that their bodies, like the parched soil, crave rainfall;

their flaking skin thirsts for it. Just as the fields will lie fallow, so too the body must rest to emerge renewed, oiled, and supple once again.

High in the sky a raptor is motionless on outstretched wings, riding the steady draft. The sky in the distance is reddish, and darker. A flash of light sends a ripple of excitement through the observers. They relish these minutes before the deluge, forgetting they will soon be wistful for clothes to dry properly and not have that mildewed, musty, last-century scent; they'll curse doors and drawers that are stuck like breech babies. For now such memories are buried. The wind blusters erratically and Philipose fights for balance. A disoriented bird tries to fly into the wind, but the gust lifts a wingtip and sends it cartwheeling.

Now Shamuel is beside him, his skin flecked with white sap, grinning at the sky. At last, the leading edge of a dark mountain of cloud approaches, a black god—oh, fickle believers, why did you doubt its coming? It seems miles away, but also already on them, because it's raining, blessed rain, sideways rain, rain from below, new rain, not the kind you can run away from, and not the kind you ward off with an umbrella. Philipose holds his face up, even as Shamuel watches him, smiling, murmuring, "Eyes open!"

Yes, old man, yes, eyes open to this precious land and its people, to the covenant of water, water that washes away the sins of the world, water that will gather in streams, ponds, and rivers, rivers that float the seas, water that I will never enter.

He hurries back to the house, Shamuel on his heels, because there's an even more important ritual that awaits them. From the other houses they come too. They're just in time.

Baby Mol, after a last glance in the mirror, waddles to the front verandah, a short child, her shoulders back despite a spine that is getting more hunched each year, her trunk swaying from side to side like a counterweight to her legs. Once they smelled rain, Big Ammachi hurriedly braided jasmine and fresh ribbons into Baby Mol's hair and hustled her into her special dress: the shimmering blue skirt with the gold border, and on top a silky half-sari that drapes over her gold blouse and is pinned to its shoulder. Elsie painted a big red *pottu* in the center of Baby Mol's forehead and applied *kajal* eyeliner that makes her all grown up.

Baby Mol smiles shyly on seeing the audience gathering, her kith and kin, here to witness her monsoon dance. She feels the weight of responsibility, for if the rains are to continue, everything depends on her. This tradition began when Baby Mol was a child, and since she will always be a child, it will always continue. She stands in the *muttam*, the watchers packing the verandah, or, in the case of the *pulayar*, leaning on the verandah wall, just under the overhang.

She begins swaying, clapping her hands to beat out a rhythm and matching it with her shuffling feet. As she warms up, the miracle occurs: the inelegant, trundling steps become fluid, and soon all limitations—her curved spine, her short stature, her broad hands and wide feet—melt away. Twenty pairs of hands clap with her and cheer her on. She thrusts her arms skyward, beckoning the clouds, grunting from the effort, while her eyes dart from this side to that. It is Baby Mol's own *mohiniyattam*, and she is the *mohini*—the enchantress—swaying her hips, telegraphing a story with her eyes, her facial expression, her hand signals, and the posture of her limbs. Her *mohiniyattam* is earthy, lower to the ground, unschooled, and authentic. Sweat mingles with raindrops in the seriousness of her dance. The message in her gyrations is one that each observer makes for themselves, but its themes are hard work, suffering, reward, and gratitude. *Lucky life*, it says to Philipose as the rain pelts down. *Lucky, lucky life! Lucky you can judge yourself in this water. Lucky you can be purified over and over* . . . When she's done, she has secured their covenant, the monsoon has pledged its loyalty, the family is safe, and all is well with the world.

CHAPTER 49

The View

1949, Parambil

Yet the day after the monsoon begins, Baby Mol is inexplicably restless and unhappy, not sitting on her bench but pacing, not relishing the downpour the way she usually does. They fear that she's ill, that her lungs and overburdened heart are troubling her. She lies with Elsie, who massages her legs while Big Ammachi cradles her head. No one can imagine that Baby Mol is now forty-one years old, not a baby at all yet always a baby. Big Ammachi pleads, "Tell me what is wrong," but Baby Mol only groans and weeps inconsolably, at times talking back sharply to whatever phantasm is whispering in her ear.

At night, husband and wife lie listening to the heavens empty on Parambil, Ninan asleep beside Elsie, and Philipose holding his wife close, both of them troubled by what ails Baby Mol.

The next morning, there's a strange lull and the skies clear. The sun comes out. People venture out cautiously, uncertain how long this will last. Uplift Master hurries over to get Big Ammachi's signature on a tax appeal form. Georgie and Ranjan decide this is the moment to talk to Philipose about a land lease with deferred payments. Shamuel and others are clustered behind the kitchen too, coming to get paid and to be given stored paddy, as is customary at the start of the monsoon. Joppan wanders up from his hut. Odat *Kochamma* takes the clothes out to hang on the line, pessimistic about the prospects of anything drying. No sooner is her task complete than a fine drizzle of tiny needles comes down. She grumbles at the skies, saying it should make up its mind.

A scream shatters the calm, a sound so terrible it arrests the drizzle. Philipose, at his desk, knows at once that it comes from the adjacent room, from Elsie's lips, even though he's never heard such a sound from her before, a full-throated shriek of terror that chills his blood. He gets to her first.

Elsie clutches the bars of their window, still screaming. Philipose thinks she's been bitten by a snake but sees no sign of one. He follows her gaze through the window to the naked *plavu*. What he sees brings bile to his mouth.

Baby Ninan. Suspended upside down, his face white, bloodless, frozen into a surprised expression, his body crooked in a manner that defies the senses.

A pointed, amputated branch of the tree grows out of his chest, blood congealed around its exit in a ragged fringe.

Philipose, screaming, charges outside and up the tree, feeling his legs slip on the wet bark, abrading his shins on the rain-soaked trunk, scraping his hands raw as he claws—how did Ninan get up at all?—but at last getting a handhold on one sharp stump. Fueled by adrenaline and desperation, he finds one foothold and the next till he has reached his son. He tries with one hand to lift him free. Shamuel, who was by Philipose's room when he heard the screams, clambers up behind him now, defying his age, willing himself up behind the *thamb'ran*. Joppan arrives in time to see his father reach Philipose. The old man's body, the color of the bark, is pressed against Philipose. He can smell Shamuel's hot breath scented with betel nut and *beedi* smoke as together—and it takes them both— they grunt and pull at Ninan, needing first to lift him clear of the spike. They heave up, and with a sickening sucking sound, the torso comes away from the pointed stump.

The body slips from their hands to Joppan and the many hands waiting below, and Ninan is laid on the ground, limp and unmoving, his spine at a crooked angle, rain now falling on his inert body and on all of them. Shamuel clambers down, and when he's clear, Philipose, not bothering to climb down, just pushes himself off the trunk from that height, and lands hard, yelling from the lightning pain that shoots through both ankles as his heels smash the ground, but in the next instant bending over his son, shouting, his voice carrying over the fields and through the trees. "*Ayo! Ayo! Ente ponnu monay!*" *My precious child!* He screams, "*Monay!* Ninan! Talk to me!" refusing to accept what his eyes show him, deaf to the cries of Elsie and Big Ammachi or the others hovering over him, deaf to the wailing, the beating of their breasts, the retching sounds. He hears none of it, because Ninan's midsection is the world caved in, a dark pit of horror, the center of a universe that has betrayed a child; betrayed the mother, father, and grandmother and all who loved him. Everything that belonged to the small body—breath and pulse and voice and thought—is gone and is dead, is beyond dead.

He gathers up his broken boy. When hands try to restrain him, Philipose fights them off, beats them away. He cradles his son in his arms, a lunatic intending to run into the gathering darkness of monsoon clouds. And if not to those healing clouds, where is he running? For a man on broken, crooked ankles seeking help for his firstborn, the nearest hospital is farther than the sun.

Shamuel and Joppan trot behind this crazed figure, Joppan's hand around his childhood friend's waist, around the hobbling creature that shouts, as if rising decibels might rouse what can never be roused again, "*Monay*, don't leave us! *Monay, ayo Ninanay!* Wait! Stop! Listen to me! *Monay*, I'm sorry!"

The men of Parambil—uncles, nephews, cousins, laborers— alerted by the wails, follow in the blood trail, falling in behind father and deceased son. Less than a furlong down the road, Philipose is still staggering forward like a drunkard on wobbly ankles, his left foot unnaturally turned inward, sobbing, and the men weep too, grown men, surrounding him but not daring to stop him, a measured march alongside a father who thinks he is running when he's barely shuffling, and finally just standing in place, swaying like an ancient.

His ankles buckle and they catch him; the strong arms of Parambil lower their brother down, ease him to the earth, to his knees, while he still clutches the terrible load in his arms. Philipose, face upturned to the heavens, screams, beseeches his God, any god. God is silent. Rain is the best that heaven can do.

It is Shamuel, the eldest and the noblest of these men, squatting tenderly next to Philipose, who alone has the courage and the authority to gently disengage the father's bloody hands. Shamuel covers the little boy with his own unfurled *thorthu*, and somehow this faded, utilitarian cloth transforms into a sacred shroud, the embodiment of the old man's love. Shamuel gathers the little *thamb'ran*'s body into his arms, cradles him carefully, lovingly, his old bones creaking as he rises; Ranjan, Georgie, Uplift Master, Yohannan, and ten other hands help old Shamuel rise, brothers one and all, every barrier of caste and custom erased in the terrible solidarity imposed by death, while Joppan alone tends to the shattered father, lifts him to his feet, ducks his head under Philipose's arm, encircles his waist, and supports him, half carries him as he limps on what are clearly broken ankles.

The wailing women have retreated to the Parambil verandah, crying, keening, or quietly weeping, cloths clutched to their mouths. Elsie is on her knees, her hands held to her chest, while Big Ammachi clutches a pillar and Odat *Kochamma* silently, rhythmically, strikes one fist, then the other to her breast, groaning, her face upturned, and they all wait. They'd last seen Philipose staggering down the road on feet that were grotesquely turned, his son's limp form in his arms; the women had hoped against all hope that somehow once he was out of sight, the father, or God, or both, could work some miracle, make the broken boy whole, make what was crooked straight.

Then all hope is shattered for the women as they see the phalanx of fathers and sons returning, a wall of mustached, fierce men, arms over each other's shoulders, brothers in heartbreak, walking as one, sobbing or clear-eyed, but every face distorted by pain, contorted with grief and anger and shock and rage. With them is the broken father, a madman, one arm over the shoulder of Joppan, held up by his childhood friend, whose muscles bulge and strain under the load until Yohannan slips under Philipose's other arm.

In the center of the phalanx is Shamuel, all but naked, wearing only his mud-colored loincloth, his *mundu* lost on that cursed tree; Shamuel, walking with great dignity, his eyes straight ahead, his the only face that is composed, his bare torso squared to the unloveliness of what he carries in his arms, which his *thorthu* cannot fully conceal; Shamuel, slowly approaching the waiting women, his pace measured, as if every minute of his toil over his lifetime, clearing this land with his *thamb'ran*, the never-ending labor that shaped the sinewy biceps and plate-like pectorals, was leading to this moment, to this sorrowful duty: to bear in his arms with great solemnity his late *thamb'ran*'s last-born's firstborn, who now joins his ancestors in the blessed hereafter.

After the burial, Philipose leans heavy on crutches, looking out the window to where the *plavu* once stood. Without asking anyone, Shamuel has cut down the remnant of the *plavu*. Shamuel vented his fury and his grief, savaging the tree with his axe, and Philipose only wishes he could have been there to take the place of the tree, so the old man's axe might have torn into his own flesh. Joppan came uninvited to join his father, to help him—indeed, to take the axe from him as Shamuel's blows became increasingly wild and reckless, and soon Yohannan was there too with others, and this time they spared none of it, attacking it viciously, digging out every last root and then filling the crater so that not even the scar of its existence showed, a brutal execution for a cursed tree. Philipose wishes they had finished him too, buried him in that spot, in that muddy soil where already the moss fed by blood and monsoon rain grows to conceal any trace of where a tree once stood in Parambil.

Shamuel tells Philipose later that they found a piece of Ninan's shirt on the penultimate branch, twice as high as where his body was impaled. He says nothing more, but both men picture the little fellow getting his shirt caught on that high branch, dangling there momentarily before the fabric tore and he plunged down onto the pointed, upturned spear of the branch eight feet below. Philipose was in his study, working. He never heard the fall, only the mother's subsequent scream.

There is far too much light in this bedroom now—obscene, hateful light. Philipose seethes with anger at himself. For not seeing Ninan begin his climb. For not hearing his son cry out. For not cutting down the tree altogether. Or leaving it be. This is all his fault. But . . . if Elsie had never bothered about the tree, *his* tree, if she'd respected his work as he had hers, then his Ninan, his firstborn, would still be alive. When Elsie stated her wish so many moons ago, if only he'd said "No!" Or said a true "Yes." In a life, it is the in-betweens that are fatal; indecisiveness killed his son. But in his grief, in his bitterness, at this moment he thinks it all began with Elsie's fateful wish: "You can cut down that tree."

Why was it all so difficult? All he ever wanted to do was love her. Since the moment of his betrothal has he not been endlessly accommodating? Changing his practices so that hers can flourish? That is what has killed little Ninan—*her* stubbornness. Some part of him must know this is unreasonable even as he thinks it. But his mind can't accept the alternative. If it's all his fault, what earthly excuse does he have to be still breathing?

He hears footsteps behind him, and he knows without turning that she's walked into the room. He and Elsie have not been alone with each other since the death. He turns to face her, hobbling on his crutches, ignoring the pain, his anger barely concealed.

He meets an anger that matches and exceeds his. Her eyes show rage, and something worse that he cannot abide: blame. Her face is as hard as the iron bars in the window and furrowed by dried tears that salt the skin.

The air between them is thick with the bile of recrimination and contempt. She dares him to accuse her, and he dares her to give words to what she's thinking.

Then she looks over his shoulder and registers that the lethal, murderous remnant of the tree is gone . . . but it is much too late. Her eyes come back to him. He won't forget her expression as long as he lives. Hers is the face of a vengeful god.

He senses her primal urge to launch herself at him, strike him, claw at his eyes, flay his cheeks with her nails. He can see the trajectory of this assault in his mind's eye, and his own feral leap to block the charge with his hands, to shove her away, curse her for wanting what she should never have wanted, accuse her of killing his son, condemn her for coming into his life and bringing nothing but tragedy.

In the next instant she looks right through him, just as for years she looked through that *plavu*, pretended that its ugliness wasn't there and that her view was unobstructed. At that moment she has made him vanish, wiped him off her canvas, so that what's left is a smeared surface that holds the false lines, the figure that did not come out right, the erroneous strokes of a marriage, and a world botched beyond repair and not what she ever imagined. She brushes past him, bumping him aside with her shoulder—the hollow, invisible, less-than-ordinary man, the husband who isn't there—as she gathers a few things.

He hears drawers opening and closing. Then he hears her say to someone, "Let's go."

Part Six

CHAPTER 50

Hazards in the Hills

1950, Gwendolyn Gardens

The scrape of Cromwell's knuckles on the kitchen door and the wet smack of gumboots being shed begin their nightly ritual. Digby's trusted comrade pads barefoot into the study, always in khaki shorts and short sleeves. And always smiling.

"Make mine a double," Digby says as Cromwell pours. Cromwell's grin widens.

One drink, and never alone, is Digby's rule. "A matter of self-preservation. An estate hazard," he might say if asked. It has been fourteen years since he acquired Müller's estate for the consortium that consisted of the friends who had gathered around the Mylins' dinner table on a New Year's Eve. Thirteen since he earned a portion of it, which he named Gwendolyn Gardens after his mother. Over that time he's witnessed the fall of three assistant managers at neighboring Perry & Co., young men who knew their way around a pint back home. It was a grand adventure at first: bungalow, servants, company motorcycle, and being the laird of more tea, coffee, and rubber than they knew existed. But they'd underestimated the loneliness and isolation of the first monsoon and found the antidote in the bottle.

His only regret about his estate is its distance from Franz and Lena. Even in fair weather it's an all-day drive south, past Trichur and Cochin, to reach the vicinity of Saint Bridget's and then several hours' climb to get to AllSuch. His family, such as it is, consists of Cromwell, the Mylins, and Honorine, who comes every summer for two months. When she leaves, a melancholy descends on him. Without Cromwell, without this nightly ritual during the monsoon, he might be lost.

Cromwell disdains chairs and hunkers near the fireplace, the glass under his nose, whisky to be breathed as much as sipped. That mix of deliberation and pleasure is in everything he does. Digby thinks of him as ageless, so he's perversely pleased to see gray creeping over his friend's temples. Digby keeps his own hair closely cropped, which makes his graying less evident. He's forty-two, but looks considerably younger; Cromwell, he guesses, is slightly older.

In this nightly ritual, they "walk" through Gwendolyn Gardens' nine hundred acres. If it were all coffee, it'd be easy, as coffee needs little labor—even less labor after they switched to robusta when leaf rust wiped out their arabica plants. On a magical morning in March, a hundred acres of Gwendolyn Gardens will look blanketed in snow because of an overnight explosion of the glorious white coffee blossoms. But competition from Brazil has driven down prices. Tea is very profitable and forms the bulk of the estate, but it's the delicate child that demands the most laborers. Being closer to the equator, their tea can be plucked all year round, unlike Assam and Darjeeling. The demand is insatiable. In the warmer, lowest reaches of the estate are the many acres of rubber trees.

"On eleven 'arpin. Sliding. Same place as before," Cromwell says at the end of his report.

I knew there was a reason I wanted a double. A landslide on the eleventh hairpin bend is a disaster. They'll run out of their stock of paddy in a week; for their laborers, the provision of rice is more critical than giving them their wages. Digby pictures the spot, the road ending abruptly in a crevasse of mud, boulders, and uprooted trees. Just above it, water springs mysteriously from the flat mountain face. A stigma. The tribals place cairns there, offerings to Varuna or Ganga, but the gods are not appeased. The treatment is painful: they must hack down parallel to the landslide through dense forest till they get below it, then cut across and back up to join the ghat road again. Every estate will pitch in. Workers will carry headloads along this U-shaped detour till the road is rebuilt. The detour could become the new road.

The next morning the monsoon ceases as though a switch was flipped, the incessant drone of rain on the roof silenced. For so many weeks, Digby's view was of swirling mist or, rarely, when the clouds settled in the valley, he'd be staring down like Zeus at the tops of cumulus and thunderheads. When he steps out, it's bright and sunny; the processing sheds and the thatch of the clinic have the soaked, bedraggled look of a pariah dog caught without shelter. Despite the landslide, his spirits soar.

Skaria, the compounder, scurries to the clinic, sporting a sweater the color of bilious boak. Tobacco smoke pours out of his nostrils and thickens in the chilly air. The man is so addicted to nicotine that he sucks on vile cheroots as though they were *beedis*. Seeing Digby, he holds his breath to conceal the smoke as he salutes. The jumpy Skaria can manage a routine sick call, but in an emergency he's worse than useless, he's an impediment.

Cromwell brings the horses around. He's bleary-eyed but grinning. Somehow he has already visited the landslide, taking every able-bodied person with him to start on the bypass. He reports that a cow is about to calve, while the polydactyl cat in the same barn has given birth to kittens. "Babies also six fingers! Good luck only!"

Digby mounts Billroth. The mud embankments flanking the driveway are green with "touch-me-not" and twitch in response to a sudden breeze, just like the skin of his colt. He gets goose bumps at the sight. He could drop a toothpick in this sod and it would soon be a sapling. From city boy to surgeon to planter. The fecund soil is what keeps him here; it is the salve for wounds that never close.

Billroth suddenly pulls back his ears and whinnies, well before
the sound reaches Digby: the rattle of a bullock cart moving at
breakneck speed, and contrary to the physics of wooden wheels,
fragile axles, rutted roads, and bovines. Then it comes into sight, the
bullocks wide-eyed, trailing ribbons of saliva, while the driver whips
them as though the devil is on his tail.

Cromwell trots forward to meet the cart. After a brief exchange,
he points to the bridle path. It ends in a squat building with the
thatch pulled down over its ears like a bonnet. The clinic.

"They coming from other side of mountain," he says. "Landslide there also. Turning and come this way. Someone told doctor is
here. Not good."

Digby experiences only the fear, not the heady excitement he
once felt in Casualty at engaging with human life reduced to its core
elements—breath, a pumping heart—or their absence. He knows
what *should* be done for most emergencies, but he doesn't have the
means. For things that *aren't* emergencies . . . well, more than a
few estate managers have discovered that if they're looking for the
friendly GP willing to drop by because Mary or Meena is off her
porridge, Digby's not their man. He has furnished the dispensary
well enough to care for his laborers, but he's a planter first. In an
emergency he'll do what he can, but he can't help feeling resentful
and apprehensive about what he might see.

"SIR, DIGBY, SIR!" Skaria shouts, emerging from the clinic, waving his arms in that ghastly sweater. Billroth trots toward the clinic;
the colt knows where duty lies even if his master is conflicted.

A baby's fist sticks into the air.

What confuses Digby's senses is that it emerges from a slit of a
wound in the belly of its very pregnant and utterly frightened mother.

The tiny, clenched hand looks intact, uninjured. The mother,
in her twenties, lies on the table, conscious—quite alert, in fact.
She's striking, with curly black hair framing a fair, oval face. Her
blouse is green, and her sari and silky underskirt white. This is no

estate laborer. The small pendant at her throat—a leaf with raised dots forming a crucifix—marks her as a Saint Thomas Christian. Her face is hauntingly familiar, beautiful in a generic way, Digby thinks. Perhaps it's her resemblance to the calendar image of Lakshmi so ubiquitous in the laborers' quarters and in shops, a print of a Raja Ravi Varma painting. His mind can't help registering these details: the wedding ring, the dark circles of fatigue around her eyes, and her admirable composure, as though she's wise enough to know the alternative is not helpful. Behind that façade, this lovely woman is terrified. And embarrassed.

The skin over her pregnant belly is stretched taut. The two-inch incision is slanted just to the left of the navel, too neat to have come about except by a knife or a scalpel. Blood trickles slowly from one edge; she's not in danger of exsanguinating. Digby pictures the blade passing through skin, then the rectus muscle . . . and then straight into the uterus, which, since she is close to term, has grown out of the pelvis, pushing bowel and bladder back and out of its way as it reaches the ribs, completely occupying the abdomen. It's the only reason she will have been spared torn intestines: the blade simply pierced the abdominal skin and muscle and encountered a bigger, thicker, and stronger muscle: the uterus. It made a slit, a porthole in the womb, and the baby reacted like any prisoner: it reached for daylight.

The infant's fingers are curled into a fist, the gossamer nails shining like glass. Digby swabs the wound and the fist with antiseptic while making these observations. The iodine stings the mother but doesn't seem to bother the baby. Had she presented to a hospital, they'd certainly have done a caesarean. In theory, Digby could do one. He has chloroform stored somewhere, if it hasn't evaporated. But lacking good abdominal retractors and with no capable assistant, a caesarean in his hands could easily endanger mother as well as baby.

He ponders his options. But he's distracted by a compost-heap, cheap-tobacco stink that reminds him of the Gaiety in Glasgow, a memory better buried. He turns to see Skaria at the window ledge, the vile cheroot on his lips. The man knows better than to smoke indoors or around Digby. But the flustered compounder couldn't help reaching for the soggy stick, like a baby seeking a nipple.

Digby's left hand, now his dominant one, moves with the precision of a pickpocket on the Saint Enoch railway platform. He snatches the cheroot from Skaria's lips and—

—in the same sweep, brings its glowing end to those infant knuckles, the red-hot tip a tenth of an inch from its skin.

The universe teeters in indecision. Then the tiny fist makes a slithery retreat into its watery world, snatched back in response to the noxious insult. The space where the fist hovered is now just shimmering air, charged by what's no longer there. In Digby's brief surgical career he's seen round worms crawl out of gallbladders; seen germline tumors containing hair, teeth, and rudimentary ears; but never anything like this.

Digby flicks the cheroot in Skaria's direction and grabs a sterile bandage, pressing it down onto the wound. "Custody of the hands," he says aloud, addressing the fetus. (He imagines the bairn raging in the womb, blowing on singed knuckles, cursing Digby and plotting revolution.) *Custody of the hands.* In his Glasgow schooldays, Sister Evangeline punctuated those words with a ruler to the knuckles.

"That baby's fist will get it into trouble one day," Digby mutters. Skaria has fled, and so he takes the mother's hand and places it over the bandage, has her apply pressure.

Outside he hears a man groaning, muttering, then letting out a bloody yell; whoever that is sounds drunk or delirious. He hears Cromwell intervening.

Digby mounts the curved needle and suture on a long holder, and signals for the mother to remove her hand from the wound, praying the baby doesn't try another escape. He spreads the wound edges just enough to see the uterine wall pressing up. Thankfully, the uterus, with its visceral nerve supply, isn't sensitive like skin. As quickly as he can he passes the needle through the wall of the womb on one side of the rent, and then through the other side, ties the knot and cuts the thread. The mother doesn't flinch. He puts in two more uterine stiches. Now the baby's only way out is the front door. He closes the skin with two stitches. She winces once but says nothing. If he used local anesthetic for every skin laceration he sutured he'd use up his precious tetracaine in a week.

"Right, then. All done," he says, looking around for Cromwell to translate. The mother is pale, exhausted, but still calm.

"Thank you so much, Doctor," she says, in English, startling him. He studies her anew: the gold earrings, the carefully trimmed fingernails. He asks for her name. Lizzi. He introduces himself.

"Are you having any contractions, Lizzi?" She shakes her head. "How far along are you?"

"I think I'm having two more weeks."

"Good. I hope you'll deliver normally. But best to be in a hospital when labor starts, all right?" She signals yes with an earnest, childlike movement of her chin. The shouting outside is distracting. Who can be drunk this early? "For now, stay here. It could be a few days before the road opens."

He turns to prepare the dressing. "Doctor," she says. "It was an accident."

How many women have said that before? And how many doctors, policemen, nurses, and children have heard those words and known differently? It's a mystery why a woman would protect a man so unworthy of it. Celeste's face flashes before him.

"That's my husband. His name is Kora," she says, pointing in the direction of the racket. "He is an estate writer." Such men are brokers who contract with the village headman down in the plains for estate labor; the appellation comes from the broker's act of writing each laborer's name in a ledger. Unscrupulous headmen often sign with several writers, leaving an estate high and dry when the season starts. Digby is lucky to have workers who return faithfully every year, because he's taken pains to ensure they have the best quarters, medical care, a one-room school, and a nursery for infants.

"My husband lost his mind suddenly last night, Doctor. He thought I was the devil."

"You mean he was fine before that?"

"Yes. But having severe asthma only. Here in mountains his asthma is very bad. He takes asthma cigarettes usually, but three days it didn't help. Yesterday he ate one cigarette. Maybe ate more. His eyes became big. He cannot sit down, hearing voices. Devils are coming to get him, he says. When I brought him food, he was hiding behind the door and attacked me. Then he is very sorry."

Digby's grandmother smoked pre-rolled stramonium cigarettes. In India he knows asthmatics roll their own using dried stramonium or datura leaves. The atropine in the leaves dilates the bronchi; but in excess it produces a characteristic poisoning with dilated pupils, dry mouth and skin, fever, and agitation. Every medical student knows the aide-mémoire to recall the signs: "Blind as a bat, hot as a hare, dry as a bone, red as a beet, and mad as a wet hen."

"It could be atropine poisoning. I'll take a look. He should get better as it wears off. Are you from around here?"

The question seems to make her sad. "No. We are from central Travancore. We used to have a house and property and loving family. But he . . . we lost it all. He borrowed from dangerous people. Much trouble. He ran away. I could have stayed. Sometimes I wish I had."

This is more information than Digby sought. He forgets that she views him not as a planter but as a physician, someone she can confide in. After her ordeal, talking about it is cathartic for her. It's no effort for him to stand there and gaze at her classical features, the idealized Malayali beauty.

They're both silent. Then, and for the first time since she arrived, her composure wavers. Her lip quivers. "Doctor, will my baby be all right?"

He regards the lovely face that looks at him so earnestly. His thoughts are interrupted by another wild yell from her husband outside. In that moment Digby has a glimpse into her future, a disturbing premonition of doom, something he has never experienced. "Baby will be fine," he says to her reassuringly. Relief washes over her features. "Just fine." He hopes that's true. "Your baby has great reflexes—that we know. He had his fist out there like Lenin," he says, trying to lighten the mood. He extends his hand over her belly, his palm down in pastoral blessing. He leans over to speak directly to the baby: "I proclaim you Lenin, evermore. If you're a boy, that is." He grins, though his scar still gives a slight snarl to that expression.

"Lenin Evermore," the beautiful Lizzi repeats, her head moving from side to side, emphasizing each syllable as though she's memorizing it. "Yes, Doctor."

CHAPTER 51

The Willingness to Be Wounded

1950, Parambil

Ninan has been dead six months, and Elsie gone from Parambil for just as long, husband and wife having turned on each other, when Big Ammachi and Uplift Master travel to the Thetanatt house in their somber finest. The last time Big Ammachi was in Chandy's house was six years ago for the engagement. On that visit, the room had echoed with Chandy's booming laughter. Now, the poor man is in a coffin in the center of the room, wreaths of jasmine and gardenia around him. His earlobes and the tip of his nose are turning dusky. If he were alive, he'd object to the cloying scents of the flowers and to being discreetly splashed with eau de cologne to mask the odors. Big Ammachi finds herself once again seated on the long white sofa in Chandy's house, her feet dangling awkwardly off the floor, wishing Odat *Kochamma* were seated beside her as she had been the last time.

Lord, in just six months how many funerals have you had me attend? If there's to be one more, make it mine. First, you took Baby Ninan. Let's not talk about that. Then Odat Kochamma. *Yes she was old. Either sixty-nine or ninety-six.* "You pick," *she'd say.* "It's one or the other. Why do I need to know?" *But did she have to die on a visit to her son's house? We prayed and slept in the same room more nights than I've slept with any soul other than Baby Mol. You should have let her be with me when you took her. After that you came for Shamuel's wife, clutching her belly one day and dead before we could get her to a hospital. Enough, Lord. You're all-powerful, almighty, we know. Why don't you sit down and do nothing? Pretend it's the seventh day for the next few years.*

Oh, it's pure blasphemy, but she doesn't care. She's like an aged rubber tree that no longer oozes in the wake of the tapper's blade, emptied of tears though not of feelings—or so she thinks. But tears come anyway when she hears the women singing "Samayamaam Radhathil." *On the Chariot of Time.* That dirge is entwined with the memory of her father's death—the worst day of her life—and reinforced by every loss that has followed. The chariot's wheels are always turning, bringing us closer to the journey's end, to our sweet home, to the Lord's arms . . . *But Lord, some, like JoJo and Ninan, just got on board. What's your hurry?*

Earlier, when she arrived at the Thetanatt house, Elsie flew into her arms, her body shaking with sobs that would not stop. All she could do was wipe the young woman's tears away and kiss her and hold her. "*Molay, molay,* Ammachi feels your pain." It had been six months since Big Ammachi had seen her daughter-in-law—Elsie had left right after the funeral. Big Ammachi was shocked to see how thin she had become, her hair suddenly white at the temples; it was such a troubling sight in one so young.

Big Ammachi had desperately wanted to say, *Where have you been,* molay? *Do you know how much Baby Mol and I ached for you?* There was so much to tell her daughter-in-law, things Elsie might have wanted to know, such as that Lizzi had finally written, but without a return address, to say she has had a baby boy . . . but of course this wasn't the occasion. Instead, Big Ammachi had held Elsie, and sat with her on this sofa for the last two hours because

Elsie wouldn't let go of her hand; the poor girl looked like a haunted child that was trying to find a place where life could not inflict more pain. And so Big Ammachi offered herself; she offered her arms, her hands, her kisses . . . and her willingness to be wounded. Isn't that what mothers did for their children? What else was a parent to do?

In the cemetery, as soon as the casket is lowered, Uplift Master says, "We must leave, Ammachi, if we're to get back tonight." Elsie clutches her mother-in-law's hand, weeping, not wanting her to go. Big Ammachi says, "*Molay*, I'd stay but for Baby Mol . . ." She wants to add, *Won't you come back with me? Parambil is your home. Let your Ammachi care for you there* . . . But of course, with so many guests at the Thetanatt home, Elsie has to remain, and it would be an unkindness to ask. Moreover, the rift between Elsie and her son is so great, it's unlikely her pleading will make any difference.

On the bus ride home she gazes in wonder at endless paddy fields, at a leper sitting on a culvert, and into houses in whose dim interiors she sees an old man reading, two girls playing, women cooking . . . Families living their lives, no one spared the pain. All these people will one day be shades, just as she too will be buried and forgotten. So rarely does she travel away from Parambil that she forgets that she's the tiniest speck in God's universe. Life comes from God and life is precious precisely because it is brief. God's gift is time. However much or however little one has of it, it comes from him. *Forgive me, Lord, for what I said. What do I know? Forgive me for thinking that my little world is all that matters.*

After a short boat ride, they walk home from the jetty. She thanks Uplift Master. She sees Parambil ahead, a faint silhouette against the sky, just as she saw it as a bride half a century ago. No lamp has been lit, and no bulb turned on, which only deepens her annoyance with Philipose.

When the messenger arrived with the news that Chandy had suddenly passed away at his estate, she'd hurried to tell Philipose. "You must go. Be with your wife," she had said. "Then maybe, after a few days, you can bring her home." He'd been reading in bed, his pupils tiny pinpricks. He'd laughed. "Go? Go how? I can't stand up for long, let alone walk any distance. And why should I go with my crutches and sit there like a pimple on her forehead that she doesn't want? She blames me. I *am* to blame." He was now so guilt-ridden that whenever she scolded him, he welcomed it. She'd given up and asked Uplift Master to accompany her. "My son has become a knife that can't slice, a fire that can't warm a pot of coffee."

Baby Mol has divined already that her mother is back without Elsie. She retreats from her bench to her mat. Big Ammachi hears her sniffles. Baby Mol so rarely cries.

Big Ammachi lights the lamp. Philipose hobbles out of his dark room, squinting like a civet cat. He's down to one crutch. The broken right ankle has healed, but the shattered left heel remains painful. No one quite understood how badly he'd hurt himself leaping from the *plavu* after retrieving Ninan's body, not till the next day when his ankles looked like Damo's, even the same gray color, but twisted. The unbearable pain of losing Ninan was compounded by physical pain.

He slumps down on Baby Mol's bench. Big Ammachi sits by him, willing him to ask about Elsie. Instead he absentmindedly roots around the tucked-in end of his *mundu*, like a monkey searching for lice, till he finds the tiny wooden box. She notes that his nails need trimming as he pries the lid open to reveal the wafer of opium. Every household has such a box, the old person's panacea for backaches, insomnia, and arthritis. Big Ammachi used it for her husband's headaches. She wishes she'd never given it to Philipose. Her son has become an opium eater.

He's preoccupied, scraping with the bamboo toothpick to get a curl of opium, then rolling it between his fingers, an annoying back and forth to shape a shiny black pearl. When she was a child, that pearl had looked beautiful to her when her grandmother ate it. Once, her grandmother had let her lick her finger; the vile bitter taste made her retch. She's tempted to slap it out of the hands of her once-handsome son, but it's already in his mouth. He says, "Amma-chi, can you bring me a little yogurt and honey?" She gets up before she says something terrible. Let him get his own yogurt.

A few weeks after Chandy's funeral, she writes to Elsie again. Her letters thus far have gone unanswered, but she needs to convey to Elsie that her beloved Baby Mol's breathing is worse than ever. Baby Mol's real sickness is her wounded soul. She hardly eats, say-ing she'll eat when Elsie comes back. Big Ammachi writes, "When people she loves leave, it's a kind of death. I beg you to visit." She leaves out so much in the letter. Lizzi has written again, but with-out a return address—she doesn't want her whereabouts known apparently. Lizzi says that while pregnant, she had an accident in which the baby's hand escaped from her belly. Miraculously, the baby, named Lenin, was born healthy. Nor does Big Ammachi mention Philipose disappearing one day, then returning with a new bicycle, having skinned his chin, his knees, and his elbows in learn-ing to ride. The purchase was triggered by Joppan refusing to buy opium for him, saying he must stop. After Ninan's death, Joppan had stayed with Philipose for weeks, sleeping in the same room. Now, because of the opium, they have fallen out. Big Ammachi suspects the bicycle's only purpose is to allow her son to purchase his own opium from the government shop by the church. None of this does she mention in her letter to Elsie.

Baby Mol's condition deteriorates further. In desperation Big Am-machi writes a last letter, a short one—it seems futile to keep writing.

> *Dearest Elsie,*
>   *I pray this gets to you. Baby Mol is dying. Call it starvation or heartbreak, they are really the same thing. As one mother to another, I beg you to visit. All Baby Mol says is "Where's Elsie?" If you come, she'll eat. Then she might live.*
>   *Your loving Ammachi*

Philipose sits shaving on the verandah, the mirror propped on the ledge. The sun is out. The so-called monsoon petered out after it started, proving to be an impostor. In the mirror's reflection Philipose sees a figure coming up the path. A beggar, he thinks. No, it's a woman in a white sari, carrying not even an umbrella. She's tall, pale, gaunt, and beautiful. His heart cavorts. A wave of gooseflesh covers his arms.

Is he hallucinating? If this is Elsie, why isn't she in the Thetanatt car? From the fog of memory he recalls Shamuel mentioning a collapsed culvert, changing the road to gushing stream. Only foot traffic can cross by clambering over a log fifty yards up.

Mouth agape, his face soapy, Philipose stares at the wife he hasn't seen for a year. At times he'd imagined she never existed, that their life together was a dream. Memories crash down on him now: the schoolgirl, the bride he brought home, their first night, the cursed tree . . . He sits paralyzed, like a stone sculpture. Not ten minutes before, Baby Mol, who hadn't risen from her mat for days, appeared at his elbow, saying, "Visitors are coming!" If he'd paid attention he could have bathed, put on a singlet and a fresh *mundu*.

Elsie stands there like the goddess Durga, her gray-opal eyes on Philipose. He worries about his appearance: the flat spot at the bridge of his nose from one bicycle fall, the cauliflower ear from another. The ground unfairly beckons his left side. Her faint flowery scent reaches him, one so different from what he remembers.

"Elsie!" he says, razor in his hand. *El-sie*. Two syllables standing in for his joy, their shared sorrow, and the forgiveness he seeks even if he's unable to forgive himself. Being bereft of speech now is a blessing—words have never served him with her.

"Philipose," she says. She looks past him and her hollowed-out face lights up as Baby Mol waddles into her *chechi*'s arms, chortling. Elsie sets her down, shocked at seeing cheekbones that were never visible, or Baby Mol's blouse hanging off the collarbones. Big Ammachi emerges hearing auspicious sounds and embraces Elsie, saying simply, "*Molay!*"

Philipose looks on with envy. The most important women in his life are one frieze of black tresses, white sari, gray hair, bright ribbons, and a turmeric-stained *chatta*. They disappear into the kitchen. In the mirror he sees the Ordinary Man's gaping mouth ready to catch flies.

CHAPTER 52

As It Once Was

1950, Parambil

Like a vengeful God, the real monsoon arrives soon after Elsie; it punishes them for being taken in by the pretender. Torrential rain and typhoon-force winds bend the palm fronds into peacocks' tails before snapping them. Wind rushing through the windows makes the eerie sound of someone blowing over the mouth of an amphora. The electric pole crashes down, silencing the radio. Shamuel ventures out and returns shocked: past the burden stone is a new lake with no sign of its far shore. The legendary floods of 1924 caused destruction all over Travancore, but never troubled Parambil. Now the swollen stream where Big Ammachi bathes threatens the huts of the craftsmen and the *pulayar*. The river spills its banks, washes away the jetty, and for the first time in Big Ammachi's memory, it can be seen from the house, stalking the dwelling that her husband made certain was out of its reach. By the fifth week, their awe at nature's violence gives way to dejection. The land begs for mercy. There's no vocabulary for their deepening sense of isolation. The newspaper hasn't graced the house since the monsoon began.

Big Ammachi worries about Elsie, who spends hours pacing the verandah, even at night, studying the sky, looking desperate like a mother who left her baby unattended across the river. There was a time Elsie could be so engrossed in her drawing that she wouldn't know if the roof blew away. Elsie planned a short visit, but all the same, why this hurry to leave?

Once Philipose realized that Elsie only came to visit Baby Mol and had no plans to stay, he withdrew, gave up any attempt to interact with her. He rarely sees her; for him the distinctions between day and night are blurred because of his little pearl, and he is increasingly a nocturnal creature. A few times he sees her patrolling the verandah, staring out at the rain as though if she looked long enough it would stop. He almost laughs when he hears her outside his window ask Shamuel if there is any way to mail a letter. The old man says the post office is submerged. Philipose is tempted to call out, *You're a good swimmer, Elsie. Why not deliver it in person?*

One night he wakes just before midnight and, out of habit, he pushes aside the curtain and peers out. He makes out a figure perched on the verandah ledge, knees drawn to chest, a stone woman, an apparition perhaps, staring at the sheeting rain. His stomach knots with fear till he recognizes Elsie. Her face, cast with shadows, looks so altered, so burdened. Seeing her weeping, he feels pity despite himself. He sits up to go to her . . . but then stops. His presence might be no comfort; it might make it worse. She's become a stranger. He knows nothing about her life in the last year. But he's puzzled. *Why such anguish? Why is it so important to leave? What is it, Elsie?* This isn't about Ninan, surely.

He must have dozed off, because when he opens his eyes, the sky is lighter. Did he imagine Elsie? He looks out and she's still there, her back to him, bent double over the low wall, retching. This time he hurries out. Seeing him, she straightens up, sways, and he grabs her before she falls. He guides her to Baby Mol's bench. She sits hunched over, clutching her belly. He brings her water. "Elsie, my Elsiamma, tell me. What is it?"

Her expression as she looks at him is so full of suffering, of torment, that it sends a shiver through him. Instinctively he holds her to him, comforts her till the spasm eases. For the briefest moment he's certain she's about to confide in him, to unburden herself. He waits . . . He sees her change her mind. She drops her gaze. "Maybe it was the pickle . . ." she mumbles.

He lets go. No pickle ever produced this grief. He says, "It didn't trouble me."

"You've hardly had a meal with us," she says, her voice hoarse.

"I know . . . I work and sleep at odd hours."

Unconsciously, he copies her posture: hunched forward, looking down. His right ankle is swollen; the left is askew, a permanent state. Her feet are as he remembers them, more tanned perhaps, the toes more flexed. An image of their feet side by side at the engagement comes to him. A chasm separates that memory from this moment. He breathes in her new scent that is utterly foreign. At one time their bodies shared the same fragrance, a function of the water, the soil, and the food of Parambil. Baby Ninan's hair, he still remembers, had a sweet, faint, puppy-dog odor on top of the family scent.

Elsie looks out with the hopelessness of a condemned prisoner. She shakes her head. If he hadn't been staring at her lips, he would have missed what she said: "I never planned to stay this long." Again, her eyes fill up.

Her words wound him. The rain picks up, as though voicing his frustration with her. How can they heal if not together? At last, he says, "It isn't just Baby Mol who needed you here." His misshapen foot twitches of its own volition.

His words give her pause. She looks at him anew. "I'm sorry," she says, brushing at her eyes. "It was hard to remain here after Ninan . . ." Perhaps it occurs to her that he didn't have that choice, because she adds, "But I didn't escape anything. It was still there with me. Every moment. As it must be with you. I knew Baby Mol needed me. Big Ammachi needed me . . ." Her voice drops to a whisper. "You needed me. But I couldn't." She puts the glass down. "I'm going to lie down, all right?" Her hand grazes his shoulder, apologetically, if not affectionately.

Two days later, Philipose sees the sun refract through orange clouds, giving the land an ethereal glow. It's gone in seconds, but by then he's in a frenzy, mounting his bicycle and pedaling furiously. He nears the end of the driveway, weaving around puddles, picking up speed, exhilarated—

When he opens his eyes, his vision is obscured. Even a lover of soil doesn't choose to embed his face in it. How long was he unconscious? Rain hammers down. He turns to one side. A pair of bare feet approach, fair at the ankles and painted bronze with mud below. Elsie helps him sit, then slowly rise. "I don't know," she says when he asks what happened. "I happened to look out and saw something on the ground. Then you moved." Skin is gone on his elbow. His left knee throbs. His shoulder aches. He leans heavily on the crooked bicycle as they head back in silence, both of them drenched. He feels for the box in the waist of his *mundu*, relieved that it's there. He needs it badly, but not in front of her. Suddenly he bursts out, "Elsie, we can start again. Build a new house elsewhere on the property. Or move away." She doesn't look at him or answer. After a while he says, more to himself than to her, "How did it get this way? It's all my fault." Rain, or tears, or both streak down her face.

In his room—once their shared chamber—he hurriedly rolls a pearl, an extra-large dose for the pain in his knee, his shoulder, his ankles, his head . . . and his heart. After bathing, he drifts off, floating in a womb, bumping gently off cushioned walls. He stirs when he feels rather than hears the creak of the wardrobe beside him. It's Elsie, her back to him, retrieving her old clothes after bathing. Usually, she sends Baby Mol on this errand, but he knows Baby Mol is under the weather. A *thorthu* corrals Elsie's wet hair, and the damp *mundu* wrapped around her torso leaves her shoulders and legs bare.

She's tiptoeing out with her bundle when, impulsively, Philipose grasps her hand. She looks startled, a mouse caught in a trap. He lets go.

"Elsie . . . please. I beg you. Sit a moment." She hesitates. She shuffles closer, then gingerly sits on the edge of the bed. "I want to thank you," he says, taking her hand again. Her gaze stays on the ground. The simple act of cradling her fingers brings him comfort. "But for you, a bullock cart might have rolled over my head. But for you . . ." His voice breaks. "It's my fault. Did I already say that?" He gently reaches for her chin and lifts her face up. "Elsie. Forgive me." Her expression startles him. The mouse looks uncomprehendingly at the trapper asking forgiveness. Is she registering what he's saying? She turns her face and her lips move. "Elsie, I can't hear you."

"I said, I'm the one that needs forgiveness."

He laughs, an awkward sound. "No, no, my Elsie! No. The world knows my dignity is gone. My legs are gone. My son is gone. My wife is gone. But as far as who did wrong, that's mine. Don't rob me of the only thing that I own." He sits up, wincing, and puts his arm with the skinned elbow around her. Pain doesn't matter. His tone is jocular. "Elsie, you were born forgiven. Can we get back to this wretch, please? He needs forgiveness, mercy."

He doesn't register that she's not responding to his attempted humor. The despair he saw the other night is cast permanently over her features, and it wounds him. If it heals him to hold her hand, surely it heals her too? The *mundu*'s knot at her chest is coming loose. He can't make himself look away. He's embarrassed by the surge of blood in his pelvis. *No, that wasn't my purpose at all when I asked you to sit, I swear by the monsoon god.* But desire has its own vocabulary, more cogent than words his tongue might shape; despite him, it comes to the forefront.

Feeling a flood of tenderness, he embraces her. She doesn't stop him. The *thorthu* slips from her hair, and when she reaches up to catch it, the knotted *mundu* comes fully undone. *I didn't make that happen. It's the universe, or fate, or the god of* mundus *and* thorthus, *the god of misunderstanding, the god I don't believe in.* She clutches at the *mundu*, but his hand gently stays hers. He kisses her cheek, then her eyelids. She trembles, her face so sorrowful that it pierces him. He wants only to console her, but he's also overcome with a familiar awe, the old wonderment that this exquisite woman is his wife. *Lord of disappointments, lord of sorrows, tell me, why bless me only to take away?* He feels her body enlarging before him, and his too—is this the doing of his black pearl? Her lips are fuller, the hollow at her throat that he so loves is wider, the dark areolae larger—all her most sensual features exaggerated and growing under his gaze.

How much pleasure their bodies used to give each other! No matter what else was happening, that never failed them. This could be the balm they need to make the unbearable bearable. After their loss, they never gave themselves the chance to weep on each other's shoulders. They'd turned viciously on each other instead. He sees it all, sees what they should have done. He runs his fingers through her wet hair, hair so thick it always felt like a living thing separate from her. He gently draws her down to lie on the bed. Not forcing her. He sees the door is wide open, so he rises slowly, painfully, and limps over to bolt it. Her head is turned from him, her thoughts far away, as though she has forgotten his presence, but as he approaches, she looks at him, taking in his scabbed, scarred body, an artist's gaze, but not free of curiosity and concern.

He climbs onto the bed. Her pupils are the opposite of his: large and bottomless. Her feet against his feel callused and rough, not the creamy, delicate feet of memory. She's been going barefoot, a sure sign of a husband's neglect. He kisses the hand that shields her breasts, and his lips encounter a hard ridge on the side of her index finger. He can imagine her working her fingers to the bone in her pain, plying her brushes day and night to reshape a world that has gone crooked. Her complexion is pale and patchy. He feels more remorse at further evidence of his neglect. "Oh, Elsie, Elsie," he says, his heart breaking. "This is mine to make right, to make whole." She doesn't seem to understand, but it doesn't matter, as long as he does. They are perfectly matched, he thinks, both of them weathered by grief and time. And what is time but cumulative loss?

His lips are on hers, but hesitantly. He doesn't want to force himself on her. He will stop if it distresses her. But weren't kisses what always resurrected them? A kiss can never say the wrong things. He wants to laugh, recalling their clumsy first kisses, pressing lips together as though sealing flaps of an envelope. They became experts. But she has forgotten. *It's for me to remind her. My duty to resurrect those lips and open our hearts.* He does so tenderly, and he imagines she responds. Yes, he tells himself, there was movement in her lips—not passion, but that will take time.

He cups her breasts, circles the nipples with his fingers. He can hardly contain himself. Her eyes are closed, tears leaking from the corners, and he understands, because how can this not remind them of Ninan? She doesn't resist, nor does she reach for him as in the days of old. *It's all right, my love. It's all right. I'll do all the work. Isn't this what we need? The balm of Gilead, the cure for what ails us.*

It used to be that when their two bodies were in motion, they became like the ecstatic temple carvings of Khajuraho, pivoting this way and that, sheets falling to the floor. *But there's time for all that*, he thinks as he takes the upper berth. This is not about his need, only his desire to convey his love, his caring. Slowly, gently he probes, explores, touches, and when he feels her readiness, he enters. Now they are one body. He moves for them both. And at once, despite his best intentions, he experiences the rise and the surge, the selfish need, the born-again feeling, and hears her name rise in his throat, speaks it so urgently that for the first time she opens her eyes, and out of the black holes of her pupils a nameless other looks back— but he is too far gone, and he collapses into her, and inside her, the only woman he's ever been with and will ever be with. What counter to death is there than this? This is forgiveness, this is the end of solitary mourning. Joy and sorrow, triumph and tragedy are the weeds and flowers of their Eden, and it will outlast the mortal blooms of this world.

* * *

After a time, he does not know how long, their still and private orchard quakes, and she moves from under him. His eyelids are as heavy as rowboats as she sits up and reaches for her *mundu*. He's floating off, sated, his heart at ease, the barrier between them dissolved. He experiences déjà vu seeing her on the edge of the bed, her back to him, her arms raised as she corrals her hair, twisting it around her palm and then into a knot, her elbows forming the points of a triangle that frame her head, the curve of her beaded spine echoing the inward curve of her waist, the outward curve of her buttocks. She turns to him, doesn't meet his gaze but puts a hand on his chest, her eyes closed, head bowed, as though praying over him, staying that way for a long moment. She stands and he knows that next she will delicately wipe the damp *mundu* between her legs . . .

Except she doesn't. She fastens the *mundu* and picks up the folded clothes she'd set down. At the mirror, she pauses to see that she's covered. Her reflected eyes meet his, and he smiles drowsily, this too a reenactment of their old ritual. But a stranger stares back at him, a soul already departed from this world but granted a backward glance at her former life. She pads out without a word.

CHAPTER 53

Stone Woman

1951, Parambil

Without the nightly disembodied radio voices, without a newspaper, without even such news as the fishmonger carries, they feel like the last humans left on earth. A terrified Decency *Kochamma* wades from household to household, shouting for the inhabitants to repent if the village is to survive. A bare-chested Philipose stops her from crossing the threshold of his house. He informs her that the families all agree that if Decency *Kochamma* alone were to sacrifice herself to the river, the magnitude of her sins are such that God would be appeased.

When they've all but given up, the monsoon tapers to a stop. It's still two weeks before the newspaper resumes delivery. They learn that hundreds have drowned, thousands are displaced, and cholera and dysentery are rampant.

When the post office reopens, Philipose is nervous, because it means Elsie could soon leave. His pride won't let him ask her, and besides, he's never alone with her again. Late that night, his bamboo spoon scrapes the bottom of his opium box. The sound is as chilling as a ship's keel striking rock. All night he rubs menthol balm over his body and groans with pain. The next morning, he rides and walks his bicycle to the opium shop, passing through slimy fields of mud, and gagging on the stench of dead fish that were marooned by receding water. Three fidgety old men wait outside the opium shop, sniffling and scratching. *I'm not like them.* Philipose struggles to corral his restless hands. Krishnankutty opens late and without apology. The sole opium licensee in the area has nummular scars of smallpox on his cheeks and dotting his bulbous nose. One eye drifts off, daring the customer to guess which to address. Krishnankutty uncovers the motherlode— a shiny lump the size of a man's head, its moist surface like the sweat-sheened back of a laborer, and giving off a musty, repulsive stink—and cuts a wedge . . . but then feels a sneeze coming on. He rubs vigorously above his lip, while the rudderless globular tip of his nose flies back and forth, until the sneeze is averted. The balance beam on his scale has hardly settled before he wraps the piece in newspaper and tosses it at his customer. Philipose bites his tongue, loathing himself for swallowing such indignities. Once outside he quickly rolls a pill thrice his usual dose. He gags on its bitterness, but his shrieking nerves sob in relief.

Soon the gnawing body aches and the belly cramps are gone. The clenched fist that was his heart now opens. He smiles at strangers who eye him warily. Already, whole volumes are shaping themselves in his head, itching to be written down. Some might imagine the black pearl is the source for such inspiration, but that's absurd. The ideas are always there! But pain is the padlocked door, the stern gatekeeper locking them inside. The little pearl merely frees them, and his pen does the rest.

Approaching the house, he hears an odd hammering sound. Elsie in her smock, forearms coated in dust, pounds on a stone in her studio. But what a stone! It's the size of a bullock, but broad at one end and tapered at the other. How did it find legs to get there? Shamuel and his helpers must have dragged it in from outside. And those tools: the mallet, big chisel, and the rasper? The blacksmith, no doubt. It pains him to think that she converses more with Shamuel and the blacksmith than with him. But the feeling passes when he realizes that the ambition of this undertaking means she's staying! He stands, mesmerized, watching her swing the heavy mallet with practiced, masculine strokes, her hips swaying to the rhythm. She's so absorbed in her task that not even a stampede of elephants would distract her. He retreats to his room to work, inspired by her example.

He intends to join the family for lunch, if not for dinner . . . but he drifts off. It's midnight when he wakes up. The house is still. He randomly opens a page in his bible, *The Brothers Karamazov*. Even when he isn't paying attention, the feel of the words, the cadence, and the reentry into the dream in Dostoevsky's head are soothing. He reads: *God preserve you, my dear boy, from ever asking forgiveness for a fault from a woman you love.* "*Chaa!*" he says and puts the book down. For once, Dostoevsky's tone is contrary to his mood.

The next morning, Elsie is neither in the kitchen nor in her workspace. When he goes to the room where the three women sleep, Baby Mol stops him, finger to her lips. "You can't go in."

"What? It's nearly ten. Is she not well?"

His mother walks by and says, "Shhh!" Has everyone gone mad? When Elsie pounds on a stone for hours, that's somehow all right, but now *he's* too loud? He opens his mouth to protest but Big Ammachi puts her fingers on his lips. "Keep your voice down," she says, smiling. "She needs the sleep of two people. That's how it was when I was carrying you."

He stares blankly at her.

"*Chaa!* Men! Always last to notice," she says, pinching his cheek before heading to the kitchen with a verve she hasn't shown for ages. His knees go weak. Since that one night that they were intimate he has hoped that Elsie might come after the others slept, her lips curved into that temple dancer's smile of desire. But she has not. And yet God—*their* God, not his—had decreed once was enough! A baby! A second chance! They'll start anew. Why didn't she tell him? He goes to his room to wait for his wife to wake up.

He falls asleep and is woken by the sound of chisel on stone. Standing in the doorway to her workshop, he sees the fine hairs on her forearms outlined in dust, glistening like silver wires in the light; there's a patina of dust on her forehead. She does a slow dance around the rock, shifting her weight from hip to hip. Watching her, he thinks, *The God who failed us is making amends, making overtures after urinating on our heads*. He feels such lightness. The weight of disappointment is lifted and—

A new thought follows, an idea so exciting, so outrageous, so full of joy and redemption . . . No, he won't let himself say it aloud. Not yet.

He appears at dinner to the surprise of all. Elsie rises to bring him a plate, but he stops her. "I ate earlier." He didn't. Big Ammachi sighs and goes to the kitchen to get him yogurt and honey—that is what he subsists on. When he's alone with Elsie he says, "I heard!"

She tries to smile. Then, without warning, her face crumples and she's fighting back tears. Of course, he understands: the blessing of a new child is also a reminder of their loss.

Two days later, Baby Mol announces from the crowded bench where the ladies gather now as a ritual, "Baby God is coming." Elsie, fresh after her bath, braids Baby Mol's hair. Big Ammachi waits for her to finish, holding a cup of hot milk for Elsie.

Ten minutes later, Philipose's very first teacher, the *kaniyan*, lopes up the path, sweating from his walk, his *sanji* across his chest. "Who sent for that fellow?" Big Ammachi says, shooting a jet of tobacco juice in his direction, inadvertently revealing the bad habit she pretends not to have.

"I did," Philipose says.

The *kaniyan*'s polished shoulders are miniatures of his bald head, a trinity that speaks of a lifetime of avoiding manual labor. Someone had mischievously told Baby Mol that the wen was a baby god living atop the *kaniyan*'s head.

"Coming on a Wednesday?" Big Ammachi grumbles. "Of all people, he knows it's inauspicious. Even a leopard cub won't leave its mother's womb on a Wednesday." She retreats to the kitchen. The *kaniyan* follows her there, his hand resting on top of the door frame, catching his breath while asking Big Ammachi for "something" for his thirst, hoping for buttermilk or tea. Scowling, she gives him water.

Squatting down on the *muttam* before Baby Mol's bench, the *kaniyan* pulls out his parchments from the *sanji*. Big Ammachi wanders back. The *kaniyan* traces a square in the sand with a stick, then divides it into columns and rows, muttering, "*Om hari sri ganapathaye namah.*"

Big Ammachi twists the crucifix on her necklace and glares at Philipose; he ignores her and puts a coin in one of the squares. He doesn't know why his mother is annoyed; isn't this the man she entrusted to teach him his letters? Now she acts as though his Vedic future-telling is nonsense, yet moments before she invoked inauspicious times. Shamuel, heading out, a folded sack on his head, squats to watch.

The *kaniyan* singsongs the parents' names, recites their stars and birth dates from memory, and then asks indirectly about Elsie's last monthly. She's taken aback. Undeterred by her lack of response, he mutters in Sanskrit, counting on his digits and casting a glance at Elsie's stomach; his finger wanders over his astrological charts, then he scribbles with a metal stylus on a tiny strip of papyrus leaf. He lets it curl back into a tight cylinder, ties it with red thread, and recites a *slokum* before handing it to Philipose, who all but rips it open in his impatience. It reads:

THE ISSUE WILL BE A BOY

"I knew it! What did I tell you? Your Lord be praised," Philipose says, in a voice that even he realizes is unnaturally loud. "Our Ninan reborn!"

Five pairs of eyes look aghast at him. Elsie gasps. Big Ammachi says, "*Deivame!*" *God Almighty!* and crosses herself. Shamuel pats his head to confirm the sack is still there and leaves. Baby Mol glares at Baby God. "Come," Big Ammachi says to Elsie. "Let's leave this foolishness."

Philipose's elation is dampened by the women's discourtesy. Don't they see they just witnessed prophecy at its best? His conviction is unshaken: the child in Elsie's womb is Baby Ninan reincarnated. This is vindication for the torment he's been through, for the recurring nightmare in which he lifts a lifeless body off the branch, and runs on broken ankles, runs nowhere. The oblivion of opium cannot stop the hounds of memory from pursuing him. Oh, but now those hounds must flee with their tails between their legs. Baby Ninan is coming back!

The weeks and months pass, and Elsie labors steadily on her great stone. She leaves its widest and heaviest end untouched, but just behind it a neck emerges, then the rosary of the spine flanked by shoulder blades. By and by, Philipose understands that it's a woman on her hands and knees. She may be turning to glance over her shoulder, although he can't be sure because the face is hidden in the broad end of the stone. Her full breasts hang down and her belly is gently convex to the earth. One hand is planted on the ground. The other arm disappears into the rock just beyond the shoulder. Is the arm signaling defiance? Surrender? Is it reaching for something?

On a night that he will later wish he could erase, while the household sleeps, he goes to Elsie's studio to examine the Stone Woman, running his hand over her. This has been his practice for countless nights. His mind picks at her like a riddle. The previous week he used a tape measure and confirmed his suspicion: she is one-fourth larger than life. Surely a deliberate choice. The four-to-five ratio paradoxically makes her *more* lifelike. Is she kneeling over a mat and sifting rice for pebbles? He's seen Elsie on all fours in such a pose, playing with Ninan, teasing him by letting her hair fall over his face. He's seen

Ammini, Joppan's wife, play with their new daughter the same way. Yet the torque of the Stone Woman's neck, the position of what is surely her emerging chin implies she might be looking back. An invitation? Might the still-hidden arm that reaches forward be clutching the headboard, bracing her body as her lover enters her? When will Elsie finish the face? The waiting is unbearable and making him anxious.

He returns to his room, takes his pen out, but first rolls a pearl to settle himself. Only after he swallows it does he recall he just dosed himself minutes earlier.

Elsie, I circled your Stone Woman tonight, just like the achen circling the altar. Three is his limit, but his rituals of witchcraft don't constrain me. Elsie, please, who is this Goddess crawling backward out of a stone womb? Is it you? Also, if this is a birth, nature agrees that headfirst is best. Tell me she's coming out, not going back in. What truth will her face reveal about you, my darling, or about us? I've waited weeks for you to finish that face! Every night I go in hoping this is the night. In the old days, when our minds were as connected as our bodies, I could just ask you. Elsie, Ninan is coming. Ninan returns. As parents we really should be closer . . .

He closes his eyes to think, pen in hand. He dozes off, head on the desk, oblivious to the thunder shower outside. This is neither the small rains nor the monsoon, just capricious weather. Half an hour later he's suddenly awake and terribly agitated. He had the most vivid dream! Such a luscious, brilliant, and meaningful dream. He looks down and he's aroused! In the dream the Stone Woman turned her head to him. She beckoned him. He saw her face clearly! Her expression revealed a profound truth about . . . about . . . he slaps the side of his head. Truth about *what*? It hovers, there just beyond recall. He groans and scrapes another pearl.

His legs carry him to Elsie's studio, but he's forgotten his slippers. Sharp shards of sandstone prick his feet. He confronts the sculpture. "Listen, I saw your face already in my dream. I'm asking for just once more . . . why hide? Are you frightened? What is it?"

The Stone Woman is silent. A bolt of lightning illuminates her. The spray of rain that blows in from outside makes her skin look moist and alive. More flashes of light animate her arms and legs. She's writhing, fighting to extricate her head! Could he still be dreaming? That stone vice imprisons her in a cowl of rock. Is Elsie her cruel jailer? Or is the Stone Woman none other than Elsie?

The next flash followed by thunder makes her terror unmistakable. He must act! *Hold on, my darling! I'll free you. I'm coming!* The next thing he knows, the biggest mallet is in his hand and raised high. It's heftier than he imagined, unbalanced and head-heavy. It descends with much more force than he'd intended, bouncing off the stone, sparks chasing it, and a shock wave surging up his elbow. On its rebound, as though with a mind of its own, the mallet strikes his collarbone, and he hears the crunching of bone. He screams as pain blankets his neck and shoulder. The mallet clatters on the floor. His left hand instinctively grabs his right and presses it to his chest, because the slightest movement of his arm or shoulder causes excruciating pain in his collarbone. He squirms in agony. His thudding heart is louder than the rain. *I am,* he thinks through the fog of pain, *quite certainly awake.* He's certain his screams and the falling mallet have woken the household. A minute passes. No one comes.

He's horrified to see that he's not only failed to free the Stone Woman, but he's ensured that no face will ever emerge. The wedge he struck loose has left a crater where eyes, forehead, nose, and upper lip could have been.

He staggers to his room, his collarbone throbbing and sending out bolts of pain with any movement of his right arm, even a wiggle of his fingers. The only way he can minimize the pain is with his right arm pressed to his chest, by his left hand. In the mirror he sees the angry swelling and the irregularity in the contour of the bone. One can go through life with no awareness of the collarbones other than they sit above the chest like a coat hanger. Then an act of stupidity brings them acutely to one's attention. With great difficulty he fashions a sling. The effort leaves him drenched in sweat.

Soon it will be morning. He can't let Elsie see what he's done. How can he expect her to understand when he barely understands himself? If it isn't murder, it's manslaughter, but in any case, there's a body to dispose of. He returns to the patio and hides Elsie's collection of mallets and her chisels behind the bookshelves in his room.

He waits on the verandah in the predawn for Shamuel. The previous night's storm has littered the *muttam* with dead leaves and palm fronds. At last Shamuel appears, standing there like a dark totem, naked from the waist up. The *beedi* scent Philipose associates with the old man clings to him, just like the threadbare plaid *thorthu* that was wrapped around his head when he walked over but is now draped over his shoulder out of respect for the *thamb'ran*. Shamuel's *mundu* is half-hitched and his kneecaps are pale saucers. He's all gray now, even the eyebrows, and there's gray in the depths of his pupils too.

"Quite a rain last night," Philipose says. He knows he's a disappointment to this man who has loved and served him since he was born. The old man studies his sling, sees the bruising. "Let's see, Shamuel . . . today . . . remember to take rice to the mill for grinding."

"*Aah, aah,*" Shamuel says automatically, though he ground the rice the previous week.

"And ask the *vaidyan* to come by." Then before Shamuel can ask why, he adds, "But before all that, get some help and move that stone that Elsie is working on."

"*Aah, a—*" Shamuel catches himself. "You mean the big woman?" So he's seen her evolution too.

"Yes. Please move it first thing. Don't wait," Philipose says, trying to sound casual, rising from his chair. "Drag it out of sight, maybe by the tamarind tree. But do it soon. She'll work on it again after the baby comes."

Philipose goes inside at once, leaving Shamuel standing on the *muttam*, scratching his chest.

In half an hour, Shamuel returns with two others, coiled ropes in their hands. Philipose is thankful that Joppan isn't in the group. They approach from the outside of the semi-enclosed patio that is Elsie's studio. They circle the Stone Woman, their feet impervious to the stone shards. Philipose watches discreetly. What do they think of the figure? Does art seem like a terrible indulgence? Especially since art has become labor for them now. They drag away the defaced stone.

Later, the *vaidyan* comes by. Philipose has little faith in his tonics and pills, but the man knows his fractures. It turns out that the sling Philipose fashioned *is* the treatment for this fracture. He must keep it on for three weeks at least.

Elsie breakfasts on plump, steamed *idli*, white as clouds. Then under Big Ammachi's watchful eyes, she applies warmed *dhanwantharam kuzhambu* to her entire body. Every *vaidyan* has his own formula, but the base is sesame and castor oils, and nightshade roots. An hour later she bathes, scrubbing off the oil with green gram powder. Before her mother-in-law lets her go, she drinks hot milk infused with *brahmi* and *shatavari* roots. It's eleven when Elsie arrives at the patio, tying an apron over her sari. Philipose is waiting. He stands, swaying from fatigue, sleeplessness, and opium.

She turns slowly from the emptiness of the patio to regard him.

"Elsie, I can explain. I put your statue safely away. Just until after our son is born."

A fly hovers in front of his face and the mere thought of swiping at it is enough to trigger pain.

She observes his sling, the ugly blue swelling, and the bony deformity with curiosity and even concern. Then she turns back to what is no longer there. She bends down to pick up the fragment that broke off when the mallet did its work. He kicks himself for leaving it there. Holding it at arm's length she turns it this way and that, trying to picture its origin. He wishes she would just explode at him, say what he deserves to hear.

"It was an accident, Elsie," he blurts out. "I had a terrible nightmare." This isn't at all what he meant to say! "I was convinced she wanted to escape. I think I was still dreaming when I came out here. I wanted to free her." He waits, expecting the worst.

"So, you meant well." Her voice is flat. Not sarcastic. Not anything.

She understands! Thank goodness. "Yes. Yes. I'm so sorry. Elsie, after our son is born, I'll bring it back. Or get you ten other stones if you like," he says.

"Our son?" Elsie says at last.

It's a blessing that she doesn't want to talk about the Stone Woman anymore. "Yes, our son! He was complaining," he says, trying for a humorous tone. "He was saying, 'Appa, I'm looking forward to coming back into the world, but all this pounding is driving me crazy!'"

Elsie says, "You're so sure it's a son."

It's not a question. He laughs nervously.

"Have you forgotten the *kaniyan*'s visit? This is our Ninan reborn!" His voice catches when he says the name, and the expression on her face flickers. A ghost has walked between them.

"God is penitent, Elsie. God asks for forgiveness. God wants to give us reason to believe again. God gives us Ninan back so we can heal."

She looks at the stone fragment in her hand, as though uncertain what to do with it, then places it on the ground carefully, like a sacred object. She looks suddenly weary. When she speaks, it's without rancor, and perhaps there's even compassion for the man she married.

"Philipose, oh, Philipose, what happened to you?" Her gaze makes him feel he's shrinking before her, becoming the size of the stone fragment. "All I wanted," she says, "was your support so I could do my work. But somehow you always seem to think you're giving it to me even when you're taking it away."

THE ORDINARY MAN COLUMN: THE UNCURE
by V. Philipose

Stop anyone on the road and once they see that it's not money, or their last plug of tobacco, but a story that you're after, they'll happily tell you the legend of their lives. Who doesn't want to recount the bad karma, the backstabbing that stood between them and greatness, kept them from being a household name like Gandhi or Sarojini Naidu? Or wealthy beyond belief like the Tatas or Birlas? Every Malayali has such a personal legend and I assure you, it is complete fiction. Invariably a Malayali also has two other tales in their possession, as constant as their belly button: one is a ghost story, and the other a cure for warts. Dear Reader, I am a collector of wart cures. I have hundreds. If you want to scare yourself collecting ghost stories, that's your business, is it not? So, whatever you think of my collecting wart cures, kindly keep it to yourself.

Why wart cures, you ask? Am I covered in warts? No. But I had one on this finger when I was a little boy. Naturally, I felt it was because of a sin I'd committed. Instead of telling my mother, I ran to my childhood friend, an older, confident fellow, my hero. He shared his secret cure: fresh goat's urine before it hits the ground, applied just before sunup. Brother, you please try to find goat piss other *than on the ground. Sister, your goat may piss all the time and look at you insolently while splashing your leg, but just try to catch some in a coconut shell in the dark without getting a head butt, or a kick in unmentionable places. Anyway, I managed. That's its own story, but I managed . . . and the wart fell off! When I told my friend, the rascal fell to the ground laughing. He'd made it up! But I had the last laugh, did I not? The cure worked.*

Families pass down wart cures like they pass down secret recipes. "Cut off an eel's head and bury it. As it rots, so will the wart." "Go to a wake and discreetly rub the wart on the corpse."

"Walk for three minutes in the shadow of someone whose face is covered with smallpox scars."

That's why I came to see DOCTOR X. (That's not his name, but it means I'm not telling you.) His specialty is warts. His name was on his board, followed by the letters: MD(h) (USA), MRVR. Such a board you would expect to be nailed to a pukka building with tile roof, not a shack next to a tire-puncture stall, with a gutter carrying smelly water in front of it. A shirtless man in a dirty mundu *stood grinning outside. I asked, Where is Dr. X. He said, I am he. Naturally, I asked about all those letters behind his name. He said the MD(h) stood for Medical Doctor Homeopathy. I said, Aah, so you attended Homeopathy College? (Between you and me, I was suspicious.) He said, Oh yes! Right here in my home I studied the* British Pharmacopeia, 1930. *I have it by-hearted. Ask me anything! I wanted to say, Surely you know there is a newer edition. Instead, I said, How is studying the* Pharmacopeia *connected to homeopathy? He said, If there's dilution, why not? Dilution is critical! Aah, I said. What about the USA after the MD(h)? (He didn't look like a man who had traveled far from above-mentioned smelly gutter.) Oh that, he said, means Unani, Siddha, and Ayurveda. All three are systems of medicine in which I have a great interest, he said. You could say I specialize.*

The nerve of this fellow! Brother, I said— He interrupted me. Call me Doctor, please. Aah, Doctor, then, don't you think people might confuse those letters with United States of America? Stop! he said, putting his hand out, like a police-man. Let me remind you that Unani, Siddha, and Ayurveda are ancient practices that existed before America. I dare Churchill or anyone to say otherwise. Aah, I said, let that be, but what about the MRVR? He said, It's for the Latin, Med-icus Regius Vel Regis, *or Physician to Royalty. I said, Wait! Did you treat someone at Buckingham Palace? No, he said.*

I successfully prescribed a purgative to a severely constipated man who was the sixth cousin of the previous Travancore Maharajah—all other treatment had failed. Instead of dilution, this time I went for concentration. I used cascara, senna, mineral oil, milk of magnesia plus my secret ingredient. I said, Does that work? (I had a personal interest because which of us doesn't struggle with constipation?) Aah! My friend, he said, laughing in a distasteful manner and dropping his voice. Does it work, you ask? Let me put it this way: If you happen to be reading a book when you take this medicine it will rip the pages right out of the binding! Anyway, my patient was very grateful. Therefore, I consulted the Malayalam–Latin dictionary to add MRVR to my name.

Aah, I said. Enough about that. I didn't come to talk about your signboard. I'm a collector of wart cures, of which there are legion. Yes, yes, he said, most agreeably, and moreover, he added, the common ingredient to all the cures is belief. When a cure works it's because the patient believes. When the cures are elaborate it's easier to believe. That's human nature. Fair enough, I said, because for once I agreed with him. So, I said. Tell me, what do you do for your wart patients? He held out his hand. I asked, What's that? Put money there, please. If a patient cares enough to put money in my hand, that means they have faith. Then my cure is sure to work.

I took my bicycle off the stand, ready to leave. I don't have warts, I said. I'm asking as a journalist. He said, You are sadly mistaken—I diagnosed warts the first moment I saw you. Where? Show me! Aah, but your warts are all on the inside, as you surely know. His hand was still held out.

Dear Reader, don't judge me harshly. Tears of understanding sprang to my eyes. I put money in the doctor's hand. Doctor, I said, I am desperate. And I believe.

CHAPTER 54

An Antenatal Angel

1951, Parambil

An uneasy truce abides during the rest of Elsie's ripening. Big Ammachi sees her avoid her husband. Who can blame her? Ever since the *kaniyan*'s visit, Philipose's behavior has grown more erratic.

In Elsie's seventh month, Big Ammachi sends for Anna, a young woman she knows from church because of her beautiful singing voice. She'd heard that Anna's husband had vanished, and that she and her daughter were struggling. Big Ammachi is sixty-three and feels every bit of it. With a new baby coming she could use some help, and if Anna is willing, the arrangement could be mutually beneficial. She misses Odat *Kochamma* terribly; the old lady's unflappable presence would have been a blessing during Elsie's delivery. She has no photograph of her beloved companion and so she keeps Odat *Kochamma*'s wooden false teeth in a jar in the kitchen. The old lady "borrowed" them from her daughter-in-law's father and wore them when the mood struck her. Big Ammachi smiles whenever her gaze falls on the leering teeth. Every night in her prayers for the departed, she cries when she comes to Odat *Kochamma*.

Anna shows up after lunch, just as Big Ammachi sits on the rope cot with the newspaper and her plug of tobacco; other than the breezeway flies, no one is around to scold her about her habit. Anna is in her late twenties, with a wide forehead, wide hips, and a smile that looks wider than both those together. For a big woman, Anna's cheeks look unnaturally gaunt since Big Ammachi last saw her in church. Hiding behind her is a frail little girl wearing oversized shorts tied with shoestring; her eyes are larger than her whole face.

"So, who's your little tail there?"

"That's my Hannah!" says her mother proudly, showing more teeth than a mouth should be able to hold. The dried stains in a concentric pattern on Anna's *chatta* do not escape Big Ammachi's notice. So it's breast milk that keeps the little bug-eyed angel from starving.

"*Aah*, I'm thinking Hannah might want to eat something," Big Ammachi says, dismissing Anna's protests and stepping into the kitchen. While the two eat, Big Ammachi asks about the absent husband.

"Ammachi, bad luck followed my poor husband like cats behind the fishmonger. He fell asleep under a palm after drinking toddy and a coconut cracked his ribs. Such bad luck." Big Ammachi ponders Anna's charitable view of her husband. "Then he lost his job and couldn't find work. He was frustrated. One morning he decided he was going to sneak onto a train going to Madras, Delhi, or Bombay, and find work. That was three months ago. There's no paddy in the house," says Anna still grinning, as if describing yet another comic turn in her marital adventure, even as her eyes get wet. "I want to find him, but how?" She dabs at her cheeks. "When Hannah grows up and asks me if I did everything to find her *Appachen* . . ."

Big Ammachi acts annoyed, but she squeezes Anna's hand. "You can't search the whole land!"

From the first moment, Anna is like four extra pairs of hands. Big Ammachi wonders how she managed before Anna *Chedethi*. That suffix gives Anna the stature of a relative, not a hired servant. Hannah trails Big Ammachi just the way JoJo once did. *Lord, I came here as a child myself, missing my mother and without a father. Now I'm mother to so many.* Hannah looks three but holds up five fingers when asked her age. It isn't long before Hannah's cheeks rise like leavened bread. Big Ammachi helps Hannah to read, using the Bible as her text. The little girl sits absorbed with the Bible long after her lesson is over.

Big Ammachi and Anna *Chedethi* ready the bedroom in the old section of the house for Elsie's delivery. It sits beside the *ara*, and above the cellar, so one could keep a close eye on the treasures of the house. The raised platform bed with corner posts that rise like church spires is cluttered with bolts of cloth. Big Ammachi delivered her children in this bed. Her mother used this bedroom in the last months of her life when she found it difficult to rise from the mat on the floor. The room has brass-studded, dark, teak-paneled walls and a decorative false ceiling. It is a museum of old Parambil artifacts, each with its own history, and she cannot bring herself to give any of it away. There's a family of long-spouted brass *kindis*, and ornate oil and kerosene lamps that sit tarnishing since electricity arrived. In one corner of the room is a ceremonial seven-tiered oil lamp as tall as Big Ammachi. They clear almost everything but the bed. Anna *Chedethi* wipes down the walls and ceiling and polishes the red oxide floor until she can see her reflection. Elsie will deliver here in this room of memory, ceremony, and transition.

Big Ammachi, in the kitchen, hears a crash and runs back to the old bedroom; she finds Philipose up a ladder, pulling down objects from the crawl space above the *ara*, which is accessed from the old bedroom.

"I'm looking for Ninan's wooden cycle," he says. "The one without pedals. Isn't it up here?"

"Are you mad? Get out!"

Later she hears him instructing Shamuel. "Elsie will deliver on the sixth. I want Sultan *Pattar* to make biryani—"

Big Ammachi pounces, furious. "What nonsense! You think this is a wedding? The moon keeps to that kind of schedule, not babies. Shamuel, you can go. No Sultan *Pattar*, nothing." Shamuel retreats slowly, so that he might hear the rest. "What's wrong with you, Philipose? Such inauspicious behavior! No celebration till we have a healthy baby."

His eyes are those of a man who has lost all reason. She might have shared with him her anxiety about Elsie's pregnancy, but this specter would not understand. What madness possessed him to drag Elsie's stone away? Big Ammachi had commiserated with her daughter-in-law, but Elsie said, "It's all right. The ideas in my head are inexhaustible. No one can move those."

Big Ammachi knows something Philipose does not: Elsie is building another sculpture out by her old bathing spot, a place her husband never visits. It began as a bundle of twigs, then grew into a curved wall, and slowly it became a giant bird's nest. Elsie roams the property relentlessly, breaking off green, malleable boughs, and dry twigs, weaving them into the nest along with found objects including rag cloth, strands of cane from the seat of an old chair, ribbons, a rusted pulley, coir rope, a doorknob. After a churchman pays a visit, Big Ammachi finds his prayer beads plaited into the nest. Elsie is like a tailorbird, swiveling her head this way and that, scanning the ground as she walks barefoot through brush and undergrowth. Her hands are blistered from the work. Big Ammachi wonders: *Is a nest really art? Has this pregnancy affected her judgment?*

One morning she notices Elsie walking stiffly, as though on stilts. She forces her to lie down. "Look at your feet! They'll be like Damodaran's soon! No more walking." Elsie's ankles have disappeared. Her toenails are dull, and her heel fissured like a dry riverbed. Yellow calluses crowd the ball of her foot. "Why aren't you wearing your slippers? I should have paid attention." But Big Ammachi has been focused on the shape of Elsie's belly, looking for the loss of height that tells her the baby's head has entered the pelvis—she has just seen that change. She hopes she's wrong because it's early. "I'm not letting you out of my sight," she says sternly. "Sit with me. Draw or paint instead of collecting *kara-bura*," she says, inventing a word on the spot.

She and Elsie move to the old bedroom, Elsie on the bed, while Big Ammachi sleeps on a mat on the floor. The first night she hears Elsie tossing and turning, her restlessness a sign of imminent labor. The waiting is over, even if it's earlier than she expected. Near dawn, when Big Ammachi opens her eyes, she finds Elsie staring at her. For an eerie moment she feels some other person occupies Elsie's body and wants to tell Big Ammachi something that she wouldn't want to hear.

"*Molay*, what is it?"

Elsie shakes her head. She admits to having intermittent warning cramps. When the sun is up, Elsie says, "Ammachi, please walk with me to my nest." They head out, Elsie's arm around the shorter woman's shoulders. They slip in through the nest's overlapping entrance that at first glance is invisible. The top of the nest reaches to Big Ammachi's chest. "I hope I can do more big pieces like this. Outdoors. That is, if I survive this labor."

"What nonsense is that? 'If I survive'?" Big Ammachi says, pretending to be annoyed.

Elsie stares at the older woman and seems about to unburden herself. Then she turns away. She sighs.

"What is it, *molay*?"

"Nothing. Ammachi, if something happens to me, please care for this baby. Promise me?"

"*Chaa!* Don't talk like that. Nothing will happen. But why even ask? Of course I will."

"If it's a daughter I want her to have your name."

By way of answer, she hugs Elsie, who clings to her. When they separate, Big Ammachi is taken aback by Elsie's grief-stricken expression. She soothes her with words, with touch. She remembers the intensity of her own emotions, her fears as labor drew near, and for Elsie it is imminent. This fragility is a sign.

Big Ammachi goes to Philipose. "Now, listen to me. Elsie has been adamant that she delivers in the house. But I don't like what

I'm seeing. I can't explain. She will deliver any moment. Arrange a car for us—"

He leaps up from the bed, alarmed. "Now? But my calendar—"

"What did I say about your calendar? We can go to the mission hospital in Chalakad. I really thought we had more time. Dear God, if only a hospital were closer."

But just then, Anna *Chedethi* calls out for her in a tone that cannot conceal her anxiety.

"Never mind," Big Ammachi says. Elsie's water must have broken.

Anna *Chedethi* has strung white bedsheets over the lower half of the windows of the old bedroom. Philipose standing outside looks uncomprehendingly at this sight. He corrals Shamuel as he walks by and says, "Looks like our Ninan is in a hurry to land, just like last time. We must slaughter a goat. And arrange for toddy—" His mother, inside the room with Elsie, overhears him and is about to go out and scold him when she hears Shamuel's voice, but not sounding like Shamuel at all.

"*Chaa!* Stop! Just keep quiet. Don't talk to me. If you want to help, go to church and pray. Take a vow not to visit Krishnankutty's shop. That's what you can do."

Silence follows.

Elsie's moans are rhythmic. Big Ammachi prepares herself, gathering her hair into a tight bun, glancing at the mirror. Her locks are thinner, and more gray than black. Just yesterday, she was the young bride writhing in pain in this very room with her first child. But it wasn't yesterday. It was the year of our Lord 1906. It feels as though she's just glanced away from this same mirror . . . and it's 1951 and she's in her seventh decade! Her earlobes are so stretched now. But the look she yearned for as a young woman means nothing to her now. She straightens her back; if she's not careful, soon her shoulders will float up to meet her ears. Already, she's tilted like a crooked palm from all the years of carrying JoJo, then Baby Mol, then Philipose, then Ninan, always on her left side so that her right hand was free to stir the pot or twitch the kindling. She sighs and crosses herself. "Lord, my rock, my fortress, and my deliverer . . . be with us now."

Elsie cries out, "*Ammay*—?" A contraction must be coming on.

"There, there, *molay*, don't worry," she says reflexively, teeth clamped around the last hairpin. "I'm coming."

Anna *Chedethi* straightens sheets that don't need straightening. The contraction is like a distant cloud, visible over treetops, then casting its shadow on Elsie's face as cramping pain twists her body, wrings it out like a washrag. Elsie grips Big Ammachi's hands so hard that her knuckles could crumble to powder. "There, there. Just breathe. You've been through this before," she says. But the truth is Elsie hasn't. Baby Ninan slipped out like a kitten squeezing through window bars.

The contraction passes and Elsie desperately sucks in air. Big Ammachi is startled to see in Elsie's eyes not fear, which would be natural, but that terrible sadness again. "Ammachi, take me to the nest."

"But we went there an hour ago, remember? Let's walk in this room if you like."

She strokes Elsie, waiting, reliving her own blessed and terrible ordeal of giving birth. She remembers she had ceased to exist anywhere but in this room. Who but a woman would understand? Just when you thought the pain couldn't get worse, it did. The thread between her and the world snapped, and she had been utterly and completely alone, battling God, battling the miraculous creation that He had allowed to grow inside her, and was now ripping her— also his creation—in two. Men like to think that women forget the pain upon seeing the blessed baby. No. A woman forgives the child, and she might even forgive the father. But she never forgets.

With the next contraction, Elsie is already bearing down. "Hold Anna *Chedethi*'s hands." Moving to the foot of the bed, Big Ammachi spreads Elsie's legs and pushes her knees toward her belly.

She doesn't understand what she's seeing. Instead of the dark, glistening hair of the baby's head framed in that oval, she sees pale flesh. And a dimple. It's the baby's bottom! That dimple is the anus. Hearing a pounding, she's distracted, wondering who's hammering at the door, until she realizes it's her own heart. This baby is upside down. This is trouble. The contraction passes and the bottom retreats, gaining no purchase. Maybe the birth canal hasn't fully softened, so perhaps if they give it time—

Suddenly, Elsie's legs shoot straight out as though unseen pulleys extend her limbs. "Elsie, don't! Bend your knees again!" But Elsie is past hearing, her legs rigid, toes pointing at the door, her arms curled against her chest in a strange posture. Atavistic grunts come through her clenched teeth, along with frothy blood-tinged saliva. "She's bitten her tongue!" Anna *Chedethi* says. Elsie's eyes roll back, showing only the whites. And then she convulses, her limbs flailing, her body rattling the bed. Big Ammachi gathers Elsie's head to her bosom, as though to deny whatever spirit is taking possession, to keep it from whipping Elsie to and fro. After an eternity, the intruder retreats. But it has taken Elsie with it: she is limp, her breathing coarse, her eyes half open and gazing to the left. She is unconscious.

Big Ammachi folds Elsie's legs once more so that her heels rest on her buttocks. To her dismay, the view hasn't changed. She washes her hands in hot water, thinking through what she should do. She removes her ring and smears coconut oil on her right hand, past the wrist.

"Anna *Chedethi*, kneel on the bed. Put your hand here on her belly and push when I say so. Lord, my rock, my fortress, my—well, you heard me before," she says in the same stern voice she used with Anna *Chedethi*. But for the convulsion, they might have waited for nature to take its course, for the baby's bottom to stretch the canal, for Elsie to push . . . but the passage looks as wide as it is going to get, and an unconscious Elsie can no longer bear down.

She gathers her gnarled fingers into a bird's beak, then insinuates them into the birth canal. Her fingertips ease past the baby's bottom, spreading out, worming their way up, the space so tight that her joints scream. She closes her eyes as if to better see in the womb's darkness. She sweeps around and stumbles onto soft stubs. Toes! And the back of an ankle? Yes! With a fingertip, she pulls on that foot, keeping its angle with the shin as she found it. Just when she thinks it might snap, the foot slips down past the baby's buttocks and is outside. She finds the other foot higher up, and eases it out, and now, with no fuss, the buttocks slip out as well, along with a loop of umbilical cord. Anna *Chedethi* looks on, her mouth gaping.

The legs dangle from the birth canal, wet and slimy, one knee flexed and the other straight, as though the baby is in mid-stride, trying to climb back inside. Its spine faces them, like a string of tiny beads under the skin. She wraps a towel around the sagging infant torso and pulls. The trunk doesn't budge, but rotates glacially, like a water wheel. She probes within once more and hooks down the crook of an elbow, and as a bonus, both shoulders deliver. Only the head remains collared by the neck of the womb. She glances up at Elsie, who hasn't moved. The froth on her lips bubbles with her rapid, shallow breaths.

She pulls, but the head is planted as if in stone. She fantasizes that if she calls the baby it will say, "Yes, Ammachi?" and come to her as so many little ones have. The sweat dripping into her eyes blinds her. Anna *Chedethi* wipes her face for her and flutters the bamboo fan. The umbilical cord dangles below the child like a white serpent, pulsating and twitching with Elsie's every heartbeat, the knots of veins under the gelatinous surface distended and angry. Seeing all of the baby but its head makes her think of Elsie's statue. Before Philipose defaced it.

"Anna, push when I tell you," she says irritably, even though it's her own wandering mind that annoys her. She squats as the next contraction begins, her knees creaking. Anna *Chedethi* presses down on the swollen belly, while Big Ammachi pulls down in the direction of the floor. But the awful angle between neck and body frightens her. "Stop! Pull up, not down," a voice clearly says. Anna

Chedethi hasn't spoken. Who was it then? Is the long-standing resident of the cellar below them trying to offer advice? She eases a finger inside to find the baby's mouth; then, with the next contraction, while keeping the head bent, she stands and pulls the baby's torso up and toward Elsie's belly, because something or someone told her that was the way. "Push, Anna!" The head comes free with a gurgle, the sound of mother and baby surrendering to nature's rule that no soul can linger betwixt and between, not if it wants purchase in this world.

Anna *Chedethi* expertly ties and cuts the cord while the newborn lies blue and lifeless in Big Ammachi's arms. She blows gently on the tiny nostrils. "Come on, precious! You're out of the water and in Parambil!" Nothing happens. She has a clear memory of Odat *Kochamma*, bending forward on her bowlegs, her arms behind her for ballast, and saying into Ninan's tiny ear, "*Maron Yesu Mishiha.*" *Jesus is Lord.* She looks up to the false ceiling and beseeches her, certain that her companion of so many years is looking down. *Say it, Kochamma! Do you want me to do it all?*

—and the child fills its lungs and squalls, a glorious sound, a universal language, the first utterance of a new life. Big Ammachi's clothes are drenched in sweat, her very bones hurt, her eyes burn, but her joy is overflowing.

There are happy noises outside the door: those waiting have heard the baby's cry.

Big Ammachi sinks to a squat with the baby. She feels she's born again. What a perfect child! She exults in the peculiar, shrill, high-pitched newborn cry, a sound that signals the end of the solitude, the return of the mother to the world, the passing of mortal danger. What was within is now without, still just as fragile, just as connected to the mother, but for the first time, separate.

"Such a good-sized child, aren't you? Praise God. I was worried that you'd be a tiny kitten." She's used to newborns squinting at the unaccustomed brightness, barely opening their eyes and if so only to peek out with an unfocused gaze. This baby stares directly at her grandmother with a serious expression.

Elsie's breathing is regular, her eyes now gazing right. Still unconscious, but alive. The afterbirth emerges, soggy and heavy, its job done. Anna *Chedethi* replaces the soiled sheet under Elsie with a thick white towel. She wraps the afterbirth in newspaper.

Anna *Chedethi* comes over to squat by Big Ammachi, both of them grinning over the new arrival, their backs to Elsie. A shattering sound comes from beneath their feet. From the cellar. It startles them, makes them look down, then turn around. They both see it at the same time: a cherry-red stream of blood pours from the birth canal, soaking the white towel and dripping to the floor. Big Ammachi hurriedly swaddles the infant and eases it down onto the mat. Anna *Chedethi* spreads Elsie's legs once more while Big Ammachi wipes away the clot at the opening, only to see another vile clot—the face of Satan—carried out in a steady, gushing river of red that joins the bloody lake under Elsie's buttocks.

Big Ammachi has never seen anything like this, but she's heard of it. *So many ways for us women to die, Lord. If it's not a labor that stalls, killing mother and child, then it's this. It's not fair!* She massages the belly, because she's heard it can help the flabby uterus get back its tone, and contract down, and stop the bleeding. But if anything, it makes the gushing of blood more pronounced. Big Ammachi staggers back, defeated, watching Elsie's life slipping away.

Philipose's voice calls from outside: "What's happening? Is my son all right?"

They don't hear him. They stare helplessly at the torrential hemorrhage. Anna *Chedethi* says, "Ammachi, let me try something."

Anna *Chedethi* oils her broad hand and eases her fingers into the birth canal. Once she is inside, in the womb, she gathers her fingers in a fist and pushes up. Her other hand on the abdomen pushes down, so that between fist within and palm without, she sandwiches the flabby womb, compressing it. Blood runs down her arm, but then it slows . . . and stops.

Speaking in short bursts, her face congested from the effort, yet somehow grinning, Anna *Chedethi* says, "This white nun . . . up past Ranni . . . she was a nurse . . . She saved a *pulayi* bleeding like a river . . . by pinching the womb like this."

"Were you there?"

"No . . ." she says, meeting Big Ammachi's eyes. "But I heard of it . . . and it just came to me."

Anna *Chedethi*'s arms quiver, the veins on her temples look ready to burst. Big Ammachi is the helper now, mopping her sweat. It's a blessing that Elsie feels nothing. But her face is as white as a bleached *mundu*. Big Ammachi glances over at the swaddled new-born; the baby looks on as its mother fights for life.

"Ammachi," Anna *Chedethi* says, "what was that sound we heard . . . from below?"

"A pickle jar must have fallen over," Big Ammachi says. "Those old shelves are tilting."

But Big Ammachi knows who it was and she's grateful. Had they kept cooing over the baby, Elsie would have been dead when they eventually turned to her. "Anna, what if you let go now?" She's worried that Anna *Chedethi* will pass out from the strain.

At first, Anna *Chedethi* seems not to have heard. Another minute goes by. Then she slowly releases pressure on the belly but keeps her balled-up fist inside. They hold their breath. There's no new trickle. After another minute, ever so gently, Anna *Chedethi* eases her hand out, cloaked dark red from fingertips to elbow. Their lips moving, both women pray silently, eyes glued to between Elsie's legs. Five minutes. Ten. Ten more. Gradually Big Ammachi feels she can breathe again.

She calls Elsie's name. She is in a deep, unnatural sleep. But she's alive. Dear God, can the poor girl survive after losing all this blood? Still the two women wait. They wait some more, now with the baby in her grandmother's arms. At last Big Ammachi places a hand over Anna's head, blessing her while looking to the heavens. "Thank you, Lord," she says. "You saw this coming. You sent me this angel."

* * *

Big Ammachi emerges from the bedroom, looking unrecognizable, wrung out, flushed and pale as if she, not Elsie, had just been through the ordeal. Her hands are clean, but her elbows are bloody, the front of her *chatta* and *mundu* is blood-soaked, and there's a blood smear across her cheek. But she is smiling dreamily, holding the new baby. She looks up, surprised to see a small crowd come to their feet. Baby Mol, Shamuel, Dolly *Kochamma*, Uplift Master, Shoshamma, and the child's father, Philipose.

"We almost lost our Elsie. Thank the Lord for bringing us through this. Such a difficult delivery," she says to those gathered, her voice hoarse. "The baby came buttocks-first. Then Elsie had a convulsion. Somehow, we got the baby out. But then suddenly Elsie was bleeding, so much bleeding . . . We almost lost her. We still might. She's very weak. Please pray she doesn't bleed again. But the baby is well. Praise God, praise God, praise God . . ."

She takes small, tired steps to her son, smiling. He'd looked dazed as she spoke, but now as she approaches, his face lights up, and he extends his arms. Big Ammachi says, "We already have a name for your daughter."

He blinks, drops his arms.

"Your daughter," Big Ammachi says.

He stumbles back. Shamuel slides a chair under him. Philipose can only stare at his mother in disbelief, his mouth open, a stupefied expression on his face. He mumbles, "God has failed us again."

She takes her time. She comes right up to his chair, standing over him. When she speaks, her words spark off her tongue, falling on him like hot oil onto water: "After the ordeal Elsie has endured . . . After what Anna *Chedethi* and I went through, that's what you have to say? 'God has failed us'?" Her voice rises. "A woman risks her life to give birth and at the end a man who's done *nothing*—less than nothing—in nine months says, 'God has failed us'?" If it were up to Big Ammachi, any man who said what her son just did should by law merit a caning. "Yes, God failed us," she says. "When he was handing out common sense, he overlooked you. If he'd made you a woman, then maybe dung wouldn't come out of your mouth in place of words! Shame on you!"

Nothing stirs in Parambil as her words hang over his head. Philipose looks up, bewildered, the disappointment now changing to hurt. But he doesn't dare speak.

Big Ammachi glares at her son. He was once a baby like the infant she holds. Does she not bear some responsibility for what he has become? "Look, an hour ago I could have come out to tell you that Elsie had convulsions and died. Forty minutes ago, I could have told you that the child was stuck upside down and mother and child had died. And ten minutes ago, I could've walked out to say Elsie bled to death. Do you understand? But I said none of those things. I said your wife lives, but barely. And what you see here is God's grace manifest in this perfect, perfect child."

Philipose doesn't say a word. He doesn't look at the baby, his face so anguished that it's as if Baby Ninan has died once more, the bloody corpse with its horrible entrails still in his arms.

"Mariamma," Big Ammachi announces in a strong voice. Elsie wanted that name. She's not waiting for her son to express an opinion. "The baby's name is Mariamma."

Yes, it is Big Ammachi's very own Christian name. *Mariamma.* A name no one has called her in the memory of anyone present, a name that hasn't been uttered since she came here as a twelve-year-old bride.

Mariamma.

CHAPTER 55

The Issue Is a Girl

1951, Parambil

Elsie is conscious but confused, and so very weak from blood loss. It is three days before she can sit up without feeling dizzy. Her recovery is painfully slow. She's in no condition to breastfeed. The smiling, gap-toothed Anna *Chedethi* nurses the baby, which to Big Ammachi is proof that Hannah is still suckling at night for comfort. If Big Ammachi had known, she'd have scolded them both. Now she says a prayer of thanks.

Only on the fifth day does Big Ammachi bring Mariamma to her mother. She's startled to see the same haunted, wretched expression on Elsie's face that she'd puzzled over before labor. Elsie looks at her daughter with great tenderness, but that sentiment is overshadowed, drowned out by inexplicable sorrow. Her hands are like floppy leaves, and she makes no attempt to reach for the child. After an eternity, Elsie closes her eyes, as though she can no longer bear to look, while tears stream out from under her lids. She turns away, her shoulders shaking, sobbing inconsolably.

The child's father sequesters himself in his room, marooned in his own home, unable to do more than observe through his window the comings and goings from the old bedroom. He doesn't come out, or if he does it is when the household is fast asleep.

Parambil is transformed once more by a newborn and the industry around it. Diaper cloths flutter on the line and Baby Mol patrols outside, shushing everyone who comes by. Big Ammachi delights in her granddaughter, her namesake. But a new baby should bring joy to its parents. This one has done just the opposite.

Big Ammachi focuses her energy on Elsie, feeding her broth, then fish and meat, to restore her blood, along with the *vaidyan*'s restorative tonics. After a week, Elsie can walk. Big Ammachi supports her as they pace the room in tandem. By the third week Elsie shows color in her cheeks, taking longer and longer walks on her own, even bathing in the stream. Though she looks in on the baby, she doesn't try to hold it, just gazes at it in Anna *Chedethi*'s arms. Big Ammachi cannot understand this, cannot shake her sense of foreboding, the sense that after all they've come through, there's one more thing waiting to happen.

Three weeks after the birth, Elsie steps outside in the early evening, in the gloaming, to bathe in the stream. Before she leaves, she asks Big Ammachi if she could please make her the sardines steamed in banana leaf again, just as she did the previous day, with no spices save for a bit of salt.

It's almost two hours before anyone realizes that she hasn't returned.

CHAPTER 56

Missing

1951, Parambil

They search the house and its surroundings. Shamuel walks along the stream and the canal; he hails the families of the blacksmith, goldsmith, and potter to ask if they've seen Elsie. Joppan cycles up and down the dark roads and to all the neighboring houses to inquire. Others walk the riverbank. By midnight, members of the extended family pack the verandah, the women's high-pitched voices a contrast to those of the men, who murmur in low registers. Caesar races around, barking. Joppan discreetly inspects every well, holding a burning palm frond torch over the mouth and peering in.

The next day, at first light, Georgie heads by bus to the Thetanatt house in the plains. If neither Elsie nor her brother is there, he'll hire a car and go up to the estate. Uplift Master assigns sectors so they can systematically scour the Parambil property in a one-mile radius of the house. Shamuel canvases all the boatmen and is assured that no one ferried Elsie the previous evening. Joppan, bravely pushing a long stick before him, wades into the tall grass of the *sarpa kavu* at the edge of the property, a spot where large rocks arranged by humans indicate an ancient temple devoted to the serpent God and where no one trespasses. Joppan establishes that there are wriggling forms aplenty, but no Elsie.

Only Baby Mol is unperturbed by Elsie's absence. When Big Ammachi asks her if she knows where Elsie is, Baby Mol says, "My dolls are hungry." Big Ammachi feels her throat tighten.

By early afternoon, Georgie returns: Elsie isn't at the family home, and her brother had just come down from the mountains an hour prior. He was certain that Elsie wasn't in the estate bungalow. Georgie said Elsie's brother had been less than gracious to him, treating him like a servant and not an elder from Parambil. Furthermore, the brother appeared drunk and had choice things to say about Philipose.

The efforts to find Elsie halt. Only Shamuel persists, going back over ground that's already been searched. Twenty-four hours after Elsie disappears, Big Ammachi, Philipose, and Uplift Master are on the verandah when Shamuel comes walking up the driveway. His somber, almost ceremonial pace gets their attention, as does what he holds in his hands like an offering. "From the boat jetty I walked along the edge of the river. I came to that place where the screw pine is so thick. I noticed one spot where it was bent back, flattened. I pushed through and came to a small clearing. Enough for one person to stand." His voice catches. "There only I found these." He extends his arms. A bar of soap sits atop a neatly folded *thorthu*, blouse, and *mundu*, and beneath those, Elsie's slippers.

Uplift Master informs the police at the substation. The best they can hope for now is word of a body being discovered downstream.

With Anna *Chedethi* nursing the baby, a sleepless Big Ammachi makes her way alone to the spot where Shamuel found Elsie's clothes. She stands there, feeling the soil between her toes as Elsie must have. She stares at the rippling brown surface of the river, whose every mood she knows, from a lifetime of giving herself to its embrace. The tethered canoes ride higher on the jetty, a sign of rain in the mountains, but a bobbing tree limb moves by leisurely. She shudders to imagine Elsie in her weakened state, disrobing here and stepping in. What got into the girl? Did she crave communion with water, a longing to be cleansed, and renewed? Elsie is a strong swimmer but that was before she nearly bled to death. The river is merciless to those who underestimate it, and it is never the same river twice. Standing here Big Ammachi feels such oppression in her chest. After a long, long time she tears herself away, but not before she kneels to kiss the soil where Elsie last stood.

Her feet carry her to Elsie's nest. She feels she is approaching a shrine, a sanctuary closed off from the world. The moss on the outside is thick, and the found objects woven into the wall appear to have been imprisoned there for decades.

Entering she spots a white, rectangular paper on the ground, held down by a polished oval stone, a river rock of the kind that Elsie used as weights on her worktable. Her heart races. Whoever had searched here had been looking for a person, not a piece of paper, and they missed it. She bends down to pick it up. It is the thick, grainy kind Elsie used for drawing and painting. There was a time before Ninan's death when such papers bred all over the house, spilling from Baby Mol's bench to the kitchen. Since her return, Elsie's strong hands had foregone charcoal and brush for the heft of the mallet and chisel before she turned to making the nest. Dew has curled the paper's edges—it has been here overnight, but not longer, because it's still pristine white. Her fingers tremble as she unfolds it. Big Ammachi sees a simple drawing, conveying with a minimum of lines on the page a familiar subject: mother and child. The faces and figures are not detailed, but with a curve here and a dash there they nevertheless allow her to see eyebrows, nose, lips . . .

"This is important, isn't it, *molay*?" The paper shakes in her hands. She studies it. There's the infant, of course. But the mother is far from young, judging by the slight stoop, by the forward thrust of the neck. "*Molay, molay*," she exclaims, her heart contracting. "*Ayo, molay*, what were you trying to say? That's *me*, isn't it? If it were you, she'd be taller, younger, and the brow wouldn't have that wrinkle. Are you telling me to care for your baby? You asked me that already. You know I will. But I'm sixty-three years old! Fathers might be dispensable, but a child needs its mother. Oh, Elsie, what have you done? Was this to say goodbye?" She's overcome and must sit on the ground.

Her body tells her with certainty that Elsie will never return; that Elsie gave herself to the river deliberately. The thought of Elsie leaving this message here, moments before she went to the river and took her life, is wrenching. She clutches the paper to her bosom and gives in to her sorrow.

She hears the distant sound of Anna *Chedethi* calling out from the kitchen. "Big Ammachi-*o*?" From the rising, musical *o* at the end, she knows that whatever it is Anna wants, it isn't urgent. But the melodic summons feels like a conclusion. It is a reminder that Parambil must go on. A householder, a mother, a grandmother has precious duties that don't cease, that go on till her dying day.

She tells no one about her find. She guards it jealously; it's a private message from her daughter to her. She stores the paper with the genealogy, in the same wardrobe where she keeps the snowy *kavani* bordered with real gold that she wears for weddings and funerals.

In the ensuing years, on Mariamma's birthday, and on other occasions when Elsie enters her thoughts, she will pull out the drawing, but always at night in the soft light of her lamp. Every time she sees it, the economy of those lines startles her anew. It could be the Virgin Mary and child. It could be many things. But she knows it's meant to be her, cradling her namesake. She never sees Elsie in it.

That rectangular sheet of paper holds the round world and its imagined corners, the remembrances of the disappeared and the dead, and the beating hearts of the faithful who pray each night that God's will be done, not knowing what that will be.

Part Seven

CHAPTER 57

Invictus

1959, Manager's Mansion in the village of M____

Lenin Evermore is a week short of his ninth birthday when the pestilence descends on the one-room shack that is their home. It comes with the suddenness of a lizard falling from the rafters. When his mother, Lizzi, said one morning that school was closed, he rejoiced, too pleased to ask why. The next morning, instead of waking to the sounds of his mother puttering in the kitchen, there is silence. His parents are still on their mats, his baby sister between them. Their faces glisten with sweat. He recalls they felt unwell the previous night.

His mother's skin is hot. When Lenin touches his baby sister, Shyla, who is just five months old, she screams as if he's pricked her with a needle. The crying rouses his father, who clutches his forehead, grimacing. Kora struggles to his feet, but sways. Lenin wonders if his father is hungover. But Kora had returned sober the previous night, unable to find food. They had filled their bellies with *kanji* water, only a trace of rice in it, and gone to bed.

"I must feed the cow," Kora says, his voice wheezier than usual and hoarse like stone scraping on stone. But he cannot stand up. He shakes his wife's shoulder but she only moans. Father and son stare at each other. Lizzi is the backbone of the family.

"Are you with fever too, *monay*?" Lenin shakes his head. "Then get water for us. And give hay and water for the cow. Please." As an afterthought, Kora says, "Everything will be all right." Then his father tries to flash his winning smile, the kind "Manager" Kora uses to persuade a headman that milk and honey will flow if villagers sign with him, and *no, no, there's no malaria up in that estate—who said?— just palatial quarters, and milk and honey—did I mention?* But his smile cannot be sustained this morning. "I've seen this before," his father says, rubbing the bumps on his skin. "If people know we have it then no one's going to help us. They won't come near." He puts his hand on his wife's cheek, also showing bumps. "Your blessed mother. What all I put her through." Lenin is surprised; this admission is unlike him. Then his father says, "Everything will be all right."

Lenin wasn't really scared till his father uttered that reassurance for a second time. It meant things were *not* all right. That bad things were about to happen because of something his father had done. There was a time, before Lenin was born, when they had a house in Parambil, a place Lenin has never seen but from his mother's stories he pictures as Eden, with loving family all around. From overhearing his parents, he knows that Kora's troubles forced them to flee Parambil. After that, his mother took complete charge. She helped her husband find employment as an estate writer in Wayanad in Malabar. Lenin has faint memories of those times. But when he was four or five, his father had got into trouble. Lizzi sold her last pieces of jewelry to buy a shack on a tiny plot; it was to ensure she was never again homeless. She forbade Kora from borrowing or doing anything but working for a wage. The shack is where they had lived ever since, the place his father calls "Manager's Mansion."

Lenin feeds the cow and brings water back to the family. He tries to get his mother to drink, but she cannot. His mother lives by "Tell the truth and tell it early," not "Everything will be all right."

Her husband cannot find work or hold down a job. It is Lizzi's skill as a midwife that brings in coin, or meat and fish. She learned from a woman in the Wayanad estates. Two weeks ago, Kora came home late at night with the cow, saying he'd won it in a game of chance. Lenin had never seen his mother so angry. She insisted he take it back. His father looked frightened; he would be beaten up if he tried, he said. The cow isn't allowed to leave the vicinity of their shack. And after all that, its udders are empty.

Lenin stays outside the house most of the day because it's disturbing to look at the family. At dusk he searches the kitchen but finds nothing but spices; he chews on a clove. His hunger is an ache. He tries smoking a *beedi* nestled in his father's box of asthma cigarettes. Before Lenin sleeps, he tries giving each of them water. He still cannot rouse his mother. Her beautiful face is marred by small swellings. Her curls are plastered down on her forehead. His father cannot raise his head; he takes one swallow, then grimaces in pain. His eyes lock urgently on Lenin's, and he squeezes his son's shoulder. The terror on his face is unlike anything Lenin has seen before. "Listen!" he whispers. "Don't do what I did. Follow the straight path." Those are his last sensible words.

Follow the straight path. There've been times when Lenin hated his father, wished terrible things on him. But he doesn't now. The lingering feel of his father's hand on his shoulder makes him sad. He's very scared now. He'd suffer school without a complaint if it would make everyone well.

The next morning, before he opens his eyes, he thinks, *Let this be a bad dream. Let me see my mother moving about, and my father holding the baby.* But his father's skin is as cold as stone. He has forgotten to breathe. His features are distorted from the blisters, and a puzzled expression is frozen on his face. His sister's mouth moves like a fish out of water, her chest heaving sporadically, and as he watches, it comes to a stop. Lenin has never seen a dead body, but he knows he's looking at two. His mother still breathes. Something breaks inside him. He flings the empty water vessel against the wall. He shakes his mother violently. "How can I manage if there's no one to care for me?" He falls on her, weeping. "I'm your baby. Please, Amma, don't leave me." Her eyes are rolled back, unseeing. She's beyond hearing.

It is hot outside, but he shivers with hunger and fear. *Follow the straight path*—that was the last thing his father said. He will do that. He will walk in a straight line till he gets food or drops dead. Nothing will stop him. If he comes to water . . . well then, he'll drown.

The straight line brings him over a fence, past a menacing bull, through a field, and soon a large whitewashed house comes into view. The Christian family living there owns much of this area. They have wanted nothing to do with Kora and Lizzi. Their house looks different to Lenin. It's because every door and window is bolted. A man's voice yells from inside: "DON'T YOU DARE COME CLOSER! GO AWAY BEFORE I UNCHAIN THE DOG!"

Lenin pauses, shocked. This family has coconut trees, *kappa*, chicken, and many cows. Can they not share? Do they not have pity? Tears stream down his face. He is committed. *Follow the straight line*. He stumbles forward. *Send the dog. If it doesn't eat me, maybe I can eat it. Either kill me or give me food.*

A face thrusts itself from the rushes on his right side, startling him. It's a thin *pulayi* woman, his mother's age, a *thorthu* covering her breasts. Does she mean him harm?

"*Monay*, move over here where they don't see you," she says. The rushes conceal her from the big house. He does what she said. "I'm Acca, from over there," she says, pointing to a tiny hut he now sees. "You're Lenin, aren't you?" She diagnoses his condition in one glance. "Wait there. I'll bring you some food."

He trembles with anticipation. She returns with a banana leaf packet and two bananas, setting them down short of him and retreating to squat twenty feet from him. Fried fish! Rice! He gobbles it down, then finishes the bananas.

"*Monay*," she says, "you don't have any sores?" Hearing her say "*monay*" brings tears to his eyes. He wants to run into her arms. He raises his arms to show he's unaffected. "And the others?" she asks.

He brushes at his wet cheeks. "Appa and the baby are dead. Amma can't see or hear me."

He hears her sharp, sucking intake of breath. "Your mother . . . you can live many lifetimes and not meet one as decent as Lizzi *Chedethi*. A heart like gold. And beautiful too." She dabs her eyes with her cloth. "*Monay*," she says, "this is smallpox. It's bad. That's why they say, 'Don't count your children till the smallpox has come and gone.' My husband and I had it. We can't get it again. Many have died around here."

"I wish I had it," Lenin says. "Then when my mother goes, I can go with her." His tears fall into the dirt.

She sniffles. "No. Don't say that. God spared you for a reason." She stands. "I'll send word to get you help."

"Acca! Wait." She turns. For a *pulayi* to give him fish and rice when they live on *kanji* and pickle is generous beyond belief. "Acca, you saved me. I promise you, if I live, I'll find a way to give back to you what you gave me many times over. Those people in the house wanted to set the dog on me. Are they not Christians?"

Her laughter has an unpleasant edge to it. "Christians, is it? *Aah*. My grandfather became a Christian, so we are too. My grandfather thought surely now his landowner will invite him inside the house to eat with him! No one told him that the *pulayar* Jesus died on a different cross. It was the short, dark cross behind the kitchen!" She laughs again.

He doesn't know what to say. "I think you are a saint."

"Listen, if it makes you feel better, *they* only sent me to market to get fish and mutton two days ago. When I returned, they were scared for me to come near. What if I carried smallpox? Or what if it was on the food? They told me to keep it. So we cooked and had a feast! You're lucky there was any left." Her expression is serious.

"No, I'm no saint, *monay*." She rises. "And I was teasing. It's the *same* cross. *Same* Jesus. It's just that people don't treat each other the same. You're praying, I hope? I'll send word for help."

As he walks home, he realizes that all this time he hasn't once prayed. It never occurred to him! Would it have made a difference?

The rancid smell reaches him even before he opens the door. His mother breathes noisily. His father's face is sunken, and almost unrecognizable. His sister is stiff, like a wooden doll.

He drags his mother to the door, toward the fresh air, by pulling on her mat. He lies next to her. Her breath is unpleasant. The mother he knows is gone, but he wants to be close to what's left of her. *One last time, Amma, hold me.* He drapes her arm over him. It exposes her belly, and he sees the scar where his father, crazed on asthma cigarettes, stabbed her, and where Lenin's hand pushed out. Doctor Digby put it back and christened him Lenin Evermore.

Lying there next to his mother, he tries to pray. Acca's face comes to him. It soothes him. Perhaps that was his Mary. A *pulayi* Mary. "God, please send another angel to save Amma. If you don't, then when you take my Amma take me too."

In the morning, the angel comes wearing a white cassock with a belt around the waist, and the black cap of a priest. His sandaled feet are white to the ankles with dust. He's rail thin, with piercing, kind eyes and a flowing gray beard. The angel looks about the shack, troubled. The smell is something one can reach out and touch. When he looks down at Lenin's mother, from the expression on his face, Lenin knows she is dead. When he fell asleep her body was warm. She's so cold now.

"Lenin Evermore? Isn't that your name?" The angel holds out his arms.

CHAPTER 58

Light the Lamp

1959, Parambil

Big Ammachi sits in the glow of the oil lamp on the verandah in front of the *ara* as she feeds her eight-year-old granddaughter.

The lamp casts their shadows on the teak wall behind them, two ovals, one larger than the other. The pebbles in the *muttam* glitter after the evening shower, and here and there a stone seems to move. Grandmother and granddaughter hear Philipose call out, "Time for prayers!"

"*Chaa!* Your father!" Big Ammachi says. "*I* used to have to remind *him* about prayers."

"My father says frogs come from pebbles." Mariamma is perched on the edge of her chair, her legs swinging, as another pebble jumps, defying gravity.

"*Aah*. That means his head is still full of pebbles. I thought I shook most of them out." The little girl's laugh displays gap teeth, and Big Ammachi slides a rice ball into her mouth. "Maybe he got that from those English books he reads only to you," she says, pretending to be jealous. Philipose even speaks to Mariamma in English, leaving the Malayalam to everyone else. "Is he reading you the one about the big white fish?"

Mariamma shakes her head, turning somber. "No. Another. This boy Oliver has no mother, no father. He's always starving. The other children are mean and make him go ask for food. The man got angry and sold Oliver to another man who makes funerals."

Big Ammachi wishes her son would choose stories without dead parents or children being sold off. "*Molay*, maybe it was just the poor boy's fate. Maybe it was written on his head."

"Like my 'specialness'?" her granddaughter says, touching the white streak in her hair to the right of her center part.

"No, your specialness is just that. Special! A mark of your good fortune." Big Ammachi thinks it gives gravity to everything little Mariamma says. "What I meant was that the boy's bad luck was being born to the wrong family, on the wrong day."

"What kind of day was I born on?"

"*Aah!* Have I not told you about the day you were born?" Mariamma shakes her head, trying not to giggle. "I told that story yesterday. And the day before, I think. Well, I'll tell you again because it's *your* story, and so it's better than that Oli or Olamadel fellow." Mariamma laughs. "On the day you were born, I sent Anna *Chedethi* to drag the big brass lamp out. In all my years at Parambil, I never saw that *velakku* lit. Because your grandfather already had had a firstborn son. Every time I went into that room, I'd stub my toe on that lamp. But the day *you* were born, I said, 'Who says we only light this lamp for a firstborn son? How about for the first Mariamma?' See, I *knew* you were special!"

Philipose appears silently, his hair slicked back. Big Ammachi still marvels that the new Philipose is as punctual as the chimes on his BBC News. He lives by routine, writing at five in the morning, walking the grounds with Shamuel at nine, having his shave and bath at ten, then off to the post office at eleven . . . and a bath before dinner, then prayers. She isn't entirely free of the worry that one day his routines will collapse like a hut in torrential rain, and he'll go back to the wretched wooden box and his black pearls. It isn't faith alone that brings him to evening prayers or to church; he needed such rituals to rebuild his faith in himself. If there were not a God, her son would have to invent one.

"Was the *velakku* my father's idea?"

"*Chaa!*" Big Ammachi says, as though he isn't standing there. Mariamma laughs. "Well, your father has many clever ideas . . . Maybe it *was* his idea. I can't remember." Philipose, eyes on Mariamma, keeps smiling.

Big Ammachi is gripped by memories of the harrowing birth, and of her son's uncharitable response. She remembers the *kaniyan* having the nerve to show up as soon as he found out the child was a girl; the man retrieved a tiny rolled-up parchment hidden under the kitchen overhang, which he handed to Philipose. It read, "THE ISSUE WILL BE A GIRL." He said he had put it there on his previous visit, because he had a strong suspicion the child would be a girl, but he had not wanted to disappoint Philipose. Big Ammachi had grabbed the parchment and tossed it at the *kaniyan*, saying, "Don't try that nonsense with us! Caesar sees the future better than you do! God gave us a beautiful girl, and it's a good thing, because more foolish men we don't need. There are too many of those standing here already." She remembers another observer, a silent old man who had held vigil outside the room where Elsie had labored, and who later looked on as the women lit the lamp; Shamuel was a stickler for tradition, but she thought he approved of the lighting of that *velakku*.

She's brusquely returned to the present by her granddaughter shaking her shoulder, saying, "Ammachi! Tell me! The lamp that night when I was born . . . What happened? Tell me!"

"*Aah*, the lamp . . ." she says. Philipose listens with the dignity of a man who has come to terms with his past. He knows just where his mother's thoughts had taken her. "I made Anna *Chedethi* polish that *velakku* until we could see our faces. It took three of them to move it over there, between the two pillars. She poured oil, put fresh wicks—four at the top, then six, eight, ten, twelve, fourteen, then sixteen. I carried you and I said to the ladies, 'This is our night!' Women came from the Parambil houses and beyond, from every direction, because they heard about it and because they saw that lamp from far away. They brought sweets, coconuts. It was your night but also our night. In the whole of Christendom, no one celebrated the birth of a girl the way we did the day you were born. I said to them, 'There'll never be another like my Mariamma, and you can't begin to imagine what she's going to do.'"

"What will I do, Ammachi?"

"God says in Jeremiah, 'I knew you before you were born.' God loves stories. God lets each of us make our own story with our lives. Yours will be unlike anyone else's. Remember that. Because you are of Parambil and because you're a woman, you can do whatever you imagine you can do."

The little girl mulls over this story that she knows so well. But tonight she asks a question that surprises her grandmother. "Ammachi, when you were a little girl, what did you imagine?"

"Me? Those were ancient times. It's so different now. I suppose I imagined what the times allowed. You know, I imagined exactly this: a home, a good husband, loving children, a beautiful granddaughter—"

"But, but, but . . . if by magic, right now, you were eight again, what would you imagine?"

"By magic, is it?" She doesn't have to think long. "If *I* were eight today, I know what I'd imagine. I'd want to be a doctor. I'd build a hospital right here." She has pestered Uplift Master for years about this: If Parambil can have a post office and bank, why not a clinic or hospital?

"Why?"

"So I could be more useful to others. Do you know how much suffering I've seen where I could do nothing to help? But in my day, *molay*, a girl couldn't dream like that. But *you*, my namesake, you can be a doctor, or lawyer, or journalist—anything you imagine. We lit that lamp to light *your* path."

"I could be a bishop," Mariamma says.

Big Ammachi is too surprised to answer.

Philipose says, "*Aah*, speaking of bishops, it's time for prayers."

CHAPTER 59

Kind Oppressors and the Grateful Oppressed

1960, Parambil

Without advance warning, Parambil receives a young visitor. The ten-year-old boy who steps onto the verandah and looks them all in the eye has a name equal to his precocious self-assurance: Lenin Evermore. It's been a year since BeeYay *Achen* wrote to Big Ammachi with the shocking news that Lizzi, Manager Kora, and their baby daughter had died of smallpox. Only Lenin survived. Big Ammachi replied at once saying she would gladly raise Lenin as her own and that he was family: the boy's father and Philipose were fourth cousins. But then BeeYay *Achen* wrote to say that Lenin felt God had spared him for one reason: to be a priest. BeeYay was sending him to board at the Kottayam seminary while attending a nearby school until he was old enough to be a seminarian. But he could spend his summer holidays at Parambil. Big Ammachi rejoiced at the thought of Lizzi's son becoming a priest. She looked forward to his first vacation.

Now, seeing Lenin in the flesh, Big Ammachi is so thrilled that it doesn't cross her mind that the holidays are far away; school is still in session. She embraces Lenin. The handsome boy has all of Lizzi's best features. Word spreads to the other houses that "Lizzi's boy, the Baby *Achen*, is here." Everyone wants to see him and talk about his mother; no one mentions Kora.

Lenin, with little prompting, recounts the story of the pestilence that descended on Manager's Mansion and took his family. His powerful voice and the vivid imagery in his speech will suit his priestly calling. Lenin says as the days passed and only his mother clung to life, he was sure he would die, but of starvation, not smallpox. His father's last words on earth were "Follow the straight path." His audience is moved by Kora's repentance and contrition as he was about to meet his maker. Mariamma looks on, a little jealous of this newcomer, her fifth cousin, but as caught up as everyone else in his tale. In desperation, Lenin says, he determined to set out on a ruler line wherever it took him. A landowner in the big house he was approaching told him to stop or he would let loose the dog. At that point, a woman appeared. "I think it was the Blessed Mary appearing to be a *pulayi*. Just as it says in Matthew twenty-five, she fed me when I was hungry." Another sigh from those listening, for who didn't know that parable? "She sent word to BeeYay *Achen* and his monks. They were caring for those with smallpox in the village. I don't know why God spared me. BeeYay *Achen* says that I don't *need* to know. He says, for everything there is a season, and a time. God saved me. I am to serve God. I know that much." Decency *Kochamma* is overcome by his testimony and hugs Lenin to her considerable bosom.

Someone asks how Lenin likes living in the seminary. For the first time the boy's confidence falters. "I liked it better in the ashram with BeeYay *Achen*. I don't like the seminary. I had some . . . misunderstandings with them." Uplift Master asks if school isn't in session now. "It is. I had some misunderstandings at the school. The principal of the seminary said it might be better for me to live here and go to school here. He only sent me."

"By yourself?" Big Ammachi says.

"An *achen* traveled with me. We . . . had some misunderstandings," Lenin says reluctantly. The answer is insufficient. "When we were on the bus, I saw we would be passing two miles from Manager's Mansion. I wanted to visit. The *achen* said no . . ." Lenin's face turns dark. "So I left him on the bus and I walked there. Then I walked here. I walked all day."

There was a *kappa* patch where his family's shack used to be, Lenin reports. The landowner from the big house—the same one who had threatened to turn his dog on him—came over carrying a stick. He had taken Lenin for a thief until Lenin explained. The landowner said the land was now his because Kora had borrowed from him using the land as surety. Lenin disagreed, saying it was his inheritance. The man said Lenin could file a case if he liked. Lenin asked to see Acca, the *pulayi* who had fed him; he wanted to give her the crucifix he was wearing, blessed by BeeYay *Achen* himself. The landowner told Lenin to keep the cross; he said Acca and her husband got big ideas from Party meetings, and felt that since they tilled the land, they had a right to it. He said they'd forgotten that the paddy in their stomachs and the roof over their heads was a result of his generosity; he said he chased the couple off his land and set fire to their hut. Lenin's face is clotted with anger as he recounts this.

Philipose asks the question that's on all their minds. Lenin says, "What could I do? If I were his size, I would have beat him with his stick. So I said, 'One day I'll find blessed Acca and give her all your land and your big house because you are a thief and one of her is better than a hundred of you.' He came after me. But with that belly of his he had no chance."

A few days later, they get a letter from the *achen* who had been assigned to escort Lenin to Parambil and had tried to stop him getting off the bus to visit Manager's Mansion. Lenin had waited till *Achen* fell asleep and then tied his sandals together. *Achen* woke up when the bus stopped to let Lenin off. He stood up to give chase and fell on his face. Lenin shouted that the *Achen* had kidnapped him. *Achen* concludes, "No doubt Lenin made it to Parambil. Give yourself two weeks and you'll be looking for a place to send Lenin, but kindly don't send that devil back to the seminary."

* * *

Lenin adapts to school and life in Parambil very quickly. But when
he discovers that Decency *Kochamma* has razored out "indecent"
pages from his favorite *Mandrake the Magician* comics in the lending
library, Lenin substitutes the missing pages with drawings of naked
men and women, labelled: ORIGINAL DIRTY PICTURES IN THE COL-
LECTION OF DECENCY *KOCHAMMA*. Once she finds out, the arthritic,
rotund woman, now almost seventy, comes after him, moving faster
than anyone thought was possible. The sight of her bearing down
on him is sufficient trigger for Lenin to "follow the straight path."
He plows through rice drying on mats, tramples a paddy field, walks
through nettles and into the young goldsmith's hut, trying to exit
through the back. The original goldsmith has passed away, and the
son is middle-aged, but is still referred to as the "young" goldsmith.
As Lenin later explains, once activated, his straight-line compulsion
ends only when he meets an insurmountable obstacle or gets a sign
from God. The young goldsmith is both, because he gives Lenin
a sound thrashing. He drags Lenin back to Big Ammachi by his
swollen ear. Lenin is covered with hives. The young goldsmith says,
"This one is just as crooked as the father." Mariamma has made her
own observation: Lenin's crookedness mostly happens in the daytime; at night he loses his cockiness, his steps become uncertain, and
she has even seen him stagger like a drunk. While she often pleads
to stay up later, Lenin can't wait to get to his mat.

As punishment for the last escapade Lenin is confined to the
house for two weeks. Mariamma says, "Why don't you try climbing
instead of this straight business? You might break your neck, but at
least you won't destroy property."

"*Aah*, but the trouble with up is that too soon you reach the
top."

A few days into Lenin's confinement, a fierce lightning storm
descends on Parambil. The walls shudder as heaven's thunderbolts
hunt for prey. In the midst of this, the "blessed boy" is missing. They

spot him outside, on the roof of the cow shed. It's a terrifying sight: Lenin's face upturned to the heavens, his arms raised, his hair plastered back, looking like Christ at Golgotha, deaf to their screams and swaying as the wind and rain buffet him. Thunder rattles the house as the clouds sparkle and glow. A lightning bolt strikes a palm twenty feet from him, its thunderclap instantaneous. It splinters the tree, and a branch knocks Lenin off his perch. The blessed boy wears the cast on his wrist like a medal. He claims to Big Ammachi that he was on the roof looking for "grace," but to Mariamma he admits he wanted thunderbolts to enter his body and give him the power to unleash lightning from his fingers, just like Lothar in *Mandrake the Magician*.

A month after his arrival, Mariamma and Podi find it hard to remember life at Parambil before Lenin. Podi is Mariamma's best friend, and about the same age. When they were boys, Podi's father, Joppan, and Philipose were also best friends. Podi means "tiny" or "dust." She and Podi agreed on most everything until Lenin came along. Mariamma resents Lenin for being "blessed" and for being fearless and for being a hero to all the children around, including Podi—though Podi denies it. Lenin is unconcerned about Mariamma's opinion, which makes it worse. She can't admit to anyone that though she detests him, she feels compelled to keep him in sight, in case she misses what he does next.

Mariamma overhears her father say to Big Ammachi, "The school sent for me again. Another fight. Because Lenin wanted to start a Communist Party chapter. He's ten! Ammachi, don't argue. Boarding school is what he needs." Mariamma should be pleased to hear this, but somehow, she isn't.

She dreams that night of Shamuel. He says, "Obey your father! He knows you break his rules. You're no different from Lenin and he might have to send you away." She wakes up troubled. What did it mean? If only she still shared a bed with Hannah she would have an answer. For Hannah, every dream had a meaning, just as for Joseph in Genesis. But Hannah has gone to convent school on a scholarship. Anna *Chedethi* doesn't know that Hannah wants to be a nun, which is why she loves fasting more than eating; Anna *Chedethi* would be shocked to learn that her daughter "mortifies" her flesh with a belt of knotted rope under her clothes. Hannah said that was what nuns did. Mariamma has no desire to be a nun.

Without Hannah, Mariamma must puzzle over her dream alone. Why was Shamuel in it? Everyone talks about Shamuel in the present tense. Can a person really be dead when he is talked about as though alive? She remembers the day Shamuel went missing. He'd gone to the provision store, and when he wasn't back well after lunch, her father went out looking. He retraced Shamuel's route. At the burden stone, he was relieved to see Shamuel, squatting down, leaning against one of the uprights while his sack rested on the horizontal slab. His chin was on his chest, as if he were sleeping. But he was cold to the touch. Shamuel's heart had stopped.

It was the first death in Mariamma's young life. She remembers her father leaving on his bicycle for Iqbal's godown, and returning with Joppan sitting sidesaddle on the horizontal bar. She'd never seen tears on the faces of grown men until that day. They laid Shamuel's body outside his hut in a coffin that rested on top of the old trestle that he loved. So many came to pay respects—it was as though a maharajah had died. Big Ammachi's grief had scared Mariamma; her grandmother wept by the casket, touching the forehead of a man who she said had watched over her from the day she arrived in Parambil sixty years before. They buried Shamuel next to his wife in the cemetery of the CSI church. Much later, her father and Big Ammachi had a brass panel set into the horizontal slab of the burden stone. Mariamma has made rubbings of the big letters with charcoal and paper. In Malayalam it reads,

"COME TO ME ALL YE THAT LABOR AND ARE HEAVY LADEN
AND I WILL GIVE YOU REST."
IN LOVING MEMORY OF SHAMUEL OF PARAMBIL

It's nearly dawn and she is no closer to the dream's meaning. She slips out of her room and ducks under her father's window. He won't hear her, but she can't let him see her shadow. Once clear of the house she races to the stream and then on to the canal. She hears footsteps behind her: Podi. They share one mind: whenever Mariamma leaves her bed, somehow Podi knows. The rules say they're not to swim without adults around. Rules are good for needlepoint and for nuns. She dives in, the water roaring around her ears. Moments later there's an explosion beside her as Podi plunges in. Swimming in the canal is their biggest secret and her greatest pleasure, even though if they're discovered the consequences are . . . well, she doesn't like to think about consequences.

Mariamma must get ready for school, but Podi lingers because Joppan is away. When her father is gone, Podi skips school and does as she pleases. If Joppan finds out, and he usually does, he thrashes her. Mariamma has heard him yell at Podi: "I was chased away when I wanted to study! Now they welcome you, and you're too lazy to go?" Joppan fascinates Mariamma. She only knows this one canal, while he knows *every* canal. Some people, no matter what they do, just seem larger, more significant, more confident than others. Joppan is like that. Lenin too. She's envious.

When she sees her father at breakfast, it hits her: the dream. Shamuel was telling her that her father knows about the canal! Maybe he always has. Before she heads to school, she goes to his room, where he's reconciling bills, muttering to himself. Seeing her, he pushes the ledger aside and looks up, smiling. She stands by his desk, straightens his pencils, ready to confess. She has a rule: she always tells the truth . . . when asked. She opens her mouth . . . but blurting out the truth when *not* asked is proving hard. She has to say *something*. She's committed. "Appa, I dreamed of Shamuel," she says at last.

"Yes?"

She nods. "Appa? Joppan is gone a lot."

"And?"

"All right, I'll see you later." *Not* confessing is much easier than confessing.

Shamuel? Joppan? Philipose sits there bewildered, then he shakes his head and chuckles to himself. Joppan *is* gone a lot. Had Mariamma stayed for more than ten seconds, and if she had really wanted to know, he might have told her that there was a moment when he thought he'd convinced Joppan to be around *all* the time. It was soon after Shamuel's funeral. His mother had summoned Joppan. He remembers that she sat, puffy-eyed, on her rope cot outside the kitchen while he and Joppan sat across from her on the low stools, like schoolboys. Big Ammachi said that whenever she paid Shamuel his wages, he'd take what he needed and ask her to save the rest for him in the strongbox in the *ara*. When the bank first opened, she put his savings into a joint account. "Now this is yours, Joppan," she said, handing him the passbook. Shamuel's house and plot were Joppan's too, to go along with Joppan's own plot. She also told Joppan she was writing over to him the long, narrow strip of land behind his plot that connected to the road. It was his to do with as he wished. She blessed Joppan, and through tears said that Shamuel was family, and Joppan, Ammini, and Podi were too.

After that, Philipose asked Joppan if he had a minute to visit with him. They sat in Elsie's old studio. Joppan lit a *beedi* and studied the passbook. After a while Joppan grinned and said, "How many cows you think are in here?" Philipose was puzzled. "Whenever I named a sum to my father that was more than a few rupees, he'd say, 'How many cows is that?' He knew what one cow was worth—that was his currency." Joppan's smile faded. "My father could have shown me the passbook before. You'd think he'd have appreciated that I know numbers and can keep accounts. If he saw me reading, he'd frown. It scared him for me to have that knowledge. He was a good man. But he wanted me to be him. The next Shamuel *pulayan* of Parambil."

Philipose felt guilty hearing this, because Shamuel had been proud of Philipose finishing high school and going to college. It bothered him to think Shamuel held Philipose to a different standard than he did his son. Father and son were often going at each other. But they had come together to save Philipose when he was at his opium-addled worst. One morning, soon after Elsie's drowning, with Big Ammachi's blessing, and after enlisting Unni and Damo, they carried Philipose out of his room. Damo had snatched him up with his trunk and swung him up on his back, where Unni grabbed him, and he sat sandwiched between Shamuel and Unni, while Joppan rode alongside on Philipose's bicycle. They went to Damo's logging camp, Philipose screaming and begging the whole way. From there Damo headed up a trail into the interior to the hut where Unni kept his pots of pungent salve, huge metal files, and sickles to keep Damo's nails and footpads from overgrowing. Whenever Damodaran decided to roam free in the jungle, that hut was where Unni waited, often drinking himself silly. Over the next six weeks, Joppan came and went, but Shamuel stayed with Philipose in that hut the entire time, putting up with his accusations and curses, nursing him through his cramps, hallucinations, and fevers until after two weeks his body was free of the grip of opium. Still they kept him there. He was ashamed. Long and heartfelt conversations with Shamuel allowed him to see how much the little wooden box had disrupted his life. The temptation never entirely vanished, but more than anything else, the thought of disappointing Shamuel, Joppan, and his mother was what kept him on the right path.

"Joppan, my mother and I want to make you an offer, though from what you just said, you will probably decline. But hear me out." Philipose said he and Big Ammachi owed Shamuel so much. Shamuel had guided him in every way in the daily running of Parambil. Without Shamuel he was lost both as a human being and as the manager of their lands, not coming close to filling Shamuel's shoes. "This is strictly a business proposition. It's *not* stepping into Shamuel's shoes. We'd like you to become manager of Parambil, make all the decisions in exchange for twenty percent of the profits from the harvest. We'd also pay a small monthly salary so that if we had a bad year, you'd still have income. If you choose to cultivate any undeveloped land, it's more work for you but more profit." Joppan was silent. "Twenty percent of the profits is substantial," Philipose added, "but it's worth it to me. I could write more. I'm not cut out for this."

The silence was getting uncomfortable. Joppan seemed to hesitate before speaking. "Philipose, what I'm about to say to you, I couldn't say to Big Ammachi. I have too much respect for her, for the love she had for my father and has for me. This will be hard for her or you to understand, but I'll say it anyway. The money in this passbook . . . ?" He paused to study Philipose.

"It's many cows?"

Joppan nodded. "Yes. But . . . also far fewer cows than my father deserved. If you think about how my *grandfather* helped your father carve out all these acres. Then consider how my father toiled here from when he was a child until the day he died. *All his life!* And at the end of it, what does he have? Yes, many cows. And his own plot for his hut—a rare thing for a *pulayan*. But just imagine if he were *not* a *pulayan*. Say he was your father's cousin. Say he worked side by side with your father. Then, after your father's time, say he continued working selflessly for Big Ammachi and for you for thirty more years. Every single day! What would be that cousin's due for his lifetime of labor? Wouldn't it be much more than what is in this passbook? It might be as much as half of all these lands."

The saliva turned sour in Philipose's mouth and glued his tongue to his teeth. "Is that what you're asking?"

Joppan looked at Philipose with annoyance, or was it pity? "I'm not *asking* for a single thing. Your mother sent for me. I wouldn't know of this passbook otherwise. And then y*ou* asked me to sit down, remember? I warned you this would be hard for you to hear. Your mother and you both said the same thing: how much you *owed* my father. He was family. I'm making a point to you as my best friend, as someone who speaks for the Ordinary Man. I thought you might *really* want to understand the truth. And the truth is that not everyone sees it the way Big Ammachi or you do. If you gave this relative of yours who worked his whole life here the same reward—a plot for a hut and his accumulated wages—everyone around would say he'd been exploited. But if it's for Shamuel *pulayan* . . . then it's generous. What you see as being generous or as being exploitation has everything to do with who you're giving it to. It helped that my father believed it was his fate to be a *pulayan*. He felt he was *lucky* to be working for Parambil! He felt rich at the end of his life, his wages adding up, and a plot for his hut and one for his son and now one more."

Philipose felt as though he'd walked into a hidden tree branch. The word "exploit" pierced him. It pained him to feel he'd taken advantage of Shamuel, a man he was willing to die for. He thought of himself and of Parambil as caste-free, above such considerations. Yet he had only to look at the face across from him and recall the *thwack!* of the *kaniyan*'s cane on Joppan's flesh and remember the humiliation of the boy who'd shown up so earnestly for school for the children of Parambil.

"Because you loved my father, this is harder for you to grasp," Joppan says. "You see yourselves as being kind and generous to him. The 'kind' slave owners in India, or anywhere, were always the ones who had the greatest difficulty seeing the injustice of slavery. Their kindness, their generosity compared to cruel slave owners, made them blind to the unfairness of a system of slavery that *they* created, they maintained, and that favored them. It's like the British bragging about the railways, the colleges, the hospitals they left us—their 'kindness'! As though that justified robbing us of the right to self-rule for two centuries! As though we should thank them for what they stole! Would Britain or Holland or Spain or Portugal or France be what they are now without what they earned by enslaving others? During the war, the British loved telling us how well they treated us compared to how the Japanese would treat us if they invaded. But should any nation rule over another nation? Such things only happen when one group thinks the other is inferior by birth, by skin color, by history. Inferior, and therefore deserving less. My father was no slave. He was beloved here. But he was *never* your equal so he wasn't rewarded as one." Joppan shook his head. "Some of your relatives here, in fact many of them, were *given* generous plots of two or three acres, more than a *pulayan* gets for a hut. It was enough land to do well. But honestly, other than Uplift Master and a few others, who has really made a success of it? Imagine if my father had been given *one* acre of his own to farm. Just think how well he'd have done."

The sophistication of Joppan's argument surprised Philipose. But even to think of Joppan's argument as "sophisticated" was exactly the kind of blindness Joppan was talking about. "Sophisticated" implied that people like Joppan or Shamuel were not entitled to use history and reason and their intellect.

Philipose said, "I take it the answer is no."

Joppan said, "I love Parambil. There's not a field here you and I didn't play on, or I didn't help my father harvest at one time. But I can't love it the way he did. Because it's not mine. But there's a bigger issue. Call me manager, reward me well, but for your relatives I'll still be Shamuel *pulayan*'s son, Joppan *pulayan*. The one whose *pulayi* wife weaves *ola* and sweeps the *muttam* of Parambil. I can't do much about being called a *pulayan*. But I can choose whether I want to *live* like one."

Soon after their first conversation, Philipose had gone back to Joppan with a second offer: they would give Joppan twenty acres of rough-cleared land that had never been cultivated, land that would be his very own. The deed would be held in escrow for ten years, during which time he would manage all Parambil lands, getting 20 percent of profits but without a monthly salary. After ten years he could move on, or they could negotiate a new contract for more land. Joppan was shocked. Big Appachen had laid claim to over five hundred acres, more than half of it rocky and steep or consisting of sunken swamps. He'd rough-cleared about seventy acres closest to the river and half of that was under cultivation. Joppan would own more land than any of Philipose's relatives.

Joppan had flashed his famous smile. "Philipose, if my father heard this, he'd call you mad." Joppan said he needed a drink and he pulled out a bottle of *arrack*. "Your offer means that you listened. You understood, painful as it must have been. It's very generous. I may regret this, but I'm going to say no." He took a large swig. "I've worked so many years with Iqbal, weathering tough times. Countless nights sleeping in the barge, looking up at the stars and dreaming of a fleet that can move in a quarter of the time it takes now. Yes, we've run into a setback with the motorized barge. Not water hyacinths tangling the propeller, but the entire proposal tangled in red tape. But we're getting closer. Even if I fail, I have to try. If I let go of my dream, something in me will die."

Philipose had felt himself shrinking, recalling *his* dreams before he went to Madras, his dreams when he met Elsie, when they got married, when she left and came back. He gulped down the *arrack* to dull the pain. He listened dully as Joppan talked about "the Party"—which always meant the Communists. That word "communists" might be anathema in many places, synonymous with treason, but in Travancore-Cochin-Malabar, in Bengal, and in more states in India, they were a legitimate party, real contenders. In Malayalam-speaking territories, the Party stalwarts were young former Congress Party members who felt betrayed once Congress came to power and gave in to the interests of big landowners and industry. The Party's membership wasn't just the disenfranchised and poor, but intellectuals and idealistic college students (often upper caste) who saw the Party as the only group willing to undo entrenched caste privilege. That year when Shamuel died—1952—the Party won twenty-five seats to Congress's forty-four. The merger of Malabar with Travancore-Cochin to form the state of Kerala was imminent, and it would bring new elections.

"Mark my words," Joppan had said as they had parted that night, "one day Kerala will be the first place in the world where a

Communist government is elected by a democratic ballot and not by bloody revolution."

As Philipose recalls this conversation of almost a decade ago, he's humbled to think that Joppan had been right: only a few years later, the Party won the majority of the seats in Kerala and formed the first democratically elected Communist government anywhere in the world.

CHAPTER 60

The Revelation of the Hospital

1964, The Maramon Convention

Malayalis of all religions doubt everything, except their faith. Each year the need to renew it, to be reborn, to drink again at the source, draws Malayali Christians to that great February revival meeting, the Maramon Convention. The Parambil family is no exception.

Ever since the first convention in 1895, held in a tent on the dry riverbed of the Pamba, the crowds have come in greater number every year. Not till 1936 did they acquire a microphone, a gift from the missionary E. Stanley Jones of America. Before that, "relay masters" stood like tent poles at intervals, stretching into the satellite tents and into the crowds on the riverbanks, repeating what the speaker said. But it is the Malayali nature that the relayers felt it their Christian duty to question and improve the translated message. E. Stanley Jones's admonition that "worry and anxiety are sand in the machinery of life, and faith is the oil" arrived at the crockery stalls as "Oh ye of little faith, your head is full of sand and there's no oil in your lamp." It nearly caused a riot.

From human relay, the Maramon Convention has gone to amplified excess, or so it seems to the Right Reverend Rory McGillicutty of Corpus Christi, United States of the Americas, as men shinny up palms, hauling up more speakers. As he waits offstage, his eardrums are threatened by hellish feedback and rifle-like pops that send the pariah dogs fleeing, leaving urine trails in the sand. The electrician lisps, "Teshting onetoothree, *kekamo?*" Yes, he can be heard at the back and even across the Palk Strait in Ceylon.

Reverend Rory McGillicutty's eyes are as overwhelmed as his ears. It began with his first glimpse of the mass of humanity and the sprawling tent city. He felt like a single locust in a plague as he struggled to keep up with the earnest *chemachen* escorting him. This crowd dwarfed anything he'd seen at the Tulsa State Fair or even the State Fair of Texas. They clutched their Bibles against their white clothes and were as serious as the business end of a .45. They were here to hear the Word, and the majority were not distracted by the food and bangle stalls, the magic shows, or the "Bowl of Death"—a huge hemisphere carved into the ground, its walls smoothed out, in which two motorcycle riders with kohl lining their eyes chased each other around at terrifying speeds, their motorcycles, defying gravity, climbing to the bowl's rim, almost parallel to the ground on which the observers stood looking in.

The biggest shock for McGillicutty was the crippled honor guard lining the approach. The lepers were on one side and the non-lepers on the other. For the latter, there was no common denominator other than misery. He saw children barely recognizable as such: one had fused fingers, a face like a pancake, and eyes where his ears might be, like an exotic fish. The *chemachen* said that these children were mutilated in infancy by their minders, who displayed them the length and breadth of India. "But," he said reassuringly, "they're *North* Indians," as though that mitigated the horror. Now, waiting backstage, McGillicutty is as nervous as a fly in a glue pot. It doesn't help that he's a last-minute replacement for Reverend William Franklin ("Billy") Graham, whose fame extends to the Maramon

Convention; his hosts are less enthusiastic about the stand-in. All the same, Rory McGillicutty's biggest worry is his translator.

His worry is legitimate. If the measure of English fluency is the ability to trot out a poorly recalled phrase from a third-form primer, like *Why ees the doug fallowing the mushter?* then many feel qualified. After all (they argue), to translate one only needed to speak Malayalam fluently, not English. Even the *achen* trained at the Yale Divinity School proved a disastrous translator, because he acted as though the speaker's words were not faithful to his translation.

Rory needn't worry; the convention has a proven translator, discovered by Bishop Mar Paulos at a Village Uplift event years ago when he saw him interpret for a grain expert from Coralville, Iowa, America. He translated just what the speaker said, while calling no attention to himself.

On the morning of the convention, this veteran translator sat before his mirror, trimming the caterpillar mustache that trekked below his nose and a quarter inch above his upper lip, owing allegiance to neither, emancipated from both. For a Malayali male past puberty, it's unmanly to be without one. The forms to choose from are legion: bottlebrush; upturned Sergeant-Major; downturned Brigadier; bushy, fascist nub ... The secret to the translator's caterpillar is to cozy up to the mirror, balloon out the upper lip, and use the naked razorblade pinched between right thumb and index finger, while the left hand pulls the skin taut. With miniscule downstrokes, one defines the upper and then—most critical—the lower margins. If he were to write a manual, the translator would say the strip of shaved skin *below* the mustache, the separation from the vermilion border of the upper lip, is the key.

Shoshamma watched her husband's punctilious edging. She said teasingly, "Uplift Master's mustache has a downlift on the left"—causing him to nick himself.

"Woman, why mock me? See what you've done?" She said sorry, but she was giggling. He struck his chest. "You've no idea of the passion burning here! *Passion!*" Her shoulders shook as she retreated. *Passion without the normal conjugal outlet because of your stubbornness!* That was his fault. He'd sworn to wait till she initiated things. He was still waiting.

The bus they took was so packed that it skipped its usual stops. Near Chenganur, a familiar figure made a death-defying leap onto the running board and pushed inside, saying, "My ticket is as good as yours! No caste system here!" Lenin was fourteen. He'd been packed off to a strict religious boarding school at ten. They'd seen him the previous holidays but already he was taller, with a faint mustache and an Adam's apple jutting as far forward as his chin. But his scalp looked as though a goat had grazed on it, and his face was bruised. He was thrilled to see them.

"A misunderstanding with my classmates," he explained. "I'm the hostel mess secretary. I decided to give our Sunday biryani to the hungry ones outside the church."

"*Aah*. And your classmates weren't prepared to fast?"

"The Sunday sermon was Matthew twenty-five. 'I was hungry, and you fed me.' Very meaningful to me. Then in Bible study my pious classmates swore to live by those principles. So . . ."

Shoshamma said, "*Monay*, you've heard the saying *Aanaye pidichunirtham, aseye othukkinirthaan prayasam.*" *Easier to control an elephant than to control desires!*

Uplift Master stared at her. Was this meant for him?

"True, *Kochamma*. Still, they're such hypocrites! What would Jesus say when there's food in one house and the neighbors starve. If Jesus returns, don't you think he'll vote Communist?"

A man behind Lenin shouted, "Bloody blasphemy! Christ voting for Communists?" The Party had made history and had many voters, but few would be on a bus heading to the Maramon Convention. In the ensuing scuffle, the bus lurched to a stop, and Lenin escaped through the driver's exit. He was laughing, arms pumping and pelvis gyrating like a Bollywood hero's, before he took off on a dead run.

* * *

Rory McGillicutty's face is pitted like a jackfruit from the acne of his youth, and he's as stocky as a *plavu*. He has a thick head of hair with each follicle looking as if it were hammered in like a railroad spike, but he has not been introduced to Jayboy's Brahmi Oil, so his hair is wild and unruly. It's a miracle that a man who grew up fishing in the flats of Aransas Bay could wind up as a fisher of men in the village of Maramon, in Kerala, India.

Uplift Master, meeting Rory backstage, is concerned: the man has no written speech, no notes, no verses bookmarked. Rory has a different concern. He has just watched a bishop deliver his speech in a monotone, his only gesture the tentative raising of a finger, like a child feeling a mastiff's nose, yet the unsmiling audience didn't mind. Rory's style, as he now explains to his translator, is the opposite. "I want my listeners to smell the singed hair, feel the heat of the eternal fires of damnation. Only then can one appreciate Salvation—you understand?"

Uplift Master's eyebrows shoot up, alarmed, though his head movement—like an egg wobbling on a counter—could mean yes or no. Or neither of those.

"I can testify to these things," McGillicutty says, "because I've been there. I'd still be in the gutter if I hadn't been saved by the blood of the Lamb." McGillicutty's fire-and-brimstone style plays well in the Deep South and as far north as Cincinnati. It was a winner in Cornwall, England, and the basis for his last-minute invitation to India. Rory has no fallback: his style *is* his message. He clutches Uplift Master's shoulders, looking him earnestly in the face. "My friend, when you translate you must *physically* convey my passion. Otherwise, I'm doomed."

Master has misgivings. "Reverend, please to remember, this is Kerala. We don't speak in tongues at the Maramon Convention. That and all is the Pentecostals. Here, we're . . . serious."

McGillicutty's face falls. He's not one to speak in tongues, but when the Holy Spirit makes the impressionable babble, who is he to object? Such a sight can transform a tentful of sinners.

"Well . . . Give it your best? *Try* to match your tone, your gestures with mine. Passion! Passion is what I am after!"

A *chemachen* alerts them that they're on after the choir. McGillicutty retreats to a corner.

Uplift Master watches him walk away. *The hubris of this jackfruit-face with no script!* But then he's humbled to see Rory get on his knees and bow his head in prayer. It should neither surprise Master nor soften his heart, but it does both. He feels like a hypocrite—didn't he just lecture Shoshamma about passion? When McGillicutty rises, Uplift Master puts his hand on the white man's shoulder—something he's never done in his life. "Not to worry. My best only I will do. Passion will be there. Mostly there. As much as possible it will be there." McGillicutty's relief makes Master feel he's done the Christian thing. McGillicutty thumps him on the back and then the reverend pours from a steel flask into its cup, offering it to his translator. Uplift Master sips and comes to a new understanding of the visitor, who motions for him to finish it. Then Rory downs a cup and sucks air between his teeth. Uplift Master feels the fiery whatever-it-is light up his chest. The passion within swells. He's a bit hungover, truth be told, and the reverend's flask is divine intervention. They have another cupful each. Uplift Master feels better than well. In fact, he has never felt better. His earlier trepidation has vanished. He loosens his shoulders. He tells himself, *If McGillicutty fails, it won't be for want of a good translator.*

The crowd murmurs with anticipation: a white priest from afar is always of interest, even if it's not Billy Graham. *We are enslaved even after we are free,* Uplift Master thinks. *We assume a white man's message is better than what our own might say.*

McGillicutty is announced, and they both walk on stage. There's pin-drop silence.

The reverend opens with a long, involved joke. When he comes to the punch line, he belts it out, one hand reaching to the sky, looking expectantly at the crowd. Several thousand smooth and expressionless faces look back at him. A red flush spreads above his collar. He turns to his translator, his eyes pleading.

Uplift Master flattens his oiled hair with his palm. He scans the crowd confidently, contemptuously, even. He holds their gaze for a long time. Then he addresses them as intimates.

"My long-suffering friends. Do you want to know what just happened? The Right Reverend Sahib Master-Rory *Kutty* just cracked a joke. To tell you the truth, I was so surprised I can't give you the details. Who expects a joke at the Maramon Convention? Let me just say it involved a dog, an old lady, a bishop, and a handbag . . ." Someone in the women's section giggles, a high-pitched ejaculation. There's shocked silence, and then the children laugh. Now ripples of laughter spread in response to Uplift Master's audacity.

"The joke isn't as funny as the reverend thinks. Besides, do any old ladies in Kerala carry handbags? At most, some coins wrapped in the kerchief, is it not? But please, let's not disappoint a guest from far, far away. Blessed are those who laugh at a visitor's jokes. Isn't that in Beatitudes? *Aah*. So, when I count to three, please, everybody, laugh—and I'm especially talking to you rowdy children sitting here in front, you masters of conniving and pretending holiness for your parents, because here's your God-given opportunity. Do it now, with the Lord's blessing. One, two . . . three!"

McGillicutty is thrilled. The old lady, the bishop, and the handbag has worked everywhere from McAllen to Murfreesboro—and now, Maramon. And *better* in Malayalam than in English!

The reverend turns serious and holds up his hand for silence. Uplift Master, his dark shadow, imitates his posture.

McGillicutty bows his head, hand still in the air. "My brothers and sisters, I stand before you as a sinner . . ."

Uplift Master translates: "Joking matters are now over, praise the Lord. He says, I stand before you as a sinner."

A murmur of appreciation ripples through the crowd.

"I stand before you as an adulterer . . . A fornicator."

"I stand before—" Uplift Master's voice stalls. His stomach feels just like that time in Madras when he had dysentery. If he uses the first-person pronoun to translate what McGillicutty said, won't everyone think *he* is the fornicator, the adulterer? He looks for Shoshamma in the crowd.

The reverend, glancing anxiously at his silent translator, says, "Friends, I'm not one to mince my words. A fornicator, I say. A man who slept with every loose woman and some who weren't till I pried them loose. That's who I was."

The bishops and priests in the front rows, who understand English all too well, glance nervously at each other.

Uplift Master smiles insincerely at McGillicutty, then at the crowd, while trying desperately to collect his thoughts. "The reverend says: Friends, my church across the sea is a big one. A huge one. Yet I've never seen as many people of faith as I see here today. And I'm proud that Uplift Master is the one to translate for me. His reputation extends from Maramon to my hometown. That's who I asked for. Thank you, Uplift Master."

Uplift Master bows his head modestly. Then he glances at McGillicutty with trepidation, trying to anticipate what might come next. When the man gets going, his mouth opens wide enough to swallow his own head.

"The number of people I need to make amends to, the number of people I led astray," McGillicutty says, sweeping his hand out, "extends from this side of the crowd to that one."

Uplift Master's eyes follow the reverend's hand, and he sees a woman in the third row keel over, overcome by humidity and the heat; he recognizes Big Ammachi as the first to minister to her, lowering her to the ground, fanning her with her program. And just outside the tent, it appears a child is having a convulsion. Adults cluster around the child.

Uplift Master sweeps his hand like Rory did: "When I look from that side of the river to this side of the river, I think of all the people here in this beautiful land who suffer from rare illness, or cancer, or need heart surgery, and have nowhere to go . . . Well, it troubles me, and I must speak openly about it."

"I broke my mother's heart when I lay in carnal knowledge with my own nanny!" the reverend says, clutching his chest. "An innocent country woman. I snuggled at her breast, and yet at thirteen I took advantage of her."

Uplift Master, barely waiting for Rory to finish, clutches his own chest and says, "If some child is born with a hole in its heart like our Papi's little child and needs an operation, where can they go?" He's inventing Papi and child, but it's in service of the Lord. "That poor boy was ten and bluer than he was brown before Papi raised the money to take him to another state, all the way to Vellore, to the Christian Medical College . . . By then, it was too late!"

Now McGillicutty catches his translator off guard by stepping off the low stage to where all the children sit cross-legged. He grabs one child. The gangly fellow he pulls up is all ears, knees, and elbows and has a gap in his teeth big enough for a tent peg to pass through. Uplift Master recognizes him as an unfortunate, a *potten*—born deaf and dumb—who always gets a choice place at the very front. Earlier, this boy laughed loudest and was last to stop. Uplift Master sees him at the convention year after year because his parents hope for a miracle. This child has never spoken an intelligible word. What misfortune for the reverend to pick the *potten* out of all the children!

"When I was a father," the reverend says, now back onstage with the grinning *potten*, "I abandoned my own boy, no bigger than this angel. He went hungry. My in-laws had to bring food because I spent my wages on gambling and on women!"

The woman who fainted is carried out. Uplift Master sees Big Ammachi looking directly at him with excitement and anticipation. He says, "Why is it that a child who is seriously ill must travel to

Madras and beyond for care? What if help were available here? I'm not talking about a one-room clinic with one doctor, and one cow by the gate. I mean a *real* hospital, many stories tall, with specialists for the head as well as for the tail and all parts in between. A hospital as good as any in the world. If one white missionary woman, Ida Scudder, God bless her soul, could build a world-class institution in Vellore, in the middle of nowhere, can we Christians in this land of milk and honey not do the same?"

"Only a devil can neglect a child like this to whisky and whoring," says the reverend, his voice breaking. "But then one day when I was lying in the gutter in Corpus Christi, Texas, the Lord called out to me. He said, 'Say my name!' and I said, 'Jesus, Jesus, Jesus!'"

Uplift Master translates: "Friends, this isn't the message I meant to preach, but the Lord seems to have brought me all the way here from Body of Christ in Texas and has put these words in my mouth to convey to you. He says, behold the suffering around you! He says, isn't it time to change it? He asks, do you really need another church? He says, glorify my name with a hospital worthy of me. I hear his voice just as I did so many years ago when I was a broken, sinful man, lying in the gutter, and the Lord appeared to me and called out, 'Say my name!' And I said, 'Yesu, Yesu, Yesu!'"

The crowd is deathly quiet. The only sound is the cawing of crows near the food stalls. Rory McGillicutty and Uplift Master wait, both hoping the audience will respond with "Jesus, Jesus, Jesus." But call-and-response is simply not the Malayali style. Uplift Master thinks the crowd looks at him without sympathy. *They want me to fail. Shoshamma will find this so funny.* Only Big Ammachi looks up at him with hope, nodding to encourage him. *I'm trying my best, Ammachi!* He feels terrible about letting her down.

All at once the *potten* shatters the silence: he says in the loud, unmodulated voice of the deaf, "Yesu! Yesu! Yesu!"

McGillicutty is lightning quick to put the microphone before the boy's mouth so that the *potten*'s "Yesu" reverberates in the tent and beyond. Rory bends down to the boy, dispensing with his trans-lator. "Say it again, son, say, Yesu, Yesu, Yesu!" he shouts.

"Yesu! Yesu! Yesu!" cries the *potten*, thrilled when his words turn into sound waves that buffet his body. He hears! He speaks! He dances with joy.

There's a crescendo of murmurs from the crowd as word spreads from front to back, then to the satellite tents and to those standing outside, to the bangle sellers, the beggars, and the daredevil motorcyclists: *A* potten *has just spoken for the first time! A miracle!*

"Say it with him, my friends," McGillicutty yells, his face red with effort, trying to flog life into the docile multitude. "SHOUT from the rooftops: Jesus! Jesus! Jesus!" But only the *potten* heeds him, shouting, "Yesu! Yesu! Yesu!"

"*Aah*," Uplift Master says, incensed by this Malayali reticence. "So God just gave voice to the dumb. A miracle! Now, through His messenger, this *plavu* stump from Body of Christ, Texas, God asks you for a sign of your attentiveness. He asks, are you listening? Are you here to receive the Holy Spirit? To be cleansed and renewed in faith? Or are you embarrassed to call the Lord's name? Are you here to sight and gossip and see who's pregnant, and which young man is being proposed for which young lady?" There's tittering from the children's section. Uplift Master senses an opportunity and turns to them. "Then you just sit there. Let your children show you what faith and courage look like. Blessed children, please show these adults how it's done. You saw the courage of one of your own who stands up here. Give him your support! Say, 'Yesu, Yesu, Yesu!'"

Blessed indeed are the children, for they will never pass up sanctioned invitations to show up their parents. They jump to their feet, and hundreds of young voices shout, "Yesu, Yesu, Yesu!" a sound that goes straight to God's ears. Uplift Master extends his hand, palm up, pointing to the children's section, while staring at the adults with a meaningful look. *Do you see?* Then he says, "That's why

Christ said suffer the little children, forbid them not unto me. Now can you say it? Yesu, Yesu, Yesu!"

The women, the mothers, rise and lend their voices: "Yesu, Yesu, Yesu!" What alternative do husbands have? The men rise: "Yesu, Yesu, Yesu!" The bishops and priests, models of Christian reticence and propriety, are in a bind, because there's something unholy about such unbridled passion, not to mention the bizarre translation. But how can they keep quiet when their Savior's name is being sung out? They join in. "Yesu, Yesu, Yesu!"

Chanting like this has never before been heard at the staid convention. The crowd is drunk with sound and cannot stop. Uplift Master feels the hairs rise on the back of his neck. Glory, glory, glory! Surely the Holy Spirit *is* here. He scans the crowd for Shoshamma's face. *Now do you see the passion?!* Rory winks at him.

After a long time, the chanting finally gives way to thunderous clapping, the crowd applauding itself. The *potten* is received back in the children's section like Jesus entering Jerusalem, and his cheering friends lift him off the ground. The audience take their seats, smiling at each other, shocked at having broken their self-inflicted decorum.

"My friends, my friends," McGillicutty says. He takes Matthew 25:33 as his text, pointing it out to Uplift Master. "The Lord will measure our lives on Judgment Day, and my dear friends . . ." McGillicutty holds the open Bible to his chest and comes to the edge of the stage, looking as if he might cry. He falls to one knee and points his trembling finger heavenward. "Mark my words, we'll have to ANSWER to him!"

Uplift Master thinks this is proof that the Holy Spirit is indeed present, as McGillicutty came up with the same verse as Lenin. Master, also clutching his Bible, falls to one knee, but artfully hiking up his *mundu* first. He translates: "God sits in a gold *kasera* like the one on your verandah, only a hundred times bigger. He will measure our lives on Judgment Day. If the Lord lets you enter His kingdom, it will be *kappa* and *meen* curry for all your days. But if not, you'll go to the other place. Do you remember the abandoned well on that property where what's-their-name fell in, and no rope was ever long enough to go that far down?" (He's confident that everyone has some version of that tragedy.) "Those depths are nothing compared to where you'll be going. The serpents that live down there have bred with fallen humans for so long that the place is populated by creatures with fangs, human hands with claws on the ends, and a serpent's body."

He has no idea where these words are coming from other than the Holy Spirit. He spots Coconut Kurian in the audience, glowering at him, arms locked across his chest, and Master continues before McGillicutty can go on: "Let's say you're there because you hoarded coconuts and jacked up the price, think of how it will feel to live with those creatures biting and clawing you and coiled around you for all eternity."

There are gasps—he's gone too far. No one's ever spoken in such graphic fashion at the Maramon Convention. On the other hand, there's little love lost for hoarders.

"Let Him in, my brethren. He is knocking," McGillicutty says in an impassioned voice, tears in his eyes. "Open your hearts to the Lord. Clothe your neighbor. Comfort him when he is in sorrow. Remember in Matthew, 'I was ill, and you cared for me, I was hungry, and you fed me . . .'"

Uplift Master, for once, translates word for word then adds: "Year after year, when our loved ones are sick, we take them by bus and train far, far away for help, and only if we have the money. Year after year, our loved ones give up the ghost for lack of a hospital like Vellore here in Kerala! Together we could build ten first-class hospitals, but we spend the money enlarging our cow sheds! The Lord says, 'Build my hospital!' Did you not hear it? Did you not call out His name? Let's make history. Each of you, take those notes out of your pocket." Uplift Master pulls out a bundle of notes from the tuck-in fold of his *mundu*. It's money from the sale of their paddy, money that he was supposed to deposit. "My wife has bid me to give generously!"

He puts the notes one by one into the donation basket on the stage, so people can see the color. Somewhere in the crowd, he's sure he hears Shoshamma gasp. The ushers jump to life, passing baskets left and right, and even those faithful outside the tent on the riverbanks find they cannot retreat, because ushers with baskets block their way.

"What are we waiting for?" says McGillicutty, who understands this phase of a meeting all too well, though he's puzzled at how his translator has gotten ahead of him. "Remember Luke 6:38. 'Give, and it will be given to you. Good measure, pressed down, shaken together, running over, will be put into your lap.'"

Uplift Master translates the verse, while McGillicutty pulls bills out of his own pocket to put in the hamper.

Uplift Master can hear the workings of the crowd's mind, the influence of Doubting Thomas. Aah, *where will such a hospital be?* Aah, *what is the hurry? Why not the government do this? Why not?*

The parents of the *potten* come on stage with their son. The wife takes off her bangles, then the gold chain on her neck, and puts them into the basket that Rory holds out. The father gives his chain. McGillicutty cries, "God bless you!"

Then, to Uplift Master's astonishment, comes Big Ammachi, all by herself, surprising her family who are still in their seats. She stands there, a tiny figure on the stage, and unscrews her *kunukku* from each earlobe. Then she unfastens her chain. Now her thirteen-year-old granddaughter, Mariamma, as well as Anna *Chedethi* rush up to join her, slipping off their bangles and necklaces.

Uplift Master says, "For with the measure you use it will be measured back to you. Do you understand? The Holy Spirit is observing! Put nothing now and reap nothing forever. Nothing!"

Now a line forms to go onstage, as if gold is being handed out and not handed in. To the astonishment of the clergy, men and women are peeling gold from ears, fingers, wrists . . . It's a day when no one holds back. Because if there's one thing Malayalis fear, it's missing out when there's reaping to be done.

CHAPTER 61

The Calling

1964, Parambil

"A miracle!" Big Ammachi says as they wait for the bus home. Her hands unconsciously flutter to her earlobes, to their unaccustomed weightlessness. "I've prayed for a clinic at Parambil for years. Today, the Lord intervened through our Uplift Master. Not only a clinic, but there will also be a hospital at Parambil. Like the one at Vellore!"

Philipose is uncertain. "But Ammachi, it doesn't mean that if they build a hospital, it will be in Parambil—"

"It *will* be!" She whips around to face him, her expression one of such conviction and resolve that he's silenced. "We must do everything to make it so! *In* Parambil!"

On the bus, Mariamma studies her grandmother with pride and wonderment; she has never seen her this excited. Mariamma can't believe what unfolded on stage, and how moved she herself was, caught up in the excitement. Those emotions are mixed up with her pleasure at seeing Lenin, who has gone overnight from boy to man, albeit a man shorn of hair. He's almost fourteen. She saw him studying her. Her thirteen-year-old body has changed too and he was tongue-tied when he came up to greet her before the speeches began. She wonders if Big Ammachi or her father noticed.

But the convention felt different for another reason this year, one that was disturbing. When they first approached the tents and walked past the usual lengthy line of beggars, the sight had unnerved her. Her uneasiness about the crippled and maimed had lingered long after they sat down. Now, on the bus, she confides this to her grandmother.

"Before, the beggars were just *there*. An unpleasant sight, a bit scary, but no more than other unpleasant things one must see."

"*Ayo!* Those are *people*, Mariamma, not things."

"That's my point, I suppose. This year, I really *saw* them as people. I was immature before. I understood for the first time that they weren't *always* blind, or *always* lame. Maybe they were born normal like me before a disease affected them. I thought, *This can happen to me!* It left me frightened, shaken, long after we sat down."

"I noticed your disquiet. But I thought it was because of our Lenin." Mariamma blushes. Big Ammachi puts her arm around her namesake. Mariamma is so much taller than her grandmother, but she loves the feeling of her grandmother's arm around her. "*Molay*, it takes a special person to see those poor beggars as human beings. Many people never notice. As though they are invisible. It speaks well of your maturity. We *should* be scared and never take our health for granted. We must pray and give thanks each day for good health."

"Ammachi, when that woman near us collapsed, I was terrified. I could hardly breathe. I wanted to run. But you . . . you went right to her. I'm ashamed."

"*Chaa!* What did I do except lay her down, fan her face? Don't be ashamed." They ride in silence for a while. Big Ammachi says, "I've seen more than my share of suffering and tragedy in my life, *molay*. I was always helpless. When your grandfather was sick, I could do nothing. When we pulled JoJo out of the water, if we had had a hospital close by . . . who knows? When Baby Mol gets ill, you know how far we go to find a doctor. *That's* why I got up on stage, Mariamma.

Because I don't want us to be helpless or frightened. Doctors know what to do. A hospital can care for the sick. That's why I want a hospital closer to our people. I'm old now, and so that's all I can do."

"Maybe it was better when I didn't notice the beggars," Mariamma says. "Now I'll be walking around frightened that I might go blind, or get fits, or collapse like that woman."

"Listen, she fainted, that's all. It was hot, she may not have drunk enough water. It happens all the time. Your father sees blood and gets faint. I've been alive long enough that I recognize fainting." After a while, her grandmother turns to her. "Mariamma, sometimes when you are most afraid, when you feel most helpless, that is when God is pointing out a path for you."

"You mean like wanting a hospital close by?"

"No, I'm talking about you. *Your* fears. Fear comes from not knowing. If you *know* what it is you are seeing, if you *know* what to do, then you won't be afraid. If . . ." Her grandmother trails off.

"You mean like being a doctor?"

"Well, some people may not be cut out for it. It's unnatural for them. I can't tell you what to do. But if I could live this life one more time, that's what I would want to do. Out of my fear, out of helplessness. In order to be less fearful, and to *really* help. You should pray about it. Only you can know." Big Ammachi hesitates. "If that is what God leads you to, I can tell you, your grandmother would be very happy."

Mariamma snuggles against the familiar shoulder, thinking over what she heard. In a year and a half, she'll leave for Alwaye College to start her pre-degree. She had planned to study zoology. But if she's moved and frightened by *human* suffering and disease, why study weaver ants and tadpoles? Why not medicine? If God is pointing her in some direction, she wishes God would point more clearly. If one *imagines* what God is saying, is that the same as God actually speaking?

She feels altered by the time they get home. Talking with Big Ammachi, addressing her fears, has brought her comfort and a curious stillness of her mind, a sensation that lingers. Could it be that God spoke to her just now through her grandmother? She feels no compulsion to talk about it further, not with Big Ammachi, nor with her father. She will pray, too, but mostly she'll try to hold on to this feeling of stillness. Whether God has spoken or has yet to speak, she's at peace.

The Hospital Fund created in the wake of the Maramon Convention carries the hopes and expectations of the thousands who attended the unforgettable sermon by Rory McGillicutty (and Uplift Master). That event, now referred to as the Revelation of the Hospital, is followed by an even bigger miracle: a generous donation of 150 acres of land at Parambil in the heart of old Travancore. It makes it hard to think of reasons to put the hospital anywhere else.

More than a year later, when the time comes for Mariamma to leave for Alwaye College, she's certain: she will set her sights on medical school. When she shares her decision with the family, her grandmother's joy is something to behold. Her father couldn't be happier. He says, "My mother wanted that for me, but I just wasn't cut out for it. You were destined for this."

Big Ammachi takes Mariamma aside to give her a gold necklace and cross. "Years ago, when JoJo died, my heart broke. In my sorrow, I prayed to God. I said, 'Please cure this, or send us someone who can.' *Molay*, I'm going to tell you something I never told you before, something I would leave out each time you wanted to hear the story of the day you were born, and lighting the *velakku*. The truth is I prayed that God would point you to medicine. But I didn't want you weighed down with my expectation. I'm glad it was revealed to you. You know that I pray for you every night and I always will. I'm too old to go with you, and besides, I can't leave Baby Mol, but your Big Ammachi will be with you every step of the way. Even when I'm long gone, you carry my name. Never forget: *I am with you always.*"

CHAPTER 62

Tonight

1967, Parambil

Not long after Mariamma's departure, Baby Mol wakes from dreamless sleep and sits bolt upright, her pudgy hands clutching at the window bars. Seeing her daughter's terrified expression, gasping for air, sweat pouring down her face, Big Ammachi raises the alarm, certain her precious baby is dying. Philipose and Anna *Chedethi* come running. The veins on Baby Mol's forehead and neck bulge like rope, and bubbly froth comes out of her mouth when she tries to cough. But what is most shocking for a mother to witness is the fear on her fearless child's face. Gradually, as Baby Mol sucks in the fresh night air, she recovers. She falls asleep on a chair by the window, propped up on pillows.

By morning, in a hired car, they're at a government clinic an hour and a half away. If only the new hospital were already finished! The lady doctor gives Baby Mol an injection to remove fluid from her swollen legs and prescribes a daily diuretic and digitalis. She thinks Baby Mol's stunted growth and bent spine have restricted her lungs; over time that has put a strain on her heart, and now fluid is damming up behind it.

After the visit, Baby Mol pees many times, and that night she rests comfortably. Only Big Ammachi lies awake, watching her little girl's breathing. The household is asleep, so she converses with the one who keeps vigil with her. "We never starved, Lord, never wanted for anything. I didn't take my blessings for granted. But there's always something, Lord, isn't there? Every year there's a new worry. I'm not complaining! It's just that I imagined there'd come a time when I *wouldn't* have anything more to worry about." She laughs. "Yes, I know it was silly to expect that. This is *life*, isn't it? Just as you intended it to be. If there were *no* problems then I suppose I'd be in heaven, not Parambil. Well, I'll take Parambil. The hospital coming here is all your doing—don't think that I'm not grateful. Still, now and then, Lord, I could use some peace. A bit of heaven on earth, that's all I'm saying."

Baby Mol recovers, but with Mariamma gone Parambil feels off-kilter again, just as when Philipose left for Madras. It's as though the sun rises on the wrong side of the house and the stream has reversed course. The reminders of her are everywhere: the impossibly fine needlepoint portrait of her hero, Gregor Mendel; the drawings she made of the human body, copied from her mother's anatomy book. Philipose even misses the unmistakable vibrations he'd sense in the early morning when his daughter snuck under his window to plunge into the canal, though it always made him anxious. She thought he didn't know. Big Ammachi sees her son reading aloud, though softly, from a novel every night, even though there is no one to read to.

Podi surprises her parents by consenting to marry, as though with Mariamma's departure, she's ready to leave Parambil. Joseph, her groom, is of the same caste, and works in a warehouse. Joppan came across him first and liked the boy's confidence and ambition, reminiscent perhaps of Joppan's youthful self. Joseph is determined to get to the Gulf and has a precious "No Objection Certificate"—NOC—through a broker. His first year's salary will go to paying this off. The marriage is over before Philipose's letter reaches Mariamma at Alwaye College. Her peevish reply asking why she wasn't invited reminds him of his own sentiments when Joppan married.

These days, when Big Ammachi stands on the canal's edge, she sees the future. On the other bank, instead of trees and shrubs she sees temporary sheds covering great stacks of brick, bamboo, and sand. The canal is being widened to allow for bigger barges to come by. Damo is overdue. What will he make of all this activity? She wishes he would come now for no other reason than that she misses him; there's much to tell him.

On a Thursday evening in late February the weather is as perfect as it gets, a gentle breeze stirring the clothes on the line. Big Ammachi sits with Baby Mol on her bench, sharing with her daughter the unchanging view of the *muttam*. "You drink the hot *jeera* water, and take your medicines, then you'll sleep well tonight."

"Yes, Ammachi. Will I snore?"

"Like a water buffalo!" Baby Mol guffaws at this. "But I *like* your snores, *molay*. It tells me my little girl is sleeping soundly and all is well with the world."

"All is well with the world, Ammachi," Baby Mol repeats.

"It is, my precious. You have no worries, do you?"

"No worries, Ammachi."

What is worry but fear of what the future holds? Baby Mol lives completely in the present and is spared all worry. Unlike her daughter, Big Ammachi, now seventy-nine, increasingly inhabits the past, reliving the memories of her years in this house. Her life before Parambil, that fleeting childhood, is like a dream that crumbles in daylight; she holds onto its edges while the middle vanishes.

This gloaming hour before they go to bed is her favorite time. Baby Mol sits sideways, while Big Ammachi unties her ribbons and combs out her thinning hair. Her daughter dangles one leg off the bench. Her adorable doll's feet of old now stay puffy with fluid, her anklebones obscured, the overlying skin thin and shiny.

Baby Mol says, "I love weddings!"

Her mother looks for a connection with the events of the day, but she finds none. "I do too, Baby Mol. One day, our Mariamma will get married."

"Why not marry now?"

"You know why! She's in college. Premedical."

"*Pre*-medical," Baby Mol says, enjoying the sound of it.

"Then she'll study to be a doctor. Like the one who helped you. *After* that, she can marry."

"We'll have a big wedding. I'll dance!"

"You must! But wait . . . we need a good groom, don't we? Not some silly boy who picks his nose. Not a tree stump who doesn't move and says, 'Bring me this, bring me that.'"

Baby Mol says, "No tree stump!" and guffaws so hard that she has a coughing spell. "What kind of husband do we want, Big Ammachi?"

"I don't know. What kind do you think?"

"Well, he must be at least as tall as me," Baby Mol says. "And as good-looking as our precious baby." By that she means Philipose. "And he must have a *good* walk." She eases off the bench effortfully, but intent on demonstrating. The walk she portrays is so reminiscent of her father's broad stride, the feet slightly outturned, that Big Ammachi gasps.

"*Aah!* So a brave, fearless fellow?" Baby Mol nods, but keeps walking because there's more to convey. "Oh, I see. A confident fellow but not *too* confident, is that it? He must be humble, yes?"

"And kind," Baby Mol says. "And he must like ribbons. And *beedis*!"

"*Chaa!* If he doesn't like ribbons, forget him. But *beedis*, I don't know . . ."

"Ammachi, *beedis* just to look at! But no little box, no black pearls!"

Perhaps their audience has been there for some time: Philipose pokes his head out of his room, his glasses on the tip of his nose and a book in his hand; and Anna *Chedethi* emerges from the kitchen, her hand stifling a laugh, taking in Baby Mol's promenading up and down, a sight so rare of late.

"Hello, hello! What're you all looking at?" Big Ammachi scolds, shaking a finger in mock anger at the audience. "Can't Baby Mol and I have a private moment? Did the *Manorama* say we're giving out free bananas to all the monkeys?"

"No free bananas for monkeys!" Baby Mol chants, delighted. The sound is so joyful that her "precious baby," now graying and towering over her, falls in step with her, taking up the refrain. "No free bananas for monkeys! No free bananas for monkeys!"

Big Ammachi's heart swells with joy to see this: her Baby Mol of old, Baby Mol of the monsoon dance, her precious, precious daughter, eternally five years old. *Such a gift, Lord. Thank you, thank you.*

At bedtime, it takes a while to settle Baby Mol against her mountain of pillows. Her pantomime has left her breathless. Her mother massages her ankles, milking them up in the hopes the swelling will recede by morning.

Outside, the frogs announce themselves and Caesar howls at the moon. In the kitchen, Anna *Chedethi* lights the lamp and a moth comes to dance around it. From Philipose's room, the radio crackles, a woman speaks but is cut off when he turns the dial to another voice. These foreigners chattering at dusk were sounds once so alien to Parambil. Now, if Big Ammachi didn't hear these voices, something would feel amiss. The world is rapidly changing, but still the house feels just like Baby Mol: timeless.

Big Ammachi lies beside her daughter on the mat, Baby Mol's pudgy fingers encircled around her mother's upper arm like an amulet, a ritual of hers from the time she was a baby. Big Ammachi hums a hymn; she hears a melodious echo from Anna *Chedethi*, sweeping the kitchen. Baby Mol's breathing slows.

Big Ammachi asks Baby Mol *the* question, the one she has asked every night for over a decade now, a question that counts on

Baby Mol's gift of prophecy. She asks it partly in jest, and always in a whisper.

"Baby Mol? Is this my night?"

For all these years, the answer has been the same. "No, Ammachi. It can't be. Then who'd be there to take care of Baby Mol?" There hasn't been a single night on which Baby Mol has failed to give that answer.

But tonight, Baby Mol is silent. Her eyes stay closed, a smile playing at the corners of her lips.

At first, Big Ammachi thinks that she didn't hear. "Baby Mol?"

Her daughter gives her mother's arm a squeeze, and her smile stays the same. Baby Mol heard. But she doesn't reply. Big Ammachi waits for a long time while Baby Mol's breathing slows, and the encircling fingers around her mother's arm relax. Big Ammachi kisses her daughter on her forehead.

What did I imagine? That I'd go on forever?

She feels some sorrow, just as when she was a twelve-year-old on the eve of a journey to marry an unseen widower, leaving her beloved mother and her home behind. That was the second-saddest day of her life. But on this occasion, her sorrow is mixed with some excitement.

She gently disentangles her arm. No, she doesn't feel sad for herself, or afraid. She only worries about Baby Mol. But she knows she can count on Philipose and Anna *Chedethi* and even Mariamma to care for this precious child. It's arrogance to think that only she can do it. Still, can anyone really replace a mother? *Nothing more I can do, is there, Lord? If it's my time, then let it be so.* This *is the moment when I can stop worrying, isn't it? So be it.*

And if so, there are two faces she must see once more. She gets to her feet.

In the kitchen, Anna *Chedethi* seeds the leftover milk with a fleck of that day's yogurt, covers it with a cloth, and moves it to a cool spot. Big Ammachi scans the darkened walls. Long ago this stopped being a kitchen, becoming instead sacred space, a faithful companion that cosseted her with its warm, scented embrace. She gives it her silent thanks.

Anna has made the *jeera* water. Big Ammachi adds an extra dollop of honey to the hot cups, a treat for herself and her son. Standing in the kitchen for the last time, she feels a surge of love for Anna *Chedethi*, the angel who came when they most needed her, and who became her companion of so many years. When Anna *Chedethi* notices Big Ammachi still standing there, cups in hand, looking at her tenderly, her smile breaks out like the sun through heavy clouds.

"What is it?" Anna *Chedethi* says.

"Nothing, my dear. Just looking at you, that's all. You were lost in thought."

"*Aah aah* . . . Was I?" Anna *Chedethi* laughs self-consciously, such a happy musical sound. Only Big Ammachi can hear the sad undertones. Hannah's decision to join a nunnery has dimmed the lamp of perpetual joy that lights Anna *Chedethi*'s face. But it has only solidified her devotion to and her affection for the family of which she is now a seamless part.

"You and your laughter have been keeping apart of late."

"Is it prayer time?" Anna *Chedethi* says, embarrassed. "Were you waiting on me?"

"We already prayed, silly! Don't you remember? You sang so sweetly."

"Goodness! Yes, we did!" Anna *Chedethi* says, laughing at herself.

"I prayed for you, as I do every night. And for Hannah. Sleep well, my dear one. Sleep well. God bless you." She doesn't trust herself to look back to see Anna *Chedethi*'s response.

She pauses outside the *ara*. Then she peeks into the old bedroom where she gave birth and where her mother spent her last days, and where Mariamma was born—it has been Anna *Chedethi*'s room for years now. Her gaze sweeps lovingly over the tall *velakku* that she lit after Mariamma's birth, again ensconced in its corner. The cellar below this room has been quiet for many years, the spirit there having found peace.

She sits for a moment on Baby Mol's beloved bench, still clutching the two cups, looking up at the rafters, then out at the *muttam*, taking it all in for the last time, her eyes misty. Then she rises and goes to Philipose. The radio is silent and he's busy writing at the small desk in his bedroom. He looks up and smiles, puts his pen down. She sits on the bed, where he joins her, and she hands him his cup. She doesn't trust herself to speak as she gazes at him. She loves her son so much, loved him even during the times when he'd been so unlovable, so enslaved by opium. She'd loved Elsie too, like a daughter. How terribly the couple had suffered. She sighs. *If I haven't said what I need to say by now, it couldn't be worth saying.* She laughs, conjuring up her husband and his silences. *I'm becoming more like you all the time, old man. Letting the spaces between words speak for me. I'll see you soon.*

Philipose says, "What is it, Ammachi?" reaching for his mother's free hand and squeezing it.

"Nothing, *monay*," she says, sipping on her cup. But it *isn't* nothing. She's thinking of Elsie, of the drawing Elsie left behind: a newborn and an older woman—herself. Drowning accidentally is terrible, but to drown oneself deliberately is a mortal sin. The drawing was Elsie's way of committing Mariamma to Big Ammachi's care. She never showed it to her son. Never shared her misgivings. He will find it in her belongings and make of it what he will.

Unlike Baby Mol, who sees things forward, she sometimes sees things only by looking back . . . but mostly the past is unreliable. She thinks of the day Elsie went into labor, much earlier than expected, and when *two* lives hung desperately in the balance. That day God in His infinite mercy gave her the two things she prayed for: Elsie's life and Mariamma's life. It could so easily have been two funerals on the same day. And then Elsie drowned.

"Forgive me," she says now.

"For what?"

"For everything. Sometimes we can wound each other in ways we don't intend."

Philipose regards his mother with concern, waiting for her to explain. When she doesn't, he says, "Ammachi. I put you through so much. And you forgave me long ago. Why would I not do the same? So, whatever it is, I forgive you."

She rises, touches his cheek, kisses him on his forehead, letting her lips linger there for a long time. From the doorway, she turns, smiles, blinks her silent love to him, and heads for her bath.

She's glad for the luxury of an indoor bathroom, but if it wasn't dark outside she'd visit her bathing spot or swim in the river one last time to take her leave. She'll miss those rituals just as she'll miss the monsoon and the way it nourishes body and soul just as it does the land. She disrobes and pours water over her head, gasping and luxuriating in the feeling as it washes over her. *Such precious, precious water, Lord, water from our own well; this water that is our covenant with You, with this soil, with the life You granted us. We are born and baptized in this water, we grow full of pride, we sin, we are broken, we suffer, but with water we are cleansed of our transgressions, we are forgiven, and we are born again, day after day till the end of our days.*

Her mat takes her weight kindly, eases the ache in her back as she stretches out. She pictures Mariamma, her namesake, far away in Alwaye, studying under a lamp, her books before her. Big Ammachi sends her a blessing and a prayer. Perhaps another matriarch with advance warning of her impending departure might summon the family from near and far. *What for? All my life I told them, "Keep going! Keep faith!"* She kisses the sleeping Baby Mol, her eternal child, hoping that she might not suffer her mother's absence too much. Her lips linger on her daughter just as they did on her son. Baby Mol in sleep automatically wraps her fingers around her mother's arm again.

She says a prayer for everyone. Her children and her grand-child. Anna *Chedethi*, and Hannah. She asks God to bless Joppan, Ammini, and Podi. She thinks of Shamuel, of the burden stone. *It's my turn, my dear old friend. I can put my burden down, too.* She prays for Lenin, the incorrigible child and future priest. She remembers Odat *Kochamma*, and smiles—maybe they can pray together once more in the evenings. She prays for Damo, who increasingly prefers his high forest paths and the company of other elephants. She'd have liked to see him again, lay her hand against his wrinkled hide. She saves her husband for the end. They have been apart for over four decades now, even though he, like Shamuel, is here in every par-ticle of Parambil. When they're together again, she'll tell him every single thing he missed, even if it takes longer than all the years she has been alive. She'll have an eternity to catch up.

The next morning when the sun rises, the hearth fires have burned down. Chickens scuff around outside. Caesar runs to the back of the kitchen and waits expectantly.

It is Philipose, putting down his pen to see why the house is so silent, who finds Big Ammachi and Baby Mol wrapped in each other's arms, unmoving, their faces peaceful.

He doesn't raise an alarm but sits cross-legged beside them, utterly still, in silent vigil. Through tears he remembers his mother's life, what he was told of it by her and by others, and what he wit-nessed of her years on earth: her goodness, her strength despite her tiny size, her patience and tolerance, but especially her goodness. He recalls their conversation the previous night. *What was there to forgive? You could never have done anything that wasn't in my interest.* He thinks of his loving sister, and the narrow, confined life she lived that never seemed that way to her, and how much she enriched their lives. He was her "precious baby," never aging for her, just as she never aged. Strangers might feel sorry for Baby Mol, but if they'd understood how happy she was, how fully she lived in the present, inhabiting each second, they'd have been envious. It will take time, he knows, to begin to trace the outlines of the massive rent in his life, in the lives of everyone who knew the matriarch of Parambil and who knew Baby Mol. For now, it is too large to comprehend, and he bows his head.

Part Eight

CHAPTER 63

The Embodied and the Disembodied

1968, Madras

On her first day, Mariamma and her classmates walk to the Red Fort, which sits apart from the rest of the medical school like the scary relative hidden away in an attic, but in this case behind the cricket grounds. Thick, muscular, gray vines form an exoskeleton holding up the crumbling red brick. The mosque-like turrets and the gargoyles staring down from the friezes remind her of *The Hunchback of Notre Dame*.

Madras has changed from her father's brief student days, when the British were everywhere, their pith helmets bobbing on the streets and most of the cars carrying white people. Now, only their ghosts linger in buildings of fearsome scale, like Central Station and the University Senate Building. And the Red Fort. Her father said these structures had intimidated him; he resented them because they were paid for by smashing the handlooms of village weavers so Indian cotton could only be shipped back to English mills and the cloth sold back to Indians. He said that every mile of railway track they built had one purpose: to get their loot back to ports. But Mariamma has no resentment. It's all Indian now—hers—whatever its origins. The only white faces around belong to scruffy tourists with backpacks who desperately need to bathe.

She takes a last glance outside, like Jean Valjean saying good-bye to freedom, as they pass under the arch that reads MORTUI VIVOS DOCENT. Inside the Red Fort, it's unnaturally cool. The yellow-lus-tered lanterns hanging down from the lofty ceilings ensure it is as dim as a dungeon. The flanking glass cabinets at the portal are like sentries, one holding a wired human skeleton and the other empty, as if the occupant has taken a stroll.

Two unshaven, khaki-clad, barefoot peons, or "attenders," watch them file in. One is tall and cadaverous, his mouth a slit, his eyes unfocused, like an abattoir worker watching the herd entering the chute. The other man is short, his mouth blood-red from betel nut, and he drools his lechery. Of the one hundred and two students, a third are female; the second attender has eyes only for the women; Mariamma feels soiled when his gaze falls on her face then drops to her breasts. The senior students warned them that in the caste structure of the school, these two, who look like the lowest of the low, have the professors' ears and can determine a student's fate.

"Stay close, Ammachi," Mariamma silently says under her breath. The night Big Ammachi died, Mariamma was away in Alwaye College, at her desk, studying her botany notes. She had the curious sensation of her grandmother being in the room, as though if she turned around, she'd see the old lady standing in the doorway, smil-ing. The feeling was there when she woke up, and still there when her father appeared in a hired car to bring her home. Her grief over the deaths of Baby Mol and Big Ammachi is fresh. She doubts it will ever fade. But through it all, her sense of Big Ammachi accompany-ing her, being embodied within her has remained—that's her conso-lation. Her grandmother lit the *velakku* the night of her birth with the hope that her namesake might shed light on the deaths of JoJo, Ninan, and Big Appachen, and the struggles of those like her father and Lenin who live with the Condition, that she might find a cure. The journey begins here, but she is not alone.

* * *

The pungent smell of formalin with an after-odor of slaughterhouse batters their nostrils even before they enter the dissection hall. The cavernous space is surprisingly bright thanks to floor-to-ceiling frosted windows and skylights that illuminate the rows of marble slabs. On the slabs, stained red rubber sheets drape static shapes that were once alive. Mariamma drops her gaze to the tiled floor. The formalin scratches her nostrils and her eyes water.

"WHO IS YOUR TEACHER?"

They come to a halt, a confused herd, panicked by this roar. Someone steps onto her heel.

The voice bellows again, repeating the question. It originates from thick lips floating under flaring nostrils. Swimmy, bloodshot eyes peer out of a fortresslike face and from under the overhanging slabs that form the brow; the cheeks resemble weathered, pock-marked concrete. This living, breathing sibling of the gargoyles atop the Red Fort is Professor P. K. Krishnamurthy, or "Gargoyle-murthy," as the seniors refer to him. His hair is neither parted nor combed but instead sticks up like a boar's bristle. But his long lab coat is brilliant white and of the finest pressed cotton, making their short, itchy linen coats look gray by comparison.

Gargoylemurthy's fingers wrap around the arm of an unlucky baby-faced fellow whose prominent Adam's apple makes him appear to have swallowed a coconut. This student's thick, wavy hair falls into his eyes and he reflexively tosses his head back, a gesture that looks insolent.

"Name?" Gargoylemurthy asks.

"Chinnaswamy Arcot Gajapathy, sir," he says confidently. Mariamma is impressed—in his place, she'd have stammered or gone mute.

"Chinn-ah!" The gargoyle is amused and bares long, yellow teeth. "Arcot Gajapathy-ah?" Gargoylemurthy smirks at the rest of them, insisting they find the name as funny as he does. Like Judases, they oblige. "So, I'm now knowing who *you* are. But Chinnah, I ask again: *Whooo-eh is, your-eh, teacher-eh?*"

"Sir . . . you are our teacher? Professor—"

"WRONG!"

His fingers flex tighter around Chinnah's arm, a python readjusting its hold. "Chinnah?" he says, but he's surveying the herd, ignoring Chinnah. "By chance have you noticed the words over the entry as you firstly walked in?"

"Sir . . . yes, I noticed something."

"Something, *aah?*" Gargoylemurthy pretends to look annoyed.

"It was some other language, sir. So, I . . . ignored—" Chinnah hastily tries to correct himself, "I think it said '*Macku*' . . . or something."

They gasp. "*Macku*" means dummy. Dunce.

"*Macku?*" The brows come together like thunderclouds. The squat neck retracts into the chest. The eyes bore into Chinnah. "*Macku* is what you are. That 'some other language' is Latin, *macku*!" Gargoylemurthy collects himself. He fills his chest. He shouts, "It says, '*MORTUI VIVOS DOCENT*'! It means, 'The Dead Shall Inform the Living'!"

He drags Chinnah to the nearest slab, snatching off the rubber sheet to expose what they've been dreading. There it is . . . A fallen log, a petrified leathery object in the shape of a woman, but the face is pancaked flat, hard to recognize as truly human. Anita, Mariamma's roommate, whimpers and leans against her. Mariamma prays she doesn't faint. The previous night, homesick, Anita asked if she could push their beds together, and without waiting for an answer she'd huddled against Mariamma, the same way Mariamma had huddled against Hannah or Big Ammachi or Anna *Chedethi*. They'd both slept soundly.

Gargoylemurthy places Chinnah's hand in the hand of the cadaver, like a priest uniting the bride and groom. "Here, *macku*, is your teacher!" A smile cracks Gargoylemurthy's features. "Chinnah, kindly shake hands with your professor! *The Dead Shall Inform the Living.* I am *not* the teacher. *She* is."

Chinnah shakes his new teacher's hand readily, preferring it to Gargoylemurthy's.

Mariamma and her five dissection mates perch like vultures on stools around their slab, with "their" body. They're each given their very own "bone box"—a long, rectangular cardboard carton—to take home. It contains a skull, its pieces glued together, the calvarium coming off like a kettle top, and the mandible hinged in place; vertebrae strung together by a wire through the neural arch to make a necklace; one temporal bone; a sampling of loose ribs; a hemi-pelvis with a femur, tibia, and ulna from the same side; one sacrum; one scapula with matching humerus, radius, and ulna; one hand and foot, fully articulated with wire; and loose wrist and tarsal bones in two small cloth sacks.

Gargoylemurthy poses Chinnah in the "anatomical position": standing with his hands by his sides, palms forward, slightly reminiscent of da Vinci's Vitruvian Man.

He says, "We are mobile, flexible creatures. But for anatomical descriptive purposes we must pretend the body is fixed in Chinnah's standing position, understand? Only then can you describe any structure in the body by its position relative to adjacent structures."

He spins Chinnah around and superimposes the scapula on Chinnah's scapula. He then defines for them its medial (closer to the midline), lateral (further from the midline), superior and inferior (or cranial and caudal), anterior, and posterior. (or ventral and dorsal) aspects. Anything nearer to the center or closer to the point of attachment is "proximal" (so the knee is proximal to the ankle), while things further out are "distal" (the ankle being distal to the knee). They need this basic vocabulary to begin. In Moore Market the previous day, her father's old friend Janakiram gifted her a used but recent edition of *Gray's*. "Mug it up, *ma*!" he said. "'Memorization and recitation' is the mantra!" When she ruffled through its pages, she heard the same mantra ring out, echoed in the meticulous underlining and margin notes of the previous owner, road signs to guide her on the journey. *Gray's* was familiar to her. In high school, once she set her sights on medicine, she spent hours with her mother's copy of *Gray's Anatomy*. It was an ancient edition even if the illustrations were largely the same. Anatomy hasn't changed but the terminology has. The Latin names are gone, thank goodness; the "*arteria iliaca communis*" is now the "common iliac artery." She'd been fascinated by the illustrations in her *Gray's*, and not just because they must have been useful to her mother. She didn't have her mother's artistic hand, but she'd stumbled onto something she *did* have. After staring at an illustration, she could close the book and reproduce the figure accurately (though not artistically), entirely from memory. She thought nothing of it, but her astounded father assured her it was a gift. If so, her gift was being able to translate a two-dimensional figure on the page into a three-dimensional one in her head. Then, like a child stacking blocks, she reproduced the figure by going from the inner layer out, till she had the whole. It had been entertaining, a parlor trick. Now she'll need to know the names of each structure and memorize the pages of text that accompany each figure.

Two hours later they file out, all one hundred and two of them, to a lecture hall at the other end of the Red Fort. Just as in college, the ladies occupy the first few rows of the sloping gallery. The boys fill the rows behind. Glaring down at them from the walls are former Heads of Anatomy—HOAs—all of them white, whiskered, bald, unsmiling, and deceased, but memorialized in these portraits.

Dr. Cowper enters quietly, the first and only Indian HOA, appointed after Independence, a clean-shaven Parsi. Cowper is small-boned, with fine, pleasant features. When his portrait eventually goes up, he'll also be the only one with a full head of hair. The two barefoot attenders and the assistant professor flutter about Cowper, but he doesn't need or expect their fawning. As the assistant calls out their names Cowper stands to one side, regarding each face with paternal interest. When Mariamma rises to say "Present, sir," Cowper glances in her direction, a welcoming look, just for her (or so she thinks, but later learns they all felt that way). She feels a stab of homesickness for her father.

The overlapping blackboards on pulleys behind Cowper shine like ebony. The shorter attender with the lecherous gaze (or "da Vinci," as the seniors call him) lines up colored chalk and duster cloth, his former sluggishness gone, as is his *paan* cheek-bulge. The class waits, pens and color pencils in hand, ready to reproduce every drawing from this legendary teacher of embryology. The only sounds Mariamma hears are the groans and sighs of the ancient fort.

"Ladies and gentlemen," Cowper says, stepping forward and smiling, "we are merely *renting* these bodies of ours. You came into this world on an *in* breath. You will exit on an *out* breath. Hence, we say that someone has . . . ? 'Expired'!" His shoulders shake silently at his own joke, his eyes glinting behind his wire glasses. "I know what happens to the *body* when it is no more, but not what happens to *you*, to the essence of you. Your soul." He adds wistfully, "I wish I did."

By confessing his doubt, he has won them over, this smiling, gentle professor.

"However, I *do* know where you came from. From the meeting of two cells, one from each of your parents—that's how you came to be. We'll spend the next six months studying that nine-month process. You could spend a lifetime and never cease to marvel at the elegance and beauty of embryology. 'Abiding happiness and peace are theirs who choose this study for its own sake, without expectation of any reward.'"

While lecturing, Cowper draws on the boards with *both* hands as naturally as he walks on two feet. He swiftly diagrams the intricate fusion of ovum and sperm to form a single cell, then becoming the blastocyst.

Toward the end of the hour, Cowper spreads out the rectangular duster cloth on the demonstration table. Delicately, he pinches up a fold down the center of the cloth duster, down its long axis, carefully shaping a long ridge. "This is how the neural tube forms, the precursor to your spinal cord. And this bulbous end," he says, fluffing up one end of the ridge, "is the early brain."

Then comes a moment none of them will forget: he lowers his body so his eyes are at the level of the surface of the table and his pale fingers carefully—as though handling living tissue—raise the long edges of the duster cloth from either side so they arch over the central ridge to meet above it in the midline. "And that," he says, pointing with his nose, and then peering at them through the hollow cylinder he has formed, "is the primitive gut!"

Mariamma has forgotten where she is, forgotten her name. She *is* that embryo. A cell from Philipose and a cell from Elsie. The two became one, and then divided.

Professor Jamsetji Rustomji Cowper drops the cloth. It's no longer a three-dimensional embryo, but a flat duster. He brushes chalk from his palms. He comes around the broad desk. He raises his hands as though in submission, his voice quiet. "We know so little. What little we *do* know leaves me in awe. Haeckel famously said, 'Ontogeny recapitulates phylogeny.' Meaning, the stages of the development of the human embryo—yolk sac, gills, even a tail— echoes the stages of human evolution, from one-cell amoeba, to fish, to reptile, to ape, to *Homo erectus*, to Neanderthal . . . to you." He has a faraway expression, his eyes full of emotion. Then he catches himself and returns to the present, smiling. "All right? That's enough for your first day."

He turns to leave, then stops and says, "Oh, and welcome to each one of you."

CHAPTER 64

The Ginglymoarthrodial Joint

1969, Madras

Every day the six of them saw and scrape at "Henrietta"—they've named her in honor of Henry Gray—beginning with the upper limbs. It's shocking how quickly their initial reticence dissipates, and soon their dissection guide, *Cunningham's Manual of Practical Anatomy*, is propped on Henrietta's belly as they work, three on each side. They feel possessive of her—they can't imagine working on any other cadaver. She's an ally in their labors. When Henrietta's shoulder is disarticulated, Mariamma carves their group number on a square of intact skin as the arms are thrown together in the formalin tank in the corridor. The next day, da Vinci fishes with his bare hands, hauls out a dripping limb, and shouts the number. Mariamma tries to carry it back with her thumb and index finger encircling Henrietta's wrist but finds she needs to hold it with both hands, like a saber; fat drops of formalin seep between her slippered toes. It's impossible to eat lunch after dissection, the formalin reek clinging to her skin. A brief letter from Lenin in the first week is a welcome sight.

> *Dear Doctor: May I be the first to call you that? But don't call me Achen because I don't know if I will ever be one. By the way, BeeYay Achen came to speak at the seminary. I told him that I am seriously thinking of leaving. After all these years, all I know is that my life was spared to serve God. But what if God meant for me to serve in some other way? BeeYay encouraged me to finish my rural student-service posting. He didn't disagree that God may have other plans for me, but he said sometimes we have to "live the question," not push for the answer.*

They became pen pals when she entered Alwaye College, by which time he was well along in seminary. His letters switch back and forth between Malayalam and English. She'd never expected him to be such a faithful correspondent. What surprises her even more is how willing he is to pour out his feelings, to explore them at length, as though he has no one else to share them with. Before she came to Madras, he'd written to say:

> *I'm a boil sticking out on smooth skin here. If my fellow seminarians share my doubts, they'll never admit to it. They'll even pretend Judges, or Chronicles—surely the most boring books in the Bible—are inspiring. But we have one or two gems whose faith burns in their every action. I'm envious. Why can't I feel that way?*

The upper limb dissection takes six weeks to complete. After the exam on the upper limb, she writes to Lenin, celebrating this milestone. "I get depressed if I dwell too long on what remains. Thorax, abdomen and pelvis, head and neck, lower limb. One more year of this. If Alwaye College was like drinking from a hose, medical school is like drinking from the raging river—and there's *so* much to memorize."

A year and two months after Mariamma first met her, Henrietta looks like the remains of a man-eating tiger's kill. At night, Mari-amma and Anita take turns being examiner and examinee, practicing for the viva voce that follows the written exam. Anita tosses a bone into an empty pillow cover and says, "Reach in, Madam." Mariamma is expecting a wrist or tarsal bone, which she must identify by feel alone.

"Easy-scapula-left-side."

"Slow down, smarty pants! Has anyone else told you you speak too fast? Name the bony features."

"Coracoid process, acromion, spine . . ."

"Take it out and show me the insertion of trapezius and the teres major . . ."

Soon she's writing to her father to remind him to send the final exam fees: the year has somehow gone by.

> *It's nice that Podi sends greetings through you but ask her why she can't write. Tell her I won't send another letter till she does. Please assure Anna* Chedethi *that I drink the Horlicks every night. I'm not surprised about what you heard about Lenin. He wrote to me that he'd rather be dissecting corpses than sitting with classmates who feel like corpses.*
>
> *Appa, after over a year of studying the body, my passing or failing will come down to six essay questions. If I fail, I join the B batch and repeat in six months. Imagine, hundreds of pages that I've memorized, diagrams practiced, just for six questions that will all be like this: "Describe and illustrate the structure of X." X will be the name of one joint, one nerve, one artery, one organ, one bone, and one topic in embryology. It's unfair!*

Six essays to judge everything I learned in over 13,000 hours. (Anita added it up.)

By the way, I told you about Gargoylemurthy and Cowper. They both like my dissections and invited me to appear for the Prize Exam in Anatomy. Only a few students dare go for it. It's a separate day, with one advanced essay and then an assigned dissection to complete in four hours.

During the study holidays she wakes from an afternoon nap to find a black-faced, wizened fellow with gray sideburns crouched on her desk, blinking rapidly. He must have reached through the window bars and worked open the bolt. When she tries to shoo him away, he bares his teeth and steps forward menacingly. The *kurangu* ransacks the desks for food and when he finds none, he pulls down the clothesline out of meanness before leaving. The monkey problem is truly out of control.

She seeks out Chinnah, their class president. He sighs. "I've pestered the dean and the superintendent for help. Hopeless! I wanted to wait till after exams, but the monkeys have declared war."

Chinnah was their unanimous choice for president, perhaps because of his coolheadedness on their first day with Gargoylemurthy. While the rest of the class is feverishly studying, Chinnah begins the Indo-Simian Campaign. He enforces the rule of no food stored in rooms; violators are shamed on the mess blackboard. He pays street urchins armed with slingshots to sit on the upper balconies to meet the regular afternoon forays the monkeys make. Then, mysteriously, a pair of monkeys gets trapped overnight in the dean's office and another in the superintendent's office, destroying and soiling these rooms in their frenzy to escape. The next day, a work crew trims overhanging branches around the hostels and repairs window screens, and now garbage is collected twice a day. The blackboard in the mess hall proclaims NO MONKEY BUSINESS WITH CHINNAH. He's a shoo-in for reelection.

But Chinnah confides to Mariamma that he's unprepared for the exam. "I'll tell you the truth. I got into medical school only because my uncle was DME." The Director of Medical Education controls all the medical school faculty postings and admissions. "Uncle 'put in a word' even though I wanted to go to law school. The buggers in the law college don't work this hard, I tell you."

In the frantic weeks leading up to the exam she gets a letter addressed in Lenin's hand but postmarked Sulthan Bathery. He's in the Wayanad District, he writes, assigned to an ancient *achen*—a widower, a good and faithful man, but very forgetful. He's at last freed from the seminary curfew, but he's in a town that pulls the bedcovers over its head at four thirty in the afternoon. The church groundskeeper, a tribal named Kochu *paniyan*, is the only person Lenin has to talk to. They've become friends. Lenin says he's still "living the question," as BeeYay *Achen* suggested. "But my faith has vanished," Lenin writes. "During the Eucharist, when *Achen* lofts the sosaffa to signal the presence of the Holy Spirit, he weeps! The poor man is overcome. Whereas I feel nothing, Mariamma. I'm lost. I don't know what will become of me. I'm waiting for a sign."

In the last days leading up to finals everyone in the hostel is glass-eyed, in a delirium of studying. They doze with lights on because collective wisdom says it's a way to get by with less sleep. A few days before the final, Mariamma dreams that a handsome man leads her to a four-poster bed and traces her profile with his finger. He kisses a spot in front of her ear. "That," he whispers, "is a ginglymoarthrodial joint."

She wakes to discover she had fallen asleep on a fibular bone. Its imprint is on her cheek. She doesn't recall ever hearing the word "ginglymoarthrodial" before. She looks it up and learns that "ginglymo" means hinge, like the joints between the bones of the fingers, while "arthrodial" means sliding, like the joints between adjacent wrist bones. But there's only *one* "ginglymoarthrodial" joint, one that both hinges *and* slides: the TMJ, or temporomandibular joint.

She mentions her dream to Anita, saying, "It's all because you left the fibula on the bed."

At breakfast, Mariamma is greeted with kissing sounds in the mess hall; her classmates stroke their ears. Anita isn't repentant, because her exploration of past exam questions tells her that the TMJ has popped up just once, seventeen years before. Never in the history of any medical school have more students memorized a certain two pages in *Gray's*.

At last the big day arrives and they break the seal on the exam. The very first question of the six reads: *Describe and illustrate the ankle joint*.

Her eyes run down to the other questions. She must describe and illustrate the axillary artery, the facial nerve, the adrenal glands, the humerus, and the development of the notochord.

But the *ankle* joint? If her dream was a clue, they'd all missed the obvious: the fibula! It was part of the ankle joint. The fact that it dug into her cheek had been a red herring. She feels her classmates staring daggers at her.

The next day, Mariamma and six others compete for the prize exam. After the essay, her assigned dissection is to expose the median nerve as it innervates the hand. She does a decent job, managing not to snap the nerve or its branches.

Chinnah is certain he's done poorly in the written exam; unless he can miraculously ace the viva voce in a fortnight, he'll be held back six months. But he has a plan: for the next fourteen days, he'll eat a kilo of masala-fried fish brains each day and have his cousin, Gundu Mani B.Sc. (failed), read select passages of *Gray's Anatomy* to him while he sleeps. Chinnah hopes Gundu's words will imprint themselves into his memory in a matrix of fish protein. The ladies' hostel is separate from the men's ("like the Virgin Islands are separate from the Isle of Man," as Chinnah says) but from her balcony Mariamma hears Gundu's chanting, like a priest reciting the Vedas.

Ten days before the viva, she receives a bulky letter from Lenin. She's hesitant to open it. If he's the victim of some serious "misunderstanding," she'd rather not know. But she can't resist. Lenin says things are better now that he's stumbled on "Moscow," otherwise known as Baby's Tea Shop, which stays open well past midnight and serves tea and liquids stronger than tea. It's a place where intellectuals gather, many of them with Party leanings. Lenin says he's learning so much, particularly from Raghu, who is his age, and a bank officer. "Raghu says I'm the third Lenin he has met in Wayanad. He's met more Stalins than Raghus. More Marxes than Lenins. No Gandhis or Nehrus. This place is the birthplace of communism in Kerala."

Mariamma tries to study, but her mind comes back to Lenin's letter. Northern Kerala—previously Malabar—is unlike the rest of Kerala. She never quite understood (till reading his letter) that in Malabar, sixty-five Nambudiri Brahmin landowners, or jenmis, held territories so vast they'd never seen them all. Their tenant farmers were the Nairs and Mappilas, who made huge profits and gave the jenmis their cut. When pepper prices tumbled, the jenmis taxed the tenant farmers and even taxed the tribals—people like Kochu *paniyan*. That, Lenin says, is why Kerala communism began in Wayanad. "At the seminary, we knew nothing about the real suffering of our own people. Call it communism or whatever you like, but standing up for the rights of the lowest caste appeals to me."

On the day of the viva, her classmate Druva goes in first. He's so nervous he trembles. Brijmohan ("Brijee") Sarkar, the external examiner, points to a cylindrical jar of formalin in which floats a malformed newborn. "Identify the abnormality." The baby's swollen head, the size of a basketball, is typical of hydrocephalus, "water in the brain," a fact Druva knows well. After he names it, it should lead to a discussion of the ventricles and the circulation of cerebrospinal fluid produced in them. In this infant, the exit of fluid is blocked, causing the ventricles, which are normally slit-like cavities in the depths of both hemispheres, to balloon out, pushing up on the surrounding brain. In the unfused, pliant skull of an infant, the head expands. But in an adult, with the bones of the skull fused, the brain would be sandwiched between skull and swollen ventricle and it would lead to unconsciousness. Druva, crippled by anxiety, manages eventually to speak, but the word that escapes his lips is "hydrocele," and not "hydrocephalus." He knows at once that he's fatally misspoken. There's a world of difference between fluid around the balls and fluid around the brain.

A stunned silence follows his utterance. Before Druva can correct himself, Brijee Sarkar bursts out laughing. It's contagious, and soon Dr. Pius Mathew, the internal examiner, is also convulsed with laughter. (Chinnah and Mariamma, waiting outside, can only hope these are auspicious noises.) Tears roll down the examiners' cheeks, and seeing Druva's expression catalyzes more howls. Each time they try to resume the questioning, they crack up. Finally, Brijee, wiping tears from his eyes, waves Druva out of the room.

Druva bravely asks, "Sir, did I pass, sir?" Pius's smile lingers, but Brijee's vanishes.

"Young man, can a hydrocele cause swelling of the head?" Brijee Sarkar says.

"Sir, no, sir, but I—"

"And there you have your answer."

"What, *da*?" Chinnah asks as Druva emerges.

"Buggered, that's what!"

Chinnah is called in. In too short a time, he emerges. He's followed at once by Dr. Pius.

"Five minutes, Mariamma," Dr. Pius says, smiling sadly, heading for a bathroom break.

Once Pius is out of earshot, Chinnah says to Mariamma, "It's B batch: brinjals, and bugger-all for Chinnah and Druva."

"What'd Brijee ask?"

"Nothing! He said, 'Your bloody uncle, the DME, blocked my promotion. And you can eat fish brain for a lifetime and perhaps grow you a dorsal fin and gills. But as long as Dr. Brijmohan Sarkar is examiner, it won't help Chinnaswamy Arcot Gajapathy pass his viva.' That bastard da Vinci must have told Brijee about my uncle. And the fish brains." Before the exam, Chinnah had declined to "tip" the attenders for good luck. It was extortion, yet everyone but Chinnah complied. He says ruefully, "I tell you, nothing good happens when family pulls strings for you. Pull becomes plug."

Before Dr. Pius can return, Dr. Brijee Sarkar pokes his head out and beckons Mariamma. She signals to Chinnah to wait. Her luck might not be any better than his.

"Madam," says Dr. Brijmohan Sarkar once the door closes behind her, "your prize exam dissection was nice, very nice." They're both still standing. "You're the only one who managed not to snap a branch nerve. Confidentially, your chances are, I'll say . . ."

He doesn't say, but he smiles and lifts his eyebrows up. Mariamma flushes, delighted.

"Ready for the viva?"

"Sir, I think so."

"Very good. Please put your hand in my pocket."

She stands before him in her cream sari and short white coat. Did she hear him correctly?

Dr. Sarkar has no sweat on his powdered face despite the oppressive heat. He stands between her and the door. Brijee Sarkar is tall, in his fifties, and his cheeks are hollowed by the loss of back molars. His thin limbs look discordant with the belly that pushes out. Rocking on his heels, his nose raised to the ceiling, his expression is now as severe as the crease in his linen pants. The sideways stance is to give Mariamma easy access to his right pants pocket.

She's studied hard. She's prepared. But not for this.

There's a ringing in her ears. The ceiling fan shoves back the sweltering air rising off the concrete floor. On the table, the hydrocephalic baby who sank Druva looks on with interest. An open tray contains the side of a head sawed down the middle with the mandible removed. A cloth bag outlines the small bones it holds.

If only he'd sit down. If only Dr. Pius would return. If only he'd ask me about hydrocephalus, or ask me to reach in the cloth bag . . . But Brijee isn't using the cloth bag, just his pocket.

A pulse flicks in Brijee's neck, a sinuous, bifid wave like a snake's tongue. "Either put your hand in my pocket or come back in September," he says softly, looking straight ahead.

Mariamma stands frozen. Why doesn't she just say no? She's ashamed to even be debating her choices. She's ashamed to see her left hand extend out, as though of its own volition—the way Brijee stands, using her left hand seems easier.

She puts her hand in his pocket. She wants to believe that whatever skeletal piece Brijee Sarkar has tucked in there—pisiform or talus—she'll identify. She so wants to believe. She doesn't want to fail.

She slides in deeper. For a fraction of a second, she's unsure of what she's feeling. Has her hand strayed? Is it her fault that she has hold of his penis? Is it her fault that no clothing intervenes? What's in her hand is a firmer, less flexible, and bonier organ than she'd ever imagined it to be. Is she meant to name its parts? The suspensory ligament, the corpora cavernosa, the corpus spongiosum . . . ?

Her brain struggles to stay in the examinee mode in the face of an organ with which she has no direct experience, engorged or otherwise; but her thoughts slip from the realm of anatomy and regress into painful memories that make the bile rise in her throat: a boatman in the canal, flashing her and Podi from his barge as they swam; the stranger pressed up against her in the bus; a turbaned snake charmer who materialized across the street from the ladies' hostel and, on noticing Mariamma studying him, made as though to remove the cloth covering his basket, but it was his lungi he had hiked up and a different sort of snake sprang up from his groin.

Why do men subject her and every woman she knows to this kind of harassment and humiliation? Is it only by forcing touch or by having an audience for their display that they know the organ exists? Earlier that year, when the ladies' hostel bus brought them back from a sari exhibition, a closed section of road forced the driver to detour through a narrow lane behind the men's hostel. A male student sat reading the paper while stark naked on the balcony. In an instant, he covered his face rather than his base. That was understandable—he wanted to spare himself the embarrassment of being recognized. But what she could not understand was his decision to stand up, face still covered but all else on display, while the bus and its passengers crawled by.

What she does next is difficult for Mariamma to later explain to herself or anyone else. It is a cornered animal's desperate instinct to survive, but also the unleashing of a primitive anger. She's reliving a familiar nightmare of a viper baring its fangs and spitting at her while she desperately clutches it under its hood, keeping it away from her face, holding on as it whips and saws and tries to strike . . . and so her fingers instinctively clamp down with murderous intent on Sarkar's penis. Her right hand leaps into the battle, coming to the left's aid, slamming into Brijee's groin from outside, buttressing her hold by grabbing anything that dangles—scrotal sac, epididymis, testis, root of penis and . . . anatomy be damned—and squeezing for dear life.

For a brief moment, Brijee's vanity permits him to think she's fondling him. He wants to speak, his eyebrows going up, but he gags on his words and turns pale. Then he steps back, the veins on his temples filling out, staggering against the table, sending the specimens crashing, the glass breaking, the hydrocephalic fetus slithering across the formaldehyde-slicked floor. Brijee drags Mariamma with him in his retreat, because whatever happens, she will not, must not let go of the snake's head. Brijee manages a scream, and she screams too, hers a bloodcurdling sound, as they tumble over the table. Her forehead meets broken glass, but nothing will distract her from choking the life out of the serpent even if she succumbs from the effort.

The door to the room bursts open, but she can't look or let go. Brijee Sarkar's face is inches from hers, the perfumed *paan* on his breath registering in her nostrils, his scream becoming silent, and his skin turning ashen. Too late, he grabs her forearms, but his strength is gone, and his touch feels gentle, pleading. Then his body sags, his hands fall away; he becomes floppy, and his eyes roll back. She can hear Chinnah pleading with her to let go, while da Vinci and Pius try to tug Sarkar free, but she cannot let go, nor can she silence her war cry. Brave Chinnah dives in to peel her fingers off one by one.

Chinnah drags, then carries Mariamma away as blood pours from her forehead. He sets her down in an empty lab room and presses a hanky over the wound. She pushes her way to the sink and scrubs furiously at her hands, then she throws up as Chinnah supports her, still compressing the wound.

Sobs and rage commingle like blood and water as she clings to Chinnah. Then she remembers—he too is a man. She strikes him on the chest, then the ears, and he suffers her blows, offering himself, willing to be wounded, while bravely keeping pressure on her cut even though it leaves him exposed, waiting till she is spent.

"I'm sorry," he whispers.

"What're you sorry about?"

"I'm ashamed for all men," he says.

"You should be. You're all bastards."

"You're not wrong. I'm so sorry."

"I'm sorry too, Chinnah."

CHAPTER 65

If Only God Could Speak

1971, Madras

The ladies' hostel is deserted. Most students have gone home for the break. A few clinical students remain. Since the mess hall is closed, they must eat in the hospital canteen.

Mariamma writes to her father that she has passed Anatomy . . . but she must delay her return to Parambil for a month or so to finish an "incomplete project." The incomplete project is herself. Outwardly, she has shrugged off the vile episode with Brijee. But her insides are still in disarray. She's ashamed to face her father. The sight of the scar on her forehead and the explanation would distress him; he'd want to see justice done. She had justice in that they believed her story—Brijee was known for this sort of thing. But Brijee's heart attack, his disgrace, his suspension from government service aren't enough punishment. He should be jailed. But she has no appetite to draw more attention to herself by pursuing this cause. Already, some medico, a frustrated poet, has immortalized her shame in verse:

Doctor Brijee once gave an exam
Offering his willy as part of the plan
But to his dismay
She obliged in a way
That left him much less than a man.

In the mornings she tags behind a senior posted to the internal medicine ward. She's excited by her first exposure to live patients and disease; it's a reminder of why she's here. In the afternoons she stays in her sweltering room, reading about the patients she encountered. Perversely, she misses the torture of a looming exam or a fat textbook to memorize—anything to distract her from what happened. She is adrift.

Three weeks later, when she returns from the hospital, she sees a man seated cross-legged on the bench under the oak tree in the hostel courtyard. A carpet-like beard runs up his throat and cheek-bones and ends in curls on his crown. A scar across his left cheek is only partially concealed by his beard. His sunrise-orange *kurta* makes him look like a man on fire. With a parrot and playing cards he could pass for a fortune-teller. But for those soft, sleepy eyes, she wouldn't recognize Lenin. He holds a hostel tea mug; soft-hearted Matron Thangaraj must have let him into this inner sanctum.

He certainly recognizes her, even though the Mariamma they both knew vanished inside the Red Fort a year and a half ago. On the inside she is someone else.

He puts the tea down and comes forward. "Mariamma?" His hands reach for hers, but she retreats.

"What're you doing here? Did Appa send you?"

"It's nice to see you too, Mariamma—"

"The hostel is off limits to men." She can't explain her outward hostility when inside she's happy to see him.

"And yet here I stand," he says defiantly.

"I'm surprised that Matron let you past the gate."

"I told her I'm your twin."

"In other words, you lied?"

"I was speaking . . . metaphorically. And Matron said, 'How sweet! You must have felt Mariamma's pain and decided to come!'"

"So, did you? Did you feel my pain?"

Lenin's expression is that of the boy who "borrowed" the bicycle he crashed, and whose curse is to tell the truth, whatever the consequences. "No," he says. "No, I didn't. You didn't reply to my letters. I assumed you were at Parambil. I just happened to arrive at Central Station a few hours ago. I looked across the street and there was Madras Medical College. I took a chance. I asked for the ladies' hostel, and here I am."

"Aren't you supposed to be at your rural posting?"

"*Aah*. I had a . . ."

This isn't the old Lenin. He's missing the righteous indignation. He can't even say that word he so often used to explain away his troubles.

"Me too, Lenin. I had a little 'misunderstanding.'"

"Matron told me indirectly. She assumed I knew," he says, eyeing her uncertainly.

"Yes, everyone knows. But they don't know what to say. 'Wishing you hearty, happy recuperation'?" Her laugh sounds strange even to her. Stranger still is that she's dabbing her eyes.

Lenin reaches again for her hand. Then he gently pulls her to him. She clings to him like a drowning woman. His *kurta* feels like sandpaper scraping her face, but no cloth has felt more welcome. If Matron sees them . . . but then, he is her twin.

"I'm ashamed to go back to Parambil."

"Why shame? I'm proud of you! The only shame is that you didn't kill the fellow."

"Let's get away from here, Lenin," she says urgently. "Let's get out of the city. Please."

He hesitates, but only for a moment. "Let's do it."

*　*　*

The ocean seems to be covered in glittering diamonds as the bus hugs the shore. With every mile she feels she's shedding soiled garments, peeling off contaminated skin. The noisy diesel and the wind through the open windows discourage conversation. Lenin has nicotine stains on his fingers. He's leaner, and his beautiful eyes have a hardness in them she's never seen before. His thick scar is more extensive than she thought, running onto the pinna of his ear, a wound that clearly wasn't sutured. They're both marked.

At Mahabalipuram, a vendor slices off the tops of fresh coconuts for them to drink. Lenin buys cigarettes, biscuits, and a string of jasmine for her hair. The scent hovers like a halo around her as they approach the stone temples.

It's not temples but the ocean that Mariamma wants most: the murmur of the waves, the restoration of water. She lets the surf wash over her ankles while Lenin holds back. The two of them are quite alone. Sanderlings line up like porters on a train platform, waiting for the next wave; they retreat smartly just ahead of the tongue of water, pecking at invisible creatures.

"Lenin, I must swim. I've never swum in the sea. The surf's too strong at Marina Beach." He looks worried. "Turn around, face away. Don't look." She sheds her sari, underskirt, and blouse, piling them by him. In just her underwear and bra, she plunges in. The ground falls off below her. The current is unpredictable, but she relishes being in the water. Lenin is still turned away. "Hey!" she says. "You can look." He turns and looks nervously at her. He calls for her to be careful. She tries to swim but struggles to get the ocean rhythm. Her eyes are burning, and salt water goes up her nose. But she's grinning. Immersion is mercy and forgiveness.

Lenin is relieved when she emerges. He turns away but hands her a *thorthu* from his cloth bag. She feels bold, reckless. After what she has been through, she's entitled to be reckless, to be any way she wants. He shields her as she sheds her wet underclothes and puts her blouse, skirt, and sari back on. The water has broken down a barrier within her.

They sit on the sand. She tells Lenin about Brijee. Even if everyone knows her story, no one really knows how *she* feels. It pours out now: her rage, her shame, her guilt—it still lingers. But with the telling comes a sense of empowerment. She has no culpability in the Brijee matter. None, other than being naïve and being a woman. During the inquiry she had tapped into the righteousness that was her due; she slapped down the least suggestion that she might be at fault. She had learned a lesson: to show weakness, to be tearful or shattered didn't serve her. One shouldn't just hope to be treated well: one must insist on it.

She feels better when she's done. She eats a biscuit. Lenin sits cross-legged, smoking, head down, tracing circles in the sand. He was visibly affected during the telling of her story, even holding her hand. Is she being self-centered by not asking about his misunderstanding, his scar, and why he is here? Or is she giving him room to decide? He can tell her when he chooses to. Or not.

The breaking waves sound louder as the light fades. The dark silhouettes of the stone temples against the sky make her feel they've slipped back in time. Her mother must have come here when she studied in Madras; she must have splashed in these same waves. This water connects the living and the dead. Perhaps the sculptures here inspired the Stone Woman. The sea breeze soothes and refreshes her. Madras feels a million miles away.

"The minutes we spend watching the waves don't count against our life spans," she says.

"Really? Maybe I should just stay here, then, if I'm to live to my thirties." He's smiling, but she doesn't like what she hears.

It's pitch dark when they leave, stumbling in the sand, holding hands. The last bus to the city has left. The old Mariamma would've panicked; this one couldn't care less.

* * *

The hand-lettered sign on the narrow, three-story lodge reads MAJESTICHOTELROYALMEELS, the letters squished together. A lone seated figure jumps to his feet, brandishing his towel like a whip, flicking dust off the chairs and dining tables. He's overjoyed to have customers. He leads the way up rickety stairs while Mariamma marvels at the steeple shape of his skull.

She lifts the thin mattress and scans for bedbugs. There's nowhere to sit other than the narrow bed. A naked bulb on the ceiling provides light. A raised door leads to a tiny bathroom with a squat-toilet, a tap, and a bucket with a mug bobbing in it. Cockroaches scurry away when she turns on the light. She fills the bucket and bathes, washing off sweat, sand, and salt. Lenin lends her a *mundu* from his bag and she ties it under her armpits. Then it's his turn.

The boy who delivers the food must be the chef's son, because his skull is also shaped like a tower. "It's called oxycephaly," she says to Lenin. He's impressed, but less so when she says there's no treatment for it.

"Good that there's a name, at least," he says.

Unwittingly, his words deflate her. Just like with "the Condition," a name cures nothing.

The banana-leaf packets of vegetable biryani exceed their expectations of RoyalMeels; the chef's cooking is better than his spelling. Lenin, bare-chested, hardly eats. She's seen him without his shirt often, but somehow this feels different. He's bemused as she wolfs down her packet and the rest of his. When she's done, he punches her on the shoulder.

"So, Mariamma*aye*," he says, "it's the usual story with you. I turn around and you're in trouble." He lights a cigarette. She snatches the cigarette from his mouth. "Hey! You could ask!"

She draws in the smoke and lets it out; the lazy spiral that rises to the ceiling is like a living being. His grin has traces of the old Lenin, but it's an effort. "So, *twin* brother. Spit it out. What's going on with you?" So much for giving him room to decide.

He stares out of the window for a long time.

"I've gone down a path," he says.

She waits, but nothing more is forthcoming. "A straight line, right? Can't stop till you must?"

He nods. "But on this one when I come to the end, it will be the end."

He has nothing more to say.

"So, how's your tribal friend—Kochu *paniyan*, was it? And Raghu, the banker? See? I read your letters."

He looks at her, his expression even more somber.

"They're both dead."

She feels a cold hand clawing at her throat. She wants to plug her ears. She should stop him from saying another word. She stands, unsure why. The naked bulb glares in her eyes and she turns it off. *There. That helps.* She paces the room, with measured steps, trying not to look frantic. Her eyes adjust. There's faint light from the window. A woman's voice drifts up from downstairs. She remembers as a girl how she hated the newly arrived Lenin for his antics, but she couldn't stop herself from trailing him. Why? She had to see what happened next. It was a compulsion. Lenin's face in the glow of his cigarette shows concern for her. And behind that expression, she sees despair. She settles back on the bed, cross-legged, facing him. She can't help herself. The old compulsion won't go away. She must know.

"When I got to Wayanad, I started remembering the strangest things," Lenin says. "I don't think I mentioned this in my letters. We had lived there when I was a young child, so my parents said, but I had no memories from then. It was only in getting to know Kochu *paniyan*, visiting his settlement in the forest, a place his family has been for three or four generations, that some of it came back. Memories of my beautiful mother. I remembered waiting for her outside huts like Kochu *paniyan*'s, shutting my ears to a woman's screams as she delivered. I can see a man just like Kochu *paniyan* coming to our house with a giant carp to give my mother. Maybe as payment. And he cleaned it for us, then he came back with cooking oil and maybe paddy. Maybe he found us alone, the kitchen fire out, and my father gone—that would be a good guess. Surely, I didn't imagine all this? What other memories are buried in my head?"

Tribals are suspicious people, Lenin said. They'd been used and abused by everyone who came. The British abolished slavery, yet they compelled the tribals to cut down their precious trees to build ships. If the British hadn't discovered tea, the mountains would be bald. Instead, they made the tribals terrace the slopes they had lived on for generations. Then more recently, it was Malayalis from Cochin and Travancore who did the exploitation, a northern migration, Lenin said. Clerks, merchants, drivers. "People like my father." The tribals didn't use cash; they bartered for what they needed. The newcomers would encourage them to build pukka houses, and to help themselves to pickaxes, wheelbarrows, shovels, pulleys, cement, clothes—no cash needed, just a thumbprint. When they couldn't pay, they forfeited land. The tribals learned painful lessons. "When you are robbed, you quickly become politically conscious. You have nothing to lose but your chains. That's Marx, by the way, not me."

"Good that you can quote Marx," Mariamma says.

Lenin pauses. "I can stop if you don't want to hear more."

She doesn't respond.

At Baby's Tea Shop—"Moscow"—Lenin liked to sit with Raghu. Lenin would occasionally see him with an older man in his forties, Arikkad, who never stayed long. Raghu said if Lenin really wanted to understand the class tensions in Wayanad, then Arikkad was the professor. Arikkad was from a middle-class Christian family. He had been to prison for participating in the coir-workers strike. Raghu said there was no better education than being behind bars. *Das Kapital* and Stalin's *History of the Communist Party of the Soviet Union* circulated among the jailed for the simple reason that they were the only ones translated into Malayalam. One went in for public drunkenness and came out a sober Communist. Arikkad became a dedicated Party man, living with the tribals, advocating for them. That was something no Congress Party worker ever did.

Lenin says, "When I was introduced to Arikkad I found him humble. Inspiring. More than my old *achen*. Here was someone actually *doing* something to improve life for the tribals. He was far more interested in *me*, in my calling to be a priest."

"*Aah!* You had a good story for that, didn't you," Mariamma says drily. It came out before she gave it much thought. "I'm sorry. Ignore that. Go on."

"No, you're right. I have a good story. That's the trouble. I used to believe my own story. But I don't now. I wasn't spared to serve God. I was spared to serve people like the *pulayi* who saved me. But I wasn't doing it, not as a seminarian. Anyway, I confided my doubts to Arikkad. He said, 'So, you're tired of dispensing opium?' I didn't get it till he explained. Apparently, Marx said that religion was the opium of the masses. It kept the oppressed from complaining or trying to change things. Arikkad also said the church didn't have to be the way it is here. He said there were Jesuits in Colombia and Brazil who lived and worked with tribals, doing just as Christ taught. When the peasants began an insurgency against a government that oppressed them, these priests couldn't help but be in solidarity with them. They joined the rebels. They disobeyed their church. One of the Jesuits had written about his cause. He called it 'liberation theology.' It was a revelation to me. I wondered if my seminary library had those texts. Probably not."

Everything changed for Lenin when Kochu *paniyan* failed to show one day for work. He came the next morning, early, knocking at Lenin's door, looking anguished, desperate. He said his younger brother had borrowed money from a businessman named C.T., then borrowed even more, pledging the family land. The loans were due. Rather than tell the family—and he must have had many warnings—the brother had disappeared. Kochu *paniyan* first knew about it when C.T. arrived with court papers saying the family had seventy-two hours to leave. Kochu *paniyan* wanted Lenin to come with him to ask *Achen* to talk to C.T., since he was a parishioner and on the church board. "People like C.T. are the opposite of Arikkad. They hate communism because exploiting the tribals is exactly how he became a rich and powerful man." *Achen* reluctantly went to see C.T. and returned right away, shaken. He'd been abused for inter-fering. *Achen* said he would pray. "I tell you, Mariamma, never have prayers felt more worthless."

Kochu *paniyan* had already been to see Arikkad, who was trying to get a stay order in court. "That's good!" Lenin said. Kochu *pani-yan* had looked pityingly at Lenin and said, "Good? Since when has court been good for our people? Court is all *their* people." The day of the eviction Lenin had gone to Kochu *paniyan's* settlement. Many tribal families had come to give support, along with Arikkad, Raghu, and other activists. Though Arikkad had filed for a stay, the judge was "one of theirs." Soon three jeeps arrived, packed with tough-looking men carrying cycle chains and bamboo sticks. Behind them a police jeep pulled up and parked at a distance. C.T. called out that the family had five minutes to leave. On Arikkad's instruction, all the assembled people sat peacefully on the ground.

"When the five minutes was up, C.T.'s *goondas* came at us. The police looked on. I saw and heard a cane break Kochu *paniyan's* jaw. Arikkad took the second blow. A woman tried to shield her head and I heard the chain snap her forearm. I was in a trance. I couldn't believe my eyes. Suddenly I felt terrible pain in my shoul-der. I turned and grabbed the chain and punched my attacker—so much for Gandhian nonviolence. But they rained blows down on me. Mariamma, they beat me mercilessly. Then those thugs tossed petrol on the thatch and set the houses on fire. I had to crawl away, the heat was so intense.

"Kochu *paniyan* was in the hospital with a broken leg and jaw. Arikkad and Raghu were beaten badly too. A few others were treated in Casualty. Someone brought me to my room on a cycle because my knee was the size of a football. *Achen* hardly recognized me; my face was like a swollen mask. Poor *Achen*: he wept as he nursed me.

He cried, looking to the heavens. He fell on his knees, calling to God to right what was wrong. Oh, Mariamma . . . if only God had answered *Achen*, who was as faithful a servant as any god might ask for . . . If only God had answered . . . my life might have taken a different path. If only God had answered . . . I was peeing blood. I couldn't walk. I just lay on that bed, brooding, licking my wounds."

A few Moscow acquaintances came to check on Lenin. They said that Kochu *paniyan* was gone from the hospital. "Self-discharge against medical advice," the hospital claimed. With a broken leg and jaw, how do you "self-discharge"? What it really meant was the police or paramilitary took Kochu *paniyan* and tortured him for information. The poor man knew nothing! His family has not seen him. They probably dumped the body in the forest where the wild animals will make sure nothing remains. He learned it was not the first time. Meanwhile no one knew anything about Arikkad and Raghu's whereabouts. The police were hunting them. They had gone underground. Rumor was they were Naxalites.

Naxalites.

A chill runs down Mariamma's spine. The room is suddenly freezing. The very utterance of that word—"Naxalite"—feels dangerous. It's enough to make her pulse race. "Stop, Lenin," she says, rising. He is not surprised. "I need to pee."

She tries to recall what she actually knows of the Naxalite movement. She knows its name came from a small village—Naxalbari—in West Bengal. The peasants there, after slaving for the landlords, were given so little back of the harvest that they were starving. In desperation they took the harvest from the land they had tilled for generations. Armed police who were in the landlords' pay arrived and fired on the peasants who had assembled for a dialogue, and a dozen or more, including women and children, were killed. That's what she recalls. It dominated the news. Outrage at the massacre in Naxalbari spread like cholera all over India, and the "Naxalite" movement was born. It was about the time Mariamma was leaving for Alwaye. Peasants in many places attacked and even killed feudal landlords and corrupt officials. The police responded just as violently. There had been a palpable fear that the country was on the verge of a revolution. If peasant groups across India coalesced, they could seize power. The government responded by charging a secret paramilitary force to go after Naxalites with no oversight, no limits on their powers. They had dragged away two innocent boys in her college who had not been seen since. The Naxalite movement had been particularly strong in Kerala. She'd worried about her father becoming a target, but he reassured her that their holdings were tiny by comparison to those of the landlords further north, who owned thousands of acres; also, they had never had tenant farmers.

Mariamma returns to sit on the bed, wrapping the sheet around her shoulders because she's shivering. Lenin asks if he should stop. "It's too late for that," she says. "Go on."

"I was in pain. It took me a long time to heal," Lenin says. "But I had another kind of pain. It was the injustice and cruelty I had witnessed. I kept thinking of Acca, the *pulayi* who saved me during the smallpox. What was her reward? To be driven away like a stray dog. The starving little boy—me—had promised her, 'I'll never forget you.' I didn't forget—that part was true. But what had I done for her? What would I ever do for her as a priest? I had 'lived the question' for a long time. In that bed, licking my wounds, I came to the answer. I had no choice.

"I told a Moscow regular that I wanted to contact Arikkad. Or Raghu. He was alarmed. He claimed not to know and left. Two days after that I had a note under my door telling me to be at a bus station at midnight. A motorcycle came. I was blindfolded and we rode away. When the blindfold came off, I was in a clearing. Three men approached, slinging rifles. One was Raghu. He tried to dissuade me. He said I could do other things with my life, if not seminary. 'Like what, Raghu?' I said. 'Banking?' There was no going back."

Lenin's voice comes from far away, it seems to Mariamma. She's in a room with a Naxalite, not the boy she grew up with. She feels terrible sadness, despair. Her body and mind are numb, in shock. She listens.

"I met Arikkad and the others in the cell I was to belong to. We desperately needed more weapons. We had only five rifles, two revolvers, and some homemade bombs between a dozen men. You can't be an armed struggle without arms. We planned two raids. One was on a police substation and armory, so we could be armed. The other raid was pure revenge. Our target was C.T., the man who took Kochu *paniyan*'s land. C.T. had an office in town, and a bungalow on his estate. The bungalow was isolated, with an unobstructed view onto any approach from below. But we had a way from the side, through thick jungle. C.T. was probably armed. But we were too, and there were more of us.

"Arikkad was to raid the armory at the exact same time that our group attacked C.T. Just as our group cut through the barbed-wire fence and entered his estate, we heard the roar of an engine and saw C.T.'s car tearing away, disappearing down the mountain. The front door of the house sat ajar. Dinner was on the table, half eaten. C.T. had clearly been warned. We found his stash of 'black' money behind paneling, only because he didn't close it flush with the wall. This was untaxed money he could never put in the bank. He must have grabbed what he could on his way out. We took two guns, then we set the bungalow on fire. We went, as we had planned, to a sympathizer's hut, stashed the weapons and money, and waited. Soon, we got word about the other raid. The police had been waiting, and they ambushed Arikkad's group as they approached the armory. Poor Raghu died on the spot. They retreated, chased by the police. Arikkad tossed a homemade bomb at the pursuing jeep, and he wounded a constable, disabling the vehicle. They split up and disappeared. Our group did the same. We left carrying no weapons so we could pass through towns without being noticed. It was a total failure.

"I spent one night sleeping outdoors. At noon the next day, I reached the rendezvous spot on a trail high up in the mountains. I was hungry, scared, and angry. I knew this meeting place could be compromised. No one was there. Just when I thought I better leave, Arikkad appeared, looking so terribly weary. He asked if I had food. All I had was water. His skin was full of bites, worse than mine. He said the police were probably not far behind, but they wouldn't leave the main road at night. Still, we couldn't stay there. We had to eat, to sleep. He said he knew of a house, a few miles further up on the edge of a corporate plantation. Sivaraman was a friend from the 'old days'—I assume, his prison days.

"It was one in the morning when we came to the edge of a clearing. When I saw Sivaraman's house, something about it bothered me. I had a vision of 'Manager's Mansion' with the bodies of my parents and sister inside. I could smell death. I tried to hold Arikkad back, but he said that if he didn't get food or sleep, he was done for. He said he'd go first and signal me if it was safe, but I told him not to. That I'd stay outside in a tree and for him not to mention my presence. When Sivaraman opened the door for Arikkad, I was watching. Sivaraman was reluctant, but he let Arikkad in. I climbed the tree on the edge of that clearing. It took all my energy. I was ten feet above ground, wedged in a fork. I used my *mundu* to tie myself to the tree so I wouldn't fall. Somehow, despite the cold, with my legs exposed and mosquitoes feasting on me, I fell asleep.

"One or two hours later, I woke up, suddenly alert. Crouching right under me was a constable with a rifle! He was unaware of me. He clicked his tongue—that was the sound that woke me. Two other constables appeared. Then I saw Sivaraman standing outside the house, waving them in.

"They dragged Arikkad out and clubbed him to the ground while Sivaraman watched. They bound his hands so tight that he cried out. I trembled with rage and fear. They marched him in my direction. I was sure my chattering teeth would give me away. They passed right under me. Arikkad kept his eyes on the ground. Something broke inside me.

"My legs had gone to sleep. It took forever for me to get down. I went to the house and pressed my mouth to the door. I called out, 'Sivaraman, you betrayed a good man. You won't live to spend the reward money. When you come out, we'll be waiting.' I heard him whimper. I hoped he would die of fright. Then on rubbery legs I went after the constables, staying far enough behind so they didn't hear me. They raced down for the ghat road and an hour later, just as the sky turned lighter, they reached it and collapsed on the ground, exhausted. They gave Arikkad a banana. I got as close as I dared, concealing myself behind a neem tree growing back over a rock. If I sneezed, they'd have heard me. I thought of one plan after another to free Arikkad. But all were suicidal fantasies, Mariamma. I had no weapons. I was so weak.

"Soon after dawn two jeeps came. A DSP—big fellow—jumped out. He was so excited, congratulating the constables. He ran up to Arikkad and slapped him viciously. Arikkad grinned and said something. The DSP cursed him and kicked him. He ordered his men to shackle his ankles and put a sack over his head. Then I heard them arguing near the jeep. The DSP shoved the constable, the same one who'd been under my tree, and pulled out his revolver. Was he going to shoot his own man? I didn't understand. But Arikkad understood, even with that hood on. '*Edo*, DSP?' Arikkad shouted. 'Be a man. Remove my hood first. Are you that much of a coward? Can't you look me in the eyes before you do it?'

"The DSP marched up the slope to Arikkad, walking so deliberately. Mariamma, it was as though he knew that this wasn't a clearing in the jungle but a world stage. Arikkad struggled to his feet, standing tall, despite the way his arms were wrenched behind him. The DSP snatched the hood away and spat words into Arikkad's ear. Arikkad laughed.

"Then Arikkad shuffled with shackled feet to turn to face the spot where I was hidden! He knew I was there. He wanted me to bear witness. 'Tell my comrades, tell the world,' was what he was trying to tell me. The DSP took three steps to square off, his right arm ruler-straight by his side, the revolver pointed at the ground. I could see Arikkad's face so clearly as he smiled at the DSP. That grin of his was more powerful than any weapon. The DSP planted his feet. Arikkad shouted, 'OTHERS WILL CONTINUE THE STRUGGLE!' I saw the DSP's arm rise. 'LONG LIVE THE REVOLUTION—'"

Mariamma can hardly breathe, watching Lenin's face, lit by the ghostly glow from the window.

"The shot was so loud. It echoed off the rocks behind me. I cried out. In disbelief. In rage. In anger. I was sure they heard me. My ears were ringing. Theirs must have been too. I saw them drag Arikkad's body down the slope. None of the constables were happy. It was cold-blooded murder. They put his body in the back of a jeep. Even after they drove off, the ringing in my ears wouldn't stop.

"I found the banana tucked under the rock where Arikkad had sat. I was sure he left it for me. I was weeping uncontrollably, I tell you. Somehow, I wrestled two stones of equal size to where the earth was stained dark with Arikkad's blood. I found a flat, long rock and lifted it to straddle the other two. I stood there for so long before this memorial, this burden stone to my comrade in arms. *It's always the same answer*, I thought to myself when I finally tore myself away from that place. *Walk the straight path to its end.*"

CHAPTER 66

The Dividing Line

1971, Mahabalipuram

Lenin soon falls asleep, as though by unburdening himself of these horrible events he has found a temporary respite. But Mariamma cannot do the same.

She looks out and sees stars. How many light-years did those pinpricks on the dark firmament travel to get to her retinae? Lenin used to know such things. The ocean is invisible, but she hears its surf as it lathers over this stretch of Coromandel Coast. The Bay of Bengal extends east from here for hundreds of miles before embracing the Andaman Islands, and then eventually the coast of Burma. If only the immensity of these elements—sky, stars, and sea—could erase the enormity of what Lenin has told her. She's saddled with knowledge that weighs heavily on her.

Lenin looks to be at peace. Big Ammachi used to marvel that a boy who was such a terror when awake could look so innocent asleep. He still does. When he had described the constables marching Arikkad out from the house and passing under the tree where he sat hidden, Mariamma had shivered uncontrollably. After Raghu's death, the failure of the raids, Lenin said he'd questioned what an armed struggle could accomplish unless all the oppressed villagers in India rose en masse. He'd barely joined the Naxalites and he was having misgivings. But witnessing Arikkad's execution, he knew he had to fight on, no matter what happened. An armed struggle needed arms, better training, to be effective, he said. He'd let slip earlier that his next stop was Vizag. Her guess is that Lenin's trip is to address these very deficiencies.

She's exhausted. She turns away from the window and stretches out beside him. The night is turning cool. She pulls the flimsy sheet over them. His body is warm. He's breathing right beside her, but she feels she's already mourning him. Lenin can never visit Parambil again, never attend a wedding, never write her a letter. Even this impulsive visit of his puts them both at risk. But she's glad he came. If she's never to see him again, at least she has some idea of what he's doing. That's better than having no news of him. The police aren't hunting him yet, or so he thinks. But from now on he'll be on the run. He will likely die or be captured while still young.

Lenin turns over in his slumber, drapes his arm over her. It's enough to spark fresh tears. She cries herself to sleep.

Well before dawn, she awakes. She watches the rise and fall of his chest, his belly moving out as hers retracts. Her thoughts feel crisp, like a cool gust after a sudden rain squall. She knows that she loves Lenin. Perhaps she always has. As children they fought and baited each other . . . and that was love. Recently, their mannered letters bared their souls—that, too, was love. "Love" isn't a word she had given herself permission to think, let alone use, because they're fourth or fifth cousins. The Condition didn't need firmer footing. But genetics now feels like a religion in which she has lost faith.

Lenin opens his eyes. For a second, the world is at bay and the word "Naxalite" lives in other rooms with other people. It's just the two of them. He smiles. Then reality intrudes.

He used to tease her by saying her eyes were devious, like a cat's. And that her piebald streak was evidence of her feline origins. Perhaps her eyes this morning reveal all the emotions that she's too shy to articulate. The hand that was draped over her now strokes her cheeks. She feels his beard, touches his scar. He draws closer. Why hold back now when she'll never see him again? She kisses, for the first time ever; kisses the man she loves. They retreat after the shock of it. The joy, the surprise on his face mirror her feelings. If she had doubts, she doesn't any longer. He loves her too. There's no holding back.

They fall asleep in each other's arms, legs intertwined, and their bodies covered with sweat. They only surface when sunlight chases the shadows out of the room and it gets hot. The world outside intrudes. But they don't move.

"I don't want anything to happen to you," she says. "Why can't it be just like this forever?" Her breasts are pressed against his ribs. She grabs a fistful of his chest hair (*what other biological purpose does it serve but as a handhold?*) and tugs till he winces. "What am I supposed to do now, Lenin? How do I live in a world without you? Never getting to set eyes on you. Wondering if I ever will. Wondering if you're alive. I can't even write to you!" She's fighting back tears.

"Oh, Mariamma," he says. His pitying tone annoys her; she wasn't asking for pity. She was mourning him. She bites her tongue. He doesn't notice. He goes on: "Mariamma. Marry me! Come away with me. How else are we to be together? If you join the movement, we can have a life together. Be husband and wife."

She digests this. Then she shoves him away, her hands scrabbling for the sheet. She feels very naked. "Listen to you!" she hisses. "Do you hear yourself? Your arrogance? You want me to give up *my* life? Follow you to a cave? Do you know why I shivered to hear your story? Shivered when the constables passed under the tree? I was terrified that the next thing you would say was that you killed Sivaraman because you felt it was justified. If you had had your gun, you would have, wouldn't you?"

"Mariamma—"

"Stop! Don't say a word. I've given everything—my strength, my sleep, my every waking hour—to study the body. To heal, not to harm, Lenin, you understand? Maybe even one day to cure the Condition. Big Ammachi prayed for that every single day. To fix *you*, you idiot! Do you know why I just gave you my body? Because I know I'm never going to see you again. But, my God, if you really thought I'd go down this path of bloodshed with you, this . . . this *stupid* path you took, not a straight path at all. If you think that, then you don't know me at all."

He rolls onto his back, chastened.

She's not done. She shakes him by the shoulder. "How come I didn't hear you say you'd give up your fight and come live a normal life with me, sacrifice your dreams for me? For the love we have . . ."

He stares at her, his face a mask of pain. "It's too late," he says at last. "If I'd known how you felt for me, I might never have gone down this path."

"You're a *macku* for not knowing. And let me tell you, there's nothing heroic about what you're doing. You want to help the downtrodden? Be a social worker! Or go into politics. Join your bloody Party and run for office. No, you're still standing on rooftops waiting for a lightning bolt, playing Mandrake the Magician. Grow up! You're no better than your father." It's vicious and she knows it. She's gone too far.

Outside they hear laughter, a woman's high-pitched voice, and a boy answering her. The sound of a tractor or diesel truck. How much Mariamma would give for *ordinary*! Ordinary would be precious. Ordinary would be extraordinary with Lenin. Anyone who disapproved of them could sit with their disapproval and make curry of it.

She brushes away tears. "Forgive me," she says.

"You're right. It was stupid of me to suggest you risk your life for something that isn't yours. And the reward is . . . There is no reward."

"My reward should have been you, Lenin. But not a Lenin in hiding. Or in prison."

"Forgive me," he says softly.

She nods. She must. She has. Forgiveness is hollow, but it's all she can offer the man she loves.

CHAPTER 67

Better Out than In

1971, Madras

She has no hope of seeing Lenin again unless it's in prison or a morgue, and still her feelings for him grow. She must hide her feelings, brine them away like the preserves under the *ara*. But ghosts abound in such places, and what's bottled can erupt.

In the second week of her posting in L&D—Labour and Delivery—she awakes feeling nausea. It recurs on successive mornings. She struggles to bathe, dress, and climb into Gopal's rickshaw. He eyes her with concern. He's perceptive, but discreet, and he won't speak unless she breaks the silence. She's hired him for the month to take her to Gosha Hospital and bring her back each evening.

Gosha is two miles from the hostel, just off Marina Beach. The only morning sounds are the squeak of the pedals, the squawk of seagulls, and the murmur of waves. At this hour it's cool. Soon, the sun will be a flame-white disc glaring off the water, and the macadam road will be hot enough to fry an egg. Gopal turns at the Madras Ice House. At one time, giant bars of ice from the Great Lakes were packed in sawdust, brought by American ships, and stored here to provide the British relief from the heat. The salt air carries scents of dried fish. It tests her stomach. In the distance, fishermen who set out in the dark now return. Their bobbing matchstick heads and the synchronous flash of wooden oars remind her of an upended insect thrashing in the water.

On the beach of a faraway land, she imagines waves keeping the exact same rhythm, sounding the same rustle and pop as they with-draw. In a place that's a mirror image of this one, another Mariamma lives, but free of this terrible apprehension. That other Mariamma is married to a Lenin who isn't a Naxalite; that doting Lenin will have tea ready for Mariamma when she returns from L&D. In her room in the hostel, she still has Lenin's *Guide to the Skies* that he forgot at Parambil. Now it sits with the precious 1920s *Gray's Anatomy* that was her mother's, an edition that isn't for studying but for treasuring. The books are her talismans, her good luck charms. But if this is what good luck feels like, then she'd hate to experience bad luck.

Her pulse rises at the sight of the bougainvillea bursting over the limestone walls of Gosha. The blossoms are placental red. Not a soul waters these plants; she believes their roots feed on a distillate from the drains of L&D, an aqua vitae richer than water and cow dung. The smiling Gurkha at the gate salutes—she's never seen him frown. The fading plaque reads THE ROYAL VICTORIA HOSPITAL FOR CASTE AND GOSHA WOMEN 1885. But it has always been "Gosha Hospital" to one and all, "*gosha*" being synonymous with "*burqa*" or "*purdah*." The British built it for high-caste Hindu women (who would not enter a hospital with untouchables) and for the Muslim women of neighbor-ing Triplicane, who are sequestered indoors and when they emerge are covered from head to foot. She's heard stories of Muslim women in obstructed labor who barricaded themselves in their bedrooms to prevent their husbands from taking them to a hospital where a white male obstetrician might touch them. Death was preferable. Times have changed. Obstetrics is no longer an all-male specialty in India. Mariamma's male classmates rotating through L&D complain they feel like pariahs because women rule. Luck has Mariamma posted at Gosha instead of Maternity Hospital in Egmore, a blessing because only Gosha can claim Staff Nurse Akila.

Outside L&D, a pale, pregnant woman paces, supported by her mother and husband. Her swollen belly exaggerates her lumbar curve as she waddles. Her contractions aren't frequent enough, so she's been ordered to walk. Mariamma sees this sight every morning and sometimes she imagines it's the same groaning woman in the same coarse white hospital sari and the absurd full-sleeved blouse. This British modification of the Victorian jacket and bodice is ill-suited for stifling heat. Now that the colonizers are long gone, why continue to wear this uniform? The woman looks right through Mariamma; the only thing on her mind is getting the baby out. "Better out than in" is the rule Staff Akila preaches. The Five-F Rule: "Flatus, Fluid, Feces, Foreign Body, and Fetus are all better out than in."

Lord, will that be me in eight months? My symptoms are unmistakable. She can confide in no one, not even her roommate, Anita.

Passing through the swinging doors of L&D, she enters a furnace; the ripe, sweetish scent smacks her in the face like a steaming wet rag. This morning, one woman's screams and curses have dominion over all the others; her husband is spared hearing her abuse because he's seated with others of the male tribe in the shade of the rain tree in the courtyard. The woman's rant is cut short by a smack like a rifle volley, followed by a nurse's shrill voice saying, "Stop it, woman! You should have cursed him nine months ago. Why bother now? *Mukku, mukku!*" Push, push! "*Mukku*" is the magic word, the "open sesame" of L&D, the chant on the staff's tongues all day and night. *Mukku!*

The daily tide of babies gives the medical students abundant experience—Mariamma reached her required twenty normal deliveries in the first four days. "Normal" labor is of no interest to the "PGs," the postgraduate trainees in obstetrics who slouch in colorful saris around the chipped wooden desk, overcoming their inertia only when things are *not* normal.

At the white pulpit, Senior Staff Nurse Akila, a short, dark, trim woman with angular features, is unruffled, writing up the medication indent, her face smoothed with powder. Her winged cap stands out against shiny black hair. Over her white uniform is a robin's-egg-blue, ironed apron, so stiff with starch that it can deflect bullets. Her tongue can scald anyone whose work she thinks sloppy, but she's a loving, nurturing soul. For Mariamma, she somehow evokes Big Ammachi, though they couldn't have been more different. The prayers to Parvati, Allah, and Jesus; the screams bouncing off tiled walls and rattling frosted windows; the miasma of blood, urine, and amniotic fluid vaporizing off sticky floors, permeating nostrils, sari, skin, hair, and brain; the labor pallets along each wall; the lime-green curtains that are always tied back, making the most private experience communal—what would her grandmother make of all this? Big Ammachi was strong and would have handled it. As for Mariamma, she simply loves it!

The L&D chalkboard resembles the board in Central Station, but with notations such as "G3P2 PROM" (third gravida, or pregnancy; second para, or live birth; and premature rupture of membranes). Mariamma approaches from behind Akila, but Staff has eyes in the back of her cap. "Listen up, ladies!" Staff shouts. "*Doctor* Mariamma's here! Don't hold back anymore, all right? *MUKKU-MUKKU!*" Akila hoots at her own joke. No one pays any attention except Mariamma, who thrills to hear "Doctor" before her name.

"Hello, Staff," Mariamma says, placing a length of jasmine on the pulpit. Mariamma patronizes an old woman near the hostel who spends her days attaching buds to a yarn, tying lightning-quick two-finger knots that would shame any surgeon. Her face and body are covered with disfiguring bumps under the skin, some the size of marbles, others the size of plums. The condition is called neurofibromatosis, or von Recklinghausen's disease; the benign fibrous tumors grow off cutaneous nerves below the skin. The famous Elephant Man, Joseph Merrick, was thought to have had a variant of neurofibromatosis.

"*Ayo!* Who has time for jasmine here?" Staff says, bringing it to her nose. But she's grinning. "Go check on three. She's a forceps

I'm saving for you only." Then she yells, "LISTEN, EVERYONE! WE'LL BE BUSY TODAY. I'M FEELING IT IN MY BONES." There's never been a day that hasn't been busy, or that Staff hasn't felt it in her bones.

The Malayali woman on pallet three has an orange mackintosh sheet underneath her buttocks and hanging over the edge. The sheet has a permanent gentian-violet stain from the innumerable women who've preceded her. When Mariamma spreads her gloved index and middle finger in a V inside the birth canal her fingers barely touch the sides of the cervix: the woman is fully dilated. The chalkboard says she has been in labor for seven hours, yet the baby's head hasn't budged past the pelvic floor. Mariamma applies the funnel-like stethoscope—the fetoscope—to the distended belly. Even with pin-drop silence, it's hard to hear the fetus. Akila says she must "*imagine* the baby's heart" to hear it separate from the mother's. *Imagine!* Suddenly she hears it, sounding like a woodpecker with a dull beak. Less than eighty is cause for alarm—this baby comes in at sixty. Now Mariamma's heart is racing.

"Staff!" she calls out, but Akila has already sent over the trolley. The forceps, fresh out of the sterilizer, have steam rising off them. The strings of the plastic apron Mariamma grabs are still wet from the previous user. She numbs the vulval skin with novocaine to one side of the midline and cuts. Tiny, pulsating gushes of blood follow the track of the angled episiotomy scissors. She's only used forceps once before. The paired forceps are like curved serving spoons with long, slim handles; when the spoons (or "blades") are positioned correctly, cupping the baby's head, the handles can be brought together and locked. But by the time one needs forceps, the baby's head is a soggy, swollen affair, with the landmarks hard to find. Using her index and middle fingers as a guide, she slides the left blade in and over the baby's head, then does the same on the right. She prays they're gripping skull, not squishing the face. But try as she might, she can't get the two handles to come together. To force it might crush the skull. Just when she despairs, the hand of the Goddess Akila appears over her shoulder, makes a small adjustment to one blade, and now the handles articulate and lock. Staff disappears.

But the traction rod Mariamma tries to affix to the handle doesn't match! She should have checked before she started. Once again, Goddess Akila's hand reaches over Mariamma's shoulder and completes the assembly despite the mismatch. Mariamma plants her feet on the floor, ready to heave. Akila positions the probationer behind Mariamma just in case she falls back when the head delivers. Mariamma tugs with the next contraction. "*Ayo*, you call that pulling, Doctor?" Akila shouts from the other side of the room without looking. "The baby will drag you back inside, slippers and all, if you can't do better." Mariamma squats and gives it everything she has. The baby's head has run aground on the promontory of the sacrum. "Staff!" she cries through gritted teeth. "It'll be fine, *ma*," Akila shouts from the pulpit, then yells at someone else: "Doctor, by the time you finish sewing up episiotomy, the baby will be walking only!"

And it *is* fine, because suddenly the head emerges. But for the backstop of the probationer, Mariamma and the baby would be sprawled on the wet floor. The limp blue creature suffers the indignity of an egg-shaped head thanks to the forceps. She frantically works the bulb of the mucus sucker in the mouth to no avail. She blows gently into the face. Nothing. The mother looks on with horror. One of Goddess Akila's ten hands reaches over and slaps the baby's bottom, and with a jerk it lets out a shrill cry. "Better, *ma*?" Akila says, grinning cheekily, the Feels-Better-Out-Than-In implied but not spoken. Mariamma is so happy she feels like bawling. The tiny fists are raised in the air . . . She thinks suddenly of Lenin and tears threaten. "Hello, Mariamma Madam!" Staff yells, now from near the autoclave. "If you won't cut the cord, kindly give the scissors to the baby. Stop daydreaming!" All-seeing Akila can even read minds. Mariamma cuts the cord and sets to work repairing the episiotomy. *As soon as I'm done today, I'll confess to Akila. I'll tell her all. I can't bear this alone.*

* * *

Hours later, at the end of their shift, she asks Akila if she can walk out with her. Hesitantly, she spills her secret. Akila bursts out laughing.

"*Ma*, every medical student who comes through L&D thinks they're pregnant. Even some foolish boys! Pseudocyesis, it's called. But I say to them, how can you be a virgin and be pregnant?" Akila cracks up again.

"Staff . . . ? I'm not a virgin," Mariamma says quietly.

Akila regards her with new interest. She takes Mariamma's chin and turns her face one way and then the other. "*Ma*, I'm working L&D before you born. Akila is knowing when a woman is pregnant. I'm knowing before God is knowing, before mother is knowing. Husbands are idiots, knowing nothing, so forget about husbands. But never is Akila wrong. Body is telling me. Cheeks, color, *ithu-athu*. I'm promising you're not pregnant. Do you believe me? Of course not! So, we'll do test, but only so you are not worrying, understood?"

In the blood bank, Akila draws the specimen herself. "I'll give to lab using some other name. But it will be normal, *ma*. Pregnancy in head, not in uterus." She stops for emphasis. "*This* time. Next time could be uterus. So, use head next time."

CHAPTER 68

The Hound of Heaven

1973, Madras

With the negative pregnancy test, her "morning sickness" vanishes. Mariamma feels like a condemned prisoner given a pardon. She'd been paralyzed by the prospect of being an unmarried mother to a child whose father was a Naxalite who'd never be seen alive again.

She's too ashamed to make a second confession to Staff Akila: that she feels let down. Why *didn't* she get pregnant? Is something wrong with her? Did her night with Lenin fail to impress the universe? Surely a love like theirs, a first intimacy, must leave its mark. It's unreasonable, she knows, but the thought lingers, even as she packs for the Christmas holidays. She's heading home at last, a visit that is long overdue.

When she gets her first glimpse of Parambil, she's struck by its serenity, so removed from the chaos of her two years away. Smoke curls up from the chimney, from a hearth that never burns out. And there stands her father, framed by the pillars of the verandah, Anna *Chedethi* next to him, as though they've been standing there keeping vigil from the day she left. He holds her so tight she can hardly breathe.

"*Molay*, without you a part of me was gone," he whispers. There's security in his embrace, just as when she was a young girl. Then it's Anna *Chedethi*'s turn to smother her. They both notice the scar on her face, even though it is fading. She blames a fall on a slippery lab floor and being cut by shattering glass. It's true enough, even if the context is missing.

The ghosts of her grandmother and Baby Mol hover close by, reminding her once more of her purpose, of why she left. Everything she is, and all that she aspires to, began in this house and its loving inhabitants. After coming home from Alwaye College for the funeral, she'd been back just once more, shortly before she started medical school. On those previous visits, the household still felt shattered from the deaths. But now she senses that her father and Anna *Chedethi* have learned to live with the loss; they've settled into a new routine. For Mariamma, this only makes the absence of those two beloved pillars of this house more glaring—like a tear in a fabric that no one else sees.

Anna *Chedethi* has made her favorite, *meen vevichathu*, the crimson liquid so thick a pencil would stay upright in it. "The fishmonger showed up yesterday. The old lady herself—not her daughter-in-law. The only thing in her basket was this *avoli*. She said, 'Tell Mariamma I brought this fellow just for her. Tell her I've a terrible ache in my neck and down my arms. The *vaidyan*'s pills are useless. If I toss them in the river, it'd be better for me, but bad for the fish.'" Mariamma pictures the old woman, her forearms dry and cobblestoned as though engrafted by the fish scales that shower down from her head basket. Now the old woman's gift sits in Big Ammachi's clay pot, transformed into a red-coated fillet, its white flesh melting on her tongue, the curry staining crimson the rice, her fingers, and the porcelain plate.

Her father is anxious to share news that isn't news to her. She feels it hover over the table, exaggerated by his efforts to pretend it isn't there. He waits till she finishes.

"*Molay*, I've to tell you something that will upset you. God knows, it's all we talk about." Anna *Chedethi*, who was clearing the dishes, stops and sits down. "Lenin has disappeared," he says. "Did you know?"

"I've been worried. He hasn't written for a while." Another half-truth.

"Well . . . believe it or not, he's joined the Naxalites," her father says.

The price of deceit is to feel like a cockroach. She listens as he recounts the newspaper stories of the raids, and of Arikkad's death while trying to escape. "The Naxalite business seemed so far away to us till now," he says. "Up in Malabar, or Bengal. Suddenly it's here in our laps."

Her father has always been a handsome man. But for the first time she notices the permanence of the dark pigmentation under his eyes, the worry lines on his forehead, the sag of his cheeks, and the shiny scalp peeking through his thinning hair. He's fifty, she realizes. A half century of living. But even so, has time sped up at Parambil since she's been gone?

When a daughter falls in love, a distancing from the father is perhaps inevitable; the first man who had her heart must now compete with another. But in Mariamma's case, it's her secrets that create the distance. Anna *Chedethi* looks at her anxiously, worried that this revelation might shatter her.

"It's terrible," Mariamma says, because she must say something. "If he joined the Naxalites, then he's more stupid than I thought. If he wanted to help the poor, why not join the Party, run for office?" She had suggested just that to Lenin. "Why this? He's an idiot. Just throwing away his life!" The vehemence of her words takes them aback. Has she overdone it?

"Well," her father says after a while, "one thing I'll say for Lenin, from the very first day he showed up here, he stated his intentions. He always felt deeply for the *pulayar*. The yoke on their necks weighed on his. We sit here and believe we are enlightened, fair. But the truth is we can be blind to injustice. He never was."

If only Lenin could hear her father defending him.

* * *

When Anna *Chedethi* goes for her bath, Mariamma sits alone in the dark kitchen that is so redolent with scent and memory. She recalls Damodaran once applying his ancient eye to the window and Big Ammachi pretending to be annoyed, scolding him. The week her grandmother died, Damo disappeared into the jungle near the logging camp. This they only learned later from Unni, who had waited in his forest hut for weeks to no avail. Damo went to keep Big Ammachi company, no doubt. Unni was a broken man. Mariamma finds the matchbox and lights one of Big Ammachi's palm-sized oil lamps, the kind that her grandmother favored, and would take with her when she went to bed. Mariamma weeps unabashedly, picturing that kindly face bathed by the lamp's soft glow. But her grandmother is with her always; these tears are for the past, for innocent times when she sat here and was fed by that loving hand, was entertained with stories, and knew she was cherished.

She composes herself before joining her father in his study. How she's missed the aroma of old newspapers and journals, and of homemade ink! And missed his familiar scent of sandalwood soap and neem toothpaste; missed this hallowed time at the end of each day when he read stories to her. Why was it one had to leave something, or have it taken away, to really appreciate it? But tonight, she's the storyteller, because he's hungry to hear every detail of her medical world, bringing his curiosity like a moth to anything that shines of new knowledge. He craves every detail. She obliges, describes it all for him . . . all but Brijee.

When they turn in, he says, "It must be so hard to see such suffering every day." He shudders. "I couldn't do it. Only luck and the grace of God keeps us free of such afflictions. We're so blessed, aren't we?"

She marvels that a man who has suffered so much can feel this way. "Appa, I'm ashamed to say I often take it for granted. I used to be frightened of the sick. Now, we're all so focused on disease that sometimes the person suffering barely registers. When I come home from L&D, or the surgical wards, I'm only thinking about dinner, or wondering if there's a letter waiting. I think all doctors have the illusion that we have some sort of bargain with God. We care for the sick and are spared in return."

"That reminds me," her father says, handing her a paper. "I came across this in my reading, the oath of Paracelsus. I said, 'I must copy this for Mariamma.'" Her father's writing is normally illegible, but this he's painstakingly printed out. "I thought, 'I want my Mariamma to be this kind of doctor.'" She reads, "Love the sick, each and every one, as if they were your own."

That night she sleeps in Anna *Chedethi*'s bed in the old bedroom near the *ara*, taking comfort in snuggling next to this woman who breastfed her, who was as much a mother to her as she was to Hannah. Anna *Chedethi* confides that Joppan has had a rough time. Iqbal had wanted to retire from the barge business. Joppan bought him out by taking out a bank loan, but to pay it off he had to work twice as hard, expanding his routes, taking on as much business as he could. Anna *Chedethi* says he paid his workers generously—he was one of them, after all. But he drove them hard. Before Onam, at his busiest time, his boatmen and loaders went on strike. They wanted part ownership of the company. Joppan tried to reason with them. Did they want a share of his debt as well? They weren't listening. He felt betrayed. "You remember that Party fellow he campaigned for and helped to get elected from that district?" Anna *Chedethi* says. "Well, he and the Party took the workers' side. Better to sacrifice Joppan's one vote than lose all the workers' votes. Joppan locked his workers out and tried to hire others. His workers sunk one barge and tried to set fire to his warehouse. Instead of giving in to their demands, Joppan closed the business. He let the bank take it. I don't know how much money he has managed to save, but I worry." Mariamma thinks at the very least they won't starve; Ammini makes an income selling her thatch panels. And they have their property. And perhaps Podi can help since she has joined her husband in Sharjah.

But this isn't how Joppan had imagined his life would be. She's surprised her father didn't mention this. Perhaps he felt protective of his friend.

In the morning, she grabs a *thorthu* and heads out. She wants to see the hospital construction, but first she stops by the nest. She breathes in its dry, woody scent. Trumpet vines romp over the sunny side. Is this what her mother intended? That nature should renew and alter the nest every year and in every season? The two tiny stools are still there, and she sits down, her knees bumping her chin, remembering Podi, who would sit opposite her. They'd play checkers or take turns sharing Can-I-Tell-You-Somethings, secrets that the adults around them didn't want them to know. Sometimes she would come by herself and pretend that her mother sat on the other stool. They'd have tea together and talk about life.

The Stone Woman is on the way to the canal. She and Podi had discovered her quite by accident when they were young, all but hidden by pepper vine and goatweed. Mariamma had been struck at once by her power, her faceless presence. She dwarfed them. She still does. Her father said it was a sculpture her mother had abandoned. She and Podi freed her, cleared the ground around her, and planted marigolds. She used to think of the Stone Woman as another incarnation of her mother, different from the one smiling at her in the photograph in Mariamma's room. As a child, she'd lie down on the Stone Woman's back and imagine her mother's strength seeping into her flesh, like sap rising in a tree. Now, she just runs her hands over the Stone Woman in silent greeting.

Across the canal, the concrete for the foundation for the hospital has been poured. Already the bamboo scaffolding lashed together with rope suggests a much bigger structure than she could've imagined. She tries to picture what the completed building will look like. It pleases her to think that the gold bracelet she peeled off at the Maramon Convention is embedded in there in some fashion, part of the hospital's bones.

The canal is newly widened and dredged all the way to its confluence with the river. The water surface is a kaleidoscope of green and brown; floating leaves move along more quickly than she recalls. She finds a spot that's secluded and strips to her underclothes. Then she scrambles down the stone incline, her soles sliding and skating on the moss, before she pushes off and dives in headfirst. The sensation of sudden transition is exhilarating, familiar, nostalgic . . . and sad. She'd hoped to slip back in time by plunging in. But there's no going back; time and water move on relentlessly. She surfaces much farther downstream than she expected. The confluence of the waters announces itself noisily ahead of her, and the current is surprisingly strong. She cuts to the side, finds a handhold, and scrambles out. No, it's no longer the same canal, and she's not the same Mariamma.

At the end of her short break, her father splurges on a tourist taxi, not to take them to the bus station but to drive them all the way to the train station in Punalur, a two-and-a-half-hour ride. They sit like royalty in the back. Her father confides to her that the task of running Parambil lands has worn him down. "I was never good at it. If I had Shamuel's or my father's passion, then we'd cultivate a lot more land and make more money." He looks sheepishly at her. "The truth is your father prefers the pen to the plow."

Mariamma thinks he's being modest. He's well known for his Unfictions. Once or twice a year he writes long investigative pieces that appear in the weekend magazine section of the *Manorama*.

"So, I've been talking to Joppan about managing all of Parambil for us. I made him an offer. I'm hopeful. He's getting out of the barge business. Too many headaches. Years ago, after Shamuel died, we made Joppan a good offer. He said so himself. It would've given him his own land, more than any of our relatives around here, and a share of the harvest in exchange for being our manager. But he had dreams of conquering the earth. Or at least the waterways. He turned it down. Also, he didn't want to be thought of as 'Joppan *pulayan*' taking Shamuel's place."

"So did you offer him something different this time?"

"You *should* ask. After my time, this will be yours, so it's good to know. I offered him ten acres that will be his outright. In return he manages our lands for ten years and takes ten percent of all our yield. Then, as he develops his land and earns money, if he wants, he can buy more land from me."

"It's generous," Mariamma says.

Her father looks pleased. "I hope he thinks so too. The offer I made long ago was much better, but so much has changed. I feel bad for him." He looks out, silent for a while. "*Molay*, Joppan was our hero, our Saint George when we were children, do you know? Destiny is a funny thing. Look at me. I finished school, had ambitions to go to college, to see the world. Instead, here I am, where I started, while Joppan is the well-traveled one. Parambil is where I feel complete. Joppan may well find that the very thing he ran away from is what will save him and make him happy. You resist fate, but the hound finds you anyway. *Lo, all things fly thee, for thou fliest Me!*"

Parting from him on the platform is wrenching. She feels a rush of guilt for all that she's held back from her father. Her secrets. Secrets that are damning. She can't imagine her father having secrets, but perhaps even he does.

Their long embrace is different from past embraces. They've reversed roles. She's the parent leaving her child to fend for itself, but the child clings to her. As the train pulls away, her father stands there waving, smiling bravely, a lone and forlorn figure.

CHAPTER 69

Seeing What You Imagine

1974, Madras

Near the end of Mariamma's internal medicine rotation, a khaki-clad peon summons her to see Dr. Uma Ramasamy, in the Department of Pathology. Mariamma's first reaction is to worry that she's done something wrong. But her pathology course is long over. Her next reaction is excitement. Uma Ramasamy is a divorcée just over thirty, a sensational teacher. Mariamma's male classmates have a crush on the professor. Chinnah says, "She's got *subject*," a phrase that in med school jargon signals mastery of a field. "Chinnah, are you sure it's 'subject' and not something else that attracts you?" "What, *ma*? You mean Madam's Premier Padmini?" he says innocently. "*Chaa!* Not at all!"

A Fiat Premier Padmini suits Dr. Ramasamy better than the stodgy Ambassador, or the cockroach-like Standard Herald. Those three rebranded foreign models are the only cars licensed to be built in socialist India; for any other car, one must be willing to pay a 150 percent import tax. Uma's Fiat is custom-painted ebony black with a red top; it has an extra bank of headlights, tinted windows, and a throaty exhaust. And, unusually, she drives herself.

When Dr. Ramasamy first lectured to their class in the century-old Donovan Auditorium, even the murmuring backbenchers were silenced when the tall, confident woman in a short-sleeved lab coat floated in. She had launched right into inflammation, the body's first response to any threat, the common denominator of all disease. In minutes she had drawn them into the thick of a battle: the invaders (typhoid bacteria) are spotted by the hilltop sentries (macrophages), who send signals back to the castle (the bone marrow and lymph nodes). The few aging veterans of previous battles with typhoid (memory T-lymphocytes) are roused from their beds, summoned to hastily teach untested conscripts the specific typhoid-grappling skills needed, and then to arm them with custom lances designed solely to latch onto and pierce the typhoid shield—in essence, the veterans clone their younger selves. The same veterans of prior typhoid campaigns also assemble a biological-warfare platoon (B lymphocytes) who hastily manufacture a one-of-a-kind boiling oil (antibodies) to pour over the castle wall; it will melt the typhoid intruders' shields, while not harming others. Meanwhile, having heard the call to battle, the rogue mercenaries (neutrophils), armed to the teeth, stand ready. At the first scent of spilled blood—*any* blood, from friend or foe—these mercenaries will go on a killing frenzy . . . Dr. Ramasamy kicked out the fuchsia-and-gold border of her red sari as she paced before the board. Mariamma was reminded of the women conjured up in her mother's sketches; the sinuous charcoal lines conveyed not just the drape of a sari but the form of the woman underneath.

A brass plaque outside her office simply reads HANSEN RESEARCH CENTER. Atypically, Dr. Ramasamy doesn't seem to need to put her name on it. The air-conditioned chill within reminds Mariamma of the sari shops in the affluent suburb of T. Nagar, where the salesclerks seated on raised platforms recklessly pull one gorgeous sari after another from the stacks, unfurling and cascading them before the client. But here chrome refrigerators, water baths, incubators, sleek lab benches, and centrifuges take the place of palisades of silk and cotton.

Mariamma's eyes fall on the sleek binocular microscope. Her mouth waters. It even has a second binocular attachment on it—a teaching head—so student and teacher can study the same slide, illuminated from below with an electric bulb. Compared to this beauty, Mariamma's one-eyed scope, which only works next to a bright window with much jiggling of its reflecting mirror, is a bullock cart.

"She's a beauty, isn't she?" Dr. Ramasamy is in an ocean-blue sari. She wears simple gold studs in her ears. She gestures to the high stools by the microscope. After preliminaries, she says, "So . . . I asked you over to see if you wanted to work on a project with me on the—"

"Yes-I'd-love-to, Madam!" she says, the words spilling over each other.

Dr. Ramasamy laughs. "Shouldn't you find out what it is first? Or do you say yes to everything?"

"No-I-mean-yes, Madam." Mariamma can't keep her head movements straight. She must look like a very silly girl. She must speak more slowly, as Anita often reminds her.

"You'd be assisting my research on peripheral nerves. On Hansen's disease."

Why not just say leprosy? Mariamma wonders.

"The task is to carefully dissect the upper limbs we've preserved from patients with Hansen's and expose the median and ulnar nerves and their branches fully. Then we photograph the gross specimens in place before we sacrifice the nerves and make multiple sections to examine microscopically. Some of those sections we will send for immunohistochemistry staining and study in Oslo."

Mariamma pictures the lepers at the Maramon Convention, or the ones who shuffled up the path to Parambil, looking like aliens from another galaxy, and stopping at hailing distance to rattle their cups. She shudders inwardly at the thought of dissecting one of their limbs. Maybe "Hansen's" is a better name after all.

"I'm honored to be asked," she says.

Dr. Ramasamy cocks her head, her smile getting broader. "But . . . ?"

"No, nothing . . . Just wondering, Madam, why me?"

"Good question. Dr. Cowper recommended you. I saw your hand dissection from the prize exam. Amazing that you did that in two hours. That's exactly what I need. But my specimens will be trickier."

"Thank you, Madam. I'm happy that you didn't pick me because of . . ."

"Because you crushed Brijee's balls?" she says, her expression deadpan. Mariamma bursts out laughing, shocked.

"*Ayo*, Madam!"

"That was an added recommendation, to be honest. I was a student here not that long ago. We had our Brijees, though no one quite as poisonous. Sadly, some are still around."

Mariamma begins the next day, retrieving a specimen from a formalin tank that seems to contain a pile of forearms with hands attached. She dissects by the window where the light is best. She has a magnifying glass on a stand if she needs it. She must find the trunks of the median and ulnar nerves in the forearm and dissect out their branches to the fingers, or rather to the stumps, since this specimen lacks fingers. The trouble is the skin is as thick as an elephant's hide, more so than the usual formalin-preserved cadaver dissection. The fat and subcutaneous tissue feel rock-hard and glued to the skin; she must be so careful not to tear the nerve. She cannot use anything as sharp as a scalpel or scissor when she might be close to the nerve. So for hours she digs, pushes, and scrapes with gauze wrapped over her finger, or with the handle of the scalpel—"blunt dissection" they call this in surgery. She's like a hunter looking for tracks. The signs are subtle, like the faint and darker ridge of earth raised by an earthworm. She sits bent over the specimen, just as when she did needlepoint as a child with Hannah. Are cloistered nuns allowed such hobbies?

It takes a week and aching wrists and a stiff neck to complete the first dissection.

"Wonderful!" Uma says when she comes to look. "I hired you because I can't spare the time to do this. But I confess, I tried. I butchered it! What's your secret?"

Mariamma hesitates. "It's partly my eyesight. I learned needle-point when I was very young. I found I could do very minute things that Hannah—the girl who taught me—couldn't, though she had normal vision. In fact, I haven't been using your magnifying glass because it makes me dizzy. Also, Madam—" She hesitates. When she tried to explain this to Anita, her roommate thought she was mad. "I don't want to sound boastful . . . or mad. But during anatomy dissection I felt I was seeing *differently*. I mean, we could all be looking down at a flat, squashed mess of formalin tissue. But I could see it in three dimensions, I could rotate it in my head. It's more than knowing what I was *supposed* to see—we had the dissection manual in front of us for that. I could see how the tissue below me differed from the figure. I could *imagine* it fully, almost see through it. After that, the challenge is to bring it out. For that I use every sense I have. I'm paying attention to the resistance of the tissue, to the feel, and even the vibration or friction as my instruments move on its surface."

Uma ponders this. "Don't worry—I don't think you're mad. You have a gift, Mariamma. There's no other way to dissect like this. Our brains have extraordinary capabilities. In our simplistic understanding, we put each function in its box—Broca's area for speech, and Wernicke's area for interpreting what we hear. But the boxes are artificial. Simplistic. The senses intertwine and spill over from one area to another. Think of the phantom limb. The leg is amputated, but the brain feels pain in what isn't there. So I can see how your brain might take the visual signal and do something different with it."

Mariamma thinks about the Condition. Already, with the knowledge of anatomy and physiology that she has, she thinks the Condition must involve parts of the brain associated with hearing and balance. Perhaps for those affected by the Condition, immersion in water causes the signals to spill over to parts of the brain that should be off limits—the opposite of a gift. She must ask Uma, but before she can, Uma speaks.

"I've seen some of your sketches. You draw well."

"Not really. I wish I had my mother's artistic gifts."

"What sort of art does she do?"

"Well, she doesn't. But she did once . . . I never knew my mother. She drowned soon after I was born."

"Oh, Mariamma!"

The sadness in Uma's voice makes Mariamma feel a rush of grief. It's not grief for her mother, exactly. How could she grieve for someone she didn't know? And she'll never get over her grief for Big Ammachi, who was mother, grandmother, and namesake all rolled into one. But being around Uma Ramasamy, given her age, and her dynamic, vibrant nature, affords Mariamma a sense of what it might have been like to converse with her mother. If she hadn't drowned.

Uma rises, squeezes Mariamma's shoulder, and goes back to her office.

Her classes, clinics, dissections, and books keep her mind occupied. Now and then she has the absurd urge to write to Lenin, who is of course unreachable. The only letters she gets now are from her father, full of the news from home. Joppan has agreed to be the manager of Parambil, and from his first day it feels as if he's been doing it forever. Her father says he can breathe for the first time. And there's drama around Uplift Master and the Hospital Fund, he reports. Podi used to work for Uplift Master, helping him with accounts. After she left, Master hired a new girl, who has apparently embezzled. The mess is being sorted out, but meanwhile poor Uplift Master is suspended, even though he's quite innocent. It hasn't affected the construction:

The outside walls are almost complete. I look at it and think I am dreaming to see such a beautiful modern building in our Parambil. I wish Big Ammachi could see this. It's her vision. Perhaps she does see it. She certainly knew we were on our way. Anna Chedethi sends love. We are so proud of you.

Your loving Appa

On a Saturday, when Mariamma catches up on her dissections, Uma drops by and they look at some of the first nerve sections together under the two-headed microscope. Uma says, "I often think about Armauer Hansen. So many scientists looked under the microscope at leprous tissue before him, but they didn't see the leprosy bacillus. It's not that hard to see! It's because they'd decided no such thing could be there. Sometimes we must *imagine* what is there to find it. That, by the way, I learned from you!"

It's flattering and inspires Mariamma to work harder. She's drawn to Uma. When she was a child, she would daydream of her mother coming home, bejeweled, always in a chariot, and with her hair flowing free, released at last from a magician's spell that kept her asleep for years. Such fantasies came to her usually when she was with the Stone Woman, or in the nest, because her mother was alive in those creations, alive in her incomplete sketches and paintings—an artist interrupted who would be back any moment. But as the years passed, the sleeping beauty never did return, the paintings remained incomplete. Uma, her living, breathing, vibrant mentor, the sort of woman who, she discovers, competes in rallies and is rebuilding an engine with her own hands, is more real than any drawing, more real than a faceless stone relic in Parambil.

She books a ticket to go home for a week during the short holidays. Two days before she's to leave, she toils in the lab, readying her dissection to be photographed.

She senses a presence behind her. She turns. Uma stands half in and half out of her office, the oddest expression on her face, her eyes wet. Mariamma's first thought is that Uma's been fishing in the formalin tank and the fumes got to her.

Uma floats toward her in slow motion like a sleepwalker and gently clasps her shoulders.

"Mariamma," she says, "there's been an accident."

CHAPTER 70

Take the Plunge

1974, Cochin

Philipose spends a rare night away from Parambil at Cochin's famous Malabar Hotel, courtesy of his newspaper. He'd proposed an article with a different take on Robert Bristow, the man viewed as a saint in this port city. His editor liked the idea.

Bristow, a marine engineer, arrived in Cochin in 1920 and saw that despite its booming spice trade, Cochin was fated to remain a minor port because of a rocky sandbar and a mammoth ridge that barred all but small boats. Ships had to berth out at sea, and goods and passengers had to be rowed to shore. Bristow pulled off an engineering feat as formidable as digging the Suez Canal: he removed the obstacles and, in the process, threw up enough silt and rock to create Willingdon Island. Ships now have a deep-water harbor that sits between Willingdon Island and the mainland; Willingdon Island is home to Cochin Airport, government offices, businesses, shops, and the magnificent Malabar Hotel.

Philipose, dining outdoors at the Malabar, looks out at the broad sea channel that runs between Vypin Island and Fort Cochin, then out to the Arabian Sea. It amuses him—given his feud with water—to be seated on land that was once water. He's here because a cranky biologist has pestered the Ordinary Man to explore what Bristow's engineering feat has done to the ecology of Vembanad Lake, which opens to the ocean at this spot. The canals and backwaters, which are the lifeblood of Kerala and feed into the lake, are exposed to salt water. "Immeasurable damage occurred to the benthic, nektonic, and planktonic communities," the man says in his letter. "And since dredging goes on year-round, the damage is ongoing. The precious rock-oyster, *Crassostrea*, is vital to a food chain that goes from fish larvae to adult fish to young children with growing brains!" Philipose is sympathetic: he's seen similar issues with building dams, denuding teak forests, or digging for ore—there are unintended consequences. The poor villagers whose lives might be affected rarely have any voice to object beforehand to such projects. Once the damage is done, what they say hardly matters.

He lingers over dinner and a complimentary brandy from the chef who, it turns out, is an admirer of the Ordinary Man. The breeze is delicate, like a woman's fingers grazing through his hair. How he wishes Mariamma could be here with him at this grand hotel.

I'm at the edge of my world, he thinks. *This is as far as I'll ever go.*

He smells history in this breeze. The Dutch, the Portuguese, the English . . . Each left their stamp. All gone now. Shades. Their cemeteries are overgrown with weeds, the names unreadable, weathered by wind. What stamp will *he* leave? What will be his masterpiece? He knows the answer: Mariamma. She is his masterpiece.

After dinner he walks to his room, stepping carefully; he's unaccustomed to brandy. The tourists seated earlier at a long table have left behind a book on the chair. No, not a book, but a small and beautifully printed catalog on the kind of heavy paper that invites touch. He picks it up. On the cover is a black-and-white photograph of a large outdoor stone sculpture.

Suddenly he's sober. The ocean is stilled, the breeze is arrested, the stars stop twinkling.

Her shoulders and arms are overdeveloped—a woman, but a superhuman one. She resembles a primitive clay figure, with her breasts full and pendulous. Her shoulder blades look like wings flattened against her body. Her skin is deliberately left coarse. She's on all fours but extends one arm. The woman's face is not revealed, still locked in the stone.

His gut coils and an equine shiver pushes out hair follicles: The magnified proportions, the posture, the attitude—it's all Elsie.

He stumbles to his room, and in a frenzy, he studies the catalog under the table lamp. The index lists this figure as "#26, Artist Unknown." The catalog is for an estate sale of the contents of the Adyar house of an apparently wealthy Englishman and "Orientalist" who'd amassed a collection of Indian paintings, folk art, and sculptures. The Madras auction house of Messrs. Wintrobe & Sons presides. He pores over each page, studying the other items. He sees nothing else that is Elsie's. Conceivably this statue could be a work of Elsie's from before they were married. Or when she went away after Ninan's death. But his gut says it isn't.

He returns to the cover. The rough, untouched stone where the face is buried is deliberate. He breaks into a sweat, feels an urge to claw at the paper, break open the stone to reveal the face.

He paces, unable to sit, trying to make sense of what makes no sense.

We never found a body. In its absence, we presumed.

He was barely present when Elsie drowned, lost in opium fantasies of reincarnation, and then sinking into recrimination. When he returned from the forest after Shamuel, Joppan, Unni, and Damo had carried him away, he was clearheaded and sober. He'd held Elise's clothes to his face, the ones she'd left on the bank. He inhaled her scent, the new scent that was hers when she returned from being away so long. The fragrance of suffering. He'd never wanted to accept that she willingly gave herself to the river, took her life, because if that were so, then he knew he'd driven her to it. No, it was an accident. In his nightmares he stumbled onto her decomposed body far from Parambil, picked apart by crocodiles and wild dogs.

But in all these years, he'd never ever considered a possibility *other* than her drowning; he'd never pictured a scenario in which her living, breathing self still existed in the same universe as his, still practiced her craft. She had cause to run away from him. But from her own child? No, surely not.

Oh, Elsie. What kind of beast were you married to if the only way you could pursue what mattered to you was to sacrifice Mariamma?

The auction is to take place the day after next. The catalog might say "Artist Unknown." But two decades of newspaper work have taught him that what is unknown is often just undiscovered.

He must go to Madras. For all these years that city has been synonymous with his failure. Not even his daughter being there could entice him to board a train. The thought of it still made him feel breathless and break into sweat.

But he will go. He *must* go. Not just for answers, but to make amends.

The next morning, the *Manorama*'s Cochin office manages the impossible. Standing at the reservations window a few hours later he collects his ticket. He's shaky, his palms sweating. He addresses his body: *We're getting on the train and that's final.* Back at the Malabar Hotel, he pens a letter to Mariamma.

> *My darling daughter, I'm boarding the train to Madras soon.*
> *I will be there by morning. I'll probably get there before this*
> *letter is delivered. But you did say that after all these years if*
> *I did show up without warning you would die of shock. Hence,*
> *these words to say I'm on my way. I have much to tell you. The*
> *voyage of discovery isn't about new lands but having new eyes.*
> *Your loving Appa*

In the afternoon, when it's time to board, he sees his name on the typed list glued to the carriage; it brings back memories of standing on this very platform with Uplift Master. It's as though his whole life has yet to unfold; he has yet to meet that adventurous girl in tinted cat's-eye glasses who is to be his wife; Big Ammachi, Baby Mol, and Shamuel are alive; and Ninan and Mariamma are unborn, waiting for the summons to appear . . .

He climbs aboard like a seasoned traveler, with nothing but the soft briefcase that holds his notebook, shaving kit, and a change of clothes. "Most welcome," he hears himself say magnanimously, helping a woman push her trunk under his bench. The train jerks forward. He laughs with the others as a *kochamma* yells from the platform, "And don't forget to wash your own underwear, *kehto*! Don't give it to the *dhobi*, you hear?" The college boys in the next cubicle shout, "What is there, *ammachi*? Let him be! For *dhobi*'s itch you simply scratch, that's all!"

The journey is off to a rollicking start. His new cubicle friends debate whether it's better to order dinner in Palakkad or wait till Coimbatore, as though life rests on such small decisions. He's astonished to hear himself offer an opinion, pretending to have experience. *You coward!* he thinks. *The fuss you made for years about visiting Madras! All you needed was for Elsie to come back from the dead.*

At dusk, the lush Malabar slopes of the Western Ghats quiet the passengers, mute their conversations. He stares out, lost. *If you changed, Elsie, I did too. I learned to be steadfast. I walked my daughter to school every single day till she forbade me. I read stories to her every night. Thank God she's a reader, and there's nothing she likes better than to be buried in a book. Wednesdays I decreed were Carnatic music night from All India Radio, but she preferred opera on the BBC—such awful sounds. Oh, Elsie, how much you missed of our daughter's life! I never accomplished very much in my life, I'll be the first to admit. But what accomplishment could be bigger than our daughter? You need say nothing to me. You owe me nothing. Elsie, I'm coming to say I am sorry. To say, I wish I could rewind the thread of our lives. I was someone different then. I'm someone else now.*

As they enter the first of the tunnels, the feeble compartment lights give the bogie a ghostly glow, and the train's hammering on the tracks is amplified into a roar.

I never stopped thinking of you. The way you looked when I first met you, and met you again, and our first kiss . . . I talk to your picture every night.

But Elsie, Elsie—what is the meaning of this statue? Could this be from the year you were away? If not, does it mean you live? Perhaps I preferred to think of you dead, so I didn't have to face how awful I had been. But Elsiamma, if you're alive and hiding, then hide no more. Let me see you, show me your face. There's so much to say . . .

Soon the train will cross over a river on a long trestle bridge that he remembers from so long ago, remembers with a shudder, because it had shaken him. He'd looked out of the window because the rhythmic clatter of the wheels on the track had changed to a high-pitched whir, and when he peeked out, they seemed to be sailing over water, with nothing holding up the train. His young self had almost fainted. Best he be asleep when it happens.

He climbs up to his berth—the topmost—and stretches out. In the confined space, the sight of the ceiling inches from his nose reminds him of a coffin. He shuts his eyes and conjures up Mariamma's face. She has made up for his thwarted ambitions, his loneliness, the imperfections of his earlier self. *We don't have children to fulfill our dreams. Children allow us to let go of the dreams we were never meant to fulfill.*

He's drifting off when he's called back by a sharp crack coming from another carriage, followed by a jolt that travels through his bogie. He feels himself rising free of the bunk. *This is strange!* The cubicle is turning around him. He observes a child suspended in space, while an airborne adult slides past. The compartment explodes with screams and the squealing of metal. He's thrown up against the ceiling, except the ceiling is the floor.

The lights go out. He tumbles in the darkness, plunging down and down, his stomach in his mouth, just as in that foolhardy ride a lifetime ago with the boatman and his dying baby.

There's a resounding crash and the compartment cracks like an egg on impact. Water gushes in. Reflexively, he takes a deep breath, ballooning his chest just moments before chilled water engulfs them all. He slides out of the cracked carriage like yolk slipping out of the egg. It's all so familiar. *Eyes open!* he hears Shamuel's voice command.

He sees a faint dark blur like a whale just under him—his carriage sinking to the deep. The air in his chest carries him up. He breaks the surface and gulps in fresh oxygen, feeling the world spin around him, clutching at a hard object next to him to steady his vertigo, but its sharp edge cuts his hand. He desperately seizes another object. It stays afloat. Eyes open, the dizziness eases.

It is deathly quiet. He looks out over a flat surface of water that is illuminated in a ghostly light and dotted with luggage, clothing, slippers, and bobbing heads. One end of a railway carriage breaks the surface, rises to point accusingly heavenward, then sinks.

On either side of him the craggy walls of a gorge press in, framing a ribbon of stars. He sees the broken remnant of the trestle bridge from which the train plunged. The water is cold. He feels no pain, but his right leg fails to respond. A light behind him! He turns slowly, but it is a gibbous moon, indifferent to what it witnesses. Now he hears a rising chorus, the cries of survivors. "Shiva, Shiva!" a woman's voice screams, and another from the opposite direction, "God! My God!" but the god of disasters is unmoved and both voices gurgle horribly into silence.

An immobile figure floats near him, facedown, a tangle of cloth and long hair, the body wrenched into an impossible shape that makes Philipose recoil.

What Philipose has managed to hook his armpit over is a soft, soggy floating cushion with a spine of something stiffer. It is barely buoyant. He paddles with his free hand, surprised to make headway. There's no current to fight, just death and debris floating in the stillness. He kicks out and now feels an electric shock of pain in the right leg.

"*Appa! Ap—!*"

The child's cry comes from somewhere behind him. A little girl, or is it a boy? Or is he hallucinating?

He flails his free arm to turn himself and his bulky float. On the mirrored surface he catches sight of hair streaked over a pair of panicked eyes that are as big as moons and losing focus, the tiny nose and lips gurgling below the water and rising briefly to try to scream while desperate little hands climb a ladder that isn't there. It's the child's struggle to breathe that galvanizes him. It is the boatman's baby all over again. The small head sinks out of sight. He hears a roar in the back of his throat as he wallows in that direction, but oh, how slowly he moves, pain searing his leg. *Appa!* It's the cry of his child, of all children. Understanding comes to him now, at the most inopportune time, that the one face he so desperately wanted to see, the face of the Stone Woman, was never meant to be seen. What did it matter? We are dying while we're living, we are old even when we're young, we are clinging to life even as we resign ourselves to leaving it.

But in the sinking child he paddles to, he, an ordinary man, has a chance to do something of true account. *Love the sick, each and every one, as if they were your own.* He wrote out those words from Paracelsus for his daughter. Here, and just out of reach, is a child, not his child, yet all are his to love as if they were his own. This child may be beyond saving, and he may be too, but it matters not and matters terribly, pedaling and paddling furiously, the one-legged, one-armed man who cannot swim, moving to a child just out of reach. His flailing hand brushes tiny fingers, but they are already sinking past him.

He takes a deep breath, pulling the skies, the stars, and the stars beyond those stars into his lungs, and *Lord, Lord, my Lord, where are you? Lord, I breathe you in, Lord breathe on me, breathe on me breath of God* . . . For once in his life, freed of indecision, freed from doubt, he is absolutely sure of what he must do.

CHAPTER 71

The Dead Shall Rise Incorruptible

1974, Madras

She holds an unopened letter from her father in her hands. Her tears fall on the address penned in her father's impossible script which somehow the postman always manages to decipher.

In this letter her father is alive.

That morning in the morgue he was not.

Outside the morgue, earlier that day, an angry crowd of relatives had clamored for news. In their contorted, tear-stained, uncomprehending faces Mariamma had seen what her face must have looked like. The same claw had gathered them all like a tuft of grass in its grip, and the same sickle had chopped them off at the knees by robbing them of their loved ones. The guards allowed a tearful Mariamma, in her white coat, to squeeze through the folding metal gates even as they held back the other bereaved: "Why should she be allowed to see the body, and not us?"

The body. That word felt like a cudgel blow.

She was to meet Uma in the morgue, but not seeing Uma, she walked around the cavernous room, no one stopping her in the bedlam, with bodies laid out on metal stretchers and on the bare floor. Then she saw a hand, as familiar as her own, peeking out from under a rubber sheet. She went to him then, held the cold hand, uncovered his face. Her father looked peaceful, resting. Unreasonably, she wanted a blanket for him in place of the rubber sheet, and a pillow too so that his head wouldn't rest on cold unyielding metal. He wasn't dead. It was a mistake. No, he just needed to sleep, that was all, then after he got some rest, he would sit up and come away with her from this noisy morgue . . . Her legs went weak, the room became dim, and sounds went soft. In a protective reflex, she sank to a squat on the floor by his stretcher, head between her knees, still clutching his hand, and sobbing inconsolably. The world had come to an end.

Slowly, the sounds of the room returned. No one paid her any attention. There was too much chaos, the wailing of others, the shouts of someone trying to restore order. After a long while she pulled herself upright. Through tears she asked her father what made him get on a train. Why *that* train? He knew she was on her way home, so why come?

Uma Ramasamy, wearing an apron, found her talking to her father. Uma and every pathologist on staff were busy helping the beleaguered coroner deal with more bodies than a morgue should hold. Uma held her, cried with her. When Mariamma asked, Uma said the rubber sheet concealed a shattered knee and a deep laceration to his left flank. She had no desire to see for herself.

She was conscious that Uma needed to leave and couldn't stay with her all day. "Uma, there's something I've been meaning to tell you. This isn't how or where I imagined I would tell you, but it has to be now. It's important. It's about my father, about my family. Please? A few minutes?"

Uma had listened, her face still, her manner attentive, her eyebrows rising in surprise.

"I'll do it," Uma said. "I'll do it personally. I'll need you to sign some papers."

* * *

Now in her hostel room, hands shaking, Anita at her side, she opens her father's letter.

> *My darling daughter.*

She reads once, twice. He says that he's en route to see her. But not why. *"The voyage of discovery isn't about new lands but having new eyes"*?

The words make no sense. She presses the letter to her lips, hoping for understanding. She catches the scent of his homemade ink: the unmistakable fragrance of home, of the red laterite earth he so loved.

At Parambil two days later, when Mariamma returns with her father's body, she and Anna *Chedethi* cling to each other like two drowning souls. Anna *Chedethi* is more than blood: she is now the last surviving member of her family.

Joppan is right behind Anna *Chedethi*, his face stony as he clutches Mariamma's hands, his eyes dark embers as though he's plotting vengeance against a God who took his best friend. Neither Anna *Chedethi* nor Joppan has any idea why her father got on the train.

She barely recognizes the bag of bones who comes forward to console her: it's Uplift Master. Her father was his only supporter after the scandal around his employee's embezzling funds, though it turned out it was the bank that had suffered most, and the Hospital Fund was largely intact. Master had judged himself more harshly than anyone else. Still, he's the man for moments like this: the needs of others, the need to organize and execute the funeral, give him purpose. "My heart is broken, *molay*," he says. He moves off to talk to the driver of the van bearing the coffin.

At the church the next day, there are so many faces she doesn't recognize, admirers of the Ordinary Man who've come to offer condolences. A woman who in appearance could be a sister to Big Ammachi, but bent over and with a cane, says, "*Molay*, we laughed with your father and cried with him for a quarter century. Our heart breaks for you." She squeezes Mariamma to her bosom.

Mariamma carries a secret that none of the mourners can know: Her father's body in the casket has had all its viscera removed; the abdomen and thorax are just a hollow shell. Uma took his entire spine out en bloc as well, inserting a broomstick in the gutter left behind. Those who earlier viewed the open casket never saw the long incision at the back of his head, running from ear to ear, just under the hairline. His scalp was peeled forward and his calvarium opened to remove his brain. Then skull and scalp were restored. A brain autopsy would not normally have been done in the setting of a disaster and with so many victims, especially if the lungs showed he had drowned. However, Uma will personally conduct a brain autopsy on this victim. But no autopsy will explain why her father got on the train.

He is to be buried next to his father; Big Ammachi; Baby Mol; JoJo; and his beloved son, her brother, Ninan, in the red soil that nurtured them and that they loved. If her mother's remains are ever found, she too will lie here. As will Mariamma herself.

She wonders what Big Ammachi would say about her son's body not being whole. *The trumpet shall sound, and the dead shall be raised incorruptible.* Did her grandmother believe that literally? Perhaps she did. If God can raise the decomposed, then God can surely reconstitute her father, even if his mortal remains are divided and on opposite coasts.

The coffin is lowered. Dirt rattles on the lid with a note of such finality that she discovers a new reservoir of tears. Later, back in the house, the extended Parambil family gathers: all the adults she knew as a child, many of them quite aged now. The twins are old men, even more alike now in their bent-over state than when they were younger, with matching canes and receding hair. Decency *Kochamma* isn't there; she's bedridden, in her late eighties, devoid of reach or venom. Dolly *Kochamma* is the same age as her co-sister; she has some wrinkles but somehow looks and moves like a spry fifty-year-old as she bustles back and forth helping Anna *Chedethi* bring out the food. Mariamma sees the faces of children she grew up with, some barely recognizable as adults. Missing are the faces of two who might have brought her some comfort: Lenin and Podi. In the Saint Thomas Christian tradition there is no graveside eulogy, but now, with the burial over, those gathered in the house look at Mariamma expectantly before *Achen* says a prayer. She stands, hands clasped together, bravely facing them. It comes to her that it's only when one's father and mother are both dead that one stops being a child, being a daughter. She has just become an adult.

"If Appa could see you now, he would be overwhelmed with gratitude. For your love for him, and for the way you have supported me in my grief. My father had so much love for Ninan, and so much love for my mother. But he never got the chance to love them for as long as he wanted. He poured all that love into me, more love than most daughters experience in many lifetimes. I was blessed. I thank each of you for being here, for giving me strength. I'll try to go on. We must all go on. That's what he would have wanted."

The morning of the funeral, her father's beloved newspaper runs his column for the last time. Under his photograph and byline the only words are: *The Ordinary Man, 1923 to 1974.* Beneath that, the column is empty, only a thick black border framing the void.

CHAPTER 72

The Disease of von Recklinghausen

1974, Madras

Mariamma writes to let Uma Ramasamy know the date of her return. Uma replies by telegram: *Bring the genealogy you mentioned. I have something to show you.*

Two weeks after the funeral, Mariamma boards the overnight train from Punalur—not the route her father took. In her berth, she cannot sleep. She finds the suspense unbearable. Why didn't Uma just say what she'd found?

She arrives in Madras in the early morning and freshens up in the hostel. By eleven o'clock she's in the gloomy and unnerving Pathology Specimen Room, waiting for Uma. The hundreds of pre-served specimens on the shelves, used by examiners to quiz students in the viva voce in anatomy, pathology, and every clinical specialty, stare at her.

Uma arrives, hugs Mariamma, then holds her at arm's length to study her, ensure she's in one piece while she struggles for the right words. She gives up and just hugs Mariamma once more. "Is that it?" Uma says at last, wiping her eyes, looking at the poster-sized sheet rolled into a tube.

"That's a copy. The original is falling apart. And it's in Malay-alam. I translated all the writing that I could decipher."

Like keepers of the faith, they pore over the lives of Parambil. Mariamma summarizes what she knows: the crucifix over wavy lines is for those who drowned; wavy lines without a crucifix indicate an aversion to water. The annotations suggest that in the fifth or sixth decade of life some of those with the Condition staggered or had dizziness. There are several references to deafness. And three mentions of weakness of one side of the face, including in her grandfather.

Uma says, "I don't see a simple Mendelian pattern of inheritance. Striking that it affects men more than women!"

"Well . . . maybe not. Since women marry and move away, there's little record of them after that. They belong to another family from then on. It's as though marriage makes them disappear." *Like my mother*, she thinks.

"Thank you for bringing it. Immensely helpful." Uma sits back. "So . . . Mariamma, on the general autopsy, there were no injuries sufficient to have caused your father's death . . . He drowned." She waits for Mariamma to absorb this. But for the Condition her father might have swum to safety.

After a while, Mariamma nods for Uma to go on. "Before I performed the brain autopsy, I spoke with Dr. Das from neurology, told him what I knew. He was with me when I removed the brain. We saw something. The truth is I almost missed the crucial finding. It was subtle, and it helped to have your story and to have Das there. Let's go to the Brain Room and I'll show you," she says, rising.

As they walk down the hall, Uma says, "The brain needs at least two weeks to harden in formalin, preferably more. I just pulled it out before I came here, and it's safe to handle but not ready for sectioning." Sectioning is the pathology ritual carried out with a bread knife and breadboard, slicing the brain much like a loaf. "Dr. Das will meet us in the Brain Room by the way. Are you ready?"

* * *

The Brain Room looks like a deep, rectangular storeroom, with shelves lining two sides and a floor-to-ceiling window at the far end. The shelves are crammed with plastic buckets, like paint in a hardware store, except these buckets hold brains, waiting to harden. A fresh brain when removed is soft and will mold itself to whatever container it is in. For it to retain its proper shape while it hardens, a string is passed through the blood vessels on its underside, then the inverted brain is suspended in formalin by tying the string to a crossbar over the top of the bucket.

Dr. Das is already there, a stooped, unobtrusive man, waiting patiently. On a tray on the table by the window, and covered by a green cloth, like dough being allowed to rise, sits her father's brain.

After introductions, Uma glances at Mariamma, then removes the cloth. Her father's brain is slightly bigger than a shelled coconut. On the underside, like the stalk below the florets of a cauliflower, is the brain stem. Dangling from it like untied shoelaces are the cranial nerves, severed by Uma in order to remove the brain from the skull. Those nerves carried signals from her father's eyes, ears, nose, and throat, allowing him to see, smell, taste, swallow, and hear. Mushrooming above the brain stem and dwarfing it are the two cerebral hemispheres. Her father's brain looks like any other brain. But it isn't. It held his unique memories, every story he wrote, and the ones he might have written; it held the love he had for her. It holds the mystery of why he came to Madras.

Uma says, "As I said, I didn't see anything abnormal at first, but then . . ." She hands a magnifying glass to Mariamma and points with a probe. "Look here, where the facial nerve and the acoustic nerve are about to enter the brain stem. Can you see this little yellow bump on the acoustic nerve? On any other brain and without Dr. Das with me, I might have thought it was nothing, especially because I saw the same thing on the other side. But given your family history, it seemed significant. I took a tiny sample of one bump before putting the brain in formalin. I did a frozen section and yesterday a more permanent stain on that sample. I saw spindle cells, stacked in palisades. It's an acoustic neuroma."

"That explains his hearing loss," Mariamma says.

Dr. Das clears his throat, and says, "Yes." The soft-spoken neurologist's body floats within his half-sleeved white coat. "Acoustic neuromas aren't malignant in the usual sense. They don't spread. They just grow very, very slowly. But, in that tight cleft between the inside of the skull and the outside of the brain stem, something the size of a peanut is like an elephant squeezed into a closet, isn't it? The tumor begins in those acoustic nerve fibers that receive balance signals from the inner ear, from the labyrinth. But as it grows, it presses on the fibers that affect hearing, as you noted. As it gets even bigger, it presses on the facial nerve sitting right next to it and causes weakness of one side of the face . . ." He pauses, to ensure Mariamma is following.

"Most patients that I diagnose in life with acoustic neuroma have them on just one side. But given that your father had them on *both* sides, and with your family history, your father probably had a *variant* of neurofibromatosis, or von Recklinghausen's disease. Do you know it?"

She does. The old woman who sold jasmine outside Mariamma's hostel had von Recklinghausen's. The profusion of bumps under her skin originated in the cutaneous nerves. The visible parts of the woman's body were completely cloaked in mushroom-like growths, though they didn't seem to trouble her.

"But my father had no skin bumps, nothing."

"Yes, I know," Dr. Das says. "But you see there is a variant of neurofibromatosis that has few or no skin lesions, and it causes acoustic neuromas on *both* sides. Sometimes it has characteristic benign tumors elsewhere. I actually think it may be a quite separate disease from von Recklinghausen's, but for now they are lumped together. There aren't very many reports of it running in families. Your family is unique."

* * *

Half an hour later, Doctors Ramasamy and Das are gone. Mariamma had asked if she could be alone in the Brain Room for a bit.

The buckets on the shelves look on like spectators. She closes
her eyes. With her feet planted firmly on the floor, she doesn't sway.
Her father would not have been able to do that; he might have fallen
over. But she can stand, eyes closed, thanks to the labyrinths, the
organs of balance buried in her bony skull—one on each side. Inside
each labyrinth, three fluid-filled circular canals, like interlocking
rings at angles to each other, register the movement of the fluid
within, and thereby register her position in space; they send that
information to the brain through the acoustic nerve. In her father's
case the signals were interrupted by these tumors.

Das spoke of the labyrinths as "proof of God." As a child, when
Mariamma spun herself around like a dervish, she'd become dizzy
when she stopped. That was because the fluid in the labyrinth, in
those circular canals, was still swirling, telling her brain that she
was turning, even though her eyes said she wasn't. The conflicting
signals made her stagger like a drunkard and even want to throw up.
Spinning like a dervish wasn't a game Lenin or her father could ever
be persuaded to play. They already lived with conflicting signals.

Since her father got unreliable signals or *no* signals from his
labyrinths, he must have compensated for this deficiency quite
unconsciously by relying heavily on his eyes to see the ground, to
find the horizon. He also relied on sensation in his feet, telling him
his feet were on the ground. In the dark when he couldn't see well,
couldn't see the horizon, or whenever his feet were in water and had
nothing to push against, he was lost.

Dr. Das said that a new advance, not yet routine—computed
axial tomography, or CAT scan—allowed incredible cross-sectional
images of the brain. Acoustic neuromas as small as her father's could
be diagnosed early in life. But, he said, even if her father's tumor
had been diagnosed in the last year, unless it was causing him major

symptoms like facial paralysis, or headache and vomiting from raised pressure in the brain, no one would consider surgery. That's because the operation is formidable and risky, and reserved for bigger tumors. For the latter, neurosurgeons would make an envelope-sized opening at the back of the skull, just above the hairline, pulling aside the cerebellum to get at the tumor, which sat buried in a minefield of critical structures—large venous sinuses, vital cranial arteries—and with other cranial nerves draped over the tumor, and with the brainstem close by.

She senses Big Ammachi with her, peering down, shocked at the sight of her son's brain on the table. Can her grandmother see past the terrible violation of his body, and rejoice at this new understanding? The Condition now has a medical name and an anatomic location, which explain its strange symptoms: deafness, an aversion to water, and drowning. They've found the enemy, but the victory feels hollow. So what if they have a name for it? What use is that unless science and surgery can advance to where a child with this disorder can live a normal life without the risk of drowning, or hearing loss, or worse symptoms as they get older?

Three generations of us are here in the Brain Room, Mariamma thinks. When Big Ammachi lit the seven-tiered lamp the night her namesake was born, she'd said to the *kaniyan,* "There'll never be another like my Mariamma, and you can't begin to imagine what she's going to do." As a child, whenever her grandmother recounted that tale, she'd always say they lit the lamp so it might show Mariamma the way for whatever she might choose to do in life. "What will I do, Big Ammachi?" Mariamma asks aloud now, just as she did so long ago, her voice echoing in the Brain Room. She hears her grandmother's reply: "Whatever you imagine."

Ammachi, I imagine taking on this enemy that drowned my father, drowned him when a train wreck couldn't kill him. I imagine conquering this cramped territory at the base of the brain, making it my battlefield, and giving myself to better understanding these tumors. It will take years

of training, but this is what I imagine, Ammachi, and I've never been more
certain—I'll be a scientist and a neurosurgeon.

Mariamma spends two more years in Madras after graduation, the
first of which is her required internship, rotating through all the
specialties. For her second year, she's a "senior house surgeon"—a
glorified intern—but on the general surgery service alone. Only
when she completes the two years is she qualified to apply for a
training spot in neurosurgery.

Deciding to be a neurosurgeon is far easier than getting a spot
in one of the few neurosurgical training programs in the country. She has excellent grades, a prize medal in anatomy, strong letters of recommendation, and by this time she has two published
papers with Uma (one on leprosy, and the other a case report on her
father's acoustic neuroma and its presentation in one family over
generations). But, even if no one says this outright, many centers
don't think women should be in neurosurgery.

At the eleventh hour, she's accepted to the oldest and best-
known neurosurgery program in the country: the Christian Medical College in Vellore, just two and a half hours west of Madras by
train. Founded by Ida Scudder, an American missionary physician, it
was first a women's clinic and then a women's medical school before
becoming coeducational. It has become an outstanding referral
center, staffed by dedicated physicians. Church missions of every
denomination support the medical school by sponsoring students.

Mariamma's admission has a caveat. Since she applied for a
"sponsored" training slot supported by her diocese in Kerala, she
must fulfill a two-year service obligation at a mission hospital *before*
she begins her training. Then, after becoming a fully-fledged neurosurgeon, she must serve for two *more* years in a mission hospital
to complete her bond.

Seven years after she first stepped into the Red Fort, she leaves
Madras, with tearful goodbyes to Anita, Chinnah, Uma, and so
many others. She will begin her two-year bond in a brand-new, but

unfurnished, four-story mission hospital that is to have the absolute best equipment. She'll be its first, and for now its only, physician.

The location of this mission hospital is a stone's throw from where her grandmother lit the lamp on the occasion of her birth: the district village of Parambil.

Part Nine

CHAPTER 73

Three Rules for a Prospective Bride

1976, Parambil

Under Joppan's watch, Parambil is becoming a lush Eden, a model farm, the plantain and mango trees sagging with fruit, and young palms sporting thick yellow necklaces of coconuts. Their thriving dairy sells milk to a cold-storage business, providing an additional source of revenue. Joppan's two young cousins serve as his permanent assistants. For the past two years, while Mariamma was in Madras, Joppan at first wrote her monthly letters, listing expenditures and income. But in just six months, at his urging, they hired a part-time bookkeeper. Parambil is doing well.

The house, however, shows its age in the spider's web of cracks on the red oxide floors; the dull teak walls cry out for a varnish. Mariamma takes Anna *Chedethi* to Kottayam to pick out a new paint scheme for the entire house, and to select ceiling fans, new sinks and fixtures, a two-burner gas range, and a backup generator. The grin on Anna *Chedethi*'s face only falters when a refrigerator is delivered. "*Ayo, molay!* What do I do with this? How will it listen to me? Does it know Malayalam?" The first time Mariamma brings her a glass of sweet lime juice, frosted on the outside and with ice cubes clinking on the top, Anna *Chedethi* becomes a believer. Now meat, fish, vegetables, and milk will keep for days.

The Mar Thoma Medical Mission Hospital is the tallest structure around for miles. The sprawling grounds around the hospital are enclosed by a whitewashed boundary wall; the NO POSTING warnings stenciled on the wall are covered by Congress and Communist Party posters. Across from the main gate is a bus stop and Cherian's tea shop. Further down the road, a new long, rectangular building holds Kunjumon's Cold Storage, London Tailors, and Brilliant Tutorials. Mariamma struggles to recall the time when all this was uncleared land with trees that she and Podi climbed.

Raghavan, the poor watchman, is hoarse from explaining to clamoring patients that yes, the hospital looks finished, but no, it's not ready for business. If they call him a liar, he shows them the unfurnished interior, the crates of equipment stacked everywhere, some donated by foreign missions. One night, Raghavan rouses Mariamma at home at two in the morning because of a child with severe asthma who he thinks is in mortal danger. He is right. Without the adrenaline in Mariamma's medical bag, the child would not have survived.

Mariamma mentions this at the weekly board meeting; the bishop who is chair of the board has ensured this one room is lavishly furnished. The members listen politely as she tries to convey the urgency of opening a casualty room with basic supplies, then without comment they move to the more urgent task of deciding the size of the inaugural plaque in the lobby and whose names should or should not be on it.

She leaves the meeting, seething, and is surprised to find Joppan outside, puffing on a *beedi*. He walks back with her in the dark as she voices her frustration. "It's comical! At this rate, the hospital might never open." They cross the gated private pedestrian bridge arching over the canal and into Parambil. When they reach the house, he says, "*Molay*, nothing is happening because Uplift Master's not there. He'll know how to deal with them. I'll send word." Only after he leaves does Anna *Chedethi* tell her that the reason Joppan had been at the hospital was to escort her home because it was dark. It's just what her father might have done.

The rumor that Master only ventures out at the witching hour and prefers the company of ghosts to that of humans must be true, because Anna *Chedethi* is already asleep when Master comes. Mariamma shares her frustrations about the hospital. She gets the sense Master is pleased to hear about the hospital's administrative dysfunction. She begs him to talk to the board.

"Never! They must ask me themselves. They still blame me for that woman who tried to embezzle the Hospital Fund." Mariamma assures him that no one faults him. "*Aah*, people *say* that. But if I drop by for tea, they count the grains of paddy in their *ara* when I leave. That's how our people are."

She pleads, invoking the names of her grandmother and her father, but he holds firm.

"I'll be your silent advisor, nothing more. Here's what you do, Mariamma. First, don't waste your time asking the board anything. *Aadariyumo angaadi vaanibham?*" *Does the goat understand the butcher's trade?* "Just make a list of medicines and supplies you need. I'll send the order to T.N.T. Wholesale Medical in Kottayam in your name, with instructions to invoice the bishop. Second, your watchman, Raghavan, is a good fellow. I only got him that job. You give him a stack of blank paper. Have him ask every person he turns away from the gate to write something, even if it is one or two lines, and sign at the bottom with their address. If they can't write, just sign. We'll mail the letters to the Metropolitan. It won't take more than ten or twenty letters before the bishop feels some pain. Lastly, I'm glad you told me about the plaque. I know where they will order it and I will find out how much it might cost. I'll call the bishop's secretary pretending to be a journalist. I'll ask, 'Is it true a child almost died of asthma because you couldn't buy ten rupees' worth of medicine, but you are spending twenty thousand rupees on a plaque?'"

"Master, in one minute you accomplish more than I could in a month," Mariamma says. "We need you."

"It's nothing," he says, but he's pleased. "Do you know, *I* only coined the name 'Mar Thoma Medical Mission Hospital'? It flows like honey off the tongue, does it not? But before the foundation was poured, people shortened it to 'Yem-Yem-Yem Hospital.'" Mariamma thinks it understandable: "M" on the Malayali tongue can come out as "Yem." And Malayalis love acronyms. "Then they began calling it '*Triple* Yem Hospital'! Can you imagine? So vulgar, *Triple Yem*! Like some ointment for piles!" She doesn't admit to him that Triple Yem has caught on—she's as guilty as all the others.

When he leaves, he says, "By the way, when the bishop questions you about the T.N.T. invoice, you just say that since he was ordering hair oil, Cuticura powder, and vitamins for himself and listing them as 'essential supplies,' you didn't think he'd mind if you added a few essentials to save lives."

With Uplift Master working behind the scenes, the part of Triple Yem she needs to function is taking shape, with electricians assembling equipment and the ground floor becoming furnished. One room at the front of the Triple Yem becomes Casualty. A large room at the back, with a waiting area outside, becomes the outpatient department. They have four hospital beds set up on a "ward" for emergencies alone. The operating theater is complete and has a state-of-the-art surgical light with so many bulbs it looks like an insect's eye. But the selection of surgical instruments—all donated—is bizarre: everything one needs for cataract surgery and for dental work, but the bare minimum for abdominal surgery. Mariamma has a night nurse, a day nurse, and a compounder presiding over a small dispensary.

The one commodity that's been abundant from the outset is patients.

When the outpatient department opens, entire families dressed in their finest come on excursions to Triple Yem, just as they might attend the Maramon Convention. One morning, a *kochamma* sits smiling and silent on the stool before Mariamma after waiting an hour in line. When asked why she's come, she makes a twisting gesture with her wrist, "Oh, *chuma!" Just like that!* "Son and wife were coming, so I thought, *What's there? Why not I come too? Aah.* Since I'm here, why not give me that orange injection?"

Mariamma is forced to inaugurate the operating room before she's ready, performing an emergency caesarean section at midnight for a baby in distress. Her night nurse gets weak-kneed the moment they enter the theater and has to sit in a corner. Mariamma turns to Joppan (who is there because Raghavan has standing orders to fetch him anytime he summons the doctor after dark or risk his wrath). With minimal instruction, Joppan calmly and competently drops ether on the gauze mask. Mariamma, operating alone, hauls the baby out. Only when she hears its shrill cry does her tension vanish. The night nurse is at least capable of receiving the baby in her lap. Mariamma closes the uterus, then muscle and skin. Joppan's awe-struck expression has changed to a silly grin by the time she's put in the last stitch. "You breathe more of that ether," she says with mock severity, "and Ammini will think you were at the toddy shop." He's still euphoric as he escorts her back. "*Molay*, what you just did . . . I have no words for it. Imagine if Podi had stayed in school. Or if I had stayed. We were smart, but we weren't smart enough to understand how important it was to study, were we?"

"Don't say that. You're what makes Parambil thrive. You put our relatives to shame. And Podi and her husband are making good money—"

He shakes his head. "Not the same thing. Anyway, I'm so proud of you, *molay*."

She's still glowing from his words when her head hits the pillow.

But every visit to the theater is nerve-racking; there's no senior surgeon to turn to and no one competent to assist. One night, for a patient who was stabbed in the belly, she promotes Raghavan to ether-mask duties, and Joppan becomes her scrub nurse and assistant. From watching her, Joppan has already picked up the basics of sterility. Now she shows him how to scrub, then don gloves and gown and stand ready, across from her. The sight of the open belly doesn't faze him. He hands her hemostat, forceps, scissors, and ligature when asked, and pulls on the retractor for her. He soon anticipates her needs. When they're done, he's elated. "*Molay*, whenever you need my help, please call me. In the daytime too. My assistants Yakov and Ousep can spare me for a few hours."

She'd rather have Joppan's help than anyone else's. He's quick to grasp her explanations of the physiology involved and how a disease has altered it. She's found him studying her surgical manual while he waits for her, his lips moving as he deciphers the English words.

Six months in, the outpatient routine wears her down with its monotony. Most complaints are trivial—body aches, pains, coughs, colds—or else they're chronic, like asthma, or the tropical leg ulcers that need to be dressed daily. The tedium is interrupted now and then by a medical or surgical emergency. Mariamma refuses to do elective surgery till she has an anesthetist and more nurses. The dream of a referral hospital with specialists is still far away, but with Uplift Master working behind the scenes and Mariamma as his amanuensis, there's more momentum. His masterful touches are hard to hide. When the bishop (pressed by the Metropolitan) breaks down and begs Uplift Master to intercede to release equipment stuck in customs, Master is officially back in the fold.

After her years in Madras with its many diversions, Mariamma's evenings and weekends at Parambil might have felt tedious if she didn't have a project that kept her busy: she's fleshing out every node and branch of the Water Tree. She especially wants to learn about the women who married and moved away and whose fate was never recorded. Her relatives—even sweet Dolly *Kochamma*—are reluctant to talk about the Condition or admit it exists. A breakthrough comes from an unexpected source.

Every afternoon, Cherian sends over a "special" tea and butter biscuits for "Doctor Madam" in the outpatient department. But he refuses payment. Early one morning, she watches him prop up the thatch awning with poles, unlock the wooden barrier, and systematically unbutton his stall for business. She walks over to thank him. Cherian insists she have a coffee. The arc of steaming liquid flies back and forth between his two mixing receptacles before it lands with a flourish in the glass that he hands to her. Her "thank you" makes him incredibly shy. She sips her coffee, and they stand awkwardly together, staring at Triple Yem as if it has just landed there and Martians might emerge. Big Ammachi once said to Mariamma, "You can confide in quiet people. They make way for one's thoughts." *But Ammachi, when they don't utter a word, how do you begin?*

She's leaving when Cherian says, "My sister drowned." She stops and stares at him. Did he speak or is she hallucinating?

"Also, my grandfather's brother. Drowned. My brother's daughters both hate water." What prompted Cherian to volunteer this? Is it common knowledge that the Parambil family has the Condition? "My poor sister had to work in the flooded paddy fields, she had no choice. When a bund broke, she was knocked off her feet and drowned in shallow water."

"Cherian, you obviously know that our family has the same . . . condition. Do you think we are related?"

"No. My family isn't from here. I was a lorry driver till I had an accident. I used to drive all over Kerala. In that time I heard of a few other families like ours. All Christians. Surely there are others."

She mulls over Cherian's extraordinary admission all day. Cherian is wrong: they *are* related. The community of Saint Thomas Christians is now quite large, but they share the same ancestors in the original families that Doubting Thomas converted to Christianity. An image of a bicycle wheel comes to her mind. If she were to place each family with the Condition along a single spoke of the wheel, then Cherian's family is on one spoke and the Parambil clan on another. The other afflicted families Cherian mentioned have their own spokes. Tracing the spokes back to the center will bring them to the ancestor with the altered gene with whom it all began. She's excited. Her task is to find many more spokes, more families with the Condition. There's one man she knows who can help.

Broker *Aniyan*'s thick gray hair is parted in the center and swept back on his temples; his intelligent eyes miss nothing as he cycles up to the house. He dismounts elegantly, swinging one leg forward and over the bar, the only option when wearing a *mundu*. In a place where mustaches are the rule, his clean-shaven face makes him look younger than his seventy years.

"*Molay*, I remember as if it were yesterday, I proposed an alliance for Elsie of Thetanatt with Philipose of Parambil."

"I thought they met on a train!"

He smiles indulgently. "*Aah*, train meeting-greeting may be there, loving-longing may be there, but without a broker how can families be introduced, or dowry discussed, or horoscopes matched?"

Anna *Chedethi* has prepared tea and jackfruit *halwa*, Big Amma-chi's specialty.

"What if the horoscopes don't match but the couple are adamant?" Mariamma asks.

Aniyan squeezes his eyes shut and opens them, a gesture that to outsiders might look like someone wincing with pain but in Kerala means something specific. "It's not a problem. We *adjust*! That's all. Most impediments are minor impediments, and minor impediments are no impediment. You see, parents often have faulty memories of the exact time of birth," he says, with the patience of a priest who must regularly recite the articles of faith. He samples the *halwa* and approves. "Ladies, before we begin today, may I share with you three lessons I've learned in doing this for decades?"

Before Mariamma can interject, Anna *Chedethi* says, "Yes! Do tell us!"

"First lesson—and don't take this wrong, *molay*—but your generation often tries to drive the bullock cart backward. In fact, the greater the education, the more someone will make this mistake," he says, eyeing her meaningfully. "The first priority is to find the *right* person, is it not? You must look at *this* proposal, then *that* proposal, then make a table of pluses and minuses, correct?"

They nod. He sips his tea, smiles. "Wrong! That's *not* the first priority." He settles back, waiting. Mariamma asks, otherwise they'll be here all day.

"First priority is: *Set the date!* Simple. You know why?"

They don't.

"Because you set a date and you're committed! Tell me, *molay*, if you decide to open a practice, will you first wait to see a patient walk by and *then* rent the building and put up a sign? Of course not! You commit! You rent an office, sign the lease for a certain date. You get furniture, is it not? *Aah, aah*. My dear God, if you only knew how much time I wasted with this doctorate fellow from Berkeley in United States of California. He comes on two weeks leave. I introduce mother and him to eight first-class, Yay-One suitable girls . . . and he goes back undecided! Why? No date! So, the first lesson is to commit to a date."

"What's the second?"

"*Aah, aah*, second lesson I already mentioned first." He grins naughtily. "Maybe you weren't paying attention earlier. I said, most impediments are . . . ?"

"*Minor* impediments," the two women say in unison.

"*Aah*. And minor impediments are . . . ?"

"*Not* impediments!" Mariamma feels she's back in primary school.

"Exactly. Adjustment is there." He looks pleased.

Anna *Chedethi* can't help herself. "Is there a third?"

"Certainly! There are ten. But these three I share because it makes my work easier. The rest will die with me. My son sees no future in this business because of the newspaper matrimonial advertisements. God help people who try that."

Anna *Chedethi* clears her throat.

"*Aah*, yes. Third rule is this. *Looks change, but character doesn't.* So, focus on character, *not* looks. And to know a girl's character you look to the girl's . . . ?"

"Mother?" they both say.

"*Aah*, correct." He nods, pleased with his pupils. "And for a boy's character you look to the boy's . . . ?"

"Father!" they say, confidently.

"Wrong!" he says, pleased to have lured them into his trap. He lights a cigarette, then returns the spent match to the match box. Mariamma wonders why smokers all do this. Is it a parallel addiction that goes with nicotine? Or is this fastidiousness meant to compensate for using the world as an ashtray? She can suddenly taste the cigarette she took off Lenin in the lodge. "Wrong, my dear ladies. For the boy's character, *again* you must look to the mother! After all, the only thing each of us can be sure of is who our mother is. Is it not?"

Anna *Chedethi* takes a second to digest this and bursts out laughing. Mariamma sees that Anna *Chedethi* is getting much too excited. She hasn't told her why she invited Broker *Aniyan*.

"*Achayan*, are you related to our family?" Mariamma says.

"Certainly! On the Parambil side, I am your great-grandfather's second cousin's granddaughter's husband's brother." He looks to the ceiling. "On the Thetanatt side—"

"Wait," Mariamma says. "'Great-grandfather's second cousin's granddaughter's' . . . That's so distant . . . In that case you can claim you're related to every family you call on."

"No! If you can't trace the relationship, you can't claim anything!" he says with some indignation. "I can. Therefore, I'm related."

"*Achine*," she says, using the respectful term for "elder." "I promise, when I'm ready to marry, I'll come to you. No newspaper matrimonial. I hope you'll forgive me, but I didn't ask you here to help me get married. I need your help with a serious medical condition, one that took my father's life. And the lives of others in our family—well, you know better than anyone. I don't know your name for it, but Big Ammachi called it the Condition."

She sits next to him and spreads out an expanded and updated copy of the genealogy, this one in Malayalam. "I copied this from the original, which our family kept for generations."

Aniyan's clever eyes dart around the sheet, a nicotine-stained fingernail traces the generations. "That's an outright lie here—he never married," he mutters. "Hmm, not three but *four* sisters here— twins—but one died as an infant, the other was Ponnamma . . ." In minutes with his pen, he has fleshed out three previous generations, working back from her grandfather. It's more than she's accomplished in weeks. He pointedly does not address the generations presently alive.

"*Achayan*, I'm trying to complete this chart." She tells him about Cherian. *Aniyan* understands her "spokes of the wheel" analogy at once. "If I can complete all the spokes in the wheel, we'll understand how the disease is inherited."

He ponders this. "*Molay*, are you able to *do* something once you find others with the Condition?"

He has homed in on the weakest link in her argument. "No . . . Not yet. For now we can only justify surgery for those with severe symptoms because it's a dangerous operation. But soon we'll be able to perform a safer one through a tiny hole above the ear. By taking the tumor out earlier, we might keep those children affected from becoming deaf, or even from drowning. Also, if we understand how it's inherited, we might for example ensure that a boy and a girl who are both unknowingly carrying this trait don't get married. Too many have suffered and died from the Condition. It's the reason I'm going to specialize in neurosurgery. To prevent it, or else to treat it earlier. This is my life's mission."

He studies her warily. Then he surprises her. "Why not? I plan to retire end of this year, so why not? It's a worthy cause. But not till then." He gathers his matchbox and cigarettes. "Two things I want to tell you before I go. Firstly, my job is to make alliances, to reduce impediments. I *always* know more than I choose to reveal about both parties. Don't misunderstand. I'll *never* suggest a match that is detrimental. I won't hide madness or mental retardation or epilepsy. But *molay*, remember this—another rule, if you like, though I'm only telling you: *Every family has secrets, but not all secrets are meant to deceive.* What defines a family is not blood, *molay*, but the secrets they share. So, your task won't be easy."

He has his foot on the pedal when Mariamma says, "Wait, you said *two* things. What's the second?"

"Set a date, Mariamma," he says, smiling. "Even if it's five years from now. Set a date."

The next evening, Mariamma returns home from Triple Yem after an exceptionally long day. Under the pedestrian bridge, the water moves lazily. The hibiscus and oleander are aflame. Two water buffalo, unyoked from the plow, stand silhouetted against the horizon, facing each other like bookends. The crickets pick up volume, sounding delirious, and soon they'll rouse the frog chorale. These everyday, unremarkable noises of her youth are now, with the passing of her cherished loved ones, an ode to memory, bearing the past into the present. It is the hour for gracious ghosts.

Her route takes her past the Stone Woman, and she never fails to acknowledge the sculptor. Elsie married into the Condition, but she didn't have it; what cruel irony that *she* should drown. Mariamma passes the barn on whose roof Lenin tried to channel lightning. Set a date. *If only I could.*

After her bath, she and Anna *Chedethi* eat in the kitchen, forgoing the new dining table and chairs for the blackened, cinnamon-scented walls, which carry the living memory of Big Ammachi. Joppan comes by to go over drawings and costs for a new building with adjoining smoke shed dedicated to their rubber trees. Here the latex will be poured into trays, mixed with acid till it hardens. Then a new manual press will turn the hardened latex into thin rubber sheets that are then hung in the smoke shed to cure before they are stacked and sold. Anna *Chedethi* ignores Joppan's protests that he's eaten, and serves him. So, just as on many other evenings, all of them are seated on the four-inch high stools, bending over their plates, which rest on the ground. Shamuel would've been scandalized to see his son *inside* the house and eating from a dish that wasn't earmarked for his use alone. Parambil has changed. The three of them are family and all one caste.

CHAPTER 74

A Mind Observed

1976, Parambil

The Ordinary Man's former editor is one of the many dignitaries at the ribbon-cutting ceremony for the new hospital. To Mariamma's surprise, he comes over to the house after the event. Other than greeting him at her father's funeral, this is her first conversation with him. He's a handsome, elegant man, older than her father. He reminisces with obvious affection about his late columnist. But he has no idea what made her father leave abruptly for Madras. "He was in Cochin writing a story about the saline contamination of our backwaters. But he barely got there before he asked our Cochin office to get him a ticket to Madras. I only found out he'd gone to Madras after the accident.

"For the longest time I was after your father to write something from Dubai, or Qatar, about all our people there. You know, when oil was discovered in the Gulf in the fifties, many daring young men went by *kalla kappal*—illegal country boats hammered together by the side of the river—or by the dhows that still go back and forth. They had no papers, nothing. But guess what? People *still* go the same way, because they can't afford the No Objection Certificates or plane tickets. They're dropped offshore and must wade or swim to the beach. If they're caught, they sit in jail. I wanted your father to travel on a dhow—legally of course—and write about the journey. Then I said I'd put him up in a fancy hotel for a week and he could write about our people laboring in the hot sun and sleeping packed together like fish to save every paisa to send home. I even promised to fly him back first-class. It was a perfect subject for the Ordinary Man. He always resisted and I never understood why."

"You mean you didn't know about my father's feud with water?" He doesn't. He's dumbfounded when Mariamma describes the Condition and shows him the genealogy. He looks queasy when he hears the details of her father's brain autopsy. "In death, my father solved the mystery."

He's speechless. "My goodness," he says. "I had no idea! You know our readers—his fans—would have loved to hear this story. Of course, my lips are sealed. Rest assured, I won't breathe a word or write about this."

"Actually, I'd be very happy if you wrote about it. The secrecy around the Condition for generations hasn't helped. Secrets kill. How do we tackle this disease if we don't know how many are affected, or how it's inherited? My relatives may not like it, but my father's story and everything I know I will happily share. The Condition is my mission. It's why I'm going to Vellore to train as a neurosurgeon."

Dear Uma,

Ever since my father's editor wrote the feature article about the Condition and how it caused the Ordinary Man's death, my relatives are suddenly willing to talk to me. I'm enclosing the newspaper cutting. I know you can't read Malayalam, but you can see the pictures. The article reads like a detective novel, with my father being one of the victims. And the detective hunting the murderer is his own daughter! "The Ordinary Man Solves the Mystery of his Own Death from the Condition" is the title. I'm glad he called it "the Condition." I think "a variant of von Recklinghausen's disease" is not only cumbersome but, as Dr.

Das said, this may not be related to von Recklinghausen's disease at all. I'm quoted as encouraging readers to write to me if they know of family members with an aversion to water. By the way, I think that's the best single screening question. Believe me, in Kerala if you don't like water, people notice. I've heard from three families. Also, thanks to my relatives, I have the stories of many of the brides who moved away after marriage—the missing element in the "Water Tree."

It's fascinating how the women with the Condition are all remembered as "eccentric." That stood out as much as their dislike of water. We girls are taught "adakkavum" and "othukkavum," or modesty and invisibility, from an early age. But these girls were anything but humble and retiring. One girl was so outspoken that potential grooms stayed away. (The same qualities in a man would be called self-confidence.) When she finally did marry, she built herself a treehouse on her husband's property. She was terrified of floods but not of heights. When the river crossed its banks, the treehouse was where she lived. Another girl was fascinated by snakes as a child, and quite fearless. In her husband's village she was the one to call if you found a serpent behind the kitchen pots. She'd grab it by the tail, then dangle it at arm's length. Apparently, a snake can't twist up and bite—it needs a surface to push against. But who wants to chance that? I found out both these women died with symptoms like my grandfather's: dizziness, headaches, facial weakness. A third girl was determined to be a priest, which is heresy. She dressed like a priest and tried to preach in church. She was thrashed for that. She took to standing outside churches and sermonizing till they chased her away. Her family forcibly put her in a convent, but she escaped and turned up in an all-male seminary, her hair short, pretending to be male. After that they locked her up in an asylum, where she died.

But I must say, as far as eccentricity goes, my grandfather, my father, Ninan, JoJo, and my cousin Lenin would all be considered eccentric, in their own ways. They had a gravitational pull that was different from others'. It was either climbing trees, or a compulsion to walk a straight line, or walking distances others couldn't imagine. I think you'd agree that these "eccentricities" aren't explained by a tumor on the acoustic nerve? So here's my hypothesis: What if these acoustic neuromas have a counterpart in the mind, some aberration that's part of the Condition and reveals itself as "eccentricity"? What if they have a "tumor of thought" (as I think of it), something that we can't see with the naked eye or with our usual tools?

I may have one tool, though, to study my father's thoughts. He had the habit of obsessively keeping journals (more eccentricity! Writing many entries each day). All those thoughts are preserved here in nearly two hundred notebooks. That's my next project: to systematically look into these journals for this "tumor of thought."

She faces one major hurdle with her project: her father's indecipherable writing. As an inquisitive child she had peeked into his journals, looking for juicy secrets, but she was stopped in her tracks by his tiny script that abhorred margins or white spaces. He wrote as though paper was more precious than gold, even if the ink was free. Writing in English gave him a measure of privacy, but his wedge-shaped letters resemble ancient Sumerian characters. Deciphering his writing will be like learning a foreign language. Besides that, her father's most valuable thoughts could be buried in a sea of trivial daily observations on mildew, on lizards falling off the rafters and the like. When Mariamma briefly scans the notebook titles she sees SMELLS, RUMORS, HAIR (FACIAL AND BODY), FEET, and POLTERGEISTS. Despite these labels, after a few pages, his entries veer off to something else and never return. He had no index or cross-reference for his entries. There's no question of Mariamma skimming through pages. The task ahead is daunting. It may be impossible.

* * *

Every night before she falls asleep, she thinks of Lenin. If only she could talk to him, tell him about her day. She'd share with him her pleasure in being home; the only drawback is that here she's robbed of any identity other than that of being the doctor. She longs to be done and begin neurosurgical training. *And how was your day, Lenin?* She shudders to imagine it. Is he even alive? If he were to die, would she know?

Uma is excited by the "tumor of thought" idea and spurs her on. So Mariamma toils away every evening, indexing entries as she goes. It's exhausting work, leaving her fingers copper-tinted from his ink. Gradually her reading speed increases. The index grows. So far, her only insight into her father's mind is its ability to flit from one subject to another, like a moth in a room full of candles. Is that the tumor of the mind? Now and then a passage leaves her breathless:

> *Last night as Elsie sketched in bed, I looked at my bride's pro-*
> *file, more attractive than any other my eyes could fall on. I*
> *suddenly had a vision, as if a portal had opened in time. I saw*
> *the trajectory of Elsie the artist as clearly as if I were seeing an*
> *arrow sailing through space. I understood as never before that*
> *she will leave her mark for generations to come. I'm nothing by*
> *comparison, blessed to be in the presence of such greatness. I felt*
> *emotional, on the verge of tears. She saw my strange expression.*
> *She didn't ask. Maybe she read my thoughts and understood,*
> *or maybe she thought she did. She put her sketch away, and she*
> *pushed me back on the bed. She took me like a Queen making*
> *use of one of her nobles, but fortunately I am the only noble-*
> *man she loves. My only real claim to lasting fame will be this:*
> *Elsie chose me. She chose me and therefore I am worthy. That's*
> *all the ambition I need: to remain worthy of this remarkable*
> *woman.*

On another evening, Mariamma stumbles onto a vastly different moment in her parents' marriage, one that feels like a cudgel
blow: in the wake of Ninan's ghastly death, her parents turned on
each other. It chills her to read her father's words, so raw on the
page: the agonizing pain from his broken ankles; his self-loathing
for not cutting down the tree; his unreasonable anger at Elsie for
fleeing Parambil—she'd been gone six months at the time of the
entry. Mariamma had never known they'd been apart! Her father's
words are rambling and disjointed, an ode to opium. Instead of a
"tumor of thought," she's peering into the cesspit of an addict's
addled mind. Yes, hers is a scientific quest, but the subject under the
microscope is her father. His thoughts can crush her.

She closes the journal, walks out of the room, tempted to abandon the project. *Please God, as I pursue my father's thoughts, don't let me
end up loathing the man I idolize and love. Don't take that away from me.*

Her feet carry her to the Stone Woman, still luminous in the
clearing, even at dusk. Embodied in rock, this manifestation of her
mother has a permanence like nothing else in Mariamma's life; in
her unmoving pose she expresses the patience of nature, of time
measured in centuries instead of minutes and hours. Mariamma sits
there for a long time.

"The Condition . . . it's just life, isn't it, Amma?" she says,
speaking to the Stone Woman. "Maybe I'm not looking to solve the
mystery of the Condition or the mystery of why I'm on this earth.
Mystery *is* the nature of life. I *am* the Condition. Maybe it isn't the
workings of Appa's mind that I'm after, the clues to an inherited disease. I think, Amma, that it's really you I'm looking for."

CHAPTER 75

States of Consciousness

1977, Parambil

For Mariamma, the empty bench outside her clinic that morning feels too good to be true. Dr. T. T. Kesavan, LMP, is her new colleague. "T.T." screens the outpatients and sends her only those with significant complaints. Soon her empty bench will fill up, but at least she's no longer hopelessly behind before she starts.

Inside her office she's startled by a very dark, barefoot man in khaki shorts and shirt, seated on the stool beside her desk and grinning at her. He has a faint Nepalese shade to his features despite his dark complexion, and a similar ageless quality to his face; only the gray eyebrows and his gray mop of hair suggest he's well over sixty.

"Good morning, Doctor," he says in English, springing to his feet. "Doctor ask Cromwell to give you!" She unfolds the paper while trying to untangle what she's heard. "I am Cromwell," he offers.

"What doctor?"

He points to a vehicle outside the front gate that's a cross between jeep and truck. On its doors in faded lettering is SAINT BRIDGET'S LEPROSARIUM. A white man sits inside, waiting. She turns to the note.

> *Dear Mariamma: I'm a physician who knew your grandfather, Chandy. I seek your professional assistance for someone who is desperately ill. Someone you know. For your safety and mine, please allow me to explain further in the car. Till then, please speak to no one. May I also ask you to discreetly bring with you a trephine and such tools as you might need to open skull and dura?*

Digby feels an indentation in the atmosphere before she comes into view. Her floating carriage is like that of a dancer, despite the heavy *sanji* she carries. She's tall and beautiful, and her coral-blue sari complements her fair skin. The flaming pale streak at the center part of her hair gives her a maturity beyond her years. He flushes with shyness as she approaches.

She slides onto the seat beside him, shaking out her sari pleats so the fabric flows to the floor. He extends his hand; hers is warm and soft, while his must surely feel rough and stiff, unable to form a concavity to match hers.

"Digby Kilgour," he stammers, and only reluctantly releases her hand. "I knew your grandfather Chandy well. And I met your mother when she was a girl—"

Mariamma takes him in, this man with blue eyes like sapphires that sparkle against his washed-out and weathered face. The back of his hands is a patchwork of rust-colored and albino-white skin. A loose cotton *kurta* exaggerates his gaunt neck. He's in his late sixties or early seventies, lean and fit, but not as rugged as his dark-skinned driver.

"Boss, we go. Too much peoples," Cromwell says, starting the engine.

"Yes," Mariamma and Digby say in unison.

As soon as they're out of sight of Triple Yem, she swivels to face him. "How is he?"

She doesn't ask who, Digby notes. "Not well. Barely arousable but worsening by the hour."

She ponders this. She slips her feet out of her sandals and brings her knees across the seat like a mermaid, tucking her bare feet under her.

"He showed up at Gwendolyn Gardens. That's my former estate way north, near Trichur . . ." Digby struggles to keep his train of thought as those translucent eyes gaze at him. "Years ago, when Lenin's mother was pregnant, she came to my estate with a stab wound and—" Mariamma nods impatiently. She knows that story. "Well, Lenin must have always known of Gwendolyn Gardens from his mother. And known of me. Part of his history. He showed up there last night, but you see I've not lived there for twenty-five years. I run a leprosarium here in Travancore. The estate is Cromwell's. There's a reward for Lenin's capture, you know. To keep him at the estate would have been dangerous, too tempting for the laborers. So Cromwell drove all night to bring Lenin down to me."

She looks nothing like a physician now; she's a young woman confronted by a ghost from her past. "Dr. Kilgour, what are we to do?"

"Call me Digby, please. Yes, that's the question. What to do? His presence puts us at risk. I didn't know how to help him. I'm a leprosy doctor, a hand surgeon. He was stuporous by the time he arrived. I wouldn't involve you. Mariamma, I'm here because he asked for you."

She becomes very still. After a bit, she says softly, "Is he giving himself up?"

Digby shakes his head. "No. Listen, I have no sympathy for Naxalites. But the police are no better. You know they'd do nothing for him medically. They'd probably murder him on sight. He's vomiting and complained of a terrible headache. He kept saying you would know what he has. I think I know too. I read about your family and the inherited disorder."

She nods. "He almost certainly has acoustic neuromas, just like my father. On both sides. But that doesn't mean I'm capable of curing him."

Her hands are clasped together in her lap; she stares ahead, lost in thought. In profile, he thinks, her features—the eyes, the brow, the long, sharp nose—are just like those of Chandy's daughter, Elsie.

"Listen, you don't have to get involved, Mariamma. For all we know, it may be too late—" The look that comes over her face makes him realize he has misspoken. Cromwell glances back in the mirror at Digby as if to say, *You made a mess of that.* "I'm sorry! What a thing to say."

Her voice is fragile, and she's speaking more to herself than to them when she says, "So he shows up suddenly and asks for me? After all these years. What am I supposed . . . ?"

She doesn't finish. Her eyes fill up. Digby roots for his handkerchief, thankful it's clean. She presses it to her eyes. Then, to Digby's surprise, she leans on him, rests her forehead on his shoulder. Digby's hand goes around her and alights gently on her scapula, holding on with the greatest care so as not to add to her burden.

CHAPTER 76

Awakenings

1977, Saint Bridget's

Digby watches Mariamma take in the grounds of Saint Bridget's as they pull past the gates. What must she think of his home of a quarter century, this quiet oasis to itself, whose high walls don't even let sounds from the outside world reach their ears? Suja, one of Digby's "nurses," brings her left palm to the stump of her right hand. Mariamma responds automatically, barely registering that Suja's "namaste" must be imagined to be complete.

The room in which they have Lenin is private and secluded from the rest of the leprosarium. Mariamma hesitates at the threshold, then follows Digby, moving like a sleepwalker. *Thank goodness he's still breathing*, Digby thinks. He watches her fingers tremble as they rise to touch Lenin's cheek. The unconscious figure on the bed has dark stubble on his face and scalp, like a devotee returning from a pilgrimage to Tirupati or Rameswaram. The sinuous veins on his thin arms stand out because of the complete absence of subcutaneous fat. His scalloped belly and the prominence of his rib cage make him look like a man on the brink of starvation, not a guerilla fighter.

Digby quietly straps the blood pressure cuff on Lenin's floppy arm. His action brings Mariamma out of her trance. Her fingers seek Lenin's pulse. "A hundred and seventy over seventy," Digby says eventually, removing the cuff. "About what it was before."

"Pulse is forty-six," she says. "The Cushing response."

When was the last time Digby heard that phrase? A half century ago in a Glasgow operating theater? He's had few occasions to remember the pioneering neurosurgeon's triad. Cushing observed that if a bleed or a tumor raised the pressure within the rigid confines of the skull, it caused the systolic blood pressure to rise, the pulse to slow, and the breathing to become irregular.

"We should sit him up," Mariamma says. "It helps lower intracranial pressure." It isn't an admonishment, but Digby knows he should have thought of it. With Cromwell's help and using a folded mattress from the other empty bed in the room, they prop Lenin up, his head lolling forward like a rag doll's.

"May I examine?" she asks.

"He's all yours!"

She looks at Digby strangely. Then she shakes Lenin's shoulders. "LENIN!" Earlier, Lenin had tried to open his eyes when Digby called his name. He'd even spoken. Now his eyes are glazed over. A patient who doesn't flinch when firecrackers go off under the bed is worse off than one who does. Mariamma grinds her knuckles into Lenin's sternum—a painful stimulus for a conscious patient. Lenin stirs, a faint furrowing of his face.

"See that?" she says. "Just the right side of his face moved." Digby missed it. She does it again, and now he sees. "A left facial nerve paralysis," she says. "The tumor on his left acoustic nerve is the issue. It must be big enough to involve the facial nerve."

She props Lenin's upper eyelids open and then rocks his head from side to side, checking for doll's-eye movements, then for a gag reflex. With a tendon hammer she compares his reflexes on both sides. She pulls an ophthalmoscope out of her bag and looks into Lenin's pupils. "Papilledema, both sides," she says. Another sign of raised pressure in the brain.

Digby watches her, seeing all the things he might have done. The body before her is the text. Soon, like a biblical scholar, she will perform her exegesis. It makes him conscious of his age—she is two generations his junior. But Digby's expertise is now in nerves that can never recover. All the book knowledge he no longer uses has vanished. In the field of tendon transfers, he's an expert, publishing a few papers on his innovations, building on Rune's work. But this patient brings him into unfamiliar territory.

Mariamma puts away her tools, her brow creased.

Digby says, "I thought we might need to make a burr hole in his skull. That's why I asked you to bring the trephine. That might relieve pressure—"

She shakes her head. "It won't help. Lenin's tumor is down near the brain stem. It's blocking the flow of cerebrospinal fluid. He has hydrocephalus. That's why he's unconscious. A burr hole is good for blood collecting under the skull, but in Lenin it would just cause the brain to herniate."

Digby digests what Mariamma has just said. He pictures the slit-like hollows—the ventricles—that sit deep within the right and left hemispheres of Lenin's brain. Cerebrospinal fluid is normally manufactured in the two ventricles, then passes down a central canal that runs like a drainpipe through the brain stem, emptying out at the base of the brain so as to bathe and cushion the outside of the brain and the spinal cord. But with the drain blocked by the tumor, fluid has backed up in the ventricles, converting them from slits to tense balloons. In infants the unfused skull would simply expand as the ventricles enlarge. But in Lenin, the enlarging ventricles are slowly squishing the brain tissue surrounding them against his unyielding skull, rendering him first drowsy and then comatose.

"But what we *could* do," Mariamma says, "is tap one of the ventricles. We would pass a needle through brain until we hit one swollen ventricle and then drain the cerebrospinal fluid. We'd have to make a tiny hole here in the skull." She points to the top of Lenin's head, off the midline. "Not a regular burr hole but just big enough to pass the needle."

"You mean you do it blind?"

"There are anatomical landmarks to follow. But it's blind, yes. But his ventricles should be so distended that the needle has a good chance of hitting a ventricle." She waits, as though she hopes Digby will talk her out if it. "I've seen it done. It's not a cure. But it might buy us time. Time is brain, they say in neurosurgery. If he improves, then if we can get him to Vellore, to the Christian Medical College, that's if he agrees to surgery . . ." She trails off, silenced by all the "ifs."

"It's the best plan," Digby says firmly.

In Digby's small theater, they prop Lenin up and bind his head to padded orthopedic frames that slot into the operating table. With a skin-marking pen, Mariamma draws a vertical line from the root of Lenin's nose straight up to the center of his skull. With a tape measure she marks a point eleven centimeters along the line. From there she draws a second line, perpendicular to the first, heading to Lenin's right ear. She marks an X three centimeters along this second line.

"Removing fluid from one ventricle will empty both, since they're connected. I chose the right to avoid the speech center in the left hemisphere. In case you're wondering."

"I should have been," Digby says.

The trephine Mariamma brought will make too big a hole. After conferring, Digby brings out the twist drill he uses for long bones. She injects local anesthetic into the skin and down to the skull at the X. With a scalpel she makes a small but deep cut down to the bone. Since he's familiar with the instrument, Digby operates the twist drill. When he feels it punch through the outer table of skull, Mariamma takes over with a rongeur to nibble at the bone till they can see the glistening membrane that covers the brain. Even through that tiny hole, the membrane bulges out, the brain seeking relief from the pressure. Digby sees Mariamma flinch: this brain belongs to someone she cares for.

She picks up the spinal tap needle. It is long and hollow with a removable inner stylet. Earlier, she'd marked the shaft seven centimeters back from the needle tip. She clamps a hemostat to the needle hub and hands Digby the hemostat. "Stand directly in front of him, Digby, and hold the hemostat. I'll be standing at his side. You must keep me pointing at the inside of the eye from your perspective. I'll be aiming for the tragus of his ear on my view. Even if I tilt the needle in the front-to-back plane, your job is to not let me deviate in the side-to-side plane, keep me pointing to the inner canthus of the eye."

God help us, this is crude, he thinks. She advances the needle into the brain. At five centimeters, she stops and pulls out the inner stylet. Nothing comes out of the hub. She reinserts and pushes the needle in another centimeter before withdrawing the stylet.

Clear fluid, like spring water, comes spurting out.

"Oh, my!" Digby exclaims. Theories are nice, but the proof is the fluid dripping steadily onto the towels.

"I can see the surface of the brain sinking back!" Mariamma says, excitedly.

When the dripping finally ceases, she slides the stylet back into the inner hollow and removes the needle, then plugs the bone with sterile bone wax. Just as she ties a knot in the single stitch she used to close the scalp wound, they feel the table shake. An ungloved hand emerges. "Hold on there," Digby shouts, whipping off the drapes.

A groggy Lenin stares out of the drapes bunched over his forehead, like a mole emerging from its burrow, squinting at the light.

"Take your mask off," Digby says quietly to Mariamma, removing his own.

Lenin's head can't move, but his eyes swivel from Digby to Mariamma. They settle on Mariamma. Digby cannot say which of them—Mariamma or Lenin—is more astonished. The theater becomes utterly still as the two stare at each other. All sounds outside vanish.

"Mariamma," says the recently comatose patient, his voice weak and hoarse. "I am so happy to see you."

CHAPTER 77

Revolutionary Roads

1977, Saint Bridget's

The resurrected Lenin has his eyes fixed on her. She cannot move. She watches Digby slice the ties that immobilize Lenin's head, speaking calmly to him as if they just met at the club. "I'm Digby Kilgour. I saw you this morning, but I doubt you'll recall that."

For a moment Mariamma imagines they'll shake hands like Stanley and Livingstone. It'd be fitting. Their last meeting was the stuff of legend: Lenin shook a fist at him, and Dr. Kilgour sent it packing with the glowing end of a cheroot.

"You're not at the estate but at Saint Bridget's Leprosarium." Lenin looks worried. "You're quite safe here. We had to smuggle you down from Gwendolyn Gardens. Too dangerous up there."

Lenin's right hand floats up to his skull. "Hold on!" Digby says. "You have a stitch there." Digby looks to Mariamma as if to say, *Go on now!*

"How's your head?" she says. *Oh, God. Are those really my first words to my one and only lover after five years apart? How's your head—after I drilled your skull and stuck a needle in your brain?* Blood surges to her face. When she was a child no one could make her blush like Lenin.

"My head is fine," he says. "I remember . . ."

They wait for him to go on. Outside, a common tailorbird chirps, *Go-on-go-on-go-on*. Mariamma holds her breath.

"I remember . . . I had a headache for so long." The words squeeze out in English, but he's out of practice. "If I cough or sneeze, my head . . . bursts. Life was being pressed out of me." He's becoming more fluent. "I had convulsions. Many. Daily. We had cyanide capsules. I was ready to take mine, then I thought . . ." Again, the pause, like a radio with a loose wire.

"Where is it?" Digby asks.

Lenin roots around the end of his *mundu*. Digby helps, extracting rupee notes held in a rubber band and a dirty ball of plastic wrap.

Lenin watches Digby. "Doctor, I know from my mother that you helped her when she needed you most. You prevented my entry into this world. Now you stop my exit!"

Digby laughs. "Both times premature. But believe me, if I hadn't tracked down Mariamma, you wouldn't have needed the cyanide."

Hearing this, something bursts in Mariamma. A few hours' delay and she'd have come to see a corpse, not this conscious, conversant being, this man who, despite everything, she loves. She sags against the table. An alarmed Digby drags a stool over for her.

Lenin's hand reaches for hers.

His smile is skewed from the facial paralysis. But the warmth, the affection and concern for her in his eyes—that's real, all Lenin. She doesn't want to be the doctor anymore. But they aren't done. She gathers herself. She wonders why he doesn't ask how they took his headache away?

"Lenin?" He looks so vulnerable, his forehead bisected by her pen and a sutured wound on his head. "You have a tumor, an acoustic neuroma. It raised the pressure—"

"I'm sorry about your father, Mariamma," he interrupts. "I read the paper. The Condition. So proud of you. Did you take my tumor out?"

It hurts to see hope extinguished in his eyes when she shakes her head. She uses the surgical pen on a piece of paper to explain what is going on. ". . . and when we put in the needle, fluid came surging out. You awoke. But it just bought us a little time."

A playful light appears in his eyes. Then he laughs, which exaggerates the immobility of half of his face, so that it looks like a snarl. She must keep her eyes on the right side of his face.

"Mariamm*aye*," he says affectionately. "My doctor. Do you remember when we were children you said something was loose in my head? And someday you'd fix it?"

They'd been in church. Lenin had caught her eye as she stood on the women's side; then, with no change of expression, he'd let a string of saliva spool down from his lip. She hadn't been able to suppress her giggle. Big Ammachi pinched her ear.

"What I said was one day I'd crack your skull and pull out the Devil."

"And you did!"

Digby brings them back to reality. "Lenin, you understand the tumor is still there. All we did was temporarily relieve the pressure above it." He looks to Mariamma for support. "The pressure will rise again."

Lenin says, "A needle into my brain? But I feel nothing."

Digby says, "It's a paradox, isn't it? Poke the brain directly, you feel no pain. Step on a nail, though, and your brain pinpoints the exact spot. Unless you're one of the patients here who feel nothing and come to harm."

Mariamma says, "Lenin, you urgently need the tumor out. But we can't do it here." She puts her hand on his chest. "We must get you to Vellore. They have experience in such operations." She sees him recoil. The fugitive calculating his escape routes.

"Why not here? I trust you—"

"I wish I could. I don't have the skills. Yet."

"Vellore? It won't take long for them to know who I am."

"But with the tumor out, you live. *Live a full life!*" She holds her breath.

He doesn't respond. He's withdrawing further. She thinks he's steeling himself for death.

Digby says gently, "Lenin? What do you think?"

He doesn't meet Digby's gaze. He looks suddenly weary. "I think . . . I'm so hungry it's hard to think."

"Oh, heavens!" Digby says. "Some doctors we are! You must be starving. And this young lady needs a cup of tea too."

Mariamma is suddenly weighed down, as though the ceiling just descended on her shoulders. She needs fresh air.

Cromwell squats outside the theater. On seeing Mariamma he smiles . . . then the smile is gone, and he leaps to his feet, rushing at her. *What now?* she thinks. *And why's the ground tilting so strangely?*

She's reclined in an armchair, her legs on an ottoman. A silk shawl covers her. Tea, biscuits, and water are beside her. She vaguely remembers being carried by Cromwell. She revived once she was horizontal, an anxious Digby hovering over her and insisting she rest. She said she'd close her eyes for five minutes. She must have fallen asleep. She has no idea for how long.

She drinks and eats greedily. Her refuge is a cool, carpeted, low-ceilinged study with bookcases built into the wall and rising up and over the door and window frames. It feels intimate and welcoming. Heavy curtains frame French windows that look out onto a small rectangle of lawn, bordered with colorful rose bushes; the garden is enclosed by a picket fence with a door cut into it on the far side. She imagines this lawn as Digby's refuge, a place to sit in the sun and read a book. She stares out, fascinated by the ruler-like edges of the lawn, the beautifully trimmed rose bushes. It's like a postcard she's seen of tiny gardens fronting row houses in England, the enclosed patches of earth far too small for the owners' horticultural ambitions, but warm and cozy all the same.

Among the bookshelves are nooks that display photographs. She's drawn to an elegant silver frame holding a black-and-white picture of a small white boy in knee-high stockings, shorts, a tie, and a V-necked sweater. In his brow, his eyes, she sees unmistakable traces of the adult Digby. The boy's shy smile as he looks at the camera doesn't conceal the trace of anxiety. His first day of school, perhaps? A beautiful woman in a skirt crouches next to him, laughing, her knees together, her hand on his shoulder. That must be Digby's mother. Her face is youthful but weary, her dark hair already showing a streak of gray. But for that instant when the shutter clicks she's gathered her best self, drawn on her experience like a veteran actor when the curtain rises, and the result is simply stunning. She's as beautiful as a movie star and blessed with a presence to match.

An unframed photograph in another alcove shows a huge, bearded white man flanked by lepers, his arms on their shoulders, like a coach with his squad. It's the same face she saw in the oil portrait hanging just within Saint Bridget's portico. This must be Rune Orqvist. She's seen that name so often in the flyleaf of her mother's ancient copy of *Gray's Anatomy*. It was his book, even if the inscription inside was from Digby. It must have made a perfect gift for a young aspiring artist. Mariamma was so preoccupied with Lenin that she and Digby never talked about this connection. Lenin! She hurriedly drains the tea, no time to dawdle.

She washes up, still marveling at the connections in her world, invisible or forgotten, but there all the same, like a river linking people upstream with those below, whether they know it or not. The Thetanatt home was somewhere close by—gone now because her uncle sold it long ago. Rune was Elsie's godfather. As a schoolboy, Philipose had been here too.

Exiting the room, she sees Digby coming down the hall: yes, the schoolboy's tinge of worry, the earnestness, and even the smile are preserved in the older man's expression. His concern for her is heartwarming.

"The tea and biscuits were magical," she reassures him. "I'm fine now." He looks relieved. "Digby, the picture in your study—that's Rune, isn't it? Same as in the foyer?" Digby nods. "His name is in my mother's copy of *Gray's Anatomy*. And you wrote the inscription. I've had the book with me all these years. It's my good luck charm!"

Digby looks touched, almost overcome. He seems to struggle to say something and gives up. Instead, he wings out his elbow, a gesture so foreign to her that she wants to laugh. She threads her arm through his. It feels like the most natural thing in the world.

They walk back to Lenin in silence, passing through a cool, shaded cloister, the brick arches giving it the feeling of a medieval monastery. The paving stones underfoot are etched by the moss pushing up in the gaps. In the shadows of the cloister, a leper in white stands against a pillar. She is so still that, for a moment, Mariamma mistakes her for a statue . . . until the *pallu* of her sari, drawn over her head, stirs in the breeze. The leper cocks one ear to the sound of their footsteps in the manner of the sightless. Mariamma shudders involuntarily, not because of the woman's grotesque features, but because the object she took to be lifeless came alive.

When this nightmare with Lenin is over, she'll write to Uma Ramasamy about this leprosarium and its living patients, such a contrast to the formalin-preserved human remnants over which she labored. She's tempted to tell Digby about Uma and their shared interest in this disease he's given himself to, his life sentence. That fortuitous assignment with Uma led her to finding the cause of the Condition, led her to Lenin. But such thoughts are indulgent. There are pressing issues to discuss.

"Digby, I think the Condition does more than produce acoustic neuromas. My theory is that it also affects personality, makes them eccentric. It's responsible for Lenin's . . . recklessness, the stupid path he took. And his stubbornness now."

"Well, it'd be a good argument before a judge, if he surrenders," Digby says. "Might shorten his time in the clink."

"I heard of this Naxalite woman serving a life sentence," Mariamma says. "She was released after seven years."

She marvels at where her mind is trying to take her. She's gone
from thinking she'd never see Lenin again to plotting a future. *You're
getting too far ahead of yourself.*

"Digby," she says, "what if Lenin won't surrender or go to Vellore, then—"

"Convince him. You must." He releases her. "I'll leave you two
together."

Lenin is back in the room where she first saw him, propped up again
and appearing to be asleep. She sits on the chair by his bed. He opens
his eyes.

"Mariamma?" He smiles at her. He picks out a biscuit from
the pack beside him and breaks it down the middle. "If we bite at
the same time, we'll have supernatural powers. Like Mandrake the
Magician. Remember? One bite, and somewhere in the galaxy, if we
two are in time . . . ?" He makes the sign of the cross over her with
the half biscuit, like a priest, but she grabs his hand.

She's laughing despite herself. "It was Phantom Comics, *macku*.
Not Mandrake." She's brought him back from the dead to call him
an idiot. "Lenin, we don't have much time. You *will* lose consciousness again, you understand? Please let us take you to Vellore."

The one-sided smile fades. He looks away. He says, "What a
waste, *ma*. These last five years. Seems like forty. Nothing changed for
the *adivasis*, the *pulayar*. And you and me? I was so stupid, so blind."

She's overcome with sadness for him—for them. A narrow
shaft of sunlight filters through leaves, touches the bed. The God
who never interferes with drownings or train wrecks likes to peer
in on the human experiment at such moments of reckoning, touching the scene with a little celestial light. She's impatient, waiting for
Lenin's answer.

"Mariamma, when it's all done, when life is almost over, what
do you want to remember?"

She thinks of their one night together in Mahabalipuram. She found him when she'd already lost him to a doomed cause. And it's happening again. Finding him only to lose him. She doesn't answer. She just holds his hand.

"What do *you* want to remember, Lenin?" she says softly.

He doesn't hesitate. "This. Here. Now. The sun on your face. Your eyes more blue than gray today. I want to remember this room, the remnant of biscuit in my mouth. Why wait for the world to show me anything better?" It's as though he's saying goodbye.

A dark cloud passes over his face—a trespasser. His breath quickens and beads of sweat glisten on his brow.

"Lenin, I beg you. Let us take you to Vellore. When the tumor is gone, then let whatever happens happen. Surrender and take what comes. But *live*! Live for my sake. Don't ask me to watch you die."

"Mariamma, it's no good. I'll die anyway. The police will kill me, tumor or no tumor." His words stumble over one another. His eyes wander and it's an effort to focus on her. She can see the veil descending. His voice is faint. "I'm glad you put that needle in. I could see you one more time, touch you, hear you. Mariamma, you know, don't you? You know how I feel about you . . . ?"

His body stiffens; his eyes roll to one side.

She cries out for Digby, and he's there, in time to watch Lenin have a seizure, rattling the bed with the violent shaking. Gradually it subsides.

Digby says, "Did he tell you what he wants?"

She bypasses the question because she won't lie. "We're going to take him to Vellore."

In a time of deceit, telling the truth is a revolutionary act. But this is her truth, her revolutionary act for Lenin and for herself. Long live the revolution.

The battered car bounces and weaves its way across the tapering waist of India from one shore to the other, racing to Vellore, Cromwell driving. Digby couldn't come—he was sad about it. She wanted him with her, but she didn't question his reasons. She sits turned sideways, checking frequently on Lenin, but he's in a post-seizure stupor—either that or the fluid has built up again. They head north to Trichur, then turn east to climb the Palghat Gap in the Western Ghats before heading down into the plains to Coimbatore. Three hours in, her neck is stiff from twisting to attend to him. She dozes off and when she wakes, she's startled to find Lenin looking at her, as if *he's* the chaperone and she's the patient being rushed to brain surgery.

She hadn't given much thought to what she'd say to him about taking him to Vellore against his wishes. She'd been sure that moment was far away, perhaps long after surgery . . . that is if he survived the ride, let alone the surgery. What does she say now? *I wanted you alive, no matter how you felt about it?* Lenin watches her squirm, amused.

"Oh, go ahead, say it," she bursts out. "Say I'm taking you to Vellore against your will."

"It's all right, Mariamma. No need. Cromwell explained."

"Don't mention," Cromwell says, glancing back in the mirror. "Two hours more," he adds. "Maybe less."

She looks out the window. The moon shines through clouds, its ghostly light illuminating an arid, pocked landscape—they've landed on a lunar crater, by the look of it. The world, and the two men in the car, are at peace. She's the one who is agitated. She wants to strangle them both.

Lenin reaches for her hand. "Cromwell says it was just this morning that we spoke, but I feel I've been gone months and months. And all that time I was thinking about our conversation. Your last words. I reflected on it for weeks, it seems like." His hand unconsciously goes to his brow to touch the bandage. "Before I woke up in this car, I'd already come to a decision. If I was ready to die for something that I don't believe in, surely, I must be willing to live for the one thing I *do* believe in."

She doesn't dare breathe. "And what's that?"

He smiles. "By now you must surely know."

A few stray dogs run around the streets of the small provincial town that is Vellore. Dawn is still hours away as they pass through the gates of the Christian Medical College Hospital. They're expected, and as interns and nurses swarm over Lenin, the neurosurgical registrar comes by, talks to Mariamma at length. He orders a loading dose of anticonvulsant and forbids Lenin from taking anything by mouth. When day breaks, Lenin is whisked away for tests.

She finds Cromwell, who'd slept in the car. She encourages him to head back—it's pointless for him to stay. He leaves reluctantly. She calls Digby. He is relieved they arrived safely. "Listen," he says, "I think it might be a good thing for you to call the editor of the *Manorama*. Tell him what's going on. If they connect Lenin to your family, your father, the Condition, it might serve notice to the police not to harm him. By the way, at Vellore they know who he is. I told them. They'll have to let the Madras state police know. They will eventually inform their Kerala counterparts." After she hangs up with Digby, she makes the call to the *Manorama*.

Lenin returns after his tests, his head fully shaved. He falls asleep. She does too, in the chair by his bed. At noon, the entire neurosurgical team returns, this time with the chief, a compact, quiet man with kind, intelligent eyes behind rimless glasses. He's still in surgical scrubs. He nods politely to Mariamma as the senior registrar presents Lenin's case in a low voice, and shares the test results. Mariamma is tongue-tied before her future boss. The chief examines Lenin quickly, but thoroughly.

"You came just in time," he says to both of them. "We discussed your case with our neurologists as well. We had to postpone a major surgical case. So we'll operate right away, no point waiting. Let's pray for a good outcome."

The orderlies arrive to take Lenin away. It's happening faster than Mariamma dreamed possible. All she gets to do is kiss him on his cheek. Lenin says, "It'll be all right, Mariamma, don't worry."

There's nothing emptier than a hospital bed to which a loved one might not return. She's overcome, slumped on the chair, her face buried in her hands. The woman caring for her son in the next bed comes over to comfort her. To Mariamma's surprise, a nurse comes and sits beside her and prays aloud. Faith at this institution is concrete, not abstract. After her father's death she'd turned her back on religion, having lost faith. But she closes her eyes while the nurse prays . . . Lenin needs all the help he can get.

Now she must wait. Three hours, then four. The wait is agonizing. All she can do is helplessly stare at her watch and look up whenever anyone enters the ward. Then, an orderly comes for her—the chief wants to see her, that's all he knows.

They walk through corridors, up stairs . . . her thoughts are a blur. She is led into a large hall outside the surgical suites where the chief waits calmly, seated on a bench. His mask dangles from one ear. He pats the bench beside him.

"He's doing well. We managed to remove most of it. I had to leave some capsule behind because it was dangerously adherent. His facial nerve may or may not recover, but I'm hopeful." His smile reassures her even more than his words.

Relief floods her being and tears spill out. He waits patiently. "Thank you! I'm sorry," she manages to say at last, dabbing at her eyes. "I'm just overwhelmed. I can't help thinking of my father. And of my father's father. And so many of my relatives who never understood what they had. This is the first time anyone in my family who suffered this disease has had it treated."

He listens, nodding, waiting. When he's sure she is done he says quietly, "I read the papers you sent us with your application. It made me wonder if some of our patients with acoustic neuromas over the years might not have been from families like yours. We're paying closer attention to the family histories now. Good work."

"Thank you. I'm honored to be coming here," she says. "What you did . . . removing such a tumor in that tiny space seems . . . impossible. A miracle."

He smiles. "Well, we don't believe we do anything alone." He nods toward a large mural on the opposite wall. It depicts gowned, masked surgeons bent over a patient, under the halo of a theater lamp. In the shadows, figures observe the surgery. One of them is Jesus, his hand resting on the surgeon's shoulder. Mariamma stares at it. She's envious of the chief's kind of faith.

"We pride ourselves here that we can do just about anything that the top centers in the world can do, but at a fraction of the cost. But the surgery we just performed, taking a rectangle of skull out just above his hairline, pushing aside the cerebellum . . . well, quite honestly, it's crude compared to another operation for acoustic neuroma that right now only two or three centers in the world are doing. It was invented by an ENT surgeon, William House, who was a dentist before he became a surgeon. He began using a dental drill to get at the inner ear, the bony labyrinth, and realized that he could, by deepening that tunnel, approach an acoustic neuroma. It's a brilliant innovation, yet incredibly difficult if you don't know what you are doing."

Mariamma has read about this surgery, but she doesn't interrupt the chief lest she come across as a know-it-all.

"*That's* what we need to offer here. It requires an operating microscope, the dental drill, and irrigation and other tools he adapted. But more than anything, it requires special training, many hours of dissecting the temporal bone on cadavers till one learns to do it. Right now only House and a few surgeons he trained perform the surgery. In time I'd like to send someone to train with him." He smiles, rising. "Who knows, maybe that's God's plan for you, Mariamma. Let's see. Let's pray about it."

Big Ammachi would have loved this man, relished his words. God had answered her grandmother's prayer: heal the Condition or send someone who can.

The chief says, "By the way, DSP Rajan of our local police talked to me. I've given him my assurance that Lenin won't be going anywhere. I know you'll help me keep my word."

CHAPTER 78

Watch This

1977, Vellore

In the recovery room, Lenin's face is puffy and swollen. His eyelids flutter, and he retches from the anesthetic. He's restless. She dabs Vaseline onto his parched lips, and wonders: Did time expand for him again, as it did after his seizure? Did the four hours of surgery feel like four years? Without this tumor that defined his whole life, will he be the old familiar Lenin or somebody new? She spoons ice chips past his lips, murmuring soothing words. He comes awake, his eyes unfocused at first. "Mariamma!" It is barely audible. She feels a fist unclench in her chest—it's been there ever since Digby showed up at Triple Yem, a lifetime ago.

The next day, Lenin is on the regular ward. He's weak but all his limbs are working, his speech and memory are intact—no damage to anything but the tumor, as far as they can tell. Mariamma feeds him, holds his urine bottle for him, cleans him, doing her best to spare the busy nurses. By watching the probationers, she's learned how to change soiled sheets under a bedridden patient, how to turn him, and give him a proper bed bath. It's humbling. Shouldn't every physician learn this? Isn't this what medicine is really about?

* * *

The *Manorama* runs the "Naxalite Priest" the day after Lenin's surgery. A saintly altar boy was bedeviled by a slow-growing brain tumor that drove him to be a Naxalite; now, after heroic brain surgery, he's whole again, repentant—that's the tale the reporter spins. Who knows, it might even be the truth. Digby had hoped that kind of publicity would keep the Kerala police from harming Lenin once he is taken into custody. It might just work.

Ten days after Lenin's surgery, Mariamma spends the entire day observing surgery at the chief's invitation. When she returns to the ward at five in the evening, she's puzzled to see a clean-shaven young man in a loose shirt and pants seated on *her* chair, next to Lenin's empty bed. All eyes are on Mariamma. The nurses are smiling mischievously.

The stranger rises on his own and turns slowly and approaches her. From the time Mariamma first set eyes on Lenin at Saint Bridget's, she hasn't seen him on his feet. He's taller than she remembers. Lenin stumbles into her embrace. He's all bones against her body, all sharp angles. Every conscious patient and all their relatives look on; Matron and the nurses have sappy expressions . . . Mariamma feels the blood rush to her face. *Dear God, please don't let them start clapping!*

At Lenin's insistence, and with Matron's blessing, they walk out to the shady courtyard behind the ward and sit on the bench. The leaves of the spreading oak in front of them make a dry rustling sound, like rice sifted in a basket. Lenin's eyes trace the branches out to their tips. He scans the skies. "If I could sleep here, I would," he says.

There's nothing slow about his thoughts. They leap like a goat from ledge to ledge, as though the words have been piling up. He says that for the last two years he and his few remaining comrades were unwanted by and unable to trust the villagers—the very people whose cause they championed. "The reward money was too tempting. A villager whom I was willing to die for could send me to my grave." The group spent more and more time in the jungle, getting increasingly disillusioned. "Do you know that a fungus called blister blight did more for the class struggle than all the Naxalites put together? It wiped out tea estates. The owners abandoned the land to the tribals. It was their land in the first place." Lenin said the immensity of the jungle silenced him and his comrades; they hardly spoke to each other.

"An old tribal in Wayanad taught me how to sling a stone with a slender leader over the lowest branch of the tallest tree. Then, by tying a rope to the leader, I could loop the rope over the branch and make a sling for my body. He showed me a special knot, a secret one, that allowed me to pull myself up little by little—the rope locks so you don't slide down. That friction knot, so hard to learn, is passed down by the tribals from generation to generation. People think of inheritance as being land or money. The old man gave his inheritance to me."

The fugitive Lenin winched himself up to the stars. He lived for days in the canopy with mushrooms, tree beetles, rats, songbirds, parrots, and the occasional civet cat to keep him company. "Every tree had its own personality. Their sense of time is different. We think they're mute, but it's just that it takes them days to complete a word. You know, Mariamma, in the jungle I understood my failing, my human limitation. It is to be consumed by one fixed idea. Then another. And another. Like walking the straight line. Wanting to be a priest. Then a Naxalite. But in nature, one fixed idea is unnatural. Or rather, the one idea, the *only* idea is life itself. Just *being*. Living."

Mariamma listens, amused and even a bit alarmed by his thoughts.

Matron sends their dinner down, with a special treat just for them—ice cream.

"Mariamma, you know the best meal I ever had? I used to think of it often. It was the RoyalMeels. Mahabalipuram? One day, I'll take you back there. To that same room."

"You promise?"

He nods. He takes her hand and kisses it, stares at her as though trying to memorize her face. He sighs. "I didn't want to ruin our evening. But earlier when you were off the ward and observing the surgeons, we learned that I'll be handed over to the Kerala police tomorrow. They'll transport me to the Trivandrum jail."

It's not grief, but primitive fear that clutches at her. Fear for his life—just as when he went under the knife. Lenin watches her, apprehensive. "Mariamma? What are you feeling?"

"I'm sad, scared—what do you expect? And I'm angry with you. Yes, I know it's too late for that. But if you hadn't insisted on being . . . being Lenin, we might have had a life." The old Lenin would have protested, blamed a misunderstanding. This one looks penitent, and she feels bad. She strokes his cheek. "But then, if you'd been a good boy and become a priest, I might have found you quite dull."

"Now that I'm an outlaw, I'm irresistible?"

She likes this Lenin. No. She loves him. As much as they've both changed, the essence of a person is formed at ten years of age—that's her theory. The "eccentric" part can't be cut out. One can perhaps learn to manage it.

"Mariamma, I know we said goodbye forever in Madras. Still, I'd have imaginary conversations with you. I saved things in a mental suitcase to tell you one day . . . What I'm saying is, I never relinquished you. I couldn't. And here I am—alive. *And* I'll be able to see you. Because you'll know where to find me—"

"But in prison!" she bursts out, bitterly. The tears won't be held back.

"Mariamma, you know that you don't *have* to wait for me?" He cannot hide the tinge of anxiety in his voice.

"Oh, stop it, would you? I'm crying because it'll be hard. But not as hard as it will be for you. I wish we didn't have to wait. But now that I found you, surely you don't think I'd let you go?"

She spends one last night in her chair by his side, her head resting on Lenin's bed, clutching his hand. As the sun comes up, she's jumpy, a nervous wreck. Lenin is unnaturally calm. Everyone on the ward knows what's coming.

At ten in the morning, DSP Mathew from the Kerala Police Special Task Force arrives with two constables, their boots sounding like hammers on the tiled floor. The DSP is a big man, unsmiling, and with a fierce mustache. His whole being, from cap to polished brown shoes to the tufts of hair winging out from his ears and even from his knuckles, is menacing. Mariamma stands up, trembling.

Lenin eases himself to his feet and steps out between the beds to face the DSP, his shoulders bravely back, but looking like a puff of wind might knock him over. The look that passes between the two men chills Mariamma's blood: two ancient enemies squaring off, men whose only desire is to tear the other's heart out, who seek vengeance for what each has done to the other. But it is Lenin who chose to surrender, and so the fleeting defiance in his eyes vanishes, as though it never existed. It only fuels the hatred in the DSP's eyes; the man's hands curl into fists. Had there been no witnesses, Mariamma feels certain the DSP would have bludgeoned and bloodied Lenin before taking him away.

Lenin doesn't protest when a constable handcuffs him. When the DSP barks an order for leg irons, Mariamma opens her mouth, but Matron beats her to it. "DSP!" Matron says in a voice that can cut interns off at the knees and cause probationers to wet themselves. "You're upsetting my patients! Your prisoner had a brain operation, do you understand? If he runs, don't you think you'll be able to catch him?" The DSP falters under her withering gaze. The leg irons vanish. "I'm giving him to you in good condition," Matron says. "Please keep him that way."

A van awaits. Mariamma is allowed to walk alongside Lenin. The back doors open to reveal bench seats along the sides, facing each other. Matron, without asking permission, tosses a pillow and blankets in, along with a big bottle of water; after that she prays over Lenin and blesses him. Before the constables help him in, Mariamma embraces him, feeling the cold metal cuffs press against her. Lenin kisses her forehead. He whispers, "RoyalMeels, the Majestic Hotel *ma*! Don't forget. Bring a bathing suit this time. I'll come for you. Be ready."

CHAPTER 79

God's Plan

1977, Parambil

Prisoners aren't allowed visitors for one month. For Mariamma, waiting that long is torture. To make things worse, every Triple Yem patient seems to know her business. Not a day goes by without someone saying, "At least in jail they get one good meal a day. How bad can that be?" A toddy tapper with a deep laceration on his forehead opines from under a surgical towel: "If only I'd gone to prison, I wouldn't be climbing trees. They learn useful things, like tailoring." Her patience vanishes and she drops her needle holder. "You're right. If you'd gone to prison, I wouldn't be stitching up a man who kissed a goat, mistaking it for his wife." Joppan takes over the suturing, something he excels at, while she storms out.

Every morning, Anna *Chedethi* fusses over her, checking the drape of Mariamma's sari before she lets her go to Triple Yem. "You've lost weight," Anna *Chedethi* scolds. "And you're not eating what I send over."

She and Uplift Master travel to Trivandrum to retain a lawyer. The man is competent and experienced. Until Lenin is formally charged, there is very little to be done, he says. He lists Naxalites who have been sentenced for seven to ten years, even life, but most have had their sentences commuted in three or four years. With

Lenin's medical history, and since he hasn't been directly connected with any deaths, he might serve only "a few years."

This is good news. Or should be. Yet by the time Mariamma gets home, the reality of what "a few years" will mean to their lives has her despondent. Soon she'll be in Vellore for her neurosurgical training. Instead of a three-hour bus ride, it'll be an overnight train journey to see Lenin. And every day she'll be worrying about his welfare in prison. She's emotionally exhausted.

Anna *Chedethi* takes one look at her face when she walks in and without a word, she sits her down. She whips chilled yogurt and water in a small bowl, adds a slice of green chili, chopped ginger, curry leaves, and salt, and serves it to her in a tall glass. She pushes Mariamma's hair back behind her ears, just as when she was a little girl, home from school. Mariamma drains the glass. This is a better invention than penicillin. She bathes, has a bit of *kanji* with pickle, then heads to bed early.

Just past midnight she's wide awake. There's no point fighting it. She heads to her father's study wanting to hear his voice in his journals. She has bookmarked those precious entries where he expresses his love for his daughter. Those passages bring her to tears every time. She marvels at the number of these odes to her at a time when she still lived under his roof; once she left for college, he pined for her even more. If only she'd come home more often.

She strokes the cover of the notebook. This is all she has left of him—his thoughts. The only notebook that's missing is at the bottom of a lake, one artifact among many in a terrible tragedy. She might never know *why* he got on the train to Madras. Thus far, the "tumor of thought" hasn't shown itself, unless the very existence of these rambling notes, the sheer volume of them, the compulsive, incessant commentary on life *is* the "tumor." But it's not a trait shared by others with the Condition. It was unique to him.

Even if she knew for sure that her hypothesis was wrong and there was no "tumor of thought," she'd keep going through every notebook. On these pages her father, the Ordinary Man, is very much alive; she dreads the day when she'll come to the last entry.

She adjusts the lamp, picks up her pen, and resumes the deciphering, the indexing, where she left off at the bottom of a page. She turns to the next page—

—and something looks off. Her eyes are jarred by the sight of white spaces, paragraph breaks, and a string of capital letters—the very things her father avoided like mortal sins. This page feels like a violation of his rule book.

> *My Mariamma turned seven today and wanted cake. No one has ever made a cake before in Parambil. She got the idea from* Alice in Wonderland. *She and Ammachi mixed the batter in a lidded tin and put hot coals above and below. I assured her that I had the* DRINK ME *potion, just in case like in* Alice, *this was an* EAT ME *cake and made her suddenly tall. Delicious! Vanilla and cinnamon. Then I gave her the birthday present: her first fountain pen, Parker 51, gold top and blue barrel. A beautiful instrument. It is what I had always promised as soon as she became a big girl. She was so excited. "Does this mean I'm a big girl at last?" I said she was. And she is!*

Mariamma sees her own childish scrawl in English on the page with the new pen.

MY NAME IS MARIAMMA. I AM SEVEN.

After another white space, her father resumes.

> *Only in meditating on Ninan's death, by suffering it anew each night for twelve years, have I come to fully understand the gift, the miracle, of my precious Mariamma. I didn't see it at once. It took time. I had to scale the highest palm, just*

like my father, to see what had eluded me on the ground, to see what I didn't want to see, what I have never put in these notes because if I did, I would be acknowledging what I knew in my bones, but I never wished to acknowledge. Thoughts can be pushed away. Words on a page are as permanent as figures carved in stone.

Tonight, prompted by my daughter becoming the big girl she wanted to be, I must be worthy of her by being truthful to myself and to these journals. I could not put these words down
UNTIL THIS MOMENT

Mariamma is disoriented by the large letters. Her father clearly stopped to fuss over each one, doodling to build a word monument, seeking to memorialize the moment. Or was he hesitating, second-guessing himself about whatever it was he was loath to put down? The three words occupy the rest of the page.

She turns to the next page:

After Ninan's death, my Elsie left. She was gone for just over a year. When she came back, Elsie was already with child.

My writing "already with child" is proof that my eyes are open. Perhaps Big Ammachi saw it all along. Perhaps that is what she meant when she said to me at Mariamma's birth, "God sent us a miracle in the form of this baby, who arrived fully formed and only herself." The baby was not Ninan reborn, but something infinitely more precious: my Mariamma! But I was a fool in the clutches of opium, unable to receive or recognize the priceless gift of my baby, who today is a "big girl."

Free of opium, my healing really only began when I undertook to love the baby girl with all my heart. I am her father—yes, I am—by my choice. Were she of my own blood, then she would be a different child, not my Mariamma, and that I shudder to imagine. I refuse to. I would never want to lose my Mariamma. My loving God didn't give me my son back. No,

he gave me something far better. He gave me my Mariamma.
And she gave me life.

She reads her father's words again and again, failing to understand at first, then refusing to understand, even as the words crash
onto her head like the roof collapsing.

already with child

When she does understand, she chokes on this terrible knowledge. She stumbles away from the desk, her mind reeling, her body
threatening to reject her meager dinner.

This room, her father's room, is suddenly foreign to her. Or
is it she herself—the observer—whom she no longer knows? She
remembers coming to this room with him after they ate her birthday
cake. She sat on her father's lap, holding her new Parker 51, filling it
with Parambil Purple ink. And writing the words now immortalized
on the page. Her father's words below that are what devastate her.

"Appa, what are you saying? My beloved father—who tells me
he is not my father—what are you saying?"

She's going mad. Who might she ask? Big Ammachi knew, or
so her father thought. But she isn't here for Mariamma to ask. She
paces the room, numb with disbelief. Where did her mother go in
that absent year? Who assuaged her grief? Did she begin a new life?
If so, why come home again? To give birth?

She's halfway through her father's journals, the entries scattered in time. But this is the only mention he's made of this. He had
the knowledge all along, but the words were too painful to write.
His every unspoken thought he'd put down except for this one. He
could not . . . until he did. Perhaps he never addressed it again in
writing, having expunged what festered inside him and found peace.

"Oh, Appa, you found your peace, but you've left me upended.
You've slashed the roots that connect me to this house, to my grandmother, to you . . ." She thinks of waking Anna *Chedethi*, crawling
into her arms. Would Anna *Chedethi* have known? No, she only came
to Parambil when Elsie was about to give birth. It would appear that

her father never discussed his suspicions, his sure knowledge with Big Ammachi. And Big Ammachi didn't talk about it with her son. She carried what she knew to her grave. As did her son . . . but for this note.

She catches sight of herself in the mirror that her father used for shaving, still there in an alcove, as though waiting for him to take it out to the verandah. She recoils because she sees a wild-eyed, anguished, insane woman staring back.

"Who am I?" she says to the apparition in the mirror. She always felt she had her father's eyebrows, his way of tilting his head to listen; definitely his nose, his upper lip—how can that *not* be true? Even their hair was so similar, thick, with a slight recession at the temples, though he didn't have her piebald streak.

Her piebald streak . . . That is her clue. That's what carries her to the top of the palm like her father, and now her vision is unimpeded.

I see.

I remember. I understand.

I have it now, this terrible knowledge I never wished for.

Part Ten

CHAPTER 80

Failure to Blink

1977, Saint Bridget's

The shrunken, ancient driver of Mariamma's tourist taxi is dwarfed by the Ambassador's large steering wheel, yet he expertly coaxes the column-mounted shifter through its changes with deft thrusts of his palm. Like many in his trade, he sits sideways, pressed against the driver's door, accustomed to having at least three family members squeezed onto the bench seat with him, in addition to the women, children, and infants in the back, transporting them to weddings or funerals.

From the rear seat, Mariamma looks out at the world with new eyes. Parambil is the home she's always claimed, but like so much she's believed about herself up to this point, that is a lie. "The only thing you can be sure of in this world is the woman who gave birth to you," Broker *Aniyan* said. Mariamma never knew her mother, and now it turns out that she never knew her father either.

The last time she came this way in Digby's car, racing to see Lenin, she wasn't thinking of the Thetanatt house. Her driver has been everywhere, and like a marriage broker, he knows just where the Thetanatt house was, before Elsie's late brother sold it. On that land now sit six "Gulf mansions"—built by Malayalis who returned from Dubai, Oman, or other outposts to construct their dream homes. The only thing Mariamma can see of her mother's past is the stately river at the edge of their former land. They press on.

"Here, Madam?" her driver says hesitantly, well before the open gate to Saint Bridget's leprosarium. In all his travels, she doubts that he has brought a fare here. Perhaps he's hoping that she'll hop out and stroll in.

"Drive to that building behind the lotus pond. I'll have them bring you tea."

"*Ayo*, thank you, Madam, not necessary!" he says, panicked. She hands him ten rupees and asks him to come back after lunch. It might be her imagination, but she thinks he receives the note gingerly.

She asks for Digby. Suja, the woman in nurse's garb whom she'd seen last time, leads the way. Suja's bandaged right foot, and her sandals, fashioned from old tires, give her a stiff, lopsided gait. They pass through the shady cloister, then the corridor leading to the theater, the disinfectant soapy odors giving way to the steamy hothouse scent of the autoclave.

Digby Kilgour is operating, but Suja encourages her to go in. Mariamma grabs a mask and cap, slips on shoe covers, and enters. Digby's assistant is short a few digits, the fingerless stalls of her glove taped out of the way. Digby looks up. He smiles above the mask. "Mariamma!" he exclaims happily.

Seeing her expression, he pauses. "Lenin . . . ?"

"He's fine."

The pale eyes study her, trying to read what he can in hers. He nods slowly. "I'm about to start. You're welcome to scrub in . . . ?" She shakes her head. "Shouldn't be much longer." The act of surgery supersedes everything. She remembers her surgical professor in Madras, a twice-divorced man, saying that in the theater the messy parts of his life—the disappointments, the debts—vanished. For a time.

Her thoughts no longer feel like her own. She struggles to stay focused. Digby makes three separate incisions on the patient's hand framed under the green surgical towels. She's tempted to rap his knuckles. *Are you a carpenter using a hammer? Hold that scalpel like a violin bow, between thumb and middle finger. Index finger on top!*

The pale lines unfolding in the wake of his blade, then the delayed blossom of blood, are just as she's used to seeing them. His movements are slow, deliberate.

"I'm not a pretty surgeon to watch," he says. He fusses over bleeding that she might ignore. After gaining his exposure, he severs a tendon from its insertion and tunnels it to a new location. "I've learned the hard way," he says, "that free grafts of an excised segment of tendon . . . don't work."

She bites her tongue. Surgeons like to think aloud. Assistants need quiet hands and quieter vocal cords. Observers, too.

"Rune was a pioneer in free tendon grafts. But I've come to believe a tendon needs to remain attached to its parent muscle, for blood supply and for function. The real enemy is scar tissue. I use the smallest incisions and I keep it bloodless."

She's grudgingly impressed at what he accomplishes with his stiff fingers—his left hand does most of the work. If she worked at this pace, Staff Akila would say, "Doctor, your wound is healing at the edges already."

Digby says, "You need the patience of an earthworm nosing between rocks . . . detouring around roots to get to where it must. Even the most rigid structures in the wrist have an almost invisible layer of slippery tissue, or so I believe. It's not in any textbook. It needs faith. You must believe without proof. I try not to disrupt that layer. Must sound like witchcraft."

She doesn't trust her voice. Every surgeon has beliefs, but also a bit of Doubting Thomas in them too. They need proof. Proof is why she is here. *Reach hither thy finger, and behold my hands; and reach hither thy hand, and thrust it into my side: and be not faithless, but believing.*

Digby sutures the tendon to its new insertion at the base of a finger. He fusses over it. "These wee fraying fibers at the cut end of a tendon are like vines, but tough as steel cables. One loose tendril can grab onto something it shouldn't and ruin your result."

He's finished. By habit she looks at the theater clock. It hasn't been as long as it has felt.

"Tourniquet off?" That came out of Mariamma's mouth, also from habit.

"Don't believe in them. The best tourniquet is one you can see hanging on the wall." He dresses the wound and immobilizes the hand in a cast. He strips off his gloves and gown.

He asks his assistant to arrange for tea to be brought to his study. "Do you mind if we pop in on one patient on our way? It's her big day and she's waited all morning."

I mind very much! I've only waited all my life.

She follows him.

In the small ward a young woman sits upright in bed. A dressing tray is at the ready. Digby puts a hand on the patient's shoulder.

"This is Karuppamma. She's in her fifties. Looks like she's twenty, doesn't she? That's lepromatous leprosy for you. It pushes out the wrinkles. Not like the tuberculoid form."

Karuppamma is shy. Her free claw of a hand goes up to cover her mouth.

"A week ago I did the same procedure on Karuppamma that you just saw. I cut the flexor digitorum superficialis tendon going to her ring finger. I can do that because she has the profundus as backup. I affixed the tendon here," he says, pointing to the root of his thumb. "She should now be able to make opposing movements. Get back the grasp function she lost. The thing is, though, to get her thumb to move, she must *imagine* she's moving her ring finger. The brain thinks it's impossible. It has to be convinced that things aren't what they seem."

Are you talking about me? Mariamma is calmer outwardly than when she first arrived, lulled into that state by waiting and by watching him at work. But her insides roil with anger, resentment, and confusion. She needs the truth. *I didn't come for surgical knowledge.* Still, she won't be rude in front of a patient.

Digby says in Malayalam, "Touch your thumb to your little finger." He butchers the language, lacking the swallowed *"errah."* Karuppamma understands. She grimaces with effort. Nothing happens.

"Stop. Now . . . move your ring finger."

Her thumb moves instead. There's a pause, and then Karuppamma bursts out laughing. Digby shares her happiness, grinning. A small crowd has gathered, sharing Karuppamma's triumph. Despite herself, Mariamma is moved. But when Digby turns to Mariamma, his expression is profoundly sad.

"This disease only takes away. Year after year, you lose something. Not from active leprosy, but from the nerve damage it caused. This is one of those rare moments when we give something back."

He tells Karuppamma that she'll get to move it more each day, till it is at full strength, but for today she mustn't overdo it. He directs Suja to immobilize the hand and wrist with a posterior slab of plaster.

Digby says, "Soon she'll move the thumb without thinking. It's astonishing. As Valery says, 'At the end of the mind, the body. But at the end of the body, the mind.'"

Mariamma follows him out. He says, "Paul Brand in Vellore and Rune here were the first to really understand that these fingers get damaged from repeated trauma. *Not* from leprosy chewing them away, but because they lack pain sensation . . ."

Her mind wanders. She's thinking of the schoolboy Philipose taking that reckless boat ride here and serving as Digby's hands, because Digby was still recovering from surgery.

". . . Paul Brand saw a patient cooking over an open fire, struggling to flip a *chapati* with tongs. She got frustrated and just reached in with her bare hand and turned it over. You and I would scream in pain if we tried that, but she felt nothing. That's when

Brand understood. Without the 'gift of pain,' as he says, we have no protection." Digby is talking to himself. "Amazing to me how few understand this. That's the nature of clinical leprosy. Not many physicians want to study it. Fewer surgeons wish to treat it." Digby gazes directly at her.

It rattles Mariamma to look at his face, seamed by age, mottled by burn scars, because it calls out to the face she sees when she looks in her mirror. Doesn't Digby see the likeness?

They enter his study, where, in what feels like a previous life, she took a nap. It's a glorious morning. She's drawn to the French windows, to see once more the jewel of a garden outside. Yellow, red, and violet roses rim the lawn, different colors than she recalls from her last visit. The gate at the far end of the picket fence is ajar. On the lawn a patient in a white sari sits in the sun and sorts roasted millet in her palms, then clumsily shovels the little pearls into her mouth. Her hands are like trees with their branches lopped off, leaving nubs. The rudiment of a thumb is what she uses for sorting. Her head is covered with the *pallu* of her sari. Mariamma sees her flattened profile, the nose leveled as if someone standing behind her is pulling on her ears. It takes a particular kind of courage to make leprosy one's calling. She must grant Digby that.

"When their facial nerves are affected, it robs them of natural expressions," Digby says, standing behind her at the window. "You think they're baring their teeth in anger when they might be laughing. It adds to the isolation of leprosy." He's still instructing. She wishes he would shut up. "I've learned to listen more than look," he says.

She hears the sadness in his voice. It would be so much easier to be angry with him if he were a boozy planter who'd gone to seed instead of this man who's given his life to those whose affliction has turned them into pariahs.

Doesn't Digby understand why she's here? He must at least know that he *could* be her father, even if he never saw Elsie again, and never knew he had a child. And if he *does* know, then he's part of the deception that hid the truth from her.

She's about to turn to him and speak when he whispers, "Notice how many times she blinks." The woman is unaware that she's being watched. "Count how many times you blink for every one of hers."

She tries not to blink. Her eyes itch, then burn. She gives in to the urge. The patient has yet to blink. The woman cocks her head toward a dog barking, the way the blind seek to localize sound. One eye is sunken, milky white, unseeing. The cornea of the other eye is cloudy.

"They fail to blink, the cornea desiccates, and blindness follows. Most of the residents didn't come here blind. When it happens, it's a sad moment."

The tea arrives. Mariamma sits down in the same chair where she had once napped. Without thinking, she removes the shawl draped over the back and places it on her lap. Digby pours.

On the bookcase she sees the silver-framed photograph of Digby as a little boy with his mother. *Your gorgeous, stunning mother, Digby. With the movie star looks. With the piebald streak in her hair. My grandmother.* When Mariamma had first glanced at the faded black-and-white photograph on her last visit, she'd thought that Digby's mother was starting to turn gray. But the woman was young. The clue had been right there, before her eyes . . . but it didn't register. And never would have if she hadn't read her father's journals.

Digby sits across from her, leaning over his cup to sip. It's clearly too hot because he sets it down, the saucer knocking against the pipe stand and making a sound like a gong.

She steels herself. "Dr. Kilgour—"

"Digby, please."

Digby, then. What I won't call you is "father." I had a father who loved me more than life.

"Digby . . ." she says, but the name doesn't sit well with her anymore. It feels like a jagged tooth scraping her tongue. "Don't you want to know why I came here today?"

He sits back in the chair and is quiet for a long time. "For years I've wondered if you would come, Mariamma. And if you would ask me what you propose to ask me." Their eyes are locked on each other. "You're the spitting image of your mother," he adds.

She takes a deep breath. Where does she begin? "D—" She can't say his name. She starts again. "How did you know my mother?"

Digby Kilgour sighs and stands. For a moment she has the absurd notion that he's about to open the door and walk out on her for asking the question he knew was coming. But no, he stands there. The eyes that meet hers are solemn, contrite, and full of compassion. "I knew one day you'd come looking for her."

She doesn't understand what he's saying. He goes to the French windows and stands there like a man about to face the firing squad, his nose almost touching the glass. She rises, teacup still in hand, to join him.

The view hasn't changed. The lawn outside is brilliant, like spilled green paint. In its center, clad in pure white, the unblinking woman still sits, sorting the millet.

"Mariamma, the woman there in the sun . . . She's probably the greatest Indian artist alive. She's the love of my life, the reason I've spent twenty-five years at Saint Bridget's. Mariamma, that is Elsie. Your mother."

CHAPTER 81

The Past Meets the Future

1950, Gwendolyn Gardens

When Digby pulled up to his club on that September afternoon, it looked like Victoria Terminus. Cars lined the side of the driveway, and suitcases were piled under the portico. It was the start of Planters' Week '50, and that year, for the first time, Digby's club—Tradewinds—had the honor of playing host.

Back in 1937, when he and Cromwell took over Müller's Madness, a serviceable ghat road was ambition enough. The road was completed just as tea and rubber prices soared, allowing the consortium with Franz and the other partners to quickly recoup its investment by selling off pieces of its nineteen-thousand-acre purchase. Soon, estates blossomed around Gwendolyn Gardens. By 1941, Digby and the other estate owners together built Tradewinds and hired an experienced club secretary who, from his first day, lobbied UPASI—the United Planters' Association of South India—for the privilege of hosting the weeklong annual meeting. That honor kept going back to the older established clubs in Yercaud, Ooty, Munnar, Peerumedu . . . Until this year.

*   *   *

Digby, as a founding club member, felt obliged to be visible. He parked himself on a sofa in the large drawing room, looking out of the picture windows that showcased the hills. On any other day, a bearer would materialize within seconds. Now the poor souls, dressed in unaccustomed turbaned splendor, ran around like harried hens.

Since Independence in 1947 and the departure of many white estate owners, Indians made up the majority at this gathering. Yet to Digby's amazement, the tenor of Planters' Week was unchanged. The cup challenges in cricket, tennis, snooker, polo, and rugby were more intense, and the beauty pageant and the dances bigger than ever. Indian national pride was at its height, but the educated, moneyed class, and certainly the ex-military officers, inevitably had English language and culture deeply enmeshed with their Indian ones.

A gust of wind sent a broad-brimmed straw hat with a blue ribbon rolling onto the manicured lawn. Digby watched its progress. A figure stepped out to retrieve it. He expected to see a sun-shy planter's wife, not the dashing, tall Indian woman in a white sari who appeared. Her thick rope of hair, draped in front of her right shoulder, shone against her brown skin. She was striking, without a touch of lipstick or face powder or a *pottu*, her arms lanky and bare. Retrieving the hat, she looked up, directly at Digby. He felt a jolt, as if she'd thrust her hand through the glass. Her haunting eyes, like those of a seer, slanted down to a sharp nose; Digby felt himself falling into their void. Then she vanished.

When he could breathe again, he felt the scents of perfume and cigarette smoke and the cacophony of voices close in on him.

"High Range was scrimmaging at the gymkhana all day. The buggers want that trophy. They—"

"I left my tails behind. Silly of me. Ritherden must have a spare—"

Digby stumbled out, feeling as if he'd seen a ghost. Had he imagined her? He heard his name being called. Was that too his imagination?

He turned to see Franz Mylin, two drinks in his big hands, coming from the bar, now packed two deep with brown and white bodies. "Did I give you a shock, Digby? We dropped off our things at your bungalow and came straight down to find you."

"Franz! I didn't expect you till much later."

"Lena's out by the courts. I say, Digs, I hope you won't mind, but we've brought a guest. What're you drinking? Here, hold these," he said, not waiting for an answer.

"It's my club, you know. I'm supposed to be—" but Franz was already diving into the crowd at the bar. Digby stood with a gimlet in each hand. Astonishingly, Franz was back almost at once with two more drinks, grinning mischievously. "These might have been for those young pups, but they were distracted."

Once outside, Franz dropped his voice. "Digby, did you ever meet Chandy's daughter? Elsie?"

So she wasn't an apparition. "Yes!"

"Lena's trying to get the poor girl's mind off the tragedy—you know how Lena is." Seeing Digby's puzzled expression, he said, "You heard, surely?"

"About Chandy's passing?"

"No, no . . . Have a snort first. You'll need it." Digby, clutching icy drinks, felt his body turn cold as Franz recounted the horrific death of Elsie's child the previous year. Elsie's fathomless look on the lawn was branded into his brain. ". . . so she fled the house, left her husband."

Digby whispered, "That poor girl! And still people believe in God?"

"Terrible business," Franz said. "Chandy's the one who brought Rune up to our hills, you know. We knew Elsie as a little girl. Went to her wedding. She's in bad shape, Digs. She won't want to be part of all the Planters' Week *golmaal*, but Lena thought it would be good to get her away."

Digby followed Franz. He'd never forgotten Chandy's pony-tailed daughter, a serious artist even then. He'd never forgotten the solemnity with which she'd taken on his "drawing therapy," as Rune had called it. It had unlocked his brain and his hand, jolted him back into the world of the living.

He'd often thought of her. He was sure she'd made good use of *Gray's Anatomy*, the gift he'd walked over to her fourteen years ago when he left Saint Bridget's. He'd expected great things of her but still was pleasantly surprised to read of her medal in a Madras art show. Now *she* was the wounded one. What did one say in the face of that kind of loss?

When Lena saw Digby, she stood, arms thrown wide. He hugged her, not letting go. There were two women in his life who'd seen him at his absolute worst: Lena and Honorine. Each had in her own way saved him.

Elsie stood up politely, watching them. White wasn't the color of summer alone, he thought. It was the color of mourning.

"Digs, do you remember Elsie?" Lena said. Elsie's eyes mesmerized him once more. He received Elsie's long, slender hand in both of his, recalling the girl who wedged a charcoal stick between his fingers and bound her hand to his with a ribbon from her hair. How effortlessly they'd skated over the paper, breaking the shackles that imprisoned him! Now he felt time dissolve, the intervening years collapsing. She'd caught up to him. A grown woman. He ought to speak, ought to let go of her hand, but couldn't do either. His mute grasp conveyed his indebtedness, and now his anguish for her.

The vacant, bottomless eyes had found focus, returning her to the present, the corners of her mouth turning up in a smile. He felt overcome by a premonition of danger ahead for her, as if she were in peril of falling off the edge of the world.

They took their chairs. There was an awkward silence. Franz said, "Well, cheers, Digby. Here's to old friendships and to new ones—"

"Renewed ones," Lena said.

A couple came over to greet the Mylins, who rose. Elsie glanced at Digby's hands. He extended his right hand, flexed the fingers, and she smiled sheepishly, caught in the act. She studied it carefully, reconciling it with what she remembered. She nodded in approval and then looked steadily at him. He couldn't look away, didn't need to. Seventeen years Elsie's senior, at that moment he felt they were equals. He was an expert on violent, tragic loss; now she had joined his ranks. He knew a simple truth: there was never anything healing one could say. One could only be. The best friends in such times were those who had no agenda other than to be present, to offer themselves, as Franz and Lena had done for him. Digby tendered himself silently.

After a while he spoke. "A few years ago, I saw your paintings at the art exhibition in Madras. I should have written to say how splendid they were." He happened to visit Madras while the exhibits were still up. Elsie's work had all been sold, but on the day of his visit he learned that one buyer had withdrawn and so Digby acquired the painting. It was a portrait of an overweight woman in her fifties or sixties, seated, empress-like, in a chair, wearing traditional Malayali Christian garb of white *chatta* and *mundu*, her large gold crucifix on a chain sitting atop her delicate *kavani*. Her hair was pulled back into a bun so severely that it appeared to lift up the tip of her nose. The viewer saw something discordant and pretentious about her pose, a disingenuousness in her smile and in her eyes. The power of the painting came from the model's unawareness that the canvas gave her away.

"I met my painting again in your living room just now," Elsie said, smiling. He waited, but there wasn't more.

"What's it like to see your work long after you let it go?"

A fleeting trace of pleasure crossed her face, an emotion that hadn't found purchase for a while. She considered her response. "It was like . . . running into myself in the wild." She laughed, a hollow sound. "Does that make any sense?" He nodded. Their voices were low. "After I got over the surprise, I was pleased with it. Usually, I want to fix things. But I was satisfied . . . I also knew that the artist was no longer the same person. If I did it again, it might be quite different."

She looked down at her hands, which were quite still in her lap.

Digby said, "Art is never finished. Only abandoned." She looked up surprised. "So said Leonardo da Vinci," he added. "Or maybe Michelangelo. Or maybe I made that up."

Her laugh was delightful to hear, like a solemn child tricked into revealing her playful side. Digby laughed too. When one lived alone, the loudest laughter went unwitnessed and therefore was no better than silence.

Elsie was, he thought, without blemishes on the outside. Flawless. Her scars, her burns, and her contractures were all on the inside, invisible . . . unless one gazed into her eyes: then it was like looking into a still pond and gradually making out the sunken car with its trapped occupants at the bottom. *You're not alone*, he wanted to say. Elsie met his gaze and didn't look away.

CHAPTER 82

The Work of Art

1950, Gwendolyn Gardens

That night his bungalow was alive, with four of them populating it, the rooms all lit up, and the red block-print Jaipur tablecloth like a blazing campfire around which they gathered. They lingered around the table once dinner was cleared, the conversation and laughter and drinks flowing. Elsie stayed silent but seemed soothed by their voices.

The next morning, Elsie didn't appear for breakfast. Lena and Franz left for the opening session. Digby stayed back. When she emerged at eleven, she drank tea, declining the eggs and sausages. "You went to a lot of trouble," she said apologetically. She had washed and loosely braided her hair, and she wore a light-green sari. The shadows under her eyes suggested the night had been difficult. Perhaps all her nights were so.

"No trouble at all." He noticed her studying the crudely shaped buns in the skillet. "That's bannock. Franz ate enough to shingle a roof, but he left you a few. It's an old Scottish recipe, just flour, water, and butter. Cromwell and I lived on it when we camped nearby, while we tore down Müller's old house. It had too many ghosts. I'd make bannock in a skillet over the campfire. Here, just try a wee piece," he said, topping it with butter and marmalade. She put it in her mouth and nodded approvingly.

"I like the big windows all around," she said. "Great light." He was enormously pleased by her approval. She took a second helping and put honey on it. He wanted to say that the honey was from his estate, but he didn't want to break the spell. "Shouldn't you be going to the meeting?" she said softly, in her low-pitched, distinctive voice.

"I won't be missed. I don't sit on committees like Franz and Lena."

"Gwendolyn Gardens?" she said, while chewing. "The name of your estate—"

"My mother," he said simply. For an instant, his mother was in the room, looking on approvingly. Elsie nodded. Digby was thinking of the portrait they drew together. His maw. Another time perhaps he might tell her.

"Elsie, I thought . . ." He hadn't thought at all; he was making it up, a surgeon with gauze over a probing finger, looking for a tissue plane. "Might you please take a walk with me?"

He led her into the west estate, through a corridor between high grasses where after the rains two species of butterfly, the Malabar raven and the Malabar rose, came to visit—but never together. His conceit was to think of them as his, as his creations. In answer to his silent plea, a Malabar rose flew before them, the vivid red of its slender body underscoring its coal-black wings. Digby stopped in his tracks and Elsie ran into him, her softness meeting his bony back. The Malabar rose was sleek, streamlined, with dark swallowtails on the wings that to Digby were like the engine cowlings of a plane. She drew closer to look.

A line of tea-pluckers, chattering away, came toward them, and the butterfly took flight. The women turned bashful and silent. Digby thought an earthy and vital life force rose off them like steam as they threaded past. Elsie seemed to drink them in. They hid their smiles with their loose, trailing headcloths, and politeness kept their eyes down. Digby, hands together, murmured, "*Vanakkam*," since his workers were Tamilians from across the state line. Elsie's hands rose too. The women responded eagerly, in bright voices, cloths falling away to reveal shy smiles as they slipped by, now stealing glances at Digby's beautiful guest. Elsie watched them as they disappeared into the sun.

"The light up here . . . is so special," she said. "As a child I thought it was because we were closer to heaven. I called it angel light."

They cut uphill, following an old elephant trail. The bungalow was at five thousand feet, and they'd climbed five hundred more. His breath was short. Should he have warned Elsie? He didn't turn to see how she was doing. Let her be. That had been Cromwell's remedy for Digby when he'd landed with his burns at the Mylins' guest cottage at AllSuch. To silently lead. To let nature do all the talking.

They were panting when at last they came to the outcrop of white rock pushing out like a hand giving its blessing to the valley below. It stood out from the brown rocks. The tribals called it the Chair of the Goddess. On its tabletop, petitioners had broken coconuts, left flowers, and smeared sandalwood paste. Digby handed Elsie his flask and she took eager gulps, her face shiny with effort, not taking her eyes away from the breathtaking view.

Whenever Digby stood here, he imagined he was perched on the goddess's belly and sighting down past her thighs to the verdant, widening valley between her knees that turned to dusty plains at her distant ankles. He hoped Elsie felt it worth the climb.

Before he could warn her (and who but a child would need warning?), she strode out to the table's edge, pausing there like a diver on the high board. *Step back!* He bit off the words, terrified that he might startle her. In all the years he'd come here he'd never dreamed of getting that close to the edge.

He inched forward on Elsie's left so she'd be aware of him. He forced himself to stay outwardly calm while battling the adrenaline surge, the fear within. Surely she heard his breathing, because he heard hers, saw her shoulders rise and fall, her scapulae wing out and return with each breath. Very slowly she leaned forward and looked over her toes, tantalized by the invitation that lay below. He stopped breathing. A breeze lifted the *pallu* of her sari so that it streamed off her shoulder, a green flag.

She turned her face to the sky, which bathed it in angel light, her expression radiant, her eyes silvery and glinting. He followed her gaze and saw a raptor rising on a thermal.

Elsie had raised her hands a few inches away from her sides, palms up as if to receive a blessing, or in imitation of the raptor. Digby had yet to breathe. He thought his heart would stop. He was a step behind her. If he tried to grab her and missed, he'd send her over. If she fought, they'd both plunge to their deaths. He called on the Goddess of the Chair, on any god listening, begged them to set aside the petitioner's disbelief, his contempt for all gods, and preserve this bereaved mother's life. Silently, he pleaded with Elsie. *Please, Elsie. I just found you. I can't lose you.*

After an eternity her left hand reached tentatively back to him, and his right shot out to meet it, as if hands knew what heads didn't. Their fingers locked around each other's. He walked her back from the treacherous edge. One step, then another. He turned her to face him, their exhalations and the breath of the valley all one now. Her legs shadowed his in a tango snatched from the edge of dying. Her body trembled.

He was certain she'd imagined stepping off, that she'd intended to shame God, shame that shameless charlatan whose hands stayed behind his back when children fell from trees, when silk saris caught fire; she'd imagined sailing out with outstretched wings just like the raptor, gathering speed and reaching that place where pain ended. He was suddenly furious with her, shaking with anger. *How do you know you go to a better place?* he thought. *What if it's a place where the horror that haunts you repeats itself every minute?*

Elsie stared at him, reading his thoughts as tears rolled silently down her cheeks. With his thumb he wiped them, smeared them on her cheekbones. He stepped down from the tabletop first. Then, as she tilted to him, her hands on his shoulders, he lifted her clear by her waist, as if she were no heavier than a feather . . . and then he held her tight, clasped her to him out of anger, out of relief, out of love. *I'll never let you fall, never let you go, not as long as I live.* She buried herself in Digby's chest, her shoulders shaking as he pressed her to him, muffling her terrible, wrenching sobs.

Walking back, they were unburdened. *Elsie, if you step away from death, that means you've chosen life.* If there was a Malabar raven to see, he wasn't looking. Nature had spoken enough that day. It was Digby Kilgour's turn, and he couldn't stop.

He told her about his school tie, biting into his mother's neck. When he spoke of his love of surgery, it was in the language of a man mourning the death of his one and only. And then he described another death, that of his lover, Celeste, an agonizing death by fire. As a boy he'd found it puzzling that the word "confessor" applied both to the one who listened and the one who admitted their sins. Now it made sense, because the two *were* one, clutching each other's hands, bound together without need for hair ribbons or charcoal sticks. Even when the path forced them to walk in single file, neither could let go, nor could he cease his story. He described his months of despair, the many times despair returned, and his desire to end it just as she had wanted to end her own. "What stopped you?" she said, speaking for the first time.

"Nothing stops me. I turn a corner and there it is again, the choice to go on or not go on. But I have no confidence that ending my life would end the pain. And pride keeps me from choosing to leave as my mother did. She had people who loved her, who needed her. Me. *I* needed her!" The last words were like an explosion.

He was silent for a few steps. Then he stopped walking altogether. He turned to her. He'd thought of Elsie often; he knew she'd grown up, married, and yet the image enshrined in his mind for so many years was that of the ten-year-old schoolgirl who unlocked his hand, a schoolgirl whose talent for art, whose genius was so evident.

The grown woman before him, now in her midtwenties, orphaned, robbed so cruelly of her child, feels to him like someone altogether different. If this is Elsie, then she's erased the seventeen years that separates them. Perhaps shared suffering did that. "Elsie, that portrait we drew in Rune's bungalow, our hands bound together? That beautiful woman was her. That was my mother's face the way I needed to remember it. Seeing the image we made together on paper released me from the grotesque death mask I'd carried around for so long in my head, the last image I had of her. Elsie, what I'm trying to say is you restored me. I'll always be in your debt."

She clutched both his hands, his mangy and mismatched paws, but still functional, doing everything they possibly could. She probed the ridge of raised scar on his left palm, the mark of Zorro, pressed down on it. She manipulated each finger like a clinician, determining the limits of its extensibility—a clinical exam, but by an artist. Then she lifted his hands, first one, then the other, and pressed the palms to her lips.

The next day she slept late but emerged looking rested. She sheepishly showed him a blister on the ball of her foot.

"What was I thinking? I shouldn't have let you walk that far in sandals."

He unroofed it with iris scissors, then powdered it with sulfa. She looked on, interested. "Does that hurt?" he asked. She shook her head. He put a pressure dressing over the fiery-red oval.

"Digby, don't you need to go to the meeting?"

He considered his answer. "I'd rather be with you," he said at last, not looking up. It was the truth. She didn't question him. They had a new way of being with each other.

Instead of taking her on a hike, he led Elsie to his indulgence: three curving terraces carved from the steep slope like an outdoor amphitheater, just in front of the bungalow. A sweet perfume met their nostrils. Digby's beloved rosebushes were planted along each terrace, like a colorful audience dressed in their play-going finery, looking down on the valley. He walked her as though past an honor guard, introducing her to the palette of discrete scents, beginning with orris, his favorite, which smelled like violets; then a clove-scented rose; then nasturtium. "I breed for scents more than for color."

They sat down. Elsie turned to point to a stone obelisk at the end of one terraced row. "What's that?"

"Ah, the Usher. He was meant to be a dancer. But the stone cracked." Her presence beside him animated Digby, made these insignificant artifacts of his life significant. "Michelangelo said every stone has a figure locked in it. This," he said, patting the bench on which they now sat, looking back at the roses, "this stone I thought was elephant. But I was wrong. Its destiny was bench."

She laughed and stood up to examine it.

"Digby," she said, and he heard the eagerness in her voice. "Where did you make these?"

Once a curing shed, his studio held stacked canvases, old welding equipment, and a fire curtain but no acetylene; in one messy corner, the floor was ridged and stained with concrete drips.

In his third year at Gwendolyn Gardens, after the ghat road was finally complete, he'd been overcome by a profound melancholia during the big rains, with little desire to leave his bed. Cromwell would have none of it. He made Digby rise, dress in rain gear, and trudge to the fields in the steady downpour, to the far side of the estate, where runoff from the slope threatened to overflow the irrigation sluice. They dug drainage ditches. Later, Cromwell brought him to the shed. "He put me to work splitting wood. 'Be useful,' he said. I cut enough for three monsoon seasons. I noticed one of the logs take the shape of a toy soldier. I tried to refine it. I ended up with toothpicks. But it didn't matter. What mattered was using my hands. Rune used to quote from the Bible: 'Whatsoever thy hand findeth to do, do it with thy might; for there is no work, nor device, nor knowledge, nor wisdom, in the grave, whither thou goest.' Cromwell doesn't know the Bible, but he's discovered the same principle. From wood, I moved to limestone. But I didn't have the patience and I moved to watercolors again."

"Digby," Elsie said. "Since Ninan's death, I've had the urge to use big tools. Like a sledgehammer, a bulldozer . . . or dynamite."

"Are we still talking about art?"

"I want my hands to do big things. As big as this view. Bigger."

He left her in the studio. Looking back from the door, he was pleased at her transformation. She was in a canvas apron, bandana, and goggles, standing before a limestone slab, swinging away with the mallet while her left hand moved the chisel. Her strokes had quickly become decisive, opening a seam, letting a sizable chunk topple free without a second glance. Already, the top of the slab formed a rough cylinder. She threw herself into it with an animation, a controlled fury he hadn't expected.

When he returned from UPASI in the late afternoon he could hear the hammer ringing. She didn't notice him at first. Fine dust coated her hair and every inch of exposed skin. When she removed apron, goggles, and bandana, her face was transformed, having shed its terrible weariness. They walked up to the house together.

She looked at her hands. "Digby, you've repaid your debt to me now, you know," she said.

The next few days he attended what was left of Planters' Week; but he skipped the evening social events.

On the eve of his guests' departure, Digby knocked on Franz and Lena's door. Lena's voice told him to come in. The couple had changed into evening regalia and were ready to return to the club. Franz was standing, while Lena, seated on the edge of the bed, was transferring things to a small purse. Their faces were turned to him expectantly. Seeing his expression, they became very still.

Digby felt blood rising in his neck. "Lena? Franz . . . ? If . . . If Elsie wants to stay here then," he stammered, "I'm happy to bring her back when she's ready. To you. Or wherever she needs." He was sure his face was red now. "The thing is . . . You see what a difference it's made. I mean the sculpting."

"It could be more than sculpting, Digs," Lena said.

A silent signal passed between wife and husband. Franz went out, thumping Digby on the shoulder as he left.

Lena said, "Digby, have you asked Elsie what she wants?" He shook his head. She chose her next words carefully. "Digs? I don't know what's best for her. And yes, I *do* see. It's miraculous. She's found a reason to go on."

"Yes, Lena! The thing is—"

"The reason might be you, Digs."

Digby sat down heavily on the bed beside her, his elbows on his knees, his head in his hands. Lena put her arm around him.

"Digby, are you in love with her?"

The question was shocking. His tongue moved to deny it at once. But this was Lena, his "blood sister," as she was wont to say. He stared at his hands as if the answer lay there. Slowly, he straightened up. He met her gaze.

"Oh God, Digs. Well, she may be in love with you too. She's so fragile, though. And vulnerable. And don't forget she's already—"

"Lena," he interrupted, not wanting to hear the word she was about to utter. "Even if I was, even if I am . . . Even if I do love her, what does it matter? I don't want . . . I'm not expecting it to lead to something. I'm forty-two, Lena, a confirmed bachelor. I'm seventeen years her senior. But if staying at Gwendolyn Gardens helps heal her wounds, I can offer her that, at least. She's rediscovering herself by working. It might be her salvation." Lena merely looked at him, not appearing to listen. "Lena. If you're worried that I won't be a gentleman, I promise—"

"Oh Digby, just stop." Her eyes were moist. She stroked his cheek, then gave him a gentle kiss. She said softly, "Don't promise. Just be you. Be good. Be true. And don't be a gentleman."

* * *

Elsie worked all the next day in the studio. He stayed out of her way. Nothing had changed. Everything had changed. They were alone.

He left it as late as he could to fetch her to dinner. As he approached the shed, he couldn't hear the clink of her mallet. Panicked, he ran the last few yards. He found her seated outside on the bench, watching the sky turn pink.

He sat next to her, out of breath but trying to conceal it. She smiled at him but looked incredibly sad. *How stupid of me. Did I expect a sculpture to erase her memory?* She leaned her head against his shoulder.

After a quiet dinner, both of them picking at their food, he said, "I want to show you one of my favorite paintings before you sleep."

He led her to the loft off the second floor and then up the ladder to the roof, where he'd set up two reclining cane chairs. He tucked a shawl around her against the chill. The cook had left a flask of hot tea, laced with cardamom and whisky. Gradually, as their eyes adjusted, the ink-black coat of night revealed jewels embroidered in the cloth. Then, after more time, the lesser stars appeared, like shy children peering around the cloaks of their parents. Above them, Orion stretched his bow. They were silent for a long time. He saw her trace a finger across the sky, as though the rising plume of the Milky Way flowed off her fingertip. She seemed to be in rapture, staring up, speechless.

He handed her the cup and poured.

"As a child in Glasgow," Digby said, "I'd go to the rooftop if the skies were clear—that wasn't often, mind. I could find the North Star. That consoled me. My fixed point. After my mother died, I couldn't believe in God. But the stars? Still there. In the same place. They made the idea of God inconsequential. I come up here in summer when the nights are clear. I look up for hours. Sometimes I wonder if this life of ours is a dream. Maybe I'm not really here at all."

"If you're not here, then I'm in your dream," Elsie said. She said quietly, "Thank you, Digby. For everything."

The next morning, he found her cross-legged on the carpet in his library, the sun streaming through the tall windows and through her hair. One of his folio-sized art books stood propped open before her.

"Digby!" she said, looking up. The pleasure in her voice gave him a catch in his throat. He sat down next to her. Together they stared at the photograph of Bernini's *Ecstasy of Saint Teresa*. "Look at the angel and Saint Teresa. Next to each other but separate. But all from *one* piece of stone. See the flowing fabric, the movement? How? How did he look at the stone when he began . . . and imagine this?" Her voice had become hushed. "He made it for this space in the church, with the sun pouring in from a skylight in the dome. It's pure magic. Oh Digby, if I could go to Rome tomorrow, I would."

"You can, Elsie." *Let's go.* She stared at him. Then she laughed. But she saw he wasn't smiling. Slowly, tears welled up in her eyes.

He rose and returned with two cups of coffee. Elsie said, "Yesterday I tried to correct what I should've left alone. One side of the stone fell away."

"Oh! I'm sorry to hear."

She smiles, amused by his expression. "It's all right, really. Whatever saint was locked in that stone was different from the one I had in mind. We must get rid of it. *I'm* sorry I wasted a good stone."

"Nothing doing. I'm keeping it. When you're even more famous, everyone will want your first sculpture. But I won't sell. And by the way, Gwendolyn Gardens sits on a mountain of limestone. I'll take you to the quarry. You can pick what you like."

Elsie resumed her work, this time with a larger, oblong stone. Digby only saw her at breakfast and at dinner. The cook took lunch over, but she hardly ate.

After dinner, their routine now was to climb to the rooftop, staying till the chill drove them inside. How much longer would the nights be clear? Digby always insisted on descending the ladder first, helping her off the last rung, holding her hand till they were outside her bedroom door, when he wished her goodnight. Every night, as he headed back to his room, he said to himself, *Be prepared, Digby. She might float off as suddenly as she arrived. Be prepared.*

One night, wispy clouds marred their view, followed soon by thicker ones, obscuring the stars. Stubbornly, they lingered, until fat raindrops drove them in. The ladder was slippery. Outside her room he said goodnight, but she held on to his hand. She walked backward, leading him into her room, closing the door behind them. *Be prepared, Digby.*

CHAPTER 83

To Love the Sick

1950, Gwendolyn Gardens

B ut he wasn't prepared to lose her. Not after that night. Not when the letter came, forwarded from the Thetanatt House to the Mylins' estate and then to his. Digby felt a chill when he saw the envelope. He'd been allowed the most blessed period of his life. *Call no man happy before he dies.*

When Elsie put the letter away her face was ashen. "It's Baby Mol. She's ill. She may be dying."

"Of what?"

"Of heartbreak, from the sound of it. On top of what ails her lungs. She saw my baby die, and then I left . . . The letter is from my mother-in-law. Ammachi says she refuses to eat. She asks only for me."

Elsie said no more about the letter, and he didn't ask. But it was like India ink dropped into the clear reservoir where they swam. It colored her mood. The mist gathered every evening, and it had turned cold with threatening gusts of wind rattling the windows at night. The rooftop was out of the question.

When they began sharing one bed, many a night he'd felt her body silently shaking next to his and he'd gather her in, hold her. On one occasion, after her sobbing subsided, she'd said, "It's only by being here, Digby, that I've felt my anger diminish a bit. My hatred, even. But it's not gone away. The sorrow will never go away. I know he loved our child. He's in as much pain as I am. He feels more guilt than I do, if that's possible. I know that it's pointless to blame him, or for him to blame me. But knowing doesn't stop it." Thinking back later, he wondered if she'd been preparing him for her leaving? There was nothing he could do.

The evening the letter came, as they sat by the fire, he knew she'd come to a decision. "I can't let Baby Mol die because of me. Not if I'm to go on living." He said nothing, waited. "Digs, we've not talked about the future. We've just lived each day. I've been able to breathe, to live and want to live, to feel love when I thought I never could again. I know I can't stay in Parambil. Too many memories, too much anger and blame. I dread going back. Even before Ninan died, even when Philipose's intentions were good, for some reason his trying to do something good for me would turn out being just the opposite." She sighs. "Digby, what I'm trying to say is I'm only going to visit. If you'll have me, I'll come back. There's no place else, no one else I'd rather be with."

He'd wished for such words. He struggled to believe her because he was an expert in disappointment. The only protection was to anticipate it. Trying to hold on to the people you loved was the recipe for disappointment. Being angry with them was just as futile.

He didn't try to pretty his thoughts, speaking as honestly as he always had with her. "I have no say in what you do, Elsie. If you feel differently when you're there, if you stay, I'll accept it. I'll have to. So the feelings I express now are not to confine you. I . . . well, I love you. There, I said it. I say that not to burden you but so you know. Yes, I want you to come back to Gwendolyn Gardens. I want to see Rome and Florence with you. I want to spend the rest of my life with you."

She covered her face with her hands. The glow from the fire played on the backs of her fingers and reflected off her hair. Had he said the wrong thing? When she took her hands away, he saw it was quite the opposite.

"Digs, I must leave tomorrow before I change my mind. And as soon as Baby Mol's better, I'll be back here . . . if you're sure."

"If you come back, I might even believe there's a God."

"There isn't, Digs. There are stars. The Milky Way. No God. But I'll come back. You can believe in that."

Digby drove her down the ghat road, their ears popping as they descended. Then they headed south through the valley and past Trichur and through Cochin and through village after village, stopping several times to eat, to stretch, until seven hours later he drove past Saint Bridget's. If it had been some other occasion, he might even have visited after getting Elsie home. But it had been too many years. The flock might be a different flock . . . and his heart was too heavy.

"Drop me just before the gate," she said as they approached the Thetanatt house; her driver would take her from here to Parambil.

She slid her fingers across the bench seat to meet his, discreetly squeezing them, conscious that they might be observed. He felt he was falling, pitching into darkness, unable to shake the premonition that despite her intention to return, she wouldn't.

For the first week, and the second, then through the best part of the endless monsoon, he held out hope. The telegraph lines were down and parts of the ghat road washed away by landslides. Even if she had summoned him, he couldn't get to her. But he felt she was trying to reach him. She called out to him at night. The destruction all over Travancore, Cochin, and Malabar was of biblical proportions. But it couldn't last forever. And it didn't. One day, the sun shone, and the telegraph lines were restored. They bypassed the landslides. At last, the mail trickled in. The monsoon was over. Weeks, and then months, went by. *She isn't coming back. Didn't I give her my blessing to do just that?* Still, he sank into a black abyss, a profound sadness. He was alive, but life felt over. He reminded himself that these mountains had saved him once before. Outwardly he was himself, even going to the club now and then. But new scars constricted his heart. The nature of the happiness that came from love was that it was fleeting, evanescent. Nothing lasted but the land—the soil—and it would outlast them all.

Eight months and three days after Elsie's departure, Cromwell came trotting out on his horse to seek Digby in the coffee fields, a letter in his hand. Cromwell, who couldn't read English, somehow knew that this letter, unlike all the others in the pile, was the long-awaited one even if Digby was no longer waiting. Digby by then was certain he'd never hear from her again. He was even thankful to her for the surgical amputation, for an ending without explanations, pleadings, or fraught correspondence that would only prolong the torture. It made him angry to see her handwriting. Why would she shatter the equilibrium he'd painfully found? A better man might have tossed away her letter, since that train had long ago left the station. He could not.

> *Dear Digs,*
>
> *I'm sorry that I did not write. It will be clear to you why when I see you. If I see you. I'm writing in haste. Could not get a letter to you early on as you know because we were cut off by floods. Digby, the reason I stayed even after the monsoon is also why I must now leave. I just had a child, Digby. I want more than anything in the world to feed, and hold, and raise, and love my daughter. For her sake I must leave now. I will tell you all in person. She is in danger if I stay. She will be better off with her grandmother and those here who will love her, even though I love her more than all of them. But my staying endangers her.*

Digby had to reach out a hand and lean on Cromwell, who stood before him. *That's my child, our daughter! It must be.* But how was the child in danger if Elsie stayed? It meant Elsie herself was in danger. He wanted to jump in the car and race to her. He read on, still leaning on Cromwell, who stood there pillarlike, patient.

> *Don't try to come here or write back. Please I beg you to trust me. Will explain when I see you. I plan to walk out of the house on March 8 at 7 p.m., around dusk. I will get into the river and float downstream to the Chalakura junction just outside the town. You can see it on a map. It's about three miles from the house. There is a bridge leading out of that junction. Wait at the north side of the bridge. There are no shops or houses there and it should be deserted at night. I will walk across that bridge by 8 p.m. at the latest. I can only hope I will see your car. Please bring dry clothes. If you come, I will explain all. If you are not there, I'll understand. You owe me nothing.*
>   *With love,*
>   *Elsie*

March 8 was the following day. He left within the hour, driving alone, over Cromwell's strenuous objections. He had told Cromwell everything.

A child. *His* child. The first time they made love they had been too caught up to think of pregnancy. After that, they'd tried to be cautious. But they were also lulled into a complacency, as though in the magical bubble of their being together at Gwendolyn Gardens, nothing could happen that they did not wish to happen.

But why hadn't Elsie come away as soon as the roads were passable? A delay of two, even three months was understandable, but why eight? Was she a captive? Why would she not bring the baby? Why such a hazardous escape? The whys kept running through his mind. Surely at some point they must return for their child. *Please trust me.* He had to.

He reached the bridge late that night, stopped, and took a quick look around. Then he checked into a government traveler's bungalow five miles away and tried to sleep. He returned to the bridge the next day at dusk. On one side of the bridge the town of Chalakura was buttoned down, its lights extinguished, just as it had been the previous night. The far side of the bridge was unlit, deserted. The river rode high, moving slowly, majestically, a full-figured goddess. He edged the car as close to the brush and reeds as he could. A laborer, head down, straining to pull an overloaded cart, came down the road, so focused on his effort that he never saw the black car or Digby in the shadow of the abutment.

Digby had no idea exactly where she would enter the water on leaving Parambil. He couldn't imagine being in the river in the dark. He'd been standing there for fifteen minutes, his eyes glued on the water, when he spotted a floating object, a resurrected Ophelia, in the middle of the river, then a flash of arm as she angled for the shore. Then nothing. Minutes passed. At last, on the far side, a silhouette separated itself from the hulking, menacing mass of the bridge. In outline it appeared to be a peasant woman in a blouse and skirt. When she came closer, he could see she was dripping wet, the clothes clinging to her. He rushed forward and wrapped her in a large towel and guided her to the passenger side of his car. She was white with cold, her teeth chattering, her body shaking, her hair bedraggled, and the scent of the river still on her. Leaning on the car she peeled off her wet skirt and blouse and dried off hastily, then slipped into the shirt and *mundu* he'd brought her. He settled her in the front passenger seat and covered her in a blanket, shocked at her appearance under the car's interior light: a pale ghost framed by black seat covers. Her face was incredibly weary, as though eight years and not eight months had passed. "Thank you for being here, Digs. Let's go, please. Quick."

As he pulled away, he saw no one in the rearview mirror. Elsie drank greedily from the bottle of water. He passed her a thermos of the hot whisky-chai they used to drink on the roof of his bungalow. Her feet were bleeding from her scramble out of the river.

"Are they looking for you?" he said.

She shook her head, biting her lower lip. "Not yet. I left my slippers and my towel by the river." She looked across at him. "They'll find it eventually. Then they'll be looking. But a body can be carried for miles." Her words chilled him. He was imagining the other reality in which she *had* drowned and wasn't seated here because her corpse was on its way to sea.

"And the baby?"

She closed her eyes, curling into her seat like a kitten burrowing into the blankets, a portrait of fatigue, grief, and loss. "Please? I beg you, Digby, please let me tell you everything when we get home." He reached under the blanket for her hand; her fingers felt stiff and rough with cold, waterlogged from her long immersion. He squeezed but she did not squeeze back. He heard a muffled "Digby," as though he'd hurt her and she was cautioning him. All too soon she was in the deep slumber of someone who had not slept for days.

At three in the morning, he negotiated the last stretch, completing the harrowing drive up the ghat road in the dark—something he'd never done before because of the real danger of wild elephants. Only when he pulled up in front of his bungalow in Gwendolyn Gardens did he register the shrieking in his shoulders and the cramp in his neck and note his fingers clamped to the wheel like limpets. He switched off the engine; the profound silence didn't wake her.

A figure peeled off from the shadows of the house. Cromwell. He'd been seated outside, wrapped in a blanket. He helped a stiff Digby out of the car, propping him up, and then shaking his shoulders, shoving him against the car as though picking a fight. "Much worrying, boss. Too much." His eyes were red and heavy with sleep.

Digby put his hands on Cromwell's forearms. "I know. I'm sorry."

Cromwell took in the sleeping form of Elsie, concealing his shock at her appearance. "Missy is all right." It was both a question and an aspirational statement.

"I don't know. She's been through hell." A hell he didn't quite understand.

Elsie came awake when he opened the passenger door. When she saw where they were, she turned to Digby with an expression of such relief that for the first time he sensed the depths of whatever horror she'd suffered. "Oh, Digby, the air feels so thin up here," she said, taking a deep breath then shivering.

She could do no more than smile wearily at Cromwell; she stumbled when she tried to walk, so Digby lifted her in his arms. She clung to his neck as he carried her inside. Digby said to Cromwell, "Thank you, my friend, for waiting. Go home, please. Your family won't forgive me for keeping you out like this."

He brought in a thermos of hot tea and chicken sandwiches that the cook had prepared. While she ate, he filled the bathtub with steaming water. He helped her out of her clothes and into the bath. Her arms were splotchy, with patches of pale discoloration like an old map. He registered her collapsed and wrinkled stomach, a contrast to her swollen breasts, the areolas stretched into dark saucers. He sat on the stool beside her. She placed her ankles on the edge of the tub and let her body sink deeper, vanishing completely under the water, save for her feet. Digby saw blood trickling from the base of her right toe; he moved closer. Her feet were studded with blisters. She emerged. He stroked her hand, which felt knobby and leathery. He studied her fingers: they had fissures, as if she'd been working with fence wire. She pulled her hand away.

He felt himself sinking.

Her hands, her blistered feet, the pale patches on her arms—he knew. He'd been with Rune at Saint Bridget's too long not to know. He wanted to scream, to shatter glass, to rail at the unfairness of a life that gave with one hand only to take away in bigger measure with the other.

She looked on, wide eyed, watched as understanding came to him, saw him clutch the edge of the tub and sway. She dared not say a word. Gradually, he composed himself. He reached in the water for her hand once more, then brought her fingers to his lips.

"Don't!" she cried, pulling away, but he wouldn't let go.

"It's too late for that," he said in a choked voice, pressing her palm to his cheek, because the love he felt was separate from the dreadful knowledge he now possessed.

"I forbid you," she said, withdrawing her feet into the tub, water sloshing over the edge.

"I forbid you to forbid me," he said, slipping to his knees, plunging his arms into the water to encircle her body, to pull her to him, this woman without whom he had no reason to go on. "There's nothing you can do to lose me," he sobbed, clutching her wet body to his. He chased her mouth as she dodged him, but he found it at last, tasting her lips and their mingled tears as she gave in, sobbing, letting him kiss her, kissing him back. Clinging to his wet clothed body, she wept, letting out what she had stifled for so long, sharing at last the terrible burden she had carried alone.

He held her tight. What did humans have in their arsenal for these moments? Nothing but pathetic moans and tears and sobs that did nothing, changed nothing. Water sloshed over the tiles: precious water, abundant water, water that could wash away blister fluid and blood, wash away tears, wash away sins if you believed, but would never wash away the stigmata of leprosy, not in their lifetime, because they had no Elisha to say, "Wash seven times in the Jordan and be cured," no son of God to touch the leprous sores and make them go away.

Elsie's letter made sense. He understood why she'd left their daughter. The reason stared at him in the curling of her fingers, the beginning of a claw hand. He knew all too well that pregnancy weakened the body's defenses, allowed a few diseases that were already in the body, like leprosy or tuberculosis, to explode. Elsie knew it too, having grown up with Rune as a neighbor and friend; she knew what laypeople would not: a newborn baby was in grave danger of contracting leprosy from the mother.

"You understand?" He nodded. Tears streamed down their faces. "I was never meant to have children, Digby."

"Don't say that."

"I *wanted* our baby, Digs! As soon as I knew I was pregnant, I wanted to come to you. But I was stuck there. I couldn't get a letter to you. And during the horrible, endless rains, my hands and feet . . . It happened so quickly. I didn't know what it was. But then I couldn't hold a pen. I knew." She stared at her cracked fingertips. "I almost died giving birth to her, Digby. Maybe that would have been better. I had a convulsion, after which, mercifully, I remember nothing. The baby was upside down. I had a severe hemorrhage. But somehow we both survived. Mariamma. That's her name, after my mother-in-law. A beautiful baby. It was days before I could even lift my head and look at our daughter. I wanted to hold her, but I could not. Rune had told me why they never allowed babies at Saint Bridget's. I knew."

Digby tried to picture his child, their child, their daughter. Mariamma. He longed for her. "I can raise her here, Elsie. I'll take care of you separately. And . . ."

"No, Digby, we can't. You can't. She's better off motherless than being the daughter of a leper." It was the first time that word had been uttered since Digby picked Elsie up. The word lingered; it would not go away. She watched Digby's face. "Yes, a *leper*, Digby. That's who I am. No one keeps a leper in their house. No one can keep that a secret." She leaned forward. "Believe me, she couldn't be raised in a better home than with my mother-in-law. Big Ammachi is love itself. And she'll have Baby Mol and Anna *Chedethi*."

"And your husband?"

She shook her head. "He's in bad shape. He took opium for his broken ankles, but he couldn't stop. Now it's his whole world." She took a deep breath and looked squarely at Digby. "He thinks the child is his, Digby. He has reason to. Just one reason, one time. He was full of opium. I didn't fight him. I could have, but I didn't. Once he knew I was pregnant, he convinced himself that it was Ninan born again. That it was God asking for forgiveness. When it was a girl, he sank deeper into the opium."

The only sound was water dripping from the tap.

Elsie said, "The only way out for me was for them to think I died. Why burden them with this knowledge of this disease? If I'd told Big Ammachi, she'd have insisted I stay. She'd have embraced me no matter what. Just like you. But I'd just drag the whole family down. Ruin their name. Ruin life for my daughter. It broke my heart that I couldn't tell Big Ammachi the truth. Better she thinks I drowned."

"But if my Mariamma lives here with us, but separate—"

"No, Digby!" she said sharply, sitting up. "Listen to me! Do you know how many nights I stayed awake to think this through? I *died* last night so that my daughter might live a normal life. Do you understand? That means I need to go where I can never be found. *Ever!* I must be where no one thinks to look, no one runs into me, no one hears rumors about me. My daughter can *never* learn of my existence. Elsie drowned. Do you understand? Gwendolyn Gardens isn't that place." Her agitation and the resolve on her face silenced him. "The only other choice I have is to walk off the edge of that Chair of the Goddess. But I'm not ready to do that. Not as long as I can still work. I want to create till I can't anymore. I can do that at Saint Bridget's."

He helped her out, dried her off. She folded a towel lengthwise and passed it between her thighs and tied a *mundu* to keep the towel in place. Once she was in bed, he brought his kit, to unroof and bandage her blisters. She tried to pull her feet away.

He remembered the blister after their first hike. She'd felt no pain. Was that an early sign he'd missed? There had been blisters on her hands when she sculpted, but that was normal—other than the fact that she hardly noticed them. Now she could step on a carpet or on a nail and the two would feel the same.

"I just wish you wouldn't touch them," she said, watching him work on her feet.

"You can't get it that way."

She laughed bitterly. "That's what Rune used to say. But Digs, *I* got it. How? From growing up beside the leprosarium? From visiting Rune? How?"

"We're all exposed, at one time or another. Some of us are susceptible."

"What if you're susceptible?" she said.

He made no answer and resumed his bandaging. "Elsie, what would you have done if I hadn't received the letter? If I hadn't come?"

"I was going to walk to Saint Bridget's," she said without hesitation. "If you came, I'd planned to have you take me straight to Saint Bridget's. But I was so very tired. And I knew we needed time to talk. I had to explain. I owed you that."

He peeled off his clothes, rinsed off, and came to her, his tiredness catching up with him. As he lowered himself to the bed, she tried to push him away. "You can't sleep with me. Why are you doing this, Digby?"

He didn't answer, pulling the sheet over his naked body and hers, snuggling against her. Her eyelids were heavy from her tears, from her ordeal, from relief, albeit temporary. He heard a mumbled, "I forbid you." Then she was out. He looked at her sleeping form, her face as white as the pillowcase. Tired as he was, his thoughts were still racing, and sleep eluded him.

An hour later, he was still awake, his arm numb under the weight of her head. He didn't care if it fell off. He could no longer separate himself from her suffering. The disease that afflicted her was now his, too. He couldn't linger on an estate that didn't need him, knowing that the great love of his life was elsewhere. Elsie had died to the world for the sake of *their* child. She couldn't make this sacrifice alone. It was now clear to him what he must do. *This is the end of one life. And the beginning of another that I could never have imagined. I have no choice, which is the best kind of choice.*

*　*　*

She awoke as light streamed in through the window, disoriented, unsure where she was. Then she realized she was in his arms. Digby's eyes were open, staring at her with tenderness. Outside she could hear the chatter of workmen going past, a foreman shouting orders. The noises of Gwendolyn Gardens. Just another day. She raised her head to look around. Digby moved his arm from under her. She studied him. He looked peaceful. Then tears came, clouding her eyes again.

"Digby. I can't stay. Not even for a night."

"I know."

"Why are you smiling?"

"If Saint Bridget's is the one place where no one will find you, then my fate has been decided. *Wherever you go, whatever happens to you, it happens to me.* No, don't argue, Elsie. It's clear to me. It couldn't be simpler. I'll always, always be with you. Till the end."

CHAPTER 84

The Known World

1977, Saint Bridget's

Mariamma feels something burning her fingers. Her tea. She drops the cup. It bounces off her body and lands unbroken on the carpet. Hot liquid soaks through and scalds her thighs.

Pain has no past or future, just the now. She leaps back from the window and pinches her sari and skirt free of her skin.

"Goodness!" Digby says. "Are you all right?"

She's very far from all right. On the other side of the French windows, the woman—the mother she has never known in her twenty-six years of life—sits oblivious on the beautiful lawn, sorting seeds in her palm. Something tells Mariamma that she has yet to blink. A lifetime passes before she can find her voice.

"How long has she . . . ?"

"She's been here almost as long as you've been alive," Digby says.

The conflicting signals in her brain clash with each other. There's a photograph at Parambil of the mother she carries in her head: those gray eyes tracked her across the room every day of her growing up—they'd even watched her daughter dress and gird herself this morning to confront the man who sired her. *That* mother stayed youthful, composed, beautiful, and elegant, her closed lips suppressing a laugh—perhaps at something the photographer had said. It was the face of a mother a daughter might confide in. How is she to reconcile that long-dead mother with this living apparition on the lawn?

"I need air," she says, turning her back to the window and fleeing the room.

She runs down a brick-lined path leading away from the main cluster of buildings; runs past an orchard, past a nursery; and arrives at the back wall of the property, hemmed in, until she spots a small gate that she flings open and races down mossy stone steps . . . and comes to a halt. Before her is the serene, slow-moving water of a canal that winds away to join a river she can hear but not see. Her feet are submerged as she stands on the last step. Every part of her, every cell wants to plunge in, to let herself be carried away as far from here as she can get.

She stands at this junction of land and water, her heart racing, breathless, and yet only now can she breathe. On the water's green, rippled surface, she sees her undulating, fragmented reflection. She came here broken, came here to question the man who fathered her but who was not her father. Instead, she found her dead mother, who somehow lives. Who has *always* lived. Who has been alive all the years Mariamma pined for her, prayed for her to come back from the dead.

The canal flows past, soaking the hem of her sari, undeterred by her distress, her new knowledge. It is indifferent, this water that links all canals, water that is in the river ahead, and in the backwaters, and the seas and oceans—one body of water. This same water ran past the Thetanatt home where her mother learned to swim; it brought Rune here to reclaim an abandoned lazaretto; and brought Philipose to save a dying baby, his hands coupled with Digby's; the same water swept Elsie away to die and then delivered her, born again, into the arms of the man who loved her more than life—and who fathered Elsie's only daughter, Mariamma.

And now that daughter is here, standing in the water that connects them all in time and space and always has. The water she first stepped into minutes ago is long gone and yet it is here, past and present and future inexorably coupled, like time made incarnate. This is the covenant of water: that they're all linked inescapably by their acts of commission and omission, and no one stands alone. She stays there listening to the burbling mantra, the chant that never ceases, repeating its message that *all is one*. What she thought was her life is all *maya*, all illusion, but it is one shared illusion. And what else can she do but go on.

She gathers herself. She walks slowly back. She pictures Elsie growing up nearby, motherless—they had that in common. Whatever else the young Elsie imagined, surely, she never imagined that she would end up *here*. Her mother did not *choose* to be a leper. With everything that Elsie had to offer to the world, how cruel that *this* is her fate: to be cloistered in a leprosarium, a place so apart from the world that it could be another planet. And all the while, an ancient, slowly dividing bacterium took away sensation, stripped her of sight, robbed her bit by bit of the ability to do the one thing she was born to do. Mariamma shudders at another appalling realization: through it all, her mother's mind must have been intact, the artist forced to witness the creeping ruin of her once-beautiful body, the progressive diminution of her capacity to make art. Mariamma cannot even begin to fathom such suffering.

Digby hasn't moved from the window, still looking out at the figure on the lawn, his unguarded expression showing sorrow and love, those two sentiments fused into one, and like a second skin for him. This scarred man stayed by her mother's side all these years, bearing witness to her suffering and suffering himself in watching her deterioration.

The change in Digby's expression when he sees Mariamma, his transition back to the present, reminds her of her father: often when she came up to him, she felt she'd summoned him back from an unfathomable place. The two men had this in common: they loved her mother. Mariamma stands beside Digby; they gaze out through the glass.

He speaks as if she's never fled the room. "Your mother suns herself here at this time in the morning." His voice is soft, wistful. "She comes through the fence gate, counts five steps to the center of the lawn. I grow these roses just for her. Her sense of smell is intact, thank goodness. She can name thirty species just by their perfume." He's like a parent bragging about a child's new skill. "When she tires of the sun, she'll take seven steps to this window and place both her hands on the glass and stay there for almost a minute, whether I'm here or not." He smiles sheepishly. "It's a little ritual of hers. Or ours. She's never explained it to me. I think it's like a blessing, a prayer she sends to me in the middle of the day, to tell me she loves me, that she's thankful for me." He smiles dreamily. "If I'm here, I put my hand on the glass, over hers. I think she knows when I do that. Then, whether I'm here or not, she leaves."

"Does she know I'm here?"

"No!" he says quickly. "No. When you came to see Lenin, I never told her. It's the only time in twenty-five years I've hidden something from her."

"Why?"

He sighs and closes his eyes. He's a long time answering. "Because her whole life has been about keeping this secret. Try to put yourself in her shoes, Mariamma. Imagine her right after Ninan's awful death. Philipose . . . your father . . . blames her, and she blames him. After the funeral, she flees Parambil. Soon after, Chandy dies. Friends of hers, concerned about her mental state, bring her up to the hills to distract her. She's full of rage and sorrow, tempted even to end her life. Quite by accident she discovers my attempts at sculpting, my tools. She takes her anger out with

hammer and chisel and I think it saves her. She stays on with me
after her friends leave. We become close . . . we fall in love. She gets
word that Baby Mol is very ill and for that reason alone she goes
to visit Parambil for a few days. She gets trapped there in a historic
monsoon. During that time, she realizes two things: she's with child.
And the leprosy makes itself known to her, becomes explosive—you
know how it can do that in pregnancy. Your father at this point . . .
wasn't at his best. Opium. She sees no way ahead, no good outcome.
Whether she comes to me or stays there, she can't be around you—
that she knows from growing up next to Saint Bridget's, from being
around Rune. It would put you in danger. She and your father keep
their distance. But he sees her in terrible distress one night, and he
comforts her, and it leads him to want intimacy. She doesn't stop
him. When her pregnancy is obvious, in his altered state, he thinks
it's his child. She comes to a decision: Once she gives birth to you,
she must vanish. She must die. You must all think her dead if she's
not to taint you forever, taint Parambil. Her only consolation is that
she knows that she can't do better than leaving you in Big Ammachi's care at Parambil."

"But if my father or Big Ammachi had known, they'd have
taken care of her, they—"

He's shaking his head. "How long before the fisherwoman no
longer brought her basket around, and your relatives avoided the
house? What this disease does to flesh is bad enough, but the fear of
contagion rips families apart. Every week we take in mothers chased
out by husbands. Fathers ejected and stoned by their sons. Only
here do they all find a home."

Mariamma wants to argue, to protest. But the truth is, if she
weren't a physician, would she even be inside these walls? She *is* a
physician, a disciple of Hansen; she's someone who has dissected
leprous tissue; she knows the enemy . . . and *still* her first reaction
was horror and repulsion at seeing her mother. Digby said, "Put
yourself in her shoes," but she finds it impossible to see herself

in those thick-soled sandals cut from rubber tires; impossible to imagine living through the nightmare her mother has lived, and still lives through. As her mother turns her sightless face to the sun, Mariamma shivers.

Digby continues, "This disease ostracizes innocent children and she didn't want you growing up tarred by the label she carries. Better you think she was dead than see your mother this way. Being here is as good as being dead," he says bitterly. "Your loved ones will never see you again. They never want to. We never get relatives visiting. Ever. You might be the first. She staged her drowning and had me pick her up downstream. I wanted to keep her at my estate, but she refused. To keep her terrible secret there was only one place she could safely be. Here. As for me, I had no choice. I wasn't going to lose her again."

"Who else knows?"

"Only Cromwell. And now you. Cromwell is a brother to me. He's made our life here possible. He was already running the estate, and now it's entirely his. My estate friends think I found Jesus and that's why I'm here. It turned out, I *was* needed at Saint Bridget's. The Swedish mission struggled to find physicians or nurses willing to work here for long. The prejudice is too great. I was already familiar with Saint Bridget's. Things had deteriorated after Rune's death. There was much to do.

"The hardest blow was when your mother's sight failed. Now I read to her every night. When we learned about your father's passing, she was heartbroken. She stopped working. Mourned for days, wept for him. For you. She lives and breathes her guilt every day, but once you were orphaned, it reached new heights. That's the only kind of pain your mother can feel now, pain of the soul. The agony of having to vanish from the earth to protect the ones she loves. All her art revolves around you, Mariamma, around the pain of giving you up. Your poor mother could only express her love by erasing herself, by becoming faceless, anonymous, unknown to her child. I see that in her sculptures, in the way they express the pain of having to hide her face, never being able to show it, being dead to you so you could live."

She weeps hearing these words. She had all the mothering and the kisses she could have wanted from Big Ammachi, her father, Anna *Chedethi*, and Baby Mol. They doted on her. Her tears are because she missed her *real* mother, who was here all this time. Yes, she misses that woman on the lawn, misses the mother that Elsie might have been, if not for the leprosy. *There's a chasm in my life of all these intervening years, our separate lives.*

Digby hands her an immaculate handkerchief. Mariamma takes it, grateful. She composes herself as best she can and she studies this man who fathered her, who came here to be with the woman he loved.

"You had to give up the world too, Digby."

"The world? Ha!" His bitter laugh is out of character. He turns to her. "No, no. I gave up something far bigger, Mariamma. I gave up *you*. I gave up the chance to know my only child. I *longed* to know you. That's not just her wound. It's mine too, you know."

Mariamma is shaken by the intensity of his emotion, by the anger and ache in his voice. She cannot hold his gaze.

"The only thing that eased the pain of not having you with us is that we had each other. And I was a surgeon of sorts again—I was paying Rune back too for what he did for me—while Elsie never stopped being an artist. Your mother and I have had a quarter century together! It's been hard. When we came here, she was still a beautiful woman. And so strong! The force of her mind, the quality of her work . . . I wish you'd seen her in her prime. My heart breaks with every setback. Look at what time and Hansen's bloody disease have done to her," he says bitterly. "But at night, in each other's arms, we try to forget. I'll take that, Mariamma."

She doesn't know what to say about this kind of love. She's envious.

"When your father's columns eventually resumed, full of wisdom and humor—and pain—she knew he'd overcome the addiction.

I dare say she was the Ordinary Man's most avid reader. She'd translate them for me. Before she became blind, that is. Then others had to read his columns to her."

"Does she know anything about my life?"

"Oh, God yes!" He smiles. "As much as we could find out. When your father's editor wrote that article explaining the mystery of the Condition, the autopsy . . . she couldn't stop thinking about it. It made her sad that the knowledge came too late for him, too late for Ninan. She felt she'd unfairly blamed him for Ninan's death—in their grief, they'd turned on each other. By the time he was freed from the clutches of opium, Elsie of Parambil was long dead. She never got to say how sorry she was."

Digby's features are highlighted by the light coming through the window; Mariamma sees profound sadness, exaggerated by the scar on his face. She even sees something of herself in this man who is almost seventy years old. She leans on his shoulder. Tentatively, he puts his arm around her, this other father of hers, embracing his daughter as together they look out at her mother.

Love the sick, each and every one, as if they were your own. Her father had copied out that quote for her; she still has it, tucked in next to the title page of her mother's *Gray's Anatomy.*

Appa, am I to love this woman who declined to engage in my life? A woman who staged her death so that I'd never think to look for her? I might understand, but can I forgive? Can there ever be sufficient reason to abandon one's child?

Abruptly, her body stiffens. She pushes away from Digby.

"Digby, I know her! Yes, lepers look alike. But I *know* her! She's the beggar who'd come to Parambil. Always before the Maramon Convention. She'd walk up and stand there, unmoving. Digby, I've put coins in her cup!"

His guilty expression confirms it.

"She hungered to see you, Mariamma. We both did. I couldn't, because as a white man, I stand out. But every year I'd drive her as close as I dared. She'd dress as a beggar and wait for hours until she

spied you before she walked up to the house. I had my own deep
yearning to see you. I was envious whenever she succeeded. If she
failed, she was distraught. It became harder as the years went on.
Once she became blind, it was all over. One year, it was Anna who
put coins in her cup. Elsie was heartbroken when she returned to
the car. Impulsively, we drove back past the house. I saw you for the
first time . . . saw you coming down the road, clear as day. I still carry
that image. I so wanted to know you . . . but you had a father. He was
the better man, a better father than I might ever—"

"Yes, he was," she says sharply. It's on her tongue to add, *Don't
you ever forget it!* But she doesn't have the heart. They've all suffered
enough.

"Digby, as much as you knew of leprosy, couldn't you preserve
her sight? Or her hands?"

He stares at her in disbelief. "D'you think I didnae try?" he
sputters. "She's my worst patient! Her active leprosy is gone, thanks
to dapsone and other treatments, but nerves—once they're deid,
they're deid! She were robbed of the gift of pain. If I could've protected her from repeated trauma, she wouldnae look like this!"
She's taken aback by his indignation, the anger in his voice, and
the flushed cheeks. It's the first time she's heard his accent twisting
through. "But all that mattered to her was her bloody art. I'd pad her
hands every morning, but if the dressing got in the way, she'd pull it
off. She might still have sight, but when her facial nerve was affected
and her cornea dried out, I'd patch the eye shut so the cornea could
heal and she'd pull it off! We battled over this. We *still* battle over it.
She says that I might as well ask her not to breathe! She says if she
stops work, then she has no life . . . That cuts me deep. I suppose I
want to hear that *I* am her life. Because I'm living for her."

Digby looks at his hands, as if the failing resides there. She
wonders if her own desire to be a doctor, to be a surgeon, to take the
world in for repairs came from this man, from his genes.

He says more softly, "Ah, well . . . I always knew I was in the
presence of genius. Your mother's kind of talent only comes along

once in a great while. Her art is bigger than me, her, or this wretched disease! Her compulsion is hard for us to understand. Believe it or not, she's still making art. When her sight deteriorated, she was in a frenzy to complete her unfinished projects, further damaging her hands. Sometimes she has me strap charcoal sticks to her fist, and then I bind my hand on top of hers, and we draw." He laughs ruefully. "We've come full circle!" Mariamma has no idea what he means. "In the dark in our bungalow, she works with soft clay. All she has is her palms. She holds the clay against her cheeks, or even her lips, to feel the shape. Unsighted, she's created hundreds of unique clay creatures, enough to populate a miniature world. Her confidence is astonishing. She knows the value of what she produces. She's always known."

"Who gets to see it?"

"Just me. Nobody else. She wanted her work to be seen, but *not* if it revealed who she was. *I* wanted it seen. Years ago, we tried cautiously. I moved several pieces to a dealer in Madras, someone I knew, a former patient. I said it was the work of an artist who never wished to be named. It sold at once at an exhibition, four of the seven pieces going abroad. Then an article about this anonymous artist ran in a German magazine. People were intensely curious. The possibility of discovery terrified her. We never tried that again. I've two sheds here full of her work. Who knows if the world will *ever* get to see it? The only thing more important to her than her art is that the world think she drowned, that no one ever finds out that she lives here as a leper. She wants her secret to die with her, even if it means her art dying too."

Mariamma thinks of her poor father, who died with his own secret, never knowing that his wife lived. Or did he know? Is that what triggered his sudden trip to Madras? Some new knowledge that came his way?

Mariamma breaks the silence. "Digby . . . Now that I know, now that the secret is out, do you think she'd want to talk to me?"

He sighs. "I don't know. The purpose of her vanishing was that you should think she died. She—we—invested a lifetime making sure of it. She thinks she's succeeded. *I thought she had too—till you walked into the theater today. So . . . would she want to talk to you? Do we shatter the illusion she worked so hard to create? I don't know."*

Mariamma thinks about her own shattered illusions. Should she thank or curse the Condition and Lenin for bringing her here? The Condition takes away, but it also gives gifts that one might not have wanted. She suddenly longs for Lenin.

She studies the woman seated on the lawn—Elsie. Her mother. She looks strangely at ease in that disfigured, broken body—or is that a daughter's wishful thinking? All her mother has of what once defined her is *thought* . . . that and the remnant of a body that barely gets around but still tries to make art. And she has this man who loves her, even as less and less of her remains.

"Mariamma," Digby says softly, "do *you* want to talk to her?"

The question makes her heart race and her throat turn dry. *No!* a voice within her says, without hesitation. *I'm not ready.* But another voice, a little girl's voice, a daughter's voice disagrees, addressing its mother: *Yes, because there's so much you should know about me. And about my father—you never knew the man he became, how he still loved you. He was the best father a girl could ever have.*

The voice that finally emerges says, "Digby . . . I can't tell you yet."

She recalls Broker *Aniyan*'s words. *Every family has secrets, but not all secrets are meant to deceive.* The Parambil family secret, which was hardly a secret, was the Condition. Her father kept another secret: that his beloved daughter was not his. If Big Ammachi knew, she kept it a secret. Elsie and Digby's shared secret was that she lived, she never drowned, but she lived with leprosy. These secret covenants kept by the adults in Mariamma's life were meant to protect her. Broker *Aniyan* also said, *What defines a family isn't blood but the secrets they share.* Secrets that can bind them together or bring them to their knees when revealed. And now she, Mariamma, who had been privy to no secrets, knows everything; they are one big, bloody, happy family.

Elsie, mother of Mariamma, gathers herself and slowly rises. Her stance is wide, her head tilted up like a visionary's and making tiny arcs as the sightless will do. She turns with small, stiff steps like a child learning to walk, until she's facing the French windows. With her palms and her finger remnants, she painstakingly adjusts the *pallu* of the white sari over her left shoulder and takes her first step, counting.

Mariamma feels her short life on earth compressed into this moment, this *one* moment that's weightier than the sum of all those that came before. Her heart pounds.

Her mother raises her hands before her to shoulder height, those strange, diminished implements held out like offerings. She approaches with her wrists cocked, palms facing forward, a heart-breaking, childlike attitude in those outstretched arms as they antic-ipate the French windows. Her brave, tragic advance transforms Digby's features; a loving, indulgent smile breaks out on his face as he watches her. Her mother comes closer, even closer, until at last both her palms touch the clear windowpane, arresting her progress. They rest there. Digby is about to place his hands on the inside of the pane, overlapping hers . . . but he stops and looks at his daugh-ter, his eyebrows raised questioningly.

Without thinking, without having to think, Mariamma feels herself drawn forward. She puts both her palms on the glass pane, pressing and overlapping her mother's hands, so that at that moment, all is one, and nothing separates their two worlds.

Acknowledgments

In 1998 my young niece Deia Mariam Verghese asked her grand-mother, "Ammachi, what was it like when you were a girl?" Any verbal answer would have fallen short, so my mother—Mariam Verghese—filled 157 pages of a spiral notebook with memories of her childhood, written in assured and elegant cursive. Mom was a talented artist, and so she interspersed quick sketches alongside her text. The fable-like anecdotes she recorded were very familiar to her three sons, though the details changed with every telling.

Mom passed away in 2016 at the age of ninety-three, but even in her last months, as I was writing this book, she would call me with some memory that had just surfaced—such as how her cousin, who kept being held back in the same grade in elementary school, was finally promoted only because his weight collapsed the bench on which he was seated, sending him tumbling into the next grade of the one-room schoolhouse. I have used several of Mom's anecdotes in *The Covenant of Water*, but more precious to me were the mood and voice that came through in her words, which I supplemented with my own recollections of summer holidays with my grandparents in Kerala, and my later visits when I was in medical school. My cousin Thomas Varghese is a talented artist (and engineer), and a favorite of Mom's. I am grateful and proud that his evocative drawings in the book have captured its atmosphere so well; Mom would be pleased.

For a story that involves three generations, two continents, and several geographic locations, I drew on many relatives, friends, experts, and resources. To anyone I have failed to acknowledge, please know that this was inadvertent.

Kerala: I am deeply indebted to the writer Lathika George (author of *The Kerala Kitchen*, Hippocrene Books, 2023), who showed me around Cochin, so generously shared priceless stories from her childhood, and was a resource for anything related to food; Mary Ganguli's long, insightful emails reflect her second calling (after psychiatry) as a writer, and were a treasure trove of Kerala tidbits, medical lore, and psychological insight; my cousin Susan Duraisamy recalled stunning details of my paternal grandmother's house and the people in its orbit; my soulmate Eliamma Rao took me to meet *Soukya*'s amazing founders, Isaac and Suja Mathai, who gave me a new understanding of healing; Eliam also took me to Sanjay and Anjali Cherian's home in Calicut and their property in Wayanad where Sanjay generously introduced me to the workings of an estate. Jacob Mathew, my contemporary at Madras Christian College, is the managing editor of the *Malayala Manorama*; he and Ammu generously welcomed me into their home and put every resource at my disposal. I hope he will forgive the liberty I've taken by having the "Ordinary Man" write for the *Manorama*; I trust he will see in these pages my admiration for his storied newspaper. Susan Visvanathan's books and writings (especially *The Christians of Kerala: History, Belief and Ritual among the Yakoba*, Oxford University Press, 1993) were invaluable. My thanks to the Taj Malabar Resort & Spa, which made my stay in Cochin so memorable; I am grateful to Premi and Roy John; my college friend, Cherian K. George; Arun and Poornima Kumar; C. Balagopal and Vinita; and the gifted architect, Tony Joseph. Catherine Thankamma, a noted Malayalam-to-English translator, pored over my manuscript and had many suggestions. Among many relatives who shared generously I thank Jacob (Rajan) and Laila Mathew; Meenu Jacob and George (Figie) Jacob; Thomas Kailath and Anuradha Maitra; and especially my godparents, Pan and Anna Varghese. My father, George Verghese, who is a great ninety-five at the time of this writing and gets on a treadmill twice a day, answered my many questions and called on his memories when asked. All errors pertaining to Kerala are my responsibility entirely.

Medical school: My Madras Medical College classmates who were enormously helpful include C.V. Kannaki Utharaj, a skilled gynecologist, whose long, hilarious, and insightful emails about labor and delivery were polished jewels and quite priceless—I owe you so much, CVK; Anand and Madhu Karnad shared hostel, classroom, clinic, and urban Madras memories and responded to countless text messages—the two of them have housed me, fed and nourished me so many times, and are my oldest and dearest friends; thanks also to Christian Medical College Vellore grads Nissi and Ajit Varki, Samson and Anita Jesudass, Arjun and Renu Mohandas, Bobby Cherayil, and my Stanford colleague Rishi Raj. David Yohannan (Johny) and his wife, Betty, hosted me, and Johny shared detailed memories of Calicut and his medical practice in Kerala and promptly responded to many subsequent queries.

Surgical matters: I thank Moshe Schein, Matt Oliver, John Thanakumar, Robert Jackler, Yasser El-Sayed, Jayant Menon, Richard Holt, Serena Hu, Rick Hodes, and Amy Ladd. Sunil Pandya's generous neurosurgical instruction was so helpful. James Chang, my distinguished Stanford colleague and hand surgeon extraordinaire, gave generously of his time, read many versions, and educated me about the nuances of hand surgery.

Glasgow and Scotland: My dear friends Andrew and Ann Elder did their best to help me understand Scottish history and dialect, took me to Glasgow again, and read the manuscript many times. Thanks also to Stephen McEwen. Once again any errors are all mine.

Manuscript: Colleagues and friends who helped with research or manuscript details or in freeing me to write include Sheila Lehajani, Mia Bruch, Olivia Santiago, Shubha Raghvendra, Katie Allan,

Kelly Anderson, Pornprang Plangsrisakul, Jody Jospeh, Talia Ochoa, Erika Brady, Donna Obeid, and Nancy D'Amico. Stuart Levitz, Eric Steel, and John Burnham Schwartz read the complete manuscript and offered invaluable comments; John is Literary Director at the Sun Valley Writers' Conference, which is for me the annual event that renews my faith in the joy and the power of the written word. Peggy Goldwyn read early versions and had sage advice; the writer and publisher Kate Jerome read several versions, and during the most trying times she shared her business insights and encouragement, for which I am deeply indebted. Two classmates from my time at the Iowa Writers' Workshop have remained my closest friends and confidantes: Irene Connelly has worked on, read, and proofread every book of mine, this one more than any other, and has always been there for me; Tom Grimes devoted countless hours to *Covenant* toward the end—my love to both of you.

Writers are nothing without editors, and the right editor makes all the difference. It was my extreme good fortune to be edited by Peter Blackstock. He shaped the book in essential ways, and did so with confidence, acuity, good humor, and humility. My agent Mary Evans found me in Iowa in 1990 and has represented me since. I owe her so much over my writing career, but especially for finding a home for this book with Peter and the incredible team at Grove Atlantic. I had the precious editorial assistance of Courtney Hodell with earlier versions; she gave this with uncommon patience, wisdom, and insight; to her and to Nathan Rostron, who read and offered such helpful advice, my heartfelt thanks.

The act of writing is a solitary one, but for this writer at least, it cannot happen without love, indulgence, support, and forgiveness from friends and family. Of my three dear sons—Steven, Jacob, and Tristan—only my youngest, Tristan, was with me during the years of writing this book, the two of us the sole occupants of the house; his forbearance, equanimity, and quiet but deep love and support sustained me through the highs and lows. My older brother, George, is the rock in my life, my true north; he is not only a beloved MIT professor, but also a brilliant proofreader and insightful reader. Each Wednesday morning for two decades I have met in person or virtually with my San Antonio "brothers": Jack Willome, Drew Cauthorn, Randy Townsend, Guy Bodine, Olivier Nadal, and the late Baker Duncan. The group was formed to support and hold each other accountable; the unconditional love of these brothers is a gift beyond any measure; and Randy and Janice lent me their Big Island retreat at a crucial point in the writing.

Stanford University has been a wonderful home for me since 2007. I am deeply indebted to Bob Harrington, my friend and the Chair of Stanford's Department of Medicine, for his unwavering commitment to his nontraditional Vice Chair. I thank Ralph Horwitz for bringing me to Stanford. Lloyd Minor, Dean of Stanford's School of Medicine, has championed my work; he and Priya Singh catalyzed the center I lead, *PRESENCE: The Art and Science of Human Connection*. Sonoo Thadaney is the wizard and conductor behind *PRESENCE*, BedMed, and all my other efforts at Stanford. I consider her, along with Errol Ozdalga, John Kugler, Jeff Chi, Donna Zulman, and every member of the BedMed and *PRESENCE* team, to be my extended family. Many other Stanford colleagues, too numerous to list, have kept me learning and growing; I thank you all. The Linda R. Meier and Joan F. Lane Provostial chair that I hold allows me the freedom to pursue interests across all the campus schools. Caring for the sick and teaching medicine at the bedside remain my foremost passions, and I am grateful to the patients, medical students, house staff, and chief residents at Stanford as well as all the other institutions where I have served who keep me humble and who keep my sense of calling as fresh as when I first began.

Finally, I can't imagine this book or my life without Cari Costanzo. She never lost faith through my ups and downs; she has read back to me every line in this book and done so through countless iterations, and also nourished my body and soul, all this while being a busy Stanford academic and a wonderful mother to Kai and to Alekos. Getting to know her older son Alekos has felt like a special gift to me these last few years. Though this book is dedicated to my mother, it owes its existence to you, Cari. *Omnia vincit amor: et nos cedamus amori.*

∼◦∾

Notes

The story in these pages is entirely fictional, as are all the major and minor characters, but I have tried to remain true to the real-world events of that time. The Japanese bombing of Madras was real; the characters of the viceroy, his first secretary, and the governor of Bombay are all imagined and bear no semblance to the actual individuals who held those positions. Longmere Hospital is fictional; I am proud to have attended Madras Medical College and to have visited Christian Medical College several times; however, the events and characters that relate to these two institutions are imagined. The Maramon Convention is legendary and I hope to visit some year; the Uplift Master scene at the Convention is fictional; Triple Yem does not exist nor does it resemble any hospital I know. The priests I knew from my childhood, as well as the one bishop—Mar Paulos Gregorios (born Paul Varghese) who was a family friend—have been inspiring, wonderful human beings. The depictions of the church and its officers are entirely fictional.

The line "father's breath was now just air" is after "Caelica 83" by Baron Brooke Fulke Greville. The material on spices and Vasco da Gama draws heavily from Nigel Cliff's wonderful book, *Holy War* (Harper, 2011) and from *Spice* by Jack Turner (Vintage, 2005). Big Ammachi and Koshy *Saar*'s thoughts on story draw from remarks of Dorothy Allison, and on maxims from Robert McKee's excellent book, *Story* (ReganBooks, 1997). Most Bible verses are italicized and are from the King James Version; the formal prayers are from the St. Thomas Christians' Evening Prayer Book or from online versions of the St. Thomas Christian liturgies. Matron's thoughts on public schools are inspired by the BBC documentary *Empire*. "Giving up the necessities but not the luxuries" is paraphrasing a similar quote ascribed to either Frank Lloyd Wright or Oscar Wilde. Celeste's description of London is paraphrasing M. M. Kaye's account in *The Sun in the Morning* (Viking, 1990), and also *Empire Families* (Oxford University Press, 2004) by Elizabeth Buettner. Honorine's saying that roses would be just weeds if they never withered and died is an idea from Wallace Stevens: "Death is the mother of beauty. Only the perishable can be beautiful." The lines by Veritas to *The Mail* about the boys of La Martinière are a paraphrase from *Paper Boats in the Monsoon* (Trafford, 2007) by Owen Thorpe. The letter writer's comments about Brahmin's failing when admitted to the highest rank is from Brian Stoddart's *A People's Collector in the British Raj: Arthur Galletti* (Readworthy Publications, 2011). "The secret of the care of the patient is in caring for the patient" is Francis Peabody's famous quote well known to all physicians (JAMA, 1927; 88:877). Celeste's observation about her husband's outward civility despite his true inner feelings is inspired by John le Carré's character George Smiley, who says, "The privately educated Englishman is the greatest dissembler on earth" in *The Secret Pilgrim* (Knopf, 1990). When Rune delivers bad news to Big Ammachi, she thanks him, "habit being so strong"; these words are from Raymond Carver's poem "What the Doctor Said" in *New Path to the Waterfall* (Atlantic Monthly Press, 1990). Rune's observations about the thumb are attributed to Isaac Newton in Charles Dickens's *All the Year Round* (1864, Vol. 10, p. 346), and later found in A. R. Craig's *The Book of the Hand* (Sampson Low, Son & Marston, 1867): "In want of other proofs, the thumb would convince me of the existence of a God." Koshy *Saar*'s recitation is from Tennyson's 1854 poem "The Charge of the Light Brigade." Digby's inscription in Elsie's *Gray's Anatomy* is from Robert Burns's "Death and Doctor Hornbook" (1785). The family with the blue tint to the whites of their eyes and fragile bones has osteogenesis imperfecta. The woman in the ENT clinic with an exophytic growth in her nostril has rhinosporidiosis. Prior to 1985 there remained much confusion around the two forms of neurofibromatosis; many patients with what is now called neurofibromatosis type 2 or NF2—"the Condition" in this novel— were lumped together with neurofibromatosis type 1 or NF1—the "classic" von Recklinghausen's disease, whose features are skin and subcutaneous nodules. It is now clear that these are separate genetic diseases with different clinical expressions, and involving different chromosomes (chromosome 17 for NF1 and chromosome 22 for NF2). "The Condition" is loosely based on a description of a large kindred in Pennsylvania (JAMA, 1970; 214:3470). The material on the famine is from public sources. The lines from the radio play that Philipose hears are from Act 5 of Hamlet. Philipose's lines, "*Lucky you can judge yourself in this water,*" and later, "*Lucky you can be purified over and over,*" are lines from the 1977 poem "Lucky Life" by the late poet (and my Iowa teacher and friend) Gerald Stern. The degree "MRVR" after the wart doctor's name is based on an anecdote in *Evolution of Modern Medicine in Kerala* by K. Rajasekharan Nair (TBS Publishers'

Distributors, 2001). The line that references "the round world and its imagined corners" is after John Donne's Holy Sonnet 7. The sin of the disastrous
translator who preceded Uplift Master is inspired by Jorge Luis Borges's
words "the original is unfaithful to the translation" in his essay *On William
Beckford's "Vathek"* in *Selected Non-Fictions* (Viking, 1999). Cowper's words,
"Abiding happiness and peace are theirs who choose this study for its own
sake, without expectation of any reward," is a tenet of Zoroastrian teaching.
"Living the question" is from Rilke's *Letters to a Young Poet* (Norton, 1993)
and it is advice I often give my mentees. "In a time of deceit, telling the truth
is a revolutionary act" is a phrase often attributed to George Orwell. Lenin
and Arikkad's escape after the failed raids in Wayanad is imagined, but the
Naxalites were (and still are) real, as is the execution of Arikkad "Naxal"
Varghese (1938–1970), who toiled for the Adivasis in Wayanad. In 1998,
Constable P. Ramachandran Nair admitted that he shot Varghese on orders
of K. Lakshmana, DSP. In 2010, a court found Lakshmana guilty of compel-
ling Nair to shoot; he was sentenced to life imprisonment and a fine of ten
thousand rupees. The fishmonger's disparagement of the *vaidyan*'s pills is
inspired by Oliver Wendell Holmes's address to the Massachusetts Medical
Society on May 30, 1860: ". . . if the whole *materia medica* as now used could
be sunk to the bottom of the sea, it would be all the better for mankind—
and all the worse for the fishes." Philipose in the chapter "The Hound of
Heaven" draws on the 1890 poem of the same name by Francis Thompson.
Philipose's letter saying that the real voyage of discovery consists not in
seeking new landscapes, but in having new eyes, is a paraphrase of a similar
thought in Proust's *À la recherche du temps perdu* (Gallimard, 1919–1927), in
Volume 5. For Broker *Aniyan*'s "*Set the date!*" I am indebted to my Stanford
Graduate School of Business colleague, Baba Shiv, who shared this memorable anecdote in his brilliant lectures on decision-making. Thank you,
Baba! Broker *Aniyan*'s statement about secrets is a quote from Sissela Bok
in *Secrets: On the Ethics of Concealment and Revelation* (Vintage Reissue, 1989).
Digby's observations while performing a tendon transfer are based on the
words of the pioneering surgeon Paul Brand: "The surgeon must practise
the patience of an earthworm feeling its way between roots and stones, and
he must not force a way through rigid structures or the tunnel will not be
lined with yielding material," in *The Journal of Bone and Joint Surgery, British
Volume*, 43-B, No. 3, 1961. "*Call no man happy before he dies*" are Solon's
words to Croesus, in Herodotus, *The Histories*, (Penguin Classics, 2003);
"*Wherever you go, whatever happens to you, it happens to me*" is a line from e. e.
cummings, "*i carry your heart with me*" (*Complete Poems*, Liveright, 1991).